EPSILON BOOK 2

DUALITY

R. JAMES STEVENS

EPSILON BOOK 2

DUALITY

R. JAMES STEVENS

Duality is a work of fiction. Names, characters, places and incidents either are the product of the author's imagination or are used fictitiously. Any resemblance to actual persons, living or dead, events, or locales is entirely coincidental.

ISBN: 0989682625
ISBN-13: 978-0-9896826-2-6

For my wife. You are the sun in my universe – for without you my world would be darkness.

ACKNOWLEDGMENTS

I'm blessed to have such a loving and supporting family. It's never easy to balance pouring your soul onto a page and taking care of everyday life plus a full-time job, but *they* get it.

To my son-in-law, Karl. Epsilon is the realization of over 10 years of evolution of our original story idea. I can't thank you enough for your inspiration in creating this world. What's next? Hollywood?

My readers and friends – thanks for the kind words of support and encouragement. I loved building Epsilon, and the fact that you all have made it a success is more than I could ever ask for.

L.R. Ryan , C.L. Davies & E.A. Thomson – a trio of fine authors that deserve your attention. I can say that they are quite honestly the nicest folks I've ever met! Thanks for your selfless support!

I like Easter Eggs.

R.

Prologue

Exodus 20:24

You shall make an altar of earth for Me, and you shall sacrifice your burnt offerings and your peace offerings on it, your sheep and your cattle. In every place in which I cause My name to be remembered, I will come to you and bless you. And if you make an altar of stone for Me, you shall not build them of cut stones. When you swing your tool on it, you defile it.

Saqqara, Lower Egypt - 2350 B.C.

Mafuane tugged heartily at the rope wrapped around his upper body; the rough anatomical lines of his muscles rose through the sheath of his crisp, brown skin. He, along with the other thirty worker-slaves in his regiment, hoisted the titanic limestone slab along the inclined ridge of the pyramid, ignoring the staggering fatigue that had set in over the day's labors. They had been working with an unwavering persistence at the structure for many days now, and even though the stone around them reflected the white-hot sunrays onto their already-tired bodies, they bullied forward, inching towards the precipice of the half-built monument.

"Steady!" the regiment captain, Fennec, barked. The group halted a minute amount, causing the stone to shift backward a few meters. Several of the men lost their footing and fell onto their backs, while the remainder grunted and picked up the slack.

"I said steady! Or you'll find yourselves working cutting duty back at the quarry!" The snap of his whip ignited their will to finish the task.

Mafuane peered out of the corner of his eye at Fennec. The captain, a strict disciplinarian by true definition of the word, did not hesitate to call out what he viewed as insubordination.

"You there! Need I repeat my command?" Fennec landed a heavy foot next to Mafuane. His nose flexed at the searing sting of their sweat.

"N-no, sir," Mafuane stammered. "Perhaps some water to quench our thirsts, sir?"

Fennec curled the side of his mouth in a disgusted sneer. He snapped his fingers. Another slave, without haste, handed him a wooden pot. Its watery contents sloshed in a spray of small droplets from the edges.

"Your refreshment," Fennec hissed, overturning the pot and allowing its quenching nectar to splash onto the ground at Mafuane's feet.

Mafuane, long past pride, released his portion of the rope, fell to his knees and began lapping up the dust-laden muck into his dry mouth.

Fennec faced the rest of the regiment. "Back to the line!" he commanded with a hearty boom.

The gracious slave wiped the muddy sand from the corners of his mouth and stared after Fennec.

I hate the man. Why does he torture us so?

Had he only Fennec to impress with his labors, Mafuane would have fallen from the line long ago. However, this construct was not about Fennec - nor any other of the regiment for that matter. The team's efforts were for Pharaoh Unas - and rightly so. Pharaoh accepted sacrifice, and in turn, offered protection for his people.

Despite the economic woes of the time, everyone loved Unas - Mafuane was no exception to that fact. Although he was a slave, Mafuane willingly sacrificed his body day after day, knowing that the Pharaoh's reward made it all worth the while.

And so he toiled. He ignored the sting of Fennec's whip at his heels. He put aside the burning of the rope against the skin of his back. He looked the other way when members of his team would fall to the ground from overwork, only to be left behind or pushed off the side of the great structure by Fennec or his minions to prevent distractions to the rest of the team.

Prior to a few weeks ago, Fennec would assemble his group just after dawn, and drive their labor until sunset. They would be allowed a generous – to them - meal and eight full hours of rest before repeating the process the next day. However, lately the team found themselves rousted several hours before the sun's rise, given their meager sustenance as nearly an afterthought, and then prodded into a long day of intense construction activities. They also found themselves working long past the sunset hours, taking away from their ability to rest before the following day's work.

PROLOGUE

In the short moments that the team had together away from Fennec, when they were not sleeping, they spoke amongst themselves about the change in their routine. While no one knew for fact, as it was not their lot in life to rub elbows with non-slaves, the rumor was that a prophecy from Pharaoh's oracle was the catalyst in the change.

According to the word coming from other circles, the oracle prophesized a 'sun event' that would happen every 4500 years - and the current cycle was almost due. The oracle warned that unless Unas completed his own tomb before that time, his kingdom, and those of his descendants, would be destroyed and wiped from the Earth.

Unas heeded religiously the warnings from his oracles - especially those that would result in his own hasty departure from this world - and set forth the proclamation that the pyramid be completed before the event.

Re, the Sun God, had become angry.

Mafuane was not the only one that had noticed it. All of the slaves, alike, had avoided looking to the sky during the daylight hours, so as not to incur His wrath. He and his team loved and feared Re, and in turn, loved and feared Pharaoh. They would do anything He commanded, and sacrificing themselves to save the kingdom in Pharaoh's name was considered a gift to them.

On what was to be the 42nd day of their labors - and after watching three others of his team succumb to the unrelenting heat - Mafuane paused, he and the rest having completed hauling the latest hulk of limestone to the ever-rising structure.

Suddenly, a crippling wave of exhaustion flowed over him, and he collapsed. He lifted his head from the chalky surface; a brilliant flash of color filled his eyes, emanating out in an expanding pattern from high upon the heavens.

Re was speaking to him.

A humbled Mafuane could not look away. He glanced at the others of his team. They, too, had collapsed - staring dumbfounded at the display. Fennec was nowhere to be found.

He gazed once again at the heavens. From within the center of the resplendent blaze, a glowing orb continued to grow until it was half the size of the afternoon sky. It morphed into the falcon-headed figure of Re himself. Two other falcon silhouettes appeared from within the colors to each side of Re: on the right, Horus, opposite him, Khonsu.

"Re!" Mafuane managed to chant with dry throat and outstretched hand.

Re looked upon the lowly slave, his falcon eyes blinking with an animalistic rapidity. Horus and Khonsu, feeling Re's intensity, knelt aside of him, bowing their heads in subservience. Re continued his pensive gaze upon Mafuane, raising his palms stretched outward.

The heat around Mafuane swelled, and the light became so fierce that he had to force his eyes into a hard squint to make out the profile of the exalted god standing in front of him. The stream of energy flow from Re's great hands down towards him; Mafuane let out a desperate howl.

However, no words came.

Upon seeing their work complete, the three gods departed, leaving behind darkness and a damp chill that rode the evening breeze.

Mafuane, blind and dumb from his encounter, lay on the ground, gazing at the heavens in ignorant stupefaction.

1:
The Event

Like a scolding parent, the nourishing star at the center of the Solar System unleashed a wicked finger of plasma into the cold of space. While normally a quick release from the surface, on this occasion the stream continued without end, forming a tidal wave of disruptive force directed at its third neighbor.

A framework of solar observing satellites, formed in a semi-circle in the safe zone between the sun and the planetary objects revolving around it, jettisoned their data back towards Earth before falling into permanent silence.

Queens, New York - October 24, 2077

The sweet aroma of sauce wafted through the kitchen of the turn-of-the-century, single-story home. Maria Dominici, awake since dawn preparing her much-loved pasta, wiped the glistening sweat from her tan forehead onto her apron. She tinkered with the band holding back her glassy black hair for a moment and grasped the wooden stirring spoon once again.

Sunday dinners were a ritual at the Dominici household, and aside from the two hours that the family would spend at their local house of worship, Maria would devote most of the daylight hours toiling away in the kitchen, delivering what her husband and five sons considered the culinary highlight of the week.

"Smells great, Ma!" a voice commented from the family room doorway.

Addison, her 16-year-old son – and eldest child – a ferocious devourer of many a plateful of his mother's cheese ravioli, jaunted into the kitchen and dipped his finger into a bowl of freshly whipped ricotta filling.

"That's for dinner!" Maria scolded, slapping the back of Addison's head. The swiftness of her swat made him spit the scrumptious concoction onto the beige tile countertop.

Addison rubbed the back of his head, taking care to coif his tussled black hair. "Aww, Ma! I spent a half hour on that..."

Maria shook her head and refocused her attention on the dinner preparations.

As his mother turned her back, he dunked his entire paw into the bowl and absconded with a mouthful of the sweet mixture. Maria wagged her head at her defiant son, grabbing the bowl away from the teen.

"You'll spoil your appetite. Now go wash your hands and get ready for supper!" she commanded, blindly whisking the stirring spoon through the pot of thick, red sauce.

"I'll be back later, Ma. Me and Eliza are gonna take the Rail over to Manhattan." He glanced over his shoulder at his mother while reaching for the handle of the patio screen door.

"What do you wanna go over there for? Can't you find somethin' to do here in town?"

Addison stopped and rolled his eyes.

"Aw, c'mon, Ma, it's not a big deal. They're havin' a viewin' for the solar flare thing in the park. All the guys are goin'." He pulled at the door. Addison had been looking forward all week to spending time with Eliza outside of school, and the viewing was the perfect opportunity to get her one-on-one.

Maria squinted at her son, her hands propped on her hips. "The hair, skipping dinner. What's up with you and Eliza anyways?"

Even in his sunlit silhouette, she could see that Addison's face had turned a bright shade of red.

He shook off the teenage embarrassment with a playful smirk and stepped next to his mother at the stove. "Nothin', Ma. Just havin' some fun is all."

With a grip that had always surprised Addison, she placed a hand on his other shoulder and pulled the teen closer to her. Maria planted a kiss on Addison's forehead.

"I love you, Addi," she said. "Don't grow up so fast!" She smacked the back of his head once more for good measure.

Addison nodded a silent agreement, as if he had a choice, smoothed his hair and headed to the door.

"And you have too much of that gunk in your hair."

He waved his hand blindly behind him.

"Addi, you and the Science Squad better be careful over there. Don't get hit by a car!" She began to stir the pot.

"Ma, they drive themselves, they ain't gonna hit us!"

1: THE EVENT

"They watch out for other cars, smart-mouth, not kids runnin' across the street where they shouldn't be!"

Addison gave a nasal grunt and exited the kitchen.

The Perimeter train - or 'The Rail' as it was commonly called - sped in silence along its raised tracks that perched twenty meters from the edge of the shoreline of South Manhattan. Designed primarily as a tourist attraction to give high-speed sightseeing tours, over the years it had evolved into the functional replacement for New York City's subway system, long-since mothballed over concerns of aging infrastructure and its proneness to flooding. Because of its high-tech design, the Rail also gave the city an icon to bridge itself from the gritty past to the technological future.

Eliza Simmons, Addison's pixie-haired crush, adjusted her left ear bud; the holo-vid on her data screen replayed an informational lecture on coronal mass ejections. She tucked a blonde lock behind her ear. Addison, alternately looking out at the sun-tipped placid water flying by in a blur and staring at Eliza's smooth, golden face, pointed at the animated image of the Sun on her screen with one finger.

"Wow, that's pretty cool," he said, indentifying the looped glob of gas illustrated within the picture. "That the CME that's gonna hit us?"

Eliza snickered and turned her molasses eyes to Addison. "CME? Addi, I didn't know you were into science."

"Oh yeah, always been." Addi tried to play up his transparent enthusiasm. "Ever since I was five and watched the Mars landing in sixty-seven with my folks."

"You wouldn't know it from the way you act all cool around your friends at school." She curled her nose and turned her attention back to the animation.

"Gotta keep up the image, ya know." Addi brushed off the sleeve of his light jacket for effect. "Not everyone appreciates us 'nerdy' types."

The train shuddered, the mechanical squawk of its braking system shattering its normal silence. The lights flickered for a brief second before extinguishing. Within seconds, the vehicle decreased its speed from a break-neck 155 kilometers per hour to a near walking pace.

"Ah, great," grumbled Addi. He glared out the window - the train had only made it halfway across the East River.

Eliza's eyes swelled. Her smile grew to where it seemed it would cover her entire face.

"It's happening!" she cried with dripping excitement.

"What?" Addi raised an eyebrow in confusion.

"The flare! This is part of it! Oooo, we're almost there!" She, too, peered out the window in anticipation of their proximity to the edge of the city.

"Never seen anyone seen anyone get excited about the Rail stoppin' before," Addi joked.

"This has never happened before!"

"A solar flare? They happen all the time, don't they?"

"Not like this one. This is once in a lifetime." She yanked the earpiece out and stuffed it into the pocket of her jacket, all the while folding the data screen into a small cube and stowing it, as well.

"Ok Suzy Science..."

"Shut up..." Eliza punched his shoulder with playful recoil.

The train lights flickered back to life; she tapped her feet with glee. The train began its rapid acceleration towards its destination.

The pneumatic doors of the train hissed open - Eliza jetted out of the entryway and onto the loading platform, and then began to skip like a carefree child down the concrete ramp that led to the street below.

"Hey, I'm here, too!" Addi called sarcastically, stepping out of the car amongst several other riders.

"Come on!" Eliza giggled, waving a hand and disappearing down the ramp beneath the floor level.

Addi waggled his head and trotted onto the ramp in pursuit.

Eliza stood at the edge of the waterfront park, bouncing on her toes, barely able to contain her giddiness. The mixture of the buttery scent of popcorn and warm, toasty aroma of Pizza Dogs tugged at Addi's attention.

"They went all out, huh?" He had not noticed that Eliza had already stepped away and into the grass. Still salaciously eyeing the food vendors, Addi followed Eliza, almost stepping on the back of her heels.

A hundred or so people, young and old alike, milled around the area, either talking spiritedly amongst their small groups, or examining digital literature from vendors and information kiosks that were set up around the park. At the center of the grassy enclave stood an enormous, holographic video unit. It depicted a countdown timer above a rotating animation of the Sun and its solar flare projections - similar to that on Eliza's data screen earlier. To each side of the colorful exhibit, several videos of various scientists demonstrating their knowledge of the subject blared over one another on smaller display units.

A strong hand tapped on Addi's shoulder.

"The End is nigh!" a male voice preached from behind him.

Addi and Eliza turned in unison to face a stranger standing just a meter from them. As if a beacon from a past century, the sun shone off a white sandwich board strapped over his shoulders, contrasting his leathery brown skin. Printed across the front side of the sign in squiggly red paint were the words 'Take us now'. The man's black eyes, buried like glistening black buttons deep within pockets of puffy flesh, seared through their souls. His wiry white hair shook as he spoke.

"It's the End! Are you prepared?" he belched with a squeaky craziness to his voice.

Addi, unable to speak, gawked with a half-open jaw at the odd man, who had decided to corner the pair of teens for his apocalyptic propaganda.

"How about you, son? Is your soul prepared for the End?" The man grasped Addi's shoulder and projected his wild-eyed insanity.

"Wha... what are you talking about?" Addi managed to stammer. He wiped the man's hand away from him.

Eliza giggled.

"It's the End, young lady." The man turned his enflamed glare to Eliza. "This is no laughing matter. Is your soul prepared to meet its judgment?"

"C'mon, Addi, let's go..." she snorted, poking at the back of Addi's shirt. She playfully rolled her eyes at the old man.

Addi nodded with an uneven bob of his head, took one last glance at the crazy man, and followed Eliza farther into the park.

The man, still rambling behind them in an incoherent tongue, continued his preaching at another unlucky fellow who had gathered his eye.

Although autumn had taken its seasonal turn, the balmy weather of late had betrayed it. The buildings beyond the park rose skyward, parsing the line between nature and the lazuline sky above, and created a stone canvas across which the sun laid its golden pigments.

A small trio strummed a bouncy Celtic tune that rode the warm air and echoed into the tourist-filled streets. While he was not certain of its ethnic roots, Addi was sure that this type of music had nothing at all to do with the gathering of this day. It did not seem to bother anyone else, however, as the playful atmosphere that the fiddling created seemed to broaden the smiles of everyone present.

"That didn't bother you at all?" Addi gave Eliza a crooked smile.

"There's always someone saying it's The End. That's nothing new," she chortled aloud. "A crazy one in every bunch."

Addi offered an apprehensive glare back at the man, who was now raising his arms in protest at something the other man had said to him. "I don't know. That was just... weird."

Eliza grabbed Addi's hand and began to trot to the gathering ahead. The excited grin on her face grew. Addi smiled, choosing instead to race past her with a playful laugh, having already decided to shake off the strange encounter.

Twenty minutes later

Having watched the bulk of the video presentations, and having perused most of the information kiosks available, Addi and Eliza strolled towards the waterfront, stopping just in front of the short sea wall. Addi dug into his Italian ice with a small, wooden spoon. Eliza gazed at the water that rolled quietly against the stones below.

"So whatcha' doin' later today?" said Addi, after chomping a large glop of his lemon-flavored dessert.

"Writing my paper on the flare, of course." Eliza flickered her mascara-caked eyelashes but did not take her focus off the river.

"You're really diggin' this science stuff, huh?"

"Yeah..." she replied.

"Even if it takes away from havin' fun doin' other things?"

"There's plenty of time for having fun."

"Even if the world ends today?"

"Oh please. That's a myth. Besides, people have been saying these things mean the end of the world for years." She tossed him a wave of her palm. "And still do..." Her eyes searched the crowd for the old man, but did not find him. She gave a dismissive shrug of her shoulders.

"Okay, okay," Addi conceded with a chuckle.

He glanced out at Ellis Island, and the Statue of Liberty just beyond. The glorious icon of freedom sat on a mammoth platform retrofitted twenty years prior, raising it an extra 50 meters and protecting it from floodwaters. The extra height, along with the colorful, digital lighting installed along its base, also enhanced its visibility - from both onshore sightseers as well as from incoming sea vessels, as if a modern-day personified lighthouse.

A playful giggle drew Eliza's attention. A small girl, no more than four, tugged at the tail of Eliza's pink shirt that hung out of her jacket. Behind her, a younger boy, whom presumably was the girl's brother as he bore a striking resemblance, stood bashfully in her shadow.

"Oh.. hi sweetie!" Eliza bent down to meet the girl at eye level with a fond smile.

The girl reciprocated the warm expression by thrusting her hand out to Eliza - a fresh, multi-colored Swizzle Pop at the end of a plastic stick within her gripped palm. "Here, you can have it."

"Why.. thank you!" Eliza cheerfully accepted the treat, pinched the girl's cheek and winked at Addi.

"I like your hair..." the little girl murmured between bouts of bashful snickering.

Before Eliza could say any more, the pair darted away, hand-in-hand, towards a couple standing in the park eyeing the proceedings.

Addi swung his head in amazement. "Kids, huh?"

Eliza shoved at Addi with a shoulder as she took a generous nibble from the Swizzle Pop.

"Here's a deal then," Addi said after a few silent moments. "How 'bout I help you with your paper if you... agree to go out with me next Saturday night?"

"Hmm," she said with a thoughtful roll of her eyes. "Well, you drive a hard bargain. You're lucky you're cute." Eliza peered over her shoulder at the park. "We better get over there and find a good spot, the timer's under thirty minutes!"

Addi snorted with a smile. *She's my type of girl.*

Hand-in-hand, the pair of friends strode back to the gathering with renewed haste.

"Attention everyone," a blaring announcement began from the loudspeakers mounted near the edges of the park. "The viewing will begin in less than thirty minutes. As with all solar phenomena, be sure..."

The PA system suddenly silenced; the massive holo-vid at the center chirped once like a throttled bird before dissipating. The moan of the crowd's disapproval raised above the murmuring of the technicians racing around the centerpiece to diagnose the ill-timed glitch.

"It's alright, just another spike," Eliza reassured Addi with a pat on his forearm.

Addi glared back at several buildings that soared above the massive skyline behind them - they were dark. "Big one this time." He pointed out the lack of illumination from any of the windows.

Eliza glanced up at the Rail platform, and then visually traced the tracks away from it. The train had once again halted over the water on its way back towards Queens.

"It'll come back... I hope." She glanced around the crowd with a disappointed frown.

"Think it's happened already?"

Eliza sighed and tapped with furious annoyance at her foldaway data screen. "Biggest day of my life and all I'm getting out of it is standing out in a park."

Boulder, CO (Capital of the United Republic of the Americas) - Four hours later

"I'm sorry for the inconvenience of no lights, folks. The blackout has affected all of us, but we've got some business to discuss." The man stood with stern authority in the doorway, squinting out at the open blinds across the room. The sun flooded the rectangular conference room, so much so that most of its occupants held one hand aloft to hold back the blinding rays.

1: THE EVENT

Vice President Seymour Timmons, an average height man with silvery-gray hair where it was not balding, had been on his annual family retreat in nearby Golden when the blackout occurred. He had not planned to make an appearance at the conference - that is, until his staff had informed him of the true nature of the event.

"Have you been able to reach the President?" he whispered behind his hand to his aide, Paulina, who stared wide-eyed around the room of military brass.

Paulina ratcheted her head with deliberate cadence, as if the rest of the room could hear her platinum tresses move. She creased her lips at the Vice President. "We haven't been able to reach anybody, sir." She tapped a French-tipped nail against her data-pad, but it remained dark.

Timmons nodded his understanding, stepped over to the empty seat at the head of the table, and then sunk silently into it. The members of the Joint Chiefs of Staff, or at least those that were in town and could make it to the Capitol Building without means of powered transportation, turned their attention to him.

"Well then," Timmons began. He glanced out at the caucus of generals and admirals. "I guess I can start by saying that it's been an odd couple of hours, and I thank you for doing what you can to make it here on such short notice."

The group, which consisted of five individuals, three men and two women, nodded at Timmons. Their thin smiles failed to mask their discomfort at the situation, however, as they normally would have had their fingers working in rapid parallel through data on their foldable e-pad screens. Without power, or the ability to use any electronics for that matter, they suddenly found themselves focusing on the humanity present in the room. They watched the Vice President, studied his gestures and the pained expression on his face.

"Vice President Timmons," one of the men, Francisco Montillo, a general from the URA South American Republic of Venezuela, chimed. He raised a heavily waxed eyebrow. "Will we be expecting the President this afternoon?"

Timmons clicked his eyes around at each of the military executives present.

"No, not today, I'm afraid, General. He's off on... other business," Timmons responded.

No one bought it, and Timmons detected the skeptical looks in their eyes. However, they kept their observations silent for the moment.

Sandra Gaillard, a flaxen-haired General from the northern, formerly Canadian, provinces of the URA, leaned forward and glared with a pair of striking slate eyes at Timmons.

"What do we know about the blackout?" she said, her words glossed in a heavy French accent.

Timmons nodded at Gaillard with a professional politeness and smiled. "General Gaillard, I'm glad you could be with us today." He clasped his hands in front of him and made his best attempt at a friendly smile to the rest of the group. "We're going to be briefed shortly by the DMST... the Department of Military Science and Technology... on what we know."

As if on cue, a slender man in a white lab coat rocketed through the doorway, clumsily dropped a handful of papers that he had clutched in his right hand, and then just as clumsily scooped them. He made his way over to the table next to the Vice President.

"S-sorry I'm late, Mr. Vice President," the man said, a shaking hand poking his thick-rimmed glasses back onto his red-tipped nose. The other hand shuffled through the mussed paperwork.

"And you are?" Timmons impatiently tapped his chubby fingers on the table.

"Oh, sorry, sir. I'm Steve Evans, Junior Associate of Nuclear Architecture over at the DMST," he answered in his best attempt at an authoritatively sounding response.

Timmons glared at Evans, and then eyed several of the gathered dignitaries. He narrowed his bloodshot eyes at the young engineer. "Where's your boss?"

"Uh, Director Fox... he's uh, he couldn't make it, sir." Evans's gulp resounded in the small room. He glared at the Vice President's aide. "I thought your aide would have told you already, sir." He avoided eye contact with Timmons by continuing to fidget through the folder in his hand.

The Vice President darted his eyes to Paulina. She widened hers and shook her head once more, the chrome-plated clip holding back her flowing hair shimmering in the sunlight. Timmons flattened his lips and turned his gaze away. "Well, have a seat, son," he said with a sudden warmth, motioning to another of his aides to free up his seat for the DMST engineer.

Evans quickly sat and readjusted his glasses, all the while still leafing through several sheets of paper dotted with graphs. A shaky hum escaped his lips; he extracted a small ream of papers and dropped them on the table.

1: THE EVENT

Timmons grunted a conciliatory chuckle and glanced around at the assembled staff, most of who failed to reciprocate; instead, they wore concerned – and impatient - frowns upon their faces.

"I take it you're prepared to give us a briefing on the blackout, Mr. um…" Timmons began, faltering when he could not recall the man's name.

"Evans… sir, you can call me Steve," Evans replied. "Yes, sir, I have all of the notes I think will be needed."

After glaring at Evans for another silent moment, the Vice President nodded and held out his hand. "Please, you have the floor."

"Thank you, sir. Well, this CME is one like we've never seen before…" Evans began.

"CME?" Gaillard interrupted, glowering at Evans across the table. Her coifed black hair only added to the mesmerizing contrast of her gray eyes.

"Uh, sorry. Coronal mass ejection. A… solar flare, if you will," Evans corrected. He could not pull his gaze away from the piercing hue of her irises.

Gaillard sneered at Evans before turning her glare to Timmons. "A solar flare caused our blackout? That doesn't seem plausible." Making her condescension strikingly apparent, she ignored Evans's attempt to clarify his statement.

"Thank you, General. Mr. Evans," Timmons interjected. His political smoothness took over. "The General has a point - we've never experienced this level of a blackout from a simple solar flare."

"Understandable, sir," Evans stammered, once again tapping at the frame of his glasses. He timidly glanced around the table like a baby lamb. "Perhaps 'solar flare' was a misnomer. Maybe 'flood' would be a more analogous term."

The group seated around the table eyed each other with speculative glances.

"Um, let me explain." Evans grabbed a water-filled paper cup from the table in front of General Montillo. "If I may, sir."

The Venezuelan nodded with one raised eyebrow.

Evans stepped to the side of the room and drew a medium-sized circle on the wall of the conference room with a black marker.

"You see, sirs… and um, ma'ams," Evans said with a docile smile. He crossed the room and stopped several meters from the drawing. Much to the surprise of everyone present, he tossed the contents of the cup in the direction of the diagram. The water, most of it missing his intended target, splashed against the wall and dribbled down to the carpet.

"Mr. Evans, please. Is this going anywhere?" Timmons asked, an irritated expression growing on his face. Gaillard wicked away a glob of the liquid from her jacket with an irritated sneer.

"Sorry, sorry, my bad. But you see, this is what a 'normal' CME, or solar flare, looks like in relation to Earth," Evans explained. "I had a decent chance of hitting the target, but it had minimal effect on it because of the relative volume of the cup."

Several around the table nodded, although their curious stares pushed Evans to elaborate.

"Your average flare ranges between one to three on the Fox CME scale – which works on exponential factors of ten per unit," the engineer continued, now engrossed in his own theorizing. "Now the one that occurred this morning... imagine the Earth as a baseball tossed into a swimming pool. It would rank on the scale outside of five, which is the maximum. However, if the scale were expanded, we'd be looking at a likely eight or nine."

The Vice President nervously eyed his advisors. "What about the communication and power disruptions. Can we expect restoration soon?"

"In my professional opinion, sir," Evans replied, "I think that is highly unlikely anytime soon."

"Are we exaggerating the situation a bit here, Mr. Evans? You even said it yourself - these types of events rarely last for very long." Timmons grasped the back of his neck with one palm.

"That's just it sir. It hasn't stopped. We're still in the flow, and it doesn't appear to be dissipating." Evans crumpled the cup and tossed it into a nearby waste receptacle.

"Are there any other experts in the DMST, perhaps with a pedigree in Astronomy or Plasma Physics that can give us a solid answer?" Gaillard interjected. "After all, why did they send a nuclear expert to brief on this type of issue?"

The others in the room, hanging on each word, turned to Evans for his response.

Evans cleared his throat and took his seat. "The CME wasn't my primary focus here today. And while the duration of the event may be speculative on my part, what I *am* here to discuss requires no speculation at all."

"By all means, Mr. Evans, don't keep us in suspense." Montillo's tone became increasingly impatient.

1: THE EVENT

"We're about to have a catastrophic failure of the PIE off the coast of New England," Evans said tersely.

"PIE?" Gaillard parroted back to him.

"Uh, yes. The Plasma Inhibitor Engines, which are used to accelerate the half-life decay of radioactive isotopes used in nuclear power plants all along the Eastern seaboard." Evans paused as several of the staff murmured their disbelief.

The engineer continued.

"The PIE is located underwater about one hundred kilometers northeast of New York City, which, as you can imagine, should be of great concern to everyone," Evans concluded.

"So, it's susceptible to power failures? That seems rather... shortsighted," Gaillard interjected, once again more than a hint of disdain in her voice.

"The PIE itself cannot lose power," the engineer explained. "Because its core is derived from plasma, it stores up a charge even without power for weeks or months on end, and the CME that is occurring now would only stand to strengthen or keep the charge alive."

Timmons frowned and wrinkled his brow. He rubbed at his forehead with a vigorous nervousness, trying painfully to absorb Evans's contradictory statements. "I'm confused then, are we talking about an overcharge situation?"

"No sir, the PIE is not really the issue in itself," Evans responded. "Overcharge dampening was built into the system, as you would expect." He glanced around the table. The look of skepticism from the dignitaries made his jaw tighten. "It's the containment unit that surrounds the PIE that is the concern. It was built to keep seawater separated from the PIE, but it is powered by standard means."

"What happens when the containment unit breaks down?" Timmons twitched his head in disbelief, already picturing the answer that was forthcoming.

"Well, sir. If seawater reacts with the PIE, it would most likely fail."

"Fail?" Gaillard groused.

"Explode."

"So we lose one of the DMST's little pet projects – where's the concern, Mr. Evans?" Gaillard rolled her eyes and tapped an impatient nail on the table.

"The explosion would be the equivalent of a fifty-gigaton nuclear bomb."

"But underwater, as you said..." Timmons added.

"Yes, sir. But the seismic shock delivered by such an explosion would be... off the scale, devastating the entire..."

Timmons bowed his head onto his clasped hands, closing his eyes in solemnity.

"There is... one other issue to worry about," Evans added. The group hung on his hesitance.

"On top of everything else?" Timmons eyes widened at the idea that anything could be worse.

Evans gulped audibly once again, grasped at the frame of his glasses and then darted his eyes around the room. He finally rested his eye contact with the Vice President.

"The spent fuel rods that get queued up for processing..." the engineer began.

The Vice President lowered his head into his palm and shook it in silence.

"...they are stored as close to the PIE as possible... in the vacated subway tunnels underneath New York City." Evans's glistening sweat, not from the lack of air conditioning in the room, raced down the sides of his pale cheeks.

"You can't be serious..." Montillo piped up, a deliberately obvious air of condescension in his tone.

"Yes, sir," Evans meekly responded. He did not take his eyes off the Vice President, who was now glaring through him. "The catastrophic devastation from the explosion and resulting tsunami would almost definitely rupture any storage facility within range of the blast."

"Why was this overlooked during design?" Timmons snarled, pounding his fist onto the table. Several cups of water rattled and fell onto their sides, spilling their contents across the wood surface before dribbling onto the floor.

Evans stared incredulously at the Vice President.

"Well... *sir*. The states west of the Mississippi River prohibit nuclear power, as well as transport and storage of spent fuel. You're familiar with the prohibition I assume, as you championed that legislation yourself when in the General Assembly. The East coast was our only option..." The meekness turned to condemnation within a nanosecond.

Timmons face became white as stone. His fuming indignancy crumbled away at the engineer's revelations.

"And as any engineer will tell you," Evans continued, "...with the prohibition against transport, it's only logical to store the fuel as close to the processing site as possible."

Gailliard huffed her overt disdain for the devolution of what the world considered the model technological society. She scribbled a few sentences on a sheet of paper, and then stuffed it into the hands of her aide. He nodded and dashed from the room.

As if in a trance, the Vice President blinked several times while ignoring the now loud muttering coming from around the table. "How long... until such an event might be possible." His vacant expression did not go unnoticed by those nearest him. "Keeping in mind that we've already been without power for several hours."

Evans glanced down at his paperwork, breaking the uncomfortable stare coming from the Vice President. A reply did not come.

"We have to get word to the New England area," Timmons suddenly said, shaking himself from his dazed stupor. "They have to be given an evacuation order!"

"Uh, sir..." Evans interrupted, "Because of the lack of power, we haven't been able to reach anyone at the containment unit. My calculations suggest that we are likely minutes away from a full breach. There just isn't enough time to execute a full evacuation of that large an area."

The room fell into a pained silence, each of the Chiefs of Staff staring away from eye contact of the others.

Timmons, finally grasping the gravity of the situation, bowed his forehead against his knuckles. Although only seconds, what seemed like hours passed until he lifted his head, sighed unevenly and then eyed each of his staff in turn. The grave expression cratered onto his face told them what was not necessary to say.

"May God save their souls..." he said above a whisper.

R. JAMES STEVENS

2:
Stricken

The flaccid waves lapped against the seawall, echoing in the silence of the park just beyond. Addi and Eliza stood and watched out over the calm harbor. Several small watercraft sat motionless; a handful of sailboats meandered a few hundred meters out.

Addi squinted from the sun's reflection on the blue waves. "So how long you been interested in science?"

Eliza spun her thumbs around each other and peered over at him through the corner of her eye. Her lip curled into a sly smile.

"Basically, like forever," she said. She turned her head, flicked her eyes up and down at him, and then spied the darkened displays at the center of the park. "I'm surprised you like science, though."

"If you didn't think that, why'd you invite me down here to this thing?" He faced her, holding one eye shut to drown out the glare of the sunlight off a nearby glass building.

With a subdued giggle, Eliza shrugged her shoulders and stretched her arms over her head. "You had to know I've had a crush on you for quite a while... didn't you? And what better chance to get to know you a little better than this?"

Addi nodded, a coy smile crawling across his face.

"And this is something I'm interested in," she continued. "Win-win, right?"

Addi let out a chuckle.

"What?" Eliza prodded, her hands on her hips.

"It's just funny," Addi answered. "That was my plan, too." The smile on his face confirmed that truth right away. Addi did not know how to follow up - everything had gone according to plan. Much better, in fact.

For the next few minutes, the pair traded glances in a flirtatious volley, while Addi mindlessly tossed small stones into the water just a few meters past the seawall.

Eliza broke the silence. "So... what do you have planned for me next Saturday?"

His smile spread even farther than before. He tossed another stone into the water. It clanked with a hollow resonance and skittered across the surface.

"It's gonna be a night you'll never forget..." he started, but then paused and focused on the water - or lack thereof - in front of him. A confused frown replaced the joyful glee of a moment prior. "Eliza... where's the water?" he asked in a monotone stupor.

Eliza, still entranced in her flirtatious moment with him, giggled. Addi grabbed her arm and spun her to face the harbor.

Both teens, speechless, gawked at the riverbed. Where there was water that flowed down the channel and out into the Atlantic just a few moments prior, now lay a muddy river bottom that stretched out into the drained ocean floor as far as their eyes could see. The steady sound of water hitting the jetties had silenced, and there was a telltale absence of the call of sea birds.

Addi glanced back at the park. Oddly, no one else had noticed the strange phenomenon, having been preoccupied talking amongst themselves in the center area around the darkened holo-vid. The Celtic melody continued to provide a solemn soundtrack to the eerie silence of nature.

They stared at each other, unable to comprehend what their young eyes were taking in.

Eliza, breaking her gaze with Addi, caught sight of a mounted police officer.

"Officer?" she yelped, to which the officer broke the horse's casual gait and steered it towards them. "Is it normal for the river water to... disappear like that?"

The officer, without fully paying attention to her query, snorted and rolled his eyes, focusing instead on a routine scan of the crowd. "Honey, it's impossible for the water to disappear. Tides don't work like..." he started, glaring down at Eliza - but then halted his condescension mid-sentence, his eyes bulging at the oddity of the dry riverbed behind them.

The muted rumble of an explosion in the distance, resembling that of thunder on a distant horizon, rent the relative quiet of the waterfront park. The crowd yelped in unison as the ground let loose a quick shudder and then became still. Unsure of the cause, or its ramifications, they wore their stunned expressions in silence. Fragmented sections of the groups stared in patient expectation. Others, their curiosity piqued at the growing numbers at the edge of the seawall, stepped forward and peered over the edge.

2: STRICKEN

A steady, hushed rumble birthed kilometers into the ocean - far beyond peering eyes, but close enough to be heard like an approaching locomotive behind a mountainside. The seconds passed; the din grew with rapid intensity to a beastly roar, and the earth beneath the crowd trembled to the point where many stumbled to their knees in their attempt to maintain their balance.

Several onlookers, including the mounted police officer nearest Addi and Eliza, took alarm.

"Earthquake! Move away from the buildings!" he shouted back at the throngs still recovering from the temblors seconds before.

The crowd quickly began to heed and disperse, fleeing in panic away from the taller structures. Their escape to safety was short-lived, as a sudden shockwave blasted the small park. It picked up and tossed nearly all that remained standing meters from where they had been before, spilling them across the grass like a handful of pebbles. The mounted police officers quickly found themselves flung from their steeds, their mounts violently twisted over onto their sides. One unlucky soul found himself crushed as his horse dropped to the ground atop him.

With a deafening clatter, windows of the surrounding buildings shattered and began a deadly rain onto the streets below. The panic level of the surprised pedestrians reached a fever pitch as razor-like projectiles thrust down upon them.

The ground, continuing its angry tirade, trembled with a mighty ferocity, shaking the foundations of the nearby skyscrapers like towers of building blocks. Massive screams erupted from one of the groups nearest the street - the stoic, stone-faced cathedral that graced the waterfront began to topple from the erratic motion of the earth beneath it. Chunks of its facade burst from the top-most levels of the building and plummeted to the ground, crushing cars and people scattering for cover.

Addi, thin streams of blood coating the sides of his neck - a result of his eardrums having burst from the shockwave - struggled to his knees. He frantically scanned the surreal scene, trying with a desperate heart to locate his partner amidst the chaos. Not ten meters from him, in the tumult of the terror-stricken that darted around him, the doomsayer stood with his arms akimbo – a wide smile of expectant relief for his visage, smiling to the heavens as if enjoying a much-needed downpour.

Addi swallowed the rising bile in his throat and squinted away the sight of the old man. "Eliza!" he screamed above the din, but no one could hear him – he could barely hear himself.

Then, he spotted her - the short, blonde locks matted around the back of her head as she lay face down at the edge of the park, her arm hideously twisted beneath her at a sickening angle. Addi gasped, shakily pushed himself to his feet and ran to her. With a gentle touch, he turned her head and breathed a sigh of relief - her eyes were open and she was awake. The sight of fresh blood on the side of her face made his body shake at its core, and he managed to whimper, "Are you ok?" in a broken cry.

She tried to turn over onto her side. Eliza let out a piercing scream - the shock of the event having dulled the realization that she had shattered her arm at the shoulder. To make matters worse, a large shard of glass protruded from her lower back, shrouded in a deep crimson stain. Addi froze. His instinct was to pull the glass from his friend's back, but fretted that it might do further harm.

A deafening whistle flooded the sky from above them to the west, split seconds before a passenger jet dropped from the heavens in a gut wrenching belly flop onto the center of the crowded street. It made impact with the hard earth and split apart, bursting into a Hellish orange fireball - its brilliant glare blinding the stunned thoroughfare. The explosion of the obliterated aircraft instantly set aflame and incinerated horrified bystanders, whom had no time to flee the devastation.

Choking off the smoke and heat from the crash, Addi raised the top of Eliza's torso in an effort to carry her to safety. The linings of his nostrils burned with the vomitous acridity of ignited jet fuel and scorched flesh, and the sounds of the mayhem around him assaulted his already-damaged ears. However, he fought off the urge to break down and cry, knowing that the slimmest chance for survival from this catastrophe was to flee the waterfront.

Before he could finish lifting her, however, an ear-assaulting bellow thundered from the east over the ocean. Addi and Eliza gawked, dumbfounded at the sight of the riverbed rolling towards the island of Manhattan like a mud-soaked carpet - its loops reaching 30 meters in the air in its approach to land like a speeding express train. The turbulent uprising plucked the Rail, still stalled in the center of its traverse across the East River, along with its tracks from the basin and flung them into the side of a nearby skyscraper.

The deafening crunch of its chassis splintering against the building echoed with a vociferous shock off the surrounding facades.

In a herculean effort, Addi scooped Eliza with both arms and dashed away from the seawall towards the other end of the park, hurdling other victims of the disaster who had fallen, or were helping others on the ground.

As he reached the park's boundary, the earth beneath their feet ruptured and tossed them into the air, flinging them into a muddled clump. The street nearest them emanated a terrible crunch and began to buckle. The magnetic rails, buried just beneath its surface, rose into a twisted ribbon and groaned. Reaching their physical limitations, they fragmented and flung outwards at breakneck speed. Their aerodynamics generated a haunting buzz as they sliced through the air, cleaving the crowd of stunned onlookers.

Buildings, lined in rows on either side of the crumbling asphalt, hopped from their foundations and burst into fragments, landing with ground shaking crashes. Other buildings simply fell over to lean on adjacent structures like oversized dominoes, before they crumbled into chunks, burying helpless victims within as well as those surrounding them. The proud Statue of Liberty, perched atop her enhanced pedestal, launched violently skyward as the ground continued to shred apart.

Addi, breathless and in tears as he pulled himself from on top of Eliza, peered down at his friend.

Her soulless gaze pierced his heart.

His eyes burned with tears of grief. He had never seen a dead person, let alone held one in his arms - to have it be someone so close made his heart ache as if squeezed in a vice. Despite his desire to be in the park on this fateful day, Addi found himself thinking of nothing more than wishing to be at home with his family while his mother prepared the Dominici Sunday dinner. His already broken heart fell into a pit of despair – the realization walloping him that Queens had most likely already taken the brunt of the devastation now raining down upon Manhattan.

From the ocean, a sound like a swarm of whispering bees drenched the humid air. Addi cranked his neck to see the latest catastrophe. His eyes filled with knowing terror, taking in the sight of a wall of water, 300 meters in height, rolling towards the city. The wind left his lungs. He bent over his deceased friend and trembled from his cries.

With the wave menacingly approaching the remains of the beleaguered city, a passenger jet suddenly skewered the center of the wall, spinning like a wingless dart and tumbling out of control onto the edge of the shore, several hundred meters north of the park. It hit the ground and began to break apart, flipping end over end and bursting into flames against a building in the distance.

The crowd, already terror stricken, wailed a stunned shriek and continued their desperate dart for cover. The sound of the advancing tsunami elevated, now to that of billions of thundering hornets. The trapped air in front of the enormous wave flooded the park in a tornadic fury, bending trees backward and snapping them like dried kindling.

In a last, desperate attempt for survival, the remaining crowd clamored away from the shore. The water, already casting its ominous shadow over the helpless horde, slammed into the city, towering over all but the tallest of buildings. Smaller structures, or at least the ones still standing in any capacity, flung from their perches and quickly washed away, sinking beneath the tumultuous surf. Countless throngs of helpless people disappeared, forcefully inundated and pulled underneath to their doom by the violent swell.

The once bustling metropolis of New York City, in a matter of a few horrific moments found itself submerged beneath the swollen Atlantic Ocean - the fractured symbol of freedom, the Statue of Liberty, the only remaining evidence of its existence. Having fallen nearly on its side some 500 meters inland, it sat on its pedestal three-quarters buried in the muddy shore of the irradiated wasteland that would be forever known as Manhattan Bay.

3:
Trust

The shadow of the mammoth jetliner flickered across the bank of clouds like a prehistoric bird, its rigid wings swept back along its sleek fuselage - roaring through the heavens on its way to deliver its passengers to their latest destination.

Golden Eagle One - or URA72, its official designation - was the ultimate in technological achievements. Proudly designed and assembled in the United Republic of the Americas, it showcased what many in the Republic felt was the realized justification for formation of the Republic in the first place.

While many a fight was waged to discourage the formation of the new union on the American continents into one super bloc of nations that became the URA - mainly by those allies of the former United States of America - no doubt could be cast upon the results of that union.

The URA's economy soared, not having to compete with other nations. While some international trade did exist, primarily with those countries that exported exotic spices, the URA flourished by allowing its own workers to create and trade amongst themselves the vast majority of its wares.

With inward-facing security from the solidification of the Republic's borders to natural boundaries of the Pacific to the west and Atlantic to the East, the collective distribution of military force was relatively simple. Never again would there be worry of enemy activities within their own hemisphere as everyone within was part of the Republic. Never had there been such a cohesive entity that prided itself on being so self-sufficient that all of its citizens resources needs were met within its own borders.

For Golden Eagle One, there was no better task than to be the official transportation of the President of the URA. Devlin Stroud, in his second full year as the landslide favorite to hold the office, sat back in his leather chair, his square chin resting comfortably upon his folded hands. His office, located just behind the nose cone section of the craft, was empty aside from him. He had just retired to the solemnity of the chamber moments before, an electronic security brief handed to him by one of his senior staff the object of his gaze. He stared forward in pensive thought, his lips flattened into an irritated scowl.

Out in the rearward passenger cabin, a woman tapped her foot nervously and glanced at the window every few moments, in-between flipping through pages on her e-pad with a disinterested finger. The sun, unusually bright this day, cascaded into the cabin and danced upon her ebony skin. A small shudder worked its way through the body of the jet, to which she grasped the armrest and inhaled a deep breath. She looked up; the sun twinkled in her jade eyes. The man across from her grinned.

"What," she asked in annoyance, showing her nerves by weaving a hand through her flowing, charcoal hair.

"You still don't like flying, after two years of flying all over the world?" the man replied, the grin growing on his youthful mug.

She pursed her lips into a tight line and then bit the end of one of her nails.

"Mags, you gotta get rid of this irrational fear!"

"It might be a fear, but there's nothing irrational about crashing into little bits on the ground." The soft bend of her accent that indicated her African roots always made those around her smile, even if it did betray her pure intensity. She continued to stare out at the clouds.

Magenta Abgomgave, two years into her stint as the President's Assistant Security Advisor, never let her 'irrational' fear interfere with her duties to the URA. However, she was still a victim of her anxiety, and anyone that had flown alongside her since President Stroud appointed her bore witness to her nervous habits once the plane would leave the ground.

"Mags! This is Golden Eagle One! It's a veritable Flying Fortress, nothin's gonna happen to us in this thing..." the other man, Press Secretary Dale Chapin, reassured her, placing a gentle hand on her forearm.

Once again, the plane lifted and dropped. Once again, Magenta gripped the armrests.

"The Flying Fortress was a twentieth century warplane," she corrected, closing her eyes and attempting to calm herself. "This is a retrofitted jumbo jet, and that doesn't make me feel any safer. I'll be glad when we're on the ground."

Chapin wagged his head with a crooked grin, his well-coifed blonde hair not moving a centimeter due to the product that shined upon its surface.

The cabin lights stuttered and then came back on. Both staffers peered up at them.

"Is that irrational, too?" Her sarcasm was not lost on Chapin, who held his retort with a silent bite off his tongue.

Another staffer, Mel Newberry, his muscles itching to relieve themselves from the tight Presidential-blue sport coat encompassing them, approached the two from the large aisle behind her. He stopped beside Magenta and placed a firm hand on her shoulder.

"Magenta, there's an urgent transmission for you in the forward comm Center," he whispered with a deep intonation into her ear.

"For me?" she asked with incredulity. "That's not protocol, and you know it..."

"They said it was someone from the Continental Space Agency." Newberry raised an eyebrow at Chapin, and continued. "And they specifically asked for *you*."

"The CSA? What do they want?" she asked.

Newberry, without another word, motioned his head towards the communications center and began to walk to the nearby staircase. Magenta quickly pushed herself from her leather seat and followed. Dale, his concern worn on his tan face, turned his head to watch Magenta scale the stairs and out of view.

Magenta and Newberry entered the forward communications center, which sat on the second deck of the aircraft in a medium-sized alcove, just above the cockpit entry foyer. The Marine stoically guarding the deck, his hand instinctively inching toward his holstered sidearm, gazed at them with a pair of intense, pale blue eyes a brief second before clicking his attention back forward.

They stopped behind one of the techs at the comm desk. Charlie Fults, a youngster whose Alabama hospitality perched on his face at all times, cocked his head sideways at her touch. Magenta leaned in and nodded at the freckle-faced lad. He waved his hand across a control panel to open the transmission.

"This is Magenta Abgomgave – whom am I speaking to?" she said, her voice suddenly presidentially stoic.

"My identity doesn't matter, what matters is what I have to say..." the man on the other end replied in an irritated yelp through bits of static.

Magenta eyed Newberry for a second, and then shook her head. "Go on..."

"It's about the CME, it's worse than what everyone was told..." the man said.

Magenta wrinkled her brow and glared in mutual confusion at Newberry.

"Solar flare..." he whispered.

She nodded her understanding. "Sir, I'm not sure how you managed to contact this station, but you can reach my office on Monday morning, and we'll be glad to hear what you have to say..."

"No!" the man on the transmission interrupted in a shout. "You need to hear this now! Everyone's lives are at stake!"

"Sir, you're not making any sense." Magenta's voice began to show her frustration.

"Listen to me!" The voice cut out more often with large amounts of static. "The DMST wanted the CSA to keep quiet about this, and we did. But I can't let this go on, you need to know what's going to happen..."

"Sir, you can stop right there. We know about the CME three months from now..." Magenta interrupted.

"It's happening now! And it's much worse than anyone was led to believe. Director Fox at the DMST was using the President as a puppet to push his agenda! You've got to warn..."

The transmission fell silent. The lights above them extinguished.

"Well, that's ominous," Magenta joked to Newberry, but abruptly stopped at the sound of someone clearing his throat behind them. "Oh, Mr. President. I'm sorry, sir." She inhaled her air of embarrassment and cleared her throat. Newberry stood up straight and stepped aside.

The President sauntered forward between Magenta and Newberry. "What's this all about?" he asked, his face with the usual stern glare.

"Claims he was someone from the CSA. You know the usual lunatic we get every now and then. The sky is falling." Magenta lifted a corner of her lips.

The techs at the console glanced nervously at one another, their workstations dark like the cabin lighting.

"Something about a solar flare?" Stroud arched a brow, waved his hand across the comm console - to no avail.

"Sir, we have nothing to worry about. This plane is fully shielded against any scaled solar flares that might..." Newberry started to explain.

The President held his hand up, cutting off the man with a silent comprehension.

Another shudder spiked through the plane, this one noticeably more violent than the last. The small group grasped onto the walls for balance.

The President abruptly made for the stairs, but then stopped and glared back at the remainder of the group. "Everyone go downstairs and find a seat, I've got some questions to ask." He disappeared down the stairwell.

The others looked to each other in silence, and then one after the other filed down onto the main deck.

Stroud approached the command deck just outside of the fortified cockpit door, his heels clanking on the metal grating. A Marine guard snapped to attention and delivered a brisk salute.

"Mr. President, sir!" the Marine barked without making eye contact.

"At ease, Charles. I need to get in to see the pilots, step aside please," Stroud commanded.

The Marine stepped sideways once into Stroud's path. The President recoiled with a look of surprise. "I'm sorry, sir. No one is allowed into the cockpit while we're airborne." Charles emitted an audible gulp. A drop of sweat appeared and dove from his youthful cheek.

"I seem to be the highest ranking person on this plane, Corporal Dodson. Not to mention, I *am* your Commander in Chief. *Stand down.*" Stroud stepped around the Marine. "In fact, I'm ordering you to go find a seat."

Charles's eyes grew, almost giving the appearance that he was about to tear up.

"For your own safety, Charles," Stroud added in a softer tone, placing a hand on the Marine's shoulder.

"Y-yes, sir," Charles conceded, lowering his hand from his sidearm at his belt, and then stepping quickly out of the command deck.

The President watched the young Corporal walk into the small corridor and out of sight, and then approached the panel next to the cockpit door. As he placed his hand on the intercom activation control, the sound of footsteps on the metal floor behind him made him pause.

"Mr. President, may I ask what you're doing?" a voice queried with stoic firmness behind him.

"Sergeant Pursely, I'm going in to talk to the pilot. I don't suppose you have any objections to that... do you?" Stroud turned his head halfway over his shoulder. He already knew that the ranking Marine onboard had his sidearm drawn and pointed at the President's back. He also knew that just behind the Marine stood at least two security agents with their own weapons drawn and most likely placed against Pursely's head.

"Sir, this isn't protocol... and you know that." Pursely's voice flayed with the edging of his nerves.

"Are you going to open this door or am I going to have to relieve you of duty, Mike?" The President made a hand gesture to call off the security agents behind the bold Marine.

Pursely bit his lip, and then holstered his sidearm to his belt. He stepped past the President, typed in his code and snugged his chin into a stirrup for retina scan. A green light illuminated above the door, followed by an audible click on the deactivating door latch.

"Now go find a seat," Stroud said, as he began to walk past the Marine.

Pursely held out his arm in front of the President, halting his entry into the cockpit - if only for the moment. The security agents took a quick step forward, their hands at their pieces. Stroud flicked an eyebrow in their direction. They relaxed their stance.

"I'll be just outside the corridor, sir. Don't make me regret this." Pursley made stern eye contact with Stroud, but the shake of his voice betrayed him.

The President patted Pursely on the shoulder with a chuckle. "You're a good man, Michael," he said, and then proceeded into the cockpit.

Sergeant Pursely shook his head at the security agents, who squinted at him as they stepped aside. The Marine stomped into the corridor beyond the command deck, the metallic echo of his footsteps fading into the forward passenger cabin just beyond.

Stroud entered the cockpit and stopped behind the two pilots. The co-pilot casually turned his head, but then did a double take at the realization of their visitor. "Mr. President! What are you doing in here, sir?"

The pilot, only taking his eyes from the controls for a split second, focused his attention back on the dash.

"Mind if I speak to the pilot for a second, Josh?" Stroud asked the co-pilot.

Josh, the youthful exuberance that normally adorned his face replaced with an unspoken tenseness, glared at the pilot for an instruction. The pilot, a solemn expression his only dialogue, motioned his head towards the cockpit door. Josh nodded with a hesitant click of his eyes, and then scurried past the President and out of the cockpit, closing the door behind him.

"Mr. Jenkins," Stroud said with charismatic warmth, turning his head forward after the door shut, "what's our situation?"

"Mr. President, this isn't a good time to be up here taking a tour of the operations," the pilot replied, his twang indicating he was a fellow Texan. He did not turn to face Stroud.

"Tom." Stroud placed a firm hand on the pilot's shoulder. Tom snapped his head to the side for a second, and then back forward again. The sun's glare illuminated the gray patch of hair that sat atop Tom's head. "We've known each other a long time. Ever since Navy Flight School."

Stroud glanced around at the massive cockpit dash, his eyes stopping on the oddly flickering instruments. "I know enough about these machines to know when something's gone wrong - and when you're holding back."

Tom's round shoulders slumped. He slowly wagged his head while pinching his pudgy nose between his fingers. "Mr. President, we've lost computer control of most of the systems onboard - including the flight surfaces. We've had to switch to analog just to keep this bird straight." His voice cracked.

With a grim nod, the President sat in the co-pilot's chair and rotated to face his friend. "But we're still up..." He ran his fingers inches above the instrumentation in front of him, his mind taking him back to a joyous remembrance of his flight days.

"Yeah," Tom answered in exasperation, "but it's definitely no picnic doing it by hand." He tapped at one of the panels a few times. "Shit." The pilot stood and gawked out the side window, back towards the wing.

"Speak to me, Tom," Stroud said, his concern evident.

"Mr. President, if you don't mind, I've got a problem I need to deal with..."

"Tom, just tell me."

"Mr. President..." Tom began. The President furrowed his brow and flashed a smirk. "Devlin," Tom corrected, "the plane's started to jettison fuel, and with no computer control I can't stop it."

"We have enough to get to anything nearby?" Stroud knew the answer before the query left his lips.

"Not likely. Even if we did, I can't tell where the Hell we are. And we lost all communications with the ground ten minutes ago - so it's not like we could raise anyone anyway. Besides, we're over the desert right now." Tom wiped the sweat from his brow with a sleeve. "I suppose I could extrapolate our position." His voice fell away in thought. "Not that it'll do us any good now..."

Stroud nodded his head and pursed his lips. "So let's get straight to it then. What are we looking at here?" Stroud's fortitude for such situations took command.

"I can keep us airborne on analog, but without fuel we're a little heavy for a glider."

"How long?"

"Ten, fifteen minutes tops." Tom released a sigh that echoed in the small chamber. "We're gonna crash, Devlin... Mr. President. But before that happens, I'm gonna burn as much altitude as I can before those tanks go dry and the engines cut out. You need to get to the escape pod." Tom turned away and clicked a couple of knobs in front of him, then focused intently on the instrument panels.

Nodding to himself, Stroud strode through the corridor outside of the command deck past Sergeant Pursely, who had re-entered the small foyer to gather a situation report.

"Mike, find a seat - now! Tell your men to brace for an emergency landing," he ordered the Marine. Stroud quickly entered the stairwell to the lower deck, two security agents in tow.

Pursely, wide-eyed at his boss's revelation, barked an order through the corridor leading to the forward passenger cabin, and then followed the group down the staircase.

Down below, the President entered the hatch to the small escape pod. He spun, gave an apprehensive stare back at the stairwell, and then closed the hatch behind him with the flick of a small lever on the wall of the enclosure. Knowing his role in what was to be, he yanked at the manual release. The lever did not budge. He pulled at it once more, but once again, it stayed in place.

"It's jammed, Mike. I can't release it from inside," he shouted through the small porthole to Sergeant Pursely, his voice muffled by the thick glass separating the two men.

Pursely, standing just outside of the pod enclosure, stepped to the manual control next to the hatch. He placed both hands on the lever and muscled it towards him. It, too, did not activate the release. He repeated the motion, but again it failed to operate. As he stubbornly began a third attempt, the hatch opened and the President stepped from the safety of the escape pod.

"Mr. President! What are you doing?" the Marine shouted.

"It's too late, Mike. We need to get back upstairs with the others." Stroud turned the Marine with a hand on his shoulder.

The four men scurried up the stairs and back into the forward passenger cabin. Like a bad roller coaster ride, the plane abruptly lurched downward. Those standing lost their balance and stumbled - some to the floor, others to seating closest to them.

The President, grabbing a nearby table to regain his footing, glared around at the cabin. "Everyone, please, take your seats. The plane is experiencing mechanical problems and we're going to have to make a... very rough landing. Please, no time to waste! Dale, make sure everyone up here is buckled in," he ordered his Press Secretary, before storming off into the corridor leading to the rear passenger cabin.

Peering at each other with a mixture of dread and fear, the others clamored for their seatbelts.

For a seemingly endless amount of time, the plane continued its tumultuous downward leaps and plateaus as the President worked his way back towards the rear of the cabin, ensuring each of his staff had found their seats and were prepared for the inevitable hard landing. A strange relief fell upon him, skimming over the heads of nearly 70 staffers now seated securely, knowing that he had accounted for all of them. He allowed a reassuring smile to sprout on his lips, looking upon Sadie Howell, whom held a small locket next to her breast. She nervously returned the President's sentiment and tightened her eyes closed. Stroud made his way back towards the front of the cabin, having to stop and brace himself several times against the nearest objects on his trek.

Just as he had reached the front row of seats, a pair of subdued backfires erupted from outside the plane. Without warning, the craft plummeted as if falling from a precipice. Stroud, unprepared for the sudden loss in altitude, rocketed from his feet and into the air. He caromed off the ceiling and then landed violently onto the cabin floor, the grotesque crack of his legs shattering echoing above the chaotic noise of the jet. He let loose a piercing scream and then slumped forward in pain.

Corporal Dodson, strapped into a seat nearby, unbuckled his belt and jumped up. Fighting the downward inertia of the aircraft, he made his way to the fallen leader.

The howl of the air flowing against the outside skin of the plane filled the cabin; the fuselage creaked and groaned with the stress of its increasing earthbound momentum.

The young Corporal grasped the President around the waist and threw him over his shoulder. In a miraculous effort, the brave Marine hauled him to the nearest seat and forced him into it while buckling him in with the assistance of a nearby staffer.

Stroud, in pain-stricken shock, grasped onto the arms of the seat. He peered up at the Marine, closed his eyes and nodded. Charles returned the acknowledgement and stumbled sideways towards his seat.

The plane jolted suddenly, as if it had struck a solid wall, shifting the craft sideways. The fuselage tore apart like tinfoil just two meters in front of the President's seat. The front-most portion of the airframe, along with the brave, young Marine and two other staffers, tumbled away in a violent storm of shattered metal. The President and his staff sitting nearest him watched helplessly and wild-eyed, as the remainder of the jet screamed out of control towards the desert floor.

4:
Gone Sovereign

The arid, desert breeze whistled through the fractured cabin. Broken wires, freed from their compartmentalized harnesses, swung unfettered amongst the hanging passenger seats that remained attached to the floor of the fuselage. A section of the mangled skin tapped against the metal floor with a muted thud. The midday sun, despite the subtle wisp of breeze flowing through the open-ended airframe, baked the atmosphere within the small dome of metal that used to be the rear passenger cabin of Golden Eagle One.

Magenta's hair floated beneath her as she hung from her seat two meters from the desert floor. The drone of a small swarm of flies, performing their dance around a fresh source of blood nearby, stirred her consciousness. She groaned, opening her eyes in a daze and unsure of how long she had been out - or whether she was still dreaming. The last she had remembered, she was having a conversation with the President in the comm center aboard the plane.

She swiped at a small tickle on her cheek, pulling back an arm smeared with her own blood. The pain traveling the side of her face awoke - something had hit her. Worse, a spike of searing heat radiated from her shoulder, as if from a flaming torch. She scanned her back with one eye and winced at the grotesque angle of her scapula protruding from the center of her back. The pungency of hot, spilled blood soured her olfactory.

Grasping her head with one hand, she shook off the dense fog surrounding her brain and peered around. She recoiled in horror and covered her eyes, leaving one peeking through the gaps between her fingers at the sight next to her. The upper torso of Dale Chapin, the President's Press Secretary and Magenta's best friend, hung in his seat next to her - the force from the violent crash having severed his body at the waist. His face looked forward, his empty eyes and blank stare frozen with the fear of the traumatic last memories of his young life – seemingly unfazed at the life's blood that spilled out in crimson flow from his tangled innards.

Ignoring the searing pain in her back, Magenta grasped mightily at the seatbelt cinched like a noose around her hips. It would not budge. She whimpered and tore at the clasp, trying with all of her being not to pay attention to what she could not ignore. Finally, the buckle gave way, and gravity yanked her from her upside-down perch. She fell with a thud into the sand below. Incredibly, the pain, which she thought could not get worse, did. She yelped and braced her shoulder with a tight grasp.

Locating a reserve of strength within, and riding her intense desire to be away from the death around her, Magenta rose and staggered to daylight outside of the wreckage.

"Hello..." she strained, the dust in her throat preventing all but a dry rasp from escaping her mouth. "Is anyone here? Hello?"

A large chunk of the center of the plane, still partially intact, lay out on the desert floor in front of her.

The galley, she thought, glancing over the spilled boxes of food and drink scattered across the dry, sandy grass.

She stood in place and rotated to take in the panorama surrounding her. Aside from the cabin in which she had just exited, and the ruptured galley, very little else remained of the mammoth aircraft. Several hundred meters to her left, a copious amount of black, sooty smoke spewed from the partial structural arc of one of the massive turbines.

To her right, and behind the disemboweled cabin, the shallow trail that marked the jet's final skid across the desert floor bled small plumes like fresh tar from a street paver. She traced the line farther towards the horizon - a rock formation stood tall with a large 'v' scar carved from its top-right corner, permanently etched where Golden Eagle One had made impact and split apart, before tumbling to a rest where she stood.

Wanting to find someone, anyone that might have survived the horrific carnage laid out before her, she began to walk the center of the trail towards more fragments of the fuselage. A partial set of seats lay a meter to her right.

A survivor! she yelled in her mind, her eyes widening at the sight of a leg protruding from underneath the broken chair.

She sprinted to the back of the seat and pushed it onto its side, finding strength she knew not that she had.

As she looked down at the ground beneath the chair, her heart dropped through her chest. A mangled limb, dismembered from the rest of its body, which was not present, lay at her feet.

Magenta turned and dropped to her knees, the vomit involuntarily finding its way across her lips and out onto the hot sand. She heaved again, and then once more at the surreality of discovering the fragments of her colleagues that she had spoken to moments prior to the crash.

She wiped her chin after spitting the last of the bile from her mouth. A groan from behind her snagged her back to reality. She pushed herself to her feet, turned towards the sound. The perilous moaning repeated itself.

From the cabin. She began to trot back to the largest remnant of the fuselage.

"Hello?" she yelled. She grunted with each step, her wounded shoulder bouncing in rhythm to her paces. She ignored the pain that threatened to darken her consciousness again.

She reached the outside of the cabin, holding her arm with a tender grasp. Heavy breaths exuded from her lungs. She bent over; the pain, now double what it was, throbbed through her entire body. Magenta rounded the rear edge of the cabin and peered in, afraid of what she might encounter next, but hopeful that someone was alive.

A movement above her drew her attention. The President, still semi-conscious and moaning in a low drone, hung upside down from a chair - still attached to the floor above him by two of its bolts. Beside him, also still fully belted, hung Kim Stewart, the Secretary of the Treasury and a newlywed by four months, her neck at a sickening angle and horribly shattered from the jet's tumble into the desert.

"Mr. President?" Magenta cried up to him, unable to believe the chances that he, of all people, would have survived the horrendous impact.

The President moaned, opened his eyes and looked down at her.

"Magenta..." he gasped, reaching for his legs with a wince of pain. "Are you... badly hurt?"

"Just my shoulder, Mr. President. I need to get you down." With a heroic burst of energy, Magenta grasped the edge of the fuselage and attempted to scale it. As she placed her weight on one of the window portals, the mass began to teeter, forcing her off-balance and back to the sand below. The pain in her dislocated shoulder intensified. She barked a grunt through gritted teeth.

"I... need to get... this belt undone, and then I should be free of this seat," Stroud said, his eyes tightened shut.

Magenta nodded her understanding and dragged a seat over to the spot directly underneath him, turning it on its face and cautiously standing on it to reach upward. All four of their hands frantically worked in unison to free the belt. Suddenly it gave way, dropping the President from his seat onto her. Magenta tumbled backward and onto the ground, her shoulder emitting a fluid pop that echoed off the insides of the fuselage. She rolled to her side and wailed a shriek that fell deaf into the hot desert air. The pain reached its peak as the ball joint of her arm miraculously found its way back into her shoulder socket.

After a few moments of recovery, she sat up, placed her head in her hands and wept in an uncontrollable quake.

The President, his legs resembling boiled noodles, swallowed his pain and pushed himself closer to Magenta.

"Magenta, dear, I'm sorry," he said. "Did I hurt you further?"

Magenta shook her head in the midst of her tears, looked over to him.

"Why... why did this happen?" she blurted through heavy sobs.

The President closed his eyes, shook his head. "It's too fresh... we need to come down from the shock for now."

He opened his eyes and scanned the area, noticing the spilled contents of the galley outside of the wreckage. "There... the galley. I'm certain there's something in there to help... a medical kit of some sort, pain killers, alcohol... anything to dull this pain..." he groaned with heavy breath.

Magenta's eyes fell to his mangled legs. The guilt wrapped her like a cold blanket, waking her from her self-pity. She wiped her tears on her ripped sleeve, nodded her head with a sober silence and scrambled towards the toppled galley.

A few hours later

The wind had shifted, bringing with it the heavy fetor of burning sheet metal and electronic components. A small grouping of Black Vultures circled overhead, awaiting their sustenance.

President Devlin Stroud, his newfound relaxation draped on his face, leaned back against the fuselage. The sun, still ruthlessly drenching the desert in its energy, perched onto the top of its downward arc. The pair of lone survivors had relocated temporarily away from the brutal rays into the miniscule shade that the shattered husk could offer. Next to him, an open bottle of prescription painkillers - a fortuitous find for certain - lay in the sand.

Magenta sat to his side, closed her eyes and pressed her weight back against the skin of the fuselage. Her own medication, a half-empty bottle of Scotch, sat by her side.

"Do you think they'll find us soon?" she asked, her eyes still closed. "This plane had to have some sort of tracker... or something, right?"

"A beacon..." he answered, his voice flat. "Normally, I'd say 'yes'. But given what's happened, I would say that's unlikely."

"Pardon my lack of protocol, Mr. President... but what the Hell does that mean?" she asked with sharp tongue.

"We'll talk later... but we've got other, more important issues," he dismissed after a brief pause. "First... it's rather warm now, but it gets a little chilly at night in the desert, so we're going to have to find some protection. Blankets. Maybe a way to start a fire."

She nodded.

"And..." he continued, and then hesitated, "...we need to get as far away from this crash site as possible. Quickly."

Magenta's eyes widened. "What? Away? Are you serious? They'll never find us... if they come looking, that is."

"Magenta..." said Stroud, his tone more serious as he locked eyes with her. "There are a lot of people... undesirables... that aren't exactly fans of mine."

She blinked in incomprehension, her brow furrowed.

"What do you think those types would do if they came across the President of the URA, helpless in a desert?"

Magenta looked out at the desert around her, having known the potential dangers of being part of the President's staff - but never to this extent.

"When civilization breaks down, there are many who would not hesitate to stab at the heart of this Republic." His forecast was as ominous as she could have imagined.

"So what do we do?" she asked. "You're in no shape to move anywhere on your own, and I have no idea where we are or how to get any help."

"You're going to have to drag me. At least out of sight of this wreckage, and somewhere where we can keep an eye on it in case someone does show up looking for us."

Magenta raked her hand through her blood-matted hair and sighed in exasperation. She scanned the surrounding desert with a hollow gaze. "If I do this for you, you promise you'll tell me what's going on here?" Her exasperation was growing.

He nodded.

An hour later

Magenta fell into a sitting position, releasing the heavy blanket on which the President sat, having dragged him several hundred meters to the other side of a nearby rock formation.

The sun had begun to sink in the western sky, projecting its grand palette through refracted rays at the edge of the horizon.

"I knew you could do it, Magenta," the President said. He cast a broken smile of approval.

Magenta shook her head. "I suppose I should go back and gather some supplies and food."

"Great idea. The sooner we get a fire started the better off we'll be."

"And then... we've got some talking to do," she added with newfound fortitude, making stern eye contact with him, before she disappeared down the embankment next to the rocks.

Thirty minutes later

Magenta plodded into the makeshift campsite, another blanket stuffed full of food and drink from the galley, and a few miscellaneous items packed into a small tin case under her arm. She let the blanket drop with a soft thud a few meters from Stroud, put her hands on her hips and stared out into the golden sunset.

"There's a road about fifty meters that way." She pointed to the northwest. "Any idea where it leads?"

He wagged his head. "We're somewhere either in the Sonoran or Mojave, but a road anywhere at this point would be a good thing. But I'm afraid I'm in no condition to travel."

"Then we'll just have to keep our eyes... and ears peeled for anyone passing by." She began to rummage through the blanket of supplies.

The President sighed.

"I wouldn't count on that, either," he said lightly.

Magenta remained silent, pulling out an extra blanket and draping it over a nearby bush. "Shelter from the sun," she informed him, as if instructing a survival class, once again picking items from the blanket sack.

"I'd say necessity breeds ingenuity... but you look like you've had experience with extreme conditions."

She ignored the comment, shaking her head with tightened lips.

"I'm going to go stand by the road for a while, maybe someone will come by." She turned away from him and stepped onto a small path into the twilight.

Several weeks later

Dusk once again arrived on the doorstep of their little section of nowhere. The small campfire crackled with yellow flame, licking its wood fuel in the silence of the approaching night.

Magenta, on a return trip from her latest foraging effort, alit from the path and into the glare of the modest fire.

The President, sitting up, his legs forced into an awkward straightness in front of him, smiled as she approached with an armful of dried bush.

"There's my little warrior." He partook of a small bite of meat, that of a snake that she had caught previously. "You never did tell me how you are so adept at survival."

"I don't have personal experience. But my Babu... grandfather," she began to explain, "he would always tell me and my siblings about the time during the wars in Africa."

The President nodded and looked away.

"After the Americas formed the URA," she continued without focusing on him, "many of the individual republics on the continent started heavier infighting - much worse than had already been present... as I'm sure you know."

She glanced at him to gauge his reaction. His eyes twinkled with the new light of the campfire, her creation from a pile of dry bush and a lighter from the small kit. He pursed his lips with a slight up curl of one side.

"The warring factions in their homeland of Nigeria cut off all access to the Atlantic ports, and thus all food and needed supplies for those living in the northern villages," she explained.

Magenta stuffed the small device back into the tin and closed the lid; she sat down onto the grassy sand and admired her handy work.

"If they wanted anything, or just wanted to escape, they had to travel up and into the Sahara, then over into neighboring provinces. He spent a lot of time with many of his friends and neighbors trekking through extreme conditions just for a basket of food or a barrel of water."

"Brave souls," the President said.

She nodded.

"They eventually left, and were one of the lucky few that were allowed entry into the URA before they... we... closed our doors to immigration for good," she added.

Magenta stared at the flames for a few moments in thought. She finally turned to face him.

"So tell me, Mr. President. What really happened here? Why did the most sophisticated aircraft in the world crash land in the desert with no warning. My suspicions tell me it wasn't an accident." Her eyes pierced his.

He hesitated, bundling the blanket up around his shoulders. The wind whistled through the campfire, making it sputter.

"It depends on how much you believe in conspiracy theory... government cover-ups and the like," he said after a long, uncomfortable silence.

"Three weeks ago I was boarding Golden Eagle One with seventy-one other co-workers in Lima. Now, I'm sitting here in the middle of a desert and there are only two of us left. You tell me what I should believe... sir." The disdain in her voice was overt.

"I... we... were misinformed, Magenta. Betrayed. By one of our own," Stroud answered in deliberate cadence, his eye contact lacking. "We knew about the solar flare, but we were misled about the severity... and more importantly, the timing."

"A solar flare caused this?" she asked, the surprise in her tone noticeable.

Stroud nodded. "But obviously much worse than what we had anticipated... or were told."

"But if a plane like Golden Eagle One could have been taken down by... oh my God." Magenta covered her mouth with sudden realization. "Regular commercial planes must have..." She stifled the comment with her hand.

"Anything that relies on electronics would have either malfunctioned to a great degree... or would have been destroyed outright. I can't even begin to imagine what's going on out there right now." The President scanned the dark horizon.

"We knew about it... wasn't there anything that could have been done?"

Stroud wrenched his lips and looked down at the ground in thought. "The projection was that this wasn't supposed to happen for another twenty-four months. Why anyone would have lied about that timeline..." He trailed off, obviously in deep pensivity.

He cleared his throat and renewed his gaze, a weak smile on his face. "But they did. We had a contingency scenario in play that would have assured the continuity of not only the government but..."

Before he could continue his explanation, the roar of a retro-bike filled the night air.

Magenta's eyes brightened. She craned her neck to spy the road.

"That's the first vehicle I've heard since we crashed..." She hopped to her feet and gawked out at the highway.

"Definitely not one that would be looking for us. Magenta... remember," Stroud cautioned in a heightened whisper, "...keep our identities a secret at all costs!"

She nodded her hesitation at the request, turned her back to him.

The rumble of the bike's motor grew closer. After a moment of exchanged glances between the pair of lone survivors, the bike stopped out on the road just at the end of the path. Its motor shut off. The desert became silent once again.

"Magenta... come sit back down, we don't know what they want. Let's not make it seem like we're waiting for them," Stroud ordered.

"We're *not* waiting for them?" she asked confusedly, taking her place across the fire from Stroud.

He jabbed her with a cold stare. They sat in silence.

The serenity of the desert night magnified the sudden sound of footsteps in the dry grass outside of their campsite. Suddenly, a shorter man, tattooed arms protruding from the sleeves of his worn leather jacket, stepped from the darkness, beyond a set of cacti that lined the campsite and separated it from the road.

"Hola," the man said in a thick Colombian accent, his eyes squinted in suspicion.

The moonlight shined off the side of his head to reveal a shaved portion. A thin mane of black hair trailed down the back of his skull.

"What are you doing out here?" He stopped and stared at the sight before him. "Don't see many people camping out this far into this area."

"Not so much camping out as stranded," Stroud offered surprisingly. "Our plane went down a few weeks back..."

Magenta's eyes saucered. She could not believe the President was about to blow their cover - after he had warned her specifically not to. She glared through the fire at him.

Without missing a beat, or making eye contact with her, he continued his story with the mysterious stranger.

"Twin engine private charter, lost the engines and navigation. I was able to glide it most of the way down, but snagged a mesa about two kilometers that way," he explained, pointing in the opposite direction of where Golden Eagle One had gone down.

"Lots of planes went down," the man replied. "But you're still out here?"

"Well, I was... seriously injured... my legs. We were hoping to either get lucky and have someone happen along, or wait until I was healed enough to hike one way or the other on the road to civilization."

The stranger eyed Magenta as he spoke to Stroud. "At least you get to be stranded with a pretty lady, that's always a good place to be..." A sickening smirk formed at the corner of his lips.

"Yes... well," the President answered, sensing the rising tension, "my name is John, and you are?"

The man darted his eyes to the sides, then down at the fire, and then approached Stroud with his hand outstretched.

"Juan Carlos," he said gruffly. "But you can call me Trujillo."

Stroud shook his hand and made strong eye contact, to which Trujillo squinted at him and tilted his head. He released the handshake.

"And this is Maria, my... assistant," Stroud continued, smiling coyly over at Magenta, before turning his attention back to Trujillo. "Please, sit with us. We have plenty to eat, thanks to her amazing skills." He chuckled.

Without a smile, Trujillo nodded his acknowledgment to Magenta and sat down on the sandy earth next to the fire.

"So tell me... Trujillo... what is it that you do that brings you out here?" Magenta asked, refusing to avert her eyes from studying the man's facial expressions.

After another long, hard stare at Stroud, Trujillo broke eye contact with him and then glared out of the corner of his eye at Magenta. "Passing through on my way up to Vegas. I seen a lot of plane crash sites over the past few weeks, and with what's goin' on I always stop to... take a look."

"So you're a scavenger..." The disdain dripped from Magenta's words.

"Maria..." Stroud scolded lightly.

"You do what you have to in order to survive," Trujillo growled at Magenta.

"You have family in Vegas, Trujillo?" Stroud asked.

Trujillo shook his head and stared into the fire. "I lost my family..." The light behind his eyes escaped on a far journey.

"Oh, I'm sorry," Stroud offered. "Because of the... disaster?"

Trujillo sneered and shook his head again. "I used to be a soldier once."

Stroud's eyes locked onto a tattoo on Trujillo's arm in the light of the flickering flames – a Greek Epsilon character ensconced between two brandished swords. "An Epsilon, I see..." He stared down at the ground in reflection of his own past.

"Then I lost it all fightin' someone else's war," Trujillo continued, still not making eye contact. The intensity of his voice rose with each word. "Got injured. Discharged. Then the fat cats up in Boulder decided to get greedy and cut off my benefits. My wife left me. Took my little girl with her."

Trujillo growled deep in his chest. To their horror, he extracted a knife from a hidden sheath on his ankle, and with a swift motion skewered a piece of snake from the fire. He ripped the smoking meat with his teeth and chewed as if a ravenous animal.

Stroud and Magenta exchanged glances in the silence.

Trujillo glared at Stroud.

"You ever have to take another man's life, John?" he asked Stroud pointedly.

Stroud shook his head, unsure where the conversation was headed.

"When it's war it's your job as a soldier. But it's different when you have to do it to keep yourself alive in the real world, eh amigo?" Trujillo cooed with smooth confidence. He placed another piece of meat on his tongue with the knife blade. "What do you do... John?"

Stroud cleared his throat and smiled at Trujillo.

"I'm an investment banker." Stroud smiled sheepishly at Magenta and continued his story. "We were heading to Dallas for a meeting when… well, the disaster happened."

"All your money couldn't save you from this, could it?" Trujillo asked.

Stroud pursed his lips, trying hard to keep the conversation positive.

"Now you know how it feels to be on this side." Trujillo fell silent. He sipped water from a cup that Magenta had handed him. "John… you look a lot like *him*."

The President's face flushed. "*Him*?"

"Yeah, you know… the head honcho. El numero uno – El Presidente." Trujillo stared daggers into Stroud's eyes.

Stroud emitted a nervous chuckle. "I get that a lot, actually. Used to use it as a party gag."

Trujillo squinted, nodding his head with a subtle inquisitiveness behind his eyes. "I've got a bike with room for one person, if you want to get out of here," he said finally.

"I don't think I can ride with my legs the way they are."

Magenta casually stood and leaned over to tuck a portion of Stroud's blanket under his legs. The President glared at her for a second, and then back over at Trujillo. Unsure if Trujillo had spotted the presidential logo emblazoned on the center of the fabric, she sat down on the other side of the fire and continued eating her dinner as if nothing was out of place.

"I guess it's me and the girl then," Trujillo hissed, placing a firm hand on Magenta's knee.

Magenta recoiled and pushed his hand away. "I'm not leaving John," she said in a sharp rebuff.

Trujillo snorted and pushed himself to his feet. "Have it your way then." He turned to Stroud with his hands on his hips. "I have access to a cargo truck. Retro type, you know. I can bring it out here tomorrow and get you and your girl back to safety if you want."

"I – we - would appreciate that," Stroud answered with a friendly nod.

"Ok then," Trujillo replied, turning to walk into the darkness. "I'll be back around noon tomorrow."

Trujillo's footsteps faded, replaced by the firing of his bike, and subsequent roar of the motor off into the distance.

Magenta glared at the President. "Are you sure you trust this guy?"

He bowed his head in thoughtful reflection. "Being in my position, you are trained not to trust anyone. But we don't have much choice. We're running out of supplies, and... my legs. I can't move them," he said in a quiet reveal, looking down with a somber gaze at the blanket covering him.

"Oh..." Magenta nodded her head in agreement of the plan.

"But if we stick together, we'll be fine." Reassuming his stoic role, he allowed his stern voice to be his reassurance.

She nodded again.

A few hours later

Magenta rolled to her side and stared into the night sky.
Damn.
She pushed herself to her feet.

Stroud, without speaking, raised an eyebrow at her from within the blankets bundled around him.

"Nature calls..." she said with a smirk. "I'm going to go and... well, use the cactus, I guess."

The President flashed a smile and closed his eyes.

The wind howled around the edges of a nearby rock formation. The campfire popped with an airy hiss, the latest batch of dry brush glowing a toasty yellow.

A twig snapped behind him. Stroud opened his eyes. Magenta was not back yet. He sat up and pricked his ears.

Suddenly, the cold steel of a blade pierced his ribcage from the back. Stroud's jaw froze open as the air fled his lungs, leaving him speechless except for a gurgle that spluttered from his lips.

Trujillo leaned over Stroud's shoulder with a sickening sneer.

"Your people came to my village looking for soldiers. We enlisted and fought your wars. I spilled my blood for your greed. You took away my family. You took away my life," he said with a guttural snarl. "Now, you know how it feels when I take away *your* life."

Stroud reached forward in a desperate attempt to crawl away from Trujillo, but the disgruntled attacker wrenched the weapon in farther and upward. He turned the handle and ripped the seven-inch blade through Stroud's chest and into his heart.

Magenta gasped.

Trujillo flung his glare towards the darkness ahead.

Magenta covered her mouth in terror at the sight before her.

Trujillo extracted the blade from Stroud's back in a spurt of crimson. Stroud fell forward, lifeless. Trujillo quickly stood and stalked the sand at Magenta, blade at his side.

"No, no, no!" Magenta cried in fear, turning to sprint away into the pitch.

Trujillo gave pursuit, entering a moonlit clearing between a grouping of brush and cacti. He stopped and scanned the darkness - Magenta had disappeared. He snorted an evil chuckle and turned away.

Magenta, hidden in a prone position just over a small embankment behind some bushes, peered into the clearing from her hiding spot. Her breath came short and heavy; her body quivered from shock. From her vantage point, Trujillo's feet were just visible, walking away and back towards the path to the campsite. To her left, the back end of the retro bike gleamed in the silvery moon, parked on the dirt next to the dark road that led away through the desert.

She stole a final glance at the road. Knowing she had only one chance at escape, she leapt to her feet and darted into the clearing. Within a meter of the bike, another man, larger than Trujillo and emitting a rancid body odor, eclipsed her path and stopped her with one forceful hand around her neck. He pulled her close to him; she flailed her arms to free herself.

"Lookie here," he grunted, an evil grin occupying the bottom third of his stubbled face.

"Let me go!" Magenta screamed, her voice strained from the man's giant hand to her throat.

"Put her down, amigo," Trujillo's voice commanded.

The man released Magenta and glared past her in surprise.

Trujillo stalked like a rabid wolf towards them, hissing with laughter, stretching his arms over his head in triumph. The other man moved backward and leaned on the bike, watching the proceedings with a sick smile. He ran his grease-black hands through his oily hair.

"You can have her when I'm done," Trujillo instructed, keeping his eyes on his prey.

Magenta stumbled and turned to run. Trujillo deftly jumped and grabbed her hair from behind, yanked her to the ground in front of him. He fell on top of her and began to nuzzle her neck, groping her with both hands.

"No! Get off me!" she yelled in a panic.

The other man snarled a perverse laugh, watching her struggle underneath Trujillo – seemingly not a new activity for the pair.

"Please... please... don't. I'll give you anything you want, just please... *no*," she pleaded.

"You had your chance to go with me, my collita negra," Trujillo snarled with angry passion.

She held her hands away from him, recoiling at the hot slobber dripping from his mouth onto her neck. She whimpered and turned her head away, closing her eyes and hoping that it was all a bad dream.

"Besides, you know how long it's been since I had a primo chica like you, huh?" He nuzzled his mouth from the base of her neck and down to the sweaty flesh between her breasts.

Magenta instinctively pounded both palms against his ears, making him growl and roll off her, holding his own hands against his head. Before he could react, she seized the knife from the sheath around his ankle and drove it into his crotch.

Trujillo howled in pain and curled into a fetal position. The other man, dumbfounded by the fact that she had bested the wily Colombian, leapt forward from his resting position against the bike and stormed at her.

Just two steps into his approach, she yanked the gun from Trujillo's pocket, turned and fired three quick shots into the other man's chest and neck. Blood spattered onto her face from the impact like a popping water balloon; the man stumbled backward onto the dirt with a thud, dead.

Shaking from the shock of the sudden attack, Magenta dropped the gun and scrambled backward on her hands until she bumped against a cactus. She shakily pushed herself to her feet and stumbled up the path towards the campsite.

She stopped as she reached its edge. It was too late.

President Devlin Stroud lay forward in a growing pool of his own dark blood, his face bent forward. The flickering of the dying campfire highlighted his cold, dead stare. As if in a final plea, his pale arm stretched outward to her.

Magenta held her hand against her mouth to hold back the instinct to vomit, and forced her eyes shut. She only had precious seconds to get to the bike before Trujillo might have a chance to recover. She whispered in a broken cry "*I'm so sorry.*"

She spun, sprinted down the path, hopped onto the bike, fired the motor and roared off into the desert blackness.

5:
Diary of a Madman

Las Vegas, Nevada - Late December, 2076

James Muldoon stood on the observation platform, the determination pressed on his patient face like a tailored suit. He glanced at his wrist-holo for the time, watching a tube car jet past into another tunnel out of sight, on its way to a distant city.

The MagnaRail - or 'Tubes' as they came to be known - were a multi-city hub of underground pneumatic tunnels that allowed high-speed travel between the east and west coasts of the URA. While not as glamorous as air travel, it did offer the opportunity for chance meetings such as today.

His partner, McGintry, leaned back on the railing, toked at a cigarette and studied the opposite direction.

"What'r we waitin fer?" McGintry's Scottish was thick as frozen gravy.

"Oh, the young McGintry. So full of questions," Muldoon replied, his own accent a smooth Irish. He tapped the railing in an uneven rhythm.

"It jes seems like an outta the way place te do business. Someone from outta town, yah?"

"Nothing gets by you, my young friend."

He glanced at McGintry, who was still staring with intense eyes at him. "If you must know," Muldoon added, "we have a government official making a visit."

McGintry raised his eyebrows. "Now why would we be seein' someone like that?"

"A deal," Muldoon said.

McGintry tossed his smoke, snuffed it with a boot heel, and then pointed an angry digit at Muldoon. "Are ye daft? Ye know that the Royals don' deal with the Feds!"

"Daft? No. I would say I'm... determined," Muldoon replied, a blind eye to McGintry's outrage. "This organization has always been one step behind in becoming truly world class. It's time to change that."

McGintry snorted and propped his hands on his hips, stared at Muldoon.

"It's time for a changing of the guard," Muldoon hissed. "It's time to sever the head of this shortsighted group."

The round face of his partner grew ever crimson; without turning to face him, Muldoon grinned.

"We will single-handedly usher in a new paradigm for the Royals, McGintry. Whether they want it or not." He smiled coyly. The latest tube whizzed by in a blur, wisping a single clump of hair across his forehead. The rest of his mane, slick and black, coiled behind him.

The Royals considered themselves kings among men, never offering a doubt as to their namesake. One would be hard pressed to find a facet of life without their elusive fingerprint stamped within the framework. Their connections ran deep: gambling, banks, law enforcement just to name a few. The genius of their operation, however, lay in their deliberate aversion to mixing their hand in government. It was this internal law that kept them away from federal prosecution, and with the formation of the United Republic of the Americas in the late Twenties, each territory managed their own law enforcement independent and sovereign to the federal government. A perfect storm.

While racketeering and money laundering had kept their organization running rich for many years, the gradual switch to a credit based system - one that was overseen by the federal Republic - was the storm on the horizon, and the organization brass were too stubborn to see the light bearing down on them in the tunnel.

"I'm not gonna let ye do that, James!" McGintry grabbed Muldoon's jacket with a ham fist.

Muldoon glanced down at the Scot's pink flesh, and then shot a vicious glare at him. "Perhaps a retraction is in order, McGintry," he said with smoothness. "You'll be the first I kill."

A chill traveled McGintry's spine. Muldoon's cold, black eyes stared through his soul. He released the Irishman.

Muldoon calmly brushed off the shoulder of his jacket. "Don't ever touch me again." He once again leaned onto the railing.

A tall, balding man in an overcoat approached them. Muldoon turned his head to look at the man with what amounted to casual disinterest.

"Stand back and watch how business is done."

"Are you the contact?" the man asked in a hushed strain, glancing around the nearly empty terminal and not making eye contact with the pair of Royals.

"Aye," Muldoon replied. "And you must be the Honorable Mr. Gates." He glanced at the man's empty hands. "It appears you don't have what you agreed to bring."

"I have something better. All you'll need," Gates answered. He reached into his jacket pocket and extracted a small, plastic object somewhat tinier than a playing card. He held his palm out to Muldoon with the card laying flat upon it.

"And what is this?" Muldoon asked.

"Root codes," Gates replied. His eyes shrunk to tiny black buttons.

Muldoon tilted his head without responding.

"For creation of credits. Unlimited credits."

Muldoon bared his teeth. "The deal was that you would give us ten billion credits."

"Credits that could easily be deactivated by the Feds," Gates said with a condescending frown. He broke his glare with Muldoon and scanned the platform, flinching at the sound of his voice echoing against the concrete walls. "This will allow you to create them without oversight. Or ability to track."

Muldoon's eyebrow rose as if a Heavenly fishhook had suddenly called it. He faced McGintry, tucking the card into his inner pocket.

"You see, McGintry... *paradigm*," he cooed. He shoved at Mcgintry's chest, causing the larger man to fall backward over the railing and land roughly onto one of the magnetic rails below. One of the departing tube cars struck him and dragged his body into the tunnel beyond.

Muldoon fixed the sleeves of his jacket, his face sporting a satisfied grin.

"What... you... sick bastard! Why did you do that?" Gates yelped, looking down in horror at the crimson stain where McGintry landed, then around the platform for any witnesses.

No one had noticed - or if they had, they were not reacting.

"Relax, my friend. It's not your blood lubricating the walls of the Tubes."

The man bit his lip in momentary terror and closed his eyes. Sweat rolled down his pale forehead.

"Let me ask you," Muldoon said. "What drove you to make such a lucrative deal?"

Gates wiped the moisture from his brow with a noticeably shaky hand, tucked the handkerchief into his pocket. "Parity..." His voice wavered. He leaned one hand on the rail, suddenly feeling the need to grip something tangible.

"Parity... indeed," Muldoon replied with a slight nod.

"But let's not pretend that it isn't because of your family's... power," Gates added with a snip, glaring with disgust at Muldoon.

Muldoon chuckled under his breath and looked past Gates. "Sometimes family comes in handy, aye?"

Gates frowned and looked away. "Just leave me out of this..."

"Then here's to your parity," Muldoon squawked. He rotated away from Gates with a gracefulness that would have made a ballerina jealous.

"I never got your name," Gates said.

Muldoon stopped, turned back to face him. "The wind."

"The wind?" Gates parroted in confusion.

"For your purposes, I came and went. I am the wind, and that is all you will ever need to know." Muldoon nodded, and then disappeared onto the exit ramp.

Several days later

The stadium roared, its foundations trembling with the zealous stomps of the fans. The local hero, a cybernetically-enhanced outfielder on the verge of setting a new record for home runs - and most balls destroyed in a single season - had just come up to bat and fouled off several pitches, before crushing the final offering over the fence some 200 meters away.

While still considered a sport by definition, baseball had become a game of the haves and have-nots. The haves were those that could afford the latest implants that would allow them to clear walls of even the most incredulous heights. The have-nots were the stalwarts, hoping that the once grand tradition would somehow find its way back to the limelight. Since the deregulation of performance enhancements, and the introduction of cybernetic implants, the outfield fences had been raised ten meters as well as moved back an additional 80. However, that only posed a temporary challenge. The implant manufacturers only needed a short amount of development turnaround to get past the latest limitations. More than ever, it had officially become a sport for the gambling industry, yet the crowds still flooded the gates to watch the spectacle.

That was not the only draw this afternoon. Underneath the stadium in a hollowed arena, hundreds gathered to take in an entirely different event. Due to the enclosed area, the noise level matched that of the stadium above tenfold. The smoky air in the space sweltered, the hint of spicy fumes coating the crowd's nostrils. The fans chanted their taunts or approvals, their t-shirts stained with sweat.

The match, one that offered the game of chance for the gambler, as well as the thrill of pure, human athleticism to all fans alike, drew everyone's attention to the small, clay ring at the center of the arena.

All but two, that is.

James Muldoon sat with his back to the goings-on, his chin rested on a fist, his expression displaying his utter lack of interest in the event.

"James, you really should watch this. This guy's in rare form tonight!" Guelph, his boss, who sat across from him, said with a juvenile enthusiasm and a nasally overtone. He pounded his fist on the table and shouted along with the rest of the crowd. Slimy sweat dripped from beneath the mottled mop atop his forehead. The light of the battle arena cast his skin in a strangely appropriate pink hue.

Muldoon rubbed the tips of his fingers against his suit jacket and rolled his eyes. "Barbarism is seldom rare." He placed his drink to his lips.

Behind him, in the arena center, and the focus of the raucous crowd, stood two men abreast of each other in crouched positions. Like two snarling tigers, each waved a shiny, hooked dagger at his opponent, slowly circling opposite the other.

One of the men took the offense, lunging forward with his weapon. The other, sitting back in anticipation of the attack, parried with his own knife, swept his opponent with an ankle hook and jumped past him. The first man fell to the ground.

The crowd erupted.

Before the first could recover, or even turn over, the second drove his dagger between the other's shoulder blades. The crowd leapt to their feet, their ear-splitting shouts reverberating off the stone walls of the underground coliseum. The second man, victorious even if it was due to an illegal move, raised his arms above his head and incited the mob to frenzy. The medics, fumbling through the chaos, knelt and tended to the fallen contender.

As if a droplet in the sea of emotion around him, Guelph stood and shook his fist, pounded it on the table once again. "Incredible! Any wonder why he packs the house every week?" he shouted with glee.

Muldoon sighed aloud, gritted his teeth. "Can we talk business now. Or is this all about... the *games*?" he asked with an eye roll and dismissive hand gesture.

Guelph smiled, shoveled a forkful of cheese-laden pasta into his mouth, and then followed by wedging half a dinner roll into his cherubic cheeks. "I thought you Micks were into this fightin' thing," he mumbled, spitting pieces of bread onto the table.

"Some of us have evolved." Muldoon wrinkled his nose as he stared at the glutton in front of him.

"You're one of a kind, Muldoon," Guelph said with a grin and a headshake. He wiped his mouth on the tablecloth and motioned to an attendant passing by. "Give me ten-to-one odds that he takes an arm off next match and you've got a wager!" Guelph barked to the man, who stopped, looked over at another standing against the wall.

After a subtle nod from the bookie's bank, the attendant reached in to shake Guelph's hand. "You have yourself a bet, Mr. Gwaleffi!" He released from the agreement handshake and disappeared into the elbow-to-elbow crowd.

Guelph gleefully chuckled and picked up his fork. He darted his eyes to Muldoon. "Great job on that *acquisition*, James."

Muldoon ground his teeth together.

"You sure it's gonna work out?" Guelph paused before piling another load of pasta into his gullet. Red sauce sloppily hung from his cleft chin.

"One can never be assured of anything, but for a wagering man such as yourself," Muldoon began, but Guelph had lost focus when the crowd bellowed it's disapproval of the disqualification of the last match due to a rules infraction.

"Damn refs!" he shouted, standing up from the table and shaking his fist in furious protest along with the rest of the fanatical crowd.

Muldoon raised his voice above the din of the crowd. "When can we see... *him*?"

Guelph blinked at Muldoon, dropped himself into his chair and leaned over his food. "You need to relax, Muldoon," he said with another mouthful of bread, overjoyed with his afternoon of watching the barbarism of the sub-games.

Muldoon maintained his cold gaze across the table.

Guelph slugged back the frothy ale in his mug and wiped his mouth on the tablecloth once more. After a table-rattling belch, he extracted a small, white stick of UberWhite - which resembled a piece of chalk - from his jacket pocket. Guelph pulverized the chunk between two of his sausage-like digits, pressed the gritty powder into his nostrils and inhaled.

For the next 30 seconds, Muldoon watched his boss's eyes roll around in his head. Guelph flopped back into his chair, drool forming at the corner of the portly man's mouth. Then, as if responding to an unseen click of a switch, he sat upright, opened his eyes and brushed away the milky residue around his nose.

"I'll take you up to him now, then," he said in a lower tone. "But watch your mouth."

Muldoon's lip curled upwards.

Moments later, the elevator doors squawked open, revealing the dingy inner car that had brought the two men some ten stories upward into the stadium. Guelph stepped out first, followed like a cat by Muldoon, whom remained to the rear his boss. The Irishman strolled with a hidden purpose behind his mask of obedience, waving away the foul stench from the elevator car.

The sweet aroma of spice hung in the closed space of the luxury skybox. Three men sat in a semi-arc around a glass table near the front window, which offered a near-birds-eye-view of the baseball game going on below. A translucent, blue billow hovered like a storm cell just below the ceiling - both men had no option but to inhale upon entering the room.

Each of the men around the table took turns puffing from their hooka tubes, their thin trails of smoke chugging upward like a trio of antique locomotives.

"Mr. Gwaleffi," the center of the three said without turning, having picked up Guelph's reflection in the windowpane ahead, "we've been expecting you."

The man lifted a hand in the air beside him and snapped once. Behind Guelph and Muldoon, a mammoth guard shoved the door shut and placed his hulking mass in front of it. His twin, smaller in stature but still gigantic by any relative nature, stood alongside of him with his arms folded menacingly across his chest.

Muldoon eyed the lesser of the two titans, whom twitched his eyes towards him and then away.

"Mr. Rayjami," Guelph said with a soft respect, bowing several times. Visible sweat beads flopped from his forehead like greasy raindrops.

Rayjami slowly rotated his chair to face the two men, the hooka tube still pinched between his lips. He sent a small ring of smoke out from one nostril, pulled the tube from his mouth. The other two men, as if by silent command, turned their chairs in unison and sat in quiet observation, puffing away while staring at Muldoon.

"I've looked over the materials you brought to me," Rayjami said without expression. For as deep as his Moroccan accent seemed, his articulation of the English language held Guelph's skittish respect.

Guelph sniggered nervously, wringing his hands in front of his belt buckle. "Sir, I can... um... explain."

Rayjami held his hand up to silence the rotund Guelph. "Brilliance," he said from the side of his mouth, sucking once again on the hooka.

"Th-thank you, sir," Guelph stammered. He held out a hand towards Muldoon. "He... procured it for me... us... you."

Rayjami floated his eyes towards Muldoon.

"But I asked him to... it was my idea... sir," Guelph added. A bit of drool squirted from the corner of his mouth.

Muldoon raised an eyebrow and titled his head at Guelph. His skin tightened around his eyes, but he remained silent.

"Very good, Mr. Gwaleffi. We knew you had the meddle to be one our upper echelon," Rayjami cooed, taking his eyes from Muldoon after a long, deliberate stare. "Congratulations."

Muldoon bit at his tongue and pushed his slick, black hair back over his head.

Guelph stepped forward, extended his hand to accept his boss's congratulatory gesture. After a few moments of nauseating sycophancy, Muldoon cleared his throat.

"Mr. Muldoon..." Rayjami began.

"James... call him James," Guelph corrected with a sneer.

"Mmm, yes," Rayjami sighed. "You may go now. Your new Regional will contact you shortly." As a conciliatory gesture, he tossed a bag of coins at Muldoon's feet. "Enjoy the games... on us," he said with a dismissive tone.

Muldoon offered a brief, if not disrespectful, nod towards Rayjami. He glared at Guelph with stabbing contempt before turning on a heel towards the door of the elevator.

"And Mr. Muldoon," Rayjami called to him. "You would be wise to learn from a man like Gwaleffi, here. Study him. His example is what advances you in this organization."

"Aye..." Muldoon snarled from the corner of his mouth, turned and entered the elevator.

Las Vegas, Nevada - October 24, 2077

"Are you certain that they have no power?" Muldoon forcefully pushed himself past the throngs of people milling about beside the roadway. Empty cars, stalled, sat on the jammed thoroughfare.

"Yes, boss," Turk answered, keeping stride with Muldoon as best he could, despite his diminutive stature and smaller step. His inflection matched his nickname. "The whole city's out!"

"Then we don't have much time. Are all the pieces in place?" Muldoon determinately made his way towards the rising structure at the end of the Strip.

"Yes... we're good to go!" Turk confirmed.

"Good. Go meet up with the others and tell them to wait for my word. We only have one shot at success, Turk. Don't let me down." The Irishman patted Turk on the shoulder and increased his gait until he was out of sight.

Twenty minutes later

Muldoon pushed open the door to the hotel suite and stepped inside with a casual stride.

"Muldoon," Rayjami said with surprise, several others standing with him turning abruptly to face the door, "this is not a good time..."

"If you spend your life waiting for the proper moment, the proper moments will fall to those that refuse to wait." Muldoon stepped to the center of the room and crossed his palms in front of him.

"What do you *want*, James?" Guelph demanded, wiping his brow on the sleeve of his sweat-stained dress shirt.

Muldoon, without as much as an eye blink, raised his right arm and fired three razor-finned rounds from a matte black weapon. As the hissing of the armament abated, Guelph bellowed and fell face-first onto the floor, grasping at his shattered knee.

Rayjami, seldom to ever show emotion, turned his eyes down at Guelph, then back to Muldoon. "What kind of weapon is this?" His eyes glowed, as if in admiration of some new toy.

Muldoon snorted. He flung the weapon onto the floor in front of Rayjami.

"A piece that I designed myself. A Ripper would be a good name for it. Amazing what it can do for a migraine."

Rayjami nodded with a raised eyebrow. "And I assume this is your statement that you deserved a promotion over Mr. Gwaleffi here?" Rayjami did not break his cool demeanor.

"You stand at the precipice of a grand opportunity, yet you choose to turn a blind eye." Muldoon straightened his jacket, and produced a small rod from an inside pocket.

He rotated towards Guelph and pressed at the tip of the rod. A shiny platinum blade, twenty-five centimeters in length and ten wide, extended from its shaft. Muldoon swung high and hard, slashing downward at the back of Guelph's unprotected neck and cleaving his head cleanly from his shoulders.

"Swine begat swine!" Muldoon growled.

The men standing next to Rayjami recoiled in horror. Rayjami, projecting an eerie calm, snapped his fingers above him.

His twin bodyguards, Castor and Pollux Webb, appeared behind Muldoon as if a brutal magic trick. Both wore similar expressions of nauseating enjoyment, their mammoth grins allowing crooked sets of yellowed teeth to peek out between their swollen lips.

Rayjami nodded to the larger, Pollux.

Muldoon glided his head and glared at the behemoth.

"Finish them. Then meet me with the others," Muldoon ordered in a preemptive command, his tone cold and calculating.

Pollux's black eyes widened. Muldoon, silent, pursed his lips. Pollux spied Guelph's headless body sprawled out on the floor in a sickening puddle of violet. A gulp came from deep within his chest.

"Pol, you don't have to..." Castor said under his breath.

Muldoon glared at the lesser Webb twin.

"Sorry... Mr. Muldoon," Castor said. He lowered his eyes to the floor.

"Finish. Them," Muldoon said to Pollux. He grinned a vicious smile at Rayjami, rotated and breezed from the room.

5: DIARY OF A MADMAN

An hour later

Muldoon stood at the entry to the bottom of the stadium tunnel ramp. The sound of chanting echoed into the concrete hall. He straightened his jacket, flicked his hair back over his head, and put his chin to his shoulder, listening to the sound of heavy clanging footsteps on the stalled escalator behind him.

"Got here... as quick as we could, Mr. Muldoon," Castor panted. His larger brother stomped along beside him until they stopped a meter from Muldoon. The larger twin dropped a plastic sack on the ground with a damp thud.

"Is it done?" Muldoon asked. He closed his eyes and took a deep breath. He had already spotted the crimson stains on Pollux's shirt. His lip kinked a silent smile.

Pollux coughed. "Uh.. yeah..." he said in a broken voice.

"Speak up, Pollux!" Muldoon barked, still facing the tunnel entryway.

Pollux choked back what sounded like a whimper and cleared his throat again. "Yes, sir, Mr. Muldoon," he cried.

"Good," Muldoon replied, ignoring the strained emotion in Pollux's response. "Where are the trophies?"

Castor glanced concernedly at his brother.

Pollux sniffled, wiped his nose on his bloody shirt. "In the bag... Mr. Muldoon." He turned his back and began sobbing.

"Oh, snap out of it you blubbering buffoon!" Muldoon raked. "After the meeting, take them to the twenty-second floor, put them in the safe room." He knelt and submerged a hand into the sack.

A few moments later

Muldoon stepped from the dark tunnel, walked to the edge of the concrete gangway and stopped at the railing. On the field, three meters below him and stretching halfway to the next seating area, stood hundreds of men and women. They suddenly turned in unison to stare at Muldoon.

"You've been mistreated..." Muldoon began.

The group murmured. Muldoon's voice echoed in the void of the stadium seats.

"You've been misled..."

His words stoked the fires in their hearts.

"And you've been mistaken for a lot that places no stock in reward for loyalty." Muldoon scanned the crowd, leaned forward onto the rail with both hands. "That ends today. The Royals are no more..."

The volume of their comments swelled.

"The stale leadership that sat in their ivory towers has been pinched from the neck of this once great organization." He reached to the ground and hoisted an object into the air beside him.

The crowd noise silenced at the sight of Rayjami's severed head, its jaw agape and staring blankly out at them.

"From this day forth, this group. This... *Syndicate*... will lead the way." Muldoon lowered the trophy down to his side. "With your strengths, your contributions, your loyalty. We will emerge as the power to be reckoned with. Across this land and all others. And you will all share in that glory!" He thrust his arms out to the crowd.

For a moment, the stunned group of mercenaries looked upon their new leader with silent reserve. One of them stepped forward and raised his weapon to the air.

"Long live the Syndicate!" he roared in an Aussie bend, squeezed the trigger and released a long volley of fire upward. The others followed suit, filling the empty stadium with an ear-splitting cascade of celebratory gunfire.

Muldoon stood back a step and surveyed. He patted the gaunt cheek of Rayjami's cold, dripping head and dropped it into the sack. A fulfilled smile crossed his lips.

6:
The Night Watchman

Rural Western Pennsylvania - September 2079

Holt Alverson crouched and stared into the dirt. An early September coolness crept about the trees and blew through the ponytail at the back of his head. He ignored the breeze, but could not ignore the telltale scent of autumn on the wind.

He rolled the sleeves on his green flannel and lightly fingered the rope trap lying on the ground. Holt squinted at the absence of the bait that usually sat in the center.

I'll be damned.

He ran his fingers through the dirt beside him, tossed it back on the ground and scanned the bare forest around him.

Holt could very easily recount the slim number of animals that had actually neared his trap in the two years since the Event: an emaciated rabbit that had happened to unluckily trip on the rope and hanged itself, and Holt, once forgetting the exact location and finding himself flung upside-down, having to wait for his wife, Chelsea, to come to his rescue.

Now, for the third time in as many weeks, something had taken the salty, dried jerky that he had routinely used as bait - without springing the trap. Something, or rather someone, had been here.

The Alverson property, sprawling upon a massive 55 acres of wooded land, was far from any real neighbors, with the closest being old man Knight, whose farm was a good ten kilometers from the couple. Knight, like many others in the small town, had died the previous winter from lack of even the basic supplies.

Holt had always prided himself on being a 'prepper', and without feeling overly ghoulish, felt vindicated on that fateful day in '77. Like the proverbial ant, he had successfully stockpiled necessities while others went on about their daily routines. He had warned them of coming hardships to be brought on by government misdeeds, but most did not heed his predictions. While the reality that his fellow countrymen were perishing bothered and prodded his guilt to a small extent, the notion of someone unknown on his property worried him more. It was a rare occurrence when they would see anyone outside of the occasional traveler working their way west, and it had been a good six months since the last.

Chelsea Alverson drove the shovel blade into the dry earth with a grunt, stopped and wiped the sweat from her brow. She had made tilling the garden behind their home a weekly routine since the Event. The results were always negative, but she still went about her task with the faint hopes that someday the plants would return, perhaps a first sign of changing times.

"We got the prettiest dirt in the county, that's for sure," Holt said.

Chelsea grabbed a handful and tossed it at him.

"Good thing I saved up all those supplies," he added with a grin, hands on his waist. "If we had to rely on your garden to feed us, we'd be in trouble!"

Chelsea dropped the shovel, turned and playfully jabbed Holt in the midsection. She gazed at the results of her toils.

"Why do you keep trying?"

"Thought maybe if I keep working, it might prime the ground for growing or something," she replied with a sigh. Holt tried to hide his smirk, but could not. "I know, I'm no scientist. What's your take on it?"

Holt rubbed the stubble on his chin with the palm of his hand. He shook his head. "Groundwater contamination? I don't know..."

"Speaking of... looks like rain tonight, and the spout needs cleaning." She pointed to their makeshift rainwater collector at the corner of their roof.

Holt turned, nodded. "I'll get that after I check out the rest of the traps."

"How's the trapping going by the way, Mr. Big Game? Got us dinner yet?"

Holt wrapped his wife in a bear hug and nuzzled his lips into her honey colored hair. "Somethin's takin' the bait. Not sure what though."

"Poachers?"

"Taking jerky? Doubt it."

6: THE NIGHT WATCHMAN

A rustling in the bare tree a hundred meters to their left near a wandering stream drew their attention. A murder of crows took wing above the treetops, quickly darting westward across the rolling hills and out of sight.

Chelsea put her hand to her mouth and coughed deeply. Holt held her out to arms length.

"Catching cold?"

She shook her head. "Dampness bringing in something I think. I'll be alright." She grasped the shovel handle and continued working the earth.

Holt plucked the snips from his tool chest. He stopped and faced the steel door of his underground bunker, having caught sight of his prized lockbox in the far corner of the dimly lit room. More resembling an oversized metal armoire, it stood from floor to ceiling and stretched three meters in width. He shook his head, pursed his lips closed.

As he emerged from the double doors up onto the grass behind their home, Chelsea glanced over from the stoop of the porch.

"You alright?" She wiped the flushed skin of her pale forehead on her sleeve.

"Yeah..." he muttered, stomped past her towards the long driveway.

"Gotta let it go, Holt." Chelsea lowered her head onto the back of her hands.

"Can't," he answered in a short tone. "Just drop it."

"Maybe I would if every time you came out of there you didn't act like someone popped your birthday balloons."

Holt stopped, placed one hand on his hip. He sighed in frustration.

"Or maybe you could crank up the HAM and make use of the one thing that survived. Stop beating yourself up about the rest."

"How can I do that, Chels?" A sneer crawled across his face. "It's because I wasn't prepared that we're as bad off as we are."

"You didn't know anything was gonna happen! No one knew!" She sighed. "At least we're still alive..."

"No excuse." He shook his head. "Being prepared is being prepared. I shouldn't have had that stuff out of there when it happened."

"You were reorganizing things, refreshing your inventory. Don't blame yourself for something that you have no control over."

Chelsea pushed herself up from the step. She stumbled, caught herself on the rail, and sat back onto the porch with a thud.

"Chels? You ok?" Holt's voice raised in alarm.

She rubbed her head with one hand. "Too much sun today. I'll be alright."

"Why don't you go back in and lie down. I'm gonna go finish fixing the front fence." He helped Chelsea to her feet, rubbing her back with a loving caress. She stepped onto the porch and into the house.

He peered back at the bunker entrance, blinked with a shake of his head, hopped off the porch and made for the front of the property.

Grasping a length of wire with one hand, Holt snipped at the slack protruding through his fist, tied the remainder around the post. He stepped back to admire his handiwork, wiping the sweat from his brow with the back of his hand. A cool zephyr blowing through the bared trees across the road near the stagnant pond chilled his spine. Holt's heart leapt.

A man stood several meters behind him, a small leather pouch strung around his shoulder hung at his side. The setting sun glowed on his weather-beaten skin, a scar across his cheek raised in contrast like a wicked lightning bolt.

"Oh... hello," Holt said slowly, brow furrowed.

"Sorry, I didn't mean to startle you or nothin'," the man said with a thick drawl.

"That's ok," Holt answered, trying not to sound alarmed. He picked up the snipped wire remnants from the ground. "Just that we don't see many folks comin' down this road."

"You live here?" The man floated a keen eye around to what he could see of the Alverson homestead.

"Mm hmm," Holt mumbled. He glared out at the approaching clouds.

"Then you might know where the nearest town is?"

Holt lifted an arm, pointed to the wind in the road a hundred meters south. "Oil City's a few kilometers that way."

The stranger nodded, flipped his scraggly mane away from his eyes. "Much obliged," he said with a squint. He turned and walked away.

Holt stared after him for a moment, until a brief roll of thunder in the distance grabbed his attention.

"Don't think you're gonna make it there before the rain comes!" he shouted to the stranger, whom had already swiftly traveled ten meters down the road.

The stranger lifted his hand in the air, waved without turning back.

The rain rattled against the metal roof of the house like firecrackers in a bucket, the clatter echoing throughout the small, single story ranch. Chelsea, standing against the sink in the kitchen, dabbed a bloodstained piece of cloth against her red nose.

Nosebleeds had been something of a common occurrence for her as of late - a small annoyance that she had chalked up to the cold, dry air flowing in from the lake up north.

Holt, while having grown accustomed to seeing his wife dealing with the issue, worried nonetheless.

"Another one?" he asked, sipping sun brewed tea from a small mug as he stepped into the room.

"Who was that you were talking to earlier?"

He placed the empty mug into the sink behind Chelsea and turned from her. "Oh, no one. Just some guy passing through."

"Anyone we know?"

"No, thank goodness."

"What's that mean?"

"Don't trust 'im." Holt's tone had never changed when it came to strangers.

Chelsea snickered, tossed the cloth into the laundry bin by the door.

"Somethin' about him, can't place it. Doesn't seem right," Holt continued.

"Is there anyone you *do* trust?"

"Being too trusting is probably what got us all into this mess in the first place."

"You don't really believe that do you?"

Holt's stern face told her all she needed to know.

"So... what. You want it to be just the two of us left in the world? Some kind of reverse Adam and Eve?" She tried to pull back on the plunging dig, but it was too late.

"Don't start on the religious BS again, Chels," Holt huffed. He turned his back to grab the jacket from a hook on the wall.

"Oh my God!" Chelsea leapt backward, hand grasped to her chest in shock. Holt spun. The stranger from the road stood at the darkened door, the dim porch light shrouding his figure. He took a hesitant step forward.

"I'm... sorry, folks. I hate to disturb you again," he drawled.

"What do you want?" A sudden tenseness rode Holt's voice, one that was not there the first time the two had spoken.

"I got lost in the rain. I wonder if it wouldn't be too much trouble... whether I could just wait on your porch until it lets up. And then I'll be on my way." The stranger offered a polite bow of his head. Rainwater dribbled from his distressed leather bomber onto the wooden floor, where it puddled next to his muddy boots.

"We can't help you..." Holt began.

Chelsea gripped her husband's elbow and glared. "*Trust...*" she said through gritted teeth.

Holt pursed his lips into a flat crease. "Sure... why not." He shook his head with an eye dart towards his wife. "Rain should let up in the next hour or so..." he added, and began to shut the door.

"Holt!" she barked in a whisper. She grasped the doorknob from him. "You can come in," Chelsea said to the stranger.

"I don't wanna be a burden or nothin'," the stranger said. His voice, in contrast to Holt's, was more like a meek kitten.

Holt stepped aside, glared at Chelsea as the stranger entered their kitchen.

"Nice place you got here, ma'am... and sir," he said, glancing between the two.

"Thanks..." Holt replied.

"Can I get you something to drink?" Chelsea said, already with a hand on the jug of tea on the countertop.

"Oh, no. Thank you anyway, ma'am, I think I've had enough drink for one day." He chuckled nervously, eyeballing the rain still pouring on the kitchen window above the sink.

Chelsea smiled, clasped her hands in front of her waist.

"Well... I'm Chelsea, and I think you've already met my hus..."

"Holt," Holt said, arms crossed on his chest.

"Ulysses Rembrandt Armwood. But people just call me Sam," the stranger tendered, shyly bowing his head again.

"Sam?" Holt furrowed his brow.

"Long story, but much shorter to say," the stranger replied.

Chelsea, meanwhile, had already sliced off a piece of homemade bread and set it on a wooden plate at the table.

"Homemade, eat as much as you'd like," she said.

"You're too kind, ma'am," Sam replied with a humbleness that made Holt scowl behind his back. Nervously eyeing Holt, the stranger sat and began to stuff the bread into his mouth like a starving pup.

Holt glared at his wife. She ignored the silent display of frustration and stood by the table in front of Sam.

"You from around here... Sam?" she asked.

"Here and there," Sam mumbled, his mouth still full of bread. "Tryin' to head out west. Wanna find somethin' better that I don't already have - which ain't much."

Chelsea widened her eyes at Holt, motioned her head towards the table. Holt reluctantly stepped over and took a seat across from Sam.

"I couldn't help but notice y'all have power," Sam observed.

Holt nodded. "Generator..."

"Mighty lucky to have a workin' piece of equipment like that, ain't it?"

"I'm fairly handy with a screwdriver and soldering iron, so that helps," Holt replied.

Sam nodded with a friendly smile, looked to Chelsea. "Ma'am, if the offer still stands, I'd like to have a glass of tea."

She grinned, walked across the kitchen to fetch another mug.

Holt stared at Sam. "So you have anything lined up once you find... whatever it is you're looking for?"

"Well, I was sorta hopin' to find someone willin' to trade my services for an agreement of room and board. I don't have no money, but I'm a hard worker, and these days education don't mean much anymore."

Holt softened his glare.

Chelsea set the mug of tea in front of Sam, turned her head towards Holt and ballooned her eyes. "Well, maybe my husband can take you into town tomorrow and introduce you to someone that might be able to help."

Sam clicked his eyes to Holt.

Holt did not fight his wife's borne trustworthiness, just nodded.

"Much obliged, sir," Sam replied.

"You can call me Holt."

Sam shook his head. "My poppa always told me when I'm a guest in someone's home to show respect. So if it's all the same to y'all, it's *sir* and *ma'am*."

Sam finished the rest of his bread, sipped the last of the tea from the mug, and set it down. "I gotta say, you folks are the nicest people I've met in a long time."

Holt snickered and smiled at Chelsea. *Maybe she's right.*

"You'd be surprised how many folks woulda just pulled a gun on me for just bein on their property," Sam added.

"We don't believe in violence, Sam. There's better ways to get through life than that," Holt said in a serious tone.

"Have you been around much... you know – out there?" Chelsea asked, her curiosity not hidden from her expression. She pressed her freckled elbows against the back of a wooden chair.

Sam stayed silent for a moment, slurping the last few drops from his empty mug before setting it down again. "I try to stay off the path. Lotta bad people out there, ma'am." He averted his gaze from her and wiped his chin on a sleeve. "But I heard stuff..."

Chelsea leaned in as if she were tuning her ears to an early 20th century radio program.

Holt's eyes lit. "Heard? From who?"

The stranger locked gazes with Holt, gave a nod of his chin towards the back door. "You know what I'm talkin' about, sir. I seen your antenna and all. I'm sure you've heard 'em all talkin'."

With a distant stare at the dense trees near the back of his property, Holt bobbed his head once. "Yeah. Right."

He had always intended to move his HAM antenna closer to the tree line, so as not to attract too much attention. He was right. But *too late.*

"I don't use it anymore, Sam." Holt scratched a fingernail at the edge of the table.

Sam nodded and politely pushed his empty plate away. "I been in the room before when they been talkin'. So I heard things..."

"What do they talk about, Sam? What's it like?" Chelsea's eyes widened.

A look of distress came over Sam's leathery face. "Nothin' good, I'm afraid. The big cities are empty. What with no power and all, and all the craziness that happened with the lootin' and riots." He cleared his throat. "Lotsa folks... died or killed each other."

Chelsea gasped and shook her head in dismay. Holt frowned at her as Sam stared down at his own hands in thought. Holt suddenly felt more vindication of his own plans.

Sam continued. "The ones that were left just took off for safer places. Atlanta, Dallas, most all the stuff on the West Coast. And I'm sure y'all know what happened up in New England..."

Holt had always assumed something disastrous had occurred, but with the island on which he had stranded him and his wife, he never truly knew the extent – until now.

"What about the rest of the world?" Holt had sat forward, his interest growing in rapid morbidity.

Sam shook his head. "Sorry, sir, I didn't stick around long enough to know all that. I only heard little bits, and it sounded like it was pretty much the same everywhere."

Holt pressed his lips together. His eyes wandered aimlessly towards the back door, which led ten yards out to the bunker he had created within the back yard. Chelsea stepped up next to him and lovingly rubbed at the center of his back. Holt sighed.

"Sam, you can sleep on the couch tonight." Chelsea wiped the crumbs from the table while grabbing the empty mug.

The stranger's face brightened. "The porch is fine with me, ma'am. Just give me a blanket and I'll be fine for the night."

A few moments later, Chelsea emerged from the hallway with a large, quilted throw nestled in her arms. Sam graciously accepted it from her, nodded his head to Holt, and stepped out onto the porch.

Through the window behind the closed door, Holt stared out at the stranger.

Several weeks later

Holt dropped the firewood into the pit at the back of the bunker entryway. The threat of winter cold had come early this year, and he worked overtime to ensure sufficient stock for what he feared could be a lean few months.

"Holt, I finished patchin' up the roof on the back porch," Sam said from behind him. He rubbed his hands together.

Holt turned, nodded to Sam. "Great job, Sam." He patted Sam on the shoulder and headed for the porch. "Seen Mrs. Alverson around?" Holt took both steps in one bound.

"No, sir. But then, I been up on the roof, so she might could be around back somewhere."

"Chels?" Holt called from the kitchen. He stepped into the short hallway and poked his head into the bedroom door.

Chelsea, wrapped in several heavy, woolen blankets, was asleep. "Chels? You awake?"

Chelsea stirred, peeked her head out from underneath the covers. "Hmm?"

"It's five o'clock. You been asleep since I left this morning?"

"Yeah... I guess. No energy today," she replied with a yawn.

"You feeling alright? You look pale..."

Chelsea sprung up, leaned over the edge of the mattress and vomited into a nearby trashcan.

"What's goin' on, Chels?" Holt sat next to her.

She wiped the caked blood from the edges of her nostrils and mouth on a cloth, set it back on the nightstand and looked up at him. Her eyes, normally a brilliant green, reflected a faded gray in the pale light from the window above the headboard.

"Just some bug that got me. I'll be ok, just need to rest," she said with a weak moan. Chelsea laid back into the pillows.

Holt rubbed her arm, pushed himself back up to his feet.

"Alright." He turned towards the door. "Gonna go help Sam with sealing the windows. Looks like winter's gonna come early..."

He glanced back – she had already fallen asleep.

Four days later

"Mrs. Alverson comin' to dinner?" Sam asked, nodding his acknowledgement of the hot bowl of stew that Holt had just placed on the table in front of him.

"She's... feelin' a little under the weather, Sam," Holt replied.

Sam grunted, picked up the spoon and began to eat.

Holt studied the hallway in deep thought. He placed the kettle back on the stove and stepped away from the kitchen. Sam watched him from the corner of an eye as he sipped the steaming mixture.

Holt stopped in the doorway of the bedroom, looked in on his wife. Chelsea, still wrapped in a bundle of heavy blankets, sat propped up against a pair of down pillows.

"You feel like eating, sweetheart?" He sat next to her on the edge of the mattress.

She shook her head, closed her eyes. He felt her forehead; a frown creased his own.

Holt had become so used to Chelsea being strong and healthy, always out and working in the garden or around the house - this version of her wrenched his gut.

"You haven't eaten in three days, Chels." His eyes fixated on the cloth she kept next to the bed, its normal beige now soaked in a deep, crimson of her blood.

"That from your nose?" he exclaimed. Holt grasped her hand.

Chelsea nodded. "And the inside of my mouth..." she said with a whimper.

"Chels, I really think we need to get some help for you."

She nodded once again, tears welling in her eyes.

He looked over his shoulder for a silent moment and sighed. "I don't feel right leaving you with... *him*... around."

Chelsea lurched forward, coughed violently into her hand. As she withdrew her fist from her mouth, the light reflected off a sticky blotch of blood on her thumb.

Holt rubbed her back; his palm unevenly brushed her protruding ribs.

"Go..." she strained.

"But..." Holt began to argue.

Chelsea grabbed Holt's hand in hers. "*Trust...*" she said softly, smiling while making strong eye contact with him.

A board in the hallway floor creaked. Holt swung around to face the doorway. Sam stood just outside of the bedroom door.

"Sorry, Holt. I'm gonna go work on that generator. 'Fore y'all need to use it and all," Sam said in nearly a whisper, his face partially shaded in the darkened hallway.

Holt nodded with a hesitance. Sam returned the nod, turned and disappeared into the kitchen.

Holt stuffed a small baggie of trail mix into his pocket, after having packed the small quilt under his arm full of supplies – a requirement for his two-day trip into Oil City. A flashlight leapt from the end of the blanket and onto the floor with a metallic clunk.

"Dammit..." He dropped the tightly wound blanket onto the countertop and stood back with a hand to his hip. He scanned the kitchen - his eyes fell upon the strap of a bag nestled next to the wooden stove in the corner. With a quick step across the creaky slats, he grasped at the handle and tugged. A small pouch flung from its wedged hiding spot behind one of the iron feet of the stove and landed on the floor behind him, part of its contents spilling from the tumble.

Within a bundle of old socks sat several large hunks of dried jerky. Holt's eyes narrowed. He glared through the windowpane above the sink, out towards the corner of the bunker in the back yard. Just visible beyond the edge was a shadow, moving in synchronous rhythm with the man greasing the generator to the side of the bunker.

"Son of a..." Holt tightened his lips and shook his head. A cough from the bedroom drew him back to reality.

It was now or never. He had no choice. He quickly tossed his necessities into the sack, along with the quilt, and made for the back door.

Two days later

The snow had arrived much earlier than anticipated that year, making travel by any means very difficult. Having made the trip into town and back, Holt rounded the corner and quickly opened the gate at the end of the dirt driveway. As he stepped onto the porch, his eye caught the flicker of light coming from the cracked door of the bunker.

"What the..." he mumbled aloud. Holt changed course and made his way to the half-open door. He descended the pair of concrete stairs and stepped into the center of the room.

His prepper supplies, all of them removed from their shelves, sat in a neat pile near the door. A rucksack, half-full and open, lay next to the cot by the desk. He hurried to it and peered inside.

Before he could ascertain its contents, he felt a thunderous crunch across the back of his neck and dropped to the cold ground. Holt turned over on his back. The outline of Sam, standing with one hand down by his side, a shovel in the other, filled the entryway.

"Look at you..." Sam growled with dripping disdain. "So smug and self-righteous with your supplies and your preparations." He slowly circled Holt, shovel propped on one shoulder. "While the rest of the world scrapes the bottom tryin' to survive."

"Take what you want," Holt groaned. He rubbed his shoulder while leaning on one elbow.

"Oh, I will. And I think I might check out that tasty wife of yours, too," Sam barked. "You're too trusting, Alverson. Shoulda never left me alone here. Your downfall is gonna be that you came back too soon." He snorted, turned and began to ascend the short staircase.

Holt, stunned, rolled over and reached under the cot.

"Sam!" he yelled.

"Yeah?" Sam snarled, turned to face Holt.

A spike of flame jumped from the end of Holt's shotgun barrel. His ears went numb with the shocking concussion of the blast in the small room.

A single slug found its way into Sam's neck just below his Adam's apple. Sam grabbed at his throat, fell back against the stone entryway with an awkward twitch, then onto the ground. His slick life's blood flowed around his fingers as he gurgled his final breaths.

Holt fell back against the cabinet and stared at Sam's astonished expression. The dense odor of burnt sulfur hung low in the air. He threw the gun off to his side, leapt to his feet and sprinted out of the bunker, his heavy breaths fogging the air.

He stumbled into the house, down the hallway and stopped outside the bedroom door.

"Chels, I'm back and I've got some antibiotics that..." A small pill bottle rattled in his hand.

Chelsea sat at the edge of the bed, hunched over. In one arm, she clenched a Bible against her chest. In her other balled fist, she held what appeared to be a good amount of her faded honey hair. He stared in confusion, suddenly noticing the several bald patches along the side of her scalp.

She turned her head to him and held up one hand to her mouth, whimpering with an uncontrolled shake. A large bloodstain marked the pillow behind her. Holt rushed to his wife's side, sat and wrapped his arms around her emaciated torso.

Together, they wept.

Several hours later

Holt stormed back into the bunker, having just disposed of Sam's corpse in a shallow grave down by the river. He rummaged through the pile of supplies still spilled on the floor next to the cabinets, pulling out a small, black box. He flicked at the switches several times, shook the device wildly and glared at the meter on its front panel.

"Damn it!" he bellowed. He threw the broken Geiger counter across the room onto the cot, where it bounced once and fell onto the ground. He had suspected it a week earlier, but he did not need the device to confirm what had become so painfully evident now.

He fell back onto the cot and held his head between his arms.

Two days later

The windows frosted at the edges, with only a small circle of clear glass remaining at the center. Already one of the strongest cold blasts before winter had even set in, the early hours of the day had produced the largest dip of the mercury yet. The air inside the house thinned and the frame of the structure creaked as the temperature plummeted overnight.

Holt held the fresh brew of hot tea between his gloved hands, let the steam waft up into his face for a moment before heading down the hallway. Thanks to the handful of painkillers he was able to barter for in town days prior, the last 48 hours had been a relatively quiet one for the Alversons. Chelsea remained in bed, where she rested while Holt kept vigil.

He tiptoed into the bedroom and stopped at the foot of the bed to look upon his wife. The cold, morning light flowed across her bundled form. Holt smiled.

"Chels," he said in a high whisper, holding the hot mug in one hand while gently rubbing her side with the other. "Some hot herbal for you."

He sat next to her.

"Chels..."

He inched the blanket down from around her head, exposing her sweat-matted honey hair - or what was left of it. He gazed upon her face.

His heart froze.

Holt let the mug fall to the floor in a smashing clamor. He climbed over Chelsea and lay next to her. He put his face into the back of her neck, pulled her into his embrace and sobbed.

Holt sifted through the scattered pile of supplies, still in the same spot that they had remained in the four weeks since Chelsea's passing. While he had spent some time in the house, mainly for purposes of sleeping, Holt had kept himself occupied since then working on the bunker. Convinced that busywork could help avoid the raw emotions that came along with her death, his focus naturally fell to what he did best.

He had expended tremendous amounts of energy and time filling the firewood pit that extended along the edge of the ground-level bunker roof. During the evenings, he rejuvenated the old, wood-burning stove in the structure, the moisture and lack of use having thrown it into a state of corroded disrepair.

The irony had not escaped him that while some little part of him felt there would be a day to put the bunker to use, he never really expected it to happen. He had always rested on the pride of knowing that he was one of the county's top preppers, and that was satisfaction in and of itself.

Chelsea's death cast the light of reality on his life that he never could have anticipated, and he came to realize it was something for which he had never prepared.

The life Holt had known had become barren and cold, and the sadness crept in like a bitter chill. He stood and pensively stared at the darkened stain at the base of the stairs - an ugly reminder of the price of blind trust he had paid with Ulysses Rembrandt Armwood.

Holt Alverson's life had changed - he did not recognize it anymore.

Holt unlatched the wall unit and began to place some of the smaller supplies onto the topmost shelf. A thin layer of dust lifted from one of the shelves, blew into his face and forced a cough. As he withdrew his hand from his mouth, he noticed a small patch of crimson on his wrist. He quickly wiped it away with a flannel sleeve.

The soft glint of light onto the HAM radio transceiver atop on the middle shelf drew his gaze. He grabbed it with a sigh of exasperation, intent on heaving it across the room to its demise. However, a small object fell off its case and onto the floor at his feet.

A crucifix, brass on wood, sat face-up by his boot. Holt tucked the radio underneath his arm and plucked the cross from the dirt. He wagged his head with a dim smirk, knowing that even without being present, *she* managed to get her point across.

After placing the remainder of the supplies back into the cabinet, Holt took the transceiver, along with an amplifier and speaker set, and mounted them back into their holders behind the small desk at the back of the bunker.

With a click of several buttons, the devices surged to life in a flickering of LED light. Holt leaned back in his chair and chuckled. After a few quiet seconds of its self-test procedure, the speakers hummed with a steady static. He leaned forward and spoke into the microphone.

"CQ Calling CQ. This is W3GRL. Whiskey-Three-Golf-Romeo-Lima."

The static returned and remained uninterrupted.

Again, he repeated the callout. Again, the void of static greeted him.

Holt folded his arms across his chest and sat back in his chair.

For the next 41 nights, after long days of toiling around the bunker, restocking shelves from fresh trips to town, and forays into the house to take occasional naps, Holt repeated his efforts. For 41 nights, he received the same result.

But he persisted.

Each night, he would take to the empty airwaves and broadcast to anyone that might miraculously be listening - offering encouragement and advice to the remnants that he was now convinced must be miniscule.

On the 42nd night, the exasperation and reality that no one was listening had long since eclipsed Holt's optimism.

As he terminated his latest transmission and static roared from the speakers, Holt pounded his fist on the desk. The crucifix rattled its way out from the bookshelf above him and landed next to his hand.

Holt gnashed his teeth, grabbed the crucifix and held it skyward in a clenched fist.

"Why?" he wailed in demand, his voice echoing with a harsh emptiness. "Why?" he screamed once again. He lowered his head onto his arms and wept.

The static lowered; a voice broke through.

"W3GRL, dies ist DPCHL. Delta-Papa-Charlie-Hotel-Lima. Konnen sie mich horen?" it said in between chunks of noise.

Holt bolted upright, yanked the microphone towards him.

"Hello? Hello? Can you hear me?" he yelled.

Again, the voice responded. "Dies ist DPCHL. Wie viele am leben sind?"

Holt frowned.

"W3GRL. Wie viele am leben sind?" it repeated several times.

"German... German!" Holt yelled to himself. He frantically ripped several books down from the bookshelf above him and began leafing through the pages at breakneck speed.

"W3GRL. Was ist ihre position?" the voice continued.

"Position... URA! URA!" Holt screamed into the mike between coughing jags. "Uh... sprechen sie English?" he added, finally locating the proper phrase in his translation dictionary.

"Ja! Ja!" the voice responded. "You are in URA?"

"Yes... yes. Oh my God..." Holt said, the irony of his excited exclamation forcing warm tears down his face.

Holt and the German conversed every night for the next several weeks, discussing everything from the aftermath of the Event to learning the German language. Holt missed only two days of talking to his distant friend when he found himself too nauseated to make it out to the bunker. However, resolving to keep in constant contact for as long as he could, he moved himself into the bunker and slept on the cot next to his radio equipment from that day forward.

As the winter reached its peak and the frigid ground hardened to near rock solid, Holt began to suffer from the same degenerating effects to which his wife had succumbed several months earlier. The linings of his nose and mouth bled heavily on a routine basis, and his appetite vanished. His skin paled and flaked away from malnutrition, and his thick, brown hair - normally bushing out from underneath his wool hat into a ponytail - had all but fallen out.

With barely enough strength to pull himself from the cot and toss a few logs into the stove, he stumbled to the desk and keyed the microphone one last time.

"CQ DPCHL. Promise me... keep talking, even if I don't respond." He released the mike.

The static burped once again.

"W3GRL. I promise, my friend." The German's English proficiency had grown over the previous weeks.

For the next few days, Holt lay in his cot, anticipating nightfall when his friend would once again broadcast his greetings.

A week after his final broadcast, Holt passed.

Outside of the bunker, beyond the driveway and past the corner of the house, the final winter snow melted away. In the barren garden beyond, where Chelsea had spent so many hours toiling away at futility, a single sprout broke through the hardened earth and stretched skyward.

7:
The Ocean

Darkness enveloped him.

The weighty tang of ozone enshrouded his body. A tempered hum filled his ears. The undulating throb at the base of his skull intensified until it was a hot dagger piercing his brain. His ribs, bruised and broken, simmered with an angry heat. The words formed at the tip of his tongue.

"What is this place?" he begged.

The words did not come. They echoed in his brain, stuck at the back of his throat like a tar-covered moth, unable to free itself from the mire. He tried again, but his mouth refused to open.

His wrist chilled at the touch of the cold steel of a metal cuff. He tried to turn his head towards whoever put it there, but his body would not let him.

"Hello?" he urged.

Again, his voice failed to launch. His hot breath queued on his tongue like a lava flow, but his teeth held back the swell. His voice grumbled deep in his chest, but he could not turn it into words.

Footsteps fled behind him, an eerie silence took their place. The hum began to surge. The rumble of thunder and the crackle of an electrical charge reverberated hundreds of meters above his head. His hair stood on end and the fillings in his teeth sent a spike of pain throughout his jaw.

As if a jet engine, the nearby structure's power increased with a thunderous roar. Wood clacked on wood in the distance - the metal on which he lay began to tremor like a jackhammer. The vibration shook him to his core. His heart fluttered in his chest, the air in his lungs rattled and his brain numbed from the shock of its force.

Just as he felt his organs would burst from the frantic resonance, a searing strobe of white flooded his eyes. He opened his mouth and forced a scream. As the sound fled his lips, the light ceased. His voice stretched, and then faded into oblivion.

His torso had spun, no longer lying face down on the metal platform as before. He opened his eyes, furiously scanned the heavens above. Lights, the size of pinholes, glossed the black canvas as far as he could see. They warped and blurred as he tumbled through the vast blackness. His breaths came short and hurried, his shock at the sensation of falling a great distance whipping at his consciousness.

A voice, British by its inflection, cascaded past his ears. Its frequency rose and dropped as it traveled, its consistency that of someone speaking into an empty drum.

"You've made a mess of things, I'm not going to deny that fact..."

He gathered a shout from his gut, but his mouth refused to part with the sound.

Another voice, similar, yet somehow different, followed.

"I believe it's your turn to live up to the terms of the arrangement..."

The muscles in his jaw tensed. A scream was there, he just could not free it.

"Furnish them with whatever supplies are necessary to fight back..." the first voice reverberated with a tinny echo.

He cried out. The muted silence of his voice squeezed at his brain until tears arrived at the corners of his eyes. The lights spun more rapidly now. He tried to reach out with his hands for anything that might break his fall, but his arms held in place as if in blocks of ice.

"Oh... Epsilons? You are telling me that they are Epsilons? They are a dangerous lot, indeed..." the voice resounded once again.

The voices fell silent. He spun himself frantically, trying from the depths of his soul to find a way to stop his freefall. His body suddenly surged forward, pulled against his will like a hook to an angler. The invisible force grabbed at his chest with a titanic grip, jerking him along like a snagged perch. The air left his lungs. He could not breathe.

Ahead of him, a tiny ring of intense, white light appeared in the pitch. It hovered for a moment, dancing at an odd pattern in the distance. He blinked and turned his head to keep his eyes focused on the mesmerizing sight. The lights around him became dimmer. The ring became larger, taunting him for what seemed forever.

This is death.

He caught sight of the bright light once again.

That's... Heaven?

His life began to replay across his conscious, all of his deeds and misdeeds suddenly coming to the forefront of his mind. He wanted to believe it was really happening. But he also did not.

But... how? Did I deserve to go there?

The reality of his apparent destination tortured his soul.

It excited him.

It saddened him.

It was happening. He was there; he could feel his own physical self. It was not a dream. Tears flowed freely now. He let it come to him.

The ring grew ever larger, its light intensifying until it drowned out everything around it. A thin layer of white pulsated around the perimeter. The familiar hum began once again, its pitch rising and lowering in synchronization with the dancing light, until it reached a deafening roar.

He turned his head, glanced behind him. The lights spun with a dizzying rapidity that made his stomach churn and his eyes flicker. He faced the light once again. His body gravitated into the center. He closed his eyes, laid his head back.

Darkness enveloped him.

Brigadier Stroud woke with a start. The acute sterility of medicine stung his nose. His arms, weighted by some unknown fluid surrounding him, hung like iron at his sides. The lukewarm, slimy gel coursed with a gentle current around his naked body, freely flowing in and out of his ears, effectively muting his hearing to all but a small gurgle. Brig could not recall falling asleep, and the pulsing knot on his neck told him he was correct in that assumption.

He attempted to lift his eyelids, but the thick, glue-like muck bonded the eyelashes to the skin of his tanned cheeks. Brig forced his arm through the gel and tore at his eyelids to force them open. He was not sure if it was the film coating his mind, or whether he was in some sort of odd dream state, but he could not see a meter in front of him. The gel, translucent with a cool, azure hue, coated him from head to toe.

Brig stabbed one hand forward. The gel continued past his reach, packed densely beyond his sight like a glowing amniotic wrap. He fought off the overwhelming urge to slumber once again, paddled his arms in a manic attempt to free himself, but found that despite his range of motion he was not able to move more than a centimeter or two.

He opened his mouth and screamed. The cry did not travel through the dense goop. After getting a small mouthful of the solution, he quickly clamped his jaw. Panic spiked his brain, realizing that he had no way of obtaining fresh air. He fell back on his Epsilon Warrior commando training, calmed himself and held his breath. After several moments of inching one way or the other, trying futilely to find an edge to the seemingly endless ocean of ooze, he stopped and forced his eyes shut.

The final molecules of oxygen flamed against his lungs. Brig's muscles ignited, their desperate last sips of sustenance failing in vain.

He would drown soon.

Using the last measure of energy in his body, Brig lunged forward. To his surprise, his hand struck against a pane of firm glass with a dulled thump. He instinctively opened his mouth and screamed. Realizing that he had ingested more of the bitter fluid, he began to cough. The gel, instead of expelling from his mouth, sucked into his throat.

Brig heaved, but it was already too late. The mixture, in one large clump, found its way into his lungs. As the last oxygen burned in his brain, his body went limp.

To his astonishment, just as all around him began to go black, the fluid in his chest evaporated. He jolted awake, his arteries rejuvenated with rich, fresh oxygen. His mind panicked, not knowing how to process the miracle that had just occurred. He flailed his arms in reaction to his sudden, second life.

Something else had made its way into his lungs within the mysterious gelatin, however. The astringent bite of medicine burned his throat. His faculties began to dim, and he lost consciousness within a few seconds.

The gurgling sound of fluid rippling into his ears gently urged him from his anesthetized stupor. Feeling that once again his eyelids were matted shut with dried gel, Brig leaned his head back. As if a new instinct, he inhaled the gel, allowing it to flow unrestricted into his lungs. Just as before, it quickly dissipated. His body quivered as the cool, oxygen-rich blood coursed through him.

A shadow moved across his eyelids.

He pawed at them, ignoring the sting of a small group of eyelashes tearing as they stuck to his cheeks. Fighting off the new dose of tranquilizer that came along with imbibing the gel, he darted his eyes around the muck.

The shadow once again moved past him, left to right, and then disappeared.

Brig pounded the glass with a fist. Nothing happened. He swung his arms several more times, each one landing with a dull thud against the thick partition.

The medicine sponged at his consciousness once again. His arms fell limp and floated in the soup. He began to close his eyes.

Suddenly, the shadow reappeared. This time, it stopped in front of him.

Brig stiffened and stared through the goo at the figure. It stood, staring back at him from a silhouette, warped through the refraction of the gel.

A girl?

Brig tried to pierce the shadowy murk with his lake blue eyes.

The shadow tilted its head to one side. Brig reciprocated as if glaring into a murky mirror.

His breathing drew shallow. He reached with one shaking hand, held it towards the figure, and then shut his eyes.

Present day (2084)

Brigadier Stroud recoiled. The irritation of the acerbic spray wafting through his nostrils and into the back of his throat made him swallow hard. He closed his throat to the bitterness. The shrill whir of a mechanical servo tickled his ears.

He opened his eyes. A thin, robotic arm receded from over his face, disappeared into a burst of static on the wall two meters away. Brig rubbed his eyes, propped himself up on one elbow and scanned the room. The cool air flowing from a high-mounted vent wandered through his toes. He peered down at his bare feet, past the plain, blue jumpsuit that covered his muscularly toned body. He ran a hand through his shoulder-length brown hair and scratched at the back of his head.

Aside from the bed that he occupied, the room contained no furniture. The sharp, white walls rounded where they met the floor to each side of him. His breath echoed in his head through the dead silence of the chamber.

Not again.

His time in quarantine seven years prior came to the forefront of his conscious. He did not want to repeat that event of his past, and he pained thinking of how he could have possibly returned to such a predicament.

"That's just great." His frustration lifted his West Texas drawl across the silence.

"What is?" replied a female voice, British, to his right.

To Brig's shock, which quickly spun into overwhelming joy, a familiar face greeted him.

Steele Fox, his childhood friend, stood next to his bed, her slender arms folded neatly across her torso. She stared in curiosity down at him. Her brunette hair flowed over one shoulder. Her piercing, emerald eyes met his.

Brig smiled. "What a wonderful place this is, that I get to see you again." He cradled her chin in his palm.

"Good to see you, too, Brigadier." Steele's steep British accent provided much needed music to his ears. "I'm surprised to see you *here*."

"Rough way to find happiness though, ain't it?" Brig lay back with his hands behind his head.

"What do you mean?"

"You know, being dead and all..."

"You're not dead, Brigadier."

Brig pushed up on one elbow again, glared with one eyebrow raised. "Right. You're alive, and we're here. Wherever this is. That's all just normal, right?"

"You're not making sense." She turned her back to him, quietly studied a holographic chart that materialized in front of her, seemingly at a silent command. "But then, that's to be expected after what you've been through, I suppose."

"What I've been through. See, you *know* then?"

Indeed, if there were any one person that knew of the pain and heartache that Brig had endured over the past several years, it was Steele. However, that pain felt light years away, as it was apparent to him that they both had moved on to somewhere much more pleasant. And together, no less.

"What I know is that you showed up here with quite a few injuries. Broken bones, contusions. God only knows what's happened to you. But you're healed now." She faced him once again, her arms crossed over her chest.

Brig sat up and rubbed at his ribs. Where there had been pain just yesterday, a result of fisticuffs in which he had partaken recently, no pain existed. His lip, swollen from the encounter with his best friend, Clive Underwood, the previous day, felt normal to his touch. He raised his eyebrows.

"How convenient," he quipped.

Without warning, the lighting of the small room extinguished. A mere second later, it popped back to life.

Brig's eyes glowed at the new sight before him. He found himself in a dirt lot, bordered along one side with a row of hedges. To the opposite side, a small Tudor style house rose up next to him. His breath left him for a moment. He squinted to gain comprehension of an incomprehensible event. Then, as if bumped into like a skipping record player, he smiled.

"Nice." He held his arms out at his sides. "You remember *this*, don't you?"

Steele, once again studying the hologram in front of her, raised her head for a brief moment to peek at the room. She nodded and then refocused on the display.

"And I suppose us suddenly being right outside your childhood home is just another sign that we're both alive?"

"It's the room. Clever optics and a very keen thought-driven algorithm," she answered, not paying much attention to her surroundings.

"Thought-driven?"

"It's what you were thinking of, and the sensors in this room pick up on the strongest thoughts present."

"So this isn't just like... my life flashing before my eyes then. That's what you're saying? Just keepin' to the script?"

The room darkened once again, and then reappeared after a quick flash of black.

Without much effort, he recognized his surroundings: the leather seating, the grand, oak mantle surrounding the oversized fireplace, the picture of his father, URA President Devlin Stroud, adorning the wall just above it.

Brig hopped from the edge of the bed, strolled to his father's dark, mahogany desk across the room. With a blind hand, he extracted a Cuban from the top drawer and lit it in one smooth motion from a lighter. He moved next to Steele.

"Look, I get it," he said with a casual drawl, puffing a ring of smoke from the side of his mouth. "You're not supposed to freak out the newbies by telling us we're dead."

She glared, her stern, but confused expression not masking her reaction. "You're not supposed to be smoking in here."

Brig chuckled. "It's ok. I know I'm dead." He scanned the room with feigned interest. "I'm not happy about it. But given everything that happened, I'm better off here anyway. We're *both* better off, don't you think?"

"*Newbies...* what the blazes?" Her exasperation was mounting. "Brigadier, for the last time. You're not dead. Now I'm thinking you may have a concussion... but you're very much alive."

He laughed, shook his head. "Alright, alright. We'll do things your way for now." Brig puffed another billow of blue smoke from his lips. "But maybe they just haven't told *you* yet," he mocked with a quick point of his finger in her direction.

As if by another unspoken command, a thin, trapezoidal opening appeared in the center of the longest wall.

After another exasperated shake of her head, Steele stepped into it. She turned towards him. "Get some rest and we'll talk more in the morning. And I'm going to have the lab technician run another brain scan to see what we missed."

Steele turned away, disappeared through the doorway. It dissipated.

Brig stared in bemusement at the vanishing door and took another puff on the cigar.

The room fluxed once again.

A warm, desert breeze traveled up from the bluff meters in front of where he stood. The setting sun cascaded across the lifeless, metal faces of the satellite dish array that sprawled out ahead. He let his eye wander to a patch of Sacaton grass on his left. The grass, partially matted from a recent visitor, danced in the quiet afternoon sunset.

A small grin tugged at his lips. His heart warmed. He could feel *her* there - again.

Brig instinctively glanced over his shoulder. Steele's motorcycle sat idly nearby, its exhaust still pinging from the heat of recent use. A tear came to his eye.

He took a deep breath. The smell of the sand around him saturated his nostrils. A subtle thud of thunder boomed in the clouds on the horizon. He rolled his eyes upwards.

"Not what I expected... but from where I thought I was goin', I guess it could be worse, huh?" he said with a knowing smirk.

He stood for a few moments more and gazed out over the array. A cool wind sprouted from the shadows below and whipped through his hair. Brig rubbed his arms to ward off the chill.

Like an unwelcome slide projector, the room once again fell into darkness.

The room illuminated; Brig's contented expression faded.

Brig ground his teeth, staring out across the dark rooftop. Rain fell in large strands from the blackened sky and stung his cheeks, quickly drenching his hair until it hung with scraggly disarray against his face. A sudden clap of thunder echoed off the façade of the building to his left.

He leapt from his spot, his replay memory pulling him three quick strides in the direction of the side wall. He stopped and growled over the tumult of the thunderstorm raging around him. Brig bit his lip and closed his eyes. He did not need to look any farther to know that *she* was standing on the ledge.

"Ok. Didn't need a reminder of *that*, though." He held his head in his hands. "Thanks."

The next morning

The vanishing doorway reappeared. Steele, looking fresh and wearing a thigh-length white lab coat that nearly matched her alabaster skin, stepped into the room. She stopped in front of the leather couch, where Brig lay with his hands rested behind his head.

"You look well rested," she observed.

"Being dead agrees with me. I'm healthy. No one's trying to kill me. And I have a pretty lady that comes to see me every day. What's not to be rested about?"

"This nonsense again? I thought we were past that." Her frustration with his insistence that he had perished had not diminished.

"We'll be past it when you admit what I already know. I don't know what this place is, but it sure isn't anywhere on Earth."

"You are currently in Recovery Room 42b, Medical Sector..." a voice, Steele's, announced through an unseen speaker in the ceiling.

Brig smirked. "That? Really? That's normal to you?"

Steele shook her head, warped her lips. "That's the central computer." She turned her back on him. "I came to tell you that your scan came back clean."

"Whew, that's a relief." He did not hide the jovial sarcasm in his tone.

"Except a small... abnormality... with your genome. But that's been corrected," she added.

"Abnormality?" Brig pricked his ears.

"Yes. But it's been rectified, so there's no cause for concern." Steele faced Brig once again.

"Just like that..." he replied with a flat smile.

"Yes."

"Now I know I'm dead..."

"What do I need to do to convince you that you. Are. Not. Dead."

"What do I need to do to convince you that you are?"

"Why do you insist on believing you are deceased?"

"Ok. Let's cut the bullshit." Brig's own frustration began well up.

"I beg your pardon?" Steele crossed her arms like an insulted child.

"No, enough of the act. I know what's going on here..."

"I don't know what you think is going on, but..."

He pointed angrily at his surroundings. "I lived my life for the past six months, so I know damn well what's real and what isn't. And this isn't!"

"Perhaps it was a dream."

"No."

"And you're sure of that fact?"

"Yes!"

"And how is it that you are this certain?"

"Because I..." Brig hesitated.

"Because you... what?"

"Because I watched you die!" Brig fell silent, his expression exposing the extreme emotional trench in his soul that had just become uncovered once again.

Steele's face became even paler as she stared into Brig's eyes.

"I held you in my arms and watched the life bleed out of you until you were gone. And then I put you in the ground..." Brig's voice broke.

"I... I don't know what to say, Brigadier."

"Just... don't say that I don't know what I'm talking about. That it was all some sort of bad dream. I lived it. And then I... died. Or something. But it was real."

7: THE OCEAN

"Then how do you explain how you are here. How I am here?" Her voice became angelically soft.

"I don't know. I don't know what the Hell is going on. Or where the Hell I am, but..."

"You are currently in Recovery Room 42b, Medical..." the voice began to announce again.

"Shut up!" Brig bellowed.

Steele grasped his hand and stared into the deep of his blue eyes. "Are you telling me you honestly don't recall how you came to be here?"

Brig shook his head with a slow incomprehension.

"Well then what I'm about to tell you is going to come as quite a shock. Brace yourself."

8:
Tabula Rasa

Flagstaff, New Mexico - Present day (2084)

Clive "Crypto" Underwood stepped onto the porch, the weathered boards creaking under his feet. He stopped and scanned the woody enclave around him; the other three cottages, abandoned long ago, sat with an empty solemnity at the end of the tree-lined dirt road. A gentle spring breeze rustled through the trees that encircled the complex, their faint 'whoosh' the only sound discernible.

Normally a weekly visit, his intense search for the truth had kept him away for the past month. He felt guilty about not having made it by since then, but he knew deep down that it was for the best - Clive had to find the answers he was looking for first.

He rapped on the door of the fourth cottage with a light knuckle, the humble echo of the wood sounding through the quiet village. He ran a quick hand through the short salt-and-pepper black hair that matted to one side of his head. The door opened a few centimeters. A slit of dim inner lighting met him along with a pair of beady, black eyes. It swung open wider. A stocky Mexican woman, nearly half his 180 centimeter height, filled the doorway.

"Hola, Senor Clive," she said with a squeaky din, her eyes squinting as they locked onto his.

"Hey, Esmerelda," Clive replied. He took a step into the doorway past her, and then stopped to meet her gaze. "Is he awake?"

"He's taking a siesta in his room." Esmerelda closed the door behind him with a gentle clunk. She looked after him, fixed her eyes on the bag under his arm.

"I brought a little something for him." Clive unstrung a medium-sized, dirty tan pouch from his shoulder. The uneven sound of his boots softly pacing across the wooden floor filled the small, dimly lit den. He set the pouch down next to a desk that held a turn-of-the-century computer.

"He was asking about you. It's been a while since you've been by. Longer than normal."

Clive pursed his lips, knelt, and extracted a small toolkit from the pouch. "Yeah... sorry about that. Had some stuff come up that I had to take care of." He paused before grasping the case of the computer and pulling it from under the desk.

"You do not need to apologize to me, Senor Clive. It's *him* that I worry about." She perched herself in a weathered rocking chair in the corner of the room and stared at him. The creak of the rocker rails flooded the tense silence.

His hands worked the screwdriver with an instinctive fever until the cover clanked loose. He let her stabbing comment slide by. "I did a little tinkering with some old parts in my workshop. Came up with a working power supply," he muttered, grunting as he forced the cover from its chassis. "I always promised him I'd get this thing working someday." A satisfied grin replaced his normally stoic mug.

"A computer's not going to replace *you*, senor."

"Just a little bit of the past - my past - to show him what life was like... *before*," Clive said, the nostalgia of days gone by biting at him as he tinkered with the technological fossil.

"Life will never be like it was before."

Clive clicked his tongue. "But we can dream..."

He flicked at the power switch on the front of the case. The computer awoke from its inactivity, beeped once, and popped before spouting a small whiff of bluish electrical smoke.

"Damn." Clive tossed the screwdriver back into the pouch in frustration. "Everything going... okay... here?" he said, looking over his shoulder at the dark-haired nanny.

"Si, just fine," she replied. Her skeptical tone told him something her words did not.

Clive nodded, yanked the failed power supply from the case. Her eyes heated the back of his head.

"There was a man."

Clive's eyebrows rose. He glared at Esmerelda. "A man?"

"Si. Some gringo a little while back. He says he was having trouble with his camion... eh... truck."

He furrowed his brow, rubbed his neck as he absorbed her disturbing news. "Then what happened?"

"I chased him away with the big gun. Bang, bang. Just like you taught me, Senor." She performed the gesture of a shotgun with her hands.

"Had you ever seen him before?"

"No. He don't look familiar. And he don't come back." She rose from the chair and busied herself with dusting a nearby table that did not appear to need it.

"Well... that's good," he said after thinking for a moment, hands on his hips. "He didn't come in, did he?"

"No."

Clive nodded, his face showing a satisfied, if apprehensive, expression.

"But hombrecito came out on the porch when he was here."

"*What?*"

"It's ok, Senor Clive. I told him to go back en la casa. So he was safe." She gave a stiff pat of reassurance on his back.

"Do you remember what he looked like?"

"I don't know. The usual gringo," she replied. "Long hair. He was... eh scruffy."

"And he hasn't been back since..."

Esmerelda shook her head adamantly.

Clive nodded again, turned his focus towards a small closed door at the back of the room.

"He had the same marking as you. You know, the tattoo," Esmerelda said after a silent pause.

Clive stopped, exhaled a revealing sigh and lowered his head. "Dammit," he murmured under his breath.

Over the years, he had taken painstaking efforts to keep the cottage hidden. The one person that he did not want to have this information had obviously found a way to get it. He pondered at the ramifications of his former Epsilon Warrior counterpart, Brigadier Stroud, knowing about his little secret. Clive had not seen Brig in a few weeks, which puzzled him, but relieved him nonetheless. Perhaps he had finally taken his advice and left town - for good.

"Do you know him, Senor? Did I do something wrong?"

"No. Doesn't matter. You did good." Clive leaned on a nearby hutch and tapped his prosthetic leg against its wood frame with a hollow clunk.

"Hombrecito has been asking about his madre, tambien."

A dagger of dreadful sorrow pierced his heart. He could not help but think of Jessica - Brig's sister - every moment of every day, and he had subconsciously avoided broaching the subject with anyone.

Clive shot a blank stare over his shoulder past her. "About that. There's something I need to tell you." His tone suddenly became serious. "And then we need to figure out how to tell him."

"Que?"

"She's *dead*, Elda."

"Aye, dios mio!" Esmerelda's eyes glazed with sadness, she held a hand to her mouth. "Miss Jessica? Que paso?"

"What happened isn't as important as the fact *that* it happened. And now she's gone."

"Oh, poor little Eli." She wiped a tear from her cheek.

"I don't know what to say to him," Clive said. He stepped towards her.

"What do we do now?"

He wrenched his lips tight again, shook his head. Clive had wrestled with Jessica's death for the past couple of months, and he had fought himself on how to handle Eli, her son.

"We keep him out of harm's way. Here... like we've been doing," he replied finally. "He's not safe anywhere else. No one knows about him, and we need to keep it that way. That ok with you still?"

"Oh yes, Senor Clive. I would never let anything happen to hombrecito."

Clive knew he was only fooling himself and buying time, however. He did not really have a plan for Eli, other than keeping him concealed at the secret cottage. He was not sure who knew about him, aside from Brig, but he could not take the chance that the Syndicate would one day show up and take him away. Deep in his heart, Clive knew that he would rather they take him away from Eli than have to lose the boy.

Clive nodded his appreciation, staring far beyond the small room in which they stood together.

"Was it them? Those... bastardos. Syndicate?" she said, pounding her fist into her other palm.

He nodded silently again.

"Senor Clive, do I need to worry about *you* being found in a ditch somewhere?"

Clive shook his head. "I know what I'm doing. I'll be free of them forever soon. Which is why I'm going to be away for a little bit longer."

"I will do my best, senor. I hope that you do find what you are looking for."

A creak from the floorboards behind them broke the uncomfortable tension between the two. Clive spun. The backlit silhouette of a slender seven-year-old boy stood, his body halfway in his room, his hands on the doorframe. The whites of his eyes glowed in the shadows as he glared out at Clive and Esmerelda.

"Is it true?" the boy asked.

"Eli... how long have you been listening?" The boy did not flinch at the authority in Clive's voice.

"Hombrecito, go back to bed," Esmerelda ordered.

Again, Eli did not budge. He had heard all that mattered.

"Is it true? Is she really gone?" Eli asked again.

Clive closed his eyes for a moment. The time had arrived for him to handle the situation, whether he wanted to or not. "Yes."

"And she's never coming back?" Eli's voice cracked.

"I'm sorry... no, Eli," Clive replied.

Eli rushed from the shadows towards Clive, wrapping both arms around his legs. He cried with a soft whimper. "I want my mommy back." He pulled away from Clive and locked eyes with him, his face red with fresh tears. "Bring her back, Daddy, bring her back!"

Clive knelt, pulled him into a firm hug. He gave Esmerelda a somber flick of his brown eyes. "I know, son. I know."

Present day (2084)

Brig and Steele strolled along the corridor, which, as with the recovery room that they had just exited, exhibited an eerily silent quality. The gentle clack of her shoes on the tile floor resonated against the matted, gray walls - but then quickly diminished, absorbed by the plasticized polymer material coating them. Even Brig's shoes, a complete wrap of soft cloth, provided a small amount of echo within the silent sterility.

"I thought it would be easier just to show you, since you're not believing much of what I told you so far," Steele said.

"This building must be really soundproofed..." Brig stared with curiosity at the walls. He dragged his fingers along it for a few meters. The tactile sensation reminded him of the titanium skin of the hover-jets that he had become so accustomed to in the Epsilon Warriors, but with the porous drag of plastic pipe.

"You could say that," Steele answered with a wink. They rounded a corner and stepped onto the platform of a waiting lift.

"An elevator? Who has an elevator anymore?" He raised an eyebrow as the doors closed.

The car shot upward with a soft whir. Concern started to grow on his face.

Within a few seconds, the lift stopped. The back wall slid upward, exposing a spacious, dark room with cool blue lighting along the ceiling.

Steele stepped off the lift, strolled to the center of the room and rotated to face Brig. "Are you coming?"

Brig exited the lift platform with both a cautious and curious gait. The door closed with a whoosh. He shook his head, exhaled audibly as he stopped in front of Steele. He peered around the room. "What is this place?"

"You are currently in the Fox Observation Tower," the central computer announced over yet another hidden speaker.

"Are you sure you're ready for this?" Steele tilted her head and flashed a half-smile.

"Nothing can surprise me more than you standing right here in front of me. So... yeah."

"Open the viewing port." Steele snapped an about-face and stepped to the far wall.

The dark wall rose upward without a fraction of sound to reveal a large, glass partition. Brig at first did not pay mind to the view - he stared at Steele, still expecting the dream to come to a sudden end. He coughed, having forgotten to take a breath while entranced by her presence. Dead or not, he still found himself magnetized by her striking beauty.

He broke his gaze and slowly stepped to the window, his hands defiantly at his hips. His unimpressed scowl faded into awed disbelief as he surveyed the grand, sprawling view set forth in front of him.

A massive complex stretched out for several kilometers in each direction, strung into a maze of corridors intersecting into small buildings. Two domes, partially transparent and roughly half the height of the observation tower, rose above the center. At the structural midpoint of the encampment, a tri-pronged set of tunnels reached out to where they met three identical, domed edifices. The opposite ends of the tunnels each spoked inward and terminated at a single, multi-humped construct.

8: TABULA RASA

The luminous, blue glow of the complex radiated upward to form a domed aura where it met the blackened, night sky. Along the horizon, a dusty, red mountain range framed the backdrop of the magnificent vista.

Brig's knees buckled. He grabbed onto the side of the viewing port to brace himself, one hand to his head. He had been many places in his life, and he thought he had seen everything - nothing could have prepared him for this. He closed his eyes.

"Where the Hell am I?"

"You are currently..." the central computer began.

"Stop. I will tell him myself," Steele interrupted.

"Very well, Dr. Fox," the voice replied with a courteous lilt.

Steele stepped forward, put a gentle hand on Brig's shoulder, and peered up at his face. "This is Red Colony One."

Brig furrowed his brow. "You mean..."

"Brigadier... welcome to Mars."

He leaned back against the glass. He put his head in his hands and rubbed his face with a desperate vigor – hoping to awaken from a bizarre dream. "But how... I don't remember how I got here."

"What's the last thing you remember before waking up?"

Brig's head spun. His mind ached when he thought about everything that happened before he awoke an hour ago. However, despite the realness of his surroundings and the cruel reality of his recent life, it all felt like a bad dream.

"I... I remember being at your father's..."

"My father's? Brigadier, honestly..."

He held up his hand in anger. "Then... I took your motorcycle to the array field."

"Then you saw it..."

"What?"

"The portal. That's how you got here."

Brig groaned and pressed the sides of his temples. He remembered the array field, but a thick haze blanketed the details of the remaining timeline.

"I think I remember that. But I didn't..."

"You were knocked unconscious by one of the guards there."

Brig squinted his disbelief. "They knocked me out? Why would they do that?"

"Be thankful that they weren't the types to do anything worse. Lucky for you, they are all mostly technicians."

Brig remained silent, glared at Steele in disbelief.

"In any case, they sent you through the portal - to here."

"I can't believe this. Why here? What is this place? How are *you* here?"

She tilted her head in incomprehension. "Brigadier, I do believe that this... whole experience is just too overwhelming for you. You're a bit delusional."

"No! It's not a delusion. It's not a dream."

"What more can I prove to you..."

"I know it was real! How do you explain my injuries when I got... here?"

"Hardly proof of what you claim. And certainly not proof that *I* was with you."

Brig pounded his fist against the thick glass. A veil of pain draped over his face as he peered out across the landscape. "I can't prove it. But I know it was real. I know it all happened..." His voice trailed off to a slight whimper. He rested his head against the viewport and closed his eyes.

She curled her lip and glanced away. "I think we need to get you back to your room. You need more rest." Steele strode like a graceful impala to the lift entrance. The door opened on silent command. She stepped inside and turned towards him.

After a few seconds, Brig rotated and stared at Steele. Like a reprimanded pet, he entered the lift with silent reluctance and stood next to her.

Brig sat forward on the recovery room couch, his head in his palms. The room had once again morphed, taking on the familiar form of Steele's apartment living room back on Earth. It provided both comfort and pain for him, but gave him the strand that he needed to keep himself grounded amongst the maddening confusion surrounding him.

"How long have I been here?" he mumbled to the empty room.

"Indeterminate," Steele's smooth voice responded through the silence.

Brig raised his eyes. "Oh... hey."

8: TABULA RASA

Steele stood a few meters in front of him, just inside the projected image of the apartment door. Brig was not sure how the lighting in this special room made her appear so crisp and beautiful, but he was not about to complain. The emerald in her eyes sparkled as he had never seen before, as if twinkling LEDs hid behind each iris. Her white jumpsuit form-fitted over her slender physique and buttoned up to her neck, where the collar disappeared under her auburn locks.

He did a double take. "What'd you do to your hair?"

She did not respond, only angled her head to the side with a mechanical smile.

He rose from the couch and approached her. "Somethin' different about you today..."

She ignored the comment. "You are not a registered citizen of Red Colony One, therefore the timeline for your residence has not been established."

Brig stared at her for a silent moment. Something was askew, and he could not place it. "Is it somethin' I said? Are you mad at me, Steele?"

A smile tore at the corner of her lip. "I'm not Dr. Fox. Although I understand your confusion."

Brig scrunched his brow.

"The central computer..." she clarified.

He reached his hand forward to touch her arm, but drew it back as it passed through to the other side. "So you're a..."

"Hologram, yes." She set a deliberate pace and rotated around him. "My designator is Darpa, named after the Defense Advanced Research..."

"Yeah, yeah. I know what it means," he interrupted. He scratched at his chin. "So is this the only room where you can..."

"I can manifest myself nearly anywhere within Red Colony One," she explained in a flat tone. "There are a few notable exceptions."

"And do you always look like Steele... um, Dr. Fox?"

"I believe Dr. Fox explained the thought algorithm process to you. Your strongest thoughts are clear to me. We've found that it's more soothing to take the form of someone that is at the forefront of your mind."

He stared past Darpa at the small kitchen, his mind replaying the events of the last night he had spent there on Earth. Steele had explained that it was all just computerized tricks and optics, but how could she believe that everything he was thinking about was not real?

The world spiraled around him. Nothing made sense, and as each second unfolded in this strange place, his head ached just a bit more. He sat back on the couch, placed his chin onto his palm.

What was the answer?

It came to him as soon as he thought it.

"Do you know about the Clarity Protocol?" It was a long shot, but something told him that if anyone was going to forthright with him now, it might as well be a computer.

"Yes."

"What can you tell me about it?"

"I'm sorry, Mr. Stroud. That data is classified, and you do not have the proper authority to access those files." She stepped forward and stood next to Brig, her hands obediently at the small of her back.

"Who does?"

"I'm sorry. That list is classified as well."

Brig rubbed his chin.

Another dead end.

He instinctively rubbed at his side, still feeling the phantom pain of the cracked ribs he had sustained back on Earth.

That's the answer.

"Am I allowed to see my medical records?" The echo of his voice immediately fell silent against the walls.

"Yes."

"Steele said that there was an... abnormality... found in my scan. Can you tell me about that?"

Darpa paused, her image appearing as if frozen. "Your records indicate that Dr. Fox deactivated gene sequence D42-19 sub 14."

"What do you know about... D42... whatever that name was?"

"D42-19 sub 14 is also known as the Clarity Protocol."

She knew. But how?

If it had all been a dream, how could it be that she knew about his condition? Worse, how could she have known how to treat it? He hated being caught between two worlds without the notion of which was real. Brig expected to wake at any moment and find himself passed out, drunk, in the sand at the array field - but that moment never came.

He studied the room - it was amazingly real. Even the sound of the rain gently tapping on the windows gave him an organic sense that he was actually there. He knew that it was a lie - at least this version of it.

His eyes fell upon his jacket, which hung upon the far wall. He crossed the room and snatched it from the hook. A small object leapt from the inner pocket and onto the floor with a light clatter.

Brig stared down at the floor in disbelief; a small plastic card lay at his feet.

"The cipher cards... the Hell?" He crouched next to it.

The strand that connected him to reality - the reality that *he* knew to be true - had presented itself. In the haze that had accompanied his journey to Red Colony One, he had completely forgotten about one of the major catalysts of recent events back on Earth. A set of cipher cards that connected Steele - the one back on Earth - to her past – and set her whole life into a downward spiral – apparently made the journey to the Red Planet along with him.

He stared at the card, not even sure if it was real, or just another image generated by the computer. The room's muted lighting reflected off the surface of the white card, exposing a dried bloodstain still on its face. He picked up the card, tapped it against his other palm. He turned to face the hologram.

"Darpa... can you read these cards?"

A panel opened on the wall with a light clunk and dropped a platter forward. She tilted her head in its direction.

"Place the cards on the tray, Mr. Stroud."

He extracted the remainder of the five cards from the jacket pocket and cautiously placed them on the platter. The panel closed with a smooth mechanical drone.

After a few moments, a display materialized in the center space of the room.

"Data card dump complete," Darpa said. "Displaying data."

"Ok then, let's see who's dreaming." As the data filled the display, Brig sat back on the couch, anxious as a young boy on the first day of school.

R. JAMES STEVENS

9:
Lost Souls

Mars. Red Colony One

The room filled with a three dimensional, rotating image. A matte-black gun, resembling a thinned artillery cannon – but with several sharp prongs at its tip that focused inward towards the snout – slowly tilted to show its cross-section. Behind the futuristic-looking gun, a seat hung from a connected chassis, upon which sat a series of small containers wired from the back of the cannon. Brig silently mouthed the nomenclature printed at the top of the display "Dark Matter Generator (DMG-42)".

Darpa had auto-dimmed the room's lighting, further intensifying the depth of the 3D effect. He peered from the corner of his eye, but the hologram of Steele's doppelganger had disappeared. He yawned and leaned his head against the couch pillow.

The digital slideshow continued, each image displaying and pointing out the equipment nuances, in both text and a subdued voice that narrated in the background. As the data exploded in front of him, slide after slide, one thing finally did catch Brig's attention - in the lower corner of each sat a designator: 'Project Architect: Steele Fox, PhD'.

Brig shook his head in disbelief. *My Steele, making heavy weaponry for the military.*

As the last weapon completed its axial rotation, the narration ceased and the hologram went dark. A single page of text, with a 3D watermark depicting the URA Eagle, came into focus.

> 'Project 42: Red Vision Mission Statement:
> To build upon the foundations of the groundwork laid by the Mars landing of 2067. We will establish a permanent colony - a foothold that will propel mankind on its exploration and discovery of the known universe.'

The page dissipated, replaced by another.

'In the past, the paradigm was a protracted effort to design, build and test rockets and associated propulsion systems that would ferry personnel and supplies to the Red Planet. Our aim is to encourage the ramping up of budgetary support in order to shorten that life cycle by an exponential degree.'

Although he was already convinced of his location, the words made his stomach drop. Brig had never heard of these plans. Why would the government have kept it all from the public? As it had been for more than seventy years, the space program had taken a backseat to politics, and news of planetary exploration was never the leading story on any news outlet.

Another thought stabbed at his brain. Did his father, the President of the URA, know about this effort? Surely, he had to have been kept in the loop, especially since it was obvious a massive amount of money must have been funneled into the project to make it a success - Brig's current surroundings were proof of that. And how did the URA manage to keep the rest of the world looking one way while they secretly made otherworldly plans?

Hide in plain sight.

The mission statement faded, replaced almost immediately with an image that grew from a pinhole of light, until it occupied the entire center of the room. A large, metal ring, mounted by several braces along its side and aimed at an angle towards the black sky, hovered within the display. The image rotated slowly, giving Brig a full view of the object within a few short seconds. A small amount of text pulsated above it: 'Long Distance Accelerating Aperture (LoDAAp)'.

Steele's voice began narration as the ring emanated a hum and began rotating around its axis.

"The DMST has developed a type of one-way portal utilizing quantum entanglement technology layered upon theoretical wormhole generation. This device permits travel along a pre-determined route in a minute fraction of the time relative to legacy space vehicles. Using a special satellite transmitter that communicates with a ground-

based quantum converter located in the southern desert of New Mexico, we have also gained the capability to piggyback faster-than-light communication into the tunnel. What used to take nearly twenty minutes for a duplex signal now takes under fifteen seconds."

The data ignited a spark in Brig's brain, and what had been a cloudy half-memory since he came to Mars suddenly cleared.

"At the array field. That's what I saw," he said aloud. "I'll be damned... it's true."

A recording of a video feed filled the hologram. A man, round-faced with glasses perched atop his nose, glared straight forward into the camera. A small readout at the bottom of the feed listed his name: William Hanley, Director URA Security Alliance.

"Fox, I just got your latest reports. We need to discuss the alternatives in case this CME is as bad as your daughter's algorithms are predicting. Project 42 is now your... our... number one priority. I'll set up a meeting with the General Assembly as soon as possible. Hanley out."

The image faded.

A queer sensation grew in Brig's gut, although the connection between the data he was seeing and the Earth Steele's actions the hours leading up to her death, was not making itself apparent.

A familiar face replaced Hanley's: Bronson Fox, Steele's father and Director of the DMST - however, a much younger version of him.

Brig recalled his final interactions with the man in recent months. "Wow. He did not age well..."

"William. I sincerely believe that Project 42 is now our only option. You must brief the GA immediately. Otherwise, the projected fallout from the CME would be... catastrophic. We must act in everyone's best interests before it's too late."

The image popped to static. A pair of emerald eyes flashed onto the display.

"Facial calibration, please," came the recognizable voice with the British intonation. The camera went fuzzy for a second, and then refocused outward, now showing her entire face.

"Father... ahem... Director Fox. I've uploaded the latest batch of mass ejection forecasts. As you can see, things are much worse than the old algorithm had foretold. Can we please meet and discuss options to circumvent the catastrophic CME. We have nearly three years to plan and implement a design - surely that is enough time."

Brig flopped back onto the couch, his head squeezed between his arms. Steele's face faded to static.

"She knew... they *all* knew."

He could not believe he was saying those words. Indeed, the proof that was perched under all of their noses had finally reared its grotesque head. The DMST, the URA Security Alliance, Bronson Fox – and yes, even Steele – were privy to the Event that essentially sent the Earth back to the feudal Dark Ages.

"Cryp was telling the truth. I can't believe it."

Something still did not seem right, however. Why would Steele fling herself off a building just because of a cover-up? Was she even involved in it other than just providing a warning ahead of time?

Brig growled. Nothing was making sense. Before he could solve the mystery of her death, he needed to figure out exactly *who* she was. Was she really Steele - or was the person here on *Mars* whom he knew to be the real Steele? How was it all possible?

"Darpa." Brig stared blankly forward, the odd set of puzzle pieces floating in his mind with no clear way to put them together.

The flawless image of his childhood friend reappeared across the room, behind the display. "Yes, Mr. Stroud."

"Where'd this data come from?"

"It appears to be a permanent archival copy removed from the DMST classified HyperNebula."

Someone didn't want this getting out. He rubbed a thumb along his bottom lip. *But who?*

"Is there anything more?" he asked.

"Yes. There are research lab audit logs. Do you wish to view them?"

"Sure..." Brig closed his eyes, trying to comprehend the swirling vortex of information that surrounded him.

A video feed began. It was Steele again, this time from an above angle as she sat at her laboratory desk.

"Audit log, October, two thousand seventy-four," a subdued computerized voice narrated in the background track of the video.

"I've completed development of the Memory Matrix," said Steele, staring directly forward at her own display, "and it is ready for testing. However, after discussions with Director Fox, it has become apparent that a valid test will not be feasible. Human testing policies and the like. Animal testing is futile. We need vocal feedback of the procedural results. To that end..." She drew a deep breath. "...I will be administering the test on myself. As well as my father, Director Bronson Fox."

The audit log blipped, as if edited for content, and then displayed Steele once again.

"I have successfully extracted a synapse nebula from my own cortex into the Matrix, and then subsequently inserted that bit of memory into the other test subject – my father." Steele's expression remained solemn. "I performed the same procedure on myself, inserting his memories into my own cortex."

Steele stopped to rub her eyes. She held her head.

"The primary side effects have been headaches and lucid dreams. I have designed a blocking procedure that effectively dims specific areas of the target's brain from being accessed. The resulting data has shown an overwhelming success of the procedure. I can liberally access the set of memories that I have extracted from the other test subject. They replay in my mind as if they were my own."

The video halted.

Brig scratched his head in distant thought. Maybe this was the reason for Steele's aberrant behavior prior to her death. Maybe it was enough to send her over the edge. He had a sense that there was still more to the puzzle.

"Darpa. Is there anything on these cards about a project named... Red Vision?"

"Yes, Mr. Stroud. There is one additional entry. Replaying now..." She turned her back as the video switched.

113

The image of Bronson Fox, showing a significant amount of age since the last transmission, stretched across the video once again. Hanley's image popped into a box lower in the display.

"William, have you any news on the budget?"

"Fox," Hanley answered, somewhat out of breath and seemingly distracted. "Good news. We got full approval for Project 42... Red Vision. Get that portal up and running at all costs."

"That is good news," Fox answered with a lilt in his voice. "And what of the plans for extraction?"

"Nothing has changed, Fox. Continuity of this Republic's government is of the utmost urgency. Show me success with the portal, and then we'll discuss who goes where."

"Marvelous..." Fox hissed, as Hanley's image faded. Fox spun in his chair in a slow semi-circle, until he was but a side profile. The room's glow highlighted a small marking at the base of his skull. The video ceased once again.

Brig was confused now more than ever. While damning evidence, it still did not seem to him a reason for Steele's bizarre behavior the final days of her life. Nor did it answer the ultimate question in his mind – how was it that he watched her die, yet she was here alive and well on Mars - and claiming complete ignorance of everything that had happened in the past three months?

He leaned forward on the couch, rubbing his temples with each set of fingertips.

The video sprung to life again.

"Gentlemen," Bronson Fox's voice announced. Brig rolled his eyes upward without moving his head. "We have some amazing progress to report on both projects. I have no doubt you will be immensely pleased with the results. I will turn over the presentation to Dr. Steele Fox."

"Thank you, Director Fox." Steele's image populated one of the larger of two squares at the top of the feed. Her eyes, normally vibrant and full of effervescence, seemed to be cloudy and altogether distant. A small conference table with several men seated, all paying close attention to their own feed, filled the bottom of the display. "From the first day that the DMST took control of this project, it has been our department's mission to determine how best to make use of this... technology... as it pertains to the military of this republic. I am pleased to announce that the Memory Matrix has been a complete success to date. We have successfully retrieved and stored selectable portions of human memory from a live patient."

The men seated mumbled amongst themselves, leaning towards one another to confer before turning their attention back to her. "Dr. Fox, can you explain the capacity in which the DMST can utilize this... technology? It doesn't seem relevant..." The air of doubt was obvious in his voice.

Steele gulped, peered down at her notes. "Right. As you are well aware, the issue of soldiers returning from battle at... less than full operational capacity has always been a perplexing one."

She stopped and licked her lips. Bronson squinted and rubbed at his chin.

"I believe what Dr. Fox is getting at, gentlemen," he interjected, "is that we have developed a method in which we can reclaim our operational assets."

"And how is that?" the man asked.

"Genetic transmutation..." Bronson explained, his hands at a point near his chin.

The man waved his hand in a dismissive swipe. "Fox, it's all been tried before. You know the failed results that have come from..."

"I'm quite aware of previous attempts. This is different. We are using... alternate hosts." Bronson's tone turned authoritatively serious.

"But how..." the man balked.

"There is an abundant source of... candidates for these types of procedures. Ones that I believe will open your eyes to the possibilities." The corners of Bronson's mouth scrolled upwards.

The feed faded into silent static.

Brig sat in silence, pondering what it all meant. The more he saw, the less he understood how it all fit together.

Another video began.

A man, apparently in his twenties, sat at a table in the center of a pallid, white room. He stared forward, devoid of expression, his hands down at his sides.

Steele's voice provided the narration.

"Subject name... Jonathan Altman Powell. Aged twenty-seven. Career criminal, given a life sentence for the murder of his parents at age fourteen."

A small inset displayed two pictures of another man. In the first, a standard photo of a URA marine in dress uniform. In the second, a man lying in a bed, missing both arms and legs.

"The original host, Corporal James Satterfield. Aged twenty-nine. Critically injured in a raid during the battle of

Southern France in 2069, and as you can see, a quadriplegic due to his injuries. Using our revolutionary method, we have spliced a complete strand of Corporal Satterfield's DNA into Powell's. Powell's mind has been effectively blocked using a technique that I have designed, which allows for the DNA transmutation to take place unfettered - as well as subduing the alternate host's state of being."

The video of the prisoner sped forward in time lapse, depicting the stunning transformation of Powell into Satterfield. Brig rubbed his eyes, unable to fathom what he had just witnessed.

"A very interesting transformation, indeed. We have found that within days of gene transplant, the alternate host begins to age at a rapid rate, slowing down as it approaches symbiosis, and then matching the pace of the original host. Although two years apart, at the end of two weeks, both men were of identical age, physiology-wise."

The white room image took over the entire display. Powell – now fully resembling Satterfield in appearance – sat up, a dazed expression on his face.

"State your name please," Steele's voice asked from beyond sight of the camera.

"James Satterfield," the man mouthed as if a waking zombie. He squinted at his surroundings.

"And do you understand how you came to be here?"

"I... I was in a car accident... I think," he responded in an uneven cadence.

"A complete synapse mapping, minus the edited out events of his actual injuries, was reprogrammed into his brain. For all intents and purposes, Jonathan Altman Powell no longer exists. He is Corporal James Satterfield."

Brig leaned forward, elbows propped on his knees, and shook his head. "What does this have to do with Red Vision?"

"I don't have an answer for you, Mr. Stroud," Darpa responded. She tilted her head at him. "Perhaps there is more information on subsequent videos?"

9: LOST SOULS

A shiver drove down Brig's spine. The presence of Darpa as a digital entity - as she had referred to herself - made him more uneasy than he could recall ever being.

Once again, the hologram popped to life - and once again, the white room filled the screen. A young man in his teens sat at the same table. The readout at the bottom of the log displayed 'Allistair Cromwell'.

Brig squinted at the man. Something seemed familiar about him – the sharp edges to his face, the crispness of his jet-black coif - but he could not determine why those stood out to him.

The man craned his neck to see around him. A small tattoo at the base of his neck exposed itself to the light.

After a few moments of watching the man sit in silence, sneering at his surroundings and the camera, lightning struck Brig's mind.

"He looks like... a young Bronson Fox." Brig's eyes wandered to the date on the video log - 2075. "Is that Bronson Fox?"

"Facial recognition algorithm indicates a potential match with Mr. Fox and this individual," Darpa offered.

"But... how?"

Darpa did not respond.

The feed jumped and depicted the white room once more. A small girl cowered in the far corner, her nightgown stretched from shoulder to ankles. Through the grainy video, Brig could see light shining off her shaved head. A small tattoo made itself clear, identical to the one seen on Cromwell just moments ago, at the base of her skull.

Brig watched in confusion.

"Who's Nadia Temple?" he asked aloud, reading the small text at the bottom of the display.

The girl glared up at the camera, as if someone had called her name. Her emerald eyes pierced into Brig's soul.

Suddenly, the form of Steele stepped through the hologram and stopped in front of Brig. Darpa's hologram dissipated.

"Nadia whom?" Steele asked.

"That's enough, Darpa," Brig commanded.

"As you wish, Mr. Stroud." The video display terminated. The lights in the room rose to their normal, subdued intensity.

"Well, I see that you are on a first name basis with the computer."

"Might as well be, she's *you* after all, right? Can't get her to call me Brig yet, though. But I'm workin' on it."

"What in the world were you watching?"

"Nothing. Just something I got from a... friend... a while back." Brig stared away in deep thought.

Steele walked towards the door, stopped and faced him. "I just thought I'd tell you that your latest scan came back clean. You're in perfect health, Brigadier."

"That's good to know, I guess." Brig could not have sounded more unenthusiastic. As was his modus operandi, getting to the bottom of the mystery staring him right in the face was ever more important than his health. "Steele?"

"Hmm?" she cooed.

"Mind showin' me around a bit. You know, somewhere other than the observation tower?"

"So, you're finally convinced you're not dead, are you?"

He would have expected an eye roll to accompany the biting sarcasm she had just imparted. "Yeah... I get that now." He scratched the back of his head with one hand. "But..." Brig fell silent.

"But... what?"

He sprung from the couch, grasped the back of her arm with a gentle touch and guided her to the door. "Walk and talk," he said as they stepped into the corridor.

The door glided closed.

10:
The Tragic Life and Death of Nadia Temple

Broad Haven, Wales - Ten years prior (2074)

Echoes of the surf's soft ramblings against the rocks, several kilometers away in St. Bride's Bay, rode upon the wind. The damp sea breeze carried their murmurs across the rolling hills and around the bend, up past the hedgerow and through the drive gate of the Temple stead.

Samuel Pence Temple, the patriarch of his small, Welsh family of three, was away at an impromptu meeting that he had deemed 'important'. Camille Adele Temple, his wife, knew all too well that simply meant he was meeting up with his bookie for the latest score.

She did not like the fact that her husband had a penchant for making wagers, especially since he tended to be unluckier than he claimed. However, she knew that there could be far worse vices for him to adopt.

There had been the period when he was involved in the shadier side of business down in Swansea, which took him away from his loved ones far too often. His late night hours during that time in their lives had kept her constantly on edge, and the mysterious phone calls at odd hours did nothing to ease her mind.

He had wisely decided to retire from his unsavory dealings - and not a minute too soon, as the combined police forces of Wales began working closely with Scotland Yard to bring about the end of their activities. While no charges had ever been formally filed against him, nor had he even been brought in for questioning, it was a commonly-held belief that it was much more than just a dalliance for him, and the authorities were circling the wagons just about the time he had made his exit from his shadowy dealings.

She stood at her stove, her platinum-blonde locks tied back in a pony, stirring the onion gravy that would adorn the bangers and tomatoes she was preparing for dinner. Samuel was never a fan of mash, so Camille had patterned her own recipe to his liking. An odd pairing, for sure, but it was just one of the many reasons for him to want to stay at home more often.

The video monitor chimed. She dabbed a small bead of sweat from her brow, set down the cleaver with which she had split the meat, and tapped at the small console beneath the wall-mounted screen.

"Well, hello dear," Samuel's voice rang.

She rolled her eyes towards the display. The video, from the perspective of the center spoke of his steering wheel, showed Samuel paying strict attention to the road, while every few seconds taking a peek into the rearview.

"Darling, I do hope you're on your way home. Dinner will be ready soon," she said. She released a sigh, but Sam did not react.

He took a few quick breaths, looked nervously in the mirror once more, and then down at the wheel-mounted camera. His razor-thin mustache glistened with fresh sweat. "Yes, yes," he chuckled. "I'm on my way now."

"Good, Nadia will be home any moment, and you know how she likes to see her Daddy as soon as she gets in."

"Of course, always." He looked in the mirror once again before focusing forward.

The sound of the engine revving filled the background of the cabin.

"Camille, dear. I have great news. Something that's going to change our lives forever!"

"Oh dear. Not another one of your get-rich-quick opportunities again, is it?"

"No, no. Not this time. This can't miss."

She had heard it before. Samuel was always trying to change their fortunes with some scheme or another. It was something that she could never understand; she never felt that their lot in life was anything of which to be ashamed. The debt that they owed to the banks for their land and home were nothing compared to the ones that he had incurred over the years doing his other 'work'. Banks did not come calling in the middle of the night to collect, either.

"Mmm hmm," she said under her breath.

"We'll talk more when I get home. I've... got to focus," he said while short of breath, taking a quick peek over his shoulder before the video terminated.

Camille giggled aloud. "He's always up to something."

The front door flew open, and then banged shut.

"Mother! I'm home," shouted a young girl's voice from the foyer.

"Nadia! How many times must I tell you not to slam that door. Your father will be home any minute now, and I don't think he cares to spend his time fixing that frame again!"

"Sorry, Mother," Nadia chirped. She pranced into the kitchen and stopped at the small island in the center. She stared at the back of her mother's head, unable to contain the smile that consumed her face.

Nadia, a spritely eight-year-old, was always a pleasant child, but something seemed to be eager to burst from her this time. She brushed her long, auburn hair aside, exposing her emerald eyes.

"Mum," she said.

Her mother did not respond. Camille stabbed at the bangers in the pan, keeping them from burning.

"Mum," Nadia repeated.

"Yes, dear," Camille finally answered over her shoulder.

"Is Dad home yet? I've got to tell him, I just have to," Nadia gushed.

"Tell him what, dear?"

"Oh he'll be so proud, Mum. I got Best Girl today. I can't wait to tell him!" She ran forward, grabbed her mother around the waist and squeezed.

Camille kissed her daughter on the top of her head, stroked her hair back to her shoulders. "Nadia, you're such a pleasure to see every day."

Nadia giggled. She looked past her mother's waist at the sizzling pan. "Bloody bangers again?"

"Nadia, mind your tongue."

"Sorry mother, but that *is* what they look like."

"No need to be fresh about it, young lady." Camille held her child at arm's length with a scolding glance.

"Yes, Mum," Nadia replied, with an innocence only an eight-year-old could muster.

"Now go and get washed up, your father..." Camille started, but the sound of a door slamming in the drive drew their attention.

"He's here! He's here!" Nadia was giddy with excitement at the prospect of sharing her incredible news with her father. She dashed to the front door.

"Nadia! Don't rush him all at once like that. Let your father unwind, dear."

"Yes, Mum."

A second set of muted thuds sounded from the front of the house. Camille unstrapped her apron, tossed it onto the island and walked to the front door. Nadia had already opened it and stood at the top step, looking on as her father faced the driveway. Camille stepped up behind her daughter and peered out at Samuel.

"Sam," Camille called. "Are you coming in, dear?"

Sam tilted his head over his shoulder at Camille, then back at the drive. Two other men in drab clothing stepped out of a second car that had stopped just behind his, one of its front wheels recklessly on the moist sod.

Camille stepped up in front of her daughter, pushed her back softly with one hand. "Sam?" she said, her voice quaking a tad.

One of the men grunted something inaudible at Sam, to which both men peered up at the porch where Camille and Nadia stood. Sam unevenly placed a hand on the man's shoulder and patted it. The man flicked away his hand and shoved at Sam's chest.

Camille started down the steps.

The other man grabbed at Sam's vest, shoved him against his car.

"Nadia, go in the house. Now!" Camille called back, as she made her way onto the damp grass towards her husband. Nadia obediently retreated into the house and glared out through the screen door at the proceedings.

"Sam, what's going on?" Camille demanded, taking a cautious step towards the three men.

Before she could say another word, the second man released Sam while the first drew a small handgun and forced it into Sam's gut. A sharp crack rolled across the hillsides. A small wisp of smoke wafted from between the two men. Sam staggered backward and fell to the ground holding his abdomen, blood finding its way around his fingertips and forming a large stain across his vest.

"No!" Camille sprinted forward to aide her fallen husband. The armed thug spun, raised his gun and unleashed a slug into her forehead. She flipped backward onto the ground in an awkward bend.

Satisfied that their work was complete, the first man stuffed the gun into his belt and strode to the car. The second grabbed his arm, rotated him to face the house, pointed at the door and mumbled an angry grunt. The first nodded, extracted the still smoking weapon and stalked up the walk to the porch.

Nadia, wearing a glazed look of terror, yelped and fled from the door. The thug scaled the stairs like a pouncing lion, tore open the door and chased her in through the foyer.

10: THE TRAGIC LIFE AND DEATH OF NADIA TEMPLE

As she entered the kitchen and rounded the small island, the thug closed the gap. He grabbed at her hair and whipped her sideways onto the floor, knocking her viciously against the cabinet. She backed against it and slowly rose to her feet. Nadia screamed in horror as the man stood over her and raised the gun to her forehead with a demonic grin.

She forced her eyes shut.

As the metallic clink of the trigger moving filled her ears, she grasped the handle of the sputtering frying pan behind her and flung its fiery contents into the face of her attacker. The thug dropped the gun and screamed uncontrollably, clawing at his blistered face with bent fingers.

Nadia unconsciously pulled her mother's cleaver from the countertop and stabbed at the man's midsection, piercing his belly with the tip. He fell to the ground with a bellow and pulled himself into a ball.

Rather than flee at the sudden opportunity of escape, Nadia instead chose to strike at the man again, puncturing him repeatedly until he no longer moved. Her primal wail overpowered his. It echoed throughout the kitchen and into the foyer, freezing the second thug that had stormed into the house.

Before he could comprehend the scene, young Nadia was upon him with the knife, stabbing with animalistic brutality until he, too, fell to the ground lifeless.

After several more moments of her relentless attack on his mutilated body, she finally ceased. Nadia dropped the cleaver onto the wooden floor with a clack and pushed herself back against the wall. She wiped a bloody arm across her nose, leaving a streak of crimson in its wake that stretched from her chin up around to one ear. The silent tears began to cascade her cheeks.

A half hour later, at the urgings of neighbors that had heard the sudden gunshots across the fields between their houses, the local police had arrived. Although not surprised to find Samuel Pence Temple and his wife shot dead outside of their modest home, they did receive quite an unexpected shock when entering the Temple stead.

Nadia sat against the wall, staring blankly forward past the mangled and bloody corpse of one of the thugs. In the kitchen, a large stream of violet blood pooled just beyond the center island, filling the crevices of the second thug's boots lying within it. Even though it was apparent to them how the scene had played out, they could not get Nadia to corroborate – or even talk.

Several weeks passed, and Nadia remained mute despite the best efforts of dozens of crisis and trauma experts. Her only living relative, her uncle Parker, had long since left Wales for the URA in search of a better life, and could not be reached.

On one particularly rainy Sunday, Nadia's fate took a rather curious turn.

"Nadia, you have a visitor," the attendant called from the doorway of her room. The staff at the asylum had, for all purposes, given up trying to communicate with the child. However, they were more than eager to rid themselves of her eerie, silent presence.

Nadia, of course, did not answer. She glared at the window, her faded emerald eyes not even registering a flinch.

The attendant shook her head, turned and pointed. A tall, lanky man stood next to the attendant and gazed a furtive glance into the room. The hallway's dim light backlit his prematurely gray hair, highlighting a small mark at the base of his neck.

"That's her. I can bring her home now," he cooed with wicked pretense, his inflection a suave British.

"Just fill out the paperwork at the front office, Mr..."

"Bryce. Parker Bryce," the man answered.

The woman nodded, ignoring the chill permeating her spine, before she disappeared into the hallway.

The man glanced at Nadia once more and cackled under his breath. "Marvelous..."

Several months later

Nadia awoke with a start, pushed herself up to a sitting position. Even with an absence of equipment, the sterility of the room made the facility's medical purpose clear. While still not her home, there was long lost hope that something had changed since the days in the asylum. She hopped to her feet and landed square on the parquet floor - her white, cloth nightgown flowing out around her.

A strange fog distorted her mind. How long had she been asleep? What day was it - and where was this place? She thought as hard as she could, but could not come up with any logical answers to her questions.

She made her way to the door, which strangely enough, whooshed open as soon as she stood in front of it. She stepped out into a hall that stretched on seemingly forever in each direction. Her toes wiggled at the tactile sensation of the crimson shag beneath her feet, and her eyes wandered to the large eagle adorning the wall several meters to her left. Its penetrating gaze frightened her, but somehow called her forward.

A man stood at the intersection of the hallway and a grand foyer, his back to her as he conversed with a woman standing in front of him. Nadia moved like a swift jungle feline along the corridor until she stood just behind him.

The woman broke conversation and offered a surprised glare. The man spun on a casual heel and met Nadia's gaze up at him. He knelt his tall frame down to meet her at eye level, ran one hand over his salt-and-pepper hair.

She had never met the man, she was certain. However, the more that she gazed into his eyes, the more she became entirely *uncertain*. Did she know him? Her brain felt soggy and pained her the harder she pressed it for information.

The man smiled unevenly and grasped her arm. "Now you know you shouldn't be out here. Time to go back to your room, Steele." He led her back to her doorway with a swiftness that told her she was not to see outside of her quarters.

Nadia cast her confusion back up at the man as she stepped inside. "Father?" Her voice was as timid as a field mouse.

"Hmm?" he cooed.

She stared at his eyes again. *Yes, that's it. Father.*

"Nothing..." she said. She spun away and entered the room.

He smiled and disappeared into the foyer.

She slowly paced the room, satisfied that she now had the answer for which she was looking. She caught her reflection in the mirror to one side of the room, stepped closer to it. Her hand unconsciously moved from her stubbled head down to the base of her neck, where a spot tingled like a carpet burn. She stared into her own green eyes, lost for a moment in their depth.

"I'm... Steele Fox," she chanted.

Outside Flagstaff, Arizona - Early 2084

The rain fell in stabbing sheets as Nadia Temple stumbled out onto the rooftop of her apartment building. She ignored the blood that still oozed from her wrist, a product of the break-in she had performed hours earlier at Clive Underwood's edge-of-town workshop. A clap of thunder shook the building, but she did not waver from her course.

She reached the edge of the side wall, pulled herself up onto the fire escape and closed her eyes. Never had things been so clear to her - never had they been so confusing and muddled. Both realities had come crashing together in one cataclysmic swoop when she viewed the data on the cipher cards, and the horrifying truth that she was never supposed to discover opened the mental block that had plagued her for years.

She was never Steele Fox, at least not in any natural sense. The cards hid the truth - the truth that destroyed both of her lives: Steele's and Nadia's.

Now, on the verge of mental collapse due to the overwhelming confusion and dread that she could not escape, she opened her eyes and looked up into the rainy sky.

"Steele!" a voice cried from behind her.

It's the storm.

Again, the voice called out to her.

"You shouldn't be here!"

As if awoken from her trance, Nadia gawked over her shoulder.

It's that man again. He took several steps. *It's Brigadier, Steele. You know him!* the other voice shouted.

"Go away, Brigadier," she sniffled through the deluge. She spun her head away.

"I love you, Steele... please! Don't do this, it was all my fault..." Brigadier pled. "I didn't think about the consequences, and I'm sorry it turned out the way it did. But please don't..."

He loves me? How is that possible? I don't know him!

"You love me? You don't know me, Brigadier." The words flowed like a script through her quivering lips.

"I know you better than I've ever known anyone in my *life*, Steele," Brig argued with a forced calm, taking another step closer to her.

"*Stop!*" Nadia cried maniacally through her tears, craning her neck to face Brig. "Don't come any closer..."

"Whatever this *is*, Steele, we can work through it. We can get through this *together*." His voice cracked.

Nadia cupped her hand over her mouth and began to sob. Her chest heaved as she turned to look down at the street below. Her two conflicting worlds were colliding in her head. She did not know in which she belonged, but she knew that she did not want to be in either. There was no safe place, and she could not go on living a lie. She remembered it all: her father's deception, her role in the grand lie perpetrated to the unsuspecting public - and her birth parents' tragic death.

"It's a *lie... it's a lie...*" she said, continuing to chant. Her voice faded.

"I don't *understand*, Steele. What's going on? *What's* a lie?" Brig shouted.

"*I'm sorry... I'm sorry...*" she cried, shaking her head, her eyes slanted almost shut. The tears flowed in a deluge.

"Sorry? You don't *have* anything to be sorry for, sweetheart. *Please...*"

Nadia closed her eyes. *And she leapt.*

As her body plummeted, she gazed into the weeping sky.

The soft ramblings of the surf, washing against the shore several kilometers out to St. Bride's Bay, flooded back to her. She dashed into the Temple stead, slamming the front door behind her.

"Mum!" she cried. "Mum, is Dad home yet?"

She waited for her mother's response, but it did not come.

"He'll be so proud, Mum. I got Best Girl today. Oh, he'll be so proud."

She coughed.

The rain washed across her face and woke her. Thunder, like a gunshot, echoed off the nearby brick façade. Brigadier was there again.

He has to know, Steele Fox's voice called to her. *He has to be told about it all.*

"You were... always there," she said weakly, trying to force a smile. "You have to... save yourself. Promise me," she demanded in a broken voice. "Red Vision..." She nodded her head with vigorous persistence, despite her broken and dying body. She pawed lovingly at his face. "Red Vision."

11:
Overburdened

Mars. Red Colony One - Present day (2084)

"And this is the entertainment sector," Steele said, pacing through an intersection of corridors that opened up into a larger, LED-adorned complex.

"Entertainment? You thought of everything, huh?" Brig glanced between the attractions and Steele.

"You can't be all work, after all," she said with a grin. "There's your standard pub or two. A small bistro over there. The food might be a little different than you're used to, however."

"A bit of home away from home then?"

"Yes. Although in this case... *home*."

He stared at her for a moment, eyeing the accomplishments of the colony. "You don't miss Earth?"

"What's to miss? Besides, this is the present *and* the future. We have to keep our eyes looking forward." Her tone lent more to the possibility that she had forcefully convinced herself of that opinion.

"That sounds a lot like your father talking."

She glared at him. "No... it's not. I believe in that vision as well."

"There's more back *there* than you think. You'd be surprised."

"What does that mean?"

"You were there."

"Not this rubbish again. Really?"

She's definitely spunky like the old Steele. And stubborn.

"I'm right here, Brigadier. I'm alive." She emphasized each word for effect.

"I'm not saying you aren't. But I know what I saw." Brig shook his head in disgusted frustration.

"Look, I'm sorry," she offered.

"Sorry... for *what*?"

"That you went through whatever you did. That you had to live back there during everything that... happened. That someone took it upon themselves to impersonate me and confuse you like this."

"No! That was no impersonator."

"That's simply delusional."

Brig crossed his arms in defiance and leaned against a nearby support beam jutting from the curved wall.

"Look," she sighed, "you've been through a lot. And quite frankly, I'm both amazed and... ecstatic that you found your way here." She grasped his hand in hers and gazed with an enticing want. "It feels like a dream."

Brig smiled, looked down at their entwined hands. "Now you know how I feel." He returned her gaze, trying to stare deep into her soul.

"I know it's difficult," she continued. "Everything is different. But you'll get used to it. In time."

Her words struck him at an odd angle. Was she talking about the fact that he was on Mars? Or was she referring to... *herself?*

"Come, let's finish the tour. I've something amazing to show you." She pulled him along as if a giddy schoolgirl.

Steele led Brig onto a wide, enclosed catwalk set in between and above two towering, semi-transparent domes. They stopped on an enclosed metal concourse and surveyed a massive forest of plants below.

Brig raised his eyebrows. "Wow."

"This... is the solarium. It provides all of the food for the colony," she bragged, leaning backward against the glass, continuing to stare at Brig.

He squinted into the relative darkness below. Several people walked through one of the rows, a small glint of lighting reflecting off their protective facemasks.

"Why do they need masks to be in there?"

"Because anyone would die within five minutes of hypercapnia without it. The atmosphere inside the domes is almost pure carbon dioxide."

He furrowed his brow at her.

"The solarium also doubles as an oxygen generator. Carbon dioxide that is expelled from the inhabitants of the colony is directed into the solarium, where it acts as natural fuel for the plants. Oxygen from the plants is filtered out, harnessed and sent to the colony for life support. Any surplus is sent to the storage reserves at the other end of the city. These simple plants provide over seventy percent of the colony's basic life support, Brigadier."

"Pretty impressive, Steele. This is all you, huh?"

She blushed. "Well, it's a team effort really. But physics is wonderful. If you're familiar with the blueprints of everything, anything is possible."

"Right... but all of this had to come from somewhere," he said, pointing out to his surroundings.

"Natural resources, of course."

"Natural? Mars has all this?"

"Well, we do have a mining facility at the base of the mountain range, but that's... not exactly... where it *all* came from."

He squinted at her hesitation. "So where then?"

She rolled her eyes away from his glare.

"Earth?" He raised his eyebrows in incredulity.

Steele pursed her lips and offered a quick nod.

Brig propped his hands on his hips and scanned around him. The bigger picture had suddenly become clear.

"So that's what the portal's for? You're all just raping Earth for the good of the colony?" He growled through his teeth.

"That's a rather vulgar way of putting it, don't you think?"

Brig shook his head.

"It was *always* the plan, Brigadier. It was always about maximum sustainability for this colony, regardless of what you might think. We built and advanced this colony so that when things like... *that*... happened on Earth, mankind could be assured of being able to survive."

Brig snorted his overt disapproval. She grabbed his hand with both of hers.

"Brigadier... let's not argue. It's obvious you have some deep-founded feelings about this, but I don't want those to spoil our time together. Do you?" she said with renewed innocence.

Her touch both warmed his heart and chilled his soul. He had missed her more than anything, and her eyes melted away his anger.

Brig examined the scale of the two domes while scratching the back of his head with one hand. "That's an awful lot of plants. How many people are here, anyway?"

"Twelve hundred and sixty," she said in an authoritative brag. "Actually, twelve hundred and sixty one." She patted his chest lovingly.

"Twelve hundred and sixty two," Darpa announced locally from a speaker above them.

Steele frowned and looked up at the ceiling. "I believe you're mistaken."

"There are twelve hundred and sixty two individuals located within Red Colony One as of last count forty two minutes ago. Twelve hundred and sixty are registered citizens," Darpa expounded.

Steele folded her lips into a crooked sneer. She glared at Brig. "Well, we know who *one* is. I don't suppose you had a mouse in your pocket when you came through?"

Her face ignited into a wide smile - Brig returned it with his own. They locked eyes for what seemed minutes without speaking. Then, without warning, she went on the offensive and pressed her lips against his.

Brig did not resist at first. He had missed the feel of her warmth next to him, and the remembrance of his pleas to have her back just once more replayed in his mind.

The familiar but strange feeling began to fester within him. He had always loved Steele - this Steele - in a brotherly fashion. He had been her protector throughout several years of her young life. But what he was feeling was not for her. It was for... the *other*.

He withdrew from the kiss and pressed his mouth to the back of his wrist.

"What's wrong?" Steele tugged his arm.

He locked eyes with her and smiled sheepishly.

"Nothing. It's just all... overwhelming," he answered. "I think I just need some more rest."

She wrapped her arms under his shoulders and laid her head on his chest. "I'm so happy that you're here."

"Me, too."

The distance in his gaze, however, described a different story.

Brig sucked a deep breath and strained against the rock walls pressing his ribs. He tilted his head upward. The small pinhole of light emanated from the distance, but something drew him downward into the abyss. A crimson-tinged light, flickering like a strobe, pulled him ever lower.

Voices from the depths filled his ears. They became louder still as he worked his way into the cold ground. The walls around him squeezed tighter, forcing the air from his lungs - but the magnet of truth yanked him farther still. The soil thumped with a rhythmic beat, as if someone were pounding a heavy hammer into the dirt beneath his feet.

The ground shook once more and suddenly he was free from the restrictive tunnel. He fell downward, freefalling meter upon meter, tumbling uncontrollably until his body landed in a soft pile of dark sand.

When he regained consciousness several hours later, the monotonous drone of trudging feet pricked his ears. Like a grand eagle, he stretched his arms outward and upward, happy to be free from the constraints of the tunnel above. He ran his hands over his stubbled head, flexing his muscles with an eager anticipation as he peered down at his nakedness.

The darkened shadows of a horde marching against him dimmed the reflection of the light ahead. He peered at their faces, squinting to distinguish them from one another, but the lack of light in the pit, and the soot that clung to their flesh, made it impossible. They marched in unison, their heads hung from exhaustion, their shoulders and backs scarred from their labors. None raised their eyes to him.

"Who are you?" Brig screamed.

Each wave passed, row by row, but did not look at him.

Brig grabbed an arm of a man that walked close to him. The man pulled it back without looking up and continued his march forward.

"Where are you going?" Brig demanded.

He spun and watched the mass of humanity file in a silent order by rows of five abreast. The line stretched on for hundreds of meters, where it met the shaded outline of a black opening ahead.

The lemmings continued their solemn stampede until they reached the aperture, where they stepped off into the nothingness and floated helplessly into the void beyond.

Brig's voice left him. He witnessed their infinite death march, five-by-five, disappearing from sight only to be followed by an endless line of replacements. He frantically grabbed at passersby, man and woman alike, but none would heed his cries. They continued on, either oblivious or apathetic to their fate, a low chorus of mumbles emanating from their masses.

A familiar warmth took seed at Brig's core. A strange, crimson glow reflected on the expressionless faces that marched nearest him, one that Brig realized came from him. He looked down; a painted, white star emblazoned across his muscular chest began to glow red. The strength of an army suddenly welled from within him.

He plucked at the arms of another man from his row, this time easily forcing him to stop and pay attention to Brig.

"Where are you going?" Brig commanded.

The man, a look of dazed defeat across his face and a white ring of chalk around his neck, glared blankly back at him. "We are the expendable. Our tasks are complete."

Brig scowled. "Don't you realize you're heading to your death?"

The man repeated his chant. "We are the expendable. Our tasks are complete."

Brig shook the man as if waking him from a nightmare. "You have to turn back!"

The star on Brig's chest glowed brighter than ever before. The man took notice. His eyes inflated, the glaze that covered them lifted like a velvet curtain. He saw Brig for the first time.

"He's a leader of men!" the man cried, his voice crackling from his years of toil in the sooty pit. He shouted to the others. They stopped their march and formed a group behind Brig. "He's a leader of men! He'll save us!"

The others quieted and listened to the hysterical old man. They witnessed Brig's emblazoned star and collectively began chanting in unison.

Strength increased exponentially inside of Brig, until it felt like his muscles would burst from their bindings. A smile of self-actualization grew upon his face.

A horrendous shriek filled the cavern behind him. Brig spun on a heel and took a silent breath.

A slime-encrusted, orange beast, ten meters in height with two gruesome heads perched atop its grotesquely bloated neck, stomped through the halted crowd, grabbing fear-stricken men and women with its bloodied fangs and rending them with the ease of a clomp of its jaws. It roared with the ferocity of a streak of enraged Bengals, tossing torn pieces of its innocent victims against the cold stone.

"Fennec!" one in the crowd bellowed with a pointed finger. "Fennec!"

Brig stepped forward with a courageous mettle in his heart and planted a heavy foot in the path of the terror.

The great fiend, Fennec, opened his maw and let loose a stone-melting roar that shook the foundations of the pit itself. Brig stood stoically in defiance, protecting the cowering horde behind him.

11: OVERBURDENED

Fennec stopped two meters in front of Brig, craned his neck downward and placed his face just centimeters from him. The demon's putrid breath wrinkled Brig's skin, but Brig fought the urge to vomit and puffed his chest at it. Fennec, momentarily taken aback by the show of fortitude displayed by this lowly mortal, looked down upon the lone warrior and snorted with disdain.

Brig's star intensified yet again.

Fennec recoiled, narrowed his eyes to slits and sized up his enemy. The trepidation in the horror's soul pulsed in Brig's veins.

Suddenly, a cobra slithered about Brig's left arm, twisting itself and showing its hooded head just in front of his face. Brig snarled at the snake, but it showed no fear, snapping at the star on Brig's chest without impunity. The crimson glow immediately ceased. Brig staggered backward.

Fennec, feeling a sense of renewed vitriol, clamped his jaw around Brig's waist. Brig howled in agony - Fennec's powerful teeth punctured his hip, sending fresh, dark blood spewing from the tear. Fennec whipped his head back and forth, swinging Brig like a wet towel.

Out of the corner of an eye, Brig caught the sight of a single man standing at the edge of the crowd, his arms crossed over his bulging chest muscles. The cavern's light backlit the shaved sides of his head and cast his shadow forward onto the cavern floor.

However, something within that shadow drew Brig's attention: a small device, winking a taunt with its red LED. Brig reached for it with each fling of Fennec's head, but it remained just beyond his fingertips.

The cobra tightened its grip on Brig's left arm.

"Brigadier, wake up," said Steele.

Brig grunted.

"You're having a nightmare, sweetheart. Wake up."

Brig opened his eyes and looked sideways. Steele, partially draped over him, sat up on one elbow, her bare shoulder peeking from underneath a white sheet, exposed to the subdued lighting of his recovery room. Brig exhaled unevenly and rubbed at his eyes.

"Mind telling me what that was about?"

"Couldn't tell you if I wanted to," he mumbled.

Steele purred. She laid her head back onto Brig's chest, her uncoiled hair flowing just under Brig's chin.

Although not Heaven, as reality had forcefully proven to him, it was certainly the closest thing to it in his recent memory. He imbibed her. Her scent was beautiful, intoxicating... *different*.

"What was she like?" Steele said in a delicate whisper.

"Who?"

"You know. Her... the other... *me*."

"I think you answered your own question." How could he *answer* that question? "She was you."

"I know you say she looked a lot like me, but..."

"No. She looked *exactly* like you. Talked *exactly* like you. She *was* you."

"Oh, rubbish." Her tone morphed from sympathetic to sarcastic in one wink.

"Steele," said Brig, using two fingers to lift her head from his chest. He peered into her eyes. "She knew everything about you, your life, your father."

"*Anyone* could have gotten that information, Brigadier."

Brig sighed. "She also knew about *us*. Our childhood together."

Steele sat up and stared away to what seemed millions of kilometers.

"How do you explain that?" This was the first time since arriving on Mars that he had pressed the issue that he knew to be the truth.

She was not budging. "I can't explain it except to say that she... was not me. *I* am me." Her eyes watered up at the corners.

"Do you know Nadia Temple?" He took a chance, hoping that if she realized he knew something that she would spill the truth... eventually.

"Who? Should I know this person?" Steele darted her eyes from his gaze. She wiped away the tear that had perched atop her cheek. "I don't know what to tell you, Brigadier."

With a gentle touch, Brig pulled her back down to him, wrapped his arms around her shoulders. He stroked her hair, stealing a casual glance around at the newly generated image of Steele's apartment bedroom. However, what was in his heart and mind was not Steele - at least not *this* one.

12:
Shadows of the Past

Mars. Red Colony One

As the blue orb of data twirled above Steele's palm, she strode like a graceful gazelle along the corridor, paying no mind to the few individuals that passed. Although she wanted to focus on the report hovering above her hand, she could not help but have Brig's comments at the forefront of her mind. Having long ago learned how to project herself in a professional manner, she had done a decent job until now around Brig.

However, her giddiness at his arrival and the increasing gravity between them was starting to show. She tried not to let it, but it did weigh on her mind that Brig continued to press about the other Steele.

Who was she?

How could she find out about someone on Earth that she knew nothing about, that until just last night she did not believe existed? The smallest seedling of doubt was germinating in her subconscious, and it bothered her... that it bothered her. Steele had always been the model of confidence, so why did she let the fact that this other girl that she did not know - and that according to Brig was dead – get under her skin? True, his insistence that she was Steele's doppelganger played a major factor in her demeanor, and probably meant that she should take this more seriously – but for different reasons.

The data orb warbled, fell from its axis and emitted a rude chirp.

"Focus, Steele. Focus! You're alive, and she's dead." A slant swelled her lips. She shook her head and rubbed her palm against the bridge of her nose. "What a ghoulish thing to say."

Steele shook off the embarrassment of her internal monologue, refocused her attention on spinning up the data orb once again.

"Could I have a word with you, Ms. Fox," a British voice called from an adjoining hallway.

Steele glanced from the corner of an eye, then back down at the hologram. "General Rossi, I'm quite busy at the moment."

"Mmm, yes. I see that," he replied with a sardonic whip to his tone, shuffling his thin arms behind his back. He relaxed his lanky, two-meter frame, bending slightly at the hips and forming what could only be described as a single parenthesis. "But I figured I might bring this to your attention before I take it... further up."

Steele sighed. She had never grown fond of the Security Chief in her time on Red Colony One, and his knack of showing up and presenting paranoid decrees involving this colony citizen or the other, left her with more headaches than she could recall.

"Darpa has informed me that we have two unregistered individuals within the colony, Ms. Fox."

"Doctor Fox," Steele corrected with a sneer.

"Ah, titles now is it?" He wrinkled his pencil-tipped nose. His amber eyes glowed with ambient lighting.

"Indeed... *General.*" She rolled her eyes upward. "But how is that my concern?"

"It should be your concern because *you've* been treating an individual in your medical facility that doesn't appear on colony manifests."

Steele flinched, albeit with a very subtle waver. She hoped that Rossi had not taken notice.

"I'm assuming that's... half... of our problem?" he continued.

"It's nothing to be concerned about, General. I treat people all the time over there."

"Security and defense of this installation is my concern, Doctor."

Steele glanced up from the orb and scrunched her nose at him. "Defense? Against *what?*"

He pursed his thin lips in aggravation. "You know quite well what I'm referring to, Doctor. We've an unfortified entry point to this colony guarded by nothing more than... technicians."

"Seems more worrisome than tracking down innocent civilians." Rossi's gaunt face flushed darker with rage by the moment. "You needn't worry, General," Steel added, "he was simply someone that had an accident at the mining facility. I had to remove his tracker to perform a life-saving procedure, which in turn removed him from the colony's registration database. The issue will correct itself in due time."

She held up a silent hand on her opposite side, away from Rossi's view, as if a signal to someone watching. Rossi, a clever bloke himself, caught the subtle motion and scanned the ceiling of the corridor. He turned his rodent-sized eyes back to Steele.

"Do you intend to report the disparity to... him?"

"I'm on my way there now," she replied, her joy almost bubbling to the surface. "I'm certain that this will be a focus of the conversation, so rest assured this matter is in good hands. Good day, General."

Steele patted Rossi's pointed shoulder with a mock smile, increasing her stride ahead of him. The General nodded silently, slowed, and then halted. He stared askance after her, his eyes squinted to small slits.

The subdued whoosh of the automatic door announced Steele's entry into the executive office of Red Colony One.

"I've got the breakdown on all of the projects we're working on. You will be quite pleased with the progress," Steele said, stopping a meter from a large, glass desk that took up the center of the room.

On the other side of the translucent slab, a man sat in a leather-bound chair, his back to her. A tuft of salt-and-pepper hair protruded above the top rim of the chair itself. "Mmm hmm," the man answered, his disinterest in the subject at hand apparent.

"General Rossi sends his regards, by the by."

"That's nice dear," the man droned.

Steele cocked an eyebrow above her scowl. She crossed her slender arms over her chest. "Are you even listening to me?"

"Oh. Yes, my darling. My apologies," the man replied with a soothing British inflection. He spun his chair to face Steele.

"Honestly, father. You were the one that called this meeting. I assumed you would have shown even the slightest interest."

"Sorry, dear. Just a bit of a distraction with another... issue," Bronson Fox replied. The wrinkles in his forehead smoothed as he looked upon his daughter. A coy smile drew up one side of his mouth. "The projects are coming along then?"

"Of course, father."

A light 'deet, deet' from the console behind Bronson drew his eye. He continued the conversation without missing a beat. "The General tells me that you have some news to share vis-a-vis the chap you are treating in the medical sector?"

"General Rossi is fond of exaggerating," Steele replied, taking a moment to look down at her finely honed nails. "Someone that had an... incident... over in the mining facility. I'm taking care of it."

Bronson nodded. "Very well. I trust you, dear." His charcoal eyes wandered to the other side of his desk before he finished his sentence. "That will be all then, I take it?"

"Well... no. The data... I thought that you wished to review it?" Steele held her palm aloft. The data orb leapt from the ether and spun, its azure glow illuminating her face and sparkling against her emerald eyes.

"That won't be necessary," Bronson replied with a wave of a palm. "I have complete faith in you to complete your tasks. Everything has gone along swimmingly thus far, so unless you have anything else to share, we will meet again next week." Bronson spun his chair away from Steele.

She wrinkled her nose, turned on a heel and exited the office.

Bronson folded his hands under his chin and stared into the empty hologram above his console. "Open a secure channel to Two Alpha." He unfolded a finger along his lips.

"Yes, Director Fox," Darpa replied with a voice that sounded as if from beyond. The subservience in her voice made a corner of his lip furl upwards.

An extended drone, followed by a few high-pitched beeps, and then a pulsating buzz emitted from the nearby speaker. After a minute of silence, intermixed with short spikes of static, Darpa spoke once again. "Two Alpha is not responding, sir."

Bronson rolled his eyes. "Are you certain? Can you try the connection again?"

"I'm positive," she replied. "I've tested the connection end-to-end, the receiver is simply not responding."

Bronson sat back in pensive reflection. "What has that old fool gone and done now?"

Steele stepped without a sound into Brig's recovery room, unsure of whether he had awoken since she had been gone. To her delight, he had.

12: SHADOWS OF THE PAST

Brig lay on top of his covers, but on one elbow, looking down at the floor in obvious thought. He raised his head at the sound of her heel clacking against the synthetic tile floor, and smiled.

"Good morning, sunshine," she offered with a lilt.

"Is it morning? I can't tell."

"I see you're not used to the Martian day yet. Don't worry, it'll grow on you. However, Darpa does adjust the lighting everywhere in the colony to reflect the current time of day to keep us from going mad. At least that's something."

Brig chuckled.

"Did you get a good night's sleep?" She winked at him and tapped a few commands into the console next to the door. The air in the room shifted, leaving a sudden sweet film on his tongue - a newfound burst of energy surged within him.

"You know I did. Where'd you head off to so early?" Her presence magnetized his eyes. Her striking beauty still made his heart flutter when she was near.

"Just tending to some things. You know, colony business."

Brig nodded knowingly and sat up. "Steele... we need to talk."

"Well, I don't like the sound of that one bit," she said playfully, but realized from the concern on Brig's face that he was all too serious. He motioned with a hand pat on the bed. She perched herself beside him.

Brig dropped the set of plastic cipher cards onto the bed between them. Steele glared at them for a second before looking away.

"Steele, you really need to look at the data on these cards."

She sprung from the edge of the bed. His eyes followed her as she paced with gruff defiance across to the other side of the room. "I *don't* need to see what's on those cards."

"You don't?"

"I don't. I recognize them. They're from my old life... back on Earth." She stood with her back to Brig. "But what's in the past, is in the past. It has no bearing on the present."

"I think if you see this, you'll feel differently."

Steele spun to face him. She softened her tone. "Is this about last night?"

Brig *knew* that she was Steele - *the* Steele. But something was off about her, too. Much like when he reunited with the other Steele, he felt there was something beneath the surface just beyond his reach – something just beyond *her* reach, as well. He needed to open her eyes to the truth, a truth that he was not sure he knew just yet - but he had to be cautious with his approach.

"Yeah, it's about last night..." he answered.

A tear formed in one of Steele's eyes. She ran her hands back through her voluminous hair and held her head. "Brigadier, I'm so sorry. I didn't mean to bring up... her."

"No, it's okay. I'm glad you did. Because we really need to figure out..."

Steele placed a finger over Brig's lips. "No. I need to say something. Something that I realized long ago – back when we were children together."

She gazed into his eyes. Brig's resolve melted for a moment, his will trapped in her eyes.

"I love you, Brigadier. I've always loved you."

A spike of chill ran across his neck. "And I love you, too, Steele. Just... not in the same way." He could not believe he was saying it. The second that it left his lips, he wanted with all of his soul to snag the words and take them back. He crunched the inside of his lip with a sharp tooth to make sure he was truly awake.

"The same way? The same way what..." Steele said, as if shocked from a slumber. "Oh... the way that you loved... *her?*" Her loving gaze became an icy glare.

Brig could do nothing but nod.

"You mean the same girl that looks exactly like me? That acts exactly like me?" Her tone became harsher with each word.

"That's just it. She's not you. You even said it yourself."

Steele turned her shoulder in anger, her arms crossed defiantly over her midsection.

"There's something different, Steele. Something about... her... attracted me to her like I was never attracted to..."

She spun and walloped Brig across his cheekbone with a palm.

"You bastard!" The tears flowed as if from an undammed reservoir.

Before Brig could assess what he had just done, Steele had jumped from the bed and stormed through the recovery room door. Brig rubbed the warm spot on his face. He shook his head in frustration and closed his eyes.

Something's wrong, I can feel it.

He stared over at the cards, still untouched on the bed. Brig scooped them in one hand, stepped across the room and placed them back in the terminal.

12: SHADOWS OF THE PAST

"Darpa, pick up where we left off."

The room morphed at Brig's silent command, once again taking the appearance of Steele's Earth apartment. Darpa appeared next to the growing display at the center of the room and glared with quiet reserve at him.

He dropped himself onto the couch and awaited the data feed.

R. JAMES STEVENS

13:
Hollow

Mars. Red Colony One

Brig stared up at the moving shadows on the ceiling of Steele's apartment - or at least the convincing illusion of Steele's apartment that Darpa had once again conjured for him. The subtle rain against the simulated building façade outside took him far away from Red Colony One, back to a time when everything was clear to him.

The metallic platter protruded from the wall a few meters away, holding within its grasp the cipher cards that he had placed after Steele had left an hour prior.

The hologram displayed the final piece of data in the center of the room: the frozen image of a young Nadia Temple staring into the camera lens, her deep emerald eyes boring through Brig's soul every time he moved his gaze.

It can't be, he tried to convince himself.

He pounded his fist down onto the fabric, disgusted about the piece of Red Vision he was not able to discern. Why was Steele being so evasive at the mention of Nadia's name? His mind ached at the prospect that she could have been so calculating with an innocent person's life. The more revealed, the less anything made sense to him. This was not the Steele that he knew.

Maybe she blocked it out of her memory. Maybe the memory block technique she spoke about on the video...

The chime on the door console rang its pleasant greeting, interrupting Brig's train of thought. He looked at the door with a queer expression.

"It's... open?" he said, his confusion honest.

Since he had arrived on Mars, his only visitor had been Steele – and she had always entered without announcement. "Darpa, that's enough," he said quietly. The video of Nadia dissipated, as did Darpa and the mirage of Steele's apartment.

The door slid open. A lanky gentleman dressed in the same crimson and gray jumpsuit as Steele, with several triangular insignias placed near his collar, stepped with an authoritative waft into the room and stopped just inside the doorway. Brig jumped to his feet and advanced a step towards him.

"Oh... if you're looking for Steele, she just left..."

"I'm not looking for Ms. Fox," the man squelched. "I was told she had a... patient... in her care here in the medical facility, and I came by to see for myself."

Brig nodded without speaking.

"Have you been here long?"

"Steele can give you all the details, she's the expert here."

The man, a Brit, smiled smartly at Brig behind a pair of amber eyes. "If you don't mind, a moment of your time is all I ask. Just a few questions?"

Brig raised an eyebrow. "And... who are you again?"

"Pardon my manners. I'm General Anthony Rossi. I'm the Security Czar and Chief Military Officer for Red Colony One."

"Military, huh?" Brig shook his head and smiled, albeit with a hidden mock. "It's a pleasure to meet you, General." He presented a friendly hand to Rossi.

"Indeed." Rossi snubbed Brig's handshake gesture, stepped past him with his own hands laced behind his back and paced the room. "Ms. Fox tells me that you're a resident of Red Colony One, and that you were treated by her. I don't seem to recall your face."

Brig snorted, shrugged his shoulders. "You remember everyone in the colony?"

Rossi turned his head to Brig. "I make it my business to remember everyone in the colony, Mr..."

"Sampson. Brody Sampson."

"Mr. Sampson. As I was saying, I don't recall seeing your face. And I'm certain I don't recognize the name."

"I've been sort of out of the public eye, so to speak," Brig replied.

Rossi shot him a suspicious eye. "And what was the nature of your injuries, Mr. Sampson?"

"Again, I think you should talk to the good doctor, she's the one with the answers you're looking for... General."

Rossi chuckled with certain derisiveness under his breath. He glared into Brig's eyes for a quick moment, and then shot a boney hand out to him. "It was a pleasure to meet you, Mr. Sampson. I hope to see more of you around the colony," he hissed.

"I'm sure you will," Brig countered, meeting the General's grasp.

Rossi's eyes fell to Brig's neck, where a tattoo of a Greek Epsilon character, ensconced between two brandished swords, met the subtle room lighting. He glanced at it, then back up at Brig's face with a curious squint.

"You're an Epsilon? I wasn't aware we had any on colony."

Brig released the handshake. "Yeah. In another life." Brig's voice fell distant.

Rossi turned his thin frame partially, and then glared at Brig. "Courageous group. Nine lives, as some would say. Birds of a feather, others..." Rossi added, his voice trailing as he stepped into the doorway.

"Those birds are kinda scattered now, General."

He watched the General turn the corner into the hallway.

"Typical brass," Brig said to himself with a grunt.

Earth. Flagstaff, Arizona

Clive stopped in front of the set of hedges that framed a pair of rod iron gates. The hedges had sprouted even farther since the last time he had been there, and being that spring had been particularly rainy this year, they had continued to overflow unfettered from their confines throughout the season with the absence of any care. He stared up at the tarnished brass 'F' that adorned the center of the fencing.

His mind wandered to his last visit to Bronson Fox's suburban estate. Clive shook off the specter of that fateful night two months ago, when he and the Syndicate strongman, Krell, plotted to nab the elderly Fox in the middle of the night. Despite the fact that Krell did not make it out alive from the operation, Clive still got the job done - he captured Fox and brought him to the safe house, as instructed.

Clive was not happy about his decision to go along with the directive from the Syndicate head, Bruno Muldoon, but he had convinced himself that it was a means to an end. He made sure that the old man did not come to harm - at least not to any extent. He also knew that if he played ball long enough with the maniac Muldoon, he just might find a way to get Muldoon's wife, Jessica, to safety. Never mind that she was the sister of his former Epsilon partner, Brigadier Stroud - she was also the mother of Clive's child.

Now she was dead.

Clive gnashed his teeth at the thought of things gone wrong. The hedge leaves whispered as he whisked through them and onto the front walk. All of his years earning an 'in' with Muldoon and his thugs had been for naught. Brig had made sure of that with his meddling over Steele's father's capture.

He strode up the dark walk. His eyes scanned the front of the mansion. Clive had not spoken to nor seen Brig since their confrontation, when their tumultuous relationship had traversed its final spiral at his workshop.

Clive stopped just in front of the porch and stared at the front door. He was not sure what to expect here tonight, and he was not relishing the idea of another showdown with Brig. He assumed, however, that he would find some combination of Brig, Steele or her father in the house.

Things are different this time.

Indeed – he was no longer worried about what Brig thought, or into what he might be sticking his nose. Surely, Steele had showed Brig the cipher cards after she lifted them from his workshop, and Brig had now discovered the same truths that Clive had previously. Surely, Brig now knew the extent of Project Red Vision – and his girlfriend's involvement in the cover-up.

This was no longer about Jessica. This was no longer about the animosity between him and Clive. This was about Clive getting what he needed, taking his son and leaving Earth - forever.

Clive pulled himself up onto the porch using one hand on a column, steadying his prosthetic leg on the creaky, wooden surface. The wind howled from the pines on the hill, as if ghosts from the past had woken. Clive lifted his collar up around his neck, reached for the door and knocked with a solid rap.

A sobering thought slammed him. What if Brig had gathered Bronson, Steele and the cipher cards, and had already... left?

He peered up at the darkened windows above the door. He turned the doorknob; the door creaked open and clunked against the frame of the cobwebbed decorative side window. Clive stepped into the darkened foyer. His hand instinctively sought out and flicked at the light switch.

The discolored oval on the floor at the base of the stairs to his right drew his eye – a faint outline demarcated the missing area rug that he used to carry Krell's lifeless corpse out of the house. He turned his gaze to the carpet leading to the living room on the left – the bloodstain from Krell's fatal injury that had saturated the short plush, was now a faint, pink hue.

Someone had most assuredly been there. But where were they?

Clive hobbled into the living room. The blanket, under which he had located the mysterious Quantum satellite device, formed a perfect, folded rectangle on the chair in the corner. On the small table next to the couch lay a neatly placed pen and pad. A musty odor hung in the stale air.

A spark of panic washed over his brain. They were gone.

Clive exhaled a sharp breath, turned and strode down the short hallway to the master bedroom. The bed was empty and made up.

"Where is it," he growled.

He tore open the linen closet at the end of the hallway and forced his arms into the pile of blankets. Clive frantically yanked shelf after shelf full of quilts, covers and sheets into a heap on the floor, grunting louder after each tumbled to the ground.

It has to be here. After all these years, there had to be a way he was charging it!

He stomped in dejection back to the front of the hallway, despite his telltale limp, and held his hands to his hips. His frustrated glare seemingly heated the air around him. He passed the final doorway; his eye caught sight of the kitchen and a small table next to the door.

A small tea set sat near the edge of the table with no chairs. At the edge of the table, where a chair should have been, sat a single teacup. He stepped into the kitchen and stopped just to the side of the table. Clive placed his hand on the side of the porcelain.

Cold. But there's still tea in it. But from how long ago?

Clive glanced around the kitchen, suddenly self-conscious that someone might be there - or watching him.

Nothing.

His eyes scanned the granite countertops that lined the edges of the grand kitchen. Aside from old appliances that dotted several areas, nothing stood out as suspicious - or used in recent days.

Clive grunted in frustration and leaned backward against the table. It wobbled sideways and tossed its contents onto the floor, spilling the cup of tea and shattering the teapot.

"Dammit..." he growled under his breath, kneeling to gather several fractured pieces of the pot. He stood with a groan of exertion, a large piece of the broken kettle in his hand, and turned towards the nearby trash receptacle. A pair of small, twin shadows in the moonlight outside, situated along side of each other underneath a tall oak, drew his gaze through the kitchen window. For a moment, he once again felt the instinctive urge to hide himself from view - the thought of prying eyes from the darkness of the back yard sending a frigid chill through him.

However, he suddenly knew it was not people that he saw - at least not alive.

Clive's growing shadow crawled across the wispy, wet grass. His feet brushed through the taller blades, flicking the evening dew onto his boots. He stopped just at the edge of the thick wood that began at the back of the property, and stood beneath its grand canopy.

Once again, the chill traveled his body.

In front of him, a somber pair of rounded, wooden grave markers stood in the cold darkness of the sprawling estate. An icy breeze penetrated his thin coat. He stared in morbid curiosity at the headstones.

He nudged the toe of his boot into the loose dirt at the bottom edge of the right-most grave.

Fresh. But who...

The subtle wind lifted one of the tree branches behind him, focusing the moonlight onto the tombstones. A small flower, a Primrose from what he could discern, lay pinned against the left marker behind a flat rock.

Clive's breath left him for a moment. He closed his eyes and bowed his head in respect, then opened them. The disbelief gripped his face.

"I can't believe it. He got them both killed."

14:
Old Foes, New Friends

Earth. New Mexico

Clive ground a fist into his eyelid, a futile attempt at trying to wipe away the bleariness of staring down another endless stretch of desert asphalt. Danil Chekushkin, his co-pilot as he had been for the past couple of months, had made numerous offers to share in the task of scouring the southwest for any sign of the elusive DMST advanced weaponry cache – the same with which he had bargained for Jessica's life with Bruno Muldoon. However, not wishing to divulge his true purpose for the search, Clive dismissed Danil's offers, citing that it kept him more alert to be the one driving.

The turn-of-the-century cargo truck that they drove - often referred by post-Event survivors as 'retro' because of its archaic reliance on petroleum-based fuel - slogged along with a weary grind, sputtering from a few patched holes in its manifold. Every so often, the exhaust would emit a resounding backfire like the reverb of a shotgun - but no one was around to hear it, and the pair had gotten so used to the obnoxious sound that it became part of the background white noise to them.

Clive glanced at Danil, who rested his head on the open window frame with one hand over his eyes, trying to benefit from the wind cascading over his sweat drenched face. His scalp glistened where his black hair thinned at the crown. The midday desert sun thrust through the grimy windscreen of the truck and simmered the close air in the cab. The air conditioning of the antediluvian relic had long ago expired and now heated engine air blustered out from the sun-cracked vents. The salty tang of day old sweat soured their nostrils.

Clive reached for his canteen and sipped at the lukewarm water, then handed it blindly to Danil. The former Russian TGB agent pushed it away without looking.

"I am used to extreme conditions... as you can imagine," Danil said with a dry wit and thick Russian accent. "I do not require refreshment." Clive shrugged an apathetic shoulder, screwed the cap into place and dropped the canteen between them on the bench seat.

Danil sat up, shielded his eyes from the sun and scanned the empty desert ahead. "Once again, no weapons cache." He did not need to look at Clive to know his face had scrunched into a sneer. "What a surprise."

Clive offered a silent nod accompanied by a low grunt. Danil gave Clive a suspicious glare. "Do you not think it is time to give up this... charade."

Clive peeked at Danil, gnashed his teeth, and then returned his eyes to the road. "It's not a charade. Those weapons exist."

"Vraki," Danil barked under his breath.

Clive rolled his eyes to the side. His proficiency in the Ukrainian tongue aside, he still did not like being told 'bullshit' in any language. "I know what I'm doing."

"Do you? I do not think that you do." Danil stared at Clive without speaking for a moment. "Even if these weapons do exist..."

"They do exist..."

"If they exist... why would you hand them over to Muldoon? He can already squash you like a petulant cockroach. Giving him this type of power would make him unstoppable."

"Why would I tell you anything like that? I can't trust you, Danil."

Danil raised his eyebrows and chuckled. "It is not about trust. I am not the person you need to worry about. It is Muldoon."

Clive tightened his lips.

"One way or another, you will lose," Danil added.

Clive continued to stare forward with a blank face. This was not Earth-shattering news to him. He knew what he was getting into, and it was a gamble he felt he had to take to ensure his safety - as well as Eli's.

Danil watched with a pondering silence at the small, sandy hills rolling by. He turned his head towards Clive once again. "Unless you are planning on not being here once you find it."

Clive flinched, albeit very subtly. Was Danil that perceptive? Did he know something that he was not letting on? "It's just weapons, Danil."

"Tell me, Underwood. What were you planning on doing once you found the portal?"

Clive's face paled. He lifted his foot from the accelerator and cranked the wheel to the right. With a squeal like that of a prehistoric beast, the lumbering truck came to a skidding stop at the side of the road. A billowing cloud of sandy dust flowed up from the front of the vehicle and the sticky odor of newly burning fluids wafted in from the engine compartment. Clive quickly faced his Russian passenger.

"How did you know about the portal?" For once Clive was doing the interrogating.

Danil continued his subtle laughter. "My friend... do you not think I do my own research when I am tasked to kidnap an old man? I know what this is all about."

Clive blinked away his own frustration. So focused on fixing his own problems and working his own plan, he had not even considered the possibility of Danil snooping and finding out what he was up to.

"How long have you known?"

The coy smile crept across Danil's face as he eyed the former Epsilon. He pulled a cigarette from the pocket of his jacket, which hung behind him, and lit it with a quick strike of a match. He puffed out a small cloud of smoke through the open window, scanning the horizon with shifting eyes.

"I told you once, Underwood – I am a student of nature. I am very interested to see what your game is."

Embarrassment bit at him more than anger. He had been careless. What else did Danil know?

"I perform my duties well. For Muldoon's benefit, I play ignorant and foolish. But do not think for once that I am a fool." Danil's scolding was solid in its intent, but smooth.

Clive belched out a heavy sigh, realizing the explosive attack on his plans by Danil's surprise revelation. He had to mitigate any further damage.

"So what now?" Clive locked eyes with Danil. "You let Muldoon know what I've been up to? You turn me in?"

Danil snorted in derision. "The ball, as they say, is in your court, Underwood. I am just curious as to why you would make a bold move against a man such as Bruno Muldoon. What do you have to gain?"

Clive remained silent, pensively staring out the windshield. Danil continued pressing.

"Is it the boy?"

Clive's face lit with incredulity. How did know about Eli?

This is getting out of control. "Do you know... everything?"

Danil smiled, took a final puff of his cigarette before flicking it out the side window. "You forget," he replied, smoke trailing from his lips, "I was Russian Intelligence. It was my job to know everything - particularly that which is held secret." On the last word, he turned a penetrating gaze towards Clive.

I've been played, Clive thought. *All this time I thought I was being so clever, and he saw right through it.*

The Russian folded his hands behind his head and closed his eyes in thought. The self-fulfilled smirk on Danil's face made Clive's stomach fold.

"He's my son, Danil," Clive finally offered. If he knows anything, he needs to know the truth.

Danil nodded knowingly. "And the mother is Mrs. Muldoon?"

Just when he thought that it could not get any worse, Danil twisted the knife even harder. Clive had no choice but to nod.

Danil kept his eyes closed, speaking as if in a meditative trance. "So this portal... if you find it... is your answer? You are going to take the boy and leave?"

Clive leaned forward onto the steering wheel with both hands. "Yeah... something like that."

Danil blinked his eyes open, clicked them towards Clive. "You do not get it yet? For Muldoon, this is one giant chess game. He is simply waiting for you to make your move." He paused to gauge Clive's comprehension. "So you had best make it a wise one, my friend."

Clive punched at the shifter; the gears ground with a heavy metallic rake. The engine moaned its pitiful song as the truck began to lurch forward.

A few hours later

Clive stretched his arms wide in a yawn; he rubbed his narrowed eyes at the dark highway rolling underneath the tired wheels. The cool, night air funneled in through the partially cranked window and lifted the short hair on the back of his head.

"So another fruitless day of searching." Danil had a unique talent for getting under someone's skin, and he played it mercilessly every moment around Clive. Clive grunted once. "Do you have any information on the actual location of this portal?"

"I did..." Clive replied. Danil raised an eyebrow at Clive. "But someone took it..."

"Your soldier friend?"

Clive nodded. "And his girlfriend."

"So we should go pay him a visit. Take back what was stolen from you."

"That's the problem," Clive replied through an exasperated breath. "I think they took that information with them and went through the portal themselves."

The sudden image of the twin gravestones at the back of Bronson Fox's estate flashed across his brain. "At least I used to think that..." he corrected with a mumble. He could feel Danil's piercing gaze. Clive stared knowingly at him. It would not have surprised him at this point if Danil knew that, too.

After a brief moment, Danil suddenly recoiled – looking forward in surprise at the road, punching his foot down onto the floor as if hitting an imaginary brake pedal. Clive quickly faced forward, stomped onto the real brake with a heavy boot. The tires locked, sending the rear of the truck fishtailing. A shriek of heated rubber peeling from the wheels into the road filled the dense, night air. With a frantic effort, Clive brought the truck under control and to a stop, three meters away from another disabled truck stopped across their path.

Two bodies, face down, lay in front of the other vehicle. Clive and Danil sat in uneasy silence, staring forward out across the hood of the truck at the unwelcome sight. Without moving his head overtly, Danil scanned the area around the truck. Clive, however, had pushed the lever to open the driver door. Danil grasped Clive's arm and pulled him towards the center of the cab.

"It is an ambush, Underwood," Danil grumbled, his eyes still focused forward.

Clive freed his arm from Danil's grip and frowned. "How do you know that?"

Danil tipped his head in the direction of the other vehicle. "Look at the bodies. There is no blood. There are no wounds." He turned his head slowly to glare at Clive. "They *want* us to go out and investigate."

The truth and gravitas of the encounter struck Clive like a hammer to the skull. *Of course it's an ambush,* he screamed in his mind.

He could not believe he had forgotten some of the most important training he had received while in the Epsilon Warriors. He rubbed at the stubble on his chin and checked both of the side mirrors of the truck. "So what do we do then?"

"Put it in reverse. We need to get away from here as quickly and quietly as we can."

Clive snorted and reached for the gearshift. "There's nothing quick or quiet about this old monster."

Danil's glare ignited farther – giving Clive the answer he already knew: they needed to escape - or be killed. Clive thrust the stick into reverse. The horrendous grinding of the gears rang out across the silent desert around them. Watching through his side mirror, Clive deftly maneuvered the unwieldy hulk backward, its engine groaning out like a dying beast. After ten meters, he yanked the wheel and forced the back end of the truck onto a dried patch of weeds at the side of the road. Without hesitating, Clive mashed the accelerator until it felt like his foot would emerge from the underside of the chassis. The motor once again emitted a sick belch as the bare rubber of its back wheels spun across the sandy asphalt.

The truck trundled to a lethargic gait; Clive and Danil glared at each of the mirrors, watching as the other truck became smaller with distance. Clive, with a silent sigh of relief, peered over at Danil. Even in the darkness of the cabin, he could see that Danil's weathered face had relaxed somewhat.

Suddenly, tiny red dots began appearing one after the other onto Danil's face and chest. Clive looked down - the same random patterns popped onto him, as well. Both men darted their attention forward in unison.

The headlights of the truck exposed a single line of people standing unbroken across the highway, their rifles aimed with efficient expertise into the cabin of the truck, the lasers of their scopes finding critical targets on both Clive and Danil. Clive forced the brake to the floor. The truck responded with a deafening shriek of its tires and came to an uneven stop.

They sat and stared; the dots continued their silent dance across their bodies. Clive's heightened pulse thumped in his ear – the short spurts of Danil's panting rode the silence of the cab. Outside, the line of men stepped slowly towards the front of the truck, the black handkerchiefs that covered the lower half of their faces absorbing the dim cone of light coming from the truck's beams. A gruff voice called from one of the men.

"Toss your weapons out the windows. And keep your hands where we can see 'em! Now!" The man, an Australian by the bend of his accent, stepped away from the others and sternly waved his rifle, a large caliber sniper model, towards the two men.

14: OLD FOES, NEW FRIENDS

Clive and Danil glanced at each other through their peripheral, continuing their silent conversation. They knew it was futile – they were outnumbered.

"Any other bright ideas?" Clive muttered through closed lips.

"We throw our weapons out the window," Danil replied dryly.

"Clever," Clive retorted under his breath, and then tossed the small pistol from the dashboard out onto the road. Danil followed suit, and both men held their arms aloft.

"Now step out of the vehicle with your hands on your head!" the man barked.

The pair dismounted from the cab onto the pavement. Clive counted their numbers. *Fourteen.*

"Turn and face the rear of the truck, put your hands on your head and walk backward towards us."

Due to Danil's diminutive stature, only the Russian's hands clasped over his head across the other side of the hood were visible. "Not good," Clive muttered. Both men converged at the front of the truck into the small stream of light.

"Stop there," the Australian ordered. Danil turned his head over his shoulder.

"You are making a big mistake..." he growled.

The Australian hefted his rifle and slammed the butt into Danil's jaw, sending the Russian tumbling to the ground, where he skidded awkwardly on his chest. "That'll be enough out of you, Ruskie..." the Australian hissed.

Clive pulled his hands from his head and leapt towards the bulky Aussie. Before he could get within one meter of the man, a metal cable looped around Clive's throat. Clive fell backward and caught himself with one hand, the other grasping futilely at his neck. He quickly found his hands bound behind his back as he was pushed forward onto his knees. The Australian slung his rifle backward and made for the side of Clive's head. Just as he launched his attack downward, another man stepped from the shadows and grasped the stock, which fell within centimeters of Clive's temple.

"Stop!" bellowed the second masked stranger, an Englishman, through his bandanna. "We need at least one of them to be able to talk, Jesse."

Jesse, the Australian, yanked his rifle from the other's grasp and glared at him. "Why? They're Syndicate scum. We'll just finish 'em off right here! That's what she'll want us to do anyway, Nye..."

Clive peered up at Jesse, squinting through the dust that drifted up into the headlight flow. "I'm not Syndicate," he said with a strain.

Jesse pulled the cloth from his face, exposing his heavily stubbled face and a pair of mismatched eyes – one blue and one white. He leaned forward and spat into Clive's eye. Nye pushed Jesse aside and tugged at the collar of Clive's jacket, until he was within the dim strobe of the truck's headlights. Not having found what he was looking for, he yanked up each of Clive's sleeves. Nye quickly dropped Clive's forearm back to his side, turned and faced the others.

"He's telling the truth, lads. He's not Syndicate."

"Are you crazy? I can spot Syndicate a kilometer away," Jesse growled into Nye's ear.

Nye pointed down at Clive. "Look at the marking on his arm. He's an Epsilon. Those chaps don't run with a lot such as the Syndicate. Do they, bloke?"

Clive bit his tongue. Nye's response was far more than he could have hoped. It was a naive lie, but he was not about to ruin his and Danil's only chance for escape now.

Jesse sneered at Clive, as Nye knelt beside Danil. The Russian returned Jesse's intent glare; blood oozed from the corner of Danil's mouth. "But this one, I recognize," Nye quipped with a wink to Clive.

A bizarre thought occurred to Clive. He suddenly had the opportunity to rid himself of Danil for good. All he had to do was go along with Nye's line of reasoning, and the cat-and-mouse game in which he and Danil participated would finally come to an end. His epiphany quickly faded, however, replaced by the image of Krell lying motionless on Bronson Fox's foyer floor with the back half of his head blown off. He could not even imagine Muldoon's response to Clive coming back from a mission with *another* of his top operatives dead. The lunatic would surely demand punishment this time.

"He's not Syndicate, either," Clive managed to choke out, the strain of the metal hoop flexed around his neck forcing a bit of froth to coat the corners of his mouth.

Nye, and several of the other men, turned their heads in surprise at Clive's revelation. "Are you sure there, chum?" Nye raised an eyebrow at Clive. "We've dealt with this joker before. He's gotten away from us several times. Like the proverbial cat with nine lives, this one." He eyed Danil. "I'd be wary of my associations."

"He used to be..." Clive added, his voice becoming raspy from lack of saliva.

"Then what're you two doin' out here in a Syndicate truck? I recognize that for sure..." Jesse barked.

Clive flicked his eyes momentarily towards Jesse, then back at Danil. "We're running from them. I helped him get away – he provided the truck. We were headed as far north and east as we could get."

Nye rose, ping-ponging penetrating glares between Danil and Clive. He extracted a small, metal case from his inner pocket, flipped it open and held it towards Clive. "Fancy a smoke?"

Clive subtly shook his head, which was not easy with the animal noose secured tightly around his throat. "Don't smoke..." he grumbled.

The Englishman grinned and reached into the tin. Dexterously perching a cigarette onto his lips with one finger, he struck a match against the truck's front bumper and fired the end of the stick. Nye inhaled the first quarter of the cigarette, and then exhaled a cloud of blue smoke into Clive's face with a pensive gaze. "Aren't you the virtuous type? A bloody commando that saves innocents from the Syndicate - *and* doesn't smoke? You're a dying breed, my friend."

Nye's sarcasm played with a heavy dose of irony in Clive's mind. *If he only knew.*

The sound of a pair of retro-bikes decelerating and coming to a stop behind the group drew Nye's attention away from Clive. Nye turned his head over his shoulder to Jesse. "Is she here?"

Jesse grunted in response.

Nye sucked the last few centimeters from his cigarette, dropped the smoking butt, and stepped aside. Several of the other men behind Nye followed suit, parting and leaving a wide berth.

A dark figure appeared in the aisle left by them and slowly sauntered forward into the headlight stream of Clive and Danil's truck, illuminating their facial features.

It was a woman - her dark skin's smoothness reflected the moon's beams; her dreadlocked hair flopped in a ponytail behind her shoulders. She stopped beside Nye and stared curiously at the pair of men on the ground.

"More Syndicate?" she said softly to Nye in what Clive recognized to be an African inflection. When she turned, the moonlight exposed a raised scar across her cheek.

Nye shook his head. "No."

Her eyes fell upon the truck, and then back onto Nye with one raised brow. "This one here claims they stole the lorry and were on the run," Nye replied.

The woman stepped forward and eyed Danil with a knowing suspicion. After a silent sneer, she crouched in front of Clive and read his face. "What's your story?"

"He's an Epsilon," Nye interjected from behind.

She grasped Clive's arm and twisted it into the moonlight, before letting it fall again. Then, rising from her crouch, waved a pair of fingers behind him. "Release him from the noose." The unseen man behind Clive loosened the metal loop and pulled it over Clive's head.

Clive, his hands also now free, rubbed the red outline at the front of his throat and glared up at the woman.

"Please forgive this rough treatment," she explained. "But you must understand that you have entered Reformation territory. This is the boundary that separates the good from the bad. Where the Syndicate rules mercilessly, and the Reformation carries on the fight to restore what once was." She turned her eyes towards Danil, pointed sternly at him. "This one, I don't trust."

"You can trust him, he's with me," Clive affirmed, his voice still as if he had just ingested a handful of sand.

The woman glared at Clive with loathing contempt. "It is hard for me to trust your word. You show up here on our land in a Syndicate vehicle – with someone we have encountered before and know to be part of that group."

"He was... he's on the right side of things now..." said Clive.

The woman continued to stare at Clive, however, her features softened. "What is your name?"

"Clive... Underwood."

"And I am..." Danil began, licking away the salty brine of blood from the corner of his lips.

"I know who you are!" the woman shouted without looking at him. "Rest assured, Mr. Chekushkin, if you turn out to be who we know you to be, you will have something much worse than a metal noose around your neck."

Clive rose to his feet and rubbed at the top of his knee where his prosthetic met his thigh. "You won't have to worry about that. So if you don't mind, we'd like to get back on the road."

14: OLD FOES, NEW FRIENDS

The woman turned, grinned a coy smile at Clive. "Oh… you're not going anywhere. You're with us for now." She walked back through the line of men.

Clive stood silently with his hands on his hips, his face expressionless.

"If you're on the right side of things, as you say, then you won't mind," she said, and faded back through the others.

R. JAMES STEVENS

15:
Bleeding Me

New Vegas, Nevada

The pomegranate sun shed its final rays of the afternoon, silhouetting the two men who stood abreast atop the roof of the colossal World's End Resort & Casino - headquarters and fortress of the Syndicate and its enigmatic leader, Bruno Muldoon.

"En garde," the Frenchman called, his nectarous voice echoing off the decorative parapet. Louis Sergeant, one of Muldoon's closest confidantes within the Syndicate Inner Circle, stood opposite Muldoon in his beginning stance.

"Etes-vous prets?" Muldoon cooed in response, querying Louis's readiness. He flashed a quick salute with a glinting epee vertically across his mask. While not a strategic meeting by any sense of the term, Muldoon never turned down an offer of a rousing duel from Sergeant to work out some of his daily frustrations.

"Allez!" Louis yelped, signaling to Muldoon that the match could begin.

Two of Muldoon's henchmen stood against the roof entryway ten meters away, their arms crossed over their bulging chests. While not showing an overt enthusiasm in the match, realizing that Muldoon frequently used them to display his skills as a fencer, they also knew their place in the organization - and how to keep it.

Muldoon began with a lunge, stretching his left arm outward in a daring opening salvo. Louis, not displaying trepidation, swiftly parried Muldoon's offering, whipping the Irishman's blade upward and away from any contact with his midsection. Muldoon emitted a subtle, disgusted grunt and dropped back into a defensive stance.

"That move rarely works, monsieur," Louis observed, executing a riposte that saw the tip of his epee tap against Muldoon's bottom rib. "I'm surprised you opened in such a manner."

"Sometimes you have to catch your opponent off guard, Louis," Muldoon replied, leaping backward, and then spinning to deliver a score on the Frenchman's upper thigh.

Louis chuckled with confident suaveness, stepping backward into a defensive posture once again. Muldoon, wanting to stay on the offensive, feinted left. Louis moved to parry, but Muldoon disengaged and quickly lunged right. His opponent, a master of the sport, circle-parried and countered, connecting with Muldoon's upper arm, knocking the shorter opponent off-balance.

Muldoon growled under his breath, his pride grazed. He righted himself and proffered a thrust at Louis's abdomen. He was met with a strong parry, but continued his volley with several additional thrusts that failed to land, finally settling on a remise met by his opponent's riposte to his own hip.

Louis relaxed and stepped backward, but before he could claim his victory in the match, Muldoon lunged once more and tapped his epee against the Frenchman's midsection.

"Victory is mine!" Muldoon proclaimed.

Louis tore at his mask, allowing his flowing, golden hair to launch into the wind. He lunged forward to argue the point, his eyes flaming a ruby red. Then, seeing the henchmen step forward in terrifying unison, he decided to err on the part of better judgment. He stepped back, snapped his feet together and bowed graciously.

"Very good, monsieur..." he said with an air of false satiation.

Muldoon, arrogant as ever, wiped his blade on a cloth from his pocket without returning the respectful bow. He returned the blade to its sheath and flipped his long, black hair over his shoulder. "If this had been an actual battle, I'd have skewered your liver, Louis!"

The Frenchman countered with a slight nod of his head - the setting sun did not offer enough light for Muldoon to witness the sneer growing at the corner of his mouth.

The rooftop door boomed open, slamming against the wall before shuddering to a rest. The ridiculously imposing form of Pollux Webb lumbered out from the dark stairway beyond. Muldoon glared at Pollux, wondering how the roof had withstood Pollux's massive weight all these years. Muldoon looked away, continuing to preen.

"Pollux, have you determined the complicity of Underwood in the freeing of the old man from the safe house?" Muldoon did not look at the behemoth.

The typical blank countenance adorned Pollux's massive, frying-pan-sized mug. He rubbed at the blonde stubble of hair along his bumpy scalp. "No, it wasn't Underwood, Mr. Muldoon. It was the other guy..."

Muldoon raised an eyebrow. "*The other guy?*" he parroted.

"Yes, sir. The one you were questioning that one night."

"The one that I instructed Underwood to get rid of?" Muldoon answered with a sharp tongue. The industry of the rusty wheels churning inside the mammoth's head was very nearly audible. He stretched his silence, musing over the sight of Pollux painfully attempting to put together a piece of logic.

Pollux, the epiphany suddenly striking him, nodded. "Yeah! Yeah! That's the one, boss!" Pollux barked with a wagging finger the size of a swollen Polish sausage link.

"So put the two together, Pollux. Underwood *did* have a hand in freeing the man, no? Particularly if that man who was supposedly dead, left with Underwood and Chekushkin."

Pollux's face flushed several shades of red before he answered again. "I'm... sorry, boss. I didn't make the connection."

Muldoon shook his head. "Why am I not surprised? You would fail to make the connection between your shoulders and that melon you call a head." Pollux's face drooped.

The door once again flung open and caromed against the wall. Another man - much smaller in stature than Pollux - emerged and hastily made his way towards Muldoon. No stranger to numerous lackeys providing non-stop status reports to him at all hours of the day, Muldoon extended no obvious reaction to the new visitor. The man stopped just in front of Muldoon and gathered his breath before speaking.

"Mr. Muldoon, sir," the man, also a lad from the Irish homeland - but with an accent as thick as pudding - said with a slight bow of his head. Muldoon nodded his head in disinterest. "Mr. Muldoon, there's something you need to see over at the highway near the old Strip."

"I'm a busy man, Davin. I don't have time for things I 'need to see'." Muldoon slipped the white gloves from his fingertips and tossed them to the Louis, who snagged them before they hit the rooftop.

"But sir," Davin insisted, "this is something you must see. One of the Regionals was... killed."

Muldoon sighed, deliberately loud enough to let Davin know he was growing bored, if not impatient, with the conversation. "Davin, death is a part of life," Muldoon answered, his words leaving a trail of ice behind them. "We shall just have to replace him."

"Sir... it's not that he was killed. It was... how... he was killed." Davin gawked at the other two men, nervously scratched his scruffy red beard, and then lowered his voice. "And there was a message."

"A message?"

"Yes, sir. You need to see it to understand."

Muldoon closed his eyes and inhaled. "Very well," he said in a breathy exhale.

Davin looked sheepishly at Pollux, and then leaned in towards Muldoon's ear. After a few, brief seconds of listening to the Irish thug's whispers, Muldoon raised an eyebrow in surprised interest. "Tasty," he hissed, landing a curious eye on Pollux.

Davin stepped backward, nodded to his boss, and exited the rooftop.

Muldoon motioned with a hand to Pollux. "Come, Pollux. Walk with me."

The pair paced towards the door - Muldoon with his hands clasped to his back, Pollux with his tree-trunk arms limp at his sides. "Pollux, you and your brother have been with me a long time."

"Yes, sir."

"You haven't told me much about your family." Pollux looked down in confusion at his boss, shook his head. "Do you have any siblings, Pollux?"

"Siblings?" Pollux scratched his head with a gigantic finger, the oft-seen expression of bewilderment growing on his face. "Oh... no, sir. Nobody but me and Cas."

Muldoon nodded knowingly. "Aye. What about your parents?"

A low growl emitted through Pollux's gnashed teeth. "I don't have any parents."

"Come now, Pollux. Everyone comes from someone."

"They're... not around. And that's all I wanna talk about... sir."

"Ahh... I seem to have broached a touchy subject." Muldoon peered upwards from the corner of an eye. "You don't wish to speak of your father?"

"I don't want to talk about my family!" Pollux's anger boomed in his voice. "...Mr. Muldoon... sir," he added with a lowering of his intonation.

"Very well, Pollux," Muldoon conceded, stretching an arm to pat the gargantuan on one shoulder, missing by half an arm's length. "We'll continue this discussion later."

"But, Mr. Muldoon..." Pollux argued. However, Muldoon had already increased his gait, holding a hand up behind him to end the conversation. He stepped into the doorway.

An hour later

Bruno Muldoon and Davin stepped from the passenger side of the cargo truck. "So... what is it that has summoned me here?" Muldoon crossed his arms defiantly across his chest and casually bit at the end of a finger.

The driver, already having rounded the front of the vehicle, reached into the cab and flicked at a switch. A set of lights atop the vehicle ignited, flooding the immediate area in front of it with a blinding, solid river of luminosity. A digital billboard rose ten meters above them, its long-defunct screen soaked from end-to-end with a blackened mildew stain.

Muldoon rolled his eyes towards Davin. "A billboard, Davin. Really? This is within my interest?"

Davin clicked his fingers at the driver and pointed upwards. The driver scaled the cab of the truck and pushed one of the light housings upward at a steeper angle. Davin and Muldoon turned simultaneously to look into its modified path.

A large bundle hung from a chain in the center of the billboard, just within the arc of light cast from the truck. Muldoon furrowed his brow and squinted. "What am I looking at, Davin?"

The driver pounded his fist onto the roof of the truck beneath the rack of lights. They flickered and increased their intensity, bringing the scene into daylight clarity.

What Muldoon thought to be a bundle showed itself instead to be a body, upside-down and draining its life's blood from a knife stuck deep in its neck. Muldoon, heavily patterned to death and its ugly incarnations, stroked his thin mustache with a macabre delight.

"And?" he asked.

Davin snapped his fingers once again. The driver aimed a pair of lights to the left of the body. For the first time since either of the two men had known Bruno Muldoon, a look of unrest crept across their boss's face. He silently read the words scrawled in blood next to the body:

'The body must bleed to rid the poison. War is coming.'

Even in the tint of night, the crimson rushing to Muldoon's face made itself apparent through the rippling of his jaw muscles.

"If the Reformation insists on making a bold statement in this game of push and shove, they have gravely underestimated their opponent," he growled through gnashed teeth. "Cut him down!" He walked away in silence from Davin and the driver.

Pollux and Castor leaned like a pair of sequoias against the parapet, gazing out over the darkened cityscape of New Vegas. The sun had made its final dive beyond the horizon and dusk had officially filled the sky. The sporadic dots of light that marked the small populace remaining in the once sprawling city twinkled in Pollux's eyes. What was left of civilization in this part of the country was right in front of them, but Pollux's thoughts were many kilometers away.

"Remember when we were kids, Cas? We'd take our desert bikes out and make our own paths through the rough?" Pollux's voice boomed, but always left the listener with the impression no one was home upstairs.

Castor snorted. "Those were good times, Pol. But that was a long time ago," he replied, his voice a gravelly Long Island raking.

"Whatever happened to those times, Cas?"

Castor, easily two meters but still significantly shorter than his brother, glared up at Pollux with curious confusion. "Why're you askin' about this stuff, Pol? We haven't talked about memories like this in years."

Pollux fell silent. Castor continued to stare at his larger twin. For someone who had always come across as big and dumb, he could tell that his brother had - in no small feat - given this a great deal of deep, intellectual thought.

Pollux turned to Castor, a small tear resting at the corner of one eye. "Mr. Muldoon asked about Mom and Dad today."

Castor contorted his face. "Why?"

"I don't know, Cas."

"He's always workin' somethin'."

Castor gazed out at the night sky, his brow scrunched into a knowing glare. Bruno Muldoon had never shown the slightest interest in the twins' parents. To him, the brothers were willing tools used for his gain. Muldoon had looked after them, kept them in his employ, and had kept them safe for the most part. In return, he simply demanded loyalty - which they handsomely paid in return. Now, something did not seem right. He was plotting - but this time it involved *them*.

Castor was not used to thinking strategically where it concerned his boss. His job was to do as told and let Muldoon handle strategy. Castor's stomach churned at the thought of what might be on the horizon for them both, and he knew that Pollux must have been feeling the same - only twofold.

Pollux clasped his gigantic paws and leaned his elbows against the roof wall in deep reflection. "Cas... didja ever think we'd be here one day?"

Castor smirked. "I guess I never really thought about it."

"We've hadda do a lotta rough stuff to get here, though," Pollux continued. "But it was worth it... right?"

Castor scowled with surprise. "Worth it?" he said with a deep yelp. "What made it worth it?"

Pollux did not answer.

"We're alive, I guess if that's what you mean."

Pollux glared at his brother with genuine concern. "You know, Cas. Maybe one day this'll all be ours." He swept his hand out towards the darkened city. "If we stay loyal..."

It suddenly occurred to Castor where Pollux was heading. He needed to stop him before it was too late - before he thought that loyalty to Muldoon was a career choice and not a necessity of the times.

"Pol... you gotta know that the only future here is keepin a roof over our heads. You don't really think Muldoon's gonna hand over the keys to the kingdom to you and me... do ya?" He placed a hand on the bigger Webb's shoulder and shook him with a subtle quake.

"But Cas... isn't that what you want, too?"

Castor gripped his brother's shoulders. "Pol... that isn't the reason why you... *do* the stuff you do... for him. *Is it?*"

Pollux withdrew from embarrassment, removed himself from Castor's grip and turned away.

"Mr. Muldoon isn't who you think he is, Pol. He's only lookin' out for himself. And no matter what you do for him, he's always gonna treat you and me the same. We're just pawns, Pol."

Pollux lowered his head into his hands. "You think he knows about Dad?" he whimpered through his fingers.

169

Castor cleared his throat with a deep growl. "I think if we just shut up about it and never mention it – we'll be just fine."

"But..." Pollux began to argue.

Castor shot a stern scowl at his brother. "Pol... you don't have to do everything he tells you to do. And just 'cause you don't, doesn't mean he's gonna find out anything he doesn't need to find out."

Pollux nodded, his rotund face pale with the overexertion of having to think too much.

"One of these days, he's gonna step past the line, Pol." Castor slapped his paw on his brother's shoulder, a good 15 centimeters above his. "I just hope you got the sense to do the right thing when it happens."

Beneath the World's End Resort & Casino, in the abandoned counting and vault areas, Bruno Muldoon and Pollux Webb strode the desolate corridor with purpose. The rooms they passed, most with barred doors or windows containing heavy portcullis-style bars, gave off the impression of a dungeon rather than the high stakes casino hotel that had once called this set of buildings home.

Pollux, although having made several trips into the underground portion of the property, had never been alone with his boss this deep into the labyrinth of hallways. A beast of a man, his turbulent nerves revealed themselves in the form of his heart pounding visibly against his comically tight sport coat. He grabbed at the edges of the jacket and pulled them taut, hoping to draw off Muldoon's discovery of his unease. Behind his eyes, the gears of his mind belched quasi-intellectual smoke, stressing over the reason for Muldoon leading him to such a remote area alone.

Muldoon, always the master of making his employees and enemies alike feel uncomfortable, had already noticed the titan's edginess.

"Pollux, there's no need for worry. I just wanted to continue our conversation from earlier... about your family."

"Mr. Muldoon, I-I'm not comfortable talking about that..." Pollux responded with a shaky voice.

"Nonsense! Just casual conversation between employer and employee. There is nothing to fear."

Upon passing one of the locked doors, a muffled, female voice called out in a muted scream. "Let me out!" Feverish pounding on the opposite side of the metal door accompanied the cries. "Castor! Let me out!"

Pollux's face contorted in surprise. He stopped and blinked at Muldoon. "Boss, wasn't that..."

Muldoon held a hand up in the air. "It was nothing, Pollux," he said calmly, still strolling along.

"But, Mr. Muldoon, that sounded like..."

Muldoon halted, faced Pollux and shot him a stern look. "You heard. Nothing. Pollux." His words shut down any notion Pollux had of pursuing the matter.

Pollux scanned the hallway in front and back of them once again before following Muldoon, who had begun walking. "What are we doing here, boss?"

"Nothing to be nervous about, Pollux," Muldoon cooed, his voice echoing along the concrete and tile corridor. Pollux took two mammoth steps and instantly matched his boss's pace once more.

"So tell me more about your father," Muldoon continued, ignoring the interruption of his thoughts.

Pollux wrung his hands together. "I-I don't want to talk about that!"

"Are you hiding something... something that I should be made aware of, Pollux?" Muldoon pressed.

Pollux remained silent, the words begging release from his sealed lips.

"Pollux... you're about to learn the finer points of interrogation," Muldoon added, apparently changing the conversation after his futile attempt at gaining information from the behemoth. "You see, for you it has always been about brawn."

The glimmer of incomprehension on the face of the colossus made Muldoon roll his eyes upward. "Muscle," Muldoon explained with an exasperated sigh. "But there are pressure points," he continued once again, "besides breaking someone's limbs to get them to talk. This... is what you will learn here tonight."

They reached the end of the hallway and stopped in front of a larger, steel door – the entry to the old casino vault back in the day. Muldoon jingled the keys in his pocket, unlocked the door and swung it open. The door hit with a thundering clang and came to a creaking stop.

If there were a spot in New Vegas with a large amount of moisture, this seemed to be its nexus. The damp air wafted out of the dark room, carrying with it the sound of a monotonous dripping.

With a blind hand, Muldoon flipped at a switch inside the doorway, illuminating the room with a dull glowing bulb that hung at the center. Pollux flinched and stepped backward, having caught sight of a man tied to a chair underneath the light.

The man closed his eyes to the sudden brightness, having been locked inside Muldoon's dungeon for an untold amount of time. His melon-shaped head wore a large amount of grayish-blonde stubble. While not nearly to scale as Pollux Webb, he was a larger brute than average.

Muldoon flashed Pollux a coy, knowing smile. "Do you know this man, Pollux?" he asked with cool calculation.

Pollux shook his head nervously. He stared at the floor.

"Are you certain?" Muldoon pried. "You act as if you've seen him before..."

"No, sir, Mr. Muldoon. I've never seen him before..." Pollux refused to meet eyes with Muldoon.

"Please, after you..." With an air of fake courtesy, he held his arm out to show the way. Pollux hesitantly stepped past Muldoon and stopped a few meters from the man. Muldoon took up a spot beside the seated prisoner. He leaned with his hands on his knees, taking turns looking at the man, and then over at Pollux.

"This man," Muldoon began in a booming pronouncement, as if he were speaking to a large group in a packed auditorium, "has betrayed us... you and I. But in profoundly different ways, Pollux. Do you understand how?"

Pollux continued to knead his fingers together with a force that would have broken the average man's digits. He glared at the concrete slab at his feet and backpedaled to the door. "Mr. Muldoon, I'm not comfortable doin' this without Cas here..."

Muldoon rose from his crouch and crossed his arms over his chest. "Tell me, Pollux..." An indignant scowl painted his face. "Who is your boss. Castor? Or me?"

Pollux halted his backward movement and lowered his head in shame. "You, boss."

"Fine, Pollux. You would be wise to listen to me, then."

Pollux nodded his head in somber agreement. Muldoon placed a forceful hand on the man's shoulder. "Do you know what this man has done?"

Pollux shook his head, still without making eye contact with either of them.

The man spun his head and shot a vicious sneer up at Muldoon, breaking his silence. "That's enough, Muldoon. Leave the boy out of this!" he barked through a dry throat.

Muldoon rotated on a heel and glared at the man. "I'll determine when it's enough, Mr... Webb," he growled. Muldoon stepped back, placed his hand on his chin and mocked an epiphany. "Webb?" he said, his voice curling upward with surprise. "Not perchance any relation to Pollux and Castor... Webb?" Muldoon ricocheted his glances between the two men as if at a demented tennis match.

Pollux began to fidget even more noticeably. The man, having grown tired of Muldoon's game playing, growled. "You know damn well that he's my son! So let's just cut the bullshit and leave him out of this. This is between you and me!"

Muldoon crouched next to the man and stared at him. "Oh... but this *is* about the boy, Mr. Webb. You see, Pollux. This man... your father... is a member of the Reformation."

Pollux flicked his eyes from Muldoon's glare.

The corner of Muldoon's lip sprouted upwards. He stood and began pacing with his hands behind the small of his back. "Oh, but you knew that already... Pollux," he continued. "That's ok. You don't have to answer. I forgive you for that. However, your father's betrayal goes far beyond working for our sworn enemy..."

"Shut up, Muldoon!" Mr. Webb bellowed. "I said leave him out of this!"

Muldoon chuckled under his breath. He continued pacing. "Do you want to know, Pollux? How dastardly this man is - what he has done. What unforgivable betrayal he has levied against you?" Muldoon stopped; a sickening grin crawled across his face. "He *killed* your mother," he added in a low, slithering tone.

"Shut up!" Mr. Webb yelled. "Stop playin' these games with him!" He rotated his head towards his son, who stared at his father with a queer expression.

"N-no, that's not true, Mr. Muldoon," Pollux said, almost as if begging for it not to be.

"Ah, isn't it?" Muldoon quizzed. "Tell him, Mr. Webb. Tell him the truth."

Mr. Webb shifted his focus away from his son. Pollux's stomach dropped several floors while watching his father's reaction, despite his legendary ironclad nerves. The grin continued to spread on Muldoon's face.

"Tell him how she didn't agree with the Reformation's tactics. How she wouldn't go along with their ill-advised plans. And how he had her *killed* because of that refusal," Muldoon prodded, twisting the painful knife further into Pollux's psyche. "He may not have pulled the trigger, mind you. But his inaction in protecting his wife... your mother... was her death sentence."

"He's twisting it, Pol!" Mr. Webb yelped over Muldoon's ranting. "Don't listen to him! That's not how it happened..."

"Dad? Is that true?" Pollux's voice cracked somewhat.

"No... it's not true," the elder Webb shot back.

"Come now, Mr. Webb. Let's not fabricate falsehoods," said Muldoon in his suave demeanor. "Tell the truth to your son. Tell him that his mother is dead."

Muldoon pointed at Pollux's father. "Who has protected you more than this man, Pollux? Who has treated you like family - kept you alive, kept you safe? Given you a purpose? Given you a life?" Muldoon threw his vicious glare towards Mr. Webb. "While who has had the one person that you love, more than your own self, killed?"

Pollux continued to stare blankly at his father, his mammoth head shaking from side to side in confused denial.

"Tell him... tell him the truth!" Muldoon needled once again.

Pollux's face, even in the dim light of the tiny alcove outside the old vault, began to grow a darker shade of violet with each second.

"Tell him! Tell him that the one person that gave him life - that allowed him to suckle from her teat during his formative years. He had her killed, Pollux. Killed!" he shouted into Mr. Webb's ear.

"That's enough!" the old man cried, spittle flinging from the corner of his mouth. He flicked his eyes up at his son, then back at Muldoon. "It's more convoluted than that, Pol. This bastard is playing you."

Pollux stood stoically in silence, his arms at his side, his hands balled so tightly that the snapping of his knuckles under his leather skin echoed in the closed room.

"Tell me the truth... Dad." Pollux said in a low grumble, like an approaching storm on the horizon - and quieter than Muldoon had ever heard him speak. A small tear trickled from the corner of one eye, and seemingly ignited and evaporated all in the same instant on his flaming cheek. "*Is Mom dead?*"

Mr. Webb glanced guiltily at Muldoon, at Pollux, then down at the floor. Without a word, he nodded.

Muldoon, giving one last smile at Mr. Webb, hid his glee at his success and faced Pollux with a stern, but understanding expression. He tilted his head and made eye contact with Pollux. "Aye, when the shroud of lies is drawn, the beacon of truth shines through."

Pollux continued his murderous glare at his father. Pollux's heart beat like a trapped prisoner in a tomb. The muffled sound of the titan's remaining teeth grinding together like concrete tablets sent a small shiver down Muldoon's spine. Pollux sprung forward and grabbed his father, yanked him from the chair by his neck - snapping the ropes that had bound his hands - and throttled him between his massive paws.

"Now now, Pollux." Muldoon gave a half-hearted attempt at wrestling the beast's arms away from Mr. Webb.

Pollux released his father and took a step backward. His father rubbed at his own throat, gasping for precious air after having it nearly choked out of him.

Muldoon pushed forward an arm and laid out his palm. A gleam of light flicked off the blade of a large hunting knife that lay upon it. "What do you know to be consistent about this organization. This... *family*... Pollux? What are our values when people levy wrongs against us?"

Pollux, his chest heaving like an overinflated balloon, wiped the saliva from his chin and glared at Muldoon with fire in his eyes. "An eye for an eye..." he grumbled from deep within his barrel-width chest.

Muldoon nodded and raised an eyebrow in approval - he had taught him well. He placed the knife, handle first, into Pollux's hand. "This man does not know the meaning of loyalty, Pollux," he hissed.

"Some things are bigger than you, Pollux, believe it or not," Mr. Webb strained, making a desperate attempt to soothe his angered son. "Bigger than me. Bigger than all of us. Decisions have to be made - for the good of everyone involved. Good for the world. This man and his organization have to be stopped at all costs!"

The sound of Pollux's gigantic knuckles popping once again filled the din of silence in the room. Almost as if able to hear the archaic machinery churning in the giant's head, Muldoon stepped back and built a coy smile at his handiwork.

"Your mother couldn't see it that way," his father continued. He gulped audibly. "But I know you're smarter than that, Pol. Everyone's always underestimated you. You can see that... can't you?"

Pollux, unable to further intellectualize his father's betrayal, stomped forward, knife in hand.

Mars. Red Colony One

"Repeat my commands, Darpa," Brig ordered, pacing like a caged jungle cat around his room. The virtual simulation presence flipped between scenes like a broken projector; Brig's mind reached high gear. The room flashed like a strobe from Clive's workshop back on Earth, to the attack outside the abandoned warehouse, Brig's seeking of sanctuary at the church, and then to the EW rescue attempt at Kaliningrad. Brig forced his head between his palms and closed his eyes.

"As you wish, Mr. Stroud." Darpa stood in the corner of the room observing, her arms crossed over her brilliant white, formfitting jumpsuit. "I am to seal your room from the inside for the next six hours, and I am to ignore any entry attempt - regardless of authority."

Brig nodded silently. While still unsure of how many days or weeks had passed since he had arrived on Mars, he was certain that a Clarity-induced episode was past due. Worse yet, he had left his only supply of the dampener serum back on Earth at Bronson Fox's estate the day that he buried Nadia. His full intention at that time was to never return - but for a different reason. Now, he found himself without a net once again. However, with Darpa's assistance, he now had assurance that no one else would be injured - or worse - when the inevitable loss of control came about.

He stopped in front of the couch, teetered backward and sagged into the plush cushions. Brig closed his eyes. He trusted Steele when she had said she corrected the issue brought about by the Clarity gene.

But is that what she really said?

His eyes fluttered open at the false security offered by his childhood friend. After all, she was very vague when she gave him the news – failing, or deftly refusing more likely, to declare anything further on the subject other than there was 'no cause for concern'. At the moment, Brig was *very* concerned. Was Steele merely looking out for his well-being, finding a 'genome abnormality' in a routine body scan and correcting it, or did she actually go looking for something specific?

15: BLEEDING ME

The unease settled on him like the thick, humid air on a windless summer night.

She couldn't have known. Could she?

He continued to doubt himself. Who in their right mind would have allowed something like this to happen - and then clandestinely render inert the monster that had lived within him for the past seven years?

Brig rattled his head, wanting to clear out the bizarre happenings of the past few days. Despite seeing the colony firsthand, he was still so unsure of what was reality anymore. Yet what he did know was that he was not willing to risk harm to anyone else should he lose control for a few hours.

As the hours passed, Brig remained motionless on the couch, staring catatonically at the blank ceiling while in wait for any sign of symptoms. He thought that he had detected a strange feeling in his gut 30 minutes prior, but it turned out to be nothing more than a gastrointestinal rumble – a result of sampling a Mars-grown eggplant from a bistro in the entertainment sector.

He drew a deep breath and exhaled. Gone was the heated twinge at the back of his skull that normally preceded an attack. Every few moments Brig peeked at the full-length mirror that adorned his open armoire, but the telltale red glint that would flood his eyes when the attack had consumed him in the past, was not present.

In the cruelest of ironies, rather than a feeling of miraculous relief, a profound sadness cascaded over him at not having the malady. His sickness had been ingrained in him so long that it had almost become a routine part of his life – his second half. His duality. Now, with that half gone, he suddenly felt incomplete.

Brig sat forward and leaned onto his knees, pressed his thumbs into his eyes. He fully expected the symptoms to force their way through the sealed door and devour his consciousness. He tapped his foot nervously against the metal foot of the couch. He glared down at his leg, watching the frantic fidgeting that could have easily been mistaken for a junkie's reaction to not having his fix. Clarity, or rather the tragic side effect that had lived within him for so long, was the monkey on his back – and now he knew not how to live without it. After another hour of unease, Brig laid his head back on the pillow and fell into a deep sleep.

A gentle breeze wisped through the long grass of the plain. At the center of a clearing, a lion lay on its belly, sniffing the air every few seconds and imbibing the sweet, dewy scent of the morning. His tail whipped in his serenity, flapping away several flies that had begun buzzing around him.

Brig approached the lion, cautiously at first, taking care to land each soft step onto the earth so as not to alarm the great beast. The lion, showing intense disinterest, turned his head in Brig's direction, sniffed once, then blinked and turned away.

The tension dropped from Brig's shoulders. He stopped and stared at the lion, fully expecting him to leap to his feet and make a run at him. However, the lion remained still, blinking away the calm that had descended upon it. Brig stared into the eyes of the grand cat, suddenly becoming aware that the red glint that he had been accustomed to was... missing.

Brig watched in silent alarm, seeing his own hand reach to the lion. He placed it on the lion's back and stroked its suede-like fur. The lion purred, taking in a deep whiff of Brig's scent, and then exhaled with a subdued grumble. As if unable to control his reckless behavior, Brig moved his hand forward and grabbed a handful of its mane between his fingers. He ran his fingertips up through the shag and onto the back of the lion's head, scratching it with a newfound love.

The lion grumbled again, then lowered its head and drifted to sleep. Brig knelt next to the giant cat and continued to stroke its mane. His fear of a brutal mauling at the claws and fangs of the wild animal traveled away with the wind through the gently swaying trees on the far ridge.

16:
Awakenings

Mars. Red Colony One

Ratel Irven bumped his padded elbow against the support beam. The replacement strut, one of the last needed to repair damage done by an errant meteorite strike a month prior, held firmly in its channel, as he worked the ion torch to attach it to the outside surface of the twin massive Red Colony One terrariums. The lambent, azure halo of the torch danced across his face shield, lighting the sweat beads perched on his forehead like tiny sparks of liquid wax.

He released the trigger on the tool and closely inspected his handiwork, snuffing the shroud of blue around him. Through the pellucid material that made up the dome itself, he spotted Steele Fox within the terrarium, on both knees tending busily to a garden. As if feeling his gaze, she glanced upward. He offered a polite wave with his gloved hand - she offered a nod and curt smirk, and he resumed his work.

Inside, a placid breeze wafted across the plain of Primrose, cascading artificial sunlit warmth over the field and through Steele's hair. She sat back on her haunches, her eyes closed, and through her breather mask inhaled the serenity of honeyed fragrance that travelled upon the wind. Within the fathomless silence of her surroundings, her mind wandered millions of kilometers for a moment, removing her from the otherwise sterile environment in which she called home. She opened her eyes, the radiant pools of emerald within reflecting the ambient light of the terrarium, and gazed upon the rocky Martian plain that rolled away to the mountains in the distance. A tear formed at the corner of one eye, and just as quickly leapt and found its way into the synthetic soil beneath her knees.

The soft resonance of footsteps pulled her back to the moment. She wiped the sadness from her cheek with a gloved palm and busied her hands around the roots of a newly planted Primrose. From her peripheral, she caught sight of her visitor - it was Brig.

She glanced over her shoulder at him without facial reaction, and then lowered her head with an annoyed sigh.

"How long have you been standing there, Brigadier?"

Brig snorted through his own mask. "I figured you'd know, or at least your... alter ego... would," he said, tilting his head over a shoulder, wondering if the omnipresent Darpa had materialized behind him.

"Did you come to needle me, or did you have something you needed to discuss?" The lack of playfulness in her voice preempted any attempt at further humor by Brig.

"I actually came to apologize."

Steele stiffened her shoulders, confirming the importance of the apology he was offering.

"I don't know if it's this place... or seeing you alive. Or everything combined," he continued, allowing a finger to scratch the back of his head, "but I shouldn't have said what I said. It was unfair."

He sighed heavily. Steele remained stoically silent.

"I'm just having a little trouble processing everything right now. But it'll get better. I promise."

Steele smirked, holding a Primrose to the end of her nose. She pushed herself to her feet. Without looking at him, she answered in what was almost a songlike melody. "So we're good then?"

Brig, incredulous to her reaction, put his hands on his hips. "Yeah. As good as can be I suppose."

She let loose a half-giggle. "Well, I suppose that was unfair to you, as well," she added while trying to stifle her giddiness. "I know that's a sensitive subject for you. So, I'll try to be more understanding in the future."

Brig nodded and kicked his foot at the ground like a shy schoolchild. He scanned the massive bed of flowers that stretched out around them. "So... your flower garden, huh? Your favorite flowers I see."

Steele nodded, a subtle giggle continuing under her breath. She looked at him with a coy upturned eyebrow. "You remembered?"

Like a flash flood, the memory awoke within of why her choice of flower stayed with him. His mind suddenly whisked back to the soul-crushing morning behind her father's estate back on Earth – the Primrose on the gravestone. It was not Steele's favorite flower that he recalled - it was Nadia's. Another fake memory - one that provided all too-real heartbreak.

Brig's face suddenly drew to alarm. He turned his focus past Steele to just outside of the massive panes of glass-like substance holding out the harsh environment of Mars.

"Cat got your tongue?" Steele jabbed.

"Uh... Steele?" Brig replied, spinning her in the direction of the dome wall. To his shock, a man in a heavy environment suit tumbled as if in slow motion along the outside of the clear wall. His arms flailed as he bounced off the curved surface and headed towards the ground.

Steele raised an eyebrow. "Use your anti-gravity, you twit..." she mumbled under her breath.

The man hit the ground in a large puff of Martian dust. Brig, already bolting past Steele and into the patch of Primrose ahead of him - snapping the heads off a good bit of them in his haste - stopped and glared wild-eyed at Steele.

"Aren't you going to do something? Doesn't he need help?"

Steele teased at the Primrose's petals in her hand. "Brigadier," she poked with a hint of mockery, "you worry too much."

She looked up into his eyes, and then to the dust cloud that stopped only a meter above the ground outside. She stepped forward once. "He's wearing a biosuit that protected him from his fall, as well as the impossible environment out there." Her voice turned to a mumble once again. "But the idiot forgot that it also has a gravity generator... and that it was on."

Brig shook his head in exasperation; Ratel stood from within the dust cloud to look at them. Steele pointed to her arm and offered a snide smile. He glanced down at his own wrist, then back at her and timidly proffered a 'thumbs-up', before using the framework of the dome to float back up to his workspace.

Brig stomped past Steele and back onto the path between the flowerbeds. "What's going on here? I don't understand this place!"

Steele grabbed him gently by the arm. "Brigadier... perhaps you'd do well with a complete tour of the colony – just to set your mind at ease?"

Brig nodded without a word.

"I'll set it up with my father..."

"Your father?" Brig's mind muddied again. "You mean... he's... *alive?*"

Steele furrowed her brow and tilted her head. "Alive? Of course he's... oh bother. You mean to tell me you saw *him* die, too?" Her voice offered more sarcasm than kind understanding, however.

Brig could only raise an eyebrow in confusion. He shook his head and closed his eyes.

Brig sauntered the length of the feeder corridor that led towards the main complex of Red Colony One, nodding disinterestedly at passersby. He had decided to forgo the 'official' tour of the colony, having decided instead to be alone with his thoughts. The fact that the tour was under the reigns of none other than General Rossi sealed off any willingness on Brig's part to participate. Having only met the man once, Brig decided that he did not want to give the General a chance to dig into his past any further. He quickly found it to be a fruitful decision, as his mind was already swirling over so many issues, and he found the peace and quiet to be exactly what he needed now.

Necessitated by his participation as a special ops commando in the Epsilon Warriors, Brig had been a world traveler once. As such, he had seen many of Earth's visual treasures. However, he could not help but feel overwhelmed at the sprawl and technological heights of what seemingly had sprung from out of nowhere.

Brig had always known about the manned missions that landed on Mars back in the 2060's, but it had always been presented to him - and the rest of the world - as small expeditions whose sole missions were to prove simply that it could be done, and then come home. What amazed him further, was that Steele - his Steele - seemed to be the root architect of it all. Was it possible that all of this was built and no one knew anything about it? Was he really just that engrossed in everything Brigadier Stroud? Or was there something more to which he was not privy? Had everyone been misled about the extent of the buildup and advancement of this installation? At this point, he was not sure whether to be impressed... or concerned.

He rolled the left sleeve of his gray jumpsuit up past his elbow, which had aggravatingly slipped down to his wrist once again. The recurring dull thud emanating from somewhere above him rattled the transparent section of the main dome of Red Colony One, and then went silent just as quickly. Brig, still not having gotten used to the oddity of the effect - which seemed to occur at regular intervals around one week apart - tilted his head and peered upward with one eye. A momentary shadow darted across his path.

What he observed was not unlike a jet contrail back on Earth - however, it was transparent and wavy, with no apparent source. He stopped and stared at the blank spot above and to the west, likening the strange sight to what he had witnessed back at the portal before his strange journey to Mars. After a brief moment, the warped space returned to normal and Brig shook his head in confusion.

Another mystery for another time I guess.

Moments later, Brig wandered through a small corridor and out onto one of the many catwalks that either connected large sections of the colony to each other, or soared above facilities that for various reasons needed to remain out of reach of normal Red Colony One citizenry.

Brig marveled at the majesty of the views afforded to anyone on this particular one, its near 360-degree vista encompassing a good portion of the colony that stretched out for kilometers in one direction. At the far west of the installation, a spire soared above all others. Brig immediately recognized it as the observation tower in which he and Steele had been a week prior. He rotated, taking in the panorama. The clay-red mountains rose up from the horizon, nuzzling the face of the dawn sky. The sun had just pulled itself up from its slumber and had rested just beyond a gap that sat between two peaks - its blue halo swelled out where it melded into a sea of pinkish hue.

The serenity of the mountain range was nothing new to Brig. Having been raised in the southwest URA, his exposure to mountains started at an early age. He had visited his father many times in the URA capitol of Boulder, and often partook in hikes during his downtime from the EWs. No, mountain ranges were nothing special in his eyes. On Mars, however, he found them to be breathtaking - clutching his eyes like the attraction of a ferrous metal each time he passed a window to a view.

The sudden nugatory feeling in his gut brought him back to reality, however. And for as lonely and lost that he was back on Earth, that sentiment magnified twofold here on Red Colony One. On an alien world - *he* was the alien.

Brig strolled forward, his strong hands kneading the fleshy meat at the base of his neck. His time in the theratank notwithstanding, Brig had still not recovered entirely from his injuries incurred during his final days on Earth. His ribs, no longer cracked, still ached when he rotated his torso, and the strain of his hideously twisted ankle projected phantom pains along his shin. The physical damage of those injuries had passed for the most part, and he knew that each day would bring him closer to full health. However, no amount of auto-massotherapy was going to extinguish the staggering disorientation clouding his mind since the first minute he had awoken on Mars.

A faint sparkle caught his eye. He stopped and scanned the horizon, the coating of the dome above keeping him from having to squint when looking directly into the sun.

Another technological innovation of Steele's team, no doubt.

Off in the distance, at the base of the 'v' that marked the chasm between the edges of two mountains, just blending into the lower arc of the sun, a small group of objects twinkled as they rose away from the surface of the planet. They floated and gyrated like tiny dominoes tossed from an invisible hand into the sky, the dust-masked sunlight glancing off their surfaces. Brig tilted his head, unsure of the source of the objects, nor their relativity to the colony.

"Some sort of trash dumping procedure..." he said aloud, albeit mumbled for only his own benefit.

However, the longer he glared into the distance, the more he doubted his initial estimation. Then, it struck him. He felt his heart drop as if it had just plummeted an empty elevator shaft.

"Bodies..." he said, aghast.

Indeed, the objects were not trash. Not useless chunks of shiny metal thrown away. Not even tiny dominoes. Brig leaned farther over the rail, as if that would bring the horrific sight to any closer resolution.

But there they were.

Groups of bodies floated away from a single point beyond the mountain range, their arms flailing, forcing their uncontrollable spin in the weightlessness of space. Without realizing, Brig had sidestepped several meters to his right, almost to the end of the catwalk where it merged with a larger, domed hallway at the intersection of the entertainment sector and the Red Colony One security enclave.

"Fancy a dig?" a Cockney-inflected voice queried from behind, his timbre more like the squawk of a parrot.

Brig spun, the surprise of his not being alone in solitary thought striking him like a wet towel across the backside.

An older man, shorter than Brig only because of his hunched physique, wavered towards him, a crooked, wagging finger outstretched. The pearlescent sclera of his eyes drowned the glimmering emerald irises within, and matched the ivory scraggle of hair that wired out around his corrugated face. The colony's cool, ambient lighting glinted from his shiny tinfoil cap. His attire was not unlike the plethora of homeless that Brig had experienced back on Earth in the years following the Event - tattered and unkempt. Oddly enough, it was similar to the same gray jumpsuit that Brig currently wore.

Brig got the distinct sensation that the man was glaring into his soul, and for a brief nanosecond, he had to convince himself that he was not staring at an advanced-age Bronson Fox. Brig scrunched his brow. "Are you... talking to me?" Brig's eyes fell to focus on a barcode tattoo that partially protruded from within the man's collar.

"I recognize ya! But ya made it out of there, didn't ya?" the man cackled.

"I... don't know who you are..." Brig glanced around to see if anyone else was in the area. "Maybe you have me mistaken for..."

"That pit's a bugger though, ya know what I'm rabbitin' about, don't ye?" the man barked over him. "But ye' made it out!"

Brig, unsure of anything of which the man was babbling, pointed hesitantly back at the stream of floating bodies, which had now trailed off to just a few barely visible dots. "Do you know what that is?"

The man raised a crooked eyebrow; his eyes seemed to glow. "Of course ye know, lad! The Expendables!" he said with a maniacal waver of his already squeaky voice.

Brig flattened his eyes farther. The man continued without hesitation.

"We're them... both of us! But ye found yer way out!"

Brig shook his head in perplexity. However, before he could untangle the old man's web of absurdity, two beefy men in security red with gold bands encircling their upper arms, appeared from within the enclave. They grabbed the man's arms and dragged him backward, ignoring his physical protests.

One of the guards belched into the man's ear as they reached the edge of a corridor "You knew we'd find you eventually!"

Just as they were to disappear around the corner, the man made eye contact with Brig one final time. "Don't let 'em take ye back!

Once you're out ye stay clear!" he screamed, the gravel in his voice muting against the absorbent plastic of the walls.

Brig took a step forward, freeing himself from the momentary trance, deciding somehow to rescue the crazy old man. Another guard, one that Brig had not noticed, stepped into his path and waved a finger in his field of vision. "But..." Brig protested, pointing past the guard at the now empty hallway.

"Sorry, sir. No one allowed past this point," the guard said. The guard sneered disapprovingly down at Brig's jumpsuit, the beryl aura of the guard's pudgy rifle snout ebbing and flowing against his own crimson clothing.

Brig glanced at the weapon. It was not much of a threat in his mind's eye - however, he knew better than to pick a fight with security at this point – especially within earshot of the security enclave, where an untold number of guards would be more than happy to assist a comrade in distress. Besides which, he was not even certain there was a reason to fight. The crazy old man might have been just that – crazy. Brig shot his palms out, his fingers outstretched, and took a step backward.

"My mistake..." Brig said, and turned towards the domed entertainment complex. He peeked over his shoulder, the guard remained – staring at him with heightened suspicion. "Where were they taking that man?" Brig mumbled, one eye upward towards the invisible, yet omnipresent, Darpa.

"I am not privy to their destination, Mr. Stroud," Darpa answered immediately, appearing next to him in stride. He realized at once that she allowed herself seen only by him, as the guard did not react to her presence. "However, beyond that corridor is the shuttle to Sector 7G."

Brig stopped and feigned interest in a pair of workers that were repairing a strut above the main section of the entertainment complex, the brilliant azure of their ion torches flashing and tossing sparks that dove harmlessly to the concourse below every few seconds. "What's Sector 7G?"

"The mining colony," she responded without hesitation.

Brig pondered in silence, every few moments glancing over his shoulder at the guard, who had apparently lost interest in him and had disappeared into an adjacent hallway. "Darpa... do you know what the term 'Expendables' refers to?"

Darpa tilted her head at an angle. She gazed at him without responding.

I'm taking what the old man said seriously? Who's crazy now?
Brig shook his head in frustration, deciding it was a mystery that
would remain as such – or simply the ramblings of a lunatic.

Suddenly, Darpa spoke once again. "'Expendables' appears to
be a slang term for the miners in Sector 7G," she explained, almost
thoughtfully - if that were at all possible.

"That doesn't help," Brig murmured.

He surveyed the enormous complex, which, at this time of the
morning, was notably devoid of patrons. A lone security guard
made his way into the main corridor of the Security Enclave, his
back to Brig as he purposefully strolled along. Brig stared with an
initial disinterest at the back of the man's head, noticing the close
shave of his hair against his skull.

"Dude could've been an EW with that buzz cut." He shot a
wide grin to Darpa, but her hologram had dissipated.

The man stopped abruptly and knelt down to tie a lace on one
of his boots that had come unfastened. The sterile light of the
corridor lit the side of the man's face. An eerie surge of electricity
sparked the base of Brig's brain. Brig's mouth hung agape as if he
had seen a ghost.

No. He *had* seen a ghost.

"It's not possible," Brig stammered in a low whisper.

Yet, the impossible had shown itself to be reality. Kneeling in a
hallway 15 meters in front of Brig - on Mars - was *Jonas Slade.*

"Jonas!" Brig called with a yelp, breaking into a quick jog at
the surprised man, whom turned to face the sound of Brig's voice.

The man glanced at Brig with a squint.

"Jonas! I can't believe it's you!" Brig eased his pace and came to
a stop a meter in front of the skeptical guard.

"Are you talking to me, sir?"

Brig guffawed. "Knock it off, man. Glad to see you!" He
playfully bumped the man's shoulder with a fist.

The guard looked confusedly down at Brig's hand. "I think you
have me confused with someone else. Do I know you, sir?"

Brig flinched. *How could he not recognize me?*

"Jonas... Jonas Slade. It's me... Brig Stroud!" He offered his
hand to the guard. "You don't recognize me?"

"No... no, I'm sorry I don't know you, sir. And my name's
Winslow. Emerson Winslow." He shook Brig's hand with a
noticeable reluctance.

Brig squinted. As the man retracted his hand from the shake, Brig spied a worn spot on the guard's forearm – a shadow of a tattoo, perhaps. He grabbed at Winslow's bicep and pulled it towards him. "C'mon, man. It's me. You gotta remember!"

The guard recoiled and pointed his other finger authoritatively into Brig's face. "You see these hash marks?" He tapped at his shoulder sleeve. "That means I can kick your ass outta here if you so much as look at me wrong, pal! Now I told ya... you got the wrong guy!"

Winslow's voice cracked just enough for Brig to hear it, and Brig was certain the slightest nervous gulp escaped from the guard's tightened throat. The man's eyes widened by the narrowest of centimeters, but enough for Brig to see the fear - like a small boy peeking from the clouded second story window of a 19th century Victorian.

"Sorry... Emerson." Brig backed and scratched at his head. "I guess I just thought you looked a lot like someone I knew back on Earth."

"It's okay... sir." Winslow broke eye contact, but his apprehension showed. He turned and stepped towards a nearby door. "It happens," he said over his shoulder, as he strode into the room. The door clicked shut.

Brig stood in silent stupefaction, his mind numb after seeing his former EW partner - that he had watched die in Russia seven years ago.

17:
Beyond the Palisades

Earth. Clovis, New Mexico

The transport truck rumbled along the pitted highway, voicing its disapproval of the moist air through a series of vociferous backfires that pierced the desolation. Clive rested his head across the back of the wooden bench where it met the metal chassis. The groan of the power plant, straining to keep up a decent speed at the driver's insistence, sung to him.

Probably an M35, he thought. *Or even a CCKW, but man that would be old.*

However, that was to be expected for any vehicle still operating in this day and age - especially after the Event. While all-electric vehicles were the norm prior to late 2077, afterwards they became obsolete - for obvious reasons. Those with internal combustion engines, and once considered a collector's item that were rarely put to any type of serious use, became the only mode of transportation going forward.

To Clive, it was no surprise that a truck used as a troop transport - and so much more - as far back as World War II was still in service, even if it did sound like it wanted to roll over and give up the ghost. He actually liked riding in these old behemoths, if only for the nostalgic feel it gave him of his days in the EWs. They did not use them for much other than field training missions, but it connected to a memory nonetheless.

The truck shuddered with a mighty defiance, tossing him over on his side. Potholes - now those he could do without, and their supply seemed to be infinite. It was apparent Danil felt the same, his disgusted grunts coming each time the massive tires rolled over a crumbling section of asphalt.

Clive pushed himself back up to a seated position and pawed at the hood over his head.

"Leave it..." a voice, Jesse's, growled from the front-most area of the cargo bed.

Clive sighed. He and Danil, led into the back of the truck several hours prior, had bounced along in darkness and relative silence the entire trip.

Must be something really important they don't want us to see, Clive pondered. *Or they're gonna throw us out in the middle of nowhere.*

As if detecting his impatience, the truck began to slow, the shrill pitch of its brakes sending a cadaverous chill up his neck. Clive and Danil pricked their ears, morbid curiosity replacing their weariness. The musty concoction of dust kicked up by the rear wheels and unburned fuel working through the worn exhaust abraded their nostrils, forcing a cough from Danil before the air finally cleared. Muffled voices near the cab of the truck preceded a loud thump on the side of the cargo bed's canvas covering.

Before Clive could discern what was going on, an unseen person plucked the hood from his head. In the pale darkness, Danil, sitting opposite him, was also without his hood. Jesse quickly reminded Clive who was in control, however, jabbing the snout of his rifle into Clive's ribs and pushing him towards the opening at the rear.

Clive grasped at the assist bar and leapt to the ground onto his good leg, did a quick hop and then gingerly regained his balance with his prosthetic. Jesse scrunched his eyes, watching the former EW rub at his lower thigh. Ignoring the glare from the bulky Australian, Clive stepped up next to Danil, who had exited the truck seconds before him. Two others that Clive had not seen, one of them he recognized as the Englishman, Nye, jumped from the steel bed and stood behind the pair.

A set of rod iron gates rose like Hell's entryway ten meters in front of Clive and Danil. The bluish moonlight flooded through the bars, illuminating a small path that wound ahead and between countless shadowy tombstones on each side. Clive glared at Nye.

"What's this?" Clive asked.

"It's a cemetery," Jesse grunted from the back of the truck.

"Master of the obvious..." Clive mocked.

Nye tapped Clive with an elbow as he passed. "But there's far more than the dead buried here, chum."

"You put a hood on our heads to keep a cemetery a secret?" said Danil.

"Still don't trust you... but you'll see why soon enough..." Jesse growled, his face now next to the diminutive Russian's.

17: BEYOND THE PALISADES

The men moved forward once again at the subtle prodding of Jesse's rifle tip. After a few minutes of stumbling through the chilled air, and curious glances between Clive and Danil, they stopped at the front of a darkened mausoleum. The blackened silhouette crept from nothingness, the moonlight blotted out by the skeleton of an elm that leaned in to tickle the front marble wall.

"This is it..." Nye announced.

Clive cocked his hands on his hips, scanned the shadows around the cemetery and chuckled. "Am I supposed to be impressed or something?"

Nye, smiling slyly, held his hand out for the two men. "You will be..."

One of the other two men from the truck, his face grimy and nearly as dark as the night, brushed past Nye and forced his shoulder into the massive stone entryway. It slid aside after a solid grunt; the grating of the marble slab on concrete echoed into the emptiness and then fell eerily silent. He stepped back into Nye's shadow. Just within the narrow corridor leading into the blackness of the mausoleum, a thin trail of light beckoned from a dug out stairwell leading down into the soft earth.

Clive and Danil gravely eyed each other. Jesse nudged them forward.

The group exited the bottom of the stairwell into a grand room, larger than the area of the mausoleum above. Wooden beams ran from floor to ceiling on each of the walls, an obvious sign that the room had been dug into the earth long after the cemetery was placed.

Clive shook off a chill at the realization that digging out this room must have involved removing the associated casket-filled vaults.

Twenty or so people, separated into several groups milling about, filled the front area of the room. As if on cue, they ceased their small chatter and stared up at the entry of the two new strangers.

Along the longest wall, and what hooked Clive's attention, sat a string of workstations that held various pieces of communications equipment: several satellite radio transceivers, a few microphones and even a radarscope. On the back wall, and drawing Danil's focus, was a walled-in section with a two-meter-tall, raised countertop that separated the back wall from the main area. Mounted within view, and just behind two men that leaned upon the counter playing cards, were an uncountable number of weapons of all sizes and power. Danil's eyes widened at the sight of several legacy-style grenade launchers, before he turned his gaze back forward without detection.

A familiar voice from behind stabbed their stunned silence.

"Impressed with what you see?" It was the woman from the ambush. She stepped between Clive and Danil.

"Not what I expected from a cemetery," Clive observed.

"Precisely," she replied, and then walked past. "Come... dine with us. We have much to talk about." She stepped into the entrance to another room off the main.

"You do not trust me, I do not trust you to break bread with. My trust must be earned as well," Danil said with an indignance that was not as surprising as it was expected.

"That's fine," the woman replied. "Then you can just stand by and watch everyone else eat." She spun away and hurried through the doorway out of sight. The group followed one-by-one into the corridor, which was only wide enough for one person at a time - and even then, they had difficulty not bruising their shoulders on the mineshaft-like beams that held up the dirt ceilings.

An hour later

The small group sat at a long, wooden table. Clive sat next to Jesse and across from the woman, who sat next to Nye. Two others filled the seats on either side of the woman and Nye. Danil, still untrusting of this group, stood behind and to the left of Clive - glaring at each of the dirty faces of the men at the table, one-by-one. Clive, on the other hand, ignored the audible laughter of the group and chewed through several dinner rolls like a ravenous fiend, before he even realized they were all staring at him. It had been years since he had a fresh meal other than scavenged or bartered cans of long-expired soups and stews back at his workshop. This was a gourmet feast to Clive.

"So, Mr. Underwood. What is it that you do?" the woman asked.

"That I *do*?" Clive bristled. "What does anyone do anymore?"

She laughed. "What is it that brought you out here... to us?"

"I told you. We're trying to get as far away from the Syndicate as possible," he replied.

She squinted her suspicion at him. "But where were you planning on going? What was your plan?"

Clive realized he was dealing with someone much more astute than his usual assortment of Syndicate lackeys, like Castor and

Pollux Webb – even more so than Danil. He was not going to be able to bluff this woman any longer. She had played her hand and opened up the Reformation headquarters to him, so it was his turn to be truthful.

"We're actually hunting…" he began.

Danil gripped Clive's shoulder and squeezed. "Underwood, what are you doing?" he growled under his breath.

Clive held up a hand to silence Danil.

A smile of realization grew on the woman's face. "I thought as much," she cooed. "Perhaps we can be of mutual assistance to each other?"

Danil grumbled behind him, as if the short Russian were about to launch. "I am going to take my own nutrition then, Underwood," he said, pulling a cigarette from inside his jacket pocket.

Nye looked up from the table, motioned silently with his head towards one of the other two men, who hopped up and led Danil from the room.

"I don't think I ever caught your name… Miss…" Clive replied.

"Magenta," she replied. "Magenta Abgomgave. But everyone calls me 'M'."

Jesse pounded a fist in anger onto the table, rattling the plates of food in front of everyone seated. "M, are you crazy?" he barked. "Don't trust them!"

Nye jumped from his seat and leaned across the table, pressing Jesse's hand harshly onto the weathered wood surface. "Jesse, mind your tongue! Show some respect!"

Jesse shot a fiery glare at Nye, then stared back at Clive.

Unfazed by Jesse's outburst, Clive glanced at him and then back at Magenta. "*The… Magenta Abgomgave?*"

"You've heard of me?"

"Well… who hasn't? Anybody that was around knows you were the President's security chief." Clive, suddenly unsure of what he had stumbled upon, glanced around. "*He's* not here, too… is he?"

Magenta lowered her gaze, and her tone. "No. He didn't survive the crash of Golden Eagle One."

Clive nodded and remained silent for a moment. "But you did?" he said, breaking the awkward silence.

She stared back blankly.

"So… all of the security and safety measures put on that plane. And you were the only one to walk away?"

Another man stepped into the room and approached Magenta, leaning in towards her ear. Clive did his best to interpret, but only came away with a piece of the hushed conversation that included the words 'ready for pickup'.

Magenta, a look of nonchalance draping her face, continued to stare at Clive. "Well, if it's been made," she said in a lowered tone out of the corner of her mouth, "why are you telling me? Where is Webb?"

The man's face twisted. He leaned in closer to Magenta, covering his mouth and whispering far too quietly for Clive to hear. Magenta's face, normally a deep ebony, and even more so in the dim lighting of the underground bunker, grew ashen at the secretive news. The light that Clive had seen in her eyes since the first moment he had encountered her on the dark, desert road, seemed to dim somewhat.

"I have to attend to some business," Magenta said, rising from her chair. "Enjoy your meal. We'll talk later." She left the room swiftly, along with Nye and the other man. Jesse stayed behind.

Clive, perplexed at the sudden exit of Magenta and her staff, refocused his efforts on cleaning his plate. After gulping a few mouthfuls, he became aware of Jesse's intense glare. Clive shifted his eyes to the side, then back to his food without speaking.

Jesse leaned onto the table closer to Clive. "Your friend's a spook, ya know," he grumbled.

Clive shook off the observation and scowled. "I know who he is. You don't need to tell me."

"Then what's that make someone who associates with 'im?" Jesse said gruffly.

Clive looked at Jesse without expression. "I already told my story," he said, palming the short glass of red juice and raising it to his mouth, without breaking eye contact. "What's it matter to you, anyway?"

Jesse slammed his fist onto the table again. "Anything that threatens the Reformation is my business... mate. Don't get it twisted," he snarled. "You just watch your back around *that* snake. He'll bite ya as soon as ya turn it."

Clive pushed himself up from the chair and grabbed his empty plate. "I'll keep that in mind." He limped off towards the empty chow line at the far side of the room. Jesse stared after him, an intense rage building in eyes.

A few moments later, Clive returned, his plate once again towering with piles of shredded meat and rolls. He dropped the dish onto the table, sat down with a dull thud and began to dig into his second helpings. Once again, Jesse's eyes burned holes into him.

"How'd you lose your leg?" Jesse squinted with an eyebrow raised.

"Who says I lost anything?" Clive answered, deadpan without taking focus from his meal.

Jesse snorted. "I can tell. You're a warrior type. What... you lose it in a war?"

The familiar steam rose within Clive's chest. "Stepped on a mine in Portugal a few years back," he mumbled through a mouthful of gravy-laden mystery meat.

"Portugal? For a country that was tryin to keep their noses out of everyone's business – ya sure found yourselves in a lot of conflicts." Jesse's sneer grew after each audible breath that he made. "But that's just like you Yanks, anyway. Bloody hypocrites!"

Clive tore a vicious hunk from another roll. "I don't want to talk about it," he replied with his mouth full.

Jesse grunted in disbelief. "But you made it out alive."

"Yeah. Obviously."

"Then there's a hero. Ya owe someone your life."

Clive took his turn snorting. "He ain't no hero," he added with a huff.

"Anyone that saves someone's life is a hero, mate." Jesse's eyes lit with a wild fire.

Clive glared at Jesse. "He's a disobedient piece of shit."

For the first time since he had seen Jesse, a smile grew on the gruff man's face – even if it was a sarcastic one. "Disobedient, mate? He saved your life. What could he have done to be disobedient?"

The dam had burst, and Clive could no longer hold the swell growing behind it. "If it wasn't for his disobedience, I wouldn't have been there to step on that mine," Clive snarled.

Jesse raised his eyebrows, giving Clive a silent signal to continue.

"He went against orders and wanted to investigate some other camp instead of heading out for extraction." Clive's voice began to trail off as he became lost in thought. "Something about... a bunch of kids..."

Jesse lurched forward, wild-eyed. "Kids? You're saying he's *disobedient*? This man's a superhero, mate!" he yelled. "You got off lucky. At least you still have your life!"

"Life? What life?" Clive balked, bits of crumbled bread expelling from his mouth with each syllable. "What do you care, anyway? What's it to you?"

Jesse, grinning and exposing several missing teeth, leaned back on his chair and yanked at his pants leg until his boot fell with a solid thump onto the table. Before Clive could say anything, Jesse pulled the camouflaged pants leg up past his boot, exposing two thin, metal cylinders where his lower leg should have been. Jesse tapped on the prosthetic with the end of his rifle and winked.

"We're kin, you and me..." Jesse dropped his leg from the table, pushed himself from his chair and leaned in at Clive, his hands on his knees. "You need to learn to let things go, mate. Next time, you won't be so lucky."

Flaming embers stoked in Clive's soul. "If you say 'you can't let it define you' I'm gonna pound on you til' you bleed," he snarled.

Jesse chuckled, sat back on the chair and whipped his hands behind his head. "Touchy, touchy."

Clive corked the bottle on his anger and grabbed another bite of meat, which had grown cold. He flicked his eyes over to Jesse, and then back down again. "How did you lose yours?" he asked quietly.

Jesse, the insanity making its appearance behind his eyes once more, leaned forward for effect. "A croc got me!"

Clive, his mouth agape exposing a wad of unchewed meat, scrunched his eyebrows. "Seriously?"

Jesse laughed and sat back again. "No, mate. But that's what you wanted to hear... right? Us Aussies are crazy. Always gettin' into trouble."

Clive shook his head and began to eat again.

"I lost it defendin' my country against that good ol' UR of A. Stepped on a mine myself."

Clive, incredibly finding room in his mouth for an additional forkful of meat - as well as his foot - remained silent.

Jesse poked his finger into Clive's shoulder. "But the difference between you and me, mate, is that I give thanks where it's due. One of my mates pulled me outta that mine field and saved my life. And I owe him *mine*... no matter what happens."

Clive's face lit with the heat of embarrassment. Before he could offer up any sort of apology, Jesse had gotten up and stormed away into an adjacent room. A few minutes later, as Clive mopped the remnants of his dinner from his plate, Jesse reappeared and dropped a sizeable half rack of charcoal-encrusted ribs onto the table in front of the surprised Epsilon.

The sweet and spicy tang of the gorgeous slab of meat was something Clive had only dreamed about for the past seven years. He forced his mouth closed, holding back the salivation that was imminent from watching the barbeque glaze ooze from the grooves of the succulent meat.

Jesse winked at Clive. "Eat up. You're gonna need your strength, mate," he said, and then walked away.

Clive leaned on the fencepost at the rear of the mausoleum, his head held low between his shoulders, resting his weight on his elbows. Although his stomach was full, more full than it had been in many years, he was still not sated. He hungered, but not for sustenance. His sights were staunchly set on completing his latest mission. But was the Reformation just the latest stepping stone in his quest - or an obstacle?

He peered out over the endless rows of headstones, their intricate geometric forms swimming out from the pitch in the silvery moonlight. What caught his eye most, however, was the alarming number of fresh graves dotting the landscape in between the standard markers. Clive slowly turned his head to glance back at the mausoleum, wondering how many of the Reformation had given their lives for their cause. Still, it could not have been anywhere near the amount that had perished since the Event in 2077. What were their stories, and why did he, of all people, survive when they could not?

A quiet presence broke his spiritual wanderings. Magenta appeared next to him and took up a leaning position mirroring his own.

"I assumed you were the thoughtful type." She smiled without making eye contact. "And I wasn't wrong. That's why I chose you."

"Chose me for what exactly?" Clive answered. "You still haven't told me *anything*."

Magenta nodded. "And to the point..."

"No... to the point would have been two hours ago when you ambushed me and my partner out on that highway and then brought us here."

"Oh... so now he's your *partner*?"

"You know what I meant. He's not my partner."

"Then what is he?"

"You tell me, since everyone around here seems to have their own uninformed opinions of him." Clive shook his head in disgust.

"He's a snake," she responded flatly. "He's one of Muldoon's go-to guys."

"So your clan knows about Muldoon?" Clive raised an eyebrow. It struck him by surprise to hear *that* name from someone outside of his normal circle.

Magenta looked forward for a few seconds before answering. "Of course. As the..." Her voice became distant as she blinked and stared at the damp patch of wild grass in front of her. "...as the head of this clan, I make it my business to know such things."

Clive turned his head forward and nodded in acknowledgment. "Sometimes things aren't what they seem, Magenta."

Magenta exhaled a heavy breath through her nose. "You don't have to tell me, Mr. Underwood." Her eyes gleamed under the moonlight and sent a spike of chill across his neck. "You're out combing the desert with Mr. Checkushkin... searching for God knows what."

She waited for a reaction. She did not get one.

"What would your boss say about that?"

Clive pointed an angry finger at her. "He's not my boss," he growled through gnashed teeth.

"Oh, that's right... he's not," she replied, the sarcasm not veiled. "But yet you *do* work for him..."

If only she knew the whole truth. The truth about what his true intentions were in infiltrating the Syndicate. *Should I tell her?*

"So how is it that you came to be the head of the Reformation? I'm assuming that's what you are now..." Clive changed the subject before she dove any farther down *that* rabbit hole.

Magenta faced Clive and melted him with her steely gaze. She knew that Clive was not the typical soldier that filled the Reformation's ranks. He showed his astute nature with every deliberately chosen word.

"They picked me up and provided me a light at my darkest hour."

"Just like that? One day you're the President's Security Chief. His plane goes down... and then you rise from the ashes to become the head of one of the two biggest organizations known?"

"It's not that simple..." she said thoughtfully.

"It never is," he replied. "But I still don't understand how a beautiful woman such as yourself..." Clive's voice chilled to a squeak as the two locked gazes. "It's a dangerous world... and yet here you are, doing something about as dangerous as dangerous can be."

"I was forced out of necessity to survive. You know how that works, Mr. Underwood..." she replied, confirming the astuteness that he had detected earlier.

"Clive..." he corrected.

Although the night was dim and the moonlight provided very little lighting, the faintest glimmer of an upturned lip appeared on her face. A small smile cracked at the corner of his own lips.

She's a tough one.

"There's more to that story about that plane crash than you're letting on... isn't there?" His gaze penetrated even deeper.

"The President survived the plane crash..." she offered.

Clive had won this round. He nodded. He had assumed as much before but did not want to make a scene in front of the other Reformation crew. The missing piece, however, was what had happened after the crash, and he was not about to let her stop talking now.

"But he was in a bad way. His legs were shattered from events during the crash." Her voice became almost mechanical as her mind drifted a thousand kilometers away. "And then..."

She paused.

"Then?"

"And then I let him down..." The moonlight reflected off a tear forming at the corner of her eye. "At the worst possible moment, I turned my back for one second. And then... he was gone."

"Gone? You just said his legs were broken. Where could he have gone to?" Clive's eyebrows announced his confusion.

She placed her hand softly onto his. While the rest of the world suffered from lack of electricity in any substantial capacity, there was plenty to be had within her touch. Clive's arm warmed and he could not help but pull within centimeters of Magenta - so close that each word from her mouth tickled his lips.

Her voice lowered.

"One of the Syndicate thugs came along and abused our trust... and killed him. It was my fault."

"I think you're being too hard on yourself." With a brashness that astounded even himself, Clive stroked the side of her face just below her scar.

She gazed into his eyes, lit from the side by the moonlight. "It was my job to protect Devlin Stroud."

Hearing the name Stroud unnerved Clive. He backed away and clenched his jaw. "But you couldn't have known. It was a horrible moment... the plane crash..."

"Regardless," she continued. "The one duty that I was sworn to perform... I failed. I let him down. I let everyone down."

Clive had gotten lucky to have her open up. However, he knew that it would be pressing his luck to try to get her to change her thinking on the matter. He placed a hand on her upper arm and rubbed.

"So how did you end up with the Reformation?"

Once again, they drew within breathing space of each other.

"I escaped with my life that night in the desert. That horrible man was going to do something as bad... or worse... to me than he did to President Stroud." She pulled away from Clive and placed her hands on the fencepost, looking out over the sleepy landscape. "I had to make a choice. I escaped on one of their retro-bikes. I ran out of fuel within the next few hours. Fortune was somehow smiling upon me – I came across a group on a desert highway in the small hours of the night." She looked over at Clive. "A lot like how you came upon us."

"Seems to be their M.O.," Clive added, his snide remark not lost on Magenta.

"We're aggressive when we need to be. But given the circumstances – what would you have us do?"

Clive did not respond.

"I swore from that day," she continued, "that I would find whoever was responsible and make them pay for what they did to him."

"But does the Reformation really have the kind of firepower needed to take down the Syndicate?"

She turned her head away once again. "We take what we can get."

"It's more than that. You don't understand the depth of that organization and the lengths that they'll go to take everything that's out there and make it theirs," he replied.

"We have benefactors," she said, and then fell suspiciously silent.

Clive raised his eyebrows. "Who?"

One of the Reformation soldiers stumbled around the corner behind them, his breathless panting breaking the intimate moment and filling the frosty air with ghostly white fog.

"There you are, M. I've been looking for you."

Magenta casually turned her eyes towards him.

"He's gone!" the man said.

Magenta scrunched her brow.

"The Russian!" he shouted, launching a suspicious glare at Clive. "He's gone."

Magenta tossed a look to Clive, as if she expected some sort of explanation. Clive tightened his lips together.

Once again, Danil had double-crossed him and left him in a precarious situation. Once again, he was powerless to do anything about it.

"Well then I guess you need to make your choice, Mr. Underwood," Magenta said.

18:
A Warrior's Call

Mars. Red Colony One

Brig stared up at the charcoal palette of sky. The pinpoint stars spread across the cloudless night and silhouetted the low-rise skyline of Flagstaff down the hill from the campsite. The resonance of cricket chirping filled the dewy air, and the crackling campfire that gave no heat flickered amongst the shadowy forest beyond. One of the taller trees pixilated for a moment, turning a deep green before it warped back to its grand self.

He sighed, the realization that it was all a Darpa-generated illusion casting a revealing light on his subconscious. However, the burned out heli-jet carcass lying next to him was the last place that he had called home on Earth. Despite that there was no tangible sense of smell of anything around him that would have tied what he was seeing to his sense memory, it still set him at ease given the recent events here at the colony.

In between a set of virtual trees at the far end of the campsite, a video projected in silence between their trunks. An hour previous, Brig had instructed Darpa to play back multiple segments of the cipher card data, deciding to split the feed and freeze frame on a grainy image of Allistair placed next to a striking front view of young Nadia.

Brig leaned back against a fallen log, his hands behind his head, and stared forward at the pair of images.

"What am I missing here, Darpa?" he said aloud.

"I'm afraid I don't know what you are referring to, Mr. Stroud." Her smooth voice boomed down from the canopy above, playing like a soundtrack to the silvery moonlight.

Darpa's presence had become organic to Brig, and he found himself holding conversations at all times of the day and night, as if second nature. He had also become accustomed to her random appearances, as they were the closest thing to his memory of Steele – or at least the other one.

"There's a connection here... and I'm just not seeing it," Brig pondered aloud. "She says that her father's alive..."

"Bronson Fox is alive," Darpa parroted.

Brig shot an eye towards the sky. "Are you just repeating what I'm saying? Or are you stating a fact?"

"I never deal in conjecture, Mr. Stroud."

"I wish I had more footage of Bronson..." Brig said, not really directing his hopes upward.

"One moment..." Darpa replied.

The images of Allistair and Nadia faded, replaced by a feed from an overhead security camera displaying a hallway just outside of the DMST lab glass doors. Allistair exited the room, the auto-lock latching quietly behind him, the pad next to the door emitting a ruby status light. He glanced up at the camera for a moment, continued on his way, and disappeared from the watchful eye of the lens.

"That looks like surveillance video. Why would that be on these cards?"

"As I mentioned previously, Mr. Stroud, most of the data on this set appears to be a permanent archive – removed from the Hyper Nebula at the Department of Military Science and Technology."

Brig frowned and sat forward. "You mean that..."

"This is the only copy of that data. It was removed permanently from that system," Darpa concluded before Brig could finish his thought.

The only person that would do something like that must have been... covering something up.

Something caught his mind's eye. "Rewind the footage of the hallway that we just saw."

Brig fixed his glare on the doorway, watching as the image worked its way in reverse - Allistair heading backward into the lab. For the next fifteen minutes, the video displayed nothing but an empty hallway, yet the timestamp on the edge of the frame clearly continued rolling.

Brig sighed heavily. *Another dead end.*

Suddenly, the lab door opened. To his surprise, however, a much older Bronson stepped out backward, swiped his card, and sauntered in reverse down the hallway and out of view.

It struck him like a mallet to the temple. Why was Allistair, for all purposes a prisoner, allowed to exit the lab on his own? And where was Bronson? At the very least, Bronson should have been escorting the troubled young man.

Brig rubbed his eyes with the heels of his palms. The pieces were there, but he still failed to see the puzzle for what it was. How could Bronson be alive, per Steele's own words just a while ago, yet Brig himself had watched the man die after he rescued him from the clutches of the Syndicate months prior? He shook his head, as if he could shake loose some piece of information that might glue it all together.

His mind wandered, for a reason unknown to him, back to the day at the satellite array field. The day that he had reunited with the woman he thought was Steele. He visualized sitting next to her. The wind tussled her hair away from her face and neck.

And there it was - the tattoo at the base of her skull.

She had said it was simply a result of blowing off steam from school – *too much partying*, she had claimed.

"Darpa, show me the side view of Allistair inside the lab from the memory matrix experiment footage. And then put a side profile of Bronson Fox next to it."

The video faded, immediately replaced by the objects of Brig's request.

Brig's eyes widened at the result. The tattoo that he had seen on Allistair's neck - an infinity symbol - was not on Bronson's. He closed his eyes and tried to picture the mark on Nadia.

"It's the same..." he murmured. He breathed in. "Darpa... do you know any details about the... memory blocking technique Steele spoke about in the video?"

"My answer is the same in regards to this as it was vis-à-vis accessing classified information, Mr. Stroud," came her succinct reply.

"And how's that fit in with regards to our conversation earlier 'vis-à-vis' your preventing people from being hurt?" Brig sat up and glared into the ether above.

Darpa did not respond.

"Let me come at it a different way, Darpa. I don't want to see the research – I just want Steele to see it. Maybe it'll jog something loose in her memory." He paused, ran his hands back through his hair. "Can you make sure that happens?"

"Will Dr. Fox's viewing of this data save the life of humans, or prevent their harm, Mr. Stroud?" Darpa's voice suddenly became curiously inquisitive.

Brig's lip twisted up at the corner. "It'll save at least one life... I guarantee it."

After a short pause, Darpa spoke again. "I will place the data in her queue, Mr. Stroud. I cannot guarantee anything further without overstepping my programming."

Brig knew exactly what he needed to do. He churned on his thoughts, glaring at the virtual campfire crackling before him.

"Darpa. How many people are in the mines?" he asked, changing the subject like speed shifting a sports car.

"Those numbers aren't kept on file in the main system, Mr. Stroud. Therefore, I have no access to that information."

"Do you know the identity of that man that I spoke to in the hallway earlier?"

"He's not a registered citizen of Red Colony One."

"Don't you find that odd?"

"It is a peculiarity," she replied after a noticeable pause.

His mind continued to ricochet from one item to the next. "Do you have a Jonas Slade registered on Red Colony One?" It was a long shot, but Brig knew what he saw. And he knew he was not hallucinating when he encountered his former EW partner in the hallway outside the security enclave.

"I'm sorry, Mr. Stroud. There is no 'Jonas Slade' registered in the colony."

"What about... Emerson Winslow?" He knew the answer, but it was worth the try.

"That record is locked, Mr. Stroud, as he is a member of the Red Colony One security enclave."

Brig's mind swirled. *Maybe I am going crazy. Maybe it's just what I wanted to see... just like Steele said.*

"How many Epsilon Warriors are registered in the colony, Darpa?"

"None registered, Mr. Stroud."

Brig nodded. It made sense.

"But there are three on station," she added.

Brig sat stone-faced, staring off into the virtual distance of the forest.

"It might interest you to know, Mr. Stroud, that the shuttle for the mining colony only arrives once a week, and the next is due later this evening."

Brig lifted a smile up at the ceiling, resolving that he must go forward with his investigation of the mines. For the remainder of the afternoon, Brig and Darpa discussed his plan of action, with Darpa providing the critical details that could potentially aid Brig to success.

Later in the evening, after pouring over the pitfalls that could lie in wait for him, it was time to execute the first phase of his plan. As he exited the room, the eerie awareness of someone watching him from around the corner pricked the skin on his arms - almost as if a ghostly hand from the past had touched his shoulder. He shook off the odd sensation and made haste towards the security enclave.

Steele stabbed her finger into the holo-display, forcing the DNA strand to spin to its opposite side, its sharp reds contrasting with the cool blues and whites. The data lining the sides of the image churned upwards, replaced by a new set that filled the blank space around the strand. To the side of the double helix sat a smaller set of molecules, together forming a multi-colored compound, the designator 'D42-19 sub 14' adorned in violet next to it.

As if in a trance, her mind deep in preponderance, she pulled her finger away from her cheek.

"Has Brigadier asked about D42-19 sub 14, Darpa?"

Darpa, standing two meters to Steele's right at another holo-terminal and dressed in identical garb, nodded. "Affirmative, Dr. Fox. As that information is part of his medical record, he is afforded access to it."

"What did you tell him?"

"Precisely what my mandate instructs, Dr. Fox."

"And nothing more?"

"Correct."

Steele pondered once again in silence, staring down at her fingernail, tapping it loudly on the clear resin desk in front of her. "I would like you to remove any record of D42-19 sub 14 from his medical history," she announced, unconsciously nibbling at her lower lip.

"Are you certain, Dr. Fox?"

"Just do it, Darpa," Steele replied. "And as always, there is to be no audit trail of this transaction."

"As you wish, Dr. Fox."

Steele let out a hefty sigh and leaned back in her chair, her slender arms gently crossed over her lap. She refocused her gaze on the blank wall at the far end of the lab.

Suddenly, the wall morphed, replaced by the familiar entryway from the DMST building in Boulder. However, a red light slowly flickered over the top ledge of the door, indicating a failed entry attempt.

"Bollocks," Steele cursed under her breath. "Why can't I remember my own authorization code for entry to that lab?"

Darpa turned to face Steele's memory-driven illusion. "I'm sorry, Dr. Fox. I am unable to assist."

"I know, Darpa." Steele's frustration was evident in her biting tone. "We've been over this hundreds of times. It's just a memory, but I just don't get... what am I missing..."

A subtle chime from the comm system behind her interrupted her thought.

"Steele, darling." Bronson's beckoning voice dripped with sweetness.

"Yes, father," Steele replied with a distant hollow tone.

"I need to see you in my quarters. Post haste."

Steele spun her chair to face the hologram of her father, standing fifteen centimeters tall on her desk. "Superb timing, father. I've something to share with you as well."

The two-tone malachite image of Bronson raised an eyebrow and folded a corner of his mouth. "Oh? And what might that be?"

"It's a surprise, father. And I'll even bring... *it*... with me." Steele flicked her finger over a control surface on her desk, forcing the hologram to dissipate. She playfully pounded her balled fist onto the desk with a light thump, hopped from her chair and strode from the lab.

Darpa angled her eyes backward over her shoulder for a moment. With an observant curiosity, she watched her creator exit the lab, and then continued with her work at the holo-terminal.

19:
Buried Alive

Mars. Red Colony One

The soft thumps of Brig's padded jumpsuit boots filled the thin corridor leading to the security enclave. He peered at the ceiling with one eye.

"Now remember, Darpa, we agreed... I need a diversion."

Darpa, once again donning the appearance of the Earth Steele, popped into focus next to him in stride.

"It is against my programming to break regulations of Red Colony One, Mr. Stroud."

"But what does your programming say about allowing humans to come to harm?" he replied, not taking his eyes from the corridor ahead.

Darpa did not respond. Even though he knew it to be just an illusion, there seemed to be something churning behind her twinkling emerald eyes.

"If I don't, there's a very good chance that something bad's going on over in that mining colony. And there might be innocents being killed."

Still no response. She continued to keep pace with Brig, the eerie sensation of her soundless footsteps keeping his neck hairs on end.

"So it's within your programming to aid me in saving those people."

After a few more seconds of silence, Darpa spoke once again. "Very well, Mr. Stroud. Give me just a moment."

Brig spied the familiar burly guard in the red jumpsuit guarding the entryway to the corridor jet way, the gold rings around his left bicep glowing with a blue hue. While not deliberately projecting such, the man's demeanor and the way in which he held his snub-nosed weapon across his chest made him very formidable indeed.

Darpa broke into a sprint, but then just as she reached the jet way, her image morphed into that of another security guard – this one in command red with several triangular shapes adorning his right shoulder. She lifted a palm and motioned to the guard.

The guard's eyes widened before he snapped his feet together to perform a crisp salute. Darpa, or rather the guard she was impersonating, barked an order that Brig could not discern, to which the guard nodded a nervous agreement. Darpa's guard increased his gait. The other guard followed suit, with both disappearing into an adjacent hallway, leaving the jet way unguarded.

Brig nodded in silent amazement.

Good girl.

He glanced over a shoulder and then stepped from the main enclave into the jet way.

"Security uniforms for the mining colony are in the far cabinet of the security antechamber - second door to your left," came Darpa's voice from a hidden speaker above him.

Brig peered upwards and winked.

Moments later

Brig sat on the shuttle, the solitary blue ring striping his left arm dulled in the muted glow of the cabin. Although a bit of nervousness spiked his stomach, a small veil of relaxation draped his mind, knowing that the face shield of his helmet completely obstructed the view of his mug. He allowed a smirk to grab one corner of his mouth, suddenly feeling like a displaced, futuristic bounty hunter from a campy science fiction flick. He had never met anyone from the guard unit at the mining colony, nor the miners themselves, but a sense of relief fell over him - that he might be able to stay anonymous during his scouting mission.

He glanced at his surroundings, moving only his eyes so as not to draw attention to himself. However, only he and two others were present in the car: a guard that stood at the front of the cabin and one other that sat a few rows behind and to the left of him.

The silence of the transport, as it pulled him to an unknown fate, was unnerving. The windows, mere slits running horizontally along the top of each wall, drew in the dim light from the Martian sunset outside. As if diving into a dark array of clouds, the light ceased and the car became murkier than it had been before. Every few seconds, a beacon whirred by the portals and disappeared just as quickly - replaced repeatedly with seemingly no end.

A lone droplet of sweat clustered on his forehead and then trickled into a brow, before it dissipated into the filter next to his cheek. With a small inhale from him, the servo on his helmet forced a gulp of oxygen into his mouth, a necessity since the tram lacked any atmosphere of its own. Brig held his breath for a few seconds, his blood absorbing the sweet elixir of life. He exhaled into the rebreather.

The lights lining the never-ending subterranean tunnel suddenly halted, and the shuttle came to a silent stop. The guard at the front of the car lifted an arm, motioned towards Brig and the other guard, and then released a lever behind him. Brig was taken aback momentarily as the entire top half of the cabin slid away out of view around the bottom of the car, exposing a small set of stairs that led up to a platform a few meters above the tram. He stood, stepped to the front of the shuttle and then onto the stairway.

His boots thumped with a light scruff on the stairs - which oddly were not metal, but apparently consisted of the same compound found in the walls of the main colony. He reached the top of the stairs and walked out onto the graded platform, squinting at the portal of light emanating from the area just over the ridge. Brig trotted up behind the other guard, whom had exited the tram before him and had swiftly made his way to the top of the rise. He fell in step with the other's pace, wondering whether the muscular brute even realized that Brig was present behind him.

As the burly guard stepped past the security checkpoint and out of Brig's view, Brig met the forceful shove from the barrel of an unseen security guard's snub-nose weapon to his chest.

"Where's your ID?" the guard grumbled.

Shit.

Brig glanced at his chest, then back at the guard. "Oh... uh, sorry." Brig fumbled for an excuse. "This is my first shift here... I'm a newbie. I must've forgotten it back at the barracks."

The guard, his grizzled face displayed with an odd, blue glow from within the edges of his face shield, eyeballed Brig with intense suspicion. He glanced at Brig's nametag and then down at a holo-pad on his wrist.

"Sampson... I don't see your name on the manifest," he growled. He tapped a hand to the side of Brig's helmet. "Face shroud off when I'm speakin' to ya, grunt!"

Brig's face shield went transparent, exposing his surprised expression. "General Rossi assigned me here at the last minute, he knows I'm here." Brig's stomach tensed. If the guard decided to follow up on Brig's claim, his recon mission was over before it ever started. Worse, he was in big trouble.

The guard glowered at him once more for a moment. He flicked off the hologram and waved Brig through the checkpoint. "Go ahead," he barked, but then held his rifle up to impede Brig's progress once more. "But I'm watchin' ya, newbie."

Brig nodded once and stepped away from the checkpoint.

The pair of guards stood at the apex of a concourse intersection that jutted out from the main walkway and overlooked the manmade cavern. Brig, on the left, gawked out across the cavern as the other, Rory Arrmslog, pointed out the finer features of the installation.

The mine, known since its opening as the Pit, operated around the clock without direct exposure to the harsh Martian environment. Hollowed out from the side of Arsia Mons, within the larger Tharsis Montes range, the artificial formation of the Pit resembled an oblong, indoor sports stadium. Mammoth, gray beams protruded from tops of the walls and held up the massive dome like a set of God's fingertips.

As Brig soon came to observe, the majority of the guards occupied the top ring of concourses. Perched just above them was a circle of high intensity floods that reached down from the center of the dome. From this superior vantage point, the security staff had a full view of operations, and could swiftly traverse the network of staircases that led down from the end and middle of each platform.

A full dispatch of 49 miners worked ten meters below, spread out in groups of twos and threes on a small lip encircling the edge of the cavernous maw. Three guards patrolled the length of each perimeter leg behind them, swapping positions every fifteen minutes as the miners went about their work. The guards held their familiar snub-nosed pulse rifles across their chests, a sure sign of oppression if Brig had ever seen one before.

The thin artificial atmosphere within the domed mine resonated with the rhythmic pulsations of 'guns' that each miner held and fired into the rock edifice. In actuality, the guns were nothing more than sonic disturbance devices that helped them chip away at the cavern walls - the resulting crystalline-laced rock fragments falling in small piles at their feet.

19: BURIED ALIVE

"What are they mining?" Brig asked, his voice a scratchy echo over the external speaker of his helm.

"Broxium. It's a special metal indigenous to Mars that was discovered after the landing and establishment of the colony," Rory answered with a Southern twang.

Brig, his face lit in a ghostly pale light from the side markers of his face shield, frowned. "Aren't you worried about having that many armed miners?"

Rory chuckled, a bit of static bleeding over his broadcast. "Those are sonic rifles - they won't do ya' no harm. Just enough to get the metal from the rock."

A belt of red lights ignited above the top of the right wall, accompanied by an obnoxious buzzer sounding from the center of the dome above. Brig furrowed his brow and glared at the guard, whom shook his head and patted Brig on the shoulder.

"You don't seem to know too much about this place - considerin' you signed up for this gig!"

Around the ledges of the Pit, the miners stopped extracting the metal and stood still, facing the center. Suddenly, a large 'clunk' moved the air throughout the mine. Thousands of small fragments of the metal leapt from the ground at the miners' feet and sailed across the Pit to the right side, where they adhered to a large panel mounted against the rock.

A cry split the air. One of the miners haphazardly flew from his position along one of the ridges and slammed against the panel. He stuck for a moment, flailing his arms as he tried to free himself from the gigantic magnet, and then tumbled into a large chute below it. Brig watched in horror as no one seemed to care - the rest of the miners casually glanced in the direction of the panel, and then back down at the ground. Another clunk followed, and the fragments released from the panel into the chute. The light strip flashed green for a second and extinguished. The miners resumed their work.

The guard shot an evil smirk at Brig, whom returned the unexpected look of glee with a disgusted sneer. "And that's why you don't wear metal here, pal."

"Where does that chute lead?" Brig asked, his voice betraying his inner panic.

"Somewhere where ya' don't wanna be, I can tell ya that much."

Brig's revealed facemask could not hide his puzzled expression.

Rory flopped his rifle over one shoulder, put the other hand to his hip. "I'm no chemist, but the metal has some special property or some such that allows it to turn from solid directly to a gas under the right... conditions. Compression or somethin'. It gets squeezed into gas, then put into containers and sent back to the colony for them to use."

Brig glanced over at the chute, wanting to ask the obvious.

"He didn't stand a chance, bud. It'll liquefy him before he even knows what hit him."

Brig's heart sunk. He knew that something bad was happening here in the mines, but he did not like how they treated the death of one of the miners with such nonchalance. Although it did not satiate his concern much, he realized that accidents had always been a part of mining dating back centuries on Earth. But thinking back to the day on the catwalk it was clear that he had seen a large group of bodies, not just one – and certainly not an accident. His investigation was far from complete.

Arrmslog led Brig to a higher, non-metallic platform just above the miner ridge. Brig peered at the miners through the grate beneath his feet, ensuring that he kept pace with his lead without making his interest in them apparent to other guards that they passed along the way.

"What about the weapons we carry?" Brig called ahead, knowing that if they had any metal in them, that the massive magnet opposite their location would have sucked them in as well.

"Boy, you really don't know much about this place, do ya?" the guard jabbed.

"Sorry, my memory ain't what it used to be, buddy."

"They're made of Broxium, too. That's the beauty of this stuff. Once it gets gasified and added to the ores and such, it loses its metallic properties with the right amount of mixin'. But it's still stronger than any metal you've ever seen."

So that's why they needed the ore I saw at the array field.

The last few moments he had spent on Earth at the portal site came to Brig's mind.

Still not making sense, though.

He failed to connect the operations that he had witnessed so far with the horrific sight he had experienced the day prior back at the colony.

Brig followed Rory down a flight of stairs. It emptied near a small tunnel bored out through one of the corners of the cavern. As the pair reappeared out of the darkness, they stood on a sizeable metal platform, which lay at the foot of a massive, arched corridor.

19: BURIED ALIVE

A small staircase jutted sharply up to their right and ended on a smaller platform that contained a miniature control panel.

"This is one of the jobs you'll be asked to do, Sampson. Extraction." Rory ascended the stairs and turned back to look down expectantly at Brig. Brig obediently followed, stopping on the small, oval scaffold.

Two switches were situated upon the small panel: one red, one green.

"What's this do?" Brig pointed at the panel.

"You'll see. You're in luck, my friend. We usually only do it once a month, but we've got some extra... trash... to take out," the guard said with a heartless chuckle.

"Trash?"

Could he have been wrong? Maybe it was his eyes playing tricks on him. After all, it was a good distance out to the mountains from the colony - it could simply have been garbage floating out into space.

The guard tapped at a recessed patch on his arm and spoke into it. "Bring 'em in."

After a few silent moments, a group of haggard looking men and women trudged onto the platform beneath them, walking five abreast. They did not look up. They avoided Brig's gaze, and instead filed in with their heads hung in defeat.

"Make sure your tether's on, friend. Or your shift is gonna be a short one. We're about to lose gravity and pressure for a bit." The guard grabbed at a pair of white, cloth ropes attached to the side of the small platform, latching one to his own belt. He handed the other to Brig.

The former EW, puzzled, attached it to himself and put his hands on the railing to watch the people below. One of the men glared up at Brig, intense sorrow and despair filtering from his eyes. He lowered his head once again.

Rory hammered the green button; the blackness of the tunnel below began to lighten. The lower platform rose at its rear, forcing the group of men and women below to scramble and fall forward. Without warning, they left their feet - sucked into the nothingness beyond.

The air rapidly escaped from Brig's lungs, along with a horrified 'No!'

He tried to step forward, but he realized the absence of gravity in the small sub-cavern when his feet left the platform. Brig grasped maniacally at his tether with one hand, just barely able to keep himself from tumbling away into the gaping void beyond the tunnel.

An emotionless, static-tainted voice blared over the guard's radio. "All clear..."

Rory smiled at Brig with a wink and jabbed at the red button. The lower platform slid back into place, the tunnel closed with a thunderous clunk and Brig landed on the platform with the newfound gravity.

"What the hell did you just do!" Brig leapt to his feet and grabbed at Rory's suit near his shoulders.

The guard brushed away Brig's hands and laughed with a snort. "You must've been asleep during orientation! What'd you think you were gonna be doing out here, pal?"

The bile swelled in Brig's throat, but he knew better than to let it go, as he would have to ride with it in his mask all the way back to the colony. He forced a swallow and leaned with one hand on the railing, his breath clouding the visor on his face.

"Don't worry, newbie. You'll get used to it after a while. Come on, I'll show you the control suite."

As they exited the extraction cave, Brig glanced over his shoulder at the dark corridor beyond. His heart plummeted, thinking about the group of people that he had just seen thrown out to their deaths in space.

"How can you just get rid of them like that?"

"They're expendables. They served their purpose... now they're used up."

The guard's callous attitude towards a bunch of fellow human beings raked Brig's soul. But more than that, the words themselves shocked him – Expendables.

"So you just take colony citizens, make them work down here until they drop – and then just... shoot them out into space?"

Rory chuckled and shook his head. They turned a corner and began ascending a much larger staircase that separated into several landings above. "No, no. Those aren't colony citizens."

Brig clomped up the stairs behind him, confused as to who the mysterious 'Expendables' could be. Rory peeked back at him, noticing Brig's confused expression. He stopped and grabbed at Brig's arm. "You mean you really don't know?" He let out a disgusted sigh. "C'mon! I think you need to take your orientation over again! They come from Big Blue..."

Brig squinted at the guard.

"You know... Earth?" Rory released Brig's arm and began his climb once again.

"Earth?" Brig's voice raised an octave. He hurried to get up next to the guard on the stairs. "Those people came from Earth?"

The guard nodded and guffawed, continuing to ascend the final few stairs before stopping on the next landing and giving Brig a look of disbelief.

Brig had discovered, through Steele's own admission, that they had been gleaning resources from Earth in order to fuel Red Colony One - but he had no idea until now that the most precious resource they had been extracting was... people.

Several hours had passed, and Brig had done his best to put the chilling events at the extraction platform out of his mind, if that were even possible, by examining every nook and cranny of the Pit – when he was not being watched intently by a specific few guards, that is.

For every step he made in any direction, he immediately felt the presence of eyes upon him - but he knew better than to raise undue suspicion by letting them know he was onto them. However, that also meant that he was not going to get any extra information out of the guards, either.

I need to get alone with some of those miners.

Too much separation between them and guards made that task easier said than done, and Brig approaching any miner on the lower level would surely raise alarm.

"Sampson!" a voice from behind him called.

Brig turned a surprised eye over his shoulder.

"Shift change!"

"Already?" Brig replied with a grunt.

"Not you, dummy... the miners! Let's go, we gotta herd 'em out and the new ones in!" The other guard grasped Brig by the shoulder material of his suit and pulled him towards the stairs.

Perfect.

As the outgoing shift of miners filed by, mindless drones following a silent cadence back towards their cramped domicile adjacent the Pit, Brig watched in silent pity. He wanted with all of his soul to stop the cycle of abuse going on before him, but he knew that his part in this mission had just begun. He had to be patient. He would have his chance.

As if on cue, Brig got his first opportunity a few seconds later.

The other guard, Wesley according to his nametag, raised his weapon from the other side of the line of miners. "Sampson! Hold this line here while I bring in the fresh crew!"

Brig nodded. Wesley's communicator clicked closed and the guard turned away down the nearby corridor.

As if by silent command, the miners halted in front of Brig. A petrifying sensation came over him, staring at the mass of workers, their suits grimy with the dusty Martian soil. Each wore a clear helmet over their shaved heads, and each stared with a grim hopelessness down at the ground.

Brig stepped forward and leaned in towards a man nearest him.

"What's your name?" Brig asked.

The man, and several nearest him, wavered as if Brig and the others were matching magnetic poles.

Brig flicked his eyes around at the downtrodden group. "You... what's your name?" he repeated, this time with more authority.

The man timidly rolled his eyes towards Brig without head movement. "M-m-me, sir?" he stammered, his Cockney inflection quite noticeable.

"Yeah, you..." Brig motioned with the end of his own weapon. The line flinched once again.

"Cummins, sir. I-I-I wasn't doing nothing, sir... I... I just finished me shift."

Before Brig could question him further, another miner stepped in front of the first and pointed a finger at Brig. "Leave 'im alone, ya tosser!" he barked. "'e didn't do nothin' wrong, just let 'im be!"

Brig took a step backward, not knowing how to react to the torrential range of emotions thrust upon him.

The man's anger quelled abruptly when Wesley reappeared with an equal amount of relatively fresh, yet still downtrodden, miners from the far corridor. With a swift set of steps, he pounced in front of the angered miner and raised the butt of his weapon. The miner took two steps backward and raised a hand in defense.

19: BURIED ALIVE

"I told ya, Emberly, you're not allowed to talk to the guards unless they talk to you!" Wesley bellowed.

"Yes, sir," Emberly muttered with feigned respect. "But 'e talked first..." He pointed at Brig before rejoining the line of exhausted miners. They began to trudge into the corridor.

Wesley cast a suspicious glare at Brig, whom turned away and worked to herd the remainder of the group out of the Pit area. Behind him, Wesley's voice raked through his external speaker. "Don't talk to the maggots, Sampson!"

Brig raised a hand without looking back.

Moments later, Brig reappeared from the corridor alone, having escorted the motley crew back to the pitiful quarters in which they remained during off-shift hours.

Wesley did an immediate about-face and motioned for Brig to follow. His hollow voice sounded over the tiny helmet speaker. "Follow me to the control tower, Sampson. Greer wanted me to bring you to him before you left for the night."

Brig frowned. *Who knows I'm here?*

"Who's Greer?" Brig quizzed, speeding up to match Wesley's pace up the multi-tiered staircase that led to a massive, glassed-in booth at the top.

"Commander Greer. He's the Commanding Officer for this entire mine." Wesley stopped and jabbed a gloved finger into Brig's chest. "And you don't want to screw around with the CO!"

Brig's stomach sunk for the second time since he had arrived at the Pit. The CO requesting an audience was not a good sign of things to come.

"So we can't talk to the miners?" Brig flicked his eyes towards Wesley as they scaled the steps.

Without making eye contact, Wesley shook his head. "Nah. You don't talk to them. They don't talk to you," he said. "Can't have 'em aspiring to anything - if ya' catch my meaning."

As the pair reached the top platform and made for the guarded door of the control room, Brig eyed the setup. Built in the style of an airport control tower, the booth sat nestled behind a mammoth glass-like panel that extended outward from the floor to where it reached the support struts tied into the rocky top of the cave. A pair of technicians sat behind the control desk just beyond the glass, each working at their own tasks in front of them. A bruising guard kept close watch over the door to the booth, as he would have expected, cradling another of the snub-nosed rifles over one arm.

The guard beamed a glare at the two men, taking particular interest in Brig, before he motioned them in and stepped aside for them to pass.

Brig ignored the man's intense glower and followed Wesley into the control room. They crossed the threshold; a man that Brig had not noticed earlier spun with a casual grace on one heel to look in his direction. The sheen on his crisp, crimson pressure suit cast a sinister aura. Brig immediately took notice of the glinting insignias attached to his muscular upper torso just beneath his thick neck.

Wesley stopped, snapping the heels of his boots together with a crisp clack and a simultaneous salute.

The officer did not return the salute, but rather mumbled a subdued 'as you were' with a harsh Australian twang, and continued his fiery gaze at Brig.

"The new shiftie that Silsbury told you about, Commander Greer." Wesley had suddenly become very stiff in his delivery.

Greer raised an eyebrow. His face lightened. "Sampson, was it?"

Brig nodded, but Wesley jabbed him with an elbow. "Yes... sir," Brig offered.

Greer rotated slowly around Brig, his square jaw firm. He examined Brig's attire from head to toe without speaking. "A little on the slight side, I would say," he observed with a gravelly voice and a wry chuckle.

"Yes, sir," Wesley pandered in reply, his own sycophantic snicker evident.

"But that can be remedied with the proper ration adjustment," Greer continued, flexing his own bulky biceps. "But for one so highly recommended by General Rossi, I'm willing to make exceptions."

Brig's flexed his eyes before he realized his reaction was becoming obvious. His earlier untruth about being sent by Rossi might just come back to haunt him.

Greer shattered the coldness of his demeanor by grasping Brig's shoulder with a solid hand and giving him a friendly nudge. "I'm expecting big things from you, Sampson. Don't let us down!"

Brig flattened his brow, and then nodded with an unsure hesitance. "Yes, Commander Greer, sir."

"Got any questions, Sampson?" Greer turned on a heel and slowly made his way to the middle of the room. He stopped behind one of the two technicians and peered over his shoulder at a colorful overlaid display of the Pit below.

"This is where it all happens, huh?" Brig had worked with brass all his military life, and he knew the proper protocol around them. But he also found his current situation grating as this man was not *his* brass.

Greer let out a sarcastic snort from one nostril that echoed from his suit's external speaker. "Yeah," he cooed, "you could say that. This console oversees the entire functionality of the Pit below." He waved a hand in front of the display. "From detection and mapping of the resources, to extraction and transport back to the storage facility," he said, as if beaming with pride over his own offspring. "This mine would be impossible to operate without this unit."

Brig nodded in mock appreciation, scanning the rest of the room while Greer admired his command post.

A blue, diamond-shaped object positioned vertically between two mounts, sparkled with intensity and emanated a deep hum from within the enclosure. Brig motioned with a nod towards the object.

"What's that?"

Without following the object of Brig's attention with his own, Greer tightened his eyelids on the newbie guard. "The computer core," he said. "But that's not your concern right now. Focus on your duties in the Pit... and then we'll see if you have what it takes to work the console later."

"You have your own computer system here? Not the same as the one in the colony?" Brig was not genuinely surprised. After all, Darpa had confirmed as much to him earlier. He was, however, more interested in how the system worked.

Greer ignored Brig's query, instead turned his gaze to Wesley, whom had obvious sweat streaks across his blue-tinted forehead. Greer nodded.

Wesley snapped a crisp salute and grabbed at Brig's arm, towing him out of the control tower.

20:
The Price of Loyalty

Earth. New Vegas, Nevada

Danil Chekushkin strode along the World's End Resort & Casino's 23rd floor, the target of the latest move of his boss, Bruno Muldoon. While Muldoon's erratic tendencies were not all that surprising – after all, someone or other was always knocking in a door or leaving a hideous bloodstain on his priceless Persian rugs – the diminutive Russian still pondered the events that precipitated this latest relocation.

As he approached the end room - the grand suite of this particular floor - he eyed the guard, Gurney, standing in front of the pair of ornate, red oak doors. The beastly, but not quite Webb-esque, guard flicked his eyes towards Danil, nodded his head and looked away. Whether the man earned his nickname from some grave circumstance, or simply had it thrust upon him by a bunch of pub mates, Danil did not know. However, he assumed it was the former rather than the latter, given his line of work.

Danil snorted in derision, albeit quietly, as he passed Gurney.

The man does not even know me, yet he lets me pass unabated to his boss.

Danil had been accustomed to standard shakedowns by the Webb twins, Castor and Pollux, and it unnerved him to not be accosted this time. He pushed at the brass lever and entered the room, closing the door with a quiet bump behind him.

The air inside the suite hit him like a blast furnace, partly due to the air conditioning units having long ago fallen into disrepair and having no one of skill to keep them maintained, but also because Muldoon always insisted on keeping the French doors of the balcony open around the clock. Danil curiously scanned the suite. His boss, who usually sat eating dinner or stood on the balcony, taking in his majestic view of the mountains on the outskirts of New Vegas as the king he envisioned himself - was not present.

His eyes stopped on the door leading to the private suite - it was partially ajar. With some reservation, he passed through the doorway and stopped. Muldoon sat in a bubble bath, buried up to his neck in foamy suds, his eyes shut in serene peace. The former TGB agent stood silently for a few moments, glaring at the mad Irishman from the beaming reflection in the mirror that adorned the entire far wall. He guffawed under his breath and stepped onto the travertine tile floor. His footsteps echoed in the grand bathroom, jarring Muldoon from his relaxation to the point it appeared he would slip beneath the foamy surface of his bath.

"Jesus Christ, Chekushkin!" Muldoon bellowed, spinning his head to look at Danil.

Danil stepped back in surprise, never having seen his boss so on edge before. Normally very in control of his faculties - and a master of making others feel intimidated – Muldoon was a man obviously very shaken by some recent event. Danil stood in silence and pondered Muldoon's demeanor.

"I told you never to disturb me in here. Where's Gurney? What is that nitwit doing that he allowed you in here?" The crimson blood in his face contrasted with the foamy, white mountain of suds floating atop the bathwater. Muldoon exhaled a heavy sigh, a bit of a nervous rattle to his breath subtly evident, and eased himself back into the soak.

"Sorry, Mr. Muldoon... sir," Danil droned, bowing his head in mock respect. "I have news that I need to share with you."

Another deep breath came from Muldoon, this time in exasperation. A single hand rose from beneath the suds - an invitation to continue.

"It is Underwood, Mr. Muldoon."

"Indeed," Muldoon retorted. "The never ending search continues, I presume?"

"This is not about the search. This is news of the man himself."
"The suspense is killing me."
Danil hesitated. "He... is dead, Mr. Muldoon."
Aside from the subtle popping of the suds atop the water, the room held a weighty silence.

"Sir... Underwood is..." Danil repeated.

"Dead... yes, I heard you the first time, Danil," Muldoon replied.

The heavy bouquet of lavender filled Danil's nostrils. He sniffed once, rubbed his nose and dropped his arm back to his side. "You are not upset about this turn of events?"

20: THE PRICE OF LOYALTY

"Upset? No." Muldoon opened his eyes and glared at Danil's reflection. "But more curious at how *you* managed to escape Death's icy embrace."

No stranger to his boss's proclivity of making his employees uncomfortable by putting them on the spot, Danil, having rehearsed the story, stood stoically and unfazed. "A matter of luck... sir."

"Luck? A man of your talents... relying on luck? Have you mellowed with age, my friend?" Muldoon's eyes fell to slits.

The Russian did not respond, aware that this was Muldoon's way of disarming his prey.

"So tell me then. How is it that my top operative is out on a routine search and recovery... and winds up dead." Muldoon rose from the frothy stew, showing no modesty as he skimmed a mound of lather from his naked form.

Danil continued to stare forward, expressionless, at the feared leader of the Syndicate in his most vulnerable form. "Poor planning on the part of the enemy."

"And that enemy would be..." The Irishman ran a bath towel over his back.

"Reformation, Mr. Muldoon. A small group of... armed... Reformation. But somehow," Danil replied, his face still stone, "I feel you already knew that."

"And *you* managed to escape... unharmed?" The Syndicate boss dropped the towel, exposing his bare back to Danil.

Danil clenched his jaw at the sight of scar remnants that trailed across Muldoon's flesh - a hideous souvenir of punishment inflicted by those same Reformation revolutionaries years prior. A satisfied grin crept over Muldoon's face, staring at Danil's discomfort in the massive mirror.

"They ambushed us and pulled Underwood out of the vehicle. Having recognized me for who I... am... they wasted no time in threatening both of our lives."

Muldoon nodded, somewhat mockingly.

"Underwood refused to divulge anything, or his true identity. They killed him on the spot. During the ensuing chaos between several of the members, I managed to knock the weapon from my captor and used it to escape." Danil dropped his eyes from Muldoon's scars. "Not without inflicting heavy casualties, as you would imagine, sir."

Pulling a white, silk shirt over his shoulders and yanking at the collar to straighten it, Muldoon turned and eyed Danil. "You truly are a survivor, my friend."

Danil eyes lit with a silent resolve, but he did not respond. His history with this man rushed to the forefront of his mind, but he promptly closed that door and swallowed the past.

Muldoon patted the Russian on one shoulder with a subdued chuckle, buttoned his shirt and seized a pair of slacks from a peg on the wall. "But no matter. I have already located what the fine... late... Mr. Underwood took so long in trying to uncover."

"You have the weapons?" Danil's voice raised an octave, betraying his apparent astonishment.

"I had Prong and Davin out looking as well." Muldoon preened at the vanity mirror, pulling his charcoal hair back over the crown of his head and down to his shoulders.

Danil took a deep, silent breath. "There were... others... searching for the cache as well, Mr. Muldoon?" he asked, cleverly masking the animosity in his voice.

"Indeed."

"But if you had someone else looking for them, why did you keep me and Underwood hunting? Are you saying that you did not believe him from the outset?"

Like a taut cobra, Muldoon stood upright in the mirror and grinned with a wicked slant back at the Russian. "Mr. Underwood was fond of the bluff. I don't truly believe that he had any approximation of the location of that weapons cache – any more than you or I, Mr. Chekushkin. *His* eye was on a different prize."

Danil studied his boss, whom had resumed his hygiene ritual at the sink. "Why then did you not let us know that it had been found a few days ago, sir?"

"Simple, my friend." Muldoon tossed a used string of waxy floss into the receptacle next to the vanity. His smile grew exponentially, as if he had ensnared a prey in his web. "Because you are a... what is the word in your tongue. Laska..."

The muscles in Danil's jaw flexed.

"Yes. A weasel, Danil. That is you. And I cannot trust you with such information. Besides," he stepped past Danil, watching him from the corner of one eye before spinning to face him, "I wanted to see how long he would keep up the ruse. And to find out what he was genuinely after."

"What do you think he was after... sir?" Danil absorbed the insult – he had been through worse, and would no doubt again someday.

The pair stood abreast of each other in silence, Muldoon with a raised brow and Danil an expression of granite.

Finally, Muldoon dashed the lull. "Come now, Mr. Chekushkin. All of the time spent alone with Underwood. You two were pomoshchniks. Mates. On the road together. Eating together. Drinking together. Day. Night. You are telling me that in all of the time over the past few months he had not confided in you - not once - about his true objective?"

Danil stood his ground. Muldoon's chess match was reaching its feverish pitch. "So what is the plan, now that you have found what we were looking for?" With his head still, Danil's eyes tracked his boss's movement towards the door.

Muldoon allowed the question to go unanswered.

"I cannot believe that those two underlings were able to decipher the location of the stash, yet Underwood was unable to. He was your best chance at success. And you used him as a pawn."

Muldoon looked past Danil and stroked his goatee in the far wall mirror. "Mr. Underwood confirmed the existence of the weapons. And that is all I required of his services. The rest was his own doing."

As Muldoon left the bathroom, Danil glared into the mirror and silently performed the signum crucis.

Dust leapt from the hooves of the black Mustang, its wiry mane dancing aside the face of its rider as the powerful filly dashed across the hilly terrain. Clive watched in pursuit from his own mount, a red dun quarter horse easily sixteen hands high - the rider's sleek form hugged her steed and prodded it along with near silent command. Magenta's horse was petite in comparison at only fourteen hands, but the stamina and strength that it displayed belied its stature and carried the Reformation leader with grace where she belonged – out front.

Clive spurred his horse with his natural leg, urging it forward in a playful display of bravado. However, as if sensing the sudden increase in the other's gait, the Mustang surged ahead several meters, keeping Clive well behind its pace. Magenta peered over her shoulder and smirked at the former commando. She swatted the rump of her steed; it responded with a whinny and kicked its legs harder than seemed possible.

The pair wound with unmatched speed through the desert, the powder between patches of scrub grass rising in response to their passing. Nye and Jesse, on a pair of thundering, tan quarters themselves, took up rear positions behind Clive and watched with knowing grins at the racers ahead of them. Suddenly, Clive slowed his mount to a trot and eased it to the side of the trail, wary that the other two men were about to overtake him. He rubbed at his lower thigh, where the prosthetic met the remainder of his leg. Magenta glanced back and, noticing that Clive had fallen drastically off pace, circled her Mustang back and came alongside the EW.

"Everything okay, Clive?" she asked over the tired plods of her filly on the soft dust of the trail.

"Yeah..." Clive replied, pulling his hand away from his leg. "Horse just got winded. Thought I'd give it a break."

Magenta skeptically eyed the young colt beneath Clive. She broke into a grin. "Good. Well, now that he's rested, let's get a move on then?"

Clive shook his head in frustration. "Heyah!" he growled through gritted teeth. His horse launched to a fast trot behind Magenta.

The group had been riding most of the day, and while not sure of their destination, it confounded Clive as to why Magenta had elected to travel on horseback rather than truck. The day had been sweltering, a typical June in southern New Mexico. The sun, drifting towards its slumber to their right, cast a glimmering sheen upon the red coat of his mount. Aside from Magenta checking on him just then, they had not spoken the entire trip, which only served to cast more confusion and mystery in Clive's mind.

However, those curiosities were secondary in his thoughts. The whereabouts of Danil Chekushkin, whom had disappeared from the Reformation compound farther north the evening prior, consumed him. The potential for disaster loomed in several of the scenarios running through Clive's brain, all of which revolved around Danil being the shifty person that Clive had come to realize about the Russian.

It would not have surprised Clive for the group to run upon a Syndicate ambush. He had made a nervous habit during their ride of glancing over his shoulder, expecting the ghostly glow of dune buggy lamps and the whistling zing of bullets. He also theorized that perhaps Danil was lying dead and decaying on the side of a deserted stretch of desert highway somewhere, vultures picking at his entrails. While he wished the man no true ill will, Clive also knew that Danil would offer no quarter when it came to keeping within Muldoon's good graces.

Clive knew the truth lay somewhere in the middle, but as to where, he was not sure – and it unnerved him at every turn.

At the base of a small crest, Magenta slowed her pace. "We're here," she called over her shoulder. Nye and Jesse, having determined the same, stopped their horses and waited at the side of the trail.

Clive painfully spurred his mount to come alongside of Magenta. "Where's here?"

"Come with me!" she shouted over a shoulder. She whipped a leg over the horse's back before hopping to the ground.

Clive followed suit, although he gingerly raised himself from the saddle. Magenta appeared at the side of his horse before he could dismount, offering up a hand to him. He flattened his lips and reluctantly took the assistance, thudding onto the dirt with his good leg. A solid moonbeam made its appearance from behind a cloud and lit the pair as they stood abreast of each other. For a silent moment, they stared into each other's eyes with deep longing. A jarring cough from Jesse broke the connection.

Magenta turned and swiftly made her way up the small rise, shuffling her boots through the small scrub grass until she reached the pinnacle. Clive stepped up beside her, wiping sweat from his brow onto his sleeve. Magenta extracted a large pair of electro-binoculars from her side bag and raised them to her eyes. After a few seconds, she blindly handed them to Clive. "It's there."

Clive glanced back at Nye and Jesse at the base of the hill standing watch over their horses, and then put the field glasses to his own eyes.

Although the sun had departed for the day, there was enough cloud-filtered moonlight cast into the dry basin below to bring forth the silhouette of a large object. Clive dropped the specs and squinted. A pair of small, red lights flashed in a silent cadence from two corners of the object, giving away its position every 30 seconds.

"What am I looking at?"

"Supplies," Magenta responded, grabbing the binoculars from Clive and turning towards the hill once more.

Clive stared in confusion at the darkened landscape ahead. After a moment, he descended the hill and met up with the rest of the group. "What do you mean supplies?" He studied the faces of each of the men, then Magenta. "From where?"

"Where isn't important," Magenta replied, clearly agitated by the query.

"You don't know?" Clive's eyes grew, visible even in the low light of the desert around them. "What kind of supplies are they?"

"Weapons mainly. But some provisions. Enough to keep us going." Magenta knowingly eyed Nye. Nye rubbed at his neck while kicking a heel into the dirt.

"So you're being supplied by someone you don't know..." Clive started to reprimand. "And where do they come from? There's parachutes attached to the side!"

Without a word, Magenta pointed upward with one finger. "Somewhere..."

"But... how? And *why*?"

Nye looked to his leader with a concerned glare. "Beggars can't be choosers, chum," he said after a moment's lull. "It keeps us on the up. Gives us what we need to fight the Syndicate."

Clive, hands to his hips, eyed each of the group individually, waiting for the explanation that never came. Finally, he snorted aloud. "Are you sure they are supplying you... or *them*?"

As if some horrible epiphany had struck them all at once, the three of them exchanged blank gazes.

Finally, Jesse broke the unspoken tension. "That's irrelevant."

"Irrelevant? How can you say that?" Clive's voice rose in pitch as he waved his hand back at the hill. "You've got God only knows who sending supplies to 'someone', and you don't know why, or how it gets there. And it's irrelevant?"

"Guns are guns, mate. No matter who sends 'em," Jesse observed, shaking his head.

"And we'll show you how relevant it is, Mr. Underwood," Magenta interjected. "This shipment, along with the others, is enough for us to make a serious dent in the Syndicate's operations. We may finally start pushing them back. That's no easy feat."

The distant rumble of thunder from the west drew Clive's attention. He gazed for a moment at the clouds that reached skyward like tendrils, brilliant flares of lightning igniting within the vertical billows. "I think you're overestimating your chances," he said, squinting back at Magenta through the pitch.

"Sounds like the man knows somethin' about those bastards," Jesse observed with a grunt.

"I know enough to know you're outmanned," Clive stared down the Australian in the darkness. "And they're crazy. They won't stop, no matter how many buildings you guys blow up."

"Then you need to see this." Magenta grasped Clive's upper arm and spun him towards the southeast. She handed him the binoculars.

Off in the distance, several kilometers downrange from where the small group perched upon the rise, stood a twinkling complex that rose from the gloom of the night horizon. Clive dropped the specs past his nose, squinting to be sure he was seeing it, then put them back to his eyes.

"A refinery?"

"Not just a refinery, Mr. Underwood," Magenta assured. "A working refinery."

Clive stood silent, the binoculars now down at his side. Finally, he spoke. "Syndicate?"

Magenta's silence told him the answer.

"What good is a refinery going to do you?" Clive did not let his frustration hide in his tone.

"Chokepoints, mate," Jesse purred in a growling whisper.

"You have no doubt wondered why we are on horseback." Magenta turned and paced towards Nye, standing opposite Clive.

Clive nodded. "It did cross my mind, yeah."

"Fuel for their vehicles is easy to come by. They can come and go as they please. They have the range to control vast stretches of land, and the population that still remains." She looked thoughtfully at Clive, the whites of her eyes glowing in the silvery light from above. "Fuel also powers their generators, runs their power plants. How do you think all of this is possible?"

Clive had not really put much thought into how the Syndicate operated. For him, it had been a means to an end – until Jessica died. Now, it was just a way to stay off the radar and keep himself alive until he found the portal – and then, he could leave it all behind.

The shroud had risen.

"Ok, so, they have a refinery..." he contended half-heartedly.

"Nye is our team's strategist. I believe he can fill you in Mr. Underwood." Magenta placed a hand on Nye's shoulder and glared at Clive.

"Very well then," Nye replied cheerfully in his proper British inflection. "This is but one of their refineries. Notably, it is the largest in the southwest URA, which makes it key. And... we believe it to be the one closest to their base of operations – wherever that may be."

The group simultaneously raised their eyes to Clive.

Clive shrugged. "I don't know what you want from me."

Magenta stepped through the small circle and took Clive's hand in hers, her eyes meeting his. "We've shown you our strategy. I know that you are the most knowledgeable of all of us about the Syndicate's inner workings." Her voice became soft as a kitten's mew. "I was hoping that you... would join us."

Clive reciprocated, grasping her other hand and peering up to the clouded night sky. The dotted canvas of stars peeked out from behind a veil of thunderheads that sprawled from the west. He stood in silence, taking in their quiet majesty. He was never a student of astronomy, but more than anything at that moment he wondered just where Mars was within the heavenly tapestry.

He gazed longingly into Magenta's dark eyes and released her hands. "I think you've got the wrong guy. I'm not that commando anymore – that was another life." He turned from Magenta. He scratched the back of his head while staring upward.

"You never leave the special forces, my friend," Nye offered, stepping forward. "Do you?"

Clive swiveled his head to look at Nye with a scrunched brow, but did not speak.

"It's always with you. It *is* you, yeah?" Nye eyed Magenta, backpedaled next to Jesse with his hands folded behind his back.

"Clive..." Magenta grabbed Clive's bicep with the intention of turning him to face her, but he did not budge. "Don't you want to see this turned around? Don't you want to put things back the way they were? The way they belong?"

Although he knew the offer was tempting, the searing reality was that nothing could ever be the same for him ever again. His life and his world had all been destroyed through a series of missteps and miscalculations – by Brig, through his own admissions.

20: THE PRICE OF LOYALTY

"You all seem to have things pretty well in hand," Clive said, not facing the group. "There's nothing I can offer you. Besides, my loyalty is with myself, my family."

"Your family?" Jesse grumbled. "Your family won't mean jack shit if these cockroaches get to go on unchecked, mate!"

Clive turned his head towards Jesse. "You don't know that. I've done pretty well staying out of their line of fire until now. Besides, I..." He fell silent, his mind on the sprawling desert ahead. "Can you just take me back now, please?"

Jesse shook his head in frustration. "Told ya," he grumbled to Nye, and then mounted his horse.

Magenta lowered her head, walked past Nye back to her mount. Nye glanced at Clive, whom remained with a determined glare, then approached his horse, as well.

The still night imploded with a burst of sand and the throaty roar of a dune buggy, the underside of its black chassis sailing over a nearby hilltop and landing a meter from the group's horses with a ferocious, ground-shaking clump. Jesse's horse, spooked along with the others, reared and dumped him to the ground before bolting to safety thirty meters away. The buggy veered at the last moment and skidded to a halt, launching a wave of sand and scrub grass divots at the frozen Reformation team. The weighty malodor of diesel and exhaust stung their throats, preventing them from any sort of reaction other than deep, hacking coughs.

Two men leapt from the vehicle and hurriedly raised a pair of AK47's towards the group. A third man stood in the back of the buggy and leaned forward onto the roll bar, the moon highlighting a wicked, toothy smile. His hands tightly gripped a mounted machine gun that he aimed in their general direction.

Jesse and Nye, finally recovering and realizing the imminent danger a moment too late, reached for their guns. One of the two men raised the rifle resting at his hip. "Don't even try it!" he barked, his accent thick with his New Jersey heritage.

The pair of Reformation commandos froze, glancing at one another, their faces grim with grave awareness.

"As a matter of fact... toss 'em forward onto the ground. No sudden moves!"

The men reluctantly tossed their rifles onto the sand, stepped backward with their hands in view.

"Righty righty ho ho ho!" the other man, his voice a squeaky Cockney, sung as he walked in front of the group. He wiped saliva from the corner of his mouth with a palm, before flinging his greasy black hair back over his head – several grimy strands fell back over his eyes. "Looks like we got some big fishies in a small pond 'ere." He poked Nye with the muzzle of his gun, turned to look at the other over his shoulder. "Worked like a charm – told ya' he'd lead us right to 'em!" He winked a crusty albino eye at Clive.

Jesse glared at Clive, having been ever suspicious of the former EW since their first encounter. He narrowed his eyes. Clive's face fell expressionless.

Cockney stepped in front of Jesse. "What ya' lookin' at 'im for, bloke? I'm the one ya' have to worry about, now ain't I?" He feigned a rush on Jesse, whom stood his ground.

"Pretty tough with that gun in your hand, aren't ya mate?" Jesse growled.

The man cackled, the back of his hand partially over his toothless mouth. He jabbed the butt of his rifle against Jesse's jaw, forcing the bigger man backward. Jesse rebounded, his arm cocked backward in a retaliatory strike. Before he could land what would have been a devastating blow on the antagonist, Nye grabbed his arm and forced him away.

"Down, boy," Nye said with a calm reassurance, continuing to push him backward. "Let's see how this plays. This may be the moment of truth."

Jesse sneered at him, but stepped back and rubbed at his jaw. He grinned, exposing a newly fractured canine. "You'll get yours. No doubt about it, friend."

Cockney snorted, waving his hands and dancing on the tips of his toes in mock fear. "Ooo, the bogeyman's gonna get me." He waved off Jesse and stepped past him. "It's not me ya' have ta worry about, scrote. It's tha' boss - an he's gonna be happy ta see ya's, I think I think!"

He peeled his eyes from Jesse and stopped, having just noticed Magenta standing just out of sight behind the bulky Australian.

"Well, 'allo 'allo," he said with a lilt and a quick step up into Magenta's face. "And where've you been all me life? In my dreams I'd wager..." Cockney tilted his head and exhaled a heavy breath; the odor of decomposing roadkill made Magenta wince. "But yet 'ere ya' are in the flesh. And what flesh it tis..." He slithered his slimy sandpaper tongue along the ridge of her cheek's raised scar. As she turned her head, eyes steeled and mouth clenched, Cockney grabbed and tore open the front of her shirt.

20: THE PRICE OF LOYALTY

Three shots rang in quick succession, rending the moist, desert air. The first found the machine gunner's neck, riving most of his head from atop his slumped shoulders in a moist spray. He fell silently to the ground behind the vehicle. The second round tagged Cockney's backup rifleman dead in the chest, the contents of which exploded out the rear of his body before he flopped lifeless to the sand. The final shot, due to his proximity to Magenta, entered above Cockney's right knee, shattering his femur before it exited from his left calf, carrying a bloody clump of stringy muscle with it. Cockney bellowed like a wounded wolf and fell to the ground.

The rest of the group, stunned, whipped their gazes to their left. Clive stood with his modified Desert Eagle down to his side - a thin trail of wispy smoke curled up from its .50 caliber, moonlight-glinting muzzle.

Cockney's eyes widened like headlights.

"You bleedin' tosser! You shot the wrong person!" he screamed, spittle streaming from his gaping maw like a rabid pit bull. "Them! Them! You're supposed to shoot them!" His voice cracked to a whimper as he held his arms around his destroyed legs.

Clive flicked his eyes towards the group. Jesse continued his vicious glare. Nye had joined him, a puzzled, yet suspicious look adorning his face.

"The boss is gonna have your arse for this, Underwood, you puke!" Cockney continued to spit. "He's gonna git all o' you!" He began to cackle incoherently, the spittle turning to full on drool as he gasped for breath.

Clive raised the barrel of the Eagle. The flash of the muzzle lit the group's faces before the desert night claimed the area once more. He tucked the gun into the back of his jacket and turned towards the horses. "Can we go now?"

R. JAMES STEVENS

21:
A Little Piece of Heaven

Mars. Red Colony One

Brig watched the reddish-amber liquid pour into the mug, its foam forming a thick head that drizzled from the edge. His eyes glazed and a crooked smile found its way onto his lips.

"Been a long time since I had a good one of these," he said to the barkeep, who held the tap nozzle above Brig's glass.

"Our specialty here," the bartender answered with a subtle Aussie twang and a friendly wink. "Red Lager."

Brig raised his glass, set it down, and sat back in his chair. The bartender replaced the tap in its holster and walked to the other end of the short bar.

It was Brig's latest visit to the entertainment sector, and he was relishing the idea of a quiet moment away from his thoughts that had constantly bombarded him back in his room. He stretched his muscular arms behind his head and released a hearty sigh.

The jaunty lilt of a light Jazz tune floated in from a small club next door that, like the pub in which he sat, contained very little population at this time of day. He tapped his fingers in rhythm on the side of his glass.

I guess nights are busier.

Brig quietly considered the irony of the sector's jovial atmosphere, which offered a stark contrast to what he had witnessed in the mining colony just twelve hours prior. He absentmindedly rapped a knuckle on the wooden bar.

Wood, he pondered with a judgmental frown. *Not from here. I'm sure they took that from Earth, too.*

He stared with no particular interest at the glass partition above the bar that separated this room from the club. A pair of overhead lights peered through the green tinted glass and cast a small cone of subdued light across the pub - mesmerizing Brig like a pleading set of helpless, emerald eyes. He drew the mug to his lips and poured a healthy pool of draft into his mouth, his eyes still transfixed on the haunting, familiar sight above him.

Brig choked on the beer, spitting most of it back into the mug – and some out through his nostrils - before dropping it back onto the bar with a hollow clunk.

"The Hell is this?" he strained, wiping the froth from his upper lip.

The bartender glanced over from the corner of the room, where he straightened a set of chairs and wiped a table. "It's an herbal brew. Takes a bit of gettin' used to!"

Brig scowled at his glass. "Got any regular beer here? You know... with alcohol in it?"

"Nah," the tapster replied with a headshake, taking up his position behind the bar once again. "No alcohol allowed on colony. Not for drinkin purposes, anyway."

Brig wiped his face with the back of a palm, pushed the mug away from him.

"You really should give it another try. Best you'll find anywhere near here."

"You an Aussie?" Brig asked, shunning the mug of herbal beer as if it were a plague-ridden rat.

"New Zealand. Well, Queensland by way of Christchurch actually. Dempsey's the name." The bartender extended a friendly hand.

Brig grasped and shook once. "Brody Sampson," he offered, then sat back onto the stool. "New Zealand, huh? They picked an awful exotic place just to find a bartender."

Dempsey chortled. "That's my secondary job, mate. Most folks here have more than one."

Brig raised an eyebrow. "Yeah? What else you do?"

"Security," Dempsey said, scrunching his eyes a bit at Brig's query. "What do you do... Brody?"

"It varies," Brig answered with his own breathy snicker, glancing around the empty bar. "You do security back there, too? You know... Earth?"

"Special Forces. Australian SOCOM - one of those elite blokes." Dempsey tossed a soft rag onto his shoulder, leaned in towards Brig with both hands rested on the bar. "You know anything about that kinda work, Brody?"

"In another life, yeah." Brig fell silent.

"You a military man?"

"Commando... just like you," Brig replied, instinctively tugging at his glass before realizing he wanted nothing to do with the swill it contained.

Dempsey's eyes fell to the tattoo on Brig's neck. He cracked a partial smile. "Yeah. One of those... what do they call 'em. Greek name..." the barkeep replied, snapping his fingers as if to recall the name from the ether.

"Epsilon Warriors..." Brig added with a muted sigh and subtle headshake.

"Right. Epsilon Warriors. Tenacious buggers, yeah?"

The former EW snorted. "Long time ago, friend. That's not me anymore."

"Never quite leaves ya' though does it, brother?"

Although an instant kinship with Dempsey was apparent, Brig had more important business on his mind besides reminiscing about his EW past.

"So you must work for Bronson Fox then?"

Dempsey stood upright and started polishing one of the taps. "We all work for him, don't ya know?"

"Yeah, yeah... I know," Brig replied, keeping up the ruse. "But you ever met the guy?"

"Nah. But I hear he's a stickler for details. Runs a real tight ship. I'd rather be here than back there any day though, if ya' know what I mean."

Brig nodded as the bartender drew another mug of the herbal fermentation and slid it towards the EW. "Told you I don't like that stuff..." Brig bristled.

"Give it another go, yeah?" Dempsey turned away from Brig and headed towards a small doorway that led into a back room. "Besides," he added, flashing Brig a wry smile and nodding his head towards the main entrance to the pub, "you don't want to turn down the pretty lady now, do ya?" He winked at someone behind Brig.

Brig spun on his stool.

"Oh, there you are, Brigadier," Steele cooed in a harmonious pitch, taking up a standing position just off his left shoulder. "I wondered where you had gotten to."

Brig blindly took a swig of the brew, winced as he forced it to the back of his throat. "I figured you'd know. What with your alter ego and all." He pointed towards the ceiling.

"Oddly enough..." Steele rolled her eyes upward, and then quickly back to Brig. "She indicated she didn't know where you were, either."

Brig swished the concoction around his mouth with a painful expression, shuddered.

"The last we spoke, I was going to arrange an official tour of the colony for you."

He clunked the mug onto the bar. "I took the tour myself. The scenic route."

"Well... good then. I think it's time you saw my father," she said with a bouncy lilt, grabbing his hand and pulling him, not against his will, from his seat.

"You know, there's actually no place I'd rather go now than to see your father," Brig said knowingly. He acknowledged Dempsey with a nod and followed her through the door.

"So, tell me. How did you like the tour? It's impressive, isn't it?" Steele asked, strolling next to Brig as they exited the Entertainment Sector.

"Interesting, to say the least. Saw some things I hadn't anticipated." He cast a curious eye down at her.

"Is that so?" Steele smiled and playfully bumped hips with him.

"Went to the mining colony." Brig stopped talking, silently urging Steele to feel the full effect of his words.

"The mining colony? What were you... how did you get *there*?" Steele bristled. "That's a secure area, they don't let just anyone visit."

Brig pursed his lips and glared at her through the corner of his eyes. "I had a friend pull some strings. Not important really. What's more important is what I saw there."

Steele chuckled under her breath. "A mine?"

Brig narrowed his eyes at Steele. The pair entered a turbo lift; the door whooshed shut behind them.

"Miners?" she continued with a facetious smirk, seeing that Brig was continuing to try to draw a different response.

"Slaves..." Brig corrected.

She contorted her face. "Slaves? Are you out of your mind?"

He shook his head, his eyes still tightened.

"The conditions are not ideal. But Brigadier, I assure you we are not enslaving our colonists to perform work in the mines," she scolded with an eye roll.

"Not *colonists*, no."

She put her hands to her hips. "Then whom?"

Brig stared at her, knowing her reaction before he even said it. "People from Earth."

"That's ludicrous!"

"Maybe we should ask your father?" He put his arms across his chest, leaned against the handrail.

Her face flushed red. "You will not discuss this nonsense with my father!" she purred like a stern tiger, jabbing a fingernail into his chest.

The anger melted from her face as she stared into his eyes. She adjusted into a more-than-friendly posture up against his midsection. "So how about we table this discussion for a later time. Like say... back at my flat tonight. We can discuss things in... private and see where the mood takes us." She caressed his chest with a soft hand before nuzzling his neck.

Brig fought the warm feeling growing in his heart and willfully ignored the intoxicating scent that was Steele. "Steele," he said, gently grasping her hand between his own, "you ever been down there?"

Her contented smile faded. "Well... yes. When it was built."

"But not since? And you haven't seen it in operation?"

"No. But..." Her tone became distantly pensive, as if Brig had possibly opened the doors to something long hidden.

The lift slowed and the shiny, slate hatch slid open with a hiss. Steele absently glanced into the alcove just beyond the doors.

"Still..." she added, turning her face towards Brig, once again a stern expression chiseled onto it, "this doesn't need to be a topic of discussion. He's not as easy going as I am about such rubbish. This line of thinking will get you nowhere with him."

Brig sighed and trailed Steele into Bronson's office suite.

"Good morning, father," Steele announced, stopping several steps in front of Bronson's sizeable, clear desk.

"Steele, my darling. This is a surprise. The weekly briefing isn't until later this afternoon," Bronson replied, his back to both of them, studying a holographic report floating just behind his desk.

"I've a surprise visitor, father."

"A visitor, eh? And just who might that..." Bronson stopped mid-sentence, casting his first look at Brig with a subdued shock. "...be." He slowly stood, not taking his eyes from Brig - even as he rounded the corner of his desk like a stalking jungle cat. He narrowed his eyes and stopped a pace away from the former EW.

Even with his slow approach, there was youthfulness to Bronson's gait that did not escape Brig's eye. Having been accustomed, albeit for a short period, to the 'other' Bronson as a frail being several months prior when he had nabbed him from the clutches of the Syndicate, Brig had to hold back his gut accusations for a bit longer. There was still something else he needed to confirm before he knew the truth.

Steele's face ignited in a fulfilled smile, looking up at Brig from the corner of her eyes. "Daddy - you remember Brigadier Str..."

"Stroud's boy?"

"Yes! It's really him, father!" Steele clapped her hands in front of her like a giddy schoolgirl, coupled with a springy bounce on her tiptoes.

Bronson slowly turned his head, tilting it and almost glaring at Brig through the corner of one eye. "I wasn't aware President Stroud's son was on station, Steele," he said, his voice cool and suspecting in tone. "I don't recall seeing his name on the staffing rosters."

Brig stood silent, a smirk lingering on his face.

"It's a long story, Daddy. But... yes, he's here!"

"And what is it that you... *do*, Brigadier?" Bronson paced around Brig, his eyes examining him from all angles.

"Just a bit of stuff here and there. Mostly in the Entertainment Sector," Brig replied. "I was thinkin' of takin' up bartending."

Bronson nodded, wrinkling his lip in thought. He finished his round of Brig and stopped in front of him. "It seems quite a trek to come here... just to tend bar, don't you think?" he asked with an air of derision. "One would think someone of your ilk would prefer something more... physically tasking. Such as security?"

"Everyone's gotta work, right?" Brig answered, winking once at Steele. "Might even wanna go work in the mining colony."

Steele stomped on Brig's left boot with a deceptive force, a fierce set of gritted teeth narrowly exposed between her tightened lips.

Bronson did not react to Steele's hushing, but continued to size up Brig with a silent eye. "If I recall, Brigadier. You went into the military at an early age, no?"

Brig nodded, raised an eyebrow. "EWs actually. Fun times."

The colony Prefect flared his nostrils.

Steele, sensing the sudden growth of tension, cleared her throat. "Daddy, I just wanted to reacquaint you with Brigadier." She looped her arm in Brig's and pulled him close. "Just in case you get word of me on the arm of some dashing stranger." She glanced up at Brig again with a telling smile. "Meet the dashing stranger."

Once again, Bronson ignored Steele's attempt at easing the tense moment. "Well, Brigadier. It was a... pleasure... to see you again." He offered his hand to Brig, whom took it hesitantly and shook once. The pair locked eyes with a ferocity that heated the air around them, before releasing their grasps.

"Likewise... Mr. Fox," Brig replied. "I'm sure I'll see *you* around."

Bronson raised an eyebrow, turned away from Brig and glared at Steele. "I've a briefing with my General to attend. Steele will show you out." He smiled flatly at the two and spun on a heel.

As he cornered the desk, an overhead cone of light fell upon the elder Fox's neck. Brig's eyes narrowed at the confirmation of his suspicions – a small infinity tattoo.

Allistair.

The turbo lift door clunked behind the pair. Brig fell against the wall of the lift and released a heavy puff of breath. He ran a hand through his hair.

"What in blazes was that?" Steele groused in a heightened whisper.

"Steele... let me explain..." Brig raised a hand in gentle opposition.

"I told you not to go toe-to-toe with my father about your delusions!"

He angrily jousted a finger at the door. "That man is not your father!"

A tear appeared at the corner of one of Steele's eyes and flowed onto her cheek. "What are you trying to do? Why do you insist on tearing all of this down?" She folded her arms across her thin midsection.

For the first time in their history together, Brig found himself able to resist the waterworks that normally made him soften. "I'm trying to open your eyes to reality, Steele! There's a lot going on here that you just aren't seeing." He tightened his lips, holding back the potentially striking truth. "Or maybe you just don't want to see."

Like an angry child, Steele stomped her foot in callow objection. "No! *This* is reality, Brigadier!" She pointed a finger at the floor. "All of this that you see around you – *that's* reality! We're on Mars. *That's* reality! Not anything you claim you saw in the mines. Not anything back... *there*. And certainly not anything up here..." Steele turned the finger and aimed it at Brig's temple.

He instinctively grasped her wrist and pulled it to her side. She exhaled a tiny whimper as the two locked eyes, their heavy breaths echoing in the quiet chamber. For a brief second, they glared in silence at each other, not having planned their next move.

Suddenly, Steele launched herself at Brig and planted a forceful kiss on his lips. Brig was strong, but the stoic resolve that he had built washed away amidst the velvet of her lips pressing against his. He pulled her close and drove his lips tighter against hers. She coiled her arms around him in a passionate embrace.

Their bodies melded into one as the lift fell away and released them to the silent vacuum of starry space. For what seemed an eternal moment, Brig found himself lost in an ocean of senses. His will to find a solution to everything that was wrong about the colony whisked away to a thin point on the horizon. He held her waist with firm hands, sliding one up and finding her flowing hair.

Her flowing... *brunette* hair.

He opened his eyes, as did she. A quick second elapsed before her searing, emerald eyes sparkled in the light of the lift car.

He pushed her away with a strong hand and pointed angrily at her. "No!" he barked.

Steele stepped backward. She furrowed her brow in confused shock.

"I have proof, Steele. And you need to see it!"

Steele stomped her foot once again. "I do *not* need to see it! Everything here is all I need to see." She turned her back to Brig and faced the lift door. "This is about the portal again."

Her angry breathing rattled the quiet air in the lift.

"There were sacrifices made. But we saved the human race. We saved technology. We saved the human race from retreating into the Dark Ages – which is where you have been the past few years. So don't tell me that I need to see *anything*..."

Brig spun Steele to face him. "Now *there's* your father!"

Steele's face flooded crimson, her gritted teeth bared through her tightened lips. She barked a loud huff as the door slid open, and wheeled around to exit the car.

Brig stepped out into the corridor after her, stopping to watch her storm speedily down the hall. "Steele! You need to see those cards! They're in my room. Go look at 'em!"

The clomp of Steele's heels reverberated with a hollow din, until she disappeared around the next corner.

22:
Requiem

Mars. Red Colony One

Brig caressed the newly minted stubble on the ridge of his skull. No stranger to having his head shaved, as it was routine from his days in boot camp, it was still an odd sensation - *that* life seemed so far away from where he stood now. He examined his surreal image in the mirror.

"Only way to get 'em to talk is to be one of 'em."

His single-shift scouting mission in the mines earlier in the week had left him with the affirmation that this was the only way to save them. It was a risk, but one that he knew to be the only choice.

It's the right thing to do, he continued to convince himself.

He strode from the small lavatory, stopping at the front of the oaken wardrobe adorning one wall of his modest suite. Brig gazed at the jumpsuit that hung within, the dull gray coloring of the material betraying the suit's central importance in the florid mission upon which he was about to embark.

Fifteen minutes later

As he stepped towards the open door of his room, Brig halted and caught the reflection of himself passing in the mirror. He absorbed a longing view, and then exited the suite. He had not gotten more than three steps into the hallway when he slowly tilted his head back to the door. A nagging specter continued to hold court on his shoulder, its icy digits reaching from beyond and grasping for his attention whenever he had steeled his resolve.

Brig shook his head and scratched the back of his neck.

"Focus, Stroud," he grunted to himself, and hastened to the Security Enclave.

Marcus Scribbs cleared his throat with a breathy scrape, rotating his shoulder with a series of audible clicks that relieved the stress of standing in one location over several hours. The momentary silvery blip of reflection sailed across the ceiling of the hollowed cavern - a sign that the latest shuttle from Red Colony One had made its appearance, dropping off a fresh set of guards for shift work at the Pit.

Scribbs rolled his eyes sideways, peering at the white tram that glided to a silent stop at the end of its rail, next to the platform on which he stood. The top slid away and a small gaggle of guards stepped from the vehicle, filing into one queue in front of him. He watched with feigned interest, his pulse rifle resting idly across his arms, and nodded through the first two guards to take on the next shift.

As the third approached him and assumed he could pass as well, the guard pressed his hand against the man's chest. Scribbs tapped at his own helmet. The man tapped his visor in response – the shield cleared to display the man's face.

"You're Sampson, right?" Scribbs grumbled, waving on the pair of queued up guards behind him.

"Yeah, is there a problem?" Brig wrinkled his forehead. He had done everything right so far - how could his plan have failed already? He glanced at the other guards, who had now reached the crest of the platform and were disappearing one by one into the bright light beyond.

"You look like you've bulked up, Sampson." The guard eyed Brig's chest and arms, noticing the extra girth that he was sure the man did not have the last time he had seen him.

Dammit.

Brig flexed a palm behind his back. He was certain he could take out this guy if he had to - but where could he go. Red Colony One was only so big, and it would not take long for Rossi's men to figure out it was him. He relaxed the fist and dropped it to his side.

"Uh... yeah. Been workin' out..." Brig began.

"That's good, Sampson. You're gonna need it down here." Scribbs smiled through his visor, the blue tint lighting his face. He waved Brig through the checkpoint.

Brig nodded to the guard and scaled the platform to the top, exhaling a silent sigh of relief as he entered the Pit. He stopped at the top of the concourse that opened into the massive cavern below and spoke silently into his helmet-mounted microphone.

"You gettin' all this, Darpa?" he whispered.

"Affirmative, Brigadier. What you see... I see."

Brig nodded and walked forward.

The first stop for Brig was the armory, which was located at the end of a short tunnel burrowed into the northwest corner of the mine, opposite the corridor that led to the miners' small barracks.

As the short line of guards coming on-shift dwindled, each accepting one of the standard snub-nosed pulse weapons from the clerk, Brig stepped forward from the rear of the queue and flashed a quick smile at him. The clerk did not reciprocate, instead pulled one of the rifles from the wall behind him without looking and forced it into Brig's outstretched hand.

Brig examined it, and then as the clerk turned away, Brig cleared his throat with a light 'ahem'. "You think I could get the other one... third from the left back there? I think I've used it before. My lucky gun."

The clerk shook his head in disgust and turned to retrieve the object of Brig's eye. As he reached, Brig slammed the butt of the rifle already in his hands against the clerk's neck. The clerk jolted forward and then poured down onto the floor, unconscious. Brig glanced around, yanked the guard's inanimate body from the floor and stuffed him into a nearby weapons locker.

Brig emerged from the armory tunnel, spied Wesley patrolling the north catwalk and swiftly scaled the steps to reach him. "Wesley, can I ask a favor?"

The guard, surprised, spun on a heel, his rifle at the ready. "Oh, it's you... Sampson. What is it?" Wesley relaxed his shoulders and turned to look over the Pit once more.

"Think you could introduce me to the rest of the crew? You know, kinda get to know them a little better."

Wesley raised an eyebrow and stared curiously at Brig, before looking back over the Pit. "Now why would you wanna do that?"

Brig propped his snub-nosed rifle over one shoulder and leaned on the rail alongside Wesley. The buzzer for the magnet cycle emitted an obnoxious drone for a few seconds, and then went silent. Brig and Wesley watched as the mined fragments sailed through the empty space at the center of the Pit and adhered to the large panel at the east end of the facility. As before, they released and fell into the extraction chute below.

"Back when I was in the service..." Brig began, as mining operations resumed. Wesley tilted his head at Brig, scrunched his brow. "Yeah... I was way back when back on... you know, Earth. Anyway... it helps with camaraderie. Makes a more efficient crew if everyone gets a little closer." He faced Wesley, his hand outstretched. "Brody Sampson, second shift. Nice to meet you."

Wesley snorted and shook his head in disbelief. "Ok. Sure, Sampson. Whatever." He met Brig's handshake, still wagging his head.

Brig's smile grew. He patted Wesley on the shoulder next to his rifle strap.

Wesley released and walked past Brig towards the staircase leading down to the first level. "If it gets you outta my hair, whatever you want."

Brig's grin expanded. He took up pace behind Wesley as the pair descended from the catwalk.

Over the next fifteen minutes, Wesley pinballed between locations within the Pit, stopping at each station to allow Brig a few seconds to shake the hand of a fellow guard. After each, Wesley made some sort of gesture behind Brig's back, either an eye roll or another derogatory motion, to the guard Brig had just met.

When they had finished with the final guard within the Pit area, Wesley stepped onto the staircase and began to climb.

"What about the guy outside the control tower. Didn't meet him yet!" Brig called from behind.

"That's enough for one night, Sampson. Get to work!" Wesley held up a gloved hand and increased his pace up the stairs, until he disappeared onto the platform above.

"Sampson! Shift change!"

22: REQUIEM

Brig peered up at the other end of the north catwalk where one of the other guards, a shift supervisor by the name of Thomson, leaned over and growled at him with an outstretched finger.

Like clockwork, Brig observed with a wry smile.

He trotted towards a line of exhausted miners already beginning to queue up outside their barracks corridor.

"Let's move it out!" Brig barked, waving an arm clockwise at the group. They began to file forward.

The line of miners, and Brig, disappeared into the tunnel.

As the retiring miners trudged into the barracks entrance, their lined boots dredging the red Martian soil, a fresh gang of men - and women, to Brig's sickly astonishment - filed out into the thin corridor. Brig fidgeted with the handle of his rifle, watching them form a double line against the wall. Much like his previous encounter with the miners, most of them hung their heads and stood in a defeated silence, awaiting the order to begin their shifts. He paced their lines, holding a stare at each one, more inviting and less daring any of them to meet his gaze. He somehow expected to fulfill his hope that there was still an ounce of humanity left in their sorrowful lives, but none lifted their eyes to him. Brig's heart plummeted further with each step.

This was the pivot. He had to act.

"You there... what's your name?" Brig called through his external speaker. He pointed at a man at the end of the line nearest him.

The man remained silent, rolling his eyes. "Granderson, sir," his voice a cool Cockney lilt. His eyes fell back at the floor.

"Another Brit?" Brig mumbled. "A lot of you fellas down here..."

"You're new 'ere... aren't ye'?" Granderson replied to the ground, not making eye contact with Brig. "Not supposed to talk to the 'elp, eh love?"

A synchronized unease fell upon the dual line of miners, as if they all knew something horrid was about to take place.

Brig stepped closer to Granderson and placed a friendly hand on the man's shoulder. Granderson flinched away as if Brig's glove were molten lava.

"It's alright," Brig reassured. "I'm here to help."

The unsure miner flicked his eyes at Brig, then back away just as quickly. "What do you want from me?"

"Just wanna know your story. How did you get here?"

Granderson raised his head, casting off the angry glares from several other miners around him. "I used to be in parliament... 'ouse of Commons..."

Brig wrinkled his brow.

"You act as if that's a surprise, sir," Granderson said, tilting his head in Brig's direction.

"A bit, yeah," Brig replied.

"Well, it shouldn't be. We were all officials of one sort or another... or family." The miner began pointing at several others. "Why, Stokes over there was in the 'ealth Ministry... and Blevins, that bloke was part of the Defense Cabinet."

"But... why are all of you... *here*?"

"You don't get it?" Granderson raised an eyebrow at Brig, a shadow cast across his weathered face. "It's all part of a vendetta. Anyone that 'as ever stood in *his* way gets put 'ere, and we're all in one way or another part of what has 'eld 'im down in the past. With what's going on back on Big Blue... we're easy pickins now."

"So you're saying you're being rounded up because of your affiliations to government?"

"You catch on quick, my friend." Granderson scanned the rest of the miners. "I'd venture to say there's even some of your country mates 'ere. You're URA, I reckon."

Brig nodded.

"That Fox doesn't discriminate one side o' the pond or the other now, does 'e? But... I've said enough. We've a job to do." Granderson fell silent and stared down at the ground once more.

Brig's jaw flexed. "Then I've got a story to tell you..."

Moments later, the oncoming shift emerged, single file - their dingy gray jumpsuits reflecting in the high intensity lights of the dome. As expected, Brig marched beside the line until they reached the edge of the Pit, where they split into two groups and took up their work positions on either side. Brig followed the smaller group to the far end of the Pit and took up a watch position just behind a pair of miners that had already begun readying their extractors.

Emberly wearily picked up his extractor, primed the battery with a loud clunk of the lever on its side, and stepped towards the rock face in front of him. Before he could engage the trigger, a shadow fell upon the rocky inner wall of the mountain. He turned his head with deliberate slowness, not wanting to give the guards any reason to think he was making an erratic move and take him out.

"Hey... Emberly." A miner stood behind him, his own extractor down by his side. He casually glanced to each side.

"What ya want?" Emberly rolled his eyes and snorted.

He suddenly caught sight of the other miner's face when the man stepped in the path of the lighting, which eliminated the glare from the man's clear, domed helmet. "You!"

The other miner moved closer to Emberly and grabbed at his arm, holding his other hand up to his face. "Don't make any sudden moves!"

Emberly yanked his arm from the man's grasp. "It's you! You're a... you're a bloody guard! You're that Sampson fella!" Emberly lowered his voice to a raised whisper. "What're ya' doin' 'ere?"

Brig, dressed in miner gray and head shaved to resemble the other miners, did another quick scan of the area behind him. He moved to stand next to Emberly. "Just act like you're doin' your normal work. I got somethin' to tell ya." Brig raised his extractor and fired a sonic blast into the rock. After a few seconds, a small chunk of rubble tumbled from the wall to Brig's feet.

Emberly stood with his mouth agape at the sight of one of the Pit guards next to him pretending to be a miner. He turned to look at the guard that had taken up a spot several meters behind them. The guard, smaller than the usual fare, tapped the side of his helmet with a bumbling awkwardness, dissipating his face shield shroud to reveal the smiling mug of Cummins, his fellow mining partner. Cummins beamed a toothless grin and waved, the heavy pulse rifle in his other hand toppling and nearly falling to the ground before he caught it.

"What in the bloody 'ell is goin' on 'ere?" Emberly glared at Brig, who released the trigger on his extractor and stepped back to admire his work.

"I'm gettin' y'all outta here." He rotated his head within his helmet to face Emberly and shot him a stern glare, his steely blue eyes igniting in the harsh lighting of the Pit. "We're shuttin' this place down. You with me?"

Emberly squinted at Brig. "This some sort of sting, Sampson. You tryin' to git us busted?"

"No joke," Brig replied before righting his extractor for another blast. "But we don't have time to argue about it."

Emberly snorted and shot a finger out towards Cummins. "What're ya, nutter! Ya got 'im playin' guard?"

Brig ignored Emberly's protests. "I needed someone with more on the ball to do the heavy work. Besides, he's already spread the word. Now... on my mark, I need you to head to the armory as quick as you can. Grab an armful of pulse rifles and bring 'em to the tunnel. Be ready to hand 'em out to the other miners when I tell you." Brig stared up at a guard on the west catwalk, just beneath the control tower.

"What about the other guards, bloke? Ya can't believe we're just gonna walk from 'ere, do ya?"

"Got that covered." Brig blasted at the rock, freeing another small pile of debris.

"That so?" Emberly fired at his own section of rock once. "And 'ow's about the guard at the armory?"

"He's napping." Brig winked at Emberly. "So. The armory on my mark." Brig turned his back, leaned in towards Emberly. "But whatever happens... do *not* grab any of the rifles off the guards. Trust me."

Movement from behind caught the eye of both men. They turned their heads simultaneously and stared in horror. Cummins, anxious for his own liberation – and not particularly bright - had fled the area and was making haste towards the stairs leading to the tram.

"Son of a bitch!" Brig growled aloud.

Emberly pursed his lips and raised a fist in Cummins's direction. "That barking numpty!"

Cummins paid no mind, however, and stumbled up the staircase like a newborn on fresh feet. His rifle left his grasp, clacked a loud din down the steps and found its way to the Martian soil at the base.

22: REQUIEM

"Oh... bloody 'ell! 'e's gone an gotten 'imself killed!" Emberly's observations were cut short - Wesley made his way from the north catwalk stairs over to the edge of the Pit, staring in their direction. Both Brig and Emberly quickly spun and shot a pulse each into the rocky face of the wall, pretending not to notice the approaching guard.

"Emberly!" Wesley stopped behind the shorter miner and glared at him.

"Yessir," Emberly grumbled, turning part way to face the guard.

"I thought I told you no more talkin'!"

Emberly did a quick take towards Brig, flicked his eyes back to Wesley before nodding once. "Righto, govna..." He glanced at Brig nervously for a nanosecond, and then focused his attention back on the wall.

"And you..."

Brig tensed, but continued to prep his extractor for the next blast, despite Wesley sharply jabbing the barrel of his pulse rifle into Brig's shoulder.

"Turn around when I'm speakin' to ya!" Wesley grabbed Brig's shoulder and forced him to about face. Security protocol promptly faded from Wesley's mind, his eyes widened to saucers as he stared up into the face of Brig. The sound of Wesley's shocked inhale sparked static on his external helmet speaker. "Sampson! What the hell!"

Before Brig could react, Wesley slammed his palm onto his own wrist and screamed "Security breach on the floor! Security breach on the floor!"

Brig glanced up at the catwalk. Several guards had now congregated near the rail and brought their pulse rifles to bear. However, they were not aiming at Brig, nor Emberly – but rather Cummins, who continued to scramble like a clumsy oaf up the staircase on the opposite end of the Pit. Two blinding beams of light escaped the lead guard's gun and drilled Cummins in the side, sending him flying from the staircase onto the cold Martian dirt - a small waft of smoke twirling up from the new hole in his torso.

Wesley took a step backward and raised his own rifle at Brig. Brig's EW instincts kicked in - he swiftly grabbed at both ends of Wesley's gun. The two locked in close melee for a moment, each tugging at the rifle, kicking up red dust around their ankles.

"Emberly! Now! Go!" Brig yelled in a strained growl.

Emberly glanced nervously between the two men, dropped his extractor, and then raced past them towards the armory tunnel, bouncing off the rock-faced corner as he disappeared from view.

Other miners had suddenly sprung to life, and despite their lack of weaponry aside from their harmless extractors, stormed their local guards with savage screams that filled the cave and echoed off the dome above. Others, also haphazardly going off plan, rushed the staircase leading to the tram platform. Strobes of brilliant alabaster lit the rock walls of the Pit like a fierce lightning storm, the beams from the guards' rifles finding their targets in groups of miners around the chasm.

Brig stared in dread as clusters of escaping miners fell to the ground, broken and smoking, their scarlet blood ebbing out onto the Martian loam. Time slowed to a crawl. Brig watched the massacre unfold in front of him. How had he not seen it beforehand?

Then, it came to him. Clarity, the piece of him that was now missing – was not present to give him the foresight he had come to take for granted. A familiar, sinking pain stabbed at his gut. His plan had failed before it even began.

Suddenly, the strip of lights above the wall opposite of him illuminated in bright red.

The magnet.

"Let go of the rifle, Wesley!" Brig cried, attempting to spin the guard's pulse rifle out of his hands, to no avail.

"You'd like that, wouldn't you?" Wesley growled, forcing Brig backward against the rock with a heavy thump. Brig stumbled and fell to the ground, catching himself with both hands. Wesley stepped back once more and raised his rifle. "This ends now!" he bellowed with a breathless boom.

The warning buzzer sounded, just barely audible over the sound of pulse bolts still raining down on the fleeing miners.

"Wesley, don't!" Brig warned, holding up a hand in front of him.

Before Wesley could pull the trigger and end Brig's attempt at liberating the poor souls of the mining colony, the telltale 'clunk' of the magnet powering up shook the air around them. Wesley's rifle lifted upwards and launched across the chasm - with the stunned guard in tow.

As Brig stared in horror, he realized *he* was moving, too. He raked his fingers into the sandy floor of the Pit to stop his momentum, but it was too late. His body sprang from the ground and sailed like a puppet over the crater at the center of the operation, his legs and arms flailing in a desperate attempt to free himself from the magnetic draw.

Within two short seconds, Brig slammed against the panel beneath the warning lights. The sickening crunch of his wrist shattering against the hard surface presaged the shrill pain that traveled up his arm a second after he jolted to a stop. Brig fought the primal instinct to lose consciousness from the sudden surge of pain and attempted to pry himself from the panel, but his arm would not budge from the wall. He peered through the fog of agony clawing up his arm, spying Wesley's rifle attached firmly to the panel next to him - with Wesley still clinging madly to it, his iron grip unrelenting.

"Let... go... of the rifle... Wes..." Brig's words stumbled over themselves, forming tinny chirps interrupted by bits of static coming from the helmet's external speaker.

Wesley sneered through the new condensation on his cracked face shield, a cascade of sweat now forming across his brow as he frantically tried to free the rifle from its magnetic mount.

Brig glanced down past his feet, where the churning grinder wheels in the waiting compression chute begged for sustenance. "You're gonna... die, Wesley. Let it go..." Brig fought with his last remaining strength to stay conscious, knowing that death was only a moment away, when the magnet would depower itself and send him and Wesley to their grisly ends.

"That's enough from... you!" Wesley screamed, his hot breath adding to the condensation clouding the silvery light within his shielded helmet.

"The rifle's not gonna let go!" Brig strained to pull his other arm and pointed at the underside of the barrel of Wesley's weapon, where a small patch of magnetic paste held the gun to the panel.

Wesley, suddenly aware of his futile attempt at freeing the rifle, took stock of his surroundings. Dotted over the panel were the pulse rifles from the rest of the crew as well, all hanging from similar blobs of the material.

"You did this!" Wesley yanked even harder at the gun, to no avail.

The sight of the magnetic goo sent a surge to Brig's brain.

The paste!

He grasped at his stuck arm, ignoring the scorching fire within that threatened to consume him. He pulled at the sleeve - the pocket on the outside edge ripped and exposed a small tube that clung to the panel. Brig freed it from the torn fabric and pushed himself from the panel, bounced off the edge of the chute wall and landed on the dirt next to the Pit five meters below with a crunching thud.

The buzzer sounded once more. Wesley made one last, frantic attempt at dislodging his weapon. Power immediately drained from the hidden magnet and Wesley dropped from the wall in a manner similar to what Brig had done. However, the back of his suit caught the edge of the wall beneath and he twirled, plummeting into the chute out of sight. The machine emitted a momentary belch and spewed a fountain of dark red fluid into the air. It fell silent once again.

Brig levered himself to one knee, fighting off the cascading pain in his right arm. His vision clouded as he strained to remain awake; sweat thundered down his chest and back within his jumpsuit. He fell face first into the dirt, finally giving in to unconscious relief.

Not ten seconds later, a pair of hands pulled him to his knees. He drearily opened one eye.

Emberly stood next to him, his clear dome pressed against Brig's. "Up now! Up Sampson! We need to get the rest of the miners to the bloody tram!"

Brig grasped weakly at the fabric of Emberly's jumpsuit. He shook his head. "No... no... we have to take... out the computer... core." He released his hand and pointed to the control room at the top of the stairs.

"Are you blinkin' mad?"

Brig shook his head once again. "It's got... all the miner records. Has to be... destroyed... or this was all for... nothing. They'll just... bring y'all back... or... worse." He bowed his head, trying feebly to regain enough strength to stand.

The graying miner glanced up towards the tower, the shrill lights above shining through his translucent silver pupils. He bit hard on his lip. "Alright then, mate. It's sixes and sevens, but you can count on me." He stared deeper into Brig's face. "You gonna be alright? Can you make it to the tram?"

Brig took a heavy breath and nodded. Emberly patted him on the shoulder, and then scaled the steps with a determined gait leading to the tower, a pulse rifle at the ready. Brig stared after him for a moment until the miner disappeared from view.

A single pulse bolt rang out, followed by the sound of a body hitting the upper platform. For what seemed like an eternal amount of minutes, Brig struggled to pull himself upright. Just as he reached a standing position, a clamor arose from the top of the stairs in the form of several muffled pulse bolts from within the control room.

Silence ensued.

Emberly reappeared, hurtling the stairs at breakneck speed. Before he had reached the halfway point, however, Greer came into view at the very top. The Commander lifted his own pulse rifle to his waist and ripped off three quick bolts, all of which found Emberly's back. The miner tripped forward and tumbled end-over-end until he hit the ground several meters from Brig - where he crumpled awkwardly into a smoking pile.

Greer placed the butt of the rifle against his shoulder and took aim at the former EW, standing near the base of the stairs. The mechanism jammed. Greer tossed the gun to the ground with a loud thud and stormed downward.

Spying Emberly's rifle in the dirt, Brig leapt over the miner's corpse and dove after it. As he grasped the handle, Greer landed with a knee into Brig's lower spine, knocking the gun out of his reach.

"Sampson was it? I knew... you... were... trouble... when I first met you!" Greer snarled with vitriol, pounding a heavy fist into Brig's kidneys with each syllable.

Brig howled, spitting globs of blood onto the clear dome of his helmet. The pain radiated through his lower extremities and far overshadowed that of his splintered wrist. He clawed the dirt in desperation to remove himself from Greer's onslaught and reach the rifle, but Greer pulled him backward and delivered several brutal kicks to Brig's side. Brig's commando training took charge once again. He grabbed Greer's booted foot with both hands and, rejecting the torturous throbbing in his own body, twisted the Commander's lower leg until the audible snap of the man's knee ligaments bursting slackened his attacker's pace.

Greer dropped to the dusty soil, grasping at his knee, briefly blinded by his own pain. Brig rolled and then launched himself on top of Greer, wasting no time in pummeling the man's midsection with a barrage of blows from his good fist while holding him down with one elbow.

After several missed attempts, Greer finally parried Brig's attacks by grasping his arm, wedging his good leg against the EW's abdomen, and twisting until both men barrel-rolled towards the edge of the precipice at the center of the Pit.

Before either could stop, their momentum carried them over the edge.

Both men dangled – Greer from both hands in the soft dirt at the edge of the chasm, and Brig hanging one-handed from Greer's injured leg. Greer turned and kicked violently with his held foot. "This is the end, saboteur!"

Brig looked beneath his feet into the dark abyss, then back at Greer. "If I'm goin' to Hell, I'm takin' you with me!" Brig barked, yanking harder at Greer's lower leg.

Seeing only one alternative to his own death, Greer climbed back onto the ledge, dragging Brig with him. Greer had already regained the advantage of attack, standing up while Brig forced himself up to a knee. He grabbed Brig by the shoulders and thrust a forceful knee into the front of Brig's helmet. While the protective material of it was nearly unbreakable, it did not protect Brig's head from jarring against the back of the dome. Greer punished Brig with three follow-ups before Brig stumbled backward and fell to the ground. The panting Commander, satisfied that he had beaten down the rogue guard, grabbed the nearby pulse rifle from the ground and hoisted it at Brig's head.

A massive shock wave jolted the mine. The control room burst outward in a hail of glass and synthetic structural components, knocking Greer forward against the rock wall. He collapsed limply to the ground, unconscious. Above, the domed edifice groaned as it shifted from the sudden loss of artificial gravity that had assisted in holding it in place for years. Skeletal struts began to twist and buckle under the enormous strain of movement, falling to the ground in a cacophony of chaos.

Brig forced himself up and staggered to the other end of the Pit, his last outstanding duty to help herd the remaining miners to the shuttle. The rag tag group, locked in a back-and-forth firefight with a small squad of guards at the other end of the Pit, ceased their volley of pulse bolts at the urges of Brig and hastily made their way up the inclined ramp.

Brig stood by the sleek, white tram as the stragglers filtered down the ramp and stepped into the vehicle. In the periphery of his vision, he caught movement. He spun to face what he expected to be a final confrontation with the leftover mine guards – or Greer himself.

A single guard stood near the back of the tram, pushing one of the last few miners into the rear of the car. He stood a good two meters tall, his chiseled arms straining against the tight fabric of his jumpsuit.

"Hey!" Brig cried, taking a step in the guard's direction.

The guard, rather than reacting with the expected attack from his rifle, merely looked up from his task, delivered a one-fingered salute to Brig and flexed his arm in a 'v' shape.

Stunned, Brig gawked in silence. "McGraw?"

Before he could confirm the unfathomable vision in front of him – the presence of Mercury McGraw, his arch-nemesis from the EW squadron - he felt the grasp at the fiber lining the elbow of his jumpsuit. He turned to face a young teen boy.

"Sir... you have to get the rest!" the boy said, a small hint of proper British accent evident in his meek plea.

Brig bent down to the boy, scrunching his brow in confusion. "Rest? Where?"

The boy pointed back towards the Pit. "In the dormitory at the other end, sleeping."

Brig glared up the ramp at the strobe of wagging high intensity lights peeking through the opening. The entire mine seemed to be shaking now, with pieces of Martian soil falling in clumps from the walls just outside and above the tram entrance.

"How many are there?"

The boy thought for a silent moment. "A full day shift's compliment plus alternates. Most likely sixty-seven."

"Dammit," grumbled Brig under his breath. "Get in the shuttle. I'll take care of it."

The teen hopped into the transport; Brig turned and limped expeditiously up the rise and back into the Pit.

Moments later, after dodging sporadic fire from the armory tunnel, Brig entered the corridor of the miners' quarters. He glanced behind him, aiming the pulse rifle in his hand backward in case any had dared follow.

Suddenly, a fierce blow met him where his neck joined his shoulder. Blackness enveloped him and he collapsed to the ground.

23:
Warrior Down

Mars. Red Colony One

The medicinal pungency of alcohol aroused Brig from unconsciousness. He opened a bleary eye, but could only peer into a backlit haze. He scrunched his eyes, wanting to wipe the sleep from his mind but found his hands bound behind him. A familiar tingle traveled his arm, a subtle reminder of the shattered wrist he had sustained in the miner revolt. A weighty, gelatinous ring tugged at his arm - the work of the miracle healing sludge he had become familiar with upon his arrival at Red Colony One.

"You needed me, Prefect?" a voice said through the fog, but away from Brig.

"Yes, General," another voice, whom Brig immediately recognized as Allistair by his suave yet authoritative British inflection, cooed. "I believe it's time for another shipment to be processed."

Brig squinted through the fog limiting his eyesight. A lanky shadow stood at the far end of the room, overlooking another who sat with what appeared to be his head resting on a palm.

Rossi.

"And, if I may ask, sir – which side will be the benefactor?" the General queried, his own softer English accent flowing like a whispering zephyr.

"Let's give the underdogs something to crow about, shall we?" Allistair's voice lost all semblance of the elder Bronson Fox for a moment, suddenly dripping with pure malevolence. "We have to pare the Syndicate's recent advances after all…"

"Very well, sir," Rossi answered with a curt nod. Brig lowered his head, detecting that Rossi had turned to face him. "And what shall we do with… him?"

Allistair sat back in his seat, his chin upon his steepled fingertips.

"I knew from the first that he was going to be trouble, sir. Epsilons aren't to be trifled with."

"Agreed, General."

"And the fact that he's involved in some... capacity... with your daughter, I..."

"Leave her to me, General. She is not your concern." Allistair stood from his desk and leaned at Rossi with both palms flat across its surface. "He, however, could help us yet..."

Brig's ears filled with the sudden whir of a mechanical servo nearby, followed by the prick of a pin in his left nostril and a wisp of medicinal vapor. He shook his head for a spell, trying to rid his olfactory of the burning stimulant he had just forcefully inhaled.

"Brigadier, my boy. Glad to see you've made it back to us." The voice of Bronson Fox had returned, as if a specter from the past.

Brig turned an eye towards the wiry frame of Allistair, who had suddenly appeared beside him. "Mr. Fox..." His eyes glided towards Rossi, who stood nearest the sliding entry door like a stalking panther. "General."

Rossi raised an eyebrow, but did not reciprocate the greeting.

The awe-inspiring view beyond Allistair's desk drew Brig's attention. He had been in Allistair's office previously, but the viewport that presented itself now had not been there – or was not active at the time. The window, which stretched from wall to wall, floor to ceiling, offered a breathtaking, panoramic view of the far end of the triple-headed power core. While elevated to where one could spy the rest of the rising colony behind it, it was evident that the executive zone sat on its own in a secured location.

"A pity about your injured arm, Brigadier. But you'll survive." Allistair's faux concern hung on each word that left his mouth. "The mining colony, on the other hand. Well... what were you thinking?"

Brig hardened his glare at the Prefect. "I know about the mine."

"Yes, I'm quite certain you do. You've done a lot of damage." Allistair paced away from Brig, his hands clasped behind his lower back. "But as the head of this installation, Brigadier, I believe that I can lessen your punishment for such a mistake..."

"It wasn't a mistake... I know about the slave labor."

Allistair chuckled. "It's hardly slave labor, my dear boy."

"What about your *extraction* procedures?"

Allistair continued to stare with an amused smile. "You're obviously looking for a reaction from me, Brigadier. What is it that you want me to say?"

"I want you to admit what you're doing down there!"

"I'll admit to no wrongdoing, my boy. It is admittedly hard work." Allistair placed his chin in his hand, feigning righteous resolve.

"Slaves... and not just any slaves," Brig growled. "Your enemies from Earth. Politicians, lawmakers... anyone that stood in your way..."

"I built this colony." Allistair allowed Brig's taunts to float by him untouched. "The naysayers may say that the Republic Space Agency did so by sending manned missions to Mars, but that sentiment is tantamount to saying Christopher Columbus created the United States – or further the United Republic of the Americas. When in fact, all he did was discover a new slice of land and plant a pennant."

"Spin it however you want – there's still innocent men and women - and children - dying down there," Brig growled.

"Dying? Yes. You saw to that, now didn't you, Brigadier?" Allistair spun to meet Brig's glare.

"I'm not the one that herded a bunch of his enemies from Earth and forced them into working to death in your mine."

"Great societies are built upon the backs of the bruised," Allistair replied, sitting at the edge of his desk and crossing his arms over his chest. "The ancient Egyptians employed slave laborers to build some of the greatest wonders of the Earth, but *that* fact has always taken a back seat to their accomplishments. The annals of history laud their efforts as 'miraculous'. What I have done here is no different and should be viewed as equal in everyone's eyes."

Brig shook his head in disgust. "You're insane."

Once again, Allistair emitted a relieved chuckle. "Brigadier. Son. There's no need for this line of discussion to continue. You made a mistake, and I'm willing to forgive if you're willing to roll up your sleeves and do some hard work to make up for the mess you've created."

"What about your daughter?"

"Steele?" Allistair guffawed. "Even she is not so love struck as to be blind to your actions, Brigadier."

"So you don't mind if I tell her?" Brig squinted. The fuse was there, he just was not sure how to light it... yet.

"My dear boy, I don't think that will be possible. You will be quite busy. After all, the mining colony won't rebuild itself."

"She'll never agree to this."

"I think you give yourself far too much credit." Allistair rounded his desk, presenting Rossi a half-smirk.

Brig followed Allistair with an unwavering eye. "I know all about you... Allistair."

Allistair halted in his tracks. He glanced at Brig without betraying his reaction to Brig's revelation. He smiled, lowered his head and walked past Rossi. "General, I would like to speak with Mr. Stroud alone for a moment."

The General started from his position against the wall. "Are you certain, sir? Epsilons are a wily bunch, and I wouldn't put anything past *him*."

Allistair raised a hand. "It will be fine."

Rossi glared at Brig, performed a half bow at Allistair before turning to walk through the door. It quietly slid closed behind him.

The Red Colony One Prefect turned his attention back to Brig, slowly approaching him with the expression of a predator about to pounce. "Now wherever did you hear such a name?" he hissed.

Brig smiled a knowing grin. "I know all about you, Cromwell. I know what you've done. And I know how you got to be where you're at. What you did to Bronson Fox. What you did to Steele..."

"What I've done *for* Steele..." Allistair interrupted, "...is merely help her realize her potential." He stretched his arms outward. "If you simply look around, I would say that is not such a bad thing."

Brig peered at the grand office and smiled in derision. "Yeah, but you blocked her memories so that she wouldn't know your master plan. Would she be ok with *that*?"

"Brigadier, my boy..." Allistair began.

"Don't call me your boy. You're not Bronson Fox, and you don't know me..."

Allistair spat an evil hiss. He placed a hand on Brig's shoulder. "Oh yes, Mr. Stroud. I know you. I know *all* about you." He leaned in towards Brig's left ear. "You. Mr. Epsilon Warrior. The prodigal son. The golden child of that glory hound Devlin Stroud. I know all about D42-19 sub 14." He moved to Brig's other ear and whispered with a chilling haunt. "*Clarity...*"

He found the fuse.

"You're a crazy son of a bitch. You sell out your entire world just for a power play. You pathetic piece of shit."

Allistair snorted under his breath again.

"You couldn't hack it with your worthless life, so you steal someone else's?"

Allistair grabbed Brig by the collar with both fists and futilely attempted to yank him up from the chair. His voice took on a maniacal fray. "*I* stole *his* life? Do you know what *he* did to *me*? He stole *my* life, and was going to make me live out the rest of my days as a simpleton with no mind of my own! How is it not fair that I just pre-empted *his* evil plot? If not for me, you would be back there with the rest – on Earth. Everyone clamoring around, scraping the bottom and killing each other for that last crumb of bread."

Brig allowed a smile to warp the end of his lips.

"He was going to play God with me! What gave Bronson Fox," he spat with disdain, "the right to take away my life and replace it with a pitiful existence?"

Allistair released the top of Brig's jumpsuit, composing himself and instantaneously reverting to the more levelheaded demeanor of Bronson Fox. "No. The man you see before you is a visionary. A man who was not afraid to take the steps necessary to ensure his own survival."

"And that makes it all ok? You think it was justified to allow millions of people to get left behind and die… all so you can prove a point?" Brig's upper lip curled into a snarl.

"You'll suffer no penance from me, my friend," Allistair seethed, his face centimeters from Brig's. "My conscience is clean. Much cleaner than yours, I presume." He backed off Brig and stood up straight once again, and once again took on an air of haughty arrogance. "Those poor, poor miners. I would think they deserved better… but you just had to – prove a point?"

"That's not what happened. We both know it," Brig grumbled through gritted teeth.

"Your word against mine, my dear boy. And whom will everyone believe – the much-respected Prefect who has led them to the grandeur that surrounds them? Or the lowly terrorist who destroyed our ability to advance our civilization the way it deserves?"

Allistair circled Brig once more, stopping next to him and glancing out at the grand view presented to them through the viewport. "Besides, Brigadier. General Rossi and his men should be rounding up the surviving miners within the hour – and they'll be promptly escorted back to the mine where they can toil day and night until that installation is back in operation. So you see, your entire effort was for naught."

"That's what you think. There's no record of who survived – the computer core was blown."

The Bronson Fox doppelganger clapped his hands together in mockery. "Bravo! You've managed to spare a few lives. Good for you. No matter... there are more where they came from."

"So we're agreed then? We tell Steele and let her decide who she believes?" Brig purred.

Allistair patted Brig on the back. "My boy, you won't be doing anything of the sort. And since you've been somewhat less agreeable to paying off your debts by working to repair the damage you inflicted in the mining colony, I suppose a little time alone to think about what you've done should change your attitude."

The sharp snap of his fingertips reverberated across the office. The door to the office slid open as if by silent command, allowing the imposing figure of Commander Greer to enter. Allistair sprouted a wicked grin and pointed at Brig.

"And I've arranged for an old friend of yours to escort you to your new quarters." He rounded his desk as Greer gruffly pulled Brig from his chair and led him to the door. "I'll be sure to give Steele your regards," Allistair cooed.

The door to the small antechamber slid open, Brig flew through the entry, bounced off a nearby table and landed chest-first at the center of the room. He futilely struggled with both arms, his wrists hopelessly bound. Brig lifted his head and surveyed the room - a small entryway with smoked glass lined the far wall. He turned his head to peer back at the door.

"That's no way to treat a family friend. Allistair's not gonna like that at all..." Brig said.

Greer stepped into the room behind him. The door whooshed shut. He cracked his knuckles against his other palm. "Allistair? Don't know 'im..." he said with a growl.

"Sure you do," Brig answered with a brash cockiness. He tried to turn himself over on his back. "He's the crazy son of a bitch we just left."

The mining colony Commander landed a kick to Brig's midsection. Brig expelled a grunt, the sickening crunch of several ribs cracking filling the small room.

"C'mon. Make it... a fair fight... let me outta these cuffs..." Brig winced.

"This ain't about a fair fight, sport. I'm here for retribution."

"You gotta be kiddin'," Brig answered between heavy breaths, levering himself onto one knee.

"Nobody comes down into my mine and gets away with sabotage." Greer fired a heavy fist against Brig's left cheek, making Brig topple onto the floor once more. Before Brig could spin himself over and attempt to get up again, the droning whoosh of a metal pole slicing the air over him preceded it slamming into his left thigh. The hideous snap of his femur splintering charged the air within the small room, followed by Brig's murderous howl. He curled into a fetal position.

Greer, not finished with his punishment, slammed the pole into Brig's ribcage, breaking several other ribs and forcing one of the bone fragments through his skin from an indentation on his side. Brig gasped for air as a heavy stream of blood flowed from the wound.

Brig watched helplessly as his life's blood poured from him. Greer extracted a large knife from his belt and plunged it into the right side of Brig's back above the broken set of ribs. With all of the air left in him, Brig screamed in agony. Greer yanked the knife from his back, drawing yet more scarlet blood from the dying man's body.

His blood pooling into a sticky puddle onto the white tile floor, Brig desperately tried to utilize his one good leg to scramble away from his attacker.

In a killing blow, Greer sent the pole in a perpendicular slant through the back of Brig's midsection, effectively impaling the EW to the floor with a nauseating spray of plasma that speckled the sterile walls of the chamber. An inhuman groan of agony escaped Brig's lips. He attempted to crawl away from his attacker, but quickly realized he was not able to move because of his grievous injury - and the pole still holding him to the cold floor.

Greer grasped Brig with one hand around the front of his neck. Rather than put him out of his misery with another killing move, Greer slid the pole from Brig's torso and shoved the end of a fabric hose into his mouth. With his other hand, Greer activated the hose with a virtual switch above the desk, sending a forceful stream of fluid down Brig's throat.

Brig gagged, desperately trying to breathe through the viscous liquid streaming into his damaged and collapsed lungs, but surrendered any attempt after a few seconds, falling limp.

"Not your lucky day... Sampson was it?" Greer taunted, yanking the hose away, pulling Brig up by the collar and shoving him through a small portal into the windowed pod.

Brig slid across the darkened space beyond.

"See... that gel heals what ails ya'. So in a week, you're gonna be as good as new. And I'll be back then to give ya' another dose of what you got just now. Your own private Hell."

Greer waved his hand over a small panel on the wall. The portal closed with an electronic buzz.

Brig, alone in the dark chamber, lost consciousness.

Earth. Flagstaff, Arizona

The rumbling Jimmy crawled to the unlit intersection. It slid to a halt with a reverberant sonance that ruptured the silent night and sent several homeless street rats scurrying for safer alleyways. Clive's intention had been to have the Reformation transport inconspicuously drop him a hundred meters or so from his workshop. However, that plan had faded with the driver's lack of familiarity with this particular neighborhood of Flagstaff, coupled with his dreariness from having driven all night from just off the Texas border in Clovis.

Clive hopped from the rear of the truck, pounded with one hand the wooden rail that lined the troop bed. The vehicle's air brakes chuffed out a hiss as the driver dropped the accelerator and forced the lumbering behemoth up to speed into the night. Clive covered the lower half of his face with his arm, avoiding the smoky cloud of diesel exhaust left behind by the retro transport.

He strode along the roadside, his prosthesis creating the subtle limp that he had lived with for the past seven years. Upon reaching the rickety wooden fence that demarcated his workshop from the adjacent properties, Clive paused and peered behind him. While not overly concerned with being noticed returning to his humble abode, he did not want anyone - notably Muldoon's thugs - seeing that the Reformation provided his transport.

As he moved forward and away from the edge post, a pair of gloved hands found him – one over his mouth and the other grasping his arm, pulling him into the shadows.

With the precision and finesse of a jungle cat, Clive extracted his Desert Eagle with a free hand. The dark stranger, also dexterous in his own right, swiftly pinned the former EW against the fence arm-first – effectively preventing any defensive moves. The minute amount of illumination from the solitary streetlamp nearby fell onto the stranger's face.

Danil, the stubble-faced Russian, glanced at the Eagle in Clive's hand, then to the man himself. "Quick with the gun, Underwood."

Clive shook free from Danil's grasp, pushing him away with both hands. "Danil! What the Hell!"

Danil held a finger to his lips, raising an eyebrow in the darkness. "You are a dead man..."

"I'm tired of your threats, Chekushkin!" Clive growled. "The best decision you ever made was crawling away from that camp like the cockroach you are. Now why don't you just keep crawling..." Clive pushed past him and stomped towards the road again.

Danil grabbed Clive by the shoulder and spun him back to face the shorter Russian. "I would not go in there if I were you," he advised in a heightened whisper.

Clive ran his fingers across through the short hair at the top of his head. "I'm tired, Danil. I went through a lot back there... but you wouldn't know that because you bugged out before... never mind. I just want to go get a good night's sleep, because I'm sure we're headed out on the road again tomorrow – right?" Clive sighed in exasperation and looked away into the darkness. A light rumble filled the night air – another storm was brewing off on the horizon.

"Muldoon thinks you are dead."

Clive holstered his gun under his jacket. "Why would he think that?"

"Because I told him so."

Clive squinted in suspicion at Danil. "What are you playing at now, Chekushkin?"

"I am not playing at anything, Underwood. You spared my life back there with the Reformation. Now I am repaying that debt by sparing yours." Danil turned away and put his hands to his hips. "Muldoon grows very weary of your delays in finding the... weapons."

"I can string him along for a lot longer if I need to, he thinks he's getting..."

Danil spun back to face Clive and pointed an angry finger. "No longer! He has the weapons you told him of. He has no need for you." Clive's silence told Danil that he had gotten his message across. "So consider us even. You would be wise to stay far away from this place for now. I am certain that Muldoon will have it watched night and day to confirm what I have told him. If you show up... alive... we will both be compromised."

"How do I know you're not playing me again, Danil? Am I just supposed to take you at your word? Do you know how crazy that would make me?" Clive huffed a breath into the cold, night air. A cloud of fog streamed from his lips.

"As I told your soldier friend before," Danil said, poking his finger into Clive's chest, "...if I wanted to turn you in to Muldoon, you would already be captured. Make no mistake." Danil shoved past Clive and stepped towards the road.

Clive glared after him. "So what are you gonna to do?"

Danil paused and looked over his shoulder. "I must keep up all appearances... for Muldoon's sake. Until such a time that he accepts that you are truly... dead. As for you," he turned away and made for a darkened portion of the roadside, "go stay at the cottage with your son. Protect him. War is coming."

Danil disappeared into the night. Clive looked on, unsure of what to do next, and equally unsure of how this latest news from the shifty Russian would alter his plans to find the portal.

24:
Reflections

Mars. Red Colony One

For the first 72 hours of his incarceration, Brig lay immobile in the very spot upon which Commander Greer had thrust him. Blood had seeped from his crusted gray jumpsuit and pooled onto the cold, silica floor. Unable at first to move due to his grave injuries, he curled himself into a fetal ball and faced the darkened barrier that curved to meet the outer glass. Between bouts of unconsciousness, in which he would attempt to push himself up to a sitting position, he realized that the gel forced down his throat by his attacker was the same that Steele had used upon his arrival on Mars. Oddly content that his injuries would soon miraculously heal, he closed his eyes and fell into a dreamless sleep.

Upon his arousal from slumber on the fourth day, Brig propped himself against the inner wall. He probed the side of his ribcage with a pair of fingers, site of the broken bone penetration just days earlier. The bone had retreated into its original location and the wound had sealed itself with a fresh layer of thick skin. Although the pain had all but dissipated, a tingling sensation accompanied the healing gel's powers – as if a small swarm of centipedes had taken up residence beneath his flesh. The sterile odor of the gel still lingered on the stale air around him.

Brig scanned the meager limits of the isolation cell. The inside wall sloped downward on each end to meet the outer glass and the ceiling made a pitched curve to connect with the floor, forming a half-hemisphere overall. While the inner glass wall was opaque, the outer was translucent and offered a dizzying view of the desolation of the Mars plains beyond its containment. He pounded on the glass, despite knowing that even the slightest crack would mean a heinous death in the harsh atmosphere of the Red Planet – it did not give.

He crawled on one knee to the inner partition, testing out the repair of his shattered thighbone and finding little to no indication of the injury. He landed several hard fists onto the glass there as well, but found it to be so thick that it did not offer a reverb from the other side. Brig sat against the inner wall, staring out at the wispy Martian sands that surrounded the outer edges of the colony. The colony itself, however, was not in within the surreal panorama – only the mountains in the short distance provided a break to the flat landscape ahead.

The noiselessness of the chamber provided a slow ticket to insanity, however. Nary a sound penetrated either side of the partitions, inner or outer, and his breath echoed within the hollow room to the point of maddening him.

The sudden whir of a servo motor pulled his attention towards one edge of the chamber. A thin glob of azure paste spurted from a slot high upon the wall and dribbled to the floor. To his chagrin, the odor within the cell changed from the medicinal essence to a pungent organic stench that wrinkled his nose hairs. Brig turned away from the putrid mass of stickiness and glared at his reflection upon the inner glass.

"Probably trying to poison me..." he said, alarming himself at the sound of his own voice within the lonely confines of his cell.

At the end of the first week, Brig's injuries had completely healed. The last effects that he recognized were simply that he had not the capacity within the finite space provided to keep himself limber after so many days off his feet.

Without warning, a burst of electricity surged throughout the chamber, coils of shimmering white and blue webbing themselves across the open space. Unable to avoid the sudden barrage of lightning, Brig's body lifted from the floor and convulsed in a horrifying spasm until the bolts stopped. He fell back to the floor, momentarily paralyzed and emitting several small wisps of smoke from his ragged jumpsuit.

The inner wall slid open. A guard, dressed in security red, stepped up into the pod, his hand grasping the same punishing rod that Greer had used on Brig a week prior. The man grabbed Brig by the collar and tossed him against the outer wall. Before Brig could recover and make it to his feet, the guard swung the rod and connected with Brig's face, sending him sprawling onto the hard surface of the chamber. Brig spat a sticky stream of crimson blood as he tried, with no success, to get to his knees.

The guard was upon him once again, slinging the rod against Brig's back and again breaking several of Brig's ribs. After several additional kicks to Brig's midsection, the guard wiped his brow and exited the chamber.

Brig, barely able to remain conscious, peered at the opening in the wall. The guard reappeared with the familiar hose in his hands and sprayed the medicinal gel onto Brig, shoving him across the floor in a river of goo up against the outside window.

"Commander Greer regrets that he wasn't able to make this week's appointment," the guard grunted in a baritone, guttural Cockney, "but he told me I could do the honors. See ya next week, scum." The guard turned away and the portal closed, leaving Brig in painful silence.

The former EW closed his eyes and lost consciousness.

Over the ensuing few days, Brig had managed to drag himself across the isolation cell and against the inner wall where he could try to blot out the eerie view outside. It had become obvious that Steele had either not known his location, or did not care to find out. In either case, a tinge of guilt edged at him for his harsh attitude towards her in the lift outside of Allistair's office, and the only one who could get word to her was apparently not within earshot of his cries.

As the sun reached its zenith, he huddled against the inner partition in order to hide from its harsh rays that magnified threefold through the outer glass. An odd sensation became suddenly apparent – the inner wall took on the properties of the outer, and began projecting that view within the chamber. Brig squinted at the brutal sunlight thrust upon him from both sides and, unable to block it with his eyelids, buried his head within his arms.

The sensation became much more dizzying at night, when the interior wall became black as the night sky and filled with mercurial dots of starlight. The strange technology that existed within the glass eliminated his own reflection and supplied him with the feeling that he was floating in space. Brig could not escape Allistair's efforts to drive him mad, and his amount of sleep lessened each night going forward. While his physical injuries soon healed again, his tenuous grip on reality faded with each revolution of the planet beneath him.

During one of his many sleepless days, Brig lay on his back staring up at the revolving sky above him, his mouth unconsciously agape with a stream of sticky drool at the corner. His thoughts wandered between various waypoints, from his lonely nights back at his campsite on Earth, to the time spent at the array field with Nadia, and back to the recent events at the mine. Immense regret about the miners that lost their lives in the failed revolt that *he* had germinated held court over his subconscious. He pondered what became of the survivors that had actually made it to safety - the crux of the plan having Darpa register them in the colony citizen database with a forged citizenry date, thereby avoiding tracking by authorities. Whether that happened or not, he was not certain.

"Darpa, can you hear me in here?" he called with a raspy tongue.

As he had anticipated, there was no answer. He sighed heavily, realizing by the minute the sealing of his fate.

"What'd I do to deserve this?" he asked himself aloud.

"What do you ever do, Brig?" a low voice responded from the ether.

With a violent flinch, Brig sprung to a sitting position. From within the shadowy void of the far chamber wall, the thin outline of a man appeared.

"Who's there?"

The voice laughed. "Like you have to even guess?" The man rose to his feet and slowly walked into the dim beam of sunlight streaming through the outer glass.

24: REFLECTIONS

It was Clive.

However, the man that Brig had once called his best friend and partner appeared as he had never witnessed previously. Hideously burned flesh caked the right side of his face and arms. The bloodstained ivory bone of his ribs poked out from beneath his torn and burnt clothing. Wrinkled, red scalp replaced his normally short and coifed hair. His eyelids were melted open.

Brig paused in silent horror. "Cryp? But... *how?*"

"Who else is there when you get your ass into a sling, Stroud? And here you are again."

Clive stopped a meter in front of Brig and shook his head in disgust. He glanced around the small chamber, spying the pile of blue glop against one wall. He knelt, grabbed a handful and stuffed it in his mouth. Clive winced and wiped his chin on his sleeve. "Never gets any better, does it?"

"What *is* that?"

"You mean you don't remember our week in the Bornean rainforest with nothing but a knife and a few tubes of protein paste?"

Brig shot a blank look at him. "That's... food?"

Clive shook his head. "Incredible, Brig. And *you're* the hero..."

"Cryp... how'd you get in here? And what the Hell happened to you?"

Clive walked to Brig and leaned into his face, his hands on his own knees. Brig's eyes widened at the sight of Clive's singed eyeballs staring at him at such close range.

"How'd *you* get here? Isn't that what's more important?" Clive stood upright and glanced out at the Martian landscape. He knocked on the glass with a knuckle. "You must've done something really shitty to end up in a place like this, Stroud."

Clive rotated his head, the charred skin remaining on his neck filling the quiet chamber with a subtle crunch like that of dried leaves. His expression showed that if he had eyebrows he would have raised them. "But let me guess, you went and did it without thinking first... right?"

Brig wagged his head in protest, pointing a finger at his former EW partner in defense. "That's not true, Cryp... those people were in trouble, I..."

"...Had to do it? *It was the right thing?*" Clive interrupted, mocking in Brig's own West Texas twang. "Am I getting close?" He laughed as he shook his head. "Yeah, yeah... no surprise there,

275

Brig. But look where it's gotten you... again." He held a hand out towards the rest of the small chamber.

"You gotta get me out of here..." Brig pled in a soft whisper, his eyes wide with maddened desperation.

Clive snorted and leaned against the glass with his arms crossed. "I *can't* get you out of here."

Brig pushed himself to his feet, grunting as he leaned against the window due to lack of strength. "What? Is this about what happened between us before I left? I'm sorry, man. I just..."

Clive dismissed the apology with a subtle wag of his head. "No. You said what you meant, Brig. I'm just a pathetic cripple blaming the world for my problems."

"Cryp, I didn't mean that... I just didn't recognize the person you had become..." Brig winced through his explanation.

"Didn't you?" Clive paused. He scratched the scorched patch of flesh at his chin for a second while looking out into the alien desolation. He stared at the resulting chunk of dripping meat and then flicked it into the darkness. "Forsaking everything else to save someone I cared about? Not caring who was hurt in the process? Sound familiar?" He stepped towards Brig and glared into his eyes. "Wake up, Stroud. We're two of a kind..."

"I lost just as much as you did when Jess died, Cryp."

"But it wasn't *my* fault, now was it?"

"You should be mad at Muldoon – he's the one that had her killed... not me!" Brig growled with a finger pointed into Clive's face.

"It's a common thread, though, isn't it? You set a plan into motion... innocents get hurt. Over and over... you never learn. Sometimes, Stroud, it's *wrong* to do the right thing."

Brig scrunched his eyebrows in disbelief. "You don't really believe that, do you?"

A crooked smile grew on Clive's charred face. "Oh no? Let's look at your track record." He peered down and pointed at his leg - which Brig had not noticed until now - was missing. "Your sister's dead... and how is the old man and your girlfriend? They doing ok?"

Brig stared at Clive, unable to defend - nor should he have. Had Clive been fabricating untruths, Brig would have laid into his former best friend – but everything out of Clive's mouth was a mounting case against Brig.

"No wait. Did he die of natural causes? No? How about your girl... did she just suddenly have an aneurism pop in her head and drop over? No?"

"That was out of my control, I did what I could."

Clive paced near the outer window. "Always an excuse. That's the way it works with you." Clive stopped and stared into Brig's eyes with a ghostly chill. "You're gonna die here, Brig. You know that, right?"

Brig raised his hands in frustration. "Then help get me out of here!"

"Where would you go? Everyone on this installation knows what you did. You're a criminal, Stroud!"

Brig wagged his head, glared outside and then up at the sky. "Help me get back to Earth."

"You don't belong there either. You've made a lot of enemies, you have to realize that."

"But I have to go *somewhere*... I don't belong *here*. Maybe I can make things right back *there*."

Clive chuckled in derision. "Make it right? There's nothing you can do to make things right, Brig. You just need to learn when to give up."

Brig, in frustration, pounded on the outer glass.

"Make no mistake, Stroud. You're gonna die here. Whether you go back to Earth or not, your fate is sealed. When the life is snuffed from the final colonist on this planet... you'll be right there with them." Clive started to walk away.

"Then help me, Cryp! Help me!" Brig shouted, taking a step in Clive's direction.

As Clive walked into the shadow of the chamber, he pointed at the pile of paste at the other end of the room. "Here's how I'm gonna help you, Brig. Eat up... you're gonna need your strength," he said with a cold emptiness, as he disappeared into the dark.

Brig hobbled forward, but with the help of a stream of the setting sun outside, he realized that Clive was not within the chamber. Brig, alone once again, fell against the inner wall, tears streaming unfettered. He buried his head in his arms.

"On your feet, soldier!" a voice barked from the darkness.

Brig stirred for a moment, lifting his head from the cold composite hardness of the isolation chamber floor.

"I said get up, Brigadier!" the voice boomed.

The confused former EW glared at the inner wall, which had cleared to expose the silhouette of a man standing in partial shadow beyond.

"...Dad?"

"I can't believe you're lying down and taking this, Brigadier. I raised you better than that, son." Devlin Stroud, his once-imposing frame now diminished, leaned one hand on a table next to him.

Brig sat up and cleared the sleep from his eyes. "I suppose this is the conversation *again* where you tell me how disappointed you are?" His father had subjected Brig to the same deprecating diatribe for most of his adult life, as well as his early adolescent years.

The light in the antechamber raised and Brig stared in consternation at his father's abated stature. His chiseled features had fallen gaunt and emaciated, and his broad chest had shrunk, leaving his shoulders slumped at the edges. A large blackened stain caked his faded dress shirt at his breastbone.

"There's no time for that son. The time has passed to argue this point further." Even his voice had weakened - a pallid echo of itself replaced what was once a strong, authoritative force that commanded any room or Presidential press conference.

Devlin's son rose to his feet and stood against the inner wall, gathering in the pitiful sight standing on the opposite side of the glass. "You've been here the whole time? Why didn't anyone tell me?"

"Focus, Brigadier!" Devlin demanded. "Listen to my words!"

"I don't understand!"

"You need to get out of here, Brigadier. You need to leave now!" Devlin leaned harder against the table and breathed several deep gasps.

"I can't, Dad. They have me locked in here... there's no way out!"

"That's always been your problem, Brigadier. You're thinking too small." Brig's father wagged a weak finger at him. "You need to take in the bigger picture. You need to get out of here fast."

"But... how? No one knows I'm in here... except Allistair."

"You'll find a way. I have faith in you, my son." He produced a small handkerchief from his pants pocket and wiped at his brow. "There will be one above and one beside that will aid you when the time comes."

Brig tightened his eyes at his father. "The Hell are you talking about, Dad?"

Devlin raised a hand up to his side and stared at its contents. Within his faint grasp was the set of cipher cards that Brig had carried with him from Earth, several smudges of dark, red blood caked on each. He turned his eyes to Brig and glared with intense rancor.

"What is the meaning of this?" he demanded.

"How did you..." Brig began.

"What's the meaning of this?" Devlin repeated, shaking the cards with pointed determination. However, his voice had morphed up several octaves. A smooth, British inflection painted each word.

"Dad?" Brig pressed himself against the glass, trying desperately to find some way of opening the portal between father and son.

Before his eyes, his father's form contorted. Where the frail form of the elder Stroud had been milliseconds prior, stood Steele Fox. She held the cipher cards within her slender hand, but shook them at Brig all the same.

"Brigadier... I demand to know the meaning of this!" She stabbed her hand to her hip.

"Steele... how did you get in here?" Brig replied, shock and confusion controlling his expression.

"How did you get these cards into my flat? No one is supposed to have access to my private suite!"

Brig shook his head. "I didn't put them there. I left them in my room."

Steele glared at Brig, the bruises that still marked his cheeks and forehead lit by the antechamber's glow. "Good lord, what happened to you?"

"Courtesy of your father's lackeys."

"You look downright dreadful!"

Brig lowered his tone and stared pointedly at her. "Steele... you need to get me out of here."

"Brigadier, do you understand what you have done? I cannot justify freeing you right now!"

"They're torturing me here, Steele!"

Steele crossed her arms and tapped her foot, continuing her skeptical glare. "Honestly..."

"They come in here once a week and beat me almost to death... heal me up, and then repeat the process a week later!" Brig's voice cracked for a second before it regained its deep intonation. "Steele, you *have* to do something!"

Steele kept silent, narrowing her eyes at Brig, as if to see into his mind to determine if he was being truthful.

"You know what happened in the mines?" he asked.

"I know enough to know that you went there and destroyed it."

"Yeah, for the reasons we talked about!"

"The slaves?" she mocked.

"Yeah. The slaves."

"I don't suppose you have any evidence of that?"

Brig pondered for a quick second. "Yeah, I do! Just ask Darpa to see the footage that we captured."

"Darpa? She has no visibility outside of the main colony..." Steele replied, her face warped in confusion.

"Don't worry about that... we arranged something."

Steele cast a skeptical eye at Brig. "Have you told my father about this?"

"Who do you think put me here?" Brig's eyes grew wide.

Steele's arms shot down straight by her side, her face flushed red. "Are you mad? My *father* put you in isolation?"

"Yeah..." Brig replied in a snort. "Dear old Dad is a laugh riot when confronted about his true identity."

The red vanished from Steele's cheeks as quickly as it came, replaced with a pale hue. "My God, Brigadier. What have you done?"

"Exactly what I said I was gonna do – expose him for who he is, and end this madness!" Brig exclaimed with an outstretched finger.

Steele held both sides of her head and mashed her eyes shut.

"But don't take my word for it," Brig continued, "view the data on those cards and watch the video Darpa has for you. Then go talk to your father."

Steele raised her eyes to Brig and listened.

"...And then if you still think I'm crazy and making things up, I'll gladly shut my big mouth, stay put where I'm at... and you can come here each night and tell me bedtime stories for the rest of my miserable life."

She glanced between the cards and Brig without speaking. Then, after several agonizing moments, gripped the cards against her breast and nodded without a word. Steele turned from Brig and moved towards the antechamber door.

"And Steele..." Brig called to her.

Steele stopped and turned.

Brig glowered at the bloody rod standing in the corner of the outside room. "Hurry please."

Tracing his stare to the instrument of his torture, Steele softened her expression, gulped audibly, and fled the antechamber.

25:
Revelations

Mars. Red Colony One

Several days had passed, by Brig's estimation, and given the amount of time he had spent ebbing in and out of sleep, he was unsure of the exact amount. His only certainty lay in the fact that he had not seen Steele in the time since their last encounter, and his doubt had risen substantially whether she could indeed secure his release - or his indefinite incarceration. His disappointment in what he presumed to be the outcome of her pleas to Allistair, the frequent hallucinations from which he suffered on a daily basis, and the impending doom of Commander Greer making another appearance to beat him into near-death submission, left Brig hopeless and bereft of energy.

Brig rolled to one side and glared out at the Martian desert stretching beyond the colony perimeter. The barren landscape that flowed in either direction without end magnified his emotional turmoil. Now, more than ever, the end had truly come.

A brief shadow from above woke him from his stupor, the unseen object from which the shadow projected sailing from horizon to horizon and vanishing as quickly as it appeared.

"Mr. Stroud," a soft voice called from the other end of the inner window.

Brig, eyes still closed, shook his head in frustrated doubt. He was tired of visitors already, and unless it was Steele, he had no interest in talking.

"Brigadier Stroud..." the stranger called again with a smooth British lilt.

Brig raised his head and looked at the reflection cast from behind him onto the outer window. "Who's asking?"

"A friend," the man replied.

The former EW turned in place to look at the inner window. The man, even more youthful than his voice had indicated, stood just on the other side of the portal, within the antechamber beyond. The lighting that did convey through the tinted glass shined upon his bleach blonde mound of hair. His adolescent looking freckles gave him the appearance of being from the Midwest URA - his Trans-Atlantic accent betrayed that sentiment.

"I only have one friend here - and you aren't her," Brig answered.

"I could be one... if you'll give me a chance."

"What good would a friend be to you that's locked up in here?"

"You and I have common interests, I believe."

Brig squinted at the stranger. "Yeah? Like what?"

"Have you ever heard of an organization called the Reformation?"

Brig's snort of incredulity echoed throughout the small isolation pod. "Would it surprise you if I said I did?"

"Not at all. Someone with your military background... I'm certain that you've heard quite a bit about them."

With a painful effort, Brig pushed himself to his feet and hobbled to the inner glass. He focused his steely blues on the stranger, who stood nearly a third of a meter shorter than Brig, with a command red jumpsuit that hung loosely on his slender build.

"Do I know you?" Brig asked suspiciously, attempting to adjust his eyes to the light within the antechamber.

"Apologies... the name is Bryce. Parker Bryce."

Brig scratched at the stubble growth on his chin with one set of fingers, while the other hand strafed the new growth of chestnut hair atop his skull. After a silent moment of thought, he raised his eyes. "Bryce? Any relation to William Bryce?"

The stranger tilted his head at Brig with an interested smile. "He's my father... do you know him?"

"I met him briefly... back on Earth before I came here."

"Excellent. As I anticipated, you *are* familiar."

Brig turned his back on Parker, staggered to the outer window and placed both palms against the glass. He glared at the harsh world outside. "I know enough about them to know that I don't want to get involved."

Parker stared at Brig, his smile still drawn on his face. "Oh come now, Mr. Stroud, we could really use a man of your talents."

"Yeah... heard that sales pitch from your father already, Parker," Brig said over his shoulder. "Told him the same - not interested."

Parker paused and stared down at his feet. "I've seen you with *her*..."

Brig rotated his head slowly to look at Parker, his brow wrinkled.

Parker caught his glare and raised an eyebrow. "We were somewhat of an item you know... until a few months ago."

Not a word came from Brig's mouth, but the clenched jaw and flexing muscles along the ridge of his skull told Parker that he was getting through.

"So you are the famous hero of hers that she went on so much about." Parker let out a disinterested grunt under his breath. "Personally, I don't see what all the fuss was about."

"Funny... I never heard anything about you..." Brig answered with a light growl.

Parker tilted his head at Brig. "But then you weren't here, were you, Mr. Stroud? Yet serendipity has led you back. And almost as if on cue, she terminates my relationship with her. That's what I would call funny... wouldn't you?" His obsidian-eyed gaze lasered through the partition between them, singing Brig's soul with jealous hatred.

"That's none of your business, Bryce. But if you're that concerned about me being the wrong influence on her... you know where the door is." Brig showed his back to Parker once again, his breath steaming from his nostrils like a woken dragon.

"What if I can get you out of this cell?" Parker responded with what seemed a polite laugh.

"I've already had that offer... and had it pointed out to me that I'd have nowhere to run," Brig replied. As he said it, however, the oddity of the realization that it had been a vision and not reality smacked him in the face.

"I'm not talking about Mars, Mr. Stroud," Parker replied, "I'm referring to getting you back to Earth."

Brig leaned back against the glass, his arms crossed. "Another reality explained to me. I don't belong *there*, either."

Parker's tone rose in astonished curiosity. "So you would rather stay here and rot in this cell for the rest of your wretched life than be back on Earth, at home... free?"

"Rotting here... or dying on a dead planet. Same choice if you ask me," Brig droned.

Parker paced the small antechamber beyond the inner glass, tapping a hand on the table next to him. He spun on a heel and made smart eye contact with Brig. "Do you have family back on Earth, Mr. Stroud?"

Brig shook his head, dropping his eye contact for a brief second.

"Are you certain?"

Brig scowled at Parker with a speculative squint. "What're you gettin' at, Bryce?"

"What if I told you that your sister is still alive?"

"I'd tell you that you're playing games, Bryce." Brig's tone deepened, his sudden anger boiling to the surface.

"No games, Mr. Stroud." Parker stared through the glass at Brig, his mouth betraying his glee at the reaction he had generated. "We have... connections in the right places, and I can assure you she is still there. But being held in seclusion by the Syndicate."

Brig pushed himself from the glass and crossed the two-meter floor before the words left Parker's mouth. He poked his finger with viciousness against the inner wall. "You better not be playing me, Bryce. That won't go well for you. Steele dumping you will be the *best* thing that happens."

"Are you a card player, Mr. Stroud?"

"Never have been. I hate games, so take note..."

"Good to know. And you'll be happy to know that my hand is fully on the table." He forced a friendly smile, approached the glass and lowered his voice. "Mr. Stroud, we desperately need someone of your ilk within our ranks."

The sigh from Brig echoed through the antechamber speaker. He rubbed at the back of his neck and glared at Parker. "You guys have weapons?"

"All we could ever need..."

"That so?"

"We have a... benefactor... that supplies us with ample firepower to take on the Syndicate."

"That's a tough group. You sure your group is up to it?"

Parker smiled once again, turned and walked to the sliding door that led back to the colony. "I'll be in touch, Mr. Stroud..." he said in a whisper, and disappeared into the corridor beyond.

Brig sat back down against the inner wall.

25: REVELATIONS

Several moments later

The sound of the inner door sliding back open reverberated within Brig's small cell – Parker had obviously left the intercom open before he left. Brig opened his eyes and peered up at the outer glass, where the contrast of the twilight sky allowed the reflection from behind him to project forward.

The backlit silhouette of a man filled the glass, the tuft of platinum hair at the top of his head glowed in the antechamber lighting.

Brig swayed his head in dismissal. "Forget something, Parker?"

Buzzing flooded the open microphone of the intercom, but no sounds from the other side of the glass came forth. Brig leaned forward and glanced back at the room. The man stood at the opposite end of the antechamber, his muscular arms coiled across his beefy chest. Brig pushed himself to his feet and leaned into the glass to see the man's face, to no avail.

"Parker?" Brig called, but the figure did not respond. "Who are you?"

The man chuckled, before pivoting on one heel and striding from the room.

Steele stormed into Allistair's office, her brunette locks sailing behind her head, her boot heels clunking with weighty determination. She approached his desk with the ferocity of a stalking lion.

"Where's Brigadier, father?" she demanded.

"Why, Steele, I didn't hear you enter..." Allistair mocked, spinning in his translucent chair to face Steele.

"Father..." Steele growled.

"Well, I'm sorry, dear. Was it my turn to keep track of him?"

Steele's face flushed with anger. "You know what I'm referring to..."

"Then you know what he did?" Allistair answered with an indignant air.

"Yes... I do," she replied, albeit with a hesitant gait.

"Then you know he was acting like a common terrorist down there, destroying my... *our* hard work!" He rose from his chair and strode around the edge of the desk, stopping in front of a holo-display projecting from the side wall. "It will take us months to fix what he has damaged!"

"So... Where. Is. He?" Steele tightened her lips into a straight line.

"Where else, my dear? He's back at the scene of the crime, helping rebuild what he so callously demolished."

Steele glared in anger.

Allistair busied himself with the hologram, and after a few moments of silence from Steele, lifted his eyes to her. "I'm certain that once he's done, he'll make his way back to you, Steele."

"Father..." she admonished.

"And if not, maybe he is not the type of man you should be associating with, darling."

"Damn it, father! That's not *your* concern, I..."

"Respect, Steele!" Allistair bellowed, to which Steele shrunk backward a step. "You will not speak to me in that tone."

"Sorry... father," she replied with a proper British politeness, and then bared her fangs. "And I know that Brigadier is in isolation..."

Allistair glared at Steele with an incredulous smirk. "What was I to do, Steele?" he relented with a sigh. "The man single-handedly set this colony back years. General Rossi and I both agreed that he is a threat as long as he is free. As the Prefect of this installation, I had to make an example of him. He needs to sit and think about what he's done before he's able to become a productive member of this colony."

"He was only doing what he perceived to be right, father."

"So now you are taking his side against mine, are you? Your own father..."

Steele stood in defiance, her arms braided across her chest.

"Steele Primrose! I'm disappointed in you. You are letting your... interest... in this man override your rationality." He brushed past her and sat at his desk, his back to her.

"When will he be able to leave that dreadful place? It's not humane, father."

"That... is entirely up to him, Steele."

"But..." she pled.

"This discussion is over, Steele. Now if you don't mind, I have work to do. As always, it's been a pleasure."

Steele wrinkled her nose in distaste, pirouetted and marched from the office. As the door slid closed behind her with a mechanical whir, she stopped in the hallway and tapped at her chin with a finger. Her other hand absentmindedly extracted the cipher cards from her pocket. She stared at them for a silent moment.

"Darpa, can you read these cards?" she said, an eye towards the ceiling.

"I already have, Dr. Fox," Darpa's voice resounded in her local airspace. "The decrypted data is ready for your viewing. Along with footage from Brigadier's time in the mining colony."

Steele stayed silent for a moment, tapping one of the cards against her cheek. "Queue up the data in my flat, Darpa. I'm on my way there now."

"Very well, Dr. Fox," the AI replied.

R. JAMES STEVENS

26:
Flight

Mars. Red Colony One

The following evening, Brig leaned against the inner wall of his solitary confinement and gazed mindlessly out at the night landscape of Mars. Phobos and Deimos, hanging high upon their stellar canvas, winked at him through a pair of dull pinhead lights in the ebony sky. With an unconscious rhythm, he thumped his back against the inner glass partition. The echo of his chest banging the window resounded throughout the cramped chamber in harmony with his labored exhales. Brig had become so accustomed to the level of silence, however, that both seemed white noise to him.

A vertical rectangle of light appeared on the glass in front of him, within it the backlit outline of a slender woman, her wavy hair flowing down past her shoulders. She held her chin low against her chest.

Brig sprung to his knees and spun to greet his childhood friend. She lifted her gaze slowly to meet his. He recoiled internally at the sight of her, and then placed his hands on the glass between them.

"What's wrong?"

Steele sobbed uncontrollably, her shoulders heaving upward with each intake of breath. Her mascara, normally applied neatly above her emerald eyes, bled from the lower edges of her eyelids and stained dark trails across her alabaster cheeks.

"I'm so sorry…" she wept.

"What happened, sweetheart? Talk to me…"

"I went to see my fath… Allistair. It's true, Brigadier… it's true. I'm sorry I ever doubted you." Steele swept a sleeve of her lab coat across a cheek, leaving a streak of soppy, black makeup on her arm.

Brig tightened his lips. Now was not the time for him to gloat, and he knew it. "I'm sorry you had to find out this way." He paused to find the right words. "Did he admit to everything?"

She lowered her head once more. "He didn't admit to anything."

"Then how…"

"I read the cards..." she answered, raising her head to look upon Brig. Her eyes glassed up again; a fresh stream of tears welled and trickled away. "I can't believe I didn't see it. I can't believe what a fool I've been all these years..."

He pointed angrily towards the hallway. "It's not your fault, Steele. That son of a bitch is the one that did all of this to you!"

Her breathing hastened. Steele held her hand to her mouth and forced her eyes closed. "We could have saved all of those people back on Earth. So many died and didn't have to..." Her voice trailed off as she finished her thought.

"Steele, you can't blame yourself for this!"

"And Nadia... I'm so sorry, Brigadier." She met Brig's sympathetic gaze and rasped a fluid breath; her eyes drooped. "That wasn't fair for either of you, and I feel so horrible for what she went through. That poor girl..."

"Steele... listen to me," Brig said emphatically. "You need to get me out of here... now!"

Steele nodded, but before she could act, the portal between them drifted open. Brig scrambled to his feet and dove out of the chamber, landing on his feet next to Steele.

"You saved my life..."

"I... I didn't do that," she replied with an air of mystified confusion. "I don't have the authority to open that cell."

"Then who..."

The answer came in the form of the antechamber door opening. Within the frame stood Parker Bryce, his thin arms folded across his slight chest. Brig nodded in sudden understanding.

"Parker? You did this?" Steele asked.

"You know this guy?" Brig put his hands to his hips and glared between Steele and Parker.

"No time to waste, Mr. Stroud. I've offered a diversion to the security in the area. You need to go... now," Parker instructed.

"Where am I going?" Brig replied.

"To the launch portal..." said Parker.

Both Steele and Brig simultaneously turned to Parker. "Launch portal?"

"Yes... there's a space elevator located in the auxiliary storage facility..."

"Yes, I know about the elevator. But I wasn't aware there was an outgoing portal in operation here," Steele said, wagging her wiry fingers at Parker.

"The portal is outside of Mars orbit on the opposite side of the planet. A launch vehicle is in areocentric elliptical orbit and passes at its low point every forty hours, at which time it intersects with the elevator."

Brig frowned and looked to Steele to see if she had comprehended Parker's explanation.

Parker raised an amused eyebrow at Brig's apparent confusion. "The elevator is essentially a tether on which we can ferry cargo to orbit, where it docks with the launch vehicle at certain intervals. From there, the launch vehicle makes its way to the portal and sends its payload through to a receiver back near Earth."

Brig pondered the information for a moment. "So you're sending me back to Earth in a box?"

"Not quite," Parker replied. "While the cargo vessels are designed to withstand reentry into Earth's atmosphere, it is not fit for live human transportation. The launch vehicle, conversely, is technically a smaller shuttle with a large payload bay. We're simply modifying its parameters so that it releases from its orbit and goes through the portal instead of the payload." He stopped for a second to ensure that Brig was grasping the information. "I presume you have some sort of piloting experience?"

"Not much, no..." Brig answered.

Parker let out a muffled 'hrmph' under his breath and raised another eyebrow. "No worries, the shuttle will be on autopilot most of the way anyway. You'll just need to handle a few reentry adjustments..."

"I thought my options were to rot here or die on a dead planet... I don't remember burning up in Earth's atmosphere being one of them," Brig said with singing sarcasm.

"I lived up to *my* end of the bargain, Stroud. I arranged for you to be released from your little playpen," Parker said, eyes squinted. "It's time you did the same..."

Brig nodded, *his* word always having meant so much to him.

"Your first trip will be as a stowaway on the cargo container sent up via the elevator. A set of throwaway thrusters will accelerate the container once you reach orbital height and match the speed of the incoming shuttle."

Brig stared at him silently, trying to hide the minute amount of trepidation growing in his eyes.

"Once the shuttle docks with the cargo unit, you will have exactly two minutes to make it into the airlock of the vehicle. Understood?"

Brig nodded again.

"Good. Dr. Fox, load these instructions into the computer of your biosuit," Parker added, and handed Steele a small, translucent chip. "And then into the ship's navicomputer. They contain all of the necessary corrections to allow the ship to break its orbit and dive into the portal."

Brig and Steele exchanged a reluctant glance.

"And now, since Dr. Fox knows the location of the elevator, I must be getting back to my post." Parker gave a defensive scan towards each end of the corridor.

"You're not coming with me, Bryce?" Brig asked.

"I cannot, Mr. Stroud. I need to keep up my appearance of being a respected member of the Prefect's team. You, on the other hand, must go forth and cement your place in history. Godspeed, Brigadier Stroud."

Brig grabbed Parker's hand and offered a half-hearted, but friendly, shake. "Thank you, Parker. And... you're just like your father. A very brave man."

"Kind words, Mr. Stroud. But I have a ways to go to live up to my father's grand legacy."

Brig narrowed his eyes at what he perceived to be a hint of sarcasm in Parker's observation, but then dismissed it as leftover snarkiness from his comments about Steele. "You won't regret this, Parker. Go, get out of here before someone connects the dots."

Parker stepped backward, glanced between the pair and bobbed his head with respect. He broke eye contact and then strode away down an intersecting hallway out of sight.

Brig faced Steele. "Now where is this space elevator thing?"

"Follow me, and for goodness sakes, don't get sidetracked!" she said with a wink.

Fifteen minutes later

The light echo of two pairs of padded boots, plodding the polished corridors of Red Colony One with desperate swiftness, broke the sterile silence normally found on the far side of the power core. Brig, following closely behind Steele, slowed as she stopped in front of a set of large, twin doors.

"This is the primary storage facility. Over there," Steele pointed at a smaller door farther down the hallway, "is the entryway to the auxiliary one. There is a corridor about two hundred meters in length, at the end of which lies the space elevator base."

An alarm claxon split the air in the distance, down one of the halls that led to the main colony.

Brig glanced over his shoulder, and then grasped Steele lovingly by the shoulders. "Thank you for believing in me, sweetheart. You've gotta go now."

Steele raised an eyebrow and grabbed Brig's hands. "I'm going with you," she said, deadpan.

"No... no you're not. You're staying here. Your life is here, Steele. You'd be throwing it all away by leaving with me."

"I don't belong here anymore than you do, Brigadier. I throw my life away moment by moment, every minute I spend with that... monster," she argued through teeth gritted.

Brig emitted a heavy sigh, pursed his lips together, looking back at the hallway where the sound of the alarm continued to flow.

"Brigadier..." said Steele, turning his face towards hers with a soft hand, "...I can be that girl, if that's what it takes for us to be together."

He frowned. "I don't want you to be... *her*."

A tear rolled down her cheek. She stared with a longing into his Terran sky blue eyes. "But I have my memory back. Things will be different back there... on Earth. I know it..."

He pushed a gentle finger across her lips. "You'll always be my Steele... and that's all I could ever ask for." He pressed his lips to her forehead.

Steele embraced him with her head against his chest; Brig reciprocated by wrapping his arms around her. After a pensive moment, he nudged her to arms length and stared into her eyes again.

"Time to go..." he said with a coy smile. He grabbed her hand and sprinted through the single door.

Having traversed the thin corridor without incident, the pair arrived at the entry to the auxiliary storage facility. Steele quietly pushed open the metal door and stepped in, Brig in close tow.

In the center of the massive room lay a large, octagonal platform. A square container filled most of the platform, its carbon-encrusted outer shell gleaming with a dull matte in the bluish lighting of the facility. An appendage resembling a silvery rope jutted from the top center of the container and disappeared through the seams of a giant hatch 30 meters above.

Steele tugged on the sleeve of Brig's jumpsuit, drawing his attention to a compartment just off the main entrance. Within, a set of two biosuits hung neatly, the gray-blue sheen of the shoulder-to-toe Broxium armor reflecting the room's blue aura. While the design held mobility in mind, it was obvious that they could protect their wearer from more than just harsh environments. She touched a control next to the rack; the clear casing around the compartment clicked and lifted away.

As she reached for the release lever that would have brought the suits down to them, a gruff voice rang out from behind.

"Hey! What are you doing here?"

Both Steele and Brig turned - a technician, dressed in an emerald jumpsuit, stood in an authoritative stance behind them. He pointed one hand at them, the other at his waist, where he presumably had some sort of weapon. He glared at Brig, ogling his miner jumpsuit, stained with blood along its midsection and sporting several fabric tears along his arms and chest.

Brig and Steele glanced at each other with alarm.

"You're not allowed in here, now what do you think... oh, Dr. Fox. I'm sorry," the man said, his voice cracking from embarrassment. "I didn't recognize you. Can I... help you?"

Steele darted her eyes to the man's credential tag hanging from his chest pocket. "Castle, is it?"

The man nodded.

"We need to... borrow these suits," she continued. "An experiment that I'm conducting with my colleague here." She held out a nervous hand towards Brig.

Castle glared at Brig once more, his skepticism glowing in his expression. "I wasn't told of any experiment, ma'am. No offense... but maybe I should speak to someone in the Prefect's office before..." He tapped at his wrist computer.

Steele stepped forward, placed a gentle hand on Castle's shoulder, pulling his hand from the computer and turning him away from Brig. "In case you've forgotten," she said in a matter-of-fact lower tone, "the Prefect *is* my father..."

A loud thump sounded from behind Castle. He fell to the floor in a heap. Steele, shocked, turned to face Brig, who stood behind the unconscious technician with a broken piece of wooden palette raised over his shoulder.

"Brigadier!" she scolded. "Was that necessary?"

"Absolutely. They already know I'm out," he answered, pointing back at the corridor. "How long til they figure out I've come *here?*"

"Too late for that, *terrorist...*"

Brig and Steele spun to face the familiar Aussie voice behind them. It was Greer, a small pulse pistol gripped in his hand.

"I told you, Sampson," Greer growled through bared teeth, "you can't get away from me."

Steele stepped in front of Brig, her arms spread wide. "You'll have to go through me first..."

Greer snickered, his malicious intent clear. "Don't think I won't do it, girl. But don't be stupid and waste your life on this scum."

"He's more man than you could ever hope to be." Her coolness made Brig grin.

The Commander raised the pistol once again, his aim sharp at Steele's midsection.

"You're gonna kill the Prefect's daughter?" Brig taunted. "I think he'll have a problem with that. Might even make *you* a new miner..." He gripped Steele's lower back, ready to push her to safety should Greer prove to be truly insane.

Greer blinked nervously and lowered the pistol a fraction of a centimeter.

With just enough of a seed of doubt in the Commander's eyes, Brig sprung into action. He deftly swiped at the lever next to the suit cabinet, sending the heavy armor down onto a surprised Greer. The Commander tumbled to the floor - his pistol discharged, sending a blinding white bolt errantly into the control panel, destroying it in a shower of brilliant sparks. The pistol ejected from his hand and skittered safely away next to a wooden crate.

Brig pounced and landed atop the man, forcing his forearm into Greer's throat. Greer agilely tossed Brig away like a soft beanbag, pushing him backward, where he crashed into a metal tool chest with a deafening clang. Greer leapt from the ground, fitting his hands around Brig's flexed neck. Brig, his arms still free, launched an uppercut into the bottom of Greer's ribcage. Greer refused to relent, gripping the EW's throat tighter with each passing second.

Brig's face flushed purple as he fought for precious air. He lifted Greer from the ground with a pair of solid knees to the Commander's groin, but still the man refused to release his crushing grip. Brig rasped for breath, his muscles burning from lack of oxygen. Reaching for a reserve of strength he was surprised he still had, Brig spiked his boot into Greer's chest. Greer launched backward at the sudden force and fell into the sparking control panel. His body convulsed with the electrical juice that poured through him, sending rivulets of thick blood-tinged drool from his gaping mouth. The safety dampener kicked in; Greer's lifeless corpse released and drooped to the floor, a thin trail of smoke spiraling from the back of his singed skull.

An hour later

Brig and Steele sat nestled within the cargo unit, waiting in quietus as the container lifted itself along the tether using a set of mechanical winches located at the center of the box. The low lighting provided by the internal emergency beacons gleamed across the skin of their armored biosuits. A pair of blue LEDs mounted within their clear facemasks cast a ghostly light across their solemn faces. An array of twinkling green indicators blinked in unison from their wristbands, indicating that the suits were indeed producing copious levels of life-sustaining oxygen.

Brig glanced at Steele, whom nervously closed her eyes in an attempt to control her breathing. "Have much experience going through these portals?"

She opened her eyes, but just stared forward. "The portal is the least of my worries." Her voice quivered. "Landing that ship is what concerns me... especially since neither of us is a spaceship pilot."

The light mechanical clunking that they had been accustomed to over the past hour ceased. The subtle pressure of thrusters shook the floor of the container - the unit separated from the tether and briefly experienced the void of space. A few seconds later, a stronger group of thrusts fired from beneath, and the container accelerated laterally.

"Well... this is it," Brig announced.

Steele closed her eyes again and inhaled.

R. JAMES STEVENS

27:
Apogee

Mars Orbit

Sweat beaded upon Brig's forehead; the helmet's internal filters quickly slurped away the moisture. Brig's stomach churned with uncomfortable nausea after only a few short minutes of floating in the emptiness of space above Mars. He peered across the dark cargo container, where Steele sat motionless against the intersecting wall two meters away. She stared with an emotionless glaze at the sliver of a window in the center of the wall, watching for any sign of the anticipated shuttle arrival.

A small series of silent bumps on the outside skin of the container rattled them to coherence. They glanced at each other with an apprehensive, shared thought.

It was time to leave.

Brig's EW training instinctively activated - he motioned with a hand for them to get up and exit. The hatch opened under a powerful twist of the release lever from the former EW, where it met the outer hull of the container without sound.

Brig poked his helmet out of the port. To his surprise, and relief, the container had successfully docked within the payload bay of the small shuttle. To his left, Mars floated like an ominous red marble beneath them, its crimson sands contrasting with the obsidian of space around it. He involuntarily inhaled with a gasp. Brig gawked for a silent moment, absorbing the amazing and surreal view.

Steele tugged at the back of his arm. "Two minutes?" Her voice provided a tinny echo in his helmet intercom.

Brig, shaken awake again, nodded and stepped out into the payload bay, Steele in tow. His eyes gravitated to the air lock, some fifteen meters away. He pointed at it for Steele's benefit. She nodded her acknowledgement and gave a thumbs-up.

He promptly realized his inexperience in zero gravity. He pushed off from the lip of the cargo doorframe, caught the armor of the biosuit on a nearby conduit and sailed into the emptiness of the payload bay. As he flailed his arms, he bounced against the far wall a few meters from the airlock entry. Managing at the last second to grab another conduit along the wall, he stopped his tumble and crawled like a frightened spider towards the airlock door.

His intercom crackled to life. "Brigadier... are you ok?"

He rotated his head within his helmet to peer at the cargo container. A familiar, searing sensation ignited at the base of his skull. Certain that his Clarity episodes were behind him, he forced his eyes shut, insisting instead on maintaining his grip with reality. The globs of sweat reappeared along his forehead, once again soaked up by the helmet filters.

Brig gripped the conduit, his arm shaking as the strength flowed from his body. A commando technique that had saved his life numerous times before, he began to regulate his heartbeat. The world around him gradually revolved back into focus; his shallow breathing reverberated within his headpiece. The angelic voice of Steele on the static-filled intercom faded back into his conscious.

He opened his eyes, clenched his jaw and turned his armored body to look across the payload bay at the cargo container. Steele, standing at the edge of the doorway, held the frame with both armored hands and stared at him, wild-eyed. His mind replayed the cipher card data where he learned of Steele's involvement in the Clarity Protocol.

A conversation for another time.

"Lesson learned... always hold on," he said, breathing heavily into his helmet mike.

The burnt orange reflection from the planet's surface lit her pale face. She nodded and peered nervously at her surroundings.

"Grab the conduit parallel on the wall to your right and then push off. But Steele..." he instructed.

She glanced up at him.

"Don't. Let. Go."

Steele blinked her eyes in a rapid strobe, taking a shuddering breath before grasping at the thin pipe a meter from the doorway. As she launched from the doorframe with a push of her foot, her hand missed its mark. She tumbled out into the payload bay with arms thrashing like a drowning child. Like Brig before her, she floated out of control across the payload bay. Unlike him, however, she panicked and failed to focus on what would save her life.

Her cries raised bumps on Brig's neck, playing like shards of glass to his ears through his helmet speaker. His eyes widened at the expression of terror on her face with each revolution of her body. Just as she was about to exit the cargo bay and into the void of space beyond, Brig plucked her from Death's embrace, pulling her up against the wall next to him.

"Oh my God, oh my God..." she cried. Her face shield filled with a cloudy condensation, and then cleared as the filters performed their task.

Brig tugged her next to him and wrapped her other hand onto one of the conduit pieces. He forced eye contact with her, instantly calming her panic and bringing her back to the moment.

She hugged the wall of the payload bay - her breathing, still rapid, roaring in Brig's helmet. Brig grabbed at the airlock door wheel, but his armored gloves failed to turn it after a few tugs. He wedged a shielded boot into a nearby handrail and applied an extra amount of force, to no avail.

Steele, watching from behind Brig, glared at her wrist computer. "Less than thirty seconds, Brigadier!" she called with a frantic shrill through the intercom.

Brig, already aware of the tight budget of time, slammed the armor along his appendages against the wheel several times. He yanked at the stuck control once again. It slowly broke loose and began to roll. After a few forceful revolutions, he pulled at the wheel - the door swung open to reveal the darkened airlock.

He gripped Steele's arm and dexterously flung her past him and into the airlock, following close behind once she landed inside. Brig slammed the door closed.

Not three seconds later, a blast of rocket thrust ignited like silent lightning from the payload bay behind them. From the small portal next to the door, they watched the cargo container eject into space towards the oncoming portal.

Brig looked to Steele. On her knees and leaning against a padded wall next to her, she glared at him with a look of equal shock.

"Guess that's why he said two minutes then..." Brig said, already working the release on the inner airlock door.

Moments later

Brig funneled himself through the narrow cockpit opening, his biosuit armor clanking clumsily against the tight bounds of the tiny compartment. As he fit himself into the pilot's chair, Steele followed suit, she occupying the navigator's spot to his right.

The cockpit, unlike the closed-in feel of a late 20th century shuttle, had the appearance of the control suite of a fighter pilot. A translucent, angular shield rose over the cramped quarters from just over the control panel back to the rear of the cockpit. While somewhat dizzying, it offered a near-360 degree view of space around them.

The amazing view of the bluish-white sun rising on the far end of Mars filled their viewport.

"So what's the plan... once we land?" Steele had regained her composure.

"The only thing that I care about right now - rescuing my sister."

"Your sister? But I thought she was... she's alive?"

"So says Parker..." Brig tilted his head within his helmet to gauge her reaction. "Does he have any reason to lie to me?"

Steele stared blankly past him and shook her head, almost as if convincing herself. "What can I do to help?"

Brig fell silent for a moment, gazing out at the stellar wonder before them. "Keep me from killing the bastard that's got her..." he answered, his voice just above a whisper.

A few reticent moments passed, both of them once again gawking at the incredible sunrise over Mars.

"This isn't going to be easy... is it?" Her smooth voice echoed a distant resonance.

"It's gonna be nothing short of a war," Brig replied. "What does Parker need us to do with this heap?"

Steele, already busy typing on her wrist computer with one padded finger, nodded her head while she completed one last sequence. "Trajectory adjustment patterns downloaded into the ship's navicomputer." She peered up at him and offered a meek smile. "The computer will handle the rest from here."

Brig pointed ahead. "Portal coming up."

An octagonal ring appeared in the darkness of space, approaching on an arc as they traversed the elliptical orbit of the shuttle. In front of them, now several kilometers away, the cargo container in which they had ridden the space elevator, glided along their same trajectory. Brig and Steele watched in nervous curiosity as it edged closer to the center-less structure. Suddenly, the container shimmered with a bright light, disappearing through the ring.

The sound of Brig gulping sounded over his helmet mike. Steele smiled at him. He grasped her hand.

Mars. Red Colony One

The door to Allistair's office suite slid open. General Rossi strode in, stopping in front of the Prefect's desk.

"Prefect..." he barked, his padded boots clicking together at the heels.

"General," Allistair responded without turning his chair to face him. The Prefect occupied himself with a holochart that hovered above his desk workstation.

"Sir, we've got a report from a technician at the elevator base. And we've confirmed it – we've tracked Stroud's movements to the portal delivery vehicle."

"Mmm, yes. Interesting," Allistair answered with mock enthusiasm.

"I can easily override the ship's navicomputer and have it brought back, I just need your authorization, sir."

Allistair perched his fingers under his chin and stared out the massive window that lined the back wall of his office. He fell silent.

"Sir?" Rossi interjected, his raised tone indicating his growing impatience.

Allistair raised a hand beside him. "No, that won't be necessary, General."

"But, sir. He's an escaped prisoner..."

"And just where do you think he's able to go, General?" Allistair answered, spinning in his chair to face the lanky man.

"Earth... sir."

The Prefect offered a chuckle and a dismissive wave of a hand. "Let him go to Earth, General. In fact, Stroud can serve us better on Earth than he ever could here. And you have to give it to him, he's a very resourceful man. I've underestimated him..."

"And... what of your daughter?" Rossi's voice flowed with a curious menace.

"Thank you for your concern of my daughter, General. But she will make her way back to me. Mark my words."

"But, sir..."

"Will that be all, General?"

Rossi inhaled deeply and tightened his lips into a vicious, downward arc. He performed a respectful nod to his Prefect and spun on a heel.

As the door slid shut behind him, Rossi typed a set of commands into his wrist computer.

"Remote command sequence completed, General," a soothing female voice announced in his hidden earpiece.

He swiped at the computer to silence it. "Old fool..." he grumbled under his breath, and then strode away.

28:
Burn

The blackness swirled about them in an infinite, invisible vortex. Sound within the small cockpit fell to less than zero, a distant blank void on a secluded island at the edge of their conscious minds. The tinny echo of their hollow breathing rattled within their helmets. The fine interior edges of the ship bled off themselves like liquid metal, alternating between fluid and vapor, before bouncing back with elasticity into cohesion.

Unable to focus, Brig shrunk into his biosuit, his eyes rolling around his head at the surreality of the unfamiliar world around him. His recall failed to produce a reality with which he could identify.

Brig pressed his hands against the sides of his helmet. *I need to... get this thing off!*

The helmet refused to detach from the armored biosuit. A hand pulled his away from its task. With a heavy motion, he rotated his head. Steele held her hand atop his. Her confused facial visage confirmed that she, too, was struggling with their current reality.

Her image blurred in and out of focus, as if a classic tube television losing sync with its signal. She kissed one of her armored gloves and clumsily pressed several fingers against his face shield. A solitary tear perched upon her cheek. Her expression, one of fearful joy, glowed within the eerie blue light of her helmet.

In the distance ahead of them, from out of the blackness, a ring ablaze with blue flame coiled its way towards them. Ghost trails drifted behind it as it moved in a zigzag pattern within the black canvas. As each second passed, the ring swelled, its light bathing the cockpit in a deathly cerulean glow.

Suddenly, the cockpit shrouded itself in immense gloom. Brig struggled to lift his arms, to find Steele in the pitch, but they would not respond to his commands.

"Steele!" he called, but no sound emerged from his lips.

His body, as if it he had left it behind, numbed. A grand weight lifted from his being. Brig lowered his eyelids and drifted from consciousness.

A tinny voice in the distance waded into the stunning silence. Growing louder in small increments, its clarity expanded. The weighty blackness around them lifted like a soft veil, replaced by a blurry, LED hue.

Brig felt a tug at his biosuit. The torso of the armored exoskeleton shifted.

"Brigadier... are you still with me?" Steele called frantically, waving the slender, armored fingers of her gloves in front of his face shield.

Brig blinked to clear his vision. He shook off the film that had encapsulated his brain. He grabbed at her hand and pulled it close to him, taking a deep breath and exhaling. A thin fog clouded the face shield of his helmet, and then dissipated with an assist from the filters.

Brig furrowed his brow in confusion. "What... happened?"

"We passed through the other end of the portal. Seems we're in one piece," she replied.

"Thought we passed somewhere else for a little while there..."

She gazed at him, her excited smile jumping from her lips. "We're going home."

An hour later

The blue marble known as Earth made its appearance against the deep slate, a semi-circle of oceans and clouds basking in the very solar light that once upon a time took its modern, technological life.

As the shuttle drifted through the silent void towards a warmer place, a feeling of intense nervous euphoria washed over Brig. The bright, blue orb centered itself in their view. He and Steele gazed forward in awe at their former home.

"You never know how much you miss it until you've been gone..." she observed, her eyes moist with emotion.

Brig pondered the finality of it all: what lay waiting for him once they land, who would be looking for him, and mostly – how he would go about rescuing his sister from the clutches of the Syndicate. There was a time when he could count on Clive to lend a hand, or least a sympathetic ear, to his cause. But it went up in smoke the day that Bruno Muldoon decided murdering his own wife - Brig's sister - was the better bargain than letting her leave with Clive.

28: BURN

"...And according to Parker's notes," Steele said, apparently having been talking while Brig contemplated his immediate future, "we should be reaching the outer layer of Earth's atmosphere in about four hours... Brigadier?"

Brig awoke from his trance and faced her. He nodded.

Steele shook her head and tapped at the console to dismiss a data screen.

"So..." said Brig, looking out at the blackness of space around them, "...you and Parker..."

"Me and Parker... what?"

"It's okay. I know about it. What did Parker say - you were an item."

Steele hushed her breathing and bit her lip.

"What exactly happened there?" Brig continued to avoid eye contact, as did she.

"We weren't compatible..."

"Compatible? Is that some fancy way of saying somethin' better came along?" Brig squinted at Steele through his face shield.

"What are you getting at?" Steele's tone became defensive.

"Just saying that you two were fine, then I show up and you dump him like yesterday's trash..."

Steele clicked her tongue against her teeth. "Not everything is about you, Brigadier."

"Fair enough. But don't you think it's odd that he's gone so far out of his way to get me off planet?"

"That's his version."

Brig chuckled and tapped his armored glove against the console.

"Since we're being truthful, what exactly was the bargain that you two worked out?"

Brig's face straightened, the subtle smirk fading in the pale blue LED light of his mask. "He wants me to help the Reformation."

"The Reformation? You can't be serious. And you accepted?"

"He gave me some additional... incentive... to accept the deal."

"Your sister..."

"I could care less about the Reformation," Brig added. "But if I have to use that as a chance to get her back safely..."

Steele nodded.

"Sure could use Clarity right about now..." he said with a vocal distance.

"What did you say?" She scrunched her brow.

"Nothing..."

Over the next few moments, their bulky biosuits provided slightly less comfort than the awkward silence in which Brig and Steele found themselves mired.

"Brigadier, I have a confession..."

Here we go.

"I... deactivated D42-19 sub 14 ... Clarity... because I was aware of the potential side effects."

Brig steeled his jaw.

"I'm sorry, I should have been forthright with you as soon as I did it... and perhaps consulted you first. I hope you can forgive me."

He snapped his head within his helmet to glare at her. "Are you serious? That's your confession?"

Taken aback, she raised both eyebrows in surprise. "What do you want me to say, Brigadier? I apologized. Isn't that enough?"

"How about... you're sorry for creating it in the first place?"

"But... I didn't..."

He held up a hand. "Don't even, Steele. This one had your name all over it. You read the data. Are you honestly gonna' sit there and lie to me about it?"

Her face flushed pale. "What are you implying?"

"That you and your father... or Allistair... or whoever it was at the time... knew what you were doing, but were too caught up in it to pull the plug!"

"How dare you accuse me of..." she shrieked, the shrillness of her voice reaching a new level over his helmet intercom.

"Do you know the Hell that we all went through with that crap? Do you know how many people died... took their own lives... took others' lives? Do you care?"

"Of course I care!" she screamed through her tears, her cry echoing as if in a tin can. She sobbed, but Brig persisted in his relentless attack.

"Then why didn't you do something?" he bellowed.

"You know my past so well, Brigadier... you tell me!" she yelped. "Why did you even bring it up?" Steele wrenched the upper torso of her biosuit away from Brig.

Brig sighed in frustration and hammered his fist against the side panel. "This is gonna' be a long trip. A really long one..." he muttered, glaring into the void around them.

Several hours later

The uneasy stillness continued to loom over the cockpit of the small shuttle like a damp cumulonimbus. Brig tinkered with several controls at the console laid out before him, trying unsuccessfully to put aside his long-buried animosity towards Steele. She, likewise, busied herself by skimming through rows of data presented to her by the ship's navicomputer. Every now and then, they would steal a peek at the other, only to turn away when chance would have them locking gazes.

A light chime accompanied a flashing LED at the center of the console, soaking the small cabin in a sparkling amber glow. A fifteen centimeter, distorted hologram of Parker Bryce leapt upon the panel between Brig and Steele.

"Congratulations on making it through the portal. Now comes the trickier part of your journey. In a few moments, you must perform braking and positional maneuvers so that the ship can make it through Earth's atmosphere properly. The ship you are in was designed for orbital use beyond planetary exospheres, and not for reentry. On the plus side, the hull of the vessel is made entirely of Broxium, which naturally can withstand extreme temperatures far exceeding two thousand degrees Celsius..."

Steele rolled her eyes sideways, and then tightened her lips as she noticed Brig glancing in her direction.

"Because of the ship's limited landing capabilities," Parker's image continued, "you will need to position it for proper insertion manually. I have included the applicable measurements that you will require on this data chip. Good luck."

The hologram faded.

Brig and Steele purposefully exchanged glances for the first time since their argument. She looked away with a haughty sigh, studied a data screen in front of her for a few seconds, and then typed in a string of commands to the console.

"Pitch and yaw information has been programmed, the ship should adjust in a moment," she said flatly, and then sat back in her seat.

Brig offered a curt nod, followed by a disgusted head shake.

With the ship engaging its thrusters to return it to its forward-facing trajectory, the white-sapphire glow of Earth's upper reaches flowed around them. An obnoxious claxon screamed from the control panel. Steele silenced it with a light tap of her armored fingers.

"That's odd…" she remarked under her breath.

"Something wrong?" Brig leaned his head forward to see Steele's face.

"The orbital maneuvering thrusters have gone offline," she replied, inching her helmet ever so slightly away from Brig's glare.

Brig wrinkled his brow. "Is there some sort of auxiliary power you can switch to?"

Steele quickly scanned the row of controls spread out in front of them, locating the power routing relay. She tapped at it as if second nature. "Auxiliary power routed. Oh bloody blazes, the thrusters aren't coming back!"

Another chime blared its presence, directing her attention to a small display at the center of the panel. "Oh dear…"

Brig leaned in and read the screen. "Manual control overridden by remote sequence. The Hell does *that* mean?"

Steele sighed, the breath leaving her mouth in a nervous quake. "It means that someone doesn't want us to make it back to Earth…"

"Parker?"

"Parker would never do that… it sounds more like…" she began.

"Allistair…" Brig concluded. "Son of a bitch!" Brig pounded the console again.

"Can we manually pitch the ship to the proper angle?" The desperation surged in the tone of her voice. She pointed at the flight stick near Brig's right knee.

"Manual flight surfaces won't work in space – no air for them to grab," Brig replied. "I sure hope Parker's right about this bird having a thick skin… because it's gonna' get real hot in here in a hurry!"

As if on cue, the edges of the glass began to glow a dark orange. Yet another indicator bawled for attention.

"Main thrusters have activated! We're… accelerating!" Steele cried.

"Dammit!" Brig bellowed. He grabbed at the flight stick.

28: BURN

The intense, building pressure of the atmosphere around them shook the vehicle like a play toy. The filters in both of their biosuits whined, swabbing the endless beads of sweat draining from their foreheads.

"I'm getting minor reaction to the stick... we're pitching a tiny bit, but it's not enough! Dammit, we'll break apart before we slow down..." Brig yelled, his voice dim over the now-deafening roar of the air grating against the hull of the ship. He glanced at the control panel. His eyes widened. "Shit!" He hammered at a control.

"What? What's happening?"

"We're starting to roll... I've lost control of the ailerons, we're gonna full-on barrel soon!"

"Oh my God!" cried Steele, her hands at her side to brace for something that bracing would very unlikely assist.

Brig released the stick and grabbed for Steele's hand, holding it tightly to his armored chest. He closed his eyes.

"Brigadier... are we going to..."

Brig squeezed her hand ever tighter.

Steele emitted a quick whimper and pressed herself into her seat. "I love you..." she squeaked.

The ship tossed violently to one side. A turbulent wave of thick atmosphere bullied it back the other way, and then rolled the chassis like a spent soda can.

Just as the heat inside the cockpit had reached its torrid zenith, the ship emerged within the lower realms of Earth's sky. It streaked far above the cloud cover like a shooting meteorite, somehow having made it through the destructive friction of reentry. The left wing of the vessel shredded and rained pieces of alien metal, which ignited and disintegrated in empty space behind them.

Hungry flames licked at the heat resistant hull, spewing gray plumes of thick gas across the cloud tops. The ship rolled once, twice and again uncontrollably above the billows and then speared downward through them. Charcoal smoke lined the thin sky behind them as the ship plummeted Earthward in a fiery ball of screaming Broxium. The nauseating drone of air striking the hypersonic vessel ruptured the serenity of the world below, followed by a shattering sonic boom that traveled behind the ship.

As its momentum carried it the final few kilometers, the fire from the lower hull extinguished, replaced by a two-tone mix of black and gray sooty smoke billowing away behind them. The ship leveled, but then ricocheted off a tall object jutting out from the mud of the ground beneath them, severing the very tip of the pillar.

The shuttle bounced upward from its trajectory, performed one final arc, and then slammed with unmatched violence into the soft earth several hundred meters away in a molten pool of flame and smoke.

29:
Sundown

Earth

The overcast sky peered into the shattered dome of the shuttle, flooding across Steele's dust-laden face shield. She exhaled a series of quick breaths and attempted to push herself upward, but the bulk of her biosuit held her within the cramped cockpit, like a child's action figure stuffed into a mismatched toy. She rocked from side to side as much as her thin frame would allow, but the alien metal would not release itself from the wedge the concussion of the crash had created.

An armored hand appeared through the broken screen - she thrust her own armored paw upward, and with a few powerful tugs, Brig pulled Steele through the opening and out onto the bent carcass of the shuttle. She stepped from the teetering hunk of Broxium onto the ground, her clunky boots lofting an echoed crunch in the moist air.

Beside her, Brig, having pulled what was surely equal to double her weight due to the suit, wiped a stream of sweat from his naked forehead.

"I can't believe we survived that..." he said, leaning over with hands on knees, sucking in precious air.

"Are you ok?" Steele asked, her voice still like grating metal over the intercom in Brig's helmet, which he now held in his hands.

Brig nodded. "Gotta thank whoever created these things... lifesavers."

She rotated the upper portion of her armored torso to scan the area behind. Not much was visible, as a blanket of fog as dense as wet concrete hung low over the land in both directions. "That would be Parker."

Brig shook his head in disbelief. "That guy must be looking at the master plan or something."

"Where in the blazes are we?" Steele wandered a few steps away from him, squinting through the white mist, trying unsuccessfully to discern any landmarks that would offer a clue as to their location.

He raked a hand through his hair, which had grown considerably in the weeks since the liberation of the mining colony back on Mars. Nothing seemed familiar – not that there was much to see.

Steele's eyes traced the black and gray tower of smoke that illustrated their perilous fall from the heavens just moments before, its lower end diving into the thick soup several hundred meters away. A semi-formed crater cradled the pair where the shuttle had skidded to a final halt into the dark soil.

The reverb of waves crashing against rocks in the distance drew Brig's attention. He inhaled deeply, taking in the thick air; the sting of salt, along with a musty tang, filled his nostrils.

"That's saltwater," he said. "We're near an ocean or sea..." He pointed in the direction of a small ridge that slowly came into focus through a lighter portion of the fog.

Steele studied her wrist-mounted computer, smacking at it several times with her other armored hand. "The computer's flaky – and it appears to have lost calibration, but it thinks that way is east." She pointed at the shadow of the ridge.

"But east where?"

After exchanging pensive glances, the pair strode forward along the burned trench that marked their arrival.

"I can't believe we're here," Steele said with a solemn gaze ahead.

"Now you know how I felt when I woke up on Mars - with you standing there right next to me."

"I always wondered if one day I would make it back to Earth. I just never anticipated it would be under these circumstances." Steele fell silent, her face expressionless as her mind wandered beyond the clouds.

Brig pursed his lips. He shifted his head awkwardly within the neck ring of the biosuit to look at her. "I'm sorry you had to find out the way you did, Steele. I know how much you loved your father."

"No apologies, Brigadier," Steele offered with a sheepish smile. "I was living a lie. And you opened my eyes to the truth that was right under my nose the entire time." She dragged an armored boot through the rock fragments that lined the trench. "It would have been truly pathetic had I never found out."

Brig released a smile and locked armored gloves with Steele; the two strode towards the eastern ridge. Their boots landed with an eerie crunch on the dirt, calling out into the emptiness of the thick fog that enveloped them.

They reached the top of the hill and stood on the packed soil, gawking out over the fog-covered water that stretched well beyond their sight. A lonely slapping of waves against the shoreline rocks below them droned like a bathtub of stagnant water.

"It's an ocean alright," said Steele. "Odd that there aren't any seabirds."

Brig looked to the gray sky, his head swiveling around to take in the limited view above him. Suddenly, his foot broke loose from the soil. He slid, feet first, down the side of the ridge, a thin cloud of dust creating a wake behind him. Just before landing in the surf below, he snagged an outcrop with the alien armor of a gloved hand.

Steele's giggle through her external helmet speaker echoed with a shrill resonance from the top of the rise. She peered over the edge down at Brig. "Watch your step there, clumsy!" she called with a playful refrain. "I believe that's two missteps since we left Mars!"

"Glad you're keeping track, sweetheart!" Brig yelled in reply. The echo of his voice fell flat in the moist soup around him.

He pushed his heavier-than-normal frame to a standing position and breathed in the damp air that wafted from the body of water behind him. He made his way to the incline, his armored boots crunching heavily on the coastal soil. With the assist of a pair of clamp-like protrusions on the wrists of the biosuit, he stepped up onto the steep side of the ridge and latched onto one.

A lifetime's worth of training flashed to mind. *Wish I had somethin' like this in EW survival.*

As the slight power assist of the suit pulled him level with the pointed rock, he recoiled in horror. Before he knew it, the grip released and he skidded downward a meter, before grabbing at another stone.

"Shit!" he cried.

"What is it?" Steele called from above.

"Thought it was a rock." He wrinkled his brow in curiosity and moved in for a closer look. "The Hell?"

A particularly loud crunch from his boots drew his attention downward. He activated a light on his wrist and aimed it at the ground.

"They're... skulls. Hundreds of them!"

"Are you mad?"

"No..." he growled, scanning more of the ground around him. "The Hell is this place?"

He clamped another set of rocks and swiftly scaled the side of the ridge, taking up a spot next to a concerned Steele. Brig glared out over the fog-lined ocean. A shadowy pillar rose from the dense clouds in the distance.

"I don't get this place," he muttered aloud. "Why it's so desolate... and the bones."

Steele raised an eyebrow at Brig. "Is this what I can expect from the rest of the world?"

"Nah," he answered with a raise of his hand. "Never been like this." He rotated himself in place. "But then, I've never been *here*. Wherever the Hell this is."

She tapped at her wrist, casting a small arc of bluish-white light in each direction. "This is as barren as it gets. Even the vegetation is... oh dear God!" Steele took a sudden step backward, saved from her own tumble over the ridge by Brig's quick hand.

"What? What!" Brig exclaimed. He aimed his light down at the spot where Steele had stood seconds before.

Buried in the soil but flush with the top layer, next to fragments of other bones, lay a human arm, its rotting blue flesh mingling with the gray around it.

Brig's eyes grew wild. He and Steele hurriedly scanned the area with their lights, finding not just one, but dozens upon dozens of similar decomposing human pieces. The sudden realization dawned on them like a steel curtain that they had been perched upon a massive open grave.

"Brigadier, I don't like this place," Steele said, her normally calm tone raising several octaves in panic.

"I'm with you, sweetheart. Let's get out of here."

He grabbed her glove within his, and they clomped away from the ridge with haste, glancing over their shoulders back at the ghostly ocean shoreline.

One of Steele's boots snagged the edge of the shuttle trench, causing her to lurch forward onto the ground.

"Who's clumsy now?" Brig chuckled in an attempt to calm her. He knelt to help her to her feet. A large object ahead, that they had both failed to notice before, caught his eye. "The Hell is that?"

The white mist ten meters in front of them swirled and revealed a massive green eye set within a stern looking face, which lay on its side. Brig focused his wrist light onto the mysterious find. Once again, his eyes grew in sudden shock.

"Oh God..." Steele said under her breath, grasping Brig's armor and pulling herself close to him.

The arc of light spraying from the end of his arm cast a panoramic pattern over the area in front of the pair, revealing something that brought their breathing to a shallow halt.

The severed head of the Statue of Liberty, lying on its side with a portion of its face entrenched in the soil, glared soullessly at them.

Steele turned and faced the ridge behind them, a look of steep consternation painting her face. "Oh no..." She glared out at the shadowy pillar rising from the foggy mist. "The PIE. It ruptured..." she said in a whisper.

"So that's what we hit on the way in..." Brig observed, now making out the headless figure of Liberty, its slanted pedestal wedged partway into the shoreline a kilometer away.

"Brigadier," Steele interrupted, her voice suddenly stern, "...we need to leave. *Now.*"

He stepped past her and glared into the fog, his hands to his hips. "And how exactly are we gonna do that?" He paused and pointed at the wrecked shuttle with one hand. "Can't exactly hop in our ship here and..."

A subtle rumble filled the air. Brig spun to face Steele.

Steele hovered a meter from the ground, a twin pair of translucent waves of air expelling from the sides of her rear pack. Concern lit her face. "Let's go..."

With sudden confusion, Brig fumbled at the minute amount of controls on his wrist, but his own pack would not sprout the thrusters that Steele's had. "How? I can't find the control..."

"It's thought controlled. Put your helmet back on." Her voice took on the intonation of a drill instructor.

Like an obedient soldier, Brig detached the helmet from his back mounted tether and placed the dome over his head.

"Now... relax. And - activate thrusters."

He sucked a deep breath.

Activate thrusters.

Not a second passed before two invisible flames jetted from the rear of his pack, and he shot upward next to Steele.

"Remind me to tell Parker 'good job'..." No stranger to high tech during his time with the EWs, Parker's ingenuity so far was humbling. "How far can we go with these?"

Steele, having already rotated to set her new trajectory, peered over at Brig. "In this configuration - about six hundred kilometers.

Remember, Brigadier, these were designed for the low gravity and minimal oxygen environment of Mars. So they will expend their energy store much quicker here on Earth. We need to move quickly."

Also no stranger to technological briefings, Brig nodded his head in acknowledgment.

"But Steele..."

She glared at him once again.

"People here aren't gonna understand seeing this kind of stuff. That can only get us in trouble. So we only travel at night - got it?"

Steele granted a final sobering glance at the desolation of Manhattan Bay. She blinked a solemn understanding to Brig. "We won't have to worry about that for a while."

With a burst of thrust and a gentle roll of thunder, the pair jetted off inland at high speed.

Several days later

Steele lounged at the edge of the serene lake, her hands stretched out behind her. The cool, late afternoon breeze floated through her hair and flicked it backward. Her eyes followed the rippling image of a large murder of crows that sailed overhead. Her breathing relaxed as she reflected on the natural beauty of their double 'v' formation.

She draped the edges of her flannel shirt over the light tee underneath, clothing that she and Brig had located earlier in the day when they arrived in the sleepy town of Trenton, deep in the rural backwoods of Tennessee.

The redolence of barbequed meat traveled the air across the lake.

Definitely a wild animal, she thought. *Perhaps boar.*

The aroma carried with it a tangy spice.

"Some sort of citrus glaze," she pondered aloud.

Her sense of smell suddenly seemed alive, being dormant for so many years on Mars. She gazed up at the sky, finding it almost surreal that just days before, they were on a spaceship headed towards Earth. And before that, at Red Colony One.

A feeling of dread and unease washed over her, her mind adrift with thoughts of Allistair and all that he had taken away. Her thoughts meandered, for the first time that she could consciously recall, to Nadia. Steele's heart ached over not only the horror that Nadia had experienced at discovering the lie of her past, but also the despair and loneliness that had overtaken her in her final hours.

29: SUNDOWN

Steele had finally come to understand Brig's trepidation at wanting to pursue a relationship with her, and deep in her heart realized that she could not blame him.

She closed her eyes and breathed deep, wanting to find a foothold here on Earth that would help her deal with her own uncertain future. The gentle song of crickets around her pricked her ears. It had been many years since she had heard them, and had taken for granted the small noises that were not present in the sterile environment of Red Colony One. A small grouping of fireflies danced at the edge of the wood. She marveled at nature and its ability to move onward, even when technology - and society, in turn - fell to the wayside to expose the raw side of life.

A twig snapped behind her, tugging her back to the moment. She flinched. A work boot landed in the plush grass beside her. She warily looked up.

Brig, a wide smile on his face, handed her a plate containing several slices of watermelon – the fruit had such a deep color of red that Steele knew she had never seen before. She grasped it with a hesitant glare on her sunlit face. He settled on the grass beside her, balancing a sweating bottle of lemonade between them.

"What's this?" She snagged the bottle from him. With a curious gaze, she set it in the grass in front of her.

"Just a little snack..."

"Isn't it about time we got moving? It *is* almost dusk."

Brig crunched a bite of the fruit and winked at her. "I think Arizona can wait an hour... don't you? Relax and enjoy the moment." He tapped her thigh with a soft palm.

"But we need to get back to that abandoned farmhouse to get our suits before..."

"Steele... relax! We'll be fine, just... wait, ok?"

For the past several days, they had followed a set pattern: travel during night hours to avoid alarming anyone that they might come upon, and then shed their biosuits in inconspicuous places for a daytime excursion into any small towns nearby. Tonight was different, however, as Brig seemed to have put on a different suit – one of relaxation that she had not witnessed in him since they had reunited.

She beamed at her plate - a smile flourished across her lips. She hungrily devoured the dark flesh of the watermelon, wiping her chin of the sweet juices before stuffing another large bite into her mouth. "Where did you get this food, Brigadier?"

"I... acquired it, just a little treat. We earned it. Don't you think?" He widened his own smile, his teeth gleaming with the setting sun across the blue lake.

An hour later

The last of the succulent watermelon devoured, the juice-soaked paper plates resting in the grass next to the spent bottles of lemonade, Brig and Steele sat back on their elbows watching the sliver of moon cast its reflection across the rippling lake.

"Time to go yet?" Steele cooed.

Brig held a finger to his lips, pointed out at the sky over the water.

The dusky azure suddenly erupted in starbursts of red and blue, followed by several earsplitting booms that rattled the air in their lungs.

Steele's eyes grew in unexpected glee. "*Fireworks*? Did you know about this?"

Brig laughed aloud. "I had a feelin'. Plus I knew the date." His face sprouted a wide grin.

"It's amazing that anyone would find cause to celebrate..." she observed with a pensive gaze at the illuminated night sky, her eyes aglow from the latest round of flares sent up for the entertainment of the townsfolk.

"The spirit never leaves 'em, Steele."

Steele smiled and leaned in against Brig's shoulder. A ray of warmth traveled his spine and settled in his chest.

The moon climbed high above the trees atop the foothills on the horizon. Steele sat forward. "Did you know that the Sun is not unlike this lake, Brigadier?"

Brig smiled without looking at her. The cicadas offered a background track to her elegant explanation.

"Its energy ebbs and flows. Sometimes, a larger amount hits our shores. But we're protected as long as we don't wade in too far." She wrapped her arms around her knees, rested her chin atop them. "Every once in a long while, however, an unexpected flow - a flood, if you will - makes its way to us. What normally provides us warmth, provides us life - shrouds us in death."

Brig, now staring blank-faced at Steele, chuckled under his breath. He slapped at a mosquito attempting to draw blood from his forearm. "That's incredible."

Steele returned the chuckle with a snort. "It's hardly incredible. It's simple physics, really."

"I'm not talking about the sun..."

She turned her eyes to him. "What?"

"It's incredible how... she..." Brig paused, tapping his fingers absentmindedly against his knee. "Nadia..." he said under his breath, "...had your same mannerisms. Expressed herself in the same thoughtful way that you do. It's just... uncanny."

Steele remained silent.

"How did you remember all of this, by the way... if it was just data on the cards?"

She gave a smug grin. "Because I reversed the memory block." She took Brig's hand in hers, stared into the depth of his curious eyes. "Brigadier, I remember everything. And it's not from just reading the cards."

"But..." His confusion was borne upon his brow. "How did you remember to undo the memory block?"

She dropped his hands and glared out at the lake. She raised one eyebrow. "The formula was encoded in the video stream on the cards. Every forty-second frame..."

Brig squinted with concern. "Allistair? But... why would he..."

Steele quickly shook her head. "It wasn't Allistair. It was Nadia."

"Nadia..." Brig whispered aloud in response.

"The encoding was added long after these cards were created. Long after the Event, in fact," she continued. Steele looked to Brig, whose gaze told her he was far away from sitting on the side of the lake with her.

"So she..." he began.

Steele nodded, and then lifted her head to the stars above. "She made sure that the secret within the secret was there for the right person to see."

A sharp jab at the center of Brig's back made him jump forward.

"As long as you two are tellin' secrets, how's about tellin' me why you're trespassin' on my property?" a voice growled.

30:
Who They Are

Earth. Trenton, Tennessee

Brig and Steele locked eyes in the dark, while the stranger with the rifle aimed at Brig's face glared down upon them from behind the bright beam of his flashlight.

"One of you gonna' speak?" the man barked with a sharp drawl from the corner of his mouth.

Brig raised his hands into the flood of light. "Don't shoot, we're not armed," he said calmly.

"Didn't ask if you were. Now why are you here?" the stranger demanded with a gruff insistence.

"We were just passin' through, sir..." Brig pushed himself to his knees, and then lifted his hands beside his head. "We just stopped to get something to eat and rest before we headed on through."

The man shined the light down onto the ground, illuminating two used paper plates and a pair of empty bottles. "I can see that..." Without moving the aim of his gun, he flipped the light back and forth along the lakeshore, then into the thin wood behind him, before turning it back into Brig's face.

Brig raised a palm between his eyes and the beam. "We're alone... sir," he said, his Texas upbringing showing his manners.

"What's your name, son?"

Brig rolled his eyes to Steele and then back. "Brody Sampson... and this is Stacy Fennec." Steele darted her eyes at Brig, her brow wrinkled in confusion.

"Brody and Stacy, not exactly foreigners. Seem to be a lot of them nowadays."

Brig stayed silent.

The man waved away Brig's raised hands, stopping his light on the vertex of the former EW's neck. "Put your hands down. Now get yourselves up."

Brig lowered his hands. Steele pressed herself against his side. "Thanks for not shootin' first," Brig said. "We'll head out now..."

"You'll go this way, Sampson. If you don't mind, I'll escort you off my land. I wasn't born yesterday." He waved his rifle once more, indicating a path with dim lighting at the end. "C'mon now, let's get it movin'."

Brig grasped Steele's hand and strode past the stranger, being careful not to raise the man's suspicions any further. The man did a final onceover of the lakeside with his beacon and turned to follow Brig and Steele.

As they traveled the narrow path, the man hastened his pace to match Brig's – catching him with several long strides. Brig turned his eyes towards him without making his glare too obvious.

The man was older, in his early 70's, and almost Brig's near-two-meter height. His bulky frame, apparently well-toned muscle at one time in his life, filled a rounded silhouette, rather than a chiseled one. His hair, or what was left of a fine crop of follicles, was worn down to gray nubs all around the crown of his head – but well groomed, neatly resembling a military crew cut. His face, weathered from a life of outdoors, emulated a leather baseball glove.

"Sampson..." the old man began, his Southern drawl livening his words, "I bet you think I'm just some crazy old man, don't cha?"

Brig respectfully shook his head. "No, sir. I don't."

"Name's Buck Rogers." The man offered his hand to Brig across his rifle barrel.

Brig took the hand and shook with a mutual firmness. A smirk grew on his face. "Really? Buck Rogers?"

"I didn't like Bo. And I sure as Hell wasn't gonna let anyone call me Beauregard. That was my daddy's name. That funny to you?"

Brig shook his head with a subtle snicker under his breath. "No, sir."

"There's a lot of bad folks in the world, son. And a lot of them that want to come in here take whatever they can. And them foreigners seem to be the root of it all."

Brig pulled Steele closer to him.

"I was a colonel in this man's army. Led my battalion into North Africa at the Battle of Cairo back in forty-two," Buck recited, looking off into the distance at the farmhouse rising from behind the trees.

"That single-handedly turned the tide of the conflict," Brig added.

Buck turned and grinned through his peppered brush mustache. "Your military school paid off..."

"How'd you know..."

"You're an Epsilon. I could see that mark of yours a mile away..." Buck chuckled. "That's right. I said mile. None of that kilometer bullshit - oh sorry, ma'am." He tipped his worn ten gallon towards Steele with a sheepish grin. "Garbage. Some things should stay just the way they were, if you know what I mean."

They approached a split in the path: the left ran up through the dim post lighting towards the house, the other led to the gate next to the main road, leading away from the property. Buck rested his gun across his arms and leaned against a fence post.

"Seventy two days in the desert fightin' guerillas pokin' their heads outta' every God damned nook and cranny in that city. That'll test your resolve, Sampson. So believe me when I tell you I ain't about to let them sons a bitches come in here and take what I got left."

"Mighty respectable of you, sir," Brig said with a flattened smile. "But you don't have to worry about us, we're just..."

"I know, I know. Just passin' through," Buck interjected. "Relax, Sampson. I know you're not one of them. A young couple neckin' down by my lake ain't what I'm worried about."

"We weren't..." Steele added with an embarrassed British lilt, the flush of her cheeks showing up even in the dusk.

Buck cackled through his teeth and dropped a friendly hand onto Brig's shoulder. A bump of thunder rolled in the clouds over the horizon. "C'mon up to the house, you two. We'll get y'all somethin' to eat."

Brig raised a hand. "Thanks, Buck. But we really need to get goin'..."

"Nonsense! Besides, somethin' bad's comin' from the east. And you don't wanna get caught out in *that* kinda rain."

Steele looked over her shoulder at the growing darkness. A cool breeze ruffled her hair. "Perhaps we should stay until it passes," she said softly to Brig.

He nodded.

"As long as we're not imposing, sir," she cooed.

"Good, and I'll make sure Tina fixes up that wound on your neck," Buck added. Buck patted Brig on the back and strode past him towards the farmhouse. "Josie!" Buck bellowed, followed by a whistle. "Josie! C'mon girl!"

A black and white Border collie sprung from a shallow set of weeds along the rear of the property, eagerly catching up to its master.

Brig placed a hand blindly on his neck, wincing as he touched a patch of boiled skin.

Steele glared after Buck, not noticing Brig's pain, and whispered from the side of her mouth. "Why did you give him fake names? Do you think it's wise to lie to someone like *that*?"

Brig watched as Buck and Josie stepped onto the wooden-railed porch. "The name Stroud probably won't sit too well with folks around these parts."

"Why would you... *oh*... your father."

Brig nodded. "And I'm not sure how much these people know about government, but I doubt they'd like hearing your father's name, either."

Steele's face straightened in sudden realization. She nodded and followed Brig to the farmhouse.

Brig and Steele sat next to each other around the worn, round dinner table. Buck and his wife, Tina, sat directly across from them. Buck's house, while small, was a comfortable ranch style home built in the late 1900's, and sat upon a small grade that offered the homeowners a grand vista in each direction.

Brig sawed at a piece of hearty venison and plowed it into his mouth, not having eaten such a delight in many years. Steele smiled as she watched the gusto with which he devoured the meal.

"...and that was the last major operation the USA... URA, pardon... conducted," said Buck.

"Last public one, anyway..." Brig added with a knowing grin, his cheek brimming outward with a hunk of meat.

"That's right, you Epsilon fellas did a lot of that black ops stuff, didn't ya?"

Brig nodded. "Had my fair share, that's for sure."

Buck sat back in his chair, a pensive look planted on his face. A small pelting of rain on the roof made its presence known. "Sampson..." Buck said, "You never did tell me where you and the little lady are headed."

Brig allowed the wad of venison to travel his throat before speaking. "Arizona - to find my sister..."

Buck wedged a small toothpick between his molars. "Anything

west of the Mississip' is bad news, son. There's a lot of bad people out there... but I'm sure you knew that."

Brig swigged the remainder of a glass of sugar-sweet lemonade and set it down on the table with a light clink. "My home's out there, Buck..."

"You're a Texan, I get that. But times have changed, Sampson. Why anyone would wanna go out there is beyond me."

"My sister's out there... somewhere. Got herself involved with some bad folks. I have to get to her..."

Buck shook his head with disbelief. "You're walkin' into a whole mess'a trouble, son."

Brig exhaled a quick sigh and lightly clunked his fork on the table. "Noted... sir," he said, not forgetting his respect for the former colonel.

"I hope you got a better plan than just you and the little missy here walkin' and hopin' for the best?" Buck glared into Brig's eyes, expressionless.

Brig did not respond, instead shoved another small piece of meat into his mouth.

A deep rumble of thunder shook the windows; the rain pounded harder.

Buck darted his eyes to Steele, then back to Brig. "Tina, get the boy some more lemonade, would ya' dear?" He rose from the table and turned his back to the group.

Tina straightened her bifocals on her nose. She glanced nervously between the two unexpected visitors and her husband, pushed up from the table and disappeared into the adjacent kitchen.

As the door whooshed shut, Buck returned to his chair. He plucked a small satchel from underneath the table and tossed it with a nod in front of Brig, where it landed with a metallic jingle. "You know what those are, don't ya?"

Brig ran his finger into the sack, paused, and then looked to Buck. "No, sir..."

"Them there are what they call Syndicate credits. It's their way of making their own money system. They use it to trade, buy... basically keep tabs on everyone under their thumb," Buck explained, focusing his eyes on rolling his palms into each other.

Brig raised an eyebrow. "So why are you givin' these to us?"

"Cuz' you're gonna need em' to fit in out there, Sampson. The less you stand out, the less you get picked on." He looked to Steele.

"You're already outnumbered. No offense to the pretty lady here..." Buck's face was suddenly wise beyond its years.

Brig hesitantly nodded. Of course he knew what Syndicate credits were. Unbeknownst to Buck, Brig had lived around and within the Syndicate's territories for years. However, he was not about to let on that it was that very organization that he was about to confront head-on.

"I also have some guns out in the shed that you're free to take with you..." Buck added.

Brig raised his hands in protest. "I can't take your weapons, Buck..."

"Take 'em, Sampson. It's not like I'm givin' ya' my best anyhow." Buck smiled, and offered a coy wink at Steele. "Now you two can stay in the guest room just through that hallway," he said, pointing to a dim corridor that exited towards the back of the house. "And you can leave at dawn if you'd like..."

"We were hoping to leave tonight, Buck..." Steele offered.

Buck shook his head. "It's not safe out there at night. We're a tight knit community. A bit of a militia set up. But even so, we can't control what goes on out there in the dark hours. I'd hate to see you get attacked along the roadside with no one to help ya' out."

Steele and Brig sighed simultaneously, realizing that arguing with Buck was pointless. Another night was not going to hinder their progress in their overall journey.

Later that evening

The pair of weary travelers, having accepted Buck's hospitality, had retired to the small guest room that sat just to the inside of the back porch. Brig and Steele, both awake, stared at the moonlight through the window. The rain had stopped, and the patterned rhythm of the water dripping from the roof onto the porch accompanied the silence coating the room. Brig lay on a small couch, his long legs propped up over the edge, creating two large silhouettes against the silver light. Steele occupied the single bed that sat against the center of the wall.

The contrasting din of the barn door rolling shut twenty meters away pricked his ears. A loud, but muffled, voice rang from outside. Brig sprang up to a sitting position. Steele propped herself up with an elbow and glared at him through the darkness.

The voices grew angrier. A thump broke the dead of night.

Brig leapt from the couch and opened the door to the porch. "Stay here!" he commanded in a loud whisper.

Within the two-story barn outside, a pair of men stood, one in front of the other. The first, a wiry framed young man with mottled blonde hair that touched his shoulders, watched from behind as the second held a long-barreled pistol on Buck.

"Come on, old man!" the second, his hair and eyes black as coal, yelled in a local accent.

Buck, on his knees in the strewn hay, looked up at him with disdain. "I'm not gonna tell you anything, you little punk!"

"Then we're gonna tear this place apart 'til we find your stash of guns, old timer!" the gunman shouted back, threatening to hit Buck with the butt of the handgun.

"You'll never get away with this."

The man laughed and wiped his mouth with a dirty sleeve. "We already have. Know who this is, Dexter?" he asked the other. "This is one of their ring leaders. We take one of 'em out, we'll show 'em who's in charge!"

The other man, Dexter, laughed nervously in return.

"Now why the Hell would you wanna go do that? We're the good guys!" Buck yelled, tilting his head to face the armed man, an incredulous glare on his leathered face.

The armed man, Gus, leaned into Buck. "Yeah... the good guys. You good ol' boys sit here in your cushy houses." Disgust dripped from each syllable like rust from a leaky faucet. "And the rest of us are out there scrapin' bottom. How you helpin' us?" He pounded the back of Buck's neck with his pistol, dropping the old soldier unconscious in the dirt.

"Gus... back off him, man! He's just an old geezer," Dexter said, showing mercy in contrast to his partner's seeming lack.

Gus jumped back up, waving the gun. "No, Dex! They don't help no one but themselves!" he bellowed. "Look around you, moron! How you think he has all this still?" Gus turned back to face Buck, leveled the gun at the old man's face. "He's out for number one. Nobody else..."

The light creak of the barn door drew their attention. Both men spun their heads and glared. A thin shaft of moonlight flowed in across the dirt. Just outside, steam slowly wafted up from the wet earth.

Gus inched towards the opening, foot crossing foot, until he stopped a meter from the door. Silence filled the barn; the pair of hoodlums anxiously listened for more noise.

Suddenly, a gunshot split the damp stillness. Gus flipped backward onto the hay-lined dirt, his gun sailing from his hands and landing several meters away. As a crimson stain grew at the front of his partner's shirt, Dexter spun to face the mystery assailant.

Brig stood at the back of the barn, smoke trailing from the barrel of the deer rifle in his hands.

Dexter turned and dove at the handgun next to him, spun and fired a round that splintered the wood beam next to Brig. The former EW ducked behind a towering bale of hay and checked the magazine of his gun. He closed his eyes, inhaled and then pressed his face against the edge of the bale.

Dexter had disappeared out the door.

A shadow grew from within the doorway. Brig raised his gun and glanced over the bale. Dexter stood with one hand holding the pistol, the other tightly grasping the neck of Steele. She whimpered, her eyes wide with terror.

"Let her go!" Brig barked.

"You made a mistake, man!" Dexter stammered, his hand visibly shaking upon the trigger. "She's dead! You're both dead!" he yelled, his voice cracking with anxious fear. He pushed the barrel of the pistol into Steele's neck.

Steele flinched. A muted cry escaped her ruby lips.

Brig raised the rifle to his cheek. "Let her go or I'll take your head off. Your choice…"

Dexter laughed maniacally. "Maybe you'll hit her? You wanna take that chance, man?"

Brig breathed in to calm his heartbeat. Deep inside, he knew Dexter was right.

Dammit, he screamed inside. *Clarity. Clarity.* He forced his eyes shut, but it would not come.

"Brigadier… it's in you," Steele cried.

Brig's eyes shot open.

"Shut up, bitch!" Dexter screamed in her ear. "You! Drop the fucking gun!" He hacked the air towards Brig with the pistol.

Brig locked eyes with Steele, his head tilted in confusion.

"Relax your senses!" she screamed.

Brig closed his eyes once more. A switch inside of him clicked;

the air around him compressed. He suddenly felt Dexter's racing heartbeat. He felt the heat coming from the man's breath.

And then... it faded.

Sweat rolled from Brig's forehead. His breathing hastened. He flicked his eyes open. "I can't! It's gone!"

Dexter cackled wildly and drew the gun up to Steele's temple.

A loud thud from the other side of the door made Dexter turn, forcing separation between him and Steele for the briefest of seconds. Brig seized the fraction, squeezing off a round that took off the back of Dexter's head. Steele's attacker fell lifeless to the floor, dark scarlet plasma oozing from his shattered skull.

Steele fell forward and moved away from him, holding her mouth with both hands in a silent scream.

Tina, Buck's wife, emerged from behind the barn door, a hammer held down by her side. Brig stood silent, his eyes freshly wet. He let the rifle drop to the barn floor. Steele grabbed him around the waist and forced her head into his chest.

31:
Falling Down

Earth. Trenton, Tennessee - The next morning

With the excitement of the intruders in the barn, and the discomfort of the burn on his neck, Brig found the rest of the night relatively sleepless. He yawned as he, Steele, Buck and Tina stood next to the gate at the end of Buck's driveway.

"Are you sure you don't wanna stay, Sampson? We sure could use a man like you here in Trenton," said Buck.

Brig grasped Buck's hand and shook. To Buck's surprise, Brig pulled Buck's arm to form the familiar 'W' of the EW handshake.

Buck grinned a toothy smile.

"That's how EWs show 'brothers for life'," Brig said. "Thanks for everything, Colonel. But I can't stay. I really have to go save my sister."

Tina stood on her toes and wrapped her arms around Brig's neck, taking special care not to disturb the fresh bandage that peeked out from his collar.

"I don't know how I can ever thank you enough for... what you did last night," she said with a waver of her voice.

Brig smiled and held her out at arm's length. "You were just as important there, Mrs. Rogers." He flicked his eyes to Buck, then back to her. "Keep him out of trouble!"

Tina chuckled under her breath. "Easier said than done."

Buck hugged Steele, then squared her shoulders and glared into her eyes, his smile wide. "Now, you two come back. You'll be welcomed with open arms!"

As Steele said her goodbyes to Tina, Buck pulled Brig aside. "You take care of that girl."

"She's tougher than she looks, Buck. You don't have to worry about that," Brig replied.

"No... seriously. They're animals out there. They couldn't care less about the sanctity of life, son."

Brig flattened his smile and nodded. Brig was no stranger to life out in the lawless west. After having spent the night with Buck and his wife - being around the types of people he had grown up with - the reality of what lay ahead suddenly struck him like a brick.

Brig smiled fondly at both Buck and his wife, before he and Steele strode through the gate, disappearing around the corner in the distance.

The late afternoon sun tossed its final rays through the rotted wood of the abandoned barn. Brig and Steele had only traveled several kilometers from Buck's property on the day, and had spent the past several hours resting for their upcoming trip. They stood over their empty biosuits, which lay on the straw at their feet, completing power-up checks on the attached wrist computers. With night nearly upon them, and with it the optimum window for undetected travel, they hurried their prep work.

Steele glanced up from her task. Brig had been noticeably introspective since leaving Buck's.

"You're being awfully silent. What's on your mind... if you don't mind my asking?" she said.

He did not make eye contact with her, continuing to busy himself with his own computer checks. "I failed. I failed you... I failed Buck. I failed everyone there last night." His voice cracked just enough to take Steele by surprise.

"What in blazes... you saved all of our lives last night!"

"That's just it, Steele." He glared at her for a second, and then dropped his eyes to the biosuit once again. "I didn't save anyone. Tina saved us by providing that distraction, I just followed up. If she hadn't been there, you... or all of us... would be dead right now."

Neither spoke for a moment.

Brig lifted his eyes to Steele. "Clarity wouldn't come to me, Steele. I reached down... and it wasn't there. And *that* made me fail." Brig released the arm of his biosuit, allowing it to thump in the straw-covered dirt. He paced to the half-hung barn door and propped his arm against it. "I've been so used to having that... ability... that it's become a part of me. And now... it's gone."

31: FALLING DOWN

Steele grasped Brig's hand and spun him to face her. "Clarity is still a part of you, Brigadier. You just have to learn how to use it." She proffered a soothing smile.

He threw his arm up and pointed into the night. "But... I don't have the catalyst! That's what makes Clarity work!"

Steele's placating smile grew. "The catalyst was simply artificial human adrenaline, Brigadier – something just to accelerate the process. Our brains don't instinctively understand what we've given them. Nor how to use it."

Brig scrunched his brow.

"The Clarity gene is still within you. You just have to know how to activate it."

"Then how do I do that? It seemed like..." He fell silent again.

"What?"

"Like something was happening last night... but then it disappeared."

"You have to relax your senses. It's quite opposite of what you would think. The more you concentrate, the less chance Clarity will work for you." She stroked the stubble on his cheek. "If you allow your senses to defocus – Clarity *will* take over."

"And I don't need a catalyst to do that?"

Steele smiled and shook her head.

"And the side effects?"

"That was the malformed gene that I removed on Mars. Clarity is still very much alive and well inside of you." She tapped lovingly on his chest with each word.

A long-missing smile sprouted across Brig's face. Steele boosted herself onto her toes and landed a peck on his lips. Brig pulled her into him by her hips and deepened the kiss. They released, smiled with loving warmth at each other, and continued prepping their suits for takeoff.

30 minutes later

The whoosh of the biosuit thrusters called like a graceful flock of doves through the thick wood nearby. A cloud of dust emanated in twin circles around their feet, as both Brig and Steele lifted off and hovered ten meters up. Without wasting another second, they tilted forward and propelled themselves over the nearby treetops.

The last remnants of the setting sun trickled through a small bank of clouds at the horizon and twinkled into their face shields. Silent moments passed along with the revolving landscape below them.

Brig's helmet speaker crackled to life with Steele's smooth voice. "Brigadier, are you certain we should be doing this alone? What if we *are* outnumbered... like Buck said?"

Brig, without looking at Steele, opened his mike. "We're gonna be outnumbered for sure. I don't doubt that," he said flatly. "But you know I saved your father before... and I was far outnumbered then."

A silent moment elapsed.

"I thought my father died during that rescue?"

Brig's gaze met hers, the blue-white of her helmet lights illuminating her face. "He didn't die because of the rescue – it was just a stray bullet."

"Precisely my point. What if that stray bullet finds your sister?"

Brig glared forward into the gloom. "She's better off dead than with Muldoon."

The pair of unearthly flyers silently navigated the night sky above the Mississippi River, Brig having chosen a particularly wood-dense crossing to avoid discovery.

Steele's eyes glowed with the majestic panorama offered by their height. In her broad experience, she had been to Mars and had seen alien landscapes, but her breath left her at the spectacular wonder of the grand river flowing beneath them.

At the west bank of the river, Steele broke the silence.

"So what's your plan then?"

Brig did not respond.

"Do you have anyone that can lend a hand. Surely you don't plan on walking in there and taking her?"

Brig thought back to the night he attempted to enlist Clive in rescuing Steele's father, particularly with how he tried to convince Steele – *Nadia* - that he had the right plan in mind. "No. Not gonna make that same mistake again. But... I don't know if anyone would be willing to help out."

"Then you *have* someone in mind?"

"A couple of people, actually."

Steele's intercom fell silent and the pair flew on for a few moments without speaking further.

"Steele... I'm sorry."

"Brigadier, you don't need to apologize for that again. It wasn't your fault..."

"I'm not talking about last night."

"Then what?"

Spotting the dull lighting of a sleepy town, Brig banked his biosuit to skirt the edge and stay out of sight. Steele followed his pattern without question.

"Back there... on the ship," he continued. "I was pretty harsh with you - about Clarity."

She shot a subdued glance over at him. "You don't have to apologize for *that*, either."

"I had no right to go off on you like that. It wasn't your fault. I know you didn't mean for things to happen that way, and if you could've done something about it before it was too late – you would've." More than a hint of sadness coated his voice.

"Not *all* my fault, anyway..." she added under her breath. "But I'm not entirely blameless, love."

The blue moonlight mixed with his face shield beacon, his steely blue eyes carved into her soul even from three meters away.

"We knew about the side effects, but the DMST - and Allistair primarily - debated that the ends justified the means with such a powerful weapon at our disposal." Her voice broke. The filter in her helmet mopped a tear from her cheek. "We were wrong. So horribly wrong. And I suppose he was using the memory blocking technique in little amounts over time."

Brig continued to stare forward, speechless.

"But I have to confess, Brigadier. I knew about it all along. I'm so... sorry." Her mike remained open. Steele's sobbing breaths echoed in his speaker. "Can you ever forgive me?"

Brig smiled, inched his suit nearer to her and took her hand in his.

On the morning of their third day aloft, and with the day's new sun poking above the horizon behind them, Steele scanned her wrist computer with a tired eye.

"Well, that just about does it," she said.

Brig offered her a curious gaze.

"The stored energy in my suit is spent."

He rotated his headpiece and surveyed the horizon about them, blocking out the rising sun to the east with one armored hand. "I saw a small town to the northeast. We can set down just over that ridge of trees and make our way into town. We'll figure out what to do from there."

Brig's thrusters sputtered just above the treetops. He fell forward, and then plummeted without warning. He flailed his arms in a hilarious attempt at flying, just before belly flopping onto the hard earth, scattering dry pine needles and dust in a small grouping of fir trees around him.

"Brigadier! Are you ok?" she called through the hollow coldness of her intercom.

Brig pricked up an armored thumb from within the dust cloud and raised himself from the ground with one arm. "I know these things are supposed to save your life... but that's gettin' old," he said with a groan.

With their tired bodies extracted from the protective confines of the biosuits, they laid the empty mechanized shells within a dry culvert. Brig visually traced the stream next to it that meandered around the outside of the small village ahead. While Steele kept a lookout near the dirt road twenty meters to their south, Brig dragged a fallen branch atop the gray-blue armor and worked to fill in the gaps with handfuls of dried leaves.

"I don't understand the need to cover these up," she called from the roadside. "It's not like we're ever going to use them again."

Brig finished concealing the last few bits of leg armor. "One thing I learned a long time ago... never say never."

Their suits neatly hidden from discovering eyes, the pair made their way out to the local highway adjacent the wood.

A few hours later

As the golden sun blasted its final beams onto the small town of Freedom, Oklahoma, Brig and Steele strode determinately along the deserted street lining the center of the village. It was quiet, and aside from only a few people that ducked into buildings here and there, the town reeked of desolation.

An eerie nervousness set in for both Brig and Steele, and they quickened their pace as a result.

Brig pointed forward to a bar nestled in between two abandoned stores. "Let's go in there..."

An incredulous glare lit her face. "A bar? Are you bloody mad?"

He smirked. "It's happy hour somewhere, right?" He grasped her hand and led her to the front entrance. "It's too far to walk to Arizona, Steele. We need to find someone that can get us at least part of the way there."

Like a scene out of the Old West, the pair stepped into the rundown pub, the floor creaking under their light steps. Steele scrunched her nose at the dusty aroma that wafted forth with the stirring of air from their entry.

A tense silence hung in the room. Brig's eyes darted to several people hidden in the corners, well within the shadows brought on by the sparse lighting. As the pair reached the center, all eyes fell upon them. Brig ignored their gazes and stepped to the bar at the back.

The uneasy feeling grew.

The bartender, a burly fellow with no hair atop his head, and a shaggy red mop clinging to his chin, glanced at Brig and then away. Brig and Steele sat in a pair of dirty, wooden stools and faced away from prying eyes.

She grabbed Brig's hand underneath the bar. "I don't like this!" she whispered through her teeth. "We need to leave!"

Brig shushed her with a hand. "It's ok, sweetheart..."

The bartender approached them with wary caution. "What'll it be?"

"A beer?" Brig's salivary glands kicked into overdrive as he said the word. Gone was the experience of Dempsey's 'herbal brew', replaced with warm thoughts of yesteryear when he would frequent pubs when not on duty. While he could not deny his kinship with Dempsey, Brig was glad that he would most likely never step foot on Mars again in his lifetime. Brig looked to Steele with a raised eyebrow.

"I'll have the same," she muttered, refusing to make eye contact with the creepy barkeep.

"Two beers then," said Brig.

Without changing his contradicting expression of suspicious apathy, the bartender ping ponged his eyes between them. He turned his back.

"I'm going to go use the ladies' room." Steele rose from her stool and gracefully disappeared down a side hall.

Brig watched her leave, and then glanced around the bar, making sure not to force eye contact with anyone or arouse additional suspicion.

The bartender returned. He clunked two large mugs of golden beer on the bar, their foamy heads flowing from the tops.

"Thanks, partner," Brig said with a facetious wink.

The bartender leaned forward, both hands on the bar, glaring at Brig. "Haven't seen you two around here before," he said gruffly in a local twang. "What's your story?"

Brig imbibed a large mouthful of beer before emitting an audible gulp. He wiped his chin with a sleeve. "Just fightin' the good fight..." he replied, a subtle squint in his eye.

The bartender's eyes flickered for a nanosecond before he stood upright. After staring for an uncomfortably silent few seconds, he nodded his head. "You're new here. I'd watch my back if I were you. Finish those up and don't hang around long." The bartender made his way towards a door behind the bar. "Let me know if you need anything else."

Steele returned to her seat, glaring at the bartender. "Well that seemed awkward. What in blazes was that about?"

"More than you know," Brig replied. "Find the restroom?"

"Let's not talk about it. In fact, let's never talk about it." Steele shuddered for effect.

Brig looked past Steele. The bartender stood silently in the doorway, studying Brig, before leaving the room.

Steele raised an eyebrow at Brig.

"Let's get out of here," Brig said, lifting himself from the stool and clanking a pair of Syndicate credits onto the bar.

Her face contorted with confusion. "But what about getting someone to take us to Arizona?"

"Somethin's not right here. We'll find a better place to search. C'mon." He pulled Steele away from the bar and nudged her through the front door, taking one last look over his shoulder as the door swung shut behind them.

Before he could turn and decide their next move, a muffled yelp called from behind him. He spun his head to look at Steele, whom had let go of his hand less than a second prior. His eyes widened in shock.

A man with a black bandana over the bottom two thirds of his face had grabbed Steele, holding a strong hand over her mouth and grasping her midsection tight with the other.

"You son of a..." Brig screamed, his attempt at defending her swiftly cut short by a wire thrust around his own neck. He flung his body in a wild buck, trying to free himself from his unseen attacker. The man behind him grunted as Brig pounded his body back against the brick of the bar, still unrelenting with the tightening of the metal noose. Veins raised above the skin on Brig's neck. He glared with a vicious eye to find Steele. With a crack to the side of his skull, Brig fell unconscious to the pavement.

R. JAMES STEVENS

32:
Nothing Comes Easy

Earth. Freedom, Oklahoma

Brig awoke to darkness. He was unsure if night had fallen - but as he regained consciousness, the cool silk of a bandana covering his eyes made him aware that something had gone horribly wrong. The odiferous sting of smelling salts bit the edge of a nostril.

He jolted his head backward, half in reaction to the strong scent, half hoping that one of his captors was within striking distance of a decent head butt. The bite of the salts faded, and the clunk of a pair of heavy footsteps on the hollowed wood floor filled his ears.

If this guy's an Aussie, I'm gonna scream.

It was déjà vu for Brig, thinking back to earlier in the year when he awoke to a similar predicament. That moment ended with his then-buddy, Clive, saving the day by offing his captor.

Not gonna get that lucky again.

"Wake up," a voice, not Australian, called from across the room.

"At least you're American," Brig groaned, welcoming the northern Texas drawl. He tried to rub the spot at the back of his head that throbbed like a war drum, but a rope bound his wrists and prevented him from any extra movement. "What'd I do to wind up here?"

"You tell me, pal," the voice replied in a sharp drawl.

The arid trace of dust in the air raked at Brig's throat. "Mindin' my own, then I get jumped and bagged. That's what." Brig pricked his ears, but did not detect what he had hoped. "Where is she?" he growled.

The man did not answer.

"I said where the Hell is she? If you hurt her, so help me I'm gonna kill you!"

The man snorted. The floorboards creaked as footsteps approached Brig. "Hmm, yeah. The girl," the man cooed. "Pretty little thing, ain't she?"

Brig pushed against his restraints, to no avail.

"Take it easy, hero. She's fine. We don't do that kinda stuff – that's the other guys."

Brig drifted his head in the direction of the man's voice. "But you attack innocent people and tie 'em up?"

The man sat on the edge of a nearby table, propped his boot on a chair with a squeak. He put a strong hand on Brig's shoulder. "What are y'all lookin' for?" His voice immediately lost all sense of levity.

The man's breath heated the side of Brig's face. "I told you, we were..."

"Cut the shit. You're tryin' to get someone's attention. Well, you got it..."

While it was not the reaction he had hoped to get when he dropped the line to the bartender earlier, it *was* something. He had to play it out and hope for the best. "We're lookin' for help gettin' to Arizona," Brig confessed with a dry voice.

The man huffed. "Droppin' an awful big callin' card just to hitch a ride." He grabbed at Brig's shirt collar and exposed the EW tattoo at the vertex of his neck and collarbone. "What's your name, dude?"

"Brody."

"Brody? Got a last name?"

"Nah. Just Brody," Brig replied with a dry candor.

"How 'bout you stop lyin' to me?"

"I'll tell you *who* I am when you take this blindfold off me and tell me *where* I am!" Brig barked.

"You're lookin' for somethin' more than a ride... Brody. So 'fess up and this gets a whole lot easier."

Brig bit his lip. *Time to drop the big name.*

"William Bryce sent me..." Brig said with slow emphasis. The table creaked as the man got to his feet. "Now show me that she's ok!" Brig bellowed into the darkness offered by the blindfold.

The man whistled twice. "Billy! Bring her in!"

A few seconds passed, when suddenly the thump of heavy boot heels, accompanied by the muffled shouts of a female, echoed in the hall. Brig smiled inside - Steele was fine.

The door swung open and the pair entered.

"Bwigadeew!" Steele hollered clumsily through a rag bound across her face.

"Steele! Sweetheart, are you ok?" Brig cried.

"Yeph!" Steele growled like a caged cat. "Take thisph dam thingw off mew!"

"Let her go!" Brig demanded, nearly lifting himself from the ground, straining again at the rope that bound him to the chair. Expecting a blow to the head to quiet him, instead Brig felt a sturdy hand on his shoulder force him back to a seated position.

"See? She's fine. So that's enough conversation outta you two..." the man said, his voice much calmer now.

"And that's enough of the cloak and dagger bullshit!" Brig growled. "You know what we're lookin' for, now take us to someone who can help us out!"

The men remained silent, the only noise in the room being Steele fidgeting with her wrist restraints.

"Take me to the Reformation!" Brig followed up, his voice booming.

A few moments of awkward silence ensued. The restraints around his hands loosened from the chair, and then were cinched tightly to each other, preventing him from what he felt like doing at the moment – cold cocking the bastard for tying him in the first place. The man looped his hand under Brig's shoulder and pulled him from the chair. Along with the other unseen man, they led Brig and Steele from the room.

Minutes later, a door opened, and Brig was tossed onto the floor of yet another room.

"Steele? You there?"

No answer.

Brig sighed, rolled over and then sat up against the wall. "The Hell..." he mumbled. The realization that he might have led both himself and Steele into mortal danger suddenly grew in his mind - that he did not think to mention the Reformation to Buck was the kicker. Buck was a leader in his town, and most assuredly would have been able to steer Brig away from trouble. Brig slammed his head backward against the soft plaster, which boomed throughout the rafters above.

"Brigadier?" Steele's muffled voice spoke through the wall.

"Steele? You're next door?" he called over his shoulder.

"Yes!" she replied with an emphatic squeak.

"Did they hurt you?"

"No. But it's not like they're being gracious hosts, either."

Brig thought for a minute. "Guess they didn't count on us being able to hear each other through these thin walls."

"Brigadier..." she said after a brief pause, "...what do you think they're going to do to us?"

He wanted with all of his soul to tell her what he was *really* feeling: that it was a mistake to not confide a bit more in Buck, that he had made another tactical error in showing his hand about the Reformation in the bar, and that this was just another misstep in a long line of decisions he had made over the years. However, he also had had enough of the 'I told you so' responses from everyone.

"They're gonna take us to someone who can help..." His tone was reluctant at best.

"And... what if they don't?"

The dagger pierced him through the wall.

"They will..." he answered, his voice trailing off to a whisper.

Several hours later

The door opened, a man stomped across the floor and picked up Brig by his shoulder.

"Now what?" Brig stuttered his feet, trying to avoid the inevitable, as the man pulled him towards the door.

The man did not answer, but as they passed through the doorway, Brig could hear the light footsteps of Steele following close behind them. A few moments later, the men assisted Brig and Steele into the flatbed of a growling truck waiting outside. From what he could tell, they sat Steele across the bed and diagonally in relation. One of the men grunted as he sat down on the metal bench next to him.

Keepin' us from talkin'.

The driver engaged the clutch; the truck's engine roared. The tires shuddered as it picked up speed on the pitted highway. He turned his head blindly to the side.

"Where we headed?" Brig asked with a smug air.

At this point, he was not even sure that someone was sitting next to him, but if they were, Brig certainly got his point across.

The hours passed as the truck rumbled along the flat Oklahoma highway. The sun had made its way into its daily descent by the time the Jimmy shrieked to a stop.

Steele coughed away the dewy stench of unburned diesel. "Where are we?"

The silent answer came in the form of the lurking guard grabbing at one arm apiece and leading them to the lip of the truck's bed. One at a time, someone on the ground beneath them assisted in their extraction.

The sharp scent of wet grass greeted them. With a shove from behind, Brig treaded unevenly on what he assumed was gravel, by the sound of it crunching under his feet. After a few steps, the small stones gave way to the soft scrunch of foliage. Dew flicked from the taller blades into the tops of his boots and onto his ankles.

A rising anxiety gripped at Brig's chest. "If you're just gonna take us out into the woods and shoot us, at least take the blindfolds off so we can see it comin!"

A forceful push from behind met him, making him stumble forward before recapturing his balance. "You talk too much," one of the men drawled. "Just keep walkin'."

The man suddenly grasped Brig by the back of his collar and halted his forward progress. The sound of a creaking door echoed with a hollow resonance from somewhere down below. The wafting odor of mildew and dust punched him in the face.

Brig turned his head and retched. "...the Hell?"

The familiar hand pushed him forward once again. However, this time another phantom hand grasped the collar of his shirt. Before he could react, his front foot stumbled downward. The strong stink of mildew quickly gave way to a dank, wet earth aroma as he caught himself from tripping.

They reached the bottom of the small, earthen staircase after a dozen steps.

Brig inhaled. *Definitely underground.*

With his shoulders bumping the narrow corridor walls, each of the wooden pillars banging painfully against him, the guard pushed him forward with one hand on his back and the other forcing his head down to prevent smacking the low ceiling beams. The claustrophobic sensation of the tiny hallway gave way into a larger space. Behind him, Steele entered with the other guard.

They brushed past him. The first guard dragged a chair across the dirt floor and shoved Brig downward onto it with a thud. The room's dense silence filled their ears, replacing the rough tire noise that had plagued them for the past few hours.

"Now what?" Brig said with more than a hint of sarcasm.

"Thought I told you to shut it," the first guard replied with a snarl. "Just sit tight. Nye will be here in a minute..." His voice trailed with his movement across the room.

The room fell into a tense closeness, with Steele's nervous breaths the only sound that he could distinguish.

"Another one of them?" a voice, soaked with a haughty British lilt, said. "Go get..." it continued, but because it came from near the tunnel entry, Brig was unable to make out the rest.

"So," the man continued, nearing Brig and taking a seat next to him, "I hear that you are looking for some assistance from us."

"I'm not gonna' say another damn word until you take these blindfolds off," Brig scolded. "We've put up with these games long enough. It's time you trust us."

"Simmsy, make our guests feel at ease," the man replied, his accent giving him a smooth, cool edge.

"Thanks," Brig replied.

"They might not make it out of here alive. The least we can do is make them comfortable."

The blindfolds lifted from their heads and the rope tying his hands fell loose. Brig quickly scanned the room, taking notice of the oak beams that held up the earthen walls and ceilings. He placed his hand on Steele's knee. The nervous cold of her flesh radiated through her worn jeans.

Brig rubbed her thigh lovingly. "It's gonna be ok," he whispered.

He was not sure he believed it, and her look of pure nausea confirmed that she did not, either.

"What is this place?" Her voice shook uncontrollably.

"I'll direct the questioning, if you please," the man interjected. "First... your names." Nye, a slender man of nearly two meters, sat with his arms crossed neatly over his lean chest. A sliver of a mustache painted his lip, the color matching the distinctive gray that adorned the strong bushel of hair atop his head.

Brig fought off his first instinct to use 'Brody Sampson'. They were already within the Reformation bunker, which was obviously a very secretive location - the last thing he wanted was to start out with a lie to a group from which he desperately needed help.

"Brigadier Stroud," he answered. "And this is Steele Fox."

Steele shot an incredulous glare at him. Brig closed his eyes and nodded away her concern.

"So what sort of assistance were you looking for? Keeping in mind that we don't normally respond to just anyone's request for help," Nye said.

"William Bryce told me that you might be able to help," Brig replied.

"Mr. Bryce... I'm not sure how you know him." Nye projected his disinterest by glancing at the ceiling. "Or whether you actually do. He is no longer with us."

"I know. I was the last person to see him alive," Brig answered.

Nye leaned forward on his chair. "Are you saying that you were somehow responsible for his death, Mr. Stroud?"

Brig shrugged off the accusation. "No. Circumstances led us to be in the same place at the wrong time."

"Where exactly *were* you when you met with Mr. Bryce?"

"That's a good question. Those bastards operate a lot like you guys. You know, knocking people unconscious, blindfoldin' 'em and lockin' 'em up before they can even figure out where they are." Brig glared at Nye with distrust.

"No doubt you're referring to the Syndicate." Nye's face remained stoic.

"One and the same."

"I was told you Epsilons were a rare breed. Yet there seems to be quite a spate of you wandering around in the desert of late."

Brig tilted his head. "I doubt that..."

"So tell me, Mr. Stroud. I'm waiting. How is it that our organization can help you?" Impatience, more than anger, coated his tone. "And this had better be worth it."

"My sister's being held. And I need some help freeing her," Brig responded, his tone suddenly lacking mockery.

Nye snorted with derision. "You're wasting our time. We don't deal in personal matters."

"You will... if you realize who's holding her." An eye roll made Brig widen his glare.

"Nonetheless... we don't grant personal favors. Especially to people we don't know, or that have no affiliation with us." Nye pushed himself up from the chair and properly placed it next to a nearby wooden picnic table.

"What if I can offer you Muldoon himself?" Brig countered.

Nye turned, raised an eyebrow and smirked. "*You* can give me Bruno Muldoon?"

Brig nodded. "I can lead you right to him."

The Brit crossed his arms over his chest, leaned onto the table and squinted his suspicion at Brig. "Are you bluffing me, Mr. Stroud?"

The former EW shook his head. Steele looked on nervously at the chess match played out before her.

"Because even with an organization as large and far reaching as ours, *that* is one of the best held secrets of our time."

"For such a large organization, the Syndicate sure makes you its bitch a lot," Brig taunted. "Are you sure *you're* not bluffing about the size of what you've got here?"

"I never bluff," Nye replied with a dead tone.

"Then we're two of a kind."

"So. We help rescue your sister." Nye got to his feet again, arms still crossed, and paced in front of Brig. "And you *say* that you can provide me with the location of our mortal enemy." He leaned on his knees with both hands and leveled his gaze at Brig. "How do I know we can trust you?"

"Bryce was pretty interested in having me join you." Nye continued his silent stare. "And so was Parker."

Nye raised a curious eyebrow. "What do you know about *him*?"

"He's the one that led me here."

The Brit's face contorted into a pensive glaze. "Alright, Mr. Stroud," he said after an exhaustive silence, "since you seem to have impeccable references... where is Muldoon?"

"Get me to Flagstaff... and we'll get our answer."

A figure came from the shadowy tunnel and stopped at the edge of the room.

"Son of a bitch!" the new visitor exclaimed.

33:
To Ashes

Earth. Clovis, New Mexico

"Cryp?" Brig yelped, his brow scrunched in amazement at the surprise appearance of Clive Underwood.

"Keep him the Hell away from me!" Clive replied, an irate finger pointed at Brig.

Nye looked back at Clive, then watched the expressions between him and Brig. "You know this man?" he asked Clive.

Clive dropped his eyes and nodded. "Yeah..."

"Is he who he says he is?"

Clive released an audible sigh. "Brigadier Stroud."

Nye nodded approvingly and turned to Brig.

"What the Hell are you doing here," Clive huffed.

"I could ask you the same..." Brig replied.

Brig's former EW partner looked past him and glared with a confused expression at Steele.

Brig, meanwhile, got to his feet and stepped into Clive's line of vision. "Cryp, we need to talk..." he began with a lowered tone.

Clive snapped from his trance and locked eyes with Brig. "No! We have nothing to say to each other anymore. Just... stay the Hell away from me!"

"But you don't understand..."

"Yeah, I know. That's what you always say, isn't it, Brig?" Clive spun away and put one foot in the dark corridor.

"Cryp... you have to listen!"

"Nope. I don't," Clive droned. He stopped and did an about face. "But there is one thing." His face contorted into a queer stare at Steele once again, noticing her brunette locks. He stepped up into Brig's face and jabbed a finger into his chest. "I don't know what kind of shell game you and your little girlfriend are playing, but there are a lot of good people here that are gonna get killed if they go along with whatever crazy scheme you got going this time!" Clive dropped his hand to his side, stared in disgust at his former partner, and plodded away.

Nye, up from his chair and standing behind Brig, patted him on the shoulder. "Well, seems this is your lucky day!" he said cheerfully. Nye watched Clive disappear into the next room ten meters away. "So much for 'brothers for life'. Do all of you Epsilons fight so?"

Brig offered a half smile to Nye.

"Anything I should be concerned with?"

Brig shook his head, and then looked away. "Although..."

Nye raised his eyebrows.

"Nothing," Brig replied. "Just get us to Flagstaff and this'll all sort itself out."

Nye grasped Brig's shoulder with gusto and paced past him. "Very well then. But first, I'd like you to attend a strategy briefing. We could use another Epsilon's input. Two heads, as they say..." He patted Brig's shoulder once more, winked and then headed into the hall.

Steele, standing silently behind Brig, gracefully inched forward next to him. "What was *that* all about?"

Brig put his hands to hips and laughed. "Believe it or not, *that's* my best friend."

With Steele in tow, her hand in his, Brig entered the large room at the fork of the corridor. Nye, his back to the hall and arms strewn across his chest, rotated his head and smiled.

"This is our war room," he said, his hand out to sweep the view.

"Impressive... considering we're... underground... where?" said Brig.

"That can wait," Nye replied. "I'd like for you to meet someone very special."

Brig scanned the room, and then stopped when he noticed Clive sitting amongst a small group of tired-looking freedom fighters of various ages. Clive made eye contact for a nanosecond, shook his head and looked away.

"M, I'm pleased to introduce you to..." Nye began from behind Brig.

"Brigadier Stroud?" a female voice announced.

Brig spun to discover who else knew of him. He squinted for a moment, unsure if the low lighting was playing tricks on his vision. Then, it came to him. "Magenta?"

Nye widened his eyes with glee. "Acquainted?"

Magenta laughed with a pleasance that no one in the Reformation had ever heard. She ambled forward and wrapped Brig in a warm embrace. "Oh my God! I can't believe it's you! Where have you been?" she said into his shoulder.

Brig laughed under his breath. "Here and there, I guess."

"Well... look at you! I haven't seen you since, when... '76?" she said, stepping back a half step and studying his face. She could not dismiss the pain in his eyes. "You've really grown up!"

Brig nodded and ran his hand through his full hair. "Forced to, I suppose."

Nye glanced curiously between the pair. Clive, still seated at a nearby table, took particular interest in the surprising reunion. "And how is it that you two know each other?" Nye quizzed.

A perpetual smile fell upon Magenta's face. "I used to be his father's..."

"...Security chief!" Brig concluded. A sudden connecting of pasts occurred in his mind. Brig glanced around the room with a morbid curiosity. "Is he... *here*?" he said in a loud whisper, almost as if Devlin Stroud himself might have overheard and disapproved.

Magenta's smile ebbed. She lowered her chin to her chest. The Reformation head took Brig's hand and tugged at it. "Come with me," she said in a whisper. "I need to have a word with you in private."

Brig glanced at Steele, picked up her hand and squeezed it with a firm assurance. Steele dropped her eyebrows and followed with her eyes. Over her shoulder, Brig caught the disturbed glare of his former EW partner.

Brig and Magenta retreated up the narrow stairs and strode out behind the mausoleum, stopping next to a broken wooden fence. Brig surveyed the sunset-baked cemetery and shook his head in amazement. "So all of that... under a cemetery. Who woulda thought?"

"It's ingenious alright..." she replied.

He leaned and jabbed her with a friendly elbow. "Look at you! I can't believe you're with *this* group."

Magenta exhaled audibly. "I'm kind of their leader..."

Brig guffawed, pushed lightly against her shoulder. "You? No way!"

She raised an eyebrow and flattened her lips.

"Really? How's that happen, Mags? The last time I saw you, you were so over your head when my father appointed you to his cabinet. How'd you wind up here leading this group?"

She lowered her head once more and stared at the ground beneath her feet. The glow of the late afternoon sun highlighted the hidden sorrow of her soul. "That's what I need to talk to you about."

Brig leaned onto the fence and crossed his arms.

"We were aboard Eagle One on our way back from a security conference in the southern URA. Me, your father... and the rest of the staff." She paused; her voice cracked. "This never gets easier."

Brig placed a soft hand on her shoulder and lifted her chin with one thumb. "What?"

"That's when it happened..." she continued, her eyes lined with salty tears.

Without further words, Brig saw the horrifying picture painted across her mind. He exhaled heavily and grabbed at the back of his neck. "The Event."

She nodded with somber slowness.

"That's rough... I understand. You hate to lose anyone like... *that*." Brig put a hand to his hip, not knowing how to move from the awkward silence of the moment. "At least it ended quickly. Right?"

Magenta grabbed at Brig's hands and held them to her heart. "You don't understand. He survived."

"I guess I don't. What happened?"

"It was after - in the desert." Her eyes escaped to a distant place. "It was just me and him." Her voice trailed off to join her thoughts.

Brig lowered his eye level to meet hers. "Mags... c'mon! Whatever happened, it's over with. What happened happened..."

"No. I failed him. It happened so fast – I didn't see it coming," she reasoned with herself aloud, tears coating her pleas. She had told the story many times over the years, but telling it to Brig turned out to be the toughest yet. "I didn't do my job. I couldn't keep him safe." She locked gazes with him; her face became stone. "Your father was murdered."

Brig's face fell white. He stood silently, his face suffused with the expression of an innocent boy adrift at sea.

"I turned my back for one moment," she continued. "I took my eye off the ball. Something I was sworn to never do. And he was gone. Murdered in cold blood by one of *their* people."

The boy's innocence in Brig's expression aged, replaced with white-hot anger – *adult* anger. Fire ignited behind his eyes. He scowled out at the horizon. "Syndicate?" he snarled.

Magenta nodded. "Yes."

Brig ground his molars with ferocity. He flexed his muscular hands at his sides. His eyes angrily scanned the rows of tombstones, suddenly wanting nothing more than to fill each and every grave with a Syndicate corpse – culminating with Muldoon's head on a pike to mark the territory.

"I swore from that day that I would make them pay for what they did to that great man... your father... and this country." Magenta dared to look up into Brig's eyes, but he was far away.

The raging hatred blistered each word. "Count me in."

Brig and Magenta reentered the bunker in a solemn parade.

Nye stood at the head of the war room, briefing the large grouping present, slowly pacing near a map pinned to the wall at the center. Next to it, an easel propped up a chalkboard.

Although his mind was ablaze at what Magenta had just imparted, Brig could not help but draw the remarkable contrast to the technology of just years prior to that of what the Reformation employed here in their bunker.

Nye halted his speech as the pair entered. In reaction, Clive craned his neck to see them. After a momentary glare at Brig, he flicked his eyes to Magenta, hoping to see some sort of friendly indication - he did not get one.

Brig took up a torn orange kitchen chair next to Steele, immediately grabbing her hand and holding it within his. Magenta joined Nye at the head of the room.

"So," Nye continued, as if never interrupted, "we'll send the primary thrust to the refinery from the northeast... with a diversionary force from the southwest. That will require us to circle around..."

Before he could finish his sentence, Brig raised his hand. "What kind of weaponry do y'all have to carry this out?"

Nye, displaying the professionalism that no doubt came with the position, barely broke stride. "All that we need, Mr. Stroud."

Brig smiled and wagged his head. "Let me guess," he said, "it's in a box that falls from the sky."

Nye, Magenta and Jesse simultaneously turned their incredulous gazes at Brig. Magenta stepped forward and placed a hand on the table at the front of the room. "How did you know that?"

"Because I know who sent it..." Brig replied. "And you're being set up to fail."

Nye chuckled. "Young man, I've been in this business long enough to know when there is a setup, or when fortune simply smiles upon you." Snobbishness glossed his words. "And this is the latter."

"I was there when it was sent – or at least when the latest one was..." Brig paused and looked to Steele - she silently nodded her approval. "From Mars."

The remainder of the members present, all except for Clive, turned their heads and took notice. Several laughed.

Nye cleared his throat with respectful impatience.

"You mean aliens are sending us weapons, mate?" Jesse croaked with a vicious smile.

"No, not aliens..." Brig shook his head. "Humans... from Earth. Or at least they used to be from here."

"Fantastical, my friend!" Nye cried, slapping his hand on the table with a hollow thud. "But I think we've had enough science fiction stories for one..."

"This here is Steele Fox," Brig interjected, placing his hand on her knee. "Anyone that doesn't know who she is - maybe saying the name Bronson Fox will wake you up."

Nye raised an eyebrow. Magenta tilted her head in sudden interest.

"M, this bloke's gone round the bend. You can't be seriously listenin' to him!" Jesse pled.

"Project Red Vision." Steele shot forward in her chair, examining Nye and Magenta with a clever eye. "Designed with the sole purpose of assuring the integrity and continuity of the URA hierarchy in the face of a predicted catastrophic event. I was the chief architect – until it was hijacked by... an unscrupulous individual with personal motives."

Magenta leaned a knee on the table in front of Steele, crossed her arms over her chest. "Project Red Vision. Explain."

Steele's expression remained stoic. Brig recognized the Red Vision mission statement from the videos as soon as she began. He fought off the cold chill that gripped him once again. "Building upon the pioneers that landed on the Red Planet several years prior, we built a portal..."

Nye and Jesse glared at each other.

"...that permitted ferrying of material - and personnel - quickly to Mars without need for expensive and time-consuming spaceflight."

"You expect us to believe this craziness?" Jesse cried.

"We don't care what you believe," Brig sniped. "This is the truth, whether you wanna accept it or not. And they're the ones sending you - and the Syndicate - weapons. But I'm guessin' that you're not gettin' the good stuff."

Jesse shook his head and snorted. "Told ya... I don't trust the lot of 'em, and you shouldn't either, M."

"It's the truth..." a voice behind Brig interjected with a solemn drone. Brig spun on his chair and stared with disbelief.

Clive closed his eyes, lips pursed tightly shut. "I can't believe I'm backing him up on this. But the part about Red Vision is true. It hadn't occurred to me about the weapons until Brig brought it up. But now it all makes sense..."

"Underwood. Maybe that was something you should have shared with us." Nye cast a chastising eye at the former EW.

"Didn't think it would ever be an issue. At least not for what you guys were trying to achieve." He offered a defensive glare at his sudden detractors. "Free weapons falling from the sky in the middle of the night. Why question it... if it advances *your* cause. Right?"

"So what's our next move, M?" Jesse glared at the Reformation leader, whom stood in stoic silence.

"Mr. Stroud, any thoughts?" Although the entire room had seen them leave, and subsequently reenter — together - she remained professional.

"You're goin' up against an enemy that has you outgunned..." He moved his eyes among those around him. "Your only chance is to divide and conquer."

"How so, Mr. Stroud? You said so yourself, we've limited resources," Nye countered.

"Keep your primary objective..."

"The refinery..." Magenta interjected.

Brig nodded. "But send another thrust at their HQ. It'll make them believe you're a far bigger threat than they ever imagined."

A simultaneous burst of laughter filled the room, its echo falling dead against the earthen walls. Jesse banged the table and howled. "And maybe we can get some of your alien friends to tell us where *that* is!"

Brig let the laughter fade without batting a lash. Nye locked eyes with him. "We'll take that under advisement, Mr. Stroud. Thank you for your input." Nye offered a slight bow.

The briefing soon disbanded, Nye having a new angle on his planned strategy, and Jesse having plenty of ammo with which to tease Brig - and Clive.

Brig and Steele had scaled the steps and were standing out on the lawn next to the mausoleum. Clive approached, his hands buried in his pockets, his gaze aimed at the ground.

"Why are you aimin' for their HQ, Brig?"

"So now we're talkin'?" Brig replied, a curious eye to his former partner.

"No. But you and I both know that's suicide." They stared each other down without speaking for a moment. "So what's in it for you?"

"I came back to help."

Clive snorted, turned his head away. "You came back to help? Is that right?"

Brig nodded confirmation.

"What else, Brig? Why else did you come back?"

Brig breathed a heavy sigh. "Jess is still alive."

"Here we go again…"

"But maybe you already knew that," Brig taunted. "Maybe you're lyin' to me again?"

Clive ignored the obvious argument bait. "Go ahead, Brig. Go ahead and do what you always do. Do things *your* way." Clive emitted a frustrated sigh. "Someone in that room back there is gonna die," he added with an accusatory finger. "And that's on you."

Brig and Steele bounced in tandem in the cab of the Reformation Jimmy. The driver, barely able to keep his eyes open let alone pay attention to their unimportant conversation, glared blankly forward.

"Better than ridin' in the back, huh?" he asked with a Texas twang.

Brig, sitting between the driver and Steele, nodded and raised his brows in agreement. He glanced to his right. Steele, silent since they had departed for Flagstaff, peered out at the passing landscape.

"Whatcha thinkin' about?" Brig asked with a lowered voice. Not that it would have mattered, since the Jimmy offered road noise at a deafening din.

"I must have seemed like an absolute ghoul to those people when I explained my role in Red Vision," she said, her coy smile absent from her alabaster face.

Brig patted her knee. "It wasn't your fault, Steele. You were manipulated into doing that project. The right reasons for you... the wrong for him."

She shook her head and bit the end of a finger. "It doesn't matter. I was still a part of it. I could have stopped it."

Brig peeled her gaze away from the window and stared into her emerald eyes. "No, you couldn't have," he argued with a caring tone. "Think of who we're talkin' about - Allistair. He woulda found a way to get it done. With or without you."

A conciliatory smile appeared on her face. "And I'm glad fate brought us together like this." He backtracked. "Not that I... believe in that sorta stuff or anything," he chuckled.

She squeezed his arm and laid her head on his shoulder.

"We'll make this right... eventually," he added, watching the truck gobble asphalt.

"So... what is your plan? Do you honestly know where this headquarters is?"

He stared out at the dark horizon. A summer storm brewed where the sky met land ahead. "No. But I have a hunch who does..."

Three hours into their ride, Brig, nearly dozing from the monotonous tire noise, perked his eyes at the sight of a half-fallen highway sign for Albuquerque. He rubbed his eyes with one hand, and then gazed at Steele. She was asleep, her head resting comfortably on Brig's jacket against the side of the truck.

He tapped the driver on the shoulder. The driver flinched, having nearly fallen asleep himself. "Think we can stop by north Albuquerque?"

The driver nodded. "Gotta stop there to refuel anyway. These beasts don't do that good on mileage."

"What's in Albuquerque?" Steele said, her eyes still closed. Before Brig could answer, she flung them open and smiled. "Your father's place!"

Brig nodded. In contrast to Steele's obvious excitement, Brig felt bittersweet about their side trip, having just learned of his father's heinous fate in the desert years prior. He was not certain what he would find there, or why he even felt the need to make the trip, but something inside drew him to it. Perhaps, given the right circumstances, it would be a fitting tribute to Devlin Stroud if Brig and Steele could one day call it home.

Three hours later

The lumbering Jimmy roared up to the end of a fenced property. A stone-pillared, rod iron fence lined the front of the massive piece of land, with several portions of the fencing having fallen into the overgrown shrubbery over the past seven years. The front lawn, normally well manicured and filled with a southwestern motif of various desert rocks and scrub grasses that lined the display, grew like a dense forest and blocked any view of the grand mansion beyond.

Brig hopped out onto the loose gravel; the driver leaned over towards the center of the truck. "I'll be back in about a half hour. Gonna go run down the road to our checkpoint and pick up some gas!" he yelled over the rumbling motor.

Brig slammed the door shut and pounded it with a fist. The transmission clunked as the driver put it in gear and drove off, leaving Brig and Steele holding their mouths from the cloud of exhaust.

33: TO ASHES

They scaled the small grade that led to the grand gates, both of which hung lifelessly from their hinges. Beyond, they could see the kilometer-long driveway, lined on each side with overgrown Cottonwoods. Twenty meters in, one of the majestic trees had fallen across the broken pavement. They strode through the gates and past the rotting Fremonts, knowing that they had to cover a decent distance and be back at the entry to meet the Reformation truck upon its return - the fallen tree eliminated any chance that the driver could come to the house to retrieve them.

"I can't believe how long it's been since I've been here." Steele gawked at the towering trees around them. "Absolutely beautiful! Although the front lawn has seen better times. I guess all things are bound to change..." she added, grabbing Brig's hand and breaking into a playful backward skip.

"And some things never change..." he replied with a smile.

Despite the overgrowth and the years that had passed, Brig found it hard to not reminisce about summers spent at the mansion. He could almost smell the sweet tang of a smoking slab of meat on his father's barbeque pit, the heavenly aroma riding the warm New Mexico air. His mouth salivated at the luxurious bitterness of a cold beer from the tap next to the pool.

"When was the last time you visited the estate?" She slowed to a walk beside him.

He arched his brow in thought. It had been *too* long. "Since the last annual barbeque... seven years? Has it really been that long? Wow..."

As they turned a small bend that led up to the house, the first sign that things were not as he remembered struck him like a bucket of ice water. A set of weathered and worn alabaster columns that marked the entrance to the main property, stood in solemn mourning in the desert sun: one cracked and pitted, the other broken in half, its top lying on its side within the Sacaton chutes that had grown up around them.

Brig's heart dropped like a freefalling elevator. The mansion that he had come to know as his first real home was gone, replaced by an enormous black stain of scorched earth, dotted in several locations with burnt husks of wooden and concrete frame.

Steele involuntarily gasped; she covered her mouth with a hand.

The pair ascended the concrete waterfall stairs that stretched three-quarters the length of the mansion itself from end-to-end. While a good portion of it had rinsed away with rains over the years, a strong layer of black soot from the blaze still coated the crevices and crept out onto the step surfaces, baked into the concrete by the unrelenting sun.

They reached the top of the staircase - Brig stopped and stared, breathless from the sight of what was once his father's proudest feature of the home. The grand, oversized oak and crystal doors that had provided an opulent centerpiece and welcoming gateway to the house itself, were nothing more than a broken skeleton of charred wood.

Although it had obviously been several years since the fire had consumed his father's estate, the heavy stench of burned wood and plastics lingered in the dry air whenever the breeze would blow.

They stepped with caution through the ruins, Brig leading the way. He stared speechlessly at the emptiness that engulfed him. Steele paused and remained just past the former entrance to the house, allowing Brig the solitude that she was certain he would require at such a moment. She had been to the estate several times as a pre-teen, when Brig and Steele had kept in close touch and made a point of seeing each other often. Her heart ached for the pain he was feeling now.

The wind provided the only ambient noise heard for kilometers - whistling with a lonesome sparseness through the desert rock formations behind the estate. Where there once stood lush green landscaping that ebbed to brown at the desert's edge, overgrown scrub grass had invaded. While the desert zephyrs offered a peaceful serenity, the sadistic wind of fate had drawn Brig to his former home and swept away any sense of connection to family that he had left in him.

He swallowed the bulge in his throat and crouched in the center of what was once the central family room. The warm memories of gatherings of years past swirled about him. They dissipated into the late afternoon sky, consumed by gloomy thunderheads that approached from the southeast. Brig captured a handful of soot and let it sift through the bottom of his hand as he glared out at the remains of the home.

The sun reflected off a small object lying in the black sediment nearby, its iridescence catching Brig's eye. He reached with a hand and dusted it with a wave. Buried within the smoky residue was a miniature video chip, which he recognized as one of the family's time capsule chips, unharmed by the blazing inferno that had devoured the estate. Brig snatched it, examined it within his fingertips and then palmed it. He bowed his head and allowed the pent up tears to flow - a piece of plastic the size of a nickel was all that he had left of his family's memories.

"Brigadier, I'm sure that everyone made it out of here safely," Steele said with a soft kindness. She stood several meters to his rear, her arms crossed over her chest. The threat of cool rain dampened the air around them. "Don't you suppose?"

Brig lifted his head and stared into the desert. He tightened his lips in frustration. "My father's dead. But it wasn't because of this fire," he said, his throat raspy from swallowing his sadness. He stood; Steele stepped forward and wrapped a loving arm around his waist. Brig pulled her close and kissed the top of her head.

They gazed at the remains of the estate, knowing there was nothing else to say. As they released, Brig stumbled and caught himself.

"Brigadier?" Steele seized one of his wrists to steady him.

"I'm fine." Brig rubbed at his eyes with a palm.

She watched as he made his way to the back of the house, where the patio would have been at one time. He stopped and glared at the pool, now filled with sludgy rainwater and burnt frame members covered with a thin film of slime. He shook his head and rubbed at the back of his neck, being careful not to disturb the bandage that Buck's wife had applied before they left Tennessee. The amount of destruction that had reigned around him, not just with his home, but also with his life, tied a knot in his stomach. He abruptly bent at the waist and vomited onto the soot-stained slab.

"Brigadier?" Steele gently rubbed his back. "What's going on?"

He wiped at his chin and shook his head. "I'm alright... I'm alright," he replied, choking off the last bit of bile in his throat. "Somethin' I ate, that's all."

The beckoning air horn of the Reformation Jimmy bellowed from the end of the driveway, blasting its call into the empty desert like a prehistoric beast. It was time to leave.

With a throaty growl, the dinosaur of a transport rolled to the end of a dark, rural cul-de-sac. Brig climbed past Steele, hopped to the pavement, and assisted her to the ground.

She stepped forward and absorbed the familiar scenery; Brig pulled himself back up to the sidestep of the truck to speak to the driver. "I need you to go back and find..." his voice trailed off as he lowered his tone.

Steele fell into a trance gazing at the front gates of her father's mansion, while Brig offered detailed instructions to the tired driver,. The hedges reached over their bounds, like fingers beckoning her forth. The tarnished bronze 'F' adorned at the center of the twin rod iron gates gleamed in the moon that drizzled down between the dark clouds above.

Brig pounced back off the side of the beast and waved at the driver. The truck rumbled a loud belch and ground off into the distance, its reverberating hulk of a motor breathing exhaust smoke into the night like a coughing dragon. The small neighborhood fell into a deathly still, the only non-vacancy being several houses down from the mansion - and that particular one was so dark it was indistinguishable in the blanket of night.

They stepped, as a couple, through the front gates and onto the short sidewalk that led to the front porch. Brig stared in curiosity at the light coming from the chandelier in the main foyer. He clutched Steele's upper arm and moved her behind him.

"Stay here... just in case," he instructed, and then hopped onto the wooden porch.

Brig cautiously turned the knob and pushed the door open with a finger. It travelled with a squeak until it tapped against the inner wall. He leaned his head through the doorway and scanned the empty foyer, taking great care to spy the top of the staircase as well as the adjacent living room. Satisfied that they were alone, he motioned for Steele to join him.

Steele stepped into the foyer beside Brig and instantly fell away from the moment, looking at the antique oak staircase that wound upwards from the right of the foyer. A numbing injection of déjà vu pricked Brig - it had only been five short months since he was standing in this very same room with whom he thought at the time was Steele, the night that she discovered her father missing. Her eyes gravitated to the carpeted floor where the foyer met the living room. The hideous, faded pink bloodstain glared at her with a relentless prodding, refusing to release her gaze.

"Oh my..." she said with a gasp. She held her hand to her mouth to stifle a cry. "Is that where..."

33: TO ASHES

"No," Brig reassured. "Your father didn't die here." He swung the door closed behind them - it echoed throughout the spacious foyer. "In fact," he continued with a sheepish grin, "that's a testament to your father's tenacity in the face of certain death."

She nodded her head, but the bewildered stare told him nothing he said would make this any easier. "I don't want to know..." she said, pulling her eyes from the macabre centerpiece. Steele advanced into the living room. Her eyes welled up at the sight of her father's favorite blanket folded on the corner chair. A small whimper escaped her lips when she spotted his favorite fountain pen and spectacles on the side table next to the couch.

Steele spun and walked briskly from the room into the foyer. She gazed at the stairway, and then at the hallway that led to the back portion of the house. She cleared her throat.

"It's disheartening when you leave a place for so long. You build up what it once was." She paced towards the hall. "The anticipation and excitement builds because you're returning to this grand world. And when you finally arrive – you realize it's much smaller than you had made it in your memory."

Brig swallowed his tongue with an agreeing nod.

She strode into the hall, Brig in tow, and entered the kitchen. She stood silently at the entrance, staring at the island that housed double, deep-well sinks. Steele blinked and then turned her head, looking over at the refrigerator built into the cabinet. Her lips moved without words as she laid eyes upon the breakfast nook at the far end of the room.

Brig rubbed at her back.

She forced a smile and shifted her head away from him, choosing instead to walk to the stove against one wall. She flicked at the burner controls with a touch of a finger. It belched to life with a flicker of blue flame. "The stove still works. Care for a spot of tea?" she said, biting her lip.

"I'd love that," Brig replied with a warm gaze. He dragged a pair of elegant wood-carved chairs from under the table and arranged them to face each other - taking up one himself as Steele readied the steaming brew. "Steele," he said, trying to grab her attention, "I think we should head out after this and take care of the first part of my plan."

"Mm hmm," she said absentmindedly.

Brig gritted his teeth. He wanted to get her out of here as quickly as possible without her seeing...

"What is that?" she cried. She stabbed her finger at the window that faced the side yard.

"What's what?" Brig said, although he already knew. His heart began to pound against his ribcage.

"It looks like..." Lightning lit part of the room like a silent soundtrack. "...markers of some sort. Over there, past the hedgerow under those oaks." She squinted and made for the door before Brig could spring from the chair.

"Steele, wait!" he barked, but she had already fled the house like a spooked feline.

He jumped through the doorway and stopped at the short concrete steps that led onto the back slab. Surely, Steele was a stronger soul than poor, misled Nadia. But what if she shared the same genetic coding that caused the latter to fling herself from a building when the emotional shock of reality hit her?

Brig's heart raced.

A strong bellow of wind tossed the branches of the nearby trees, its voice echoing like phantoms in the short wood at the top of the hill.

"Steele!" he called, but she had already arrived at the solemn reminder of those lost. Brig fell against the rock siding of the house, his vision blurred. He held his head with one hand and slowed his breathing. "Can't be the side effects... she said they were gone..."

Steele slowed and approached the twin grave markers. She wiped the hair that folded across her face in the strong breeze. A light mist cascaded across the overgrown backyard. She stopped at the foot of the first pile of rocks. The word 'who' had nearly left her lips when she recalled it, realizing the answer already.

"*Father...*" she said in a whisper.

Steele blinked at the sudden actuality lying in the dirt at her feet - tears wet her face more than the drizzle around her. "I'm so sorry," she wept. "I was so wrapped up in what I thought you wanted from me that I... I left you behind. I was too focused to see clearly. I should have known better." She lowered her head. Her shoulders shuddered with her sobs.

As the rain flattened her hair, she lifted her gaze to the second stone. Steele tilted her head in confusion, suddenly ignorant as to who would have been placed alongside of her father. A chill raced the length of her spine. She inhaled with a sharp squeak, catching sight of the shriveled Primrose, wedged by a pair of flat rocks at the base of the headstone.

33: TO ASHES

Words left her. A sudden surreality grabbed her, as if she were standing at her own grave.

"You poor girl..." she managed to rasp. "I'm sorry for what you went through. If only I could have seen what..." she paused and scrunched her eyes shut. "I pray that you are finally at peace. And that you can forgive my naivety."

She remained silent for another ten minutes before the rain strengthened, pouring down from the oak above her in rivulets and drenching the back of her clothes.

A voice called to her from the downpour.

She turned to find Brigadier standing a meter to her right. He closed the gap and wrapped his coat around her in a protective embrace. The pair stood in the rain and paid their silent respects.

R. JAMES STEVENS

34:
The Past, Present

Earth. Flagstaff, Arizona

The echo of whispers in the tiny, darkened pub tickled Steele's ears. She scanned the near-deserted room. "What makes you so certain that you'll find him here?"

"I'm not..." Brig answered, his eyes wandering around the room, as well.

As was the norm for this bar - the very same in which Brig recalled various confrontations - several patrons hid like cockroaches in the corners of the room, seeking the shadows for their conversations and dealings - mainly, however, just to not be seen.

Brig leaned forward and held a finger to his lips. Steele glanced around with trepidation, suddenly frightfully aware that this was no ordinary watering hole. She had been accustomed, even if it had only been a few days, to being within friendly territory – whether that was at Buck's ranch, or behind Reformation lines. Now, darting her eyes around the darkened pub, she realized this was a much more dangerous place to be.

Brig watched her rub her arms with a nervous twitch. He glared at the bartender, the familiar gruff bloke with the eye patch, whom wore a perpetual sneer on his mug as he leaned his elbows on the far side of the bar. It had crossed his mind, albeit as a passing blip on his mental radar, whether Syndicate henchmen actually talked to each other. Did they share news of what was going on in the world? Within their own organization? How would this man feel if he knew that there was a former EW sitting just across the room that was personally responsible for the deaths of several of his teammates?

The thought faded just as swiftly as it came. He spun his thumbs around each other. "I just wanna get out of here... go back to the mansion and get a good night's sleep for once in my life," he said with a raspy whisper.

"Brigadier, if it would be ok with you," Steele asked like a meek kitten, "I'd like for us to go to my flat instead. There are just too many ghosts at my father's place for my liking."

Brig blinked, and then offered a conciliatory grin. The much larger specter haunting *her* apartment loomed for him, but not having elaborated the circumstances behind Nadia's unfortunate death to Steele, he knew it was more important to set her mind at ease. He fidgeted in his seat, groaning as he touched the bandage that hid beneath his collar.

"And when we get there, let me take a look under that bandage. That should have healed by now."

Brig nodded, his discomfort borne upon his sneer.

"How did you get that, by the way?"

Brig's attention fell to the front door. He motioned his chin at Steele. She slowly shifted in her chair.

Danil Chekushkin, the stubble-faced, diminutive Russian, entered and discreetly placed himself in a stool at the bar. He motioned to the bartender with two fingers. Brig pushed himself from his chair and made his way over to the ex-TGB intelligence agent, dropping onto the stool next to Danil and leaning onto his elbows.

Danil remained quiet and unresponsive to Brig's presence, his only motion the slow sipping from a double shot of vodka that the bartender had set in front of him. He swallowed and stared forward.

"Underwood's friend..." he said with a deep drone. "I am surprised to see you here. I was under the impression that you had... what is it that you Americans say... left for greener pastures?"

"Sometimes the chickens have to come back to roost," Brig replied.

Danil exhaled a light chuckle. He sipped another gulp of his drink. "If you are looking for your friend, I do not believe that he wants to be found by you."

Brig shook his head. "Nah... I've already seen him."

"Visited the Reformation bunker, have you?"

Brig tilted his head at the Russian. "You know about that?"

A sly smile etched itself on Danil's face. He remained silent, imbibing the remainder of the clear liquid in his glass. He clunked it onto the bar - the bartender immediately replaced it with another. "Then why is it that you came to see me?"

"What?" Brig patted Danil on the shoulder. "I can't just come to talk to my favorite Russian buddy?"

"We are friends now?" Danil's intonation raised an octave.

Brig dropped the act, and his smile. "No, I suppose not..." He paused. "But I do need to thank you... for the information you gave me on the old man."

Danil nodded subtly. "Did you accomplish what you set out to do?"

"For the most part."

"Ah..."

Brig knew that the Russian was very astute, and that one sound from Danil's mouth told Brig volumes of what he already knew of *that* particular quest.

"Muldoon's men are a tenacious group, for certain." Danil gulped another swig of vodka.

Brig nodded his agreement of Danil's observation. For a moment, Brig replayed the events of that fateful night. He closed his eyes and blinked away the horrid sight of Bronson Fox's lifeless eyes, and of an emotionally distraught Nadia draped over what she thought was her father's bloody corpse in the back of the escape van.

"I find it difficult to believe that you came all the way back here just to thank me," Danil growled.

"See, Danil? That's why I like you," Brig said with a mock smile. "You cut through the crap."

Danil stared blankly forward again. "So what is it then?"

"I'm lookin' for some information."

Danil remained reticent.

"I need to know where the Syndicate HQ is..." Brig added.

Danil laughed with a hearty boom and peered at Brig through the corner of an eye. "I gave you a gift once. But that was because I did not agree with Muldoon's treatment of the old man. Why should I give you another?"

Brig bored his gaze into the side of the Russian's face. "Because he murdered my family."

"Your sister... Mrs. Muldoon?" Danil replied with no emotion. "Yes, so I have heard."

"And my father," Brig added through gritted teeth.

Danil shook his head. "Sorry, my friend. I have been sworn to secrecy. Doing otherwise would endanger *my* life."

Brig pounded his fist on the bar. The bartender snapped from his sleepy trance and glared his good eye at Brig. Several others in the bar, making themselves suddenly visible, glanced in his direction as well. Brig leaned into Danil and jabbed a finger into his shoulder. "You know what it's like to lose your whole family to a crazy bastard like Muldoon for no reason?" he growled in an intense whisper.

Danil slanted his head and squinted at Brig with a knowing pain. "You do not know what I have been through, or you would not make such a bold - and ignorant - statement," he hissed. The Russian glared past Brig into the corner, where Steele sat with a studious gaze at them. He swallowed the rest of the vodka in one gulp and slammed the glass onto the bar. Danil hopped from the stool and determinately strode towards her table.

Brig, remembering too late Danil's threat against Nadia the last time they had met in this very same spot, jumped from his seat and positioned himself in front of the angry Russian.

Danil pushed past Brig and stopped at the table, glaring down at Steele with curious eyes. "I want to say you are the girl. But you are not." He tilted his head, grabbed the overhead light and shone it into her face.

Steele held up a palm to block the light.

"You are a remarkable clone of her. But you are *not* her." He released the lamp, letting it swing like a dying pendulum over her head. Danil turned and stalked through the front door into the damp night.

Brig shook his head and sighed, sat back next to Steele.

"Well, that didn't go over so well, now did it?"

Brig did not answer, his wrinkled scowl doing the talking for him.

"Can anyone else provide the location besides him?"

He tightened his lips and drummed his fingers against the edge of the table. After a second, he nodded. "Yeah... but he's not gonna tell me, either."

The misting rain dampened the thinning black locks of hair at the crown of Danil's head. Darkness shrouded him.

"I have not seen you for several years." He lowered his gaze. "It has broken my heart to think about coming here and being with you again after what I have done."

He closed his eyes and burrowed his chin into his chest for a brief second.

"I have been on this journey... a very dark path. I cannot tell what my final destination is, but I have arrived at a split in the road."

34: THE PAST, PRESENT

Danil placed a fist over his mouth and cleared his throat. He shuffled his feet in the dirt. "I am not sure whether one path leads to redemption... or the other." He paused and glared forward. "Or whether redemption is even possible. But I need to make a decision. I have come here to ask your advice."

New Vegas, Nevada - Four years prior (2080)

Danil Chekushkin rocked back onto his haunches and glared up at a scowling Bruno Muldoon.

"Why have you refused to pay tribute?" Muldoon barked.

"I do not pay for my freedom," Danil replied.

Muldoon cackled. "Everyone pays for their freedom... yet they are naïve enough to believe that freedom is theirs for the taking - and is free."

"I have no money to pay your silly tribute..." Danil kept his gaze deathly cold and distant.

"Then we will have to come to some sort of arrangement... sooner or later, everyone pays." Muldoon snapped his fingers above his head.

A Syndicate goon appeared from the small hallway in the abandoned split-level ranch house, his meaty palm around the neck of a flaxen-haired woman, whom wore a grimace of fear.

Danil lurched forward. "Vladlena!" he cried in Russian. "I told you to stay back, I will handle this! Look what you have done!"

Muldoon forced Danil back to his knees with a strong hand to his shoulder.

Vladlena trembled; tears tumbled along her rosy cheek. "I'm sorry, I'm sorry," she sobbed. "I love you and I didn't want to see you hurt!"

Danil glared maniacally up at the Syndicate leader. "Let my wife go, she is innocent in this..."

Muldoon's eyebrows arched in mock astonishment. "I'm surprised at you, Chekushkin!" he cooed. "You, being the master interrogator - you know how this works."

Danil squinted. "You have to let her go now! We will figure out a way to make this work, but she is not to be involved."

Muldoon paced with a demented, casual gait to Danil's terrified wife. He turned his torso and smiled evilly back at the Russian, and then ran a finger along the woman's tear-stained face. He pulled his finger back and tasted the tip.

"Salty..." he said with a slimy whisper. "But oh so sweet..." Muldoon made his way back to Danil, humming in a joyful stride. "Perhaps your... services... could be of use to me in exchange for the tribute you owe to me?"

Danil spat on the bare wood floor next to him. He glared disgustedly up at Muldoon. "I will never work for a scum like you!" he growled.

Muldoon crouched and locked eyes with the former TGB agent. "You do not make the rules here, my friend," he declared through a wicked sneer. "Besides," he added, rising to a standing position once again and wiping a speck of invisible dust from his coat sleeve, "why would I let her go when I can have two for the price of one?"

He nodded at the goon, whom immediately released Vladlena's neck. She gave a surprised gawk at Muldoon, rubbed at her reddened neck for a second and dashed towards her husband. Muldoon produced his now-infamous Ripper from his side and fired two silent rounds into the woman's chest. Vladlena plunged backward onto the ground and died within an instant.

Danil's eyes bulged. Enraged, he leapt from his knees and launched at Muldoon – but met a brick wall in the mountainous form of Pollux Webb, a meter before he reached his target. The mammoth of the Webb twins grabbed Danil by the shoulder, using only three of his baseball-bat-sized digits to hold him in place.

"The boss ain't done talkin' to ya, Ruskie," he bellowed, his booming, obtuse voice seemingly rattling the windows of the vacant home. "Now how's about you just sit down!" Without much effort or force - but still a great amount by anyone else's standards - he shoved the Russian backward onto his behind three meters away.

Danil fought back the rare tears that perched upon his cheekbone. He ground his teeth until his jaw ached and his gums oozed angry blood. Then, a glaze fell over his eyes. Gone was the veil of fiery anger - replaced by a steely glare of icy resolve. He lowered his eyes.

"Take my life too, Muldoon," he said with a grave cold. "You have taken the life of an innocent. But here I still refuse to pay your tribute."

The room fell into weighty silence. Muldoon crossed his arms over his chest and chewed at a fingernail with disinterest.

"You have lost..." Danil added. "Dead men pay no tributes, either."

Muldoon laughed aloud. "Touché, Mr. Chekushkin. Touché!" he lauded in jest. "But know this... I never do anything without a plan. You are far more useful to me alive."

Danil maintained his dead stare. "Then I will spend my days ensuring that I avenge the wrong that you have done here today."

"Oh, my friend," Muldoon hissed. The Irishman knelt next to Danil with his hand upon a shoulder. "Do you not think that I have already anticipated that?" He placed his face within centimeters of the side of Danil's. "I know where you have come from, Chekushkin. You will work for me - or I will find your family."

Danil closed his eyes. "You know nothing. I have no family."

Muldoon hummed under his breath and rolled his eyes back in his head. "Maksim, Pytor..." Muldoon began in flawless Russian, much to the chagrin of Danil, whom instantly recognized the names of his elder siblings.

Danil kept an unwavering eye forward, the sickening gurgle of Vladlena's blood effusing from her punctured chest filling the void between Muldoon's words.

"...your brother, Yevgeni, in Kolomna." Muldoon's hot breath moved the hairs atop Danil's head. "Your whore sister, Diana, in Bryansk. Tell me when I'm getting warmer..."

Danil lubricated his dry throat with a swallow of saliva.

"...or perhaps your little boy, Nikolas. Living out in Mozhaysk with his great-dedushka. How old would he be, Danil? About seven now?"

Danil's breathing became increasingly audible.

"All cozy in their warm little homes... until I have them dragged out into the frozen night, and end their wretched lives. I believe I'll let the boy watch the rest die first – before I let him know it was all in the name of his father, Danil Chekushkin." He grabbed at the back of Danil's coat collar and growled through his teeth. "And then I will grind their bones to ash for use as fertilizer in my wife's herb garden!"

A glob of glistening sweat beaded upon Danil's forehead.

Muldoon wiped it with a swipe of his finger. "Why so tense, my friend? Or are you realizing that I never bluff? I know that's what you were thinking." He stood and brushed his hands together.

Danil lowered his head and bellowed a wailing howl. After the echo of his cry faded, he opened his teary eyes and glared at the floor beneath him. "Da..." he said with quiet reserve.

Muldoon smiled.

Flagstaff, Arizona. Present day (2084)

With the heavy drops pasting the salt-and-peppered hair to the sides of his head, Danil glared forward into the pitch.

"For years, I have spent my life with an eye always looking behind me," he said softly. "And now I see, thanks to you, that I need to look forward. I know what I must do. I will see you soon, my Vladlena."

A lily leapt from his palm and floated down, coming to rest in the mud at the base of Vladlena Chekushkin's weathered wooden headstone.

Brig and Steele strolled the empty boulevard that ran past her apartment. The rain had stopped 30 minutes prior, leaving small clouds of mist that rose from the heated ground.

"So what do we do now? Does this throw your plans in the air?" she asked.

Brig shook his head in frustration and sighed. "I don't know. We have a couple of days til the truck comes back to pick us up..."

She grasped his hand in hers and offered a conciliatory grin. "Perhaps we use this opportunity to... dare I say it... live happily ever after?"

Brig huffed a subtle laugh. "There's never gonna be happy ever after as long as that bastard's around. As long as I know my sister is still out there alive somewhere, under his thumb."

She rested her head upon his shoulder. "It was worth a shot..." she replied dreamily.

Brig spun at the sudden sound of footsteps splashing carelessly through the puddles behind them.

It was Danil.

Brig pushed Steele to safety at his back with one arm. "What're you doin' here?"

Danil stopped in front of Brig, his hands in his jacket pockets. "Muldoon can be found at the World's End hotel in New Vegas," he said in an emotionless drone.

Brig tilted his head in suspicion. He narrowed his eyes.

"He keeps his prisoners in cells within an underground tunnel attached to the properties around it. If you are looking for someone, they will be in there. But you will be hopelessly outgunned - and outnumbered," the Russian added. "Consider this my final gift to you, Underwood's friend." He quietly turned and began to stride away.

"Danil!" Brig called.

The Russian stopped and dropped his chin to a shoulder to listen.

"Come with us," Brig offered. "We could use someone like you."

Danil pondered silently for a second. "No, I have done my part," he said with an air of finality.

"Don't you wanna see how this ends? Help make it right?"

Danil returned to stand in front of Brig. "When I looked into the face of your girlfriend earlier this evening, I saw terror and innocence." His voice became melancholy and hollow. "It was a look that I had not seen in many years. And it reminded me of what I had lost and had sworn to avenge. I had lost my way, but now I know that what I have done here tonight is my way of 'setting things right', as you say."

Brig tightened his lips and nodded his acknowledgement.

"I must go and meet my fate, as do you. Good luck to you, Underwood's friend." He shifted his eyes to Steele with a silent glare, and then spun on a heel.

"Danil..." Brig called once more.

The Russian stopped, sighed and held his head up to the heavens.

As Danil rotated, Brig grabbed his hand and shook. "Brigadier Stroud..."

Danil nodded and offered a faint smile. "Godspeed to you, Brigadier Stroud."

R. JAMES STEVENS

35: Dawn

Earth. Flagstaff, Arizona

Bronson Fox had always been in control, from the workers that he handpicked to be on his team at the DMST, to the special shrubbery on his estate that he had imported from the Middle East. The positioning of his front porch was no exception, as it provided a grand vista of the night sky over the cul-de-sac that no other home in the neighborhood could offer.

Brig and Steele sat on said porch of the lonely mansion, staring out at the canvas of stars laid out above the iron gates. Steele, her head comfortably on Brig's shoulder, smiled with silent contentment.

For what was about to happen, Brig displayed a remarkable amount of calm. For the first time in ages, a sense of happiness draped over him that he thought had been long lost.

"Brigadier, I'm afraid..." she said. "Are you sure you can trust the Russian?"

His jaw tensed. "Don't you mean - are you sure we can trust Parker?" He ignored the queer glance that she offered in return. "He's the one that told me Jess was alive. Danil just gave me the location." He grasped her shoulder. After planting a kiss on her ear, he reassured her. "It's gonna be alright, I promise."

"You know me, I was a tough little girl, wasn't I?"

Brig chuckled, remembering the spunky eight-year-old British girl sitting in the dirt, attempting to defend herself against a pack of bullies. "You sure were. And still are..."

"I graduated from college at nineteen." She sat up and leaned forward, looking to the dark heavens, trying unsuccessfully to scan the sky for her home of the past ten years. "I led a team of engineers to Mars, for goodness sakes. But for once in my life, I'm deathly afraid of what the future has in store for me. For *us*..." Her voice trailed off to a crackly mutter.

He nodded his head in silent understanding. "Starin' death in the face has a tendency to do that to you."

She shifted her watery eyes to him.

"You've always been in control, Steele." He took her slender fingers in his strong palms. "Everything you've done, you knew the risks and could control the outcome. With this, you don't have any more control over it than I do. It's like fate is draggin' us along, and that scares the Hell outta you." He kissed the back of her hands, one after the other. "It scares the Hell outta me, too."

She grinned and choked a laugh at her own expense. "I love you." Her voice grew to a warm tone.

Brig laughed and squeezed her hands between his. "And I didn't even have to pull you out of a raging river to get that one outta you!"

Steele playfully pushed at his chest with both hands. "I didn't think you'd remember that. I'm so embarrassed!"

"How could I forget? That moment told me everything I needed to know about you, Steele Primrose Fox."

They fell silent for a moment, and then leaned in to connect with a tender kiss.

"I don't ever want to forget a thing about you," she said, gazing into his steely blue eyes. "The good or the bad."

"Don't ever change, promise me?"

She nodded and fell into his arms once again.

The throaty grumble of the Reformation Jimmy hailed from over the hill in the distance. Brig and Steele gazed forward into the night, knowing the fate that of which he had just spoken was barreling along the highway at a cool 90 kilometers per hour. They rose from the porch and strolled along the small walk, hand-in-hand, enjoying the cool night air. What fate had in store for him, or both of them, he was not sure of – but he found the ride suddenly enjoyable.

As they cleared the overgrown hedges along the front of the estate, the Jimmy rumbled to a stop five meters from the small curb. Its brakes let out a piercing hiss that called into the night like a 19th century locomotive. Brig and Steele waved away the choking stench of diesel and approached the cab. Brig jumped forward and grasped at the door handle, swinging the weathered metal door open for Steele.

The driver leaned from his seat. "Just her, sir," he yelled over the idling beast's power plant. "You need to get in back... with the others."

Brig glared with bewilderment at the tail end of the massive truck. He nodded, lifted Steele with one arm onto the side of the cab, and closed the door behind her. Steele widened her eyes at him from inside the cabin - he shrugged his shoulders and made for the back of the vehicle.

The olive drab canvas covering the bed swung open with a 'thwip' from the bottom corner - Jesse poked his head through the dark opening and shot his hand outward to Brig. The former EW hesitantly grasped the Australian's meaty palm, accepting the assist into the blackness of the truck bed.

Brig stood for a silent moment, adjusting his eyes to the pitch. Even with the miniscule trail of moonlight seeping in, he could see that he and Jesse were not alone. The whites of at least seven other pairs of eyes met him from seated positions on the benches parallel to both sides. Brig squinted as Jesse flicked on a small beam attached to his shoulder, illuminating enough of the enclosed transport in a reddish hue to see that it was a full house.

"Welcome to the party, mate..." Jesse growled, his own multi-colored eyes glowing from behind the beacon. The gruff Aussie glared down at Brig's clothing. "Although it looks like someone didn't dress for the occasion." Several others, including at least two women, filled the quiet with light laughter.

"If I'd known we were headin' somewhere nice, I would've worn my Sunday best," Brig retorted.

Jesse sneered in return. "This here's Alpha Squad. Me, you know. There's Simms, Crocker, Davis..." As he introduced each name, he briefly aimed his light around at the respective group member - each nodded a brief greeting to Brig. "...Abelline, Searider, Kazmer and Pursely." He sat back against the bench. "And you already know our distinguished leader... M." Jesse tapped his shoulder. The light extinguished.

Another light, amber in hue, flicked on across and diagonal from Brig. Magenta Abgomgave, her cocoa skin absorbing the small beacon like a calm rill, flicked her eyes up at Brig.

Brig took the only spot available, nearest the back of the truck wedged next to a larger brute, who he remembered as Kazmer. Brig sat forward. "Magenta? Why the full turnout just to pick us up and take us back to Clovis?"

"We're not going back to Clovis, Brig," she answered with a soft, but all too real, authority. "After much debate, and soul searching... we've decided that we cannot pass up an opportunity to strike directly at the Syndicate's heart." She fell silent. "That is... if you have the information you promised."

"I do..." Brig offered. He felt the expectant eyes of nine others piercing him in the dark. "New Vegas. World's End hotel." A cold sweat gripped him. Brig plopped hard against the back of the bench and wiped at his forehead to clear the moisture that had accumulated.

"Who's your source?" a voice called from the other end of the truck, nearest the cab.

Brig snapped out of his momentary nausea and leaned forward once again. "Cryp?"

"Who's your source, Stroud?" Clive repeated.

"Oh yeah," Jesse quipped, "Underwood's here, too..."

Brig pressed his lips together. No matter how he put it, no one was going to feel great about the name he was about to utter. "Chekushkin," he said flatly.

"Jesus Christ! The Ruskie!" Jesse bellowed. "M, c'mon!"

Magenta looked to Brig. "We've never had any reason to trust him. Why do *you*?"

Brig glanced around the group of glaring freedom fighters. "Normally I'd say in this day and age you can't trust anyone..." He stopped and licked his dry lips, glared with knowing distrust at Clive across the darkened compartment. "But he's never lied to me. In fact, he's gone out of his way to help me in the past."

Jesse snorted his disgust.

"And this time I could see it in his eyes. If he says it's New Vegas, I'm willin' to take that chance."

"He's leadin' us to our deaths, M! You can't be serious with this one! This ain't the Epsilon Warriors!" Jesse pled, a finger jutted in Brig's direction, standing with his head scraping the canvas ceiling.

Magenta held up a hand to Jesse, silencing him. The huffing Australian sat. "Brig, you truly believe he's being honest and not running us into some sort of trap?" She locked eyes with Brig in the darkness.

Brig nodded. "It was definitely some sort of hotel that they had me in."

Jesse jerked his head towards Brig.

"I guess now's the time to start believin' the little guy..." Brig added.

Magenta paused in deep thought, and then nodded.

"But just us? Ain't that kind of a light force to be headin' into the eagle's nest?" Brig touched at the oozing bandage on his neck and winced.

"It's not just us, mate," Jesse grunted. He leaned to pull aside the canvas sealing the compartment from the outside.

Just behind them, their engines idling in harmony with the truck beneath him, sat a line of two transports and a fuel truck bringing up the rear.

Brig sat back as the canvas dropped again. "You're givin' up on the refinery for this?" he asked Magenta.

"This is roughly half of our western force," she replied. "The other portion will strike the refinery at a predetermined time. But this... is now our *primary* objective."

"*And* my sister..." Brig made sure they remembered *his* reason for coming along.

"If she's there... yes," Magenta replied with cool detachment. She peered at the back window of the cab. "Where would you like us to drop your friend?"

Brig thought for a moment – this was not the deal. But there was no way he was going to allow Steele in the middle of a warzone. "Her apartment. She'll give the driver directions."

The man closest to the front of the truck, Simms, pounded on the metal cab with a closed fist. "New Vegas... and bring the girl to her place!" he shouted. The shadow of the driver's hand rising in acknowledgement preceded the livening of the truck's engine.

The convoy lurched forward into the night.

30 minutes later

The convoy waited back at the main highway as the lead truck, carrying Brig and Steele, split off and made a detour into the quiet residential streets of Flagstaff. As it reached the empty avenue that led past Steele's apartment and thundered to a stop, Brig leapt from the rear of the truck and strode to the front of the vehicle. Steele, already a step out of the cab, bounded from the side of the truck and landed like a sleek panther in front of him. Brig grasped her hand in his, and together they walked to the main stairwell just beyond the courtyard of her apartment complex.

The moon had risen from its slumber behind the mountains, casting a bluish hue across the stonework façade. The pair stopped at the bottom step and faced each other, a longing grin fading from their faces. Steele boosted herself to her toes and planted a peck upon his lips. She held her chin up in defiance of her loneliness.

A lone roll of thunder echoed from a distant cloudbank. A gentle wisp of breeze lifted a patch of hair from her shoulders and placed it across her cheek. Brig drew it from her face and held her cheek in his palm.

She furrowed her brow and held the back of her hand to his face. "Brigadier, you're burning up!" She tilted his head to meet the brilliant moonlight. "You're absolutely pallid! Are you feeling ok?"

He chuckled and closed his eyes. "Flu," he replied with a whisper.

"Oh dear..." She wept, pulling his head down against the soft skin of her neck. "Please be careful. I don't want to lose you."

"Don't worry," he said, "after all I've been through, it's gonna take more than a few EurAsian thugs to do me in." He laughed to ease her anxiousness.

Steele locked gazes with him, her glassy, emerald eyes seeking out and gripping his soul for the moment. A chill passed through her like an icy zephyr. She shivered.

He rubbed her arms. "You ok?"

"I just..." she began, but her voice failed.

"What is it?"

"Why do I feel that this is the last time I'll see you alive..." But she did not cry. She glared at the idling Jimmy at the end of the courtyard.

He wrapped his arms around her and held her close. "Before I leave, go up to your place - lock the door and keep the lights as low as you can stand them." He stared at her with a grave seriousness. "Get your cricket bat and keep it handy. Don't open the door to anyone but me. Understand?"

She nodded.

"And I mean nobody..." he reiterated.

"Brigadier... please come home," she whispered.

"Go..." He smiled as she passed him and disappeared up the dimly lit stairwell.

After a few silent moments, the light clunk of her door on the fourth floor closing and locking echoed through the stairwell. Brig walked solemnly to the back of the truck. A bolt of nausea doubled him over; he retched and vomited onto the curb next to him.

Jesse poked his head through the canvas. "You gonna make it, mate?"

Brig wiped the bile from his chin and glared up at him.

"Thought you black ops commandos were game. Got the nervous stomach, do ya?"

"Just the flu..." Brig growled. "Now let's go."

Jesse snorted and retreated into the truck bed.

Brig put a hand on the grab bar; a cone of light in the distance caught his eye. A dagger pierced his heart as he looked upon the solitary streetlamp that lit the corner of Steele's apartment building – the cold slab of asphalt where Nadia had left him.

Fifteen minutes later

The lead truck lumbered onto the highway, its aged motor groaning its disapproval of the mission into which its owners had forced it. The remainder of the convoy quietly awaited the arrival of their leader, forming a chuck wagon semi-circle with their engines shut down to preserve precious fuel. A shrill wail emanated from the moving truck as its driver slowed the ancient monstrosity to a halt in front of the others.

The tarp flipped open. Jesse and Magenta exited and made their way to the front. Jesse aided Magenta up onto the creaking front fender of the truck, where she faced her Reformation counterparts. She cast a somber gaze out at her compatriots, their eager faces lit by the pulsing headlights of the Jimmy beneath her.

"Seven years ago..." she began, her voice reaching into the darkness beyond. The crickets seemed to quiet in the hollow night, awaiting her rally speech. "I was cast into a cruel new world - alone and hopeless."

Her eyes scanned the crowd. As much as she had missed her own family, the ragtag group of freedom fighters assembled for the pre-dawn raid was as much part of her as anyone had ever been. Her eyes watered, but she knew that this was not the time to show weakness.

"Those that I loved were lost to me, and I was forced to face a bleak future - or shrivel and die." A light cough filled the silence from the crowd. "I was fortunate enough to have a guardian angel on my side. You knew him, my brothers... and sisters..." Magenta forced a smile, looking upon the scattered few women in the group. "William Bryce."

A few offered up whistles and cheers at the mention of the legend's name.

"He saved me. Offering me something that I thought I had lost... life. I didn't know at the time that the dark road ahead led to freedom." She paused and stared down at the cracked asphalt that flowed beneath them. "And now... here we stand. All of us... on that same road. A darkness has fallen on our land. It threatens our very basic freedoms, it threatens our birthright. The hallowed ground of our once proud nation is staked by terrorists that wish to enslave us all. And those that do not wish to be enslaved - they simply extinguish."

The silence peaked to the point that not a breath leaked amongst the rebels present.

"This is our chance. Ours, my... *family*..." Magenta held her hands out in a grand gesture. "...to take back what has been taken. To right what has been wronged. To strike at the heart of evil that has plagued this land! Seven years ago, we planted the wary seeds of the Reformation. Today..." Her voice rose to a fever pitch. "Today, we are no longer the Reformation. Today, we choose to travel that road to New Vegas..." She pointed with a gutsy determination into the night. "While our brethren carry out their mission on the oil refinery at Artesia, we choose to make our biggest stand in our short history at the feet of the very terrorist that needs to be driven from our soil! Today, we become... the Revolution!"

Cheers arose from the group.

She screamed over the din. "The Syndicate has told us the streets will run red with our blood. Today, we make our stand. Whether we emerge unscathed or otherwise, we will have made the biggest statement in almost three hundred years of this proud country's history. In the immortal words of one Patrick Henry..."

Her warm smile faded. She glared at the crowd and raised her rifle to the night sky. The crowd silenced themselves as if turned down by a volume control. They hung on the words they knew to be next.

"Give me liberty... or give me death!"

A raucous howl erupted from the group of freedom fighters, overpowering the grumble of the Jimmy's engine beneath her feet. They raised their rifles to the sky in kind, filling the night with a tri-pronged chant of 'Revolution!'

Magenta, tears welling in her jade eyes, hopped to the pavement and disappeared into the back of the Jimmy.

Jesse hoisted himself by one foot onto the fender and glared at the celebrating crowd of rebels. They quieted.

"As of ten kilometers ago, we're now in Syndicate territory." He drew a deep breath of moist air. "That don't mean much around these parts... but Vegas pulls us deeper into their well. Which means we can expect hostiles at any time. Be prepared for anything. And be ready to dismount and assume guerilla tactics if pressed."

He silently studied the crews before him.

"Listen mates." Jesse lowered his voice to a steady growl. "They may not know we're comin'... but they'll sure as Hell know we were there! Lock and load. Saddle up!"

The group gave one last cheer with a skyward thrust of their guns, and then disbanded into their respective vehicles. The trucks came to life in a chorus of groans, belching thick plumes of exhaust into the starlit, desert sky.

The convoy arrived on the outskirts of New Vegas in the small hours before dawn. The moon cast a ghostly pall across the landscape of buildings. From the perspective of several of the freedom fighters present, the panoramic view of a darkened New Vegas offered a direct contrast to their memories of the past. Vegas had always been an exhilarating feast of lights for the eye - now, it rose from the dark, desert floor in the void like a cemetery crypt. The trucks stopped, their engines silenced, and groups of the rebels dismounted in the gloom.

The air around them vibrated their lungs; a sound like that of a disembodied helicopter blade pierced the silence of the night. The small army of Revolution fighters forced their hands to their ears. The fuel tanker, which had remained at the rear of the line of trucks, lit up in a blinding ball of phosphorescent light like a midnight sun. With an ear-splitting shriek of searing metal, it melted to the ground into a pool of molten plasma. The nearest transport, parked three meters in front of the disintegrated tanker, caught fire and lifted from the pavement, burning a bright white from the plasma runoff of the initial explosion behind it.

Several unfortunate freedom fighters, in the process of dismounting from the transport, caught the brunt of the wave of glowing flame. Their bodies twisted with unearthly pain as they burned - white coils of wispy smoke rotating around their scorching flesh and streaming from their charred eyes. As the brilliance of the fire receded, the final corpse - actually just the remaining charred skull - came to rest on the shoulder of the highway. The breezy, desert air gave way to the choking stench of broiling flesh.

The surviving members of the squad scattered like disturbed ants, casting their bodies with reckless abandon behind the nearest objects they could find. A large grouping of them took temporary refuge behind a concrete walkway that spanned the nearby Strip, pressing themselves against the wall in the darkness.

"What the fuck was that?" screamed Simms, his breath thundering from his nostrils.

"Too big to be artillery fire," replied Abelline, a Texan, and one of several women on the team.

"Tank?" questioned Kazmer.

Simms craned his neck around the corner. He stared at the scorched pool of metal that used to be two trucks at the end of the convoy. "Never saw a tank do anythin' like that..." he drawled in his Arkansas meter.

They stared wild-eyed at each other in the night.

"That was a dark matter cannon..." a voice from the edge of the pillar chimed.

"A what?" Simms squawked in confusion.

"What the Hell's a dark matter cannon?" another asked.

Clive looked to the confused crew. "Why don't you ask *his* girlfriend, she knows all about it..." Clive nodded his head in Brig's direction.

Brig, kneeling behind a pedestrian bench, glared at his former EW partner.

Jesse fingered the barrel of his rifle and stared at the pair with disgust. "Anything else you wanna tell us, Underwood?" he growled, spittle flinging from his lip. "We're gettin' our arses handed to us here!"

Clive wiped the sweat from his brow with a quick motion of his arm. He darted his gaze back at the darkened Strip. "Probably a lot worse than that. No telling," he replied with tense forethought. "I didn't think it was anything to worry about. Thought it was a bluff. But now that I'm seeing it..."

"Fucking Christ! You two are gonna get us killed!" Jesse roared his disapproval and pounded a fist against a darkened ad kiosk. The remaining glass shattered and fell to the pavement, its echo flowing into the empty street beyond like a wave through a pipe.

The air heated once again, just before a large portion of the overpass erupted into concrete powder around them. Choking back mouthfuls of dust, the Revolution soldiers sprinted for cover at the corner of a strip plaza across the road.

Brig grabbed Jesse by the collar. "Who's gettin' *who* killed?" he growled under his breath.

Jesse's eyelids spread back over his feral eyes.

Brig released the Aussie and shook his head. Never one to bark about discipline, as he had always flown by the seat of his pants regardless of the mission, Brig suddenly found himself longing for the days of being under the structured echelon of the Epsilon Warriors. He glared at Clive, passed him in the darkness and leaned against the side of the building.

Jesse grumbled and checked the magazine of his rifle. "Anyone see where that came from?" he belched.

"On it..." Simms replied, his M2Z heavy machine gun already spitting tracer fire from its barrel into the gloom, ripping large portions of the facade from a building four hundred meters up the street.

"Hit and run, Simmsy!" Jesse admonished, "With those tracers, you'll be a sittin' duck when they return fire!"

Simms nodded and released the trigger. The area fell into darkness once again. The grizzled soldier hefted the smoking rifle over his shoulder with a grunt and jogged to the other side of the street. With flawless precision, he lit the dark streets of New Vegas once again.

Abelline took up a parallel position along the opposite side, alternating fire with Simms, and then relocating to a different spot every few minutes. The strobing flashes of gunfire from the pair of weapons glistened in the sweat on her muscular arms.

In a bygone era, Vegas was alit with neon and LED – but this fateful morning, flaming laces of ammo strung across the building tops like brilliant orange spider webs, violently tearing chunks of a once-grand resort hotel and dropping them to the ground with distant echoes. In the momentary lulls of heavy fire from the pair of M2Z's, blind return arms fire cropped from smaller buildings several blocks away.

The war had begun.

The night air quickly saturated with the pungency of burnt gunpowder, and gray billows of smoke lingered above the streets like nighttime thunderheads. The chaotic shouts of enemy soldiers barking tactical orders replaced what was once a tourist-filled avenue of sights and sounds.

Satisfied that he had adequate cover fire in place, Jesse faced the rest of the group. "Alright... three squads!" he bellowed. "Searider, you take seven with you. I'll take M and those six." He glared at Brig. "Stroud... you and Underwood take the rest of Alpha."

Brig steeled his nerve and gripped his rifle.

"We split here," Jesse continued, sweeping the gathered grouping of freedom fighters, "take both sides of this one, and then another squad up the other avenue." He pointed in the darkness beyond their current location. "RV up just before those twin towers... that seems to be the line. Any questions?"

Several members squinted into the pitch. A pair of shadowy, monolithic behemoths rose above the city, straddling either side of the road like a pair of underworld guardians. Every few moments, a brief flash of muzzle fire illuminated the shattered black glass that lined the facades of each tower.

The air exploded once again with the terrifying din of a dark matter volley. Nanoseconds later, the center of the street ruptured and collapsed inward, leaving a massive crater in its wake. Davis, and two others who had strayed too close to the edge of the road, disappeared within the destruction.

The remainder of the team, with the exception of Brig, Clive, Jesse and Magenta, retreated to safety behind a pair of abandoned semi trailers. Brig eyed the men and women that cowered in the darkness meters away. His heart coiled, the sudden realization hitting him like a sharp stone to the chin - these so-called soldiers were neither grizzled, nor even battle tested. Aside from Jesse and Clive, he now doubted if any had ever been near live rounds. With eye whites glaring like saucers back at him, it was certainly evident that they most likely had never seen a compatriot killed.

"Get up you maggots!" Jesse barked, stomping a foot in the frozen group's direction.

Brig grasped at Jesse's shoulder and turned him. "That's not gonna work..." Brig informed the angered Australian.

Jesse whipped Brig's hand in anger.

Brig held up a hand to clarify his intentions. He stepped towards the group and knelt to the pavement. After wiping his brow of sweat and steadying himself from a swirling dizzy spell, he eyed each of the team. "This is what you've trained for..." His voice was a sudden calm in a terrifying storm that gripped them all.

"But it's nothing like you've ever seen, or ever will. It's war. It's Hell. It's beyond Hell."

One of the men, more resembling a late teenager than anything else, sniffled and hid his eyes.

Brig flattened his lips. "It's inhuman," he continued. "You have to turn it off... and leave the humanity back there..." he pointed towards the trucks. "Every moment from here out determines whether you walk out of here as a team, a hero... or get carried out. Or worse." He lowered his tone to a more solemn resonance. "Nothin's gonna bring them back. But I promise you... if each of you goes out there knowin' that you're responsible for the buddy next to you, and you keep it in your head that nothin's gonna keep you from gettin' back home safe – then you're halfway there."

He scanned the team. Their shocked demeanors slowly melted into hesitant resolve. Brig patted the young man's knee, rose from his crouch and motioned for his squad to follow.

The group split into its ordered groupings and dispersed into the night, attention to their movements cleverly distracted by the on-and-off glowing barrage from Simms and Abelline. Gunfire from adjacent streets and parking lots provided a steady backdrop as Brig and Clive trotted at the lead of their pack.

Neither of the two former EW partners exchanged words, but then, nothing had to be said. They were professionals at the game of war, and they knew what the stakes were in this incursion. Not that they felt they had anything really to say to each other, anyway.

The small group halted at a bright flash that silhouetted the strip plaza across the street, along with the second squad making their way in the darkness in front of it. A resounding boom followed, rattling the remaining glass in the windows along the boulevard.

"The Hell was that?" exclaimed one of the fighters to Brig's rear.

Brig, without pausing his gait, tensed his jaw. "Plasma rifle."

"You sure?" the young man retorted.

"Pretty sure..." Brig replied. The former EW commando had seen enough of the weapons to know their signature orange and yellow fireball - and he wanted none of it.

The constant soundtrack of stuttering gunfire tapered to a halt, with only single cracks heard every few moments from the adjacent streets. Brig and Clive glared at each other with trepidation through the gloom. They had also seen enough battle to know what that potentially signified, particularly in concert with the plasma explosion of a few seconds prior.

Moments later, having not spent a single cartridge, Brig's squad stealthily crept to the rendezvous point. Within seconds, Jesse followed close behind with Magenta and the rest of their crew. They pressed themselves thin against another road-spanning walkway, keeping themselves in darker pitch than that which enveloped the city itself.

The pair of ebony monoliths soared above them and met the starry sky with chiseled points that hovered over the Strip. Jesse leaned his head slowly around the edge of the façade and eyeballed the buildings. Two nasty looking barrels jutted from several divots carved out from midpoints of each tower. The Aussie turned his sights to the ground ahead, 100 meters from their current position. Even in the murk, the heavily fortified intersection in which the towers waded was clearly marked - dozens of armored soldiers held positions, prone and kneeling alike, awaiting whatever force the Revolution had mustered.

"Where's bloody Charlie Squad?" Jesse growled under his breath.

As if on cue, footsteps drug along the asphalt behind them. Jesse and Magenta spun, rifles at the ready. Two men, both recognized by Jesse as being from the third squad, stumbled forward from the side street that intersected the walkway. The first propped up the second, whom held a hand across his upper arm, the lower portion of his sleeve in tatters where his forearm used to be. His head drooped onto the shoulder of his partner as they limped into the group.

"Where's the rest of your team, Moser? Where's Searider?" Jesse squinted into the blackness behind them.

Moser closed his eyes and sighed, shook his head with a telling silence. "Too much firepower. We don't stand a chance against these guys..." he said in a cracked whisper. The sandy-haired Moser winced and pressed his hand to his side.

Jesse narrowed his eyes to slits, noticing the stream of chunky blood that squirted between the man's darkened fingertips. "Ah Hell..." Jesse grumbled. "Russell!" he said with a gruff snort.

"Sir!" came the reply from behind, as a ginger-topped young man, who could have been no more than nineteen, scrambled up to stand next to the Aussie.

"Get these two back to the trucks, they're no good to us like this."

"Yessir," Russell answered, slinging his rifle over his back and grabbing under the limp arm of the wounded soldier propped against Moser. They swiftly disappeared into the darkened streets of New Vegas, leaving a trail of sporadic gunfire in their wake.

Jesse scowled at their last location, wiped the sweat from his brow and breathed a heavy breath. "Well, M. Now what? We're bleedin' manpower here..."

Magenta, her arms crossed over her chest, flicked her eyes towards him from the shadows.

Brig, whom had taken several steps away from the group, stood quietly and stared into the night past the barricaded intersection ahead, where his eyes seemingly bored into the front entrance of an abandoned casino.

"As much as I hate to say it, Brigadier," Magenta said, more than a hint of regret in her soft tone, "we can't afford these types of casualt..." she broke off, rotating her head in Brig's direction and discovering that he had begun to walk away from the group into the deep shadow of the nearby walkway.

"Where are you going?" Clive barked, just above a whisper.

Brig did not respond.

"Stroud! Get back here!" Clive ordered, his voice carrying alarmingly far into the night air.

Brig slowed, but did not face his former partner.

With an amazing agility that showed very little impedance from his prosthetic, Clive dashed like a hobbled gazelle after Brig. He grasped Brig by the collar of his jacket and pinned him against the concrete wall of the staircase. "Where the Hell do you think you're going?" He glared into Brig's eyes.

Brig brushed Clive away and pointed at the darkened building. "There's a tunnel entrance in there."

Clive flicked his eyes sideways and tightened his brow.

"That's where they're keepin' Jess," Brig added.

"Are you nuts?" Clive yelped. "Jess is dead! Have you lost it?"

"I don't know if she's alive or not... but that's where they keep their prisoners." Brig's voice maintained a flat tone; he continued to look past Clive.

"How would you know that?" Clive asked through short, panting breaths.

The corner of Brig's lip curled up in a revealing smile. "Because I can see it."

Clive stayed silent, unsure what Brig was intimating.

"Clarity..."

Clive shook his head in disgust. "Man, now I know you've gone over the edge. What... need some more serum or something?" He grabbed at the elbow of Brig's coat again. "Let's get the Hell out of here before you get yourself - or them - killed," he said with a finger pointed back at the squads.

Once again, Brig pulled away from Clive's attempts to hold him, and stepped towards the casino.

"You're not goin' anywhere, Stroud!"

"I'm goin' in there, Cryp. You can either come in there with me. Give me backup or whatever." Brig spun and stuck a finger in Clive's face. "Or you can go back with them. Either way's fine by me. But I'm goin' after her."

Clive sighed and put his hands to his hips.

Brig showed teeth in a sneer and turned away. "Oh," he added over his shoulder, "and I'll be sure to let Jess know how much you *didn't* want to help out."

Clive watched as Brig paced away from him. "Wait..." he said with a dead tone.

Brig stopped and tilted his head to the side.

Clive, his hands still on his hips, glanced back at the group. "If we get down there, and she's not there - you promise we'll turn around and leave with the group?"

Brig mulled the offer for a second without speaking, and then nodded.

"Wait here..." Clive instructed with a stern gesture. He retreated to the group ten meters away.

"He thinks his sister is down in one of those tunnels under the casino over there," Clive said to Magenta, offering her an expression of relenting frustration.

Magenta blinked and maintained her stance next to Jesse. "I'm sorry, Clive. We can't go any farther. We've already lost too much. We're in over our heads." She gazed past Clive towards Brig, whom stood with his back to them, still staring at the building. "I'm afraid he's on his own."

Clive rotated his head to look at Brig. "Well... I'm going with him."

"I'm going with 'em, too," Jesse interjected.

"Jesse, no..." Magenta ordered. "I need you here."

Jesse stepped closer to Magenta. "I don't trust these two, M. What if this is a trap and they're gettin' ready to send out the dogs on us?"

She widened her eyes until the whites glowed in the moonlight. "But what if you get killed?"

"Better me than you, M. We can't afford to lose you. At least you'll have time to get the team away." He glared at Clive, then pointed at Magenta. "Get set to arm those charges on that line we set. And be ready to bug out in case this goes south."

She pursed her lips together and stepped away from Jesse, her arms wrapped at her waist.

Jesse and Clive gathered themselves and caught up to Brig, who had already made his way to the boarded entrance of the abandoned casino. Jesse deftly removed a large piece of the plywood from the doorway, discarding the board with ninja-like precision and silence. As the two EWs entered before him, Jesse followed in reverse, the sight of his M60 against his cheek.

Brig stood in the massive foyer, squinting into the dark.

"Well?" Clive prodded from off Brig's left shoulder.

Brig shook his head and closed his eyes. He thought back to what Steele had told him. He gritted his teeth - dulling his senses was harder than he had anticipated. Brig drew in a deep breath and allowed his surroundings to melt into the background.

Suddenly, an unnatural harmonic, like a softly squealing harp, filled his ears. He opened his eyes. Across the far end of the casino, over scattered piles of broken slot machines and overturned card tables, a single door pulsated with a golden aura. Brig rubbed his eyes, certain that his recent sickness was toying with his eyesight.

"There..." he said, pointing.

Jesse and Clive glanced at each other, without a clue as to what Brig was referring. Brig darted forward, slaloming through the darkened piles of debris. With no recourse, they sped after him, their boots clunking on the cracked marble floor like bats in a massive cave.

Brig slowed as he approached the doorway, allowing the others to catch up to him. He turned the handle and pulled the door towards him. It opened with a creak to reveal a staircase that led downward and around a corner. A small stream of light beckoned forth from beyond. Brig pointed at Clive.

"You two stay here. We don't need them coming in and blockin' us off."

Clive nodded in agreement.

As Brig disappeared down the stairwell, Jesse started forward. Clive blocked him with a hand to his chest. Before Jesse could protest, several raps of gunfire sounded from below. The Aussie gripped at the stock of his rifle and took a step towards the stairs. Clive pushed him back again. "Don't worry," Clive said assuredly, "he can take care of himself."

After a few moments listening to intermittent cracks of weapons fire, Jesse slung his weapon over his shoulder. "I'm tryin' hard to trust you, Underwood," he said with a grumble. "But do you trust *him*?"

Clive did not return the larger man's glare, choosing to keep his eyes pasted on the stairwell instead. "Trust isn't the issue."

Jesse snorted. "What then?"

"Just pray that you never have to find out..."

Downstairs, Brig crouched behind a toppled money cart. Every few seconds he angled his M4 carbine over the top of it to squeeze off a lethal lob of bullets towards a pair of Syndicate thugs that had taken up defensive positions along the corridor ahead of him. The gunfire fell silent. The thud of a metal object falling next to him made him flinch. Without hesitating, he grabbed what he already knew to be a live grenade and launched it down the hallway back at its source.

A deafening roar cascaded the corridor, carrying with it debris that included the remains of both thugs. Brig rose from his hiding spot and yanked at the reload mechanism of the rifle - but it merely emitted a lethargic clunk. He ripped at it again, but once more, it locked in place.

"Jammed..." he growled, and then slammed the gun against the wall. Instead of releasing the magazine, as it should have, the stock cracked and fell in two pieces at his feet. "The Hell. Mysterious benefactors, my ass."

He tossed the useless remainder onto the floor behind him. The master plan of the puppet master back on Mars was coming into focus, and he knew that it did not bode well for those that were relying on shipments of intentionally defective weaponry.

From within the light mist of falling dust, the gleam of an axe blade, hanging from a partially destroyed safety board, caught his eye. Brig pressed at the oozing wound on his neck, glanced down the hallway at the scattered pieces of his foes. He yanked the axe from the wall and spun it in his hands.

"Better than nothing, I guess."

The piercing harmonic returned. Brig fell against the wall and covered his ears, but he came to realize that the sound was within his own head. He righted himself and opened his eyes. Once again, a glowing amber aura presented itself around a doorway three meters ahead along the left wall. He sucked in a calming breath and stepped forward. In the distance ahead, he could hear the clomping of footsteps along an adjacent corridor - no doubt his little gunfight with the Syndicate had drawn the attention of someone on the other end of the tunnel. Although he had very little time before they would arrive, the harmonic heightened its call; the aura pulsed in rhythm. *This was the door* - he could feel it.

He pounded his fist on the dense steel with a hefty resonance. "Jess?"

The light scuffling of footsteps behind the door filled the silence.

He rapped once again. "Jess, are you in there?" he called through the metal door.

"Brig? Is that you?" the muffled reply came from the other side.

"Yeah! I'm gonna get you out of there." He turned his head towards the growing sounds of enemy footsteps. "Gonna break down the door - stand back!"

He heaved a mighty swing of the axe at the door, but the head merely glanced off with a resounding metallic boom. Gritting his teeth and shaking off the sting that traveled his arm, he let loose another herculean stroke, to no avail.

"Dammit!" he growled. Sweat spilled from his damp forehead.

"What happened?" Jess called from within the former counting room.

Before Brig could proffer a response, the terrifying rising whine of a charging plasma rifle pricked his ears.

"Shit!" he cried, as he sprung from the door and sprinted several steps, before diving behind a pile of rubble.

The hallway erupted in a fiery cloud of orange and white heat that warped the structural beams overhead with a menacing groan. The bolt from the Syndicate soldier's weapon tore a hole into the opposite wall of Jess's cell and brought down onto Brig the structure of the ceiling in a thunderous clamor.

As the rain of destruction came to a crumbling halt, the first of two Syndicate troopers stepped forward and kicked at the rubble that blocked the corridor.

"Got that son of a bitch!" he chuckled to his partner, whom slung his own plasma weapon over his shoulder and beamed a barbarous smirk.

As the first continued to kick at the debris, toppling a hunk of concrete and a splintered section of drywall, Brig sprung from within the wreckage. With a dexterous motion and primal howl, he swung the axe with a thrust from his back foot, landing the deadly blade square in the first soldier's sternum. The man swelled his eyes and choked back a frothy gurgle, before falling limp with the axe still planted in his chest. The second, aghast at the sudden momentum shift, yanked the rifle from his shoulder and plucked the trigger with a quivering finger.

The shrill whine of the plasma power plant flooded the broken corridor.

Brig lifted the fallen soldier with the axe handle and swung the corpse at the firing trooper. With a blinding flash and a spray of slushy embers, the body of the deceased soldier disintegrated at the midsection and dropped away in two horrendous pieces. Brig's commando training took charge, allowing him to sense the fraction of a second hesitation by his enemy. He pounced forward and pummeled the stunned trooper about the head with the broken axe handle before the man could recharge his deadly weapon and have another go at the former EW. With one final brutal stroke, Brig buried the splintered shaft in the abdomen of the trooper. The man heaved forward and fell to the ground at Brig's feet, his life's blood spilling around the handle into a syrupy sheen that spread away from his body.

Brig stepped over the fallen soldier and stumbled to the cell door. He leaned against it with one hand while mopping the globules of perspiration that gathered at his brow. "You... ok, Jess?" he said, his breath flowing in heavy spurts.

"What happened out there?" Jess's voice squeaked at an octave much higher than normal. "Are you ok?"

"Need a cleanup on aisle seven out here... but yeah, I'm ok." He breathed in a calming breath, nabbed the still smoking plasma rifle from the dead soldier nearest him, and put several steps in between himself and the door. "Get to the other side of the room, and shield yourself behind something big!"

He waited until her footsteps faded. After a quick count to three, he aimed the gun to a spot right of the door, closed his eyes and depressed the trigger. The telltale squeal of the charging mechanism preceded a concussing blast that covered the opposing wall in a waterfall of liquid flame. He choked back the barbed stench of brimstone and waved away the cloud of smoke that hung in the air. Where the wall was a second before, a gaping hole that stretched from floor to ceiling took its place.

Brig stepped forward and into the gap. Jessica sprung from behind a counting machine and sprinted to her brother, flinging her arms around him and gripping him with a grasp tight enough to strangle a crocodile. "How did you know I was here?" she said in a muffled cry against his shoulder.

"Long story," Brig answered, exhaling both in relief and pain. "Let's get out of here."

She released him and glared at the crimson-stained bandage on the side of his neck, and then nodded. "What about Bruno?"

Brig's jaw tensed. As much as he wanted to scale the stairs and take care of the bastard once and for all, he knew that the most important objective of this mission was within his grasp.

With only moments to spare until a good portion of the Strip ignited in a fiery volcano of explosives, he grabbed her hand. "I don't think we need to worry about him anymore. He'll never hurt you again."

As she backed from him, her eyes broadened in surprise. Brig, continuing in commando mode, spun and took aim at the hole in the wall behind him.

Clive stood in the center of the breach, his arms at his side, looking on in astonishment at the mother of his child. Jessica fled past Brig and dashed towards his former EW partner. Clive lifted her midstride and wrapped her in a full embrace, his tears intermingling with her flowing locks against his face. He pressed his nose against her neck, euphorically inhaling the scent. Jess sobbed with a joyous spasm, kissing Clive about the forehead and cheek.

Brig looked on in silence, his expression borne of skeptical concern for his sister.

A few moments later, the trio emerged from the stairwell beneath a thin trail of smoke. Brig eyed the dark expanse that once welcomed throngs of gamblers from the world over. "Where's Jesse?"

"Probably guarding the front entrance," Clive replied.

They stopped and squinted into the cavernous room, but could not make out the beefy form of their Australian counterpart. The small group moved with quiet trepidation to the foyer of the former casino. As they reached the end of the grand marble slab that led out to the plaza, and before they could react in defense, a trio of Syndicate troopers raised their laser-sighted weapons to them.

"Drop your weapons right there and walk out slowly!" the leader of the enemy squad ordered with a vicious bark.

Clive shot a menacing glare to Brig and threw his M4 to the travertine with a heavy clank. Brig closed his eyes and breathed a frustrated sigh, before dropping the plasma rifle at his feet. Jessica, unarmed, quietly stepped behind Clive. Ahead of them, Magenta, Jesse and the rest of the Revolution invaders knelt at gunpoint in front of their captors, their hands clasped on their heads.

As the troopers converged on the trio, a scream of screeching tires echoed behind them. Nearly all of the enemy troops turned in time to witness a retro pickup truck speeding their way. It fishtailed, presenting its open bed to the group. A large, mounted M60 stood in the cargo area, opening fire on the surprised men. With surgical precision, the gunner downed seven of the enemy squad before the rest sprinted for cover to offer retaliatory fire.

Four additional trucks, two pickups and two passenger, arrived within seconds to flank the first, their own guns blazing into the group of retreating soldiers. The Revolution group, lying prone on the ground and in shock about the turn of events, glared at the pack of trucks with astonishment.

Buck Rogers lifted himself from behind the first pickup's mounted gun. Brig, a sudden sense of warmth flowing over him, smiled a broad grin.

"Son, looks like you done pissed on a hornet's nest!" Buck yelled from the truck, waving his ten gallon to his side. "What're you waitin' for? Get in!"

Clive, Magenta and Jesse offered Brig an apprehensive glare.

"You heard the man, let's move!" Brig pulled several of the team to their feet.

The Revolution freedom fighters swiftly loaded into the trucks – those that could not fit within the cabs hopped into the open beds of the pickups. The passenger trucks, filled to their limit with Revolution soldiers, fled the scene in a haughty cloud of burning rubber.

Brig, alone with one last fighter, leapt into the back of one of the remaining two pickups. With a whoop from the first driver out his window, the pair of vehicles stormed away from the abandoned casino towards the transports. Buck's pickup took up the rear, the fiery ex-Colonel still pouring hot metal into the Syndicate troops flowing into the street to pursue.

As the last of the trucks zoomed through the empty pre-dawn New Vegas Strip, a chorus of fireballs ignited the gray twilight. One by one, and in succession, groups of buildings behind them shattered apart with ear-splitting force.

The air vibrated once again. A dense dark matter projectile screamed down from a gunner perch in the left tower, ripping a gaping crater in the asphalt and flipping Buck's pickup forward end-over-end. The truck landed in a shrieking skid of sparks that lit up the dark street around it.

Brig pounded on the back window of his pickup. "Stop now! Stop!"

His truck, along with the one ahead that carried Jesse and Clive, squealed to a halt in the center of the war-torn boulevard. Brig, Jesse and Clive sprung from their vehicles and quickly made their way to Buck's overturned truck.

Brig's eyes widened as he located the old army colonel, his lower extremities pinned beneath the bed of the smoking retro. Brig skidded to a stop on his knees next to Buck.

"Time to get you out of here, sir..." he shouted to Buck in the din of small arms fire coming from the pursuing horde.

"Don't be God damned ridiculous, son!" Buck barked like an injured, but riled, lion. "Forget this old war horse and get the Hell out of here before you git yourselves all killed!"

Brig, ignoring Buck's stubborn protests, shook his head while he threw a shoulder at the bed of the truck. "Not about to let you die in the hands of the enemy, Colonel!"

With the heroic assistance of Jesse and Clive, the three soldiers craned the bed of the truck enough for Buck to slide his wounded legs from underneath the twisted metal. They released the truck and let it fall to the ground; Clive scooped up Buck and flung him over his shoulder. The former EW hobble-sprinted to the lead truck and placed Buck inside. Jesse dove in next to them and slammed the door shut before the vehicle tore away towards the transports.

Brig grabbed Roberson Crocker, a Revolution soldier, and sprinted at top speed to their pickup. The air around them caved once more - the pickup disintegrated in front of them, along with the driver and another of Buck's cavalry.

Behind them, a gaggle of Syndicate troopers advanced and opened fire upon the pair, their armament peppering the ground with bright sparks at their feet. Focusing ahead, Brig scanned through the fog of war and identified Magenta's vehicle, its taillights illuminating the neighborhood in a red glow. Several freedom fighters emerged from the stopped truck. The muzzles of their guns resembled fiery crosses in the darkness, laying down cover fire for the pair to make their escape.

Having no choice but to take an evasive route, Brig and Crocker took to a shadowy side street, dodging machine gun fire at each turn, weaving their way towards the transport staging area. They maneuvered a corner and reached an alley situated behind a small strip plaza; a lone Syndicate trooper intercepted them at the next turn.

"On your knees, scum!" the trooper commanded, expelling heavy breaths from the pursuit. "And drop that rifle!"

Crocker reluctantly skidded his M4 into the dark alley.

While a quick escape was first on his mind, Brig realized that facing such a heavily armed soldier with no weapons of their own was certainly suicide for at least one of them. The pair put their hands to their heads and lowered themselves to a kneel.

"You don't wanna do this, pal," Brig explained, his eyes scanning his surroundings in hopes of finding a way out of the deadly predicament.

The trooper spat out a disdainful laugh and squeezed the trigger of his AK47, releasing a heavy volley of searing metal into the chest of Crocker. The shocked Revolution freedom fighter flipped backward into a pretzel-like bend and bled out onto the cold pavement next to Brig.

Brig relaxed his breathing. He had escaped death so many times in his life - but he knew that it was unavoidable this time. The Syndicate soldier turned the barrel of his gun to the Epsilon.

Suddenly, a blur swept across from Brig's right side. As the muzzle of the trooper's piece came to life once more, Magenta leapt from the intersecting alley and across Brig's path, shoving him from harm. Before she could fire her 9MM sidearm, the Revolution leader absorbed a volley of rounds to her abdomen, mid-flight, dropping her to the ground face first.

Without hesitation, Brig snagged Magenta's gun and emptied the clip on the Syndicate trooper. With lethal efficiency, the rounds all found a tight pattern on the soldier's neck, severing his head from his shoulders. The trooper's lifeless corpse fell backward and twitched its final essence, still gripping the assault rifle.

"Everyone onto the transports, we're heading out!" Jesse shouted above the flurry of activity outside the row of remaining trucks.

The vehicles roared to life. Clive grabbed Jesse by the shoulder. "There's still a few folks who haven't made it back yet, Jesse." He looked to the darkened street corner a block away, where only two hours before the courageous crew had begun their incursion. "Magenta's one of them..."

Jesse continued his preparations for departure, tugging at one of the M2Z's and tossing it into a nearby transport. "She gave us standing orders. We leave if she doesn't make it back by sunrise."

Clive's eyes fell to the first hint of daylight breaking over the mountains to the east.

Jesse, having already realized the deadline was upon them, pounded his fist against the hood of the transport. "Alright, let's move it out Revolution!"

"Jesse! Over there!" Abelline shouted, her grimy hand outstretched towards the street corner.

Within the smoke of war and the twilight of the early morning, a silhouette of a man carrying someone across his shoulders appeared. Brig stepped into the headlights of the waiting transports, Magenta hanging in a lifeless heap over his back, a blackened violet stain down his jacket where she lay.

Simms and Pursley rushed to assist their fallen leader. Brig powered through them and placed her on the open bed of the nearest transport. "Need a medic over here. Now!" he bellowed.

Kazmer, busy loading a crate of ammo onto his transport, leapt from the back and scrambled forward around a gathering crowd. He scaled the bed of the Jimmy and knelt next to Magenta, quickly tearing at the front of her shirt to expose her wounds. His face flushed white.

Brig entered the transport bed and knelt next to his friend. He placed a hand against her forehead. "Mags. Mags, it's gonna be alright," he said with as much calm as he could muster.

Magenta sputtered, trying to sit upright before Kazmer pushed her back flat.

"That was one helluva raid, Mags," Brig continued, his voice beginning to break. "Couldn't have done it better myself..."

She forced a smile. "So now we're... even," she said with a nod of her eyelids.

"No! I'm not gonna accept that, Mags." Brig clutched at her pale hand. He clenched his teeth together. "You never owed me anything. It's those Syndicate bastards that have to pay up."

Magenta opened her eyes. The sunrise lit the bed of the transport. Her gaze fell upon Clive, whom stood at the back at the group interlocked with Jessica in a tight embrace. Magenta's expression morphed to one of resolve. She squeezed Brig's palm with her remaining energy.

"Fight the good fight..." she gasped.

Amidst the war torn Mecca of New Vegas, the solemn group of freedom fighters formed a semi-circle around the back end of the Jimmy. The sudden death of their revered leader left them in stunned silence.

Their trance was short-lived. Another volley from one of the twin dark matter cannons ruptured the street just twenty meters away from them. With a hasty effectiveness, they completed their mounting of the transports and retreated away from New Vegas as the sun began its crawl across the desert.

36:
Going Home

Earth. New Vegas, Nevada - Later that day

Bruno Muldoon cocked his arm at an angle behind his back, defending his position against his favorite fencing partner, Louis Sergeant. One of the Syndicate leader's most trusted advisors, Keegan McDowell, a Scotsman with a flaming red Mohawk and a pair of mutton chop sideburns, stood off to the side of the match – once again held on the roof of the World's End Resort & Casino.

Keegan casually glanced down towards the Strip, where a line of smoke columns still rose skyward from the decimated city blocks.

"...And have a full squad trail them into the desert," Muldoon said while waving his epee in the air at Louis. "I want no one left alive."

The advisor blinked, not from the setting sun on the horizon, nor the stirring breeze flowing across the rooftop carrying with it the strong pungency of burning asphalt, but from his consternation at his boss's orders. "But, sir, that's nearly half our troops," the advisor balked, but with a reserved tone. "Is that wise?"

Muldoon, in the midst of a lunge, glared at the advisor from within his screened mask. "They learned a harsh lesson last night, Keegan." Muldoon's air dripped with a conceited cunning. "Now they know what they are up against."

"And what of the Strip defenses?"

Muldoon whipped away Sergeant's advance with a smooth parry. "Our defenses are more than they can handle, and they won't soon make another mistake like they made here. It's time to send the mice back into their holes."

Keegan flicked his eyes towards one of the other guards, then at the ground. He bowed his head, the tall swath of hair along his scalp tussling in the wind. He turned and disappeared into the roof stairwell.

Castor Webb passed Keegan on the way out of the small roof door, bending and squeezing his massive frame through after the advisor darted inside. The large, but still smaller of the two Webb twins, took several strides across the roof and stopped behind his boss.

The Syndicate head grunted his aggravation as he performed an overly aggressive lunge at his opponent. Sergeant deftly dodged and riposted to Muldoon's midsection. Muldoon snarled and swiped his epee in disgust across the gravelly surface.

"Sorry to bother you during your match, boss." Castor cleared his throat and hooked his massive arms behind his back.

Muldoon halted his advance on Sergeant and backed away. Sergeant bowed, his blade tucked under his arm.

"Actually, Castor," Muldoon replied with a breathy grumble, "your timing is perfect." He snagged the mask from his head and wedged it under his arm.

Castor scrunched his brow. "Boss? We goin' somewhere?"

A gust of wind whipped Muldoon's flowing black hair around his face. He casually swiped it away.

"Is that a good idea, you know... with everything that went down last night?"

Muldoon allowed a non-humorous laugh to escape his lips. "This isn't about going anywhere, Castor. And since you and your dimwitted oaf of a brother seem to want to question my motives at every turn..." He wiped the tip of his blade on his vest. "Perhaps it is once again time to demonstrate to you both how business is run in *my* organization."

The mammoth's stomach plummeted a level. It struck him that Bruno Muldoon must have had something on them. With a horror in his gut, Castor thought back to his private conversation with his brother weeks prior - on the very same roof.

The door to the roof squeaked open. Castor averted his eyes from his boss and watched as one of Muldoon's lackeys, Davin, drug a familiar, diminutive figure from the stairwell behind him.

With his wrists tied by rope behind his back, Danil Chekushkin worked to keep up with the stride of his captor. Davin grabbed Danil by the short hair on the back of his head and slammed the Russian down to his knees with a grunt.

Danil narrowed his eyes and glared forward away from everyone present. His fate nearly upon him, he showed no remorse, and moreover, appeared to be in a very calm state.

"Mr. Chekushkin," Muldoon began with a cursory bow. He lifted his eyes to the Russian and smirked. "You've looked better."

Muldoon rose and sleeved his epee at his side. "Loyalty, Castor," he continued, "has always been of utmost importance to me. Which makes the price of disloyalty so great..." He knelt next to Danil, placed his hand on the Russian's shoulder. "Our little Russian friend here is about to learn such a lesson."

Danil sucked in a deep breath and calmly exhaled.

"It seems that the Reformation's little attack on us overnight was no accident, nor was it a stroke of luck that they knew of our whereabouts." Muldoon tilted his head and tried to lock eyes with the kneeling Danil.

The Russian, still steadfastly staring forward at a distant point on the horizon, did not react to Muldoon's revelations.

"Someone gave us away, Castor."

Castor held his hands up in defense. "It wasn't me or Pol, boss, I swear..."

"Relax, Castor," Muldoon assured. "I'm referring to Mr. Chekushkin here."

"Chekushkin?" Castor balked, his eyes bulged. "I know the Ruskie ain't too smart sometimes. But, boss, I don't think he'd do somethin' like that..."

Muldoon cleared his throat and stepped away from Danil, his hands behind his own back. "Wrong kind of loyalty, Castor." He spun on a heel and stared down at Danil with disgust. Muldoon grabbed at a tuft of hair upon the Russian's head, pulling his eyes up to meet his glare. "You've foolishly decided to try my patience, my friend."

Danil maintained his silence.

"Have you forgotten the circumstances of your employ with me?"

Danil snorted once, but still refused to speak.

Muldoon released Danil's hair, rotated with deliberate forethought and walked a few steps away. With a graceful spin, he swung his epee at Danil's face, slashing the kneeling man's cheek. Blood spurted from the jagged wound.

The former TGB agent closed his eyes and shed the pain. "My conscience is clear," he said with stoic resolve. "And I am not afraid to die. Are you?"

Muldoon emitted a crooked laugh, one that betrayed the edge of his nerves.

Sergeant nervously cleared his throat and took a step backward.

The Syndicate leader lifted his blade once more and aimed it at Danil's throat. "My kingdom demands greater than you, treacherous serf!"

Danil lifted his eyes to Muldoon with an intense glare. "But what false kingdom is this, when thy own king's name is treachery?"

Muldoon, perceptibly taken aback, lowered his epee. His face flushing red, he grabbed Danil and pulled him to eye level with a throat grasp.

Danil sneered and breathed through his nose, his diminutive stature overshadowed by his defiant stance against "Brutal" Bruno Muldoon.

"You've chosen an ill moment to be brave, cockroach," Muldoon growled through clenched teeth.

Dark blood spilling from his lacerated cheek, Danil granted Muldoon an otherworldly smile. "You have witnessed your last sunrise, Bruno."

Muldoon's eyes grew to saucers.

Danil kept his iron gaze. "And the next sunset you see will be your own..."

Muldoon dropped Danil back to his knees and spun away from him. He glared to the mountains on the horizon. "Your hour is nigh, Danil. What say you?" he announced with a flat resonance, his voice like a distant echo in the wind.

Danil remained stoically silent.

His chin tucked to his shoulder, Muldoon spied Danil with one eye to its corner. "Your loyalty is penniless..." he snarled.

"And justice is merciless..." Danil responded without hesitation.

Muldoon twisted and in one motion lifted an onyx-handled revolver from his side. With a crack that reverberated throughout the desert sky, he unleashed a shot that drilled Danil in the center of his forehead.

A dribble of deep crimson blood flowed like a stream of sludgy motor oil from the hole above his eyes. The Russian hovered on his knees for a brief moment before bending backward onto the rooftop. A rookery of Albatross took wing from the next roof over, soaring on a trajectory that took them above the small gathering, and then dove below roof level and out of sight.

Muldoon lowered the gun to his side, a thin strand of wispy smoke oozing from its barrel, and breathed an audible release of tense air through his flaring nostrils.

Castor, Sergeant and Davin flinched at the sudden turn of events. Muldoon tossed the gun onto the rooftop beside Danil's dead body. Sergeant quickly snagged the piece and buffed the handle before tossing it to one of the guards. Muldoon tugged at the vest of his fencing jacket, wiping away the invisible stains of battle. "Castor," he said with a calm air, contorting his face to examine his coat, "get that diseased worm out of my sight."

Castor, his eyes wide with percussed stupor, stared down at the deceased former TGB agent. While not friends of the Russian by any measure, his heart filled with melancholy for another in the long line of fallen victims of his boss. His gaze hooked on the dead man's peaceful visage of death and would not relent. For someone who had just succumbed to such a violent end as had Danil Chekushkin, his face, normally tightened behind a veil of intense mystique, showed little else than blissful release.

"Castor..." Muldoon barked, "Whenever you have the time."

The smaller Webb twin shut his eyes and stowed away the confused sadness he held in his heart for Danil, and then, flicking an apprehensive eye towards Muldoon, scooped up the lifeless form and carried him from the rooftop.

"En garde!" Muldoon cried, once again back in his defensive stance. Sergeant held a nervous breath, watching Castor disappear into the stairwell, before he placed the mask back over his face.

Brig stared through the shutters of the cottage at the setting sun. Without warning, he belched a cough into his hand. He withdrew his arm, revealing a splotch of deep red blood where he had touched his hand to his mouth.

"Let me tell you, you are one stubborn son of a bitch..."

Brig blotted the syrupy fluid with a sleeve and dropped his hand to his side.

Buck Rogers lay in a bed across the room, a makeshift traction device holding up his hideously wounded leg.

The Epsilon chuckled under his breath. He tilted his head over his shoulder to catch a glimpse of Buck leaning forward in his bed, the pain evident on his scrunched face.

"I told you to leave me there and get the Hell away."

Brig shook his head. "Now you know I wasn't gonna leave you there." He stepped next to Buck and placed a hand on the old man's shoulder. "There's still a lotta fight in this ol' warhorse."

Buck snickered with a boyish glee.

"Besides, my old man always told me I never paid much attention to the big picture, so that wasn't unexpected."

"Well on the bright side," Buck interjected, "our counterparts up in the Great White North have agreed to lend the Reformation a hand in this little soiree."

Brig glared at the last sunbeams of the day, flowing through the cracks in the window boards. "It's Revolution now..."

"So it is..." Buck said with a crooked smile. "What's in a name anyhow."

Brig nodded in silent agreement without looking back at Buck.

"So tell whoever's in charge of this outfit that they've got an entire Canadian regiment comin' down to help even things out against those bastards."

"I doubt anyone has anything to even out against what the Syndicate showed us," Brig said with a distant groan. He rubbed at the stubble on his chin.

Buck snorted. "Never underestimate the will of a people, Sampson."

Brig darted his eyes towards the old man.

"You're talkin' about a displaced nation of individuals with over three hundred years of proud history behind 'em. And the seeds of that nation sprouted from the very word that this group adopted." Buck paused to ensure Brig was receiving his message. "Don't corner the dog if you ain't willin' to get bit."

"See? And you wonder why I wanted to save you?"

Buck's smile spread. He leaned to the side of his bed and spit a cheekful of dark juice into a can. "So this is what you're gonna do? Stay on and show these boys and girls how to fight?"

Brig thought for a moment in silence, shook his head. "I got what I came for. And I gave them something they needed."

"Well that's pretty short-sighted." Buck's tone became stern. "And *dimwitted.* They could use someone with your experience and leadership skills, Sampson."

Brig chuckled aloud. "Now you're sounding like my dad."

"That's not what he said, Brig. And it didn't help that you had such a hard head," a soft voice offered from the dimly lit doorway.

Brig squinted at the silhouette standing across the room in the setting sun. "Jess..."

Jessica strode the room with an airy grace and hugged her brother.

Buck leaned back with his hands clasped behind his head. "Somethin' you wanna tell me... *Sampson?*"

Brig's face, very gaunt even in the dim lighting of the cottage, flushed a meek red. He clicked his eyes at Jessica, then down at the floor with an ashamed nod. "My name's not..."

"...Sampson, I know..." Buck countered. "I was just wonderin' when you'd finally fess up."

"How long have you known?" Brig asked, nervously fiddling with the oozing bandage on his neck - unsure of whether to offer a conciliatory smile or make a quick exit from the room.

Buck closed his eyes and flattened his smile. "How much of an old fool did you take me for that I wouldn't recognize the President's son?"

The air in the cottage became still as night. Jessica, her face ghostly white, stood in silence behind her brother.

"Did you forget where I came from, Brigadier?"

"No, sir," Brig replied. "I'm sorry, I didn't mean to deceive you, it's just that with a name like Stroud, I..." He exhaled heavily. "Does this change things between us, Buck?"

"Well Hell no it doesn't change anything!" Buck barked, his eyes flipping open. "Does it change anything if you knew that I'm a sixth generation Grant? As in Ulysses S. Grant?"

Brig raised his eyebrows.

"You think people back in Trenton would take kindly to someone with *that* lineage in their midst during times like this?"

"I don't think it matters to them, you're who you are, Buck..." Brig replied.

"Exactly my point, son. Don't be afraid of who *you* are. *You're not your father, and he's not you.*"

Brig nodded. "He's definitely not me," he muttered. "And we don't get along."

With an audible huff, Buck shook his head and lay back on his pillow. "So what else is new?"

"You don't understand. He busted my chops every chance he got. And shoved me out of sight when it was inconvenient for his needs." A familiar anger broiled in Brig's gut.

"Brigadier, we're talking about the leader of the God damned free world," Buck interjected. "A man like that deserves just a bit more than an ounce of respect."

Brig shook his head with adamant fervor. "You have kids, Buck?"

Buck's face straightened, as if his mind had flown thousands of kilometers from the room. He looked down and clasped his hands together. "Two boys." He paused. "Lost them both outside of Rome in fifty-three..."

"The Tiber Skirmish..." Brig said.

Buck raised his eyes for a second at Brig, nodded, and then dropped them again. "Tina and I raised those boys with all the discipline and love that we could muster. When they were teens, they were just about the most obnoxious little bastards that ever walked in my sight." A distant smile crossed his lips. "We used to say I put them through school, and they put me through Hell." He lifted his gaze and squinted wisely at Brig. "And since I lost them, there's not a God damned day that goes by I don't wish they were right back there at the farm with me and the wife. Bad attitude and all. I still love 'em."

Brig blinked and tightened his lips.

"Don't let that happen to you son. Your daddy meant well."

Jessica stepped around Brig and stood at the foot of Buck's bed. "I can't thank you enough for what you..." she said, smiling widely. "...all of you... did for me."

"My pleasure, ma'am," Buck said, tilting his hand forward, as if he had his trusty ten-gallon within his leathery palm. "I figured what Brigadier was gettin' into," he continued, nodding at Brig, "but when I got his message, I knew it was more serious than any of us thought." He fell silent and looked down at his clasped hands again. "And I owed him as much."

Brig pursed his lips in humility. "Well you more than made up for it today, Colonel."

Buck snorted. "And then you went and saved me again. Boy, how in the Hell am I ever gonna break even with you?"

"First thing you can do is get your rest," Brig instructed with a stern finger wave. "They worked on that leg for five hours this afternoon."

Buck tented the worn gray blanket away from his body and peered down at his bandaged thigh. He raised an eyebrow and scratched at his bald head. "Well if that don't beat all. I guess my days of walkin' the trails in the fall are done with."

Brig narrowed his eyes and dropped them to the floor. It was an all too familiar situation for him, and he did not want to have another friendship dashed to the rocks by offering false hope. He nodded without speaking.

"Brig, I got what you asked for, too," Buck said, grasping Brig's forearm between his fingers, and squeezing at a drip bag hanging next to his bed with the other hand. "Go find Ricky and tell him to let you see the truck."

Brig smiled and winked knowingly at Buck.

"Can I speak to you outside?" Jess asked, tugging at Brig's sleeve.

The former EW nodded and faced the old man. "Get your rest, Colonel..."

Buck, his head back and eyes closed, had drifted off.

As the last of the sun's dying embers beamed through the waving trees that lined the small dirt road, Brig and Jess strolled across the mini cottage compound. Four crows sat atop a branch, taking turns cawing as they scoured the ground below for sustenance. On the opposite end of the grass circle that marked the center of the village, Clive and Jesse stood next to the Jimmy that had brought the group to the secluded enclave. The pair did not show interest in Brig and Jess's exit from the far cottage - at least Jesse did not. Clive, on the other hand, stole subtle glances in their direction, as he and Jesse held a conversation that the wind carried as droning murmurs.

"You know Dad would have been proud of you today..." Jess tucked her hands partially into the torn pockets of her black jeans.

Brig snorted a mild 'hrmph' and squinted away the glare from his eyes. "Would he?"

"Mm-hmm," Jess hummed. "That was amazing."

"I think if he were here, he'd make every effort to point out what I did wrong." Their feet crunched through the gravel at the edge of the drive. "That I just let the leader of this country's last chance at bringing things back to normal... die..."

Jess grabbed at Brig's elbow. "Brig, that wasn't your fault. She made the choice to step in front of that bullet."

"Doesn't really matter though, does it? Not to him."

"Brig... c'mon. You know he loved you more than anyone else in this world."

"He had a funny way of showin' it, Jess." He paused while they passed near a small grouping of Revolution fighters, perched upon the porch of one of the empty cottages playing a quiet hand of Texas Hold 'Em. "I was never his favorite person."

"You were an obnoxious teenager, for Christ's sake!" Jess's Texas twang jumped to a squeaky octave.

Brig stopped and turned fully towards his sister, looking past her to the last remnants of the sun that flowed like lava over the mountains in the distance. "You know the last conversation I had with him?"

Jess shook her head in silence, her hands to her hips.

"He told me how disappointed he was in me. He told me how he had me removed from active duty because..." Brig exhaled with a gruff rasp. "I was locked in a quarantine room with no doors... and he stood on the other side of a window telling me how God damned disappointed he was in me. In *me*, Jess!"

She blinked her incomprehension.

Brig shook his head.

"You gotta let it go, Brig." Her voice smoothed. "He's gone. But you have to believe me... he loved you more than life. More than himself and any of his grandiose dreams of running the world."

Brig placed his hands behind his neck and arched his back in exasperation.

"You couldn't see it the way I did. I know how he did everything in his power to help you out. Everything he did was to make you successful. He wanted you to be better than him."

He blinked twice in thought. Brig had never considered that possibility.

"Brig," Jess placed a hand on Brig's cheek and forced his gaze towards her, "if he was tough on you... it was because he saw the potential for you to be something very special." Her mouth turned up in a loving smile. "And he was right."

He put his hands to his hips and surveyed the small village around him, his eyes stopping at the small group of soldiers they had passed, then to Buck's cottage, and then to Clive. "Where do I go from here, Jess? What's next?"

Jess's smile grew. "I have a couple of ideas. But first things first. There's someone I want you to meet." She grasped his hand and pulled him towards the fourth cottage.

"Hi, Elda," Jessica said, entering the cottage with Brig in tow.

"Hombrecito has been waiting for you, Miss Jessica," Esmerelda answered.

Brig furrowed his brow in confused curiosity.

"Can you get him for me?" Jess touched Esmerelda's arm with a hand while flicking her eyes over to Brig, her excitement barely contained.

Esmerelda tightened her gaze on Brig for a moment, looked to Jess, and then vanished into a doorway at the back of the room.

"What's this about?" The telltale whine of a Jimmy's brakes echoed in the enclave outside of the cottage. Brig glanced over his shoulder before returning his curious glare at his sister.

"So do you think Buck's gonna to be alright?" Jess pulled his attention away from the moment. "That was a pretty nasty injury."

Brig nodded. "Yeah, he can't go anywhere for a couple of weeks. But once he's past the initial shock of the injury and surgery, he should be fine to leave."

The front door of the cottage creaked open. Both Brig and Jess lifted their heads.

Steele, her footsteps on the wooden floorboards like a cat, strode into the room.

Jess's face brightened. "Steele! Oh my god!" she called, closing the final gap between the two with a loving hug.

"Jessica... I'm so glad that you're ok," Steele answered with a shortness of breath. "We'd heard the worst! I'm happy that's not the case."

The two parted. Jess smiled at her brother. "You can thank Brig."

Steele smiled at him with warmth that filled the room. "You don't have to sell me... he's amazing," she said, looping one arm through Brig's and around his back.

A cough from behind them grabbed their attention. "Hi," a small voice called. Eli, his arms crossed over his chest and hands tucked into his armpits, stood just beyond the door that Esmerelda had gone into moments before. Jess stepped over to him and placed a loving hand on his shoulder.

"Brigadier," she said, "I'd like you to meet Elijah."

Brig tilted his head and scrunched his brow. He instantly recognized the boy from the last time he had been to the village, months before.

Jess went down to one knee next to the small boy. "Eli, this is your Uncle Brigadier."

A few seconds passed before the reality registered with Brig. His eyes widened. He took a step forward and stopped. "Uncle? You mean..."

Jess, with an elated smile, nodded. "This is my son, Eli."

Wise beyond his years, Eli cocked his head and stared back up at Brig. "I've seen you before."

Brig knelt onto his haunches a few steps in front of Eli. A growing smile adorned his face, accompanied by a welling of tears at the corners of his eyes. "Yeah..." he said with a cracking voice, "I've seen you, too. It's nice to finally meet you, Elijah."

Jess rubbed her son's shoulder with a glee that needed no further words from her.

"It was that day..." Eli added.

Brig nodded. "Yeah, that day..." His face contorted as a thought struck him like a bolt. "That day that... Clive..." he muttered, standing suddenly. Anger tugged at the corner of his upper lip, baring several teeth. "He knew..." he growled. Brig spun and forced the door open, banging it against the wall with a loud clatter. He stormed through it. "That son of a bitch!"

He took a step and leapt from the porch; Jesse turned his head. "Here we go..." he said, watching Brig approach like an angered jungle cat. "Here's your mate, Underwood. And looks like he's out for blood!"

"I've got it..." Clive answered with a calm grunt.

Brig pounced between the pair and grabbed Clive by the shoulder. With a fluid motion, he delivered a crushing blow across his former EW partner's chin. Clive tumbled backward and onto the patchy grass.

"Brigadier! Stop!" Steele shouted from the small porch behind him.

Jessica exited the cottage behind her and swiftly made her way towards the clearing at the center of the enclave.

"You knew!" Brig snarled, jabbing a furious digit downwards at Clive. "He's my blood, and you kept him from me! Who the Hell do you think you are?"

Clive spun and swept Brig's legs from underneath him. Brig fell to the ground awkwardly, knocking the wind from him as he landed on his face.

"Jesse, stop them!" Jessica ordered.

The brash Aussie snorted and crossed his arms over his bulging chest. "Not my fight, lady." He spat a wad of tobacco juice off to the side of the group. "So this is how brothers for life show respect?" He shook his head in mocking disbelief.

Clive levered himself and stepped back from Brig. He brushed off the front of his shirt. Brig lifted himself onto his knees, his breath coming in large, audible rasps.

"He's my flesh and blood, too, Stroud," Clive hissed, wiping the small trickle of blood from his lower lip.

Brig tilted his head sideways at Clive. "The Hell are you talking about?"

Clive glanced hesitantly at Jess, and then back at Brig. "Eli's my son."

Brig, confused, flung his eyes to Jess. The sincerity of her eyes told him the truth. Brig slowly got to his feet, wiping away caked dust from his mouth. "Why didn't you tell me?" he snarled.

"For the same reason I didn't tell you about Jess being alive," Clive shouted back. "He needed protected!"

"From me? You had no right!" Brig barked, taking an aggressive step at Clive.

Jessica wedged herself in between the two. "I think what he's trying to say..." she said, pushing Clive backward away from Brig, "is that the less people that knew about Eli, the better."

"Jess, seriously? I'm his uncle for cryin' out loud!" Brig's voice resounded off the wooden cottages around them.

Jess imparted a sheepish upturn of her lip. "Clive... you really should've told him."

Clive emitted an audible sigh and looked to the darkening skies. He nodded and pursed his lips. "I'm sorry I kept that from you, Brig."

Brig, his anger doused by the sudden remorse from his former friend, ran a hand through his hair. He closed his eyes and gathered his composure. "And I'm sorry I ran at you."

"Great... now can we get past this stupidity?" Jessica rolled her eyes between the two.

Clive cast a fiery glare at Brig, spun and began to stride towards the cottage, before Jessica grabbed his arm to stop him. Brig shook his head and turned away.

"What the Hell?" Jess yelped. "What's going on here? You two used to be best friends - what's changed?"

Clive clicked his eyes towards Brig, then at Jessica before casting his gaze beyond the trees. "Eli wasn't the reason..."

Jess narrowed her eyes. "Then what?" Clive tightened his lips in silence, snorted under his breath with a nod of his chin at Brig.

"Brig?" Jess said, her eyes boring into the back of her brother.

Brig propped his wrists onto his head and let out a sigh. "Best just to let the past lie, Jess. Nothin' you can say right now's gonna change that..." He paused. "He's made his choices, and for some reason he thinks he can't trust me anymore."

Clive stomped forward and thrust his finger at Brig in fury. "Bullshit, Stroud! You know damn well what you did to cause all this!" Clive, suddenly aware that everyone had halted their own conversations around the enclave and were taking a silent interest in them, tightened his jaw. Jess massaged Clive's arm and forced eye contact.

"Clive... what's this about?" she with a soft purr.

"I'll tell you what it's about, Jess," Brig said, spinning and facing them. "He blames me for everything that's ever gone wrong in his life."

Clive narrowed his eyes at his former partner.

"Is this about..." Jessica began, inhaling sharply in silent horror, realizing she was focusing her gaze on Clive's prosthetic. She yanked her eyes back up to meet his. "...What happened in Portugal?"

Before Clive could proffer a defense, Brig stepped up next to Jessica. "Yeah, it's about Portugal," he snarled. "That was my fault, right? So was me getting promoted while you got discharged. Huh?"

Clive's face flushed red, but he retained his composure.

Brig bared teeth through the corner of his mouth and jabbed his finger down at Clive's leg. "Maybe it was me who forced you to head to Russia to trade your soul for some cheap surgery?" He turned and rubbed at the stubble on his chin.

Clive tensed his jaw in seething anger.

Brig snorted in disgust and turned back to face Clive. "Or maybe..." he wagged his finger in mock thought at the former EW, "it's because he thinks I orchestrated you two breaking up... because he thinks I'm a racist, Jess. Can you believe it?" Brig put a foot forward and jabbed the air in front of Clive. "He thinks I'm a God damned racist that didn't want my sister hanging around someone with a black father."

The camp fell into an eerie silence, with the cicadas providing the only audible noise in the dusk.

"Go ahead, Underwood. It's out there now, tell her!"

Without a verbal response, Clive wound and decked Brig across the cheek with an iron fist. Brig stumbled backward, but did not fall. Steele gasped behind a slender hand to her mouth.

Brig smeared a stream of blood onto the back of his sleeve, peered wickedly at Clive. "Bingo..." he growled in a thick drawl.

Jess grabbed at Clive's wrist and forced him to look into her face. "Oh, no... no, no, no," she said with a sympathetic coo. "Honey, you don't really believe that, do you?" Clive forced his eyes from her gaze. She placed his chin between her hands and looked up into his eyes. "Clive... that's not what happened at all. Brig had nothing to do with us breaking up."

Clive shook his head with a sneer and backed away from Jess. "So it looks like the Stroud's are sticking together on this one, huh?"

"Clive, please believe me! When I found out I was pregnant, I thought it was Davis's."

Clive rolled his eyes at the thought of Davis, her late husband.

Jess fell into deep thought. "Our relationship had fallen apart... but I thought... foolishly... the pregnancy would have been a way to put it back together. A new beginning."

She turned her back from Clive and stepped away, her hand to her forehead as she relived the arduous past.

"And you weren't in any state of mind to handle that, Clive. You really weren't. You needed to find yourself, and it wasn't fair of me to ask you to be with someone carrying another man's child."

"I told you it wasn't me!" Brig shouted.

"Brig, stop!" Jess barked. She spun back around and grasped at Clive's collar with both hands. "You have to believe me, sweetie. I had no idea Eli was yours. Not until long after we broke up and you... disappeared." Clive lowered his head in silence. "And then it was too late..." She dropped her head onto Clive's chest.

Clive wrapped his firm arms around Jessica's torso and pulled her into him. "I don't know what to say," he muttered next to her ear.

"An apology would be nice..." she replied after a moment's hesitation.

Clive released the strength of his embrace and focused on her eyes. Her stern air left him without words. "I'm sorry..." he stammered, "I didn't know... and I assumed wrong."

"No, not to me," Jess corrected. "You owe Brig an apology."

Clive's consternation turned to disbelief. He backed from Jess, glared at her, straightened his collar with both hands and cleared his throat. "I'm sorry, Brig. I'm sorry that I assumed the worst."

Brig stood expressionless.

"My world was coming down around me, and I assumed you were just stepping in line with everyone else. And..." Clive paused and kicked the dirt at his feet. "I shouldn't have done that."

Brig nodded hesitantly. "So you're done with the Syndicate?"

Clive scrunched his eyes at Brig. "The only reason I was with them was because of Jess. She's here now, so I have no reason to be with them anymore. *This is the end.*"

Brig offered a slight bob of his head in Clive's direction, borne half of approval and half of experienced mistrust.

Jess faced Brig and pointed a stern finger in Clive's direction. "You owe him an apology, too, Brig!"

Brig widened his eyes, but then seeing Jess's resolve, softened his scowl. Like a pair of schoolyard adolescents scolded for a scuffle, Brig mimicked Clive's movements, scraping his feet at the dirt. "I should've been more patient with you too - more understanding that you weren't gonna do something that I thought you would." He met Clive's glare. "I'm sorry, too. But I'm glad you realize now that I wouldn't have done somethin' like that to you. We're brothers, Cryp. And that's forever."

Clive nodded and looked away. The ugly past seemed to be resolved, but both found it difficult to bury it completely. "So we're done here?" he grunted, a quick flick of his eyes to Jess.

"And a handshake..." Jess added.

With Brig leading - albeit reluctantly - both men held their hands out for a brief, single shake.

They released. Jess shook her head, grabbed both of their arms. "No, no... that's not how EWs shake, now is it?" She shot a grin to the former partners.

The corner of Clive's mouth turned upwards in a rare grin. Grasping Brig's palm together with his, Clive mirrored his elbow with Brig's in the form of the familiar 'W'.

Brig scanned the small crowd of Revolution and Trenton militiamen that had hung on their conversation. "Ok, show's over," he sniped, which was met with a few subdued chuckles.

As the group dispersed, and the former EWs embraced their loved ones, Brig with Steele, Clive with Jessica, a retro bike rumbled into the center of the enclave and skidded to a stop. The engine backfired once, rolling an echo that caromed off the empty buildings in the nearby desolate city blocks. A solo rider, a Revolution fighter as identified by his black bandana covering the bottom two thirds of his face, climbed off the mount.

Jesse tilted his head at a curious Brig. "One of our scouts..."

The man swiftly made his way to the Australian, small puffs of desert sand flowing from his leather jacket. "Convoy comin' in from the west," the man said through the bandana, with a thick Alabaman drawl.

"New Vegas?" Jesse grunted.

"Yeah, it's Syndicate alright..." the man replied.

Jesse panned the scattered group. "You heard the man! Time to saddle up and get back to Clovis," he barked. "The Syndicate's on the move and headed our way, mates."

The group did not wait for further instructions - instantly scurrying like a horde of ants, preparing and stowing their gear in the Jimmies sitting parallel to each other at the center of the compound.

Jesse stepped between Brig and Clive and twirled his finger in the air. "Ok, you two. Time to go..."

Clive nodded.

Steele darted her eyes at Brig, her face drawn in surprise.

"I'm not leavin' the camp," Brig said. "Buck can't travel, and the women can't defend themselves against those monsters."

Jesse stared at him in apathetic silence. "We'll send a truck in two weeks," he replied, and then spun to help with preparations.

"You sure you're going to be ok alone?" Clive said.

Brig coughed with a deep rasp twice and regained his balance. "I'll be alright. Just leave me some weapons and ammo." He focused his gaze on the dirt road that led from the enclave into the edge of town. "But y'all need to get out of here. No tellin' who's seen those Jimmy's hangin' around. The faster you leave, the safer it'll be for everyone left back."

Fifteen minutes later

The two remaining Revolution Jimmies lined up nose-to-tail along the dirt road, their covered cargo beds restocked with fresh supplies from the Trenton militia and their motors grumbling in unison. Clive held Jessica by her shoulders, placed a loving kiss on her forehead.

"I'll see you in two weeks," he said, lifting her chin with a pair of fingers.

"You be safe." Her glassy eyes met his.

"Nothing fancy here, just heading back to Clovis. We have to stay ahead of that convoy and keep out of trouble."

As the pair broke from their embrace, Jessica turned and stepped onto the small wooden porch, where Eli watched the parade of Revolution fighters flow into their respective vehicles. Clive approached the passenger side of the lead truck and suddenly stopped. Brig stood several meters from him, watching his former EW partner in silence.

Clive switched directions and approached him. "You know, Stroud," he began with a gruff air, "I'm not saying everything's under the bridge with us. But I *am* glad we straightened that part out," he said with a subtle finger motion back at the cottage.

"I understand everything, Cryp," Brig replied. "And I'm glad to have you back." He offered a hand outward to Clive. "Fraternitas Aeternus..."

Clive, for the first time in several long years, continued his smile, grasping Brig's hand to again form the signature EW handshake. "Brothers forever..."

Brig, rather than releasing from the tight grip, yanked Clive towards him and embraced his brother for life. Both men, their eyes closed and sealed with subtle tears, silently acknowledged the gravity of the moment and then parted. Clive wiped his eyes on his sleeve. Brig draped his arm back over Steele's shoulder.

As the door of the Jimmy slammed closed and the engine growled to move the beast away from the camp, Brig pressed his lips onto the side of Steele's head.

"Maybe the sun's gonna shine again," he said.

Outside of Clive's workshop, the Revolution Jimmy thundered its approach into the small neighborhood. The shrill squeal of its brakes preceded the short slide of its bare tires on the cracked asphalt, piercing the serenity of the night.

"Just a few minutes..." said Clive. He jumped from the cab of the truck onto his good leg and ambled a few steps. Jesse poked his head from inside the cargo bed, wrapping his torso around the back of the truck to get a good view of Clive.

"Underwood, what's this about?"

Clive waved without looking back. "Just give me a few minutes, I need to pick up something important." He continued to walk. "Something that should help us all out..."

Jesse shook his head and mindlessly lit a cigarette, the embers at its tip glowing in the darkness. He puffed a cloud into the moist air.

Clive halted a few steps before the workshop front door, surveying the neighborhood and the small building in front of him. For the past six years, this had been his home, and although it was not much to brag about, it was something he could call his own. He allowed another smile to crack at the corner of his lips.

Suddenly, he had a future that did not seem like the dark tunnel that it had been. Jessica and Eli were waiting for him back at the cottage, and he found himself eagerly anticipating his hopeful return to the quiet enclave after a short stint at the Revolution headquarters in Clovis.

He peered up at the stars above and thought of his last conversation with Brig. Against all odds, his relationship with his former best friend was apparently on the mend. The anger that had amassed over the years towards his EW partner still existed in some respect, but for once in a long time, the rough seas that separated the brothers for life seemed calmer.

He reached into his jacket pocket, jingling the set of keys that he knew he would be using for the final time, and forced them into the lock of the front door. The heavy air around him dampened the sound of the cylinder's click and the ensuing scrape of the sliding door pushing open. Clive peeked back at the Jimmy and stepped into the darkened workshop, closing the door behind him.

The driver of the Jimmy yawned and tapped his fingers with an impatient rhythm on the worn plastic of the oversized steering wheel.

The night exploded, along with the workshop in front of him, sending a blinding fireball of liquid flame outward and upward that doused the front end of the idling truck. The dull olive paint on its hood ignited in an opaque sheet of blue flame; the concussion of the blast shattered the windscreen inward, sending heated fragments of safety glass into the face of the shocked driver. His clothes ignited in a horrific shroud of orange, forcing him out of the cab and onto the ground. The dying man's discordant wail echoed hauntingly into the night.

The flames launched from the cab and onto the canvas covering of the truck bed, traveling with unimpeded fury over the length of the vehicle. Like a swarm of panicked wasps flying from their imperiled hive, the small team of freedom fighters launched from the flaming bed of the Jimmy and took flight from the overtaking blaze.

While two of the team doused the flaming Jimmy with a pair of fire extinguishers they snagged from the cockpit, Jesse, wide-eyed, absorbed the frightening scene that had unfolded before them. A small structure to begin with, made of not much more than stucco and concrete block, Clive's workshop ceased to exist within a matter of a few seconds.

"Son of a bitch..." he grunted in disbelief.

37:
Endgame

Earth. Flagstaff, Arizona - Early the next morning

A pair of nightingales alit upon a branch above the cottage enclave and whistled out their song to the rising sun. They halted their tune for a moment as a loud rapping on the door of the third cottage filled the dewy air.

Steele appeared after a soft squeak of the door's hinges.

Jesse, the boisterous Australian, leaned against the wooden support beam on the porch.

"Oh... did you forget something?" she said.

"I need to talk to Stroud," Jesse replied in a gruff tone.

"Who is it?" Brig's voice called from within, sounding as if he had just completed a marathon.

Steele stepped aside and glanced at Brig, whom sat upright on the couch along the back wall of the small living room. He raised his head from his hands, the table lamp next to him highlighting his peaked and drawn face. Brig warily pushed himself to his feet and stumbled to the door, utilizing a nearby chair for balance. He stopped next to Steele.

She placed herself behind Brig, poking her head around him to stay within sight of Jesse. Brig squinted with one eye, holding back the morning sunrise from Jesse's silhouette. "Has it been two weeks already?"

Jesse maintained his flat stare. "There's been an accident."

"Don't tell me." Brig sighed and ran a hand through his sweat-matted hair. "Y'all got attacked on the way back to Clovis?"

Jesse shook off the suggestion with a hand wave. "Nah... nothin' like that. Underwood wanted to go back to his place to get somethin' important."

Brig raised a curious eyebrow. "Important? Like what?"

"His words, Stroud." A subtle shrug of his shoulders was offered. "Anyway, as soon as he stepped inside, the place went up like a factory full of firecrackers..."

"Oh bloody..." Steele gasped, cupping her hand over her mouth.

Brig, squinting through the morning sunlight, gazed past Jesse's shoulder to the truck outside. His eyes fell to the charred, bare metal front of the frame, and then to the blackened skeleton of the cargo bed that normally held the green tarp.

"The Hell happened?" Brig strained, taking a quick visual inventory of the Revolution force hunkered in the back of the truck. "Where's he at?" he said with a lowered timbre. "Was he hurt?"

Jesse stared blankly at the former EW. "I never seen anyone survive a blast like that. There was nothin' left."

A creak in the floorboards behind them abruptly stopped their hushed conversation. Brig and Steele turned to see Jessica, one arm tightly across her midsection, the other with her hand held to her mouth, fighting back a heaving sob.

Brig faced Jesse. "Take me there..."

Jesse held up a hand to Brig's bare chest. "There's nothin' left, Stroud. Your mate's gone..."

Brig, baring his teeth, pushed Jesse backward onto the porch and pointed into the Australian's face. "Take me there! I need to see it for myself!" he shouted in a fierce whisper.

Steele, already having fetched Brig's threadbare flannel shirt, handed it to him with a sorrowed expression. Jesse eyed the blood-soaked bandage on Brig's neck. Brig braced himself against the wooden pillar to pull the shirt painfully over his broad shoulders, buttoning the front without caring whether each button met its eye, and glared at Jesse.

"Stay here with Jess, she needs you..." Brig said over his shoulder to Steele.

She nodded and closed the cottage door behind her.

"Let's go..." Brig growled, before launching forward and off into the grass.

The truck rumbled into the familiar neighborhood along the edge of the industrial section of town; Brig spied the small property that he knew to be nestled between two wooden fences.

However, one of the fences now dipped in its center, with portions of it reduced to cinders. A curling contrail of black smoke spiraled into the morning sky from between the pair of fences, marking the spot that used to be Clive's modest workshop.

The brakes squealed on the Jimmy. Brig glowered through the empty portal where the windscreen used to be, the destruction in front of them jarring him like a sledge to his skull. He hopped from the cab and staggered up to the edge of the scorched skeleton of toppled concrete blocks.

A strange sense of gut wrenching déjà vu gripped him, having just stood in a similar husk of his father's estate in recent weeks. However, he did not feel the same distance that he had felt when seeing the remains of his father's mansion. This felt like someone had personally struck out at his heart with a blazing dagger.

He stepped through the blast-widened opening that used to be the front door. His eyes penetrated the smoke.

Maybe he escaped out the back door.

He scanned the scattered fragments of his workshop; a blackened piece of metal that caught his eye vanquished the thought. At the end of a twisted rod hung a tattered and shredded boot. Brig knelt and mindlessly grabbed at the object. The stored heat within the metal singed his fingers, and he tossed it back to the burnt ground.

He fought off a bout of dizziness and stood once again, wiping the soot from his hand onto his shirt. His eyes meandered along the exploded side wall of the workshop, and stopped at a gut-wrenching sight that confirmed his worst fears.

Lying along the bottom crease of the wall, wedged with its grotesquely burnt back towards him, was Clive's body – half in a fetal position with his arms outstretched. Attached to one charred flesh hand was a melted glob of plastic and wires that used to be some sort of communications device.

Brig inhaled deeply through his nose. He stoically stared down at the remains of his best friend and brother for life, wiping away the water that had built at the corner of his eyes.

With a growing scowl and a flexed jaw, he took in the final sight of the ruins of Clive's home. He spun on a heel and made for the waiting Jimmy.

Moments later, with Clive's burnt remains wrapped in a blanket in the bed of the truck, Brig determinately climbed into the cab and slammed the door shut.

"Take me back to the cottage..." he snarled, without making eye contact with Jesse.

30 minutes later

The Jimmy arrived back within the enclave. Before the lumbering beast had even rolled to a stop, Brig leapt from the cab and landed like a rabid cat on the grass.

Steele stepped onto the small wooden porch of the third cottage and crossed her arms over her chest to ward off the cool morning chill. "Brigadier? Where are you going?"

Brig, his eyes glassy and seemingly focused kilometers away, strode past the cottage without response, moving swiftly towards a pair of pickups that Buck's men had brought from Trenton the previous morning. He rounded the first and dragged the tarp from its bed, exposing the pair of biosuits that he and Steele had worn on their trip back to Earth. Brig waved his hand over the wrist computer of the nearest suit. The biosuit responded with a set of chirps, before it lit the familiar ghostly ring of blue LEDs around the helmet mount.

New Vegas, later that day

A small grouping of Syndicate heavies, two soldiers and two troopers, busied themselves repairing a set of fortifications along the battered Strip. The asphalt, already worn from years of no maintenance, wore its newly minted craters like a hideous black eye - several of them swallowed the road at random intervals as far as the eye could see.

Not normally bustling with activity in any recent year, the street was unusually serene, with only Syndicate troops present. The residents of the area either had opted to hide out in their meager homes, or had fled the immediate area for the safety of some other shelter, away from the war zone of the previous day.

37: ENDGAME

"It's gonna be a long time before those bastards show their faces in New Vegas again," one of the soldiers bragged with a wide smile. "If ever."

The other three placated their group leader with sycophantic snickering, continuing their work at a leisurely pace.

The whining whoosh of a plasma rifle obliterated the deceptive peace. The blue-white bolt from nowhere landed in the center of the small group, disintegrating two of them, and sending the others off in a hail of asphalt fragments and body parts.

Brig, a plasma rifle down at his side, a thin contrail of smoke curling from its heated barrel, hovered 20 meters to their south. The nearby Syndicate troops and lesser henchmen, wide-eyed with awe, lifted their AK's and M16's, and emptied their clips in his direction. The Artificial Intelligence of Brig's biosuit deftly moved him from harm's way - dodging the speeding metal projectiles with ease. He recharged his plasma weapon.

He raised it once again and unleashed a blinding glob of fluid death upon the defenders, smashing their ranks and crashing down upon them a defunct digital billboard that straddled the Strip. Their shock keeping them from processing any rational thought of a superior defense, the troops continued to return fire with their conventional weapons. While most of their armament missed the mark - mainly because the AI of the biosuit offered advanced technology that no conventional weapon could consistently match - some did hit Brig's suit and ricocheted away from him in a shower of blue-orange sparks.

As the last of the nearby troops fled to safety, Brig commanded the suit to land. He hit the ground running, the clamorous clank of alien metal reverberating with each thunderous footstep onto the hard asphalt. With a scoop of one armored hand and a single motion of his other, he grabbed an AK47 from one of the fallen and took to the air like a wingless demon.

He showered retribution from above, strafing the terrified troops that scattered like gasoline-doused ants. His rifle and plasma fired in horrific tandem, leaving no hiding place untouched, and no visible survivors among the already thin defense that Muldoon had laid in the aftermath of the Revolution's first strike. At random intervals, Brig commanded the alien suit to hop onto the sunset-lit pavement, where he would mercilessly run down a troop or two that had unwisely decided to stay and engage.

A volley of bullets ripped into the pavement around Brig's armored feet as he finished off a pair of unlucky henchmen. Brig rotated and fired, but the soldier had already disengaged and bolted into an abandoned restaurant situated within a small parking lot. Brig gave chase, his footsteps thundering heavy enough to rattle the windows on the front of the building.

Brig kicked his foot through the heavy steel frame of the doorway and squinted into the darkness beyond. The LEDs mounted within the shoulder armor of the biosuit flicked on with a silent command from its wearer, illuminating the interior of the dank former eatery in a ghostly glow.

The soldier, his M16 nervously aimed at Brig, cowered at the sight of the metallic monstrosity standing over him. He jammed his finger onto the trigger. A small burst came forth from the end of the barrel, along with a stream of muzzle flame that lit the blackness in orange light.

Amidst the pitchy twang of armament ricocheting from his chest plate, Brig stomped forward and grabbed the weapon from the soldier's hand. With the aid of a pair of powerful actuators mounted at the wrists of the biosuit, he snapped the rifle into three mangled pieces and dropped the useless pile of scraps to the floor with a hollow series of clanks.

The alarmed soldier scrambled backward until he met the wall.

Brig lifted his assault rifle to the man's forehead. "World's End!" he screamed with a tinny echo through the external speakers of his helmet.

"P-p-please... oh God! Don't kill me!" the soldier cried.

Brig narrowed his eyes and commanded one of the LEDs to focus on the man's face. The Epsilon softened his scowl, seeing in detail the face of the soldier at his feet, whom appeared to be no more than youth in his late teens. "World's End! Where is it?" he repeated with a ferocious rasp.

The soldier shakily pointed to his left. "Two... blocks past the... towers..."

Brig coughed. The biosuit filters wiped the sheen of blood from his face shield.

The soldier, peering out from behind his shaking hands, looked up at Brig. "Are you... gonna kill me?"

Brig sneered. "You Syndicate?"

The soldier nodded. "B-but... I didn't have a choice. They forced me and my brother to join. Said they'd... k-kill our dad if we didn't."

Brig growled his frustration. "Consider this your pink slip."

The soldier sealed his eyelids in fear.

"Go south on the Strip and don't look back." He paused in silence. "Get out of here!"

Before the teen could get to his feet and take his surprise leave, the air in the empty room compressed with a violent outward surge. The building exploded in a thunderstorm of concrete and glass particles, the result of a direct hit from one of the Syndicate's dark matter cannons.

A Syndicate troop, manning one of the twin dark matter cannons mounted adjacent to each other in the towers, raised his fist in victory and howled to his compatriot across the street. He pointed down at the crater that used to be a restaurant. "Got that son of a bitch!"

The other motioned his acknowledgement with frantic thumbs up.

Suddenly, Brig appeared in front of the gunner, hovering several meters from the tower's glass facade. The trooper, dumbstruck, fumbled for the trigger mechanism. Brig squeezed a lightning burst from his refreshed assault rifle – this one an M60 - the deadly spray tearing the face off the trooper's head in a bloody splash of pulp.

As the deceased man's last action, his hand fell upon the trigger and released the armament. The windows of the building flexed inward as the projectile hurled from the barrel of the dark matter cannon. Although the biosuit reacted with unearthly dexterity, dodging the main impact of the cannon's force, the tail of the speeding comet of destruction whipped Brig's shoulder and spun him to the ground.

Like a meteor striking the fragile shell of a newborn planet, the projectile slammed the second tower - directly onto the second cannon emplacement. The tower groaned and twisted midway upon its axis, and then teetered forward with the deafening roar of splintering steel beams. Like a felled giant, it toppled forward and into the side of the first. The supporting tower grimaced and shuddered its disdain before absorbing the shock of the extra weight, whilst mounds of debris from both structures rained to the pavement.

Pandemonium ensued beneath the fallen pair of towers, which still quaked like a pair of wavering dominoes under the abnormal angle and weight presented by the partially devoured skyscraper.

Syndicate troopers and henchmen, alike, scrambled away from the scene, disregarding any attempt at firing upon their attacker.

Brig, like an armored angel of death, stomped from the debris field in a swirling cloud of dust, mowing a bloody path through the fleeing enemy with a flaming pulse rifle in one hand, a screaming M60 in the other. Blue electrical sparks danced from the shoulder of his suit where the dark matter cannon had nicked it moments before, illuminating Brig's soulless expression. Wads of blue flame railed from the barrel of his pulse rifle, finding abandoned storefronts and lighting the smoke-filled New Vegas Strip with blinding flashes of destruction.

After several more moments of his march of terror, he reached the brick-paved entryway of the majestic World's End Resort & Casino. Brig stopped just beyond the defunct fountain that graced the center of the grand driveway, a spot just to the left of its gigantic bronzed globe marquee. He focused his eyes on the darkened front doors while ignoring the sporadic gunfire that met him from a group of open windows several floors above street level.

The former EW, approaching his date with destiny and unfazed by the hail of gunfire raining down upon his armor, stormed forward, crushing the fragile brick beneath his heavy feet. The M60 halted as it used up its seemingly endless magazine, instead choking out a cloud of barrel smoke. Brig tossed it to the broken pavement.

He raised the plasma rifle onto his forearm and released a stream of bolts at the facade of the hotel, setting it aflame in a dazzling sheet of blue that licked upwards, morphing into black flame-laced smoke. Moments later, the plasma rifle froze and fell silent. Brig glared at the base of the stock, not having realized the damage it had sustained in the dark matter cannon blast. With ferocity unborn of anything seen in regular combat, Brig slammed the plasma rifle onto the ground, severing it with the impact.

In a blinding flash, a bolt from a Syndicate plasma rifle plowed into Brig's chest, lifting his entire frame from the pavement and tossing him backward ten meters, until he skidded noisily to a halt. Slowly, he pushed himself up to a seated position and gathered his wits. Rattling breaths flowed from his compressed chest, echoing within his helmet. But something more dire than enemy bullets concerned him now – his biosuit, already fractured from the dark matter cannon, was now on fire with a phosphorescent glow from the direct hit of the plasma bolt.

37: ENDGAME

"Release! Release!" he commanded the AI of the biosuit. It complied by jettisoning the armor from around his body.

Within the rain of enemy fire, Brig leapt to his feet and found nearby cover at the base of the hotel's main tower, behind a pair of gargantuan stone planters. Brig pulled a pair of 9MM side arms from his belt – courtesy of Buck's militia - steeled himself, and sprinted forward while laying down a spray of cover fire that shattered a row of windows along the front of the building.

He vaulted into the entryway - two Syndicate henchmen met him, their own rifles at the ready. Brig dropped them with two intricately placed rounds to each of their throats. They fell backward and twitched to a silent death on the cold tile. With the efficiency of a highly trained death machine, Brig scooped their AK's and continued into the darkened lobby.

Cross-shaped muzzle flashes lit the casino just beyond the grand foyer, and the heavy stench of sulfur wafted upwards into the tiled dome above. Brig, possessed far beyond concern for his own well-being, plowed forward. He took out both gunners from behind their perches with a steady stream of hot metal that made the tips of his weapons glow like twin hellhounds.

More gunfire erupted at Brig from another pair of henchmen, taking turns ducking behind a heap of decomposing slot machines. Brig focused beyond the cowardly duo at a third henchman, disappearing into a small corridor at the far end of the darkened casino. He dropped to his haunches and awaited the curiosity of his attackers.

After a moment of unreturned gunfire from the henchmen, they cautiously wove their way through the mounds of old equipment, poking their barrels at each turn in anticipation of their enemy's reappearance. As one made his way along a glinting stretch of broken metal, Brig silently rose to his feet behind the man and glided a field knife across his throat. The henchman fell to the floor in a gurgling pile. Brig sheathed Clive's charred field knife back onto his calf.

The second henchman stood in the dark, sweat beads leaping from his forehead. He squinted at the bulky shadows around him, shallowing his breath as he turned from side to side. A wicked hiss, like that of a coiled cobra, caught his ear. He stood erect and dropped his gaze to his chest, where a fragment of light gleamed off the handle of the knife protruding from his chest. He coughed a torrent of chunky blood from his lips and dropped to his knees.

Brig emerged from the darkness, slid the blade from the man's chest with a moist yank and wiped it on his pant leg before moving on. He steeled his gaze on the stairwell that stood at the end of the corridor ahead.

Brig approached the passage, stepping through the frame of the door that had long since fallen to the wayside. He stopped at the edge; flickering lights from above hummed an uneven buzz, lighting the tiled path to the stairwell. A scuffling of boots echoed from behind him. With barely a thought or a turn of his head, Brig lifted an AK and waved the barrel twice across the width of the hall. As the deafening din of the gunfire died away, another pair of henchmen fell to the ground behind him. He checked the magazines of his twin death dealers – they were dry. Brig dropped them to the tile in a clattering cacophony of heated metal.

Brig unfocused his senses, rolling his eyes backward into his head and listening for Clarity to tell him of dangers higher up in the stairwell. He could hear the nervous breathing of a henchman, several floors up, waiting for the intruder to make his approach. Brig thought he detected a whimper from the unseen enemy, but there would be no mercy today. He stepped forward.

A loud slapping of heels on the tile inside the alcove preceded a surprised henchman that slid out from around the corner, making a futile attempt at escaping Brig's sight.

Brig launched forward and grabbed the man by the back of his neck, yanked his head backward. "What floor is Muldoon on?" he grimaced in a throaty rasp.

The man did not answer, instead unwisely choosing to glare with a fierce defiance – and display loyalty to the wrong cause.

Brig placed his other hand at the front of the man's neck and squeezed at the bulge in his throat. The man's eyes began to swell from their sockets. "Tell me where he's at, and I promise I'll make your death that much easier," he growled.

With an expression borne of electrified panic, the man fell limp. "Twenty third floor..." he muttered with a thick EurAsian inflection.

His eye to the stairwell, Brig spun his hands together, snapping the henchman's neck with a sickening crunch that echoed beyond the hallway. Brig dropped the lifeless form and stepped through the doorless frame. A rhythmic metallic clunk filled the dead air above him. Brig spun and dove out of the doorway towards the hall, as a bouncing grenade cratered the frame and a good portion of the wall in a thunderous outpouring of powdered concrete and metal fragments.

As the cloud of debris filtered its way upward, Brig warily levered himself and staggered into the destroyed alcove. The stairs, or what remained of them, crumbled and hung from the floor above him. He leapt and barely snagged a gnarled piece of rebar protruding from the fractured concrete, and then pulled himself up to solid flooring with the small amount of strength remaining within him. He exuded a painful grunt and leaned his weight on the loosened railing between the staircases, glancing upward.

After a brief second, the shadowy form of the other henchman appeared above. With lightning efficiency, Brig flooded the narrow opening with the contents of a clip from a 9MM. The shots hit their mark, exploding the man's chest in a dark spray that rained a light mist. The dead henchman fell forward, bouncing recklessly against the railings on his death spiral downward, until he landed with a crunchy thump on the landing above Brig.

A few moments later, after a draining climb, Brig emerged from the stairwell on the 23rd floor. Upon exiting the doorway, a cascade of bullets decorated the wall next to him. Once again, without regard for his safety, he strode forth into the barrage. With his twin 9's leveled in front of him, belching flame from their short muzzles, Brig hammered the pair of Syndicate thugs awaiting his arrival. They crumpled to the floor as their knees burst apart from the shots, their bellowing wails leaving a haunting calling call for whom Brig knew to be waiting just beyond one of the doors ahead.

He stopped and narrowed his focus, allowing Clarity to guide his path once more. At the end of the hallway, a pair of dual doors that led to the primary suite of the floor glowed with an amber aura. Fully expecting further resistance, Brig maintained the aim of his guns while he swept the hallway with a fiendish glare. The sting of gunpowder hanging in the stagnant air forced a rasping cough from his lungs. He stopped and leaned with one hand against the wall and gathered a shallow breath. He moved forward.

The silence did not break.

Brig checked the chambers of both handguns, but found them to be vacant. He dropped the pieces to the floor with a hollow thump and straightened his shoulders. He approached the doors of the grand suite and stopped, the thin sliver of light from within painted across his sweaty and pallid face. He drew his lungs deep with a sudden serenity.

His journey's end was behind the doors, and it was calling to him. The warm air cascading off the mountains beckoned him forward.

With a swift ferocity, he buried his boot in the center of the doors. The decorative frame that adorned them splintered and they slammed against the inside walls. Once again expecting a final push of enemy resistance, but getting none, Brig strode determinately in through the entryway, his blazing azure eyes fixated on his prey.

Bruno Muldoon, non-reactive to the brutal intrusion of his personal suite, stood on the opposing balcony with his back to the room. The heated desert air lifted his glossy black locks behind his head as he gazed into the final embers of the day. He pushed away from the railing, turned and straightened his dinner jacket before casually strolling in through the French doors.

Brig stopped in the center of the room and breathed a heavy sigh through his teeth.

"Ah, Mr. Sampson..." Muldoon cooed, "I'd say what a surprise it is to see you here, but you left no doubt of your impending arrival." He pointed over his shoulder with a disinterested roll of his eyes. A row of small columns of black smoke drifted up from the broken Strip behind him.

"Your time is up, Muldoon," Brig growled.

"Is it now?" Muldoon's mouth curled up at the corner. He scanned Brig from head to toe, stopping momentarily at the crimson-black bandage that hung at his neck. "By your appearance, I'd say your clock is winding much faster than mine."

Brig barked a fluid cough, wiped the resulting blood on his darkened sleeve. "I don't care about me... I'm already dead. You're the one going down here tonight."

Muldoon's smirk grew.

"You've taken everything from me, so there's nothing else I have to lose," Brig continued through bared teeth.

"From you?" Muldoon waved an angry finger through the air. "The man that strategized and executed the kidnap of my wife..."

"My sister!" Brig snarled like a rabid jungle beast, taking a step forward.

"I grow tired of you, Mr. Sampson. But that's not your name either, now is it?" He placed an arm at the small of his back and raised the other in the air. "Mr. Stroud, your reward for making it so surprisingly far through my defenses..." he said with a crisp snap of his fingers.

37: ENDGAME

Before Brig could react, a fist the size of a bowling ball slammed against his cheek; he stumbled sideways and fell to the floor with a truncated grunt. The imposing form of Castor Webb stood over him like a concrete slab atop a pair of Sequoia trunks, darkening Brig's vision. Brig's head spun as he attempted to rise to his knees.

Only slightly more surprising to him than Castor's sudden appearance from seemingly ether, was the titan's catlike agility in pouncing at the former EW without detection. Brig pawed at his shattered cheekbone and groaned out his pain.

"You didn't really believe that I'd let just anyone in here without some sort of final defense, did you?" Muldoon clicked his tongue rapidly in succession.

Castor rained another balled fist down onto Brig's ear. Brig wailed in agony and rolled onto his side.

"All you've truly accomplished is pointing out my folly in the hiring of incompetence. But you've culled the ranks, and I'll not make that mistake again." Muldoon shifted to face the crumpled soldier in the center of the room. He pointed a casual finger at Castor. "That, Mr. Stroud, is what's called loyalty."

Muldoon propped himself on his haunches a meter from Brig and narrowed his eyes to slits. "And... it's what loyalty proffered incorrectly earns *you*."

Brig closed his eyes and breathed an uneven rattle. He swallowed the salty blood drizzle at the back of his throat.

Muldoon tilted his head and leaned closer. "How is that little hellion from the Dark Continent, by the by?"

Brig angled his eyes to Muldoon.

"No need to respond. I know the answer," he chuckled. "A pity." He raked his manicured nails across the plush shag at his feet. "But tell me, Mr. Stroud. How did you ever forgive her?"

Brig slowed his breathing.

"She allowed the leader of the free world... *your father*... to die. Surely, that must have weighed mightily upon you." Muldoon flicked his eyes at Castor and then back at Brig, whom did not raise his eyes in return. "Your father. He died bravely, spilling his life's blood at the end of a rogue's dagger... while that little bitch coward ran for her life. So tell me – do you forgive her? Or is there vitriol in your heart?"

Brig lifted his gaze and snarled at Muldoon.

"Ah... pressure points," Muldoon whispered with a nauseating smirk.

"What the Revolution did you to was the beginning of your end..." Brig hacked a violent spasm, spilling more precious droplets of blood onto the carpet.

The Irishman snickered and stood from his crouch. "The only surprise, my friend, was the timing of their ill-fated attempt at relevance." He paced past Brig and then stopped to look upward at the ceiling. "Thanks to that sorry excuse for counterintelligence. That degenerate Russian worm. But that leak has been plugged."

Brig shut his eyes and wobbled to his knees. He did not need to be an oracle to know that Danil's fate had sealed the night he revealed Muldoon's ultimate secret.

"Yes, loyalty, Mr. Stroud." Muldoon crouched beside Brig, this time close enough to feel the heat radiating from him. "Just ask the fine Mr. Underwood." He laughed with deliberate cadence. "Life is a fencing match. You feign, you stab, you parry, riposte... and then when your opponent aims to declare victory... you strike... and extinguish him."

He pushed Brig's shoulder with a finger, toppling the former commando painfully onto his side once again.

Brig lifted his head with a wary swagger. "You son of a bitch. You're... gonna hafta... kill me..." he snarled. Foam, intermingled with a small stream of blood from his ear, dripped from the side of his swollen jaw.

Muldoon smiled a wide grin and nodded to Castor. "That..." he said with nauseating glee, "is a request I can fulfill. Castor, finish him." As he stepped away from Brig and admired himself in the mirror above the bar, he raised a finger. "And make it quick, I'd like to eat dinner sometime tonight."

Castor rubbed his palms together, stepped forward and reached his massive hand to Brig's neck. Before he could close his grip, however, he strained a groan through tightened lips. The lesser giant stepped back in a clumsy stumble, grasping at his abdomen, where a violet stain quickly spread from around a protruding knife. He fumbled to gain a grip on the slick handle, but shock overcame him and he hit the floor like a felled oak.

As Castor lay gasping in panic, his brother, Pollux, stormed from the adjacent room and plucked Brig from the floor with one gargantuan mitt. Brig gurgled as his breath left him. Pollux ground his teeth together and bored his red eyes into Brig's. "I told ya' I was gonna git ya," he screamed, his voice offering a hint of unevenness. "You shoulda killed me downtown when you had the chance!"

Muldoon, avoiding the unease of seeing Castor lying at his feet in a growing pool of his life's essence, swallowed hard and stepped back from the fray. "Finish him, Pollux. Finish him now!" he cried with a rare hesitation.

"Pol... Pol..." Brig gasped. "Don't... listen to him..."

However, Pollux, the bloodlust blinding his brain, continued to close his palms around Brig's throat.

"He doesn't care... about you or your... family..."

Pollux's fists loosened. He clicked his eyes towards his boss ever so slightly, and then glared at Brig. "I'm gonna kill you!" he roared into Brig's face.

Brig, as pale as he had been in recent days, blinked his eyes. "Look at your br... brother," he choked out, "he's... dying. Muldoon doesn't... care..."

Once again, Pollux's grip slackened.

"Your job is not to think, you overgrown imbecile!" Muldoon screamed. He smacked Pollux across the back with a balled fist. "Kill him now, or I'll do it myself and God help me, you'll be going over the railing when I'm done!"

As Brig's eyes flickered their final gleam, he parted his lips. "You still... have a chance to save... your brother, Pollux."

Suddenly, Pollux released Brig, whom fell awkwardly to the floor into a limp pile. He took a step backward and looked to his boss with an expression comprised of confusion - and final realization.

"Don't just stand there, idiot!" Muldoon barked with a mad glare, spittle heaving from his mouth. His trademark suaveness had fled him. "Kill. Him!" He grabbed at Pollux's jacket lapels and shook the beast.

Pollux wiped Muldoon's grasp away with a flick of his palm. The mammoth glanced down at Brig before exhaling a whimper. He scooped his brother into his arms, carefully slid the blood-caked knife from Castor's abdomen and tossed it on Muldoon's Persian rug. Castor, his face a pallid white, tapped Pollux lovingly on the side of his face, and then closed his eyes. Pollux, hefting his twin like a limp doll, lumbered from the room.

Muldoon, a dumbfounded expression painting his face as his eyes followed the flight of his loyal subjects, bellowed "Pollux! Get back here this instant!"

The pair had already disappeared through the broken doorframe and into the corridor beyond without a response, the boom of Pollux's thundering hooves dying out near the stairwell.

"Castor! Tell your brother to return at once!"

Brig pushed himself to a standing position, a renewed vigor embracing his beaten and broken body.

The Syndicate head unfocused from the empty doorway and switched his gaze to the former Epsilon Warrior in front of him. "Bravo, Mr. Stroud..." he cooed with a mocking clap of his hands. He swiped at his slick forehead. "Bravo. You've rid yourself of both of them at once. Something that no one has ever managed to do. I'm truly impressed." He pulled at the lapels of his jacket once again. "You've passed the test."

Brig, grinding his teeth in silent anger, locked his heavy glare on the back of Muldoon's head.

Muldoon scanned the starry palette above the mountainous horizon and folded his hands behind the small of his back. "You'll make an excellent right hand man, Mr. Stroud." He craned his neck to eye Brig. "Assuming you survive your injuries from tonight..."

Brig growled. "You're goin' on about loyalty. You don't know the meaning of the word." He swiveled his head and scanned the empty room behind him. "No one's comin' to save you this time. I told you this is the end, Muldoon."

Muldoon spun on a heel and wore his best surprised glare. His eyes gravitated for a brief second on the bloody field knife lying a few meters away. "Are you going to run me in with that knife, too?" Muldoon released an involuntary chortle. "How workaday..."

Brig snorted his disdain and slid something from within the back of his belt. A powerful silhouette of a large caliber handgun appeared within his left palm. Brig stepped forward and tilted the charred barrel into Muldoon's line of sight. He narrowed his eyes and bared a set of teeth from one side of his mouth.

"Know what this is?"

Muldoon raised his eyebrows and flared his nostrils. "A weapon that's seen better days, I presume."

Brig breathed a laugh that showed anything but humor. "I pulled this from the fire."

Muldoon did not speak.

"You know the one... the one that took the life of my best friend." Brig caressed the barrel of the gun, lifting a thin film of soot that clung to his index finger. "My brother for life..." He raised his eyes to Muldoon.

"Are you going to shoot me now, Mr. Stroud?" Muldoon's eyes widened. He took a step forward. "Revenge killing? Put me in my place? Teach me a lesson?" He paused. "Or all of the above?"

Brig, his breath flowing heavily through his teeth, tapped his finger against the trigger guard.

"Be true to yourself, Stroud. You're not a killer."

Brig shook his head once. "Not like you, Muldoon."

"None are..."

Before the Syndicate boss could utter another syllable, Brig raised Clive's modified .50 caliber Desert Eagle and fired a shot into Muldoon's left knee. A wad of flesh and bone exploded from the side of his leg. He toppled to his other knee.

"That's for my sister..." Brig snarled.

Muldoon bit into his lip; blood spurted from the split skin. He madly gnashed his teeth and glared up through several strands of mussed hair that covered his face. He cackled with a demented squeak and gripped the bloody hole in his leg. "Mistakes can be made," he said, his voice an insane caricature of its former self. "All is forgiven then?"

Fire shot from the barrel of the Eagle; Brig released another round – this one finding Muldoon's opposite knee.

Muldoon flipped over backward and wound his arms around both legs.

"That's for my father..." The intensity in his voice carried into the desert night.

His eyes glazed in madness, Muldoon rolled to his side to face Brig. "Do you know what you've done?" he screamed. "You're condemning the world with your condemnation, Stroud! Tread wisely!"

Brig twitched the end of the barrel to the left and squeezed the trigger once more, plowing a scorching piece of metal into Muldoon's right shoulder. The force of the blast pushed Muldoon to his back on the balcony. "That was for Nadia..."

Muldoon narrowed his eyes in confusion, while he alternated holding the wounds on his knees and shoulder.

Brig stepped forward and placed the barrel against his prey's drenched forehead. "And this is for everyone else you've had a hand in destroying..."

With a steady stream of intermingled froth and blood flowing from his broken lip, Muldoon flexed his jaw and glared up at Brig. "Go on then, you coward!" he wailed. "Finish the job for which you came. Drive the nail, Pilate!"

Brig flicked a finger on his trigger hand; Muldoon flinched. However, instead of another deafening blast from the powerful handgun preceding the Syndicate head's gruesome fate, the hidden magazine dropped from the blackened grip into Brig's other hand.

Without taking his eyes from Muldoon, Brig emptied the mag into his back pocket, slammed it back into the Eagle and leaned forward.

"What do you think you're doing?" Muldoon crowed. "Finish me!"

Brig smiled with stern resolve and cocked the action on the weapon. He tilted the broken chamber into a stream of silvery moonlight so that Muldoon could view the single bullet that sat snugly within. "They say everyone has one with their name on it..." Brig growled. He stood upright and clicked the action closed before turning away into the room.

"I knew you weren't a killer! Come back here you sniveling coward!" Muldoon bellowed.

Brig held the Eagle out to his side for Muldoon's benefit, and then clunked the heavy piece of metal onto the edge of the dinner table several meters away. The former EW glared at Muldoon with narrowed eyes.

"Do the right thing..."

Breaking Muldoon's scowl of incredulity, Brig strode from the room.

"Come back here!" Muldoon's voice echoed like a rabid coyote into the corridor. "Castor! Pollux! Stop him!"

The 23rd floor of the World's End Resort fell into silence as Brig reached the stairwell door. He hunched his tired body over the rail and began descending the concrete steps.

A clap like the thunder of doom rang out and reverberated throughout the hallway above. Brig flickered his eyes shut for a brief second and then continued his slow exit.

Allowing gravity to assist his descent, Brig found himself on the second floor, just above the fractured set of stairs that would lead him from the tomb that the hotel had become. He hooked an arm onto the bent rail and leaned forward, tumbling awkwardly down the broken concrete, before falling into a combat roll at the base of the stairwell.

He lay for a moment, his eyes closed tightly. He gathered his remaining energy that would carry him home and staggered from the gaping hole, leaning one hand against the wall. The desert night's hot breeze wafting in from the open lobby ahead called him forward from the depths of Hell.

"Brigadier? Are you okay?" Steele's angelic voice called from behind him.

He did not respond - he continued to stagger towards the end of the corridor that led into the darkened casino floor.

"Brigadier! Sweetheart... are you okay, can you hear me?"

As he reached the base of the World's End Resort's iconic globe marquee, Brig stopped and tilted his head through his brain's dense fog to look at her. The horror of the previous seven years washed from his expression like a melting candle.

Steele hurried forward and placed her slender hands on his cheeks. Brig dropped to his knees and embraced her with weakened arms around her waist, and then looked up through a sheet of hot tears.

"It's over... it's all over," he managed to strain from his dry throat.

She stroked the hair over one of his ears and met his gaze. "What's over? What happened up there?"

Through a cascade of heavy sobs, Brig coughed and slumped to the shattered drive. As the flickering lights of the New Vegas welcome sign dimmed from his vision, Brig released a sigh.

"Jesse!" Steele's voice echoed distantly. "He's over here, come quickly!"

38:
Family

Earth. Flagstaff, Arizona

Brig opened his paling blue eyes. The afternoon sun poked its curious rays through the cottage shutters on the other side of the room.

In a head shattering déjà vu moment, he gazed upon Steele Fox standing a few meters from him, a shroud of sunlight surrounding her. He tried to speak, but his weakened condition left him barely able to mutter a word.

"Hello beautiful," he managed to force out.

Steele turned to face him with a fractured smile. She stepped to his bedside and placed her hand on his. "Glad to see you awake," she said in a quiet whisper.

"Where..." Brig started, before devolving into a deep cough. He attempted to push himself to his elbows, but she held him down with barely a light hand on his chest.

"Brigadier, lie down. You need to keep your strength."

Brig closed his eyes and did his best to breathe deeply.

"You're at the cottage. You've been asleep for three days." Her voice cracked. "Brigadier, I need to tell you something."

Steele scraped a chair across the wooden floor, placed it at the side of the bed and propped herself upon it. She peered down at her feet, the back of her hand to her mouth without speaking, holding back the urge to vomit.

In what seemed an enormous task, Brig grabbed her hand with two fingers and pulled it close to his chest. "I know... I'm dying."

She raised her eyes and smiled a weak grin.

"After everything I've... *we've*... been through, this flu's gonna kill me."

Steele's expression sunk. She blinked several times in rapid succession. "Brigadier, you don't have the flu. You have radiation poisoning."

Brig, struggling to comprehend her diagnosis, raised his head from the pillow. "How?"

Steele moistened her lips with a flick of her tongue. "When we crashed outside of New York City. You were exposed to an extreme dose of radiation. Likely more than we've ever measured before as humans."

Brig shook his head. "Then why weren't you affected?"

He interrupted his own thought, recalling their short time at the desolate shoreline of the once bustling metropolis. The moment he replayed the events immediately after the crash, he realized his fatal mistake – he had removed his helmet upon leaving the shuttle and before pulling Steele from the wreckage.

The pair sat in close silence for a moment. Steele raised her head once again. "I'm so sorry, Brigadier, I should have realized when we were there... But the computers in our biosuits weren't operating properly and didn't detect anything..." Her voice trailed, and then reappeared in a sullen tone. "I should have done something. I'm so sorry."

She glanced at the last rays of sunlight flowing through the window. A distant thunder rolled across the clouds, shaking the ground.

"It seems lately all I'm doing is apologizing for my missteps..."

"You have nothing to apologize for, Steele."

Steele faced Brig. She took his hand in hers. "You are quite simply the bravest man I've ever known."

Brig closed his eyes and winced as he adjusted his position on the bed. "A lot of good that's done me..."

The screen door sprung open and one of the Revolution medics, a boy more than a man, strode in with a clear bag of fluid under his arm.

"Should I give him some morphine to ease his pain a little bit?" he said with a heavy Texas drawl.

Steele raised her hand to halt him. The medic clicked his eyes to Brig, then back to her, before he turned with a nod and left the room. Steele refocused on Brig.

"Brigadier, you've singlehandedly changed the direction of this conflict. Do you realize the importance of that?"

Brig forced a smile that washed away when he began coughing again. Steele swabbed a copious stream of violet blood from the corner of his mouth.

"You need to listen to that young lady, Brigadier," a familiar voice added from the doorway.

Neither had to turn - they knew who it was. Steele smiled and rose from the chair before turning to see Buck Rogers, his usual toothpick hanging from his lip. He leaned on a pair of crutches.

"That's the craziest damn thing I ever seen anybody do." He plucked the toothpick from his mouth and squinted. "And the bravest..."

"Buck... glad to see you up and around," Brig said with as big a smile as he could muster.

Buck placed the pick back between two molars and nodded at Brig. "You'll be up and about in no time, too."

Steele looked away.

"So, Buck – you gonna stay a while then?" Brig laid his head back on the pillow.

"Nah," Buck said with a small head shake, "the word is that the Canadians just showed up over in Clovis." He tapped his ten-gallon backward on his head. "These boys think I can offer some strategy for 'em."

Brig chuckled. "They need you, Buck."

"Just gonna be a mop-up operation, Brig," Buck replied.

"Well they have the best leadin' them."

Buck tapped his index finger in the air at Brig. "It's all because of you, Brigadier. You rest on that a while. An' when you get better, you come back an' join us."

Brig stayed silent, not wishing to divulge the grave secret that he and Steele had just been discussing. He nodded and then painfully lifted his right hand to his forehead to offer a weak salute.

Buck's face fell, more than he had intended to let on, before he returned the gesture with a crisp salute of his own. He lifted his hat to Steele, bowed his head with a Southern respect, and hobbled through the screen door.

Before it could offer its wood-on-wood clack to the remaining two in the room, the door stretched open with a scream of its spring. Two silhouetted figures appeared, drenched in the afternoon sunlight.

The faces of Jessica and Eli materialized, each wearing smiles that provided all the light necessary in the small cottage living room. Jessica, hand-in-hand with her son, quickly crossed the room and draped herself across Brig. He dug deep into his empty energy store and lifted his arm to her shoulder.

She tilted the lampshade to expose the pale skin of her brother's face.

"Jess... I'm sorry about Clive," Brig said, just above a whisper.

Jessica held her tears and nodded. "He always made his own choices, Brig..."

"Yeah, but..."

Jess wagged her head. "I don't know what he was thinking, either. But it's gonna be okay." She turned her eyes to her son, whom stood at the foot of Brig's cot. A tear rolled from the corner of her eye. A long lost smile grew on her lips.

"You look sick, Uncle Brig..." Eli offered in a small voice.

Brig, fighting down a heavy cough, lifted a thumb in Eli's direction with a wink. "I'm gonna be alright."

Steele stood silent in the shadow of the oak front door. She darted her eyes to Jess and then down at the wooden floorboards.

"So are you going to be staying here now that..." Eli started before his voice trailed off. He looked to his mother and then stepped towards Brig. "...Dad's gone?"

Brig drew in an uneven breath and forced his eyes shut. He winced out a smile. "I'll try, buddy. I'll try." No longer able to hold it back, Brig shook and belched a raking hack from deep in his lungs.

Steele subtly cleared her throat and stepped from behind the door. "He really needs to get his rest..." she said with a subdued lilt.

Jess snagged another tight hug from Brig. "Thank you..." Jess whispered into Brig's ear, and then kissed him lightly on the cheek. She gathered Eli with a motion of her hand, smiled unevenly at Steele, and the pair left the cottage.

As Brig's cough increased in both depth and fluid production, Steele stepped to the doorway and motioned for the medic to return. With a nervous shake, he tapped the IV into the back of Brig's hand and left the room without a word.

Steele turned away and eyed the growing billows of storm clouds forming just over the trees, her arms crossed in a tight bow around her midsection.

"It's gonna be okay, sweetheart..." Brig said, his voice struggling to maintain an even pitch.

The screen door clapped shut. Steele clamped her eyes closed and fought off a sob.

Like a gravelly monster roaring from the depths of a cavern, Brig hacked before lying back on his fluid-soaked pillow with a groan. "Sure could use... some of that magic gel..."

Steele lifted her eyes to the rising tower of clouds in the distance with renewed interest. She nodded to a conversation in her head.

"That's it!" she said in an exclaimed whisper. She swung around to face Brig, but he had already faded off to a deep slumber. Steele spun back to the window. "That's our only chance..."

An hour later

The miles of desolate desert highway disappeared beneath the chassis of the Jimmy, replaced by an endless supply that flowed forth like a cracked charcoal ribbon.

Jesse, without looking at Steele, whom sat next to him, rubbed at his eyes. "I've been all over these areas out here, and I never seen anything like what you described. You sure you know what you're lookin' for, mum?"

Steele flexed her jaw. "Positive. Just follow the clouds."

Jesse scrunched his brow. "The clouds? That'll be a sandstorm... don't wanna get caught up in that."

Steele scoured the skies ahead of them. "It's not a sandstorm. Trust me."

As the truck rolled along a rising hill of rocky scrub grass to their left, Steele leaned across the dashboard and pointed. "That's it! Just follow along that ridge..."

Jesse eyed the dark line of clouds, their murky depths drawing a black sheet that prevented viewing anything beyond the foothills. "We're goin' into that?" His voice did not mask his trepidation.

Steele nodded.

Suddenly, the wall of darkness dissipated, falling away in a misty sheen to reveal the dusky desert sky. He lifted his foot from the accelerator. The engine burped a backfire as the truck shuddered to a slow gait.

"Now what?"

"No worries, Jesse," Steele replied with a sudden confidence. "You'll know when we're there."

He shook his head and stomped the pedal once again. "But where's that..." he muttered under his breath.

The sun had disappeared from the sky and the Jimmy's lone working headlight plowed through the darkness ahead.

"I'm tellin' ya, there's nothing out..." Jesse started, but swallowed the rest of his complaint when the headlight caught on the remaining fragment of a muddy florescent military base sign, buried partially in the sand. He slapped the brake pedal to the floor, bringing the rumbling vehicle to a halt meters from a chain link gate crossing the highway.

The pair squinted into the night, but the headlight failed to give them visibility past the fence.

"Looks deserted, mum."

"There's got to be someone here..." she whispered.

Before Jesse could react, the snubbed hardness of a .38 muzzle warped his left cheek. He dropped his right hand, but the hidden gunman jabbed the gun with increased force against his face.

"You made a mistake coming here..." the stranger announced.

"You're the one makin' a mistake puttin the gun in my face, mate," Jesse growled.

The man pulled at Jesse's collar, pressed the gun harder against the bulky Aussie. "This is a secure installation," the gunman barked. "Might I ask what you're *doing* here?"

"Secure cargo, mate. Why don't you just open the gate for us... and we'll be on our way."

Steele leaned into the moonlight. "Please. He's telling the truth! Just open the gate!"

The man wagged the gun in Steele's direction. "Why don't you just shut up!"

"Hey! You don't talk to the lady that way..." Jesse snarled.

Another hand reached from outside the passenger window, grasping Steele by her shoulder and pulling her tightly against the seat. Steele struggled against his grip, but could not free herself. He recoiled at the sight of her face.

"Dr. Fox? Is that you?" His light voice betrayed his young age.

"Yes... it is," she replied, flinging his hand away from her shoulder.

"But... what're you doing here? I thought you were..."

"Yes..." Steele interrupted, "...but I'm here now. And we need to get to the portal."

The man nodded.

"Get your friend to drop his gun..." she ordered.

"Back off him, Lake!" the second ordered, hopping from the side of the truck and trotting towards the empty guard shack.

"You sure, Jason?" the first asked, cautiously releasing Jesse's collar.

Jason waved his hand behind him. He pounded a fist onto the gate release. As the gate finished dragging across the sandy asphalt, Jesse prodded the Jimmy forward. The pair of guards watched as the Jimmy disappeared into a cloud of dust, illuminated in an eerie red from the taillights of the roaring retro beast.

38: FAMILY

Jesse guided the lumbering transport around a tight curve that led between two hills. Loosely placed timbers lined the walls of the path, and shrubbery growing between them held them together – giving the appearance that the path was hastily carved. The hill on the left gave way to a large metal wall that towered over them. On the right, a long line of stacked wooden crates several rows deep pointed the way forward. Another wall, equal in height to the first, lined the back row of crates and stretched on into the night.

As the Jimmy cleared a break in the crates, a large object towered in an ominous height over them. Mounted by several large braces at its base, a circular vertical ring rose from an elevated platform into the night sky. The structure tilted upward at an angle with a single row of slowly pulsating red lights around its circumference.

Jesse, his mouth agape, slowed the Jimmy to a crawl. "If I didn't see it with my own eyes, I wouldn't believe it..." He turned his eyes to Steele. "You sure about this, mum?"

Steele shook her head as she stared at the portal. It had been years since she had seen it in person, and although she had been the principal architect on the project, the mechanical behemoth placed against the contrast of the night sky still evoked a shudder. "I'm not sure about anything anymore, but we've got to. Help me get him out."

Jesse stopped the truck with a defiant squeal of its brakes, hopped from the cabin and circled around the back of the bed. Steele met him around the other side and watched Jesse mount the cargo bed.

A moment later, he reappeared at the edge of the bed, Brig draped over his back like a worn carpet.

"What do you think you're doing here?" a man's voice barked from behind them.

Steele spun to face him.

"We don't have any shipments scheduled today!" he added, reaching one hand behind his jumpsuit at the waist.

Jesse, ignoring the man's authoritative stance, dropped from the cargo bed and readjusted Brig across his shoulder.

"I'm Dr. Steele Fox..." Steele said with firm command, "...and I'm authorized to be here."

The technician, not hiding the shock at the recognition of her identity, darted his eyes to Brig's motionless form across Jesse's back, and then back at Steele. "But... you're at the colony..."

Steele nodded with a smart tilt of her head. "Good, you know who I am then. I need to get this man through the portal. He needs medical assistance immediately. Stand down."

The man stepped forward and pressed a hand to her shoulder. "I can't let you do that, ma'am."

"Are you mad? I said step aside, this is colony business!"

He glared at Jesse, whom towered over the technician by a clear fifteen centimeters. "I'll have to clear it with the Prefect," he said with a shaky voice, his eyes darting nervously between the surprise visitors.

"No. I'll talk to him," Steele interjected. "After all, he is my..." She paused and swallowed her disgust. "...*Father*."

The technician nodded and stepped from their path. "Help get him to the platform," Steele ordered, pointing towards the portal.

He reached for Brig's arm, but Jesse swung the Epsilon's lifeless form away and stomped towards the platform's flat set of stairs.

With several gazelle-like strides, Steele entered the small glass-fronted control room nestled at the vertex of two steel backstops. She exhaled a steady breath as her fingers glided over the panel. It came to life with myriad LEDs in bright blue and green that danced across her face; the cobwebbed speaker in the corner of the hut spurted a series of droning buzzes and metallic chirps. Steele focused her attention on the activity out at the platform.

Jesse had already finished climbing the elongated steps and watched the sweaty technician lug a pair of large crates into the center of the oval. He grasped at Brig's legs and assisted Jesse in laying the former EW prone across the crates, before turning and offering a crooked smile and hesitant thumbs up to Steele.

"One Alpha, what is it now?" a tinny voice projected over the speaker.

Steele severed her longing gaze and glared down at the display. "Father... it's me."

The audio went silent for a long moment. "Steele?" the voice finally responded, an increasing rush of circumambient noise haloing the reply. "What is this about?"

"I want..." She stopped herself and stared out at Brig's motionless form atop the twin crates. "I *need*... to come back."

Barbs of static filled the transmission, but no reply came.

"I've made a mistake, father. I know that now..."

"And I'm supposed to trust you at your word?" came the disdainful response.

"I chose poorly. But I don't belong here, father. I don't. There's nothing for me here." She feigned a sob. "The colony is my home."

Again, a delay preceded Allistair's reaction. "I'm pleased that you've come to your senses, my dear. But..." He paused and cleared his throat for effect. "How am I to allow you to return in the company of a terrorist?"

"He's dead..."

"Pardon?"

"He died when the shuttle crashed on reentry. Brigadier's dead, father."

Steele twinkled her fingers over an auxiliary panel. A surrounding wall of charcoal clouds formed from nothing, taking their place along the top ridge that bordered the facility on each side. They rose with a rapid expansion until their end was no longer in sight, and began rotating within themselves. Small rumbles of thunder echoed in the artificial cylinder that cradled the portal, accompanied by fingers of electrical bolts that leapt from cloud to cloud along the billowy enclosure.

"My condolences on your loss, darling. I know you were quite fond of Brigadier."

Steele gnashed her teeth. "Will you *please* transmit the activation codes, father? I need to return to the colony at once." She choked back her anger.

The transmission ebbed into nothingness.

Steele could picture Allistair, his spindly hands steepled under his chin as he pondered the ramification of allowing her back after betraying him.

"Perhaps this is a teachable moment, my flower..."

Her stomach cringed at the once-endearing term.

"A chance for you to rediscover your responsibilities. Where's the girl that I raised? Hmm?"

The bastard's not going to let me come back!

Steele raised her eyes and gazed upon the platform. To her dismay, Jesse hovered over Brig, shaking him about the collar as the technician stood with a helpless expression behind him. She furrowed her brow, unsure of why either would be tending to Brigadier.

Suddenly, Jesse, as if he detected Steele staring at him, turned and waved his arms to gather her attention. She tilted her head in confusion. Jesse motioned in desperation for her to come to him.

As she pulled her eyes away from the burly Australian, she noticed the reason - Brig was lurching from his prone position on the crates in a throe of a death convulsion. She gulped her fear and glared down at the console once again.

"Father, I need the codes now. Please transmit them at once!"

After the standard silence of the communication traversing the portal circuit to Mars and back, he spoke with a suspicious tongue.

"Steele... what is it that you're not telling me here?"

Steele inhaled a deep breath and held it. "They're... going to kill me!" she said in a panic, not all feigned.

"*They*? Who exactly are *they*?"

"There's no time to explain father," she said, watching as Brig's convulsions continued.

A thick stream of bloody froth flowed from the corner of his mouth. The clock had wound down.

"They've been tracking my movements for the past few days. If they find me here, the entire operation... could be compromised!" It was her last hope; she closed her eyes tightly in hopes that he would bite.

A defeated sigh preceded his response. "Very well, Steele."

The console lit in a bright pattern, as a stream of encrypted codes flowed from the remote end.

"I'll expect you in the executive suite immediately upon your arrival..."

Steele did not respond, as she had already fled the control hut. Her thin legs carried her without haste up the flat stairs, where she slid to a stop on her knees next to Brig.

"Doesn't look good, mum," Jesse said.

"Jesse, go to the control room. Our half of the codes have been entered. Append what was just transmitted and activate the portal. Now!" she screamed over the din of the artificial storm raging around the installation, pointing wildly with one hand while looking over Brigadier's condition.

"Yes, mum," he barked in reply, and then sprinted away down the stairs.

She watched Jesse study the panel in front of him, dumbstruck, before he began working the controls. Steele placed her hands on Brig's chest and began what she hoped would be a lifesaving procedure - pumping a multitude of times before stopping and listening for any sign of breath from him. She swept his mouth with a pair of fingers, scraped the caked froth from his face and pressed her lips to his. After several unsuccessful repetitions, she withdrew and looked into his sullen eyes.

"No, no, no! You can't be... you can't leave!" she cried, huffing several more breaths into his mouth before sitting back on her knees in defeat. She released a shrill wail that carried over the tumult around her. With a body-quaking sob, she fell over Brig's lifeless form.

A calm melancholy fell over her like a wet sheet. The world around her turned dark. She peered up at Brig's dead eyes, his empty stare at the portal behind him. She lifted her glare to the ring towering over her – the night sky behind it was still visible.

"Jesse!" she yelled like a panicked child in a thunderstorm. "Activate the portal!"

Jesse flung his hands in the air behind the glass. "I can't find the bastard, mum! There's nothing labeled 'activate' here!"

"The button! Press the bloody green button!" she replied with a piercing shriek.

Jesse nodded in shocked comprehension. He pounded his fist onto the console.

As the technician leapt from the platform and took cover in the small control hut, the ring's sleeve of red lights began pulsating in rhythm with the roaring hum that saturated the air. The lightning in the cloud walls jumped in violent arcs across to opposite sides, sending blinding blue flashes of light that flickered like a strobe.

Steele covered her eyes and draped herself across Brig's vacant husk.

Just as the roar began vibrating the very foundations of the platform and portal itself, a blinding aura surrounded them. With the deafening boom like that of dynamite exploding in a closed room, Steele, Brig and the crates... were gone.

The air turned deathly silent and the clouds fell to mist. Jesse, his jaw ajar, shook his head in disbelief.

"Now there's somethin' you don't see every day..."

39:
Unas and Fennec

Mars. Red Colony One

"This one's deceased," announced a female Scot, reading the chart as though it were a humdrum news article.

"The transport got him?" another woman, a Cajun by her accent, asked.

"Nah, looks like he was dead long before that. Poor bastard."

The sensation of heat on Steele's skin brought to her senses the feeling of bathing in liquid fire. She knew it not to be true, however - nonetheless it was an uneasy feeling. She forced her eyes open to slits and glared through the fog that shrouded her vision.

"She's awake. Hook her up to a stabilizer stat before she goes into defib," the Scot ordered.

Steele's mind swirled in a dizzying vortex of blackness, but the pinhole of light at the end urged her conscious to take control. She flung her arms in front of her, knocking the stabilizer cuff and electrode ring from the second technician's grasp and onto the tile floor.

"No..." Steele grunted through stiff lips.

"Dr. Fox, you've just been through the portal. You need to lay back and let the stabilizer do its job," the Scot assured, pressing at Steele's shoulder to hold her down.

"Don't tell me..." Steele growled, "...about the portal, Celia. I've been through... it before. I'm fine. And I need to..." She laid her head back onto the soft cushion of the medical cot underneath her, trying to reign in the vertigo that clamped her brain.

Celia McTavish, her short fiery locks swept out in sharp points, stepped back and put her hands to her hips.

Steele shifted herself and dropped her legs to the side of the cot. Without a word, she pushed up and stood, hiding the obvious effects of the portal traversing like a wily seadog.

"Dr. Fox, I wish you'd take your own advice and sit back," McTavish chastised.

"No time," Steele fired back, and pushed past her.

The technician tugged at Steele's sleeve, halting her hasty exit from the portal receiver hub. "The Prefect has instructed me to escort you to his office."

Steele brushed McTavish's hand away and stepped over to Brig's body. "I know what my father wants, thank you." She darted her eyes to the second tech, who stood with an observant eye behind McTavish. "I need you to bring him to my lab immediately, I'll meet you there."

"But Dr. Fox, it's my orders to take you..."

Steele spun on the spot and glared fire into McTavish's icy blue eyes. "Are you going to apprehend me, Celia? Do you have that authority?"

Celia withdrew, placing her hands obediently down at her sides. "No, ma'am."

Steele flung an eyebrow upward and nodded once. "Then I suggest you two do as I instructed." She pointed at Brig's body. "Take him to my laboratory at once. And do not let this happen again."

"Yes, ma'am," Celia responded with a flick of her eyes to the other tech.

"Darpa..." Steele said under her breath, striding towards the exit of the domed enclosure.

"Yes, Dr. Fox," came the familiar reply of Darpa, whose digital entity materialized in stride with Steele.

"Prepare the Vat."

Darpa nodded and then faded away.

Moments later, in Steele's lab

Steele looked on at the theratank - or the Vat, its common moniker amongst the colony's lab technicians - with a mournful tear that strolled her cheek.

The backlight from the room-width tank projected a teal flood of light that worked its way through the translucent bacterial gel. The gel wove its miraculous web about Brig's naked corpse, attaching itself to his ashen skin and finding its way in through his partially open mouth.

Steele knew that it was too late. The Vat was designed to heal injuries, not raise the dead. She gazed upon Brig's vacant stare, the broken windows to a soul no longer present. She allowed a faint cry to escape her lips, and then, gathering her resolve, turned her chin to her shoulder.

"Vitals, Darpa..."

Darpa, her hologram blazing behind Steele as it stood at a console to the other side of the quiet laboratory, without turning replied "Flat, Dr. Fox."

Steele closed her eyes and sent a wish off to the cosmos, but opened them knowing that it would go unfulfilled.

"He's not responding to the treatment, Dr. Fox," Darpa added, her voice eerily melancholy. "How tragic. I'm sorry for your loss..." she said just above a whisper.

Steele nodded, but then tilted her head to the side. "You're... *what?*"

"And whom are you talking to, Doctor?" General Rossi interjected from the now open door of the lab.

Steele stealthily swept away the tears from her porcelain face and lifted her gaze back to Brig's darkened shadow. "General..." she said without visually acknowledging him.

Rossi scanned the room, pacing with his arms folded neatly behind him. He stepped next to Steele with a sharp click of his boot heel and joined her in studying the teal tinted gel - although with a mocking half interest. His eyes stopped at Brig's pale face; a smile tugged at the corner of his lips.

"Now is not a good time, General."

"That is not *your* decision to make, Doctor," he riposted. "As I'm sure you are aware, your father has requested an immediate audience."

"My father can wait. I have more pressing issues with which to attend."

"He didn't ask. And neither did I..."

"Be gone, General. We have nothing left to discuss!"

Rossi contorted his face into a disgusted sneer. "No amount of your pathetic weeping will bring back your precious Epsilon," he hissed, inching close enough for her to feel his searing breath on her neck. "Nor should it. Why the Prefect doesn't have you up on treason isn't so much a mystery as a crime in itself."

He rotated his torso to face the dead EW, floating like a leaf in a stagnant pond. Rossi spat on the floor at the Vat's base. "But you were mistaken if you thought you would escape with *that* terrorist."

"How dare you speak to me in that manner?" she bellowed, a finger jabbed at him. "Need I remind you *I* am the Prefect's daughter, and I will not be treated with such disrespect." Steele stomped her foot onto the tile. "Especially in my laboratory! This is *my* domain!"

Rossi bared his teeth and stooped his two-meter frame over Steele. "And this colony is my domain, doctor. Need. I. Remind. You."

Her eyes locked with his. "Will that be all, General?" she snarled.

"No..."

As quickly as the word left his lips, both of Steele's hands lifted involuntarily from her sides and whipped together, melded with the blue pulsating radiance of a pair of powered shackles.

Steele, her eyes widened in horror, tried to push herself away from Rossi, but the associated restraining bridle protruding from his hand kept her tied to his presence like a human magnet.

"This way, *Ms.* Fox..." he cooed, escorting Steele against her will from the lab.

The door to Allistair Cromwell's executive suite slid open with a gentle whoosh - but a less than gentle display from two very familiar faces followed. General Rossi tilted his head to navigate the doorway and towed Steele behind him – the souls of her boots scraping the floor as she fought like a marlin on a line.

"Prefect..." he said with an evil malice that doused each syllable.

Allistair blinked a silent acknowledgement to Rossi and then glared at Steele. "You're late," he said with a foul sting. "I said immediately upon arrival, Steele."

Rossi slung the restraining bridle across his body, deftly flinging Steele with it into a waiting chair at the foot of Allistair's glass desk. She gathered her breath and pushed herself upright, hammered the shackles against her seat, to no avail.

"Father," she seethed, "order this boorish pustule to release me at once!"

Rossi let loose a defiant crow, his head cocked back in an arrogant slant.

"Steele Primrose!" Allistair cawed, "you will show respect to the General. I will not warn you again!"

"Respect? He deserves nothing less than a swift kick in the..."

"That's enough!" screamed Allistair.

"It's alright, sir," Rossi interjected, a hand raised calmly in front of him. "I understand her anger. After all, she is in mourning for her... *friend.*" With pouting lips and a fake sympathy pasted on his face, he paced across Steele's path. "It was almost pitiful, Prefect. Your sweet little flower standing there... gazing longingly at his corpse wishing that he would come back."

Allistair raised an eyebrow. "He's here?"

The General turned halfway to face the colony leader, nodded once. "In the Vat."

"Steele? What exactly *was* your plan?" Allistair rose from his chair and prowled around the corner of his desk. "Revival?"

Steele lowered her gaze and gulped once. "I... I had hoped... but. It was much too late."

Allistair's voice lowered to a hiss. "The agreement to allow your return was that you came back alone."

"He's dead, father."

"Irrelevant. His presence in my colony - dead or alive - was something I wanted to avoid. And was *not* part of our arrangement! You lied to me."

"I did no such thing! What difference does it make when he's dead?" The words left an icy patch across her soul.

The Prefect leapt from his perch at the edge of his desk. "I don't want him here! He's an Epsilon, and I don't want him in my colony!"

Steele feigned recoil but showed her classic reserve. "Father, you're being much too irrational about Brigadier. He is no longer a threat..."

Allistair inched uncomfortably close to Steele's cheek. "Let's drop the charade, Steele. You and I both know the score in this little game."

"I don't know what you're getting at, father. And frankly, I..."

"Enough. Enough!" He circled around her chair, and then gripped her throat with one angry hand.

"Fath..." she gagged, her eyes widened.

"What's my name?" The words slithered from his tongue.

"B...Bron...son Fox..." she managed to strain from her lips.

"What is my name?" he growled, purple blood gathering under the skin around his fingertips.

"Br...onson..."

Allistair clenched his jaw and bared his teeth in fuming anger. "What. Is. My. Name!"

"...Allistair," she said with vitriol.

He released his hand from her throat and stood back upright with a fulfilled smile. "See how simple that was?"

General Rossi stood silently to the side of the doorway, a knowing grin on his lips.

"So you have it then," Steele said with dripping disgust. She massaged the scarlet ring around her neck. "Now what? Send me to the mines to keep me quiet?"

"Oh, my dear," Allistair replied, making his way back around his desk with a lilt in his step, "you are much too valuable to be put on a shelf... for long."

Steele flicked her eyes towards Rossi, but he had not budged from his post. "For long? What are you working at?"

Allistair floated down into his chair. "First, you will be punished for your treachery. I had hoped that you would have stayed back on Earth for a while longer, so that you could better appreciate the hierarchy of things. But that opportunity has passed."

Steele shook her head and sneered. "You disgust me..."

Allistair grinned and waved his hand over a section of his desk. A bright blue and red hologram materialized a meter above it. "I'm certain you recognize this..."

Steele drew in a breath at the sight of the hovering detention cell diagram. "No... you can't be serious!"

"You will be placed in isolation..."

She shrieked her disapproval, once again banging the shackles, this time against his desk.

"Once your sentence is up... you will undergo the memory block procedure."

The General, suddenly standing next to Steele, jerked the restraining bridle upward and pulled her from the chair. Steele kicked violently with both legs, knocking over the chair, but failed to gather traction against Rossi.

"You can't do this to me!" she cried in a maniacal wail.

"Oh, I assure you - I can," he replied with a calm tilt of his head. "But you'll be back. And you can take solace in the fact that you won't remember a thing." His sickening smile grew wider as he motioned at the door.

Rossi bowed once and dragged Steele from the room.

Later

Steele pulled her knees to her chest, tucking her arms underneath. The reflection of the starry sky around her was a dizzying illusion for sure, but she paid no mind to it. In just a few short months, she had lost the two men that mattered most in her life: her father, and equally important, Brig. Soon, the entire host of memories of them both would be gone in one dizzying swoop.

With a somber irony, she surveyed the barren Martian landscape, stretching from end to end of the viewport afforded to anyone entombed in Allistair Cromwell's isolation chamber. The desert outside seemed so filled with promise earlier in her life, but now seemed bleak, desolate - and alone. Steele allowed a tear to escape unfettered from the corner of her eye – not only for what had been lost, but for what soon would be.

An amber rectangle of light opened on the reflective portion of the glass in front of her.

"You ok, sweetheart?" Brig's voice asked through the tinny sounding loudspeaker mounted in the ceiling.

For a fraction of a moment, Steele's heart leapt. She spun her head to look upon what would be her innermost desire – Brig stood within the small viewing portal of the antechamber, his lean but chiseled frame inviting her with an outstretched hand. The cold realization hit her, however, as she looked down where his shadow should have been cast forward into the chamber – and her hopes fell back from soaring heights.

"Darpa, that's not a good illusion," Steele droned. She leaned back against the wall and closed her emerald eyes.

"It's very near perfect, Dr. Fox," Darpa responded in Brig's west Texas twang, an incredible mimicry by any stretch.

Steele buried her head against her knees. "That's not what I meant, Darpa. It's... just not what I needed to see right now."

"I'm sorry, Dr. Fox," replied Darpa, still in Brig's voice. It morphed to Steele's. "I thought that the image of him would soothe you."

Steele paused in pensive thought. "The only thing that would soothe me, Darpa, is that if you could open the door to this chamber and release me."

"I do not have access to the circuitry in this wing of the colony, Dr. Fox."

"I know, Darpa," Steele responded in a flat tone, "I created you, after all. It seems my fath... Allistair... was very deliberate in his review and editing of your programming, and deleted very select areas from your omnipresence."

"Is there anything else I can do for you, Dr. Fox?"

Steele stared forward, not wiping away the stream of tears that now flowed down from her glassy eyes. "You could locate Parker and let him know of my predicament."

She looked out at the starry sky, realizing that it was not long ago that Parker had sent her and Brig back to Earth.

"Although I'm not sure he would believe you. Or care." She sighed. "But what I really want more than anything right now is to..."

She turned, but Darpa had already gone.

Two days later

Parker Bryce gnawed at the corner of his lip in thought, staring through the dazzling LED display that danced about the cabin of the turbo-lift.

"And you're sure of that report?" he asked, his soft British inflection flowing like a quiet babbling brook.

"It's confirmed," his counterpart, Damon, another Brit that stood next to him, replied.

Parker furrowed his brow. "I'd ask why he would detain her... but just the fact that she's back on colony answers any concerns – especially after she betrayed him."

Damon drummed his fingertips on the smoky plastic material of the back wall. "Think he's going to... terminate her?"

Parker wagged his head. "No chance. She is his bread and butter – without her this colony wouldn't be half what it is today. No, Damon – she's alive, and that speaks volumes about his willingness to protect her." He flicked his eyes to Damon and squinted like a scheming fox. "But this opens up a marvelous opportunity."

"How so, Parker?"

Parker wiggled his finger in the air about him. "I don't know his intentions, but you can be assured he will go to great lengths to keep her safe. And I think that she might serve as the perfect distraction for the old man."

He waved his palm over his wrist computer, and then swiped a complex pattern. The computer responded with a subtle chirp and a soulless voice. "Task sequence enabled and scheduled for plus Sol 2 at eighteen hundred Martian Coordinated Time."

Damon fidgeted with the sleeves of his jumpsuit. "You think they'll bite?"

Parker smiled and deactivated his wrist unit. "We have no choice, we have to make them now."

The lift came to a fluid stop and the doors whooshed open to reveal the inviting confines of the Observation Tower. Both men stepped from the car and strode into the quiet room.

"Gentlemen, please pardon my tardiness," Parker offered with a stiff sincerity. "But after you see what I have to offer you, I'm certain that you'll feel it was worth the wait."

Two men sat aside one another in the padded silence, both staring out at the architectural majesty of Red Colony One through the floor-to-ceiling observation glass. The first, a burly hulk whose muscular girth overflowed from the lounge chair on which he perched, rotated his head ever so slightly. Upon his head sat a strip of platinum plush that stretched from the lines of his leathered forehead to the base of his skull. The second, a boyish youth to his face, craned his neck to watch as Damon escorted Parker into the quiet room, taking particular notice of their command red jumpsuits. He ran his hand nervously through his fresh, curly locks and darted his eyes to his counterpart.

"An amazing vista, is it not?" Parker said, new warmth to his voice.

"You invited us here for sightseeing?" the larger man grumbled, his voice a strong baritone.

"Hardly," Parker responded with an amused chuckle.

The man thumped his digits with a heavy stroke on the crimson fabric of the chair. He glanced at his partner, and then squinted at Parker in suspicion. "Do we know you?"

Parker tilted his head forward in a respectful nod. "Allow me to introduce myself." He turned and surveyed the colony below them. "I am Parker Bryce, Viceroy of Communications for Red Colony One. This," he waved his hand at Damon, "is Damon Churchill, my Chief Communications Technologist."

Damon, his eyes a brilliant azure, proffered a smile to accompany a bob of his head. A lock of charcoal hair flicked across his forehead. He swiped at it with an unconscious motion.

"And you can say that we share a common... thread," Parker added. He leaned against the glass and crossed his arms over his thin chest.

"So you know *us* then?" the first man countered.

"I know of you, yes." He pushed off the glass and paced in front of the seated men, a palm wrapped around his chin. "You are Mercury McGraw, a former commando with the vaunted Epsilon Warrior Squadron. Your partner," he said with a slow twirl to face

465

them, "is one Mr. Jonas Slade, also a former Epsilon. Although until a few days ago, you were living your existence as Emerson Winslow."

Jonas lowered his head and shook it, more from apparent confused exhaustion than anything else.

"Thanks to Darpa's uncovering of the memory mapping protocol..." Parker continued.

"Darpa?" McGraw parroted with an impatient sarcasm.

"Maybe another time," Parker replied. "I've asked you here tonight because I have necessity of your assistance. A mission, if you will - and I know how well that suits you Epsilons." He paused to allow the former EWs to absorb the moment. "Interested?" Parker cooed.

"I'm still here, ain't I?" McGraw replied.

Jonas raised his bloodshot eyes but did not speak.

"Very well then." Parker flicked a pair of fingers over his wrist. A bluish hologram sprung to life against the observation glass. "Do you know this man?"

"That's Bronson Fox," Jonas chimed.

"Seemingly," Parker replied with a flat expression. "However, the man you know as Bronson Fox is an imposter. A ruthless dictator - and a mass murderer."

"Now wait, wait, wait..." Jonas balked. "He's a tough boss... a stickler for the rules. But a mass murderer? C'mon."

"Says the man who has spent the past eight years under a forged... and *forced*... identity," Parker parried.

McGraw remained stoically reserved, his hands layered upon the arms of the chair.

"Right, but..." Jonas said. He rubbed his eyes and careened them around the room. "...that doesn't make him a killer. Or a dictator."

Parker nodded with a pursed lip smile. "I understand your loyalty, and that is admirable, Mr. Slade. However..." He rubbed a finger over his wrist once more.

A second hologram took its place next to the rotating image of the Bronson impostor.

"This image is from a surveillance camera outside of the Leeds Festival at Bramham Park in twenty seventy two." Parker fixed his glare on McGraw, whom stared back without speaking. "Allistair Cromwell. Aged thirteen." He paused. "Fourteen minutes later, young Mr. Cromwell brutally stabbed a newlywed couple on their way from a remote parking lot. Seventy-four times."

Jonas tossed his palms to his sides. "What's this have to do with..."

Parker raised his hand. "After a thorough investigation, it was presumed that Cromwell acted out of revenge for the untimely death of his older brother two years earlier. His body was found savagely beaten and dumped into an abandoned mineshaft."

"Ok, so this Cromwell character just snapped and offed two people. I don't see the connection here, Bryce," McGraw said, his voice conveying his disinterest in the subject.

"Scotland Yard reopened the investigation a year later and determined that *Cromwell* killed his own brother." The pair of EWs raised an eyebrow in unison at Parker. "And he was then linked to the savage - and senseless - killings of four others over a span of fourteen months."

"And?" McGraw gruffed, twirling his hand in front of him as if to speed along the explanation.

"Normally, despite his young age, Cromwell should have been locked away in an asylum at the very least." Parker slung his hands behind his back and paced the floor nearest the window, his eyes scanning the floor in thought. "However, he was intercepted and put in a special - highly secretive - program within..." He turned his eyes to the men. "The Department of Military Science and Technology."

Jonas scrunched his brow. "The URA took him? But... why?"

"Why indeed..." Parker mused, keeping a keen eye on McGraw's flat expression. "He was one of many in an experimental program run by the esteemed Dr. Steele Fox and her father... her *real* father." He turned to face the slowly rotating holograms of Allistair Cromwell and Bronson Fox. "Gentlemen, the two men you see before you are the same person – Allistair Cromwell."

"That's some makeup job..." McGraw said, not hiding the skepticism in his deep voice.

"No makeup. Genetic transmutation. Within a few short months of his interment under the watchful eye of the DMST, the now fifteen-year-old was... *modified*... to become the much older Bronson Fox that you see on the right."

Jonas shook his head in confusion once more. "But why would Bronson Fox... the real one, I mean... turn Cromwell into himself? That doesn't make sense."

"From what we've gathered of classified data retrieved from Dr. Fox's private quarters, the original intention of the program was to provide alternate hosts for critically wounded URA soldiers returning from the battle field. However..."

McGraw turned a suddenly interested eye towards Parker.

"...That plan changed midstream... sometime around twenty seventy-four. The new direction was to replace key leaders of the URA government with doubles – clones - that offered little to no differentiation from their original host. All the while, the leaders ferried themselves to Mars in the face of an impending global catastrophe. Commonly known as..."

"The Event..." Jonas whispered aloud.

Parker nodded. "Or at least, that was the plan. Coupled with stolen surveillance in Dr. Fox's possession, it didn't take a mathematician to deduce that Cromwell realized what was about to happen to him before he underwent a memory blocking procedure, and took the real Bronson Fox's place."

"Dr. Fox, too?" Jonas asked.

"No, by no surprise she came to Red Colony One... but left behind an alternate host in her stead."

McGraw rubbed at his square chin, one finger massaging the deep cleft in the center. "You're here, Bryce. Maybe you're someone we shouldn't trust, either?"

"I was hand selected by Dr. Fox because of work that I had done for the DMST as a contractor. Nothing more."

"How convenient..."

"And you would be wrong, Mr. McGraw. As I mentioned at the start of this conversation, there is a point where our threads converge."

"Don't keep me in suspense then..." A sneer crawled onto McGraw's face.

"What Cromwell doesn't know is that I am a senior leader of the Reformation. My father, William Bryce, was one of the founders of the organization and led them up until earlier this year. Before he lost his life at the hands of the Syndicate."

McGraw leaned forward onto his knees. "That's a great story, Bryce. Mind gettin' to the reason why I would give a damn?"

Parker fell silent, pursing his lips with a determined fire. "Allistair Cromwell and his regime must be removed from power."

"A coup?" Jonas cried, springing to his feet. "Merc, you believe this? No way, Parker! That's not what the EWs are about. You've got the wrong guys..."

Parker locked eyes with McGraw.

"Tell him, Merc. Tell him we don't need to hear any more," Jonas pled.

McGraw narrowed his eyes, but remained silent.

"Not entirely true, now is it, Mr. McGraw?"

Jonas ping ponged his confused glare between Parker and McGraw. "Merc?"

"Sit down, Slade..." McGraw ordered.

Jonas lowered himself back onto the couch in shock. "What are you saying, Merc?"

"He's saying that *mercenaries* have a different outlook on such... operations."

"Mercenary?" Jonas widened his eyes. His voice rose to a higher pitch. "Since when are you a mercenary, McGraw?"

McGraw slowly ticked his eyes to their corner, then back at Parker without a word.

"For the past several years, Mr. Slade," Parker replied.

Jonas, a hurt look replacing the confusion, curled an eyebrow.

McGraw jabbed a finger into Jonas's shoulder. "Don't judge me, Slade! You don't know what it's like back there!"

Parker sat back against the window once again, a fulfilled grin on his mug.

"You do what you have to do to survive..." McGraw turned his glare back to Parker. "Not that I have to explain myself to anyone - even you, Bryce."

"Even when your employer is the Syndicate?" Parker inquired, his voice not wavering. Damon smiled at Parker's adeptness in playing the pair of Epsilons.

"Just because they threw me some credits, doesn't mean my loyalty is to anyone but myself. No one else is lookin' out for me, so I do what I have to."

"Very well then, Mr. McGraw," Parker replied, standing upright once more and nodding to Damon. "So I take it that I've got your interest?"

"I'm pretty comfortable here right now. Why would I want to stir up a mess like that, Bryce?" McGraw answered, pointing at the pair of twirling digital images.

"Because I can assure you that your comfort will be short lived. *Very...* short lived."

"That so?"

"Allistair Cromwell doesn't like Americans," Parker explained.

469

McGraw snorted and shook his head.

"...And he has a particular distaste for Epsilons. He likens them to terrorists. Just ask your former squad mate, Stroud. Something about the mining colony?"

"I was there, and I saw what happened," McGraw said. "Stroud may be a fuck up, but he's no terrorist."

"Brig? A terrorist? You're reaching, Parker," Jonas interjected.

"Gentlemen, you've convinced me! But it's not my opinion that matters."

Jonas dug deep in his broken memory with a crooked frown. "So Brig's here? I thought it was a dream... or something." He turned to McGraw with the air of an excited child.

"He's gone, Slade," McGraw grumbled.

"You sure? Because we could really use his help."

"Stroud departed for Earth some time ago, Mr. Slade," Parker confirmed with a nod.

McGraw continued his perpetual sneer. "Just because Stroud got his ass in a sling with Cromwell doesn't mean we're all marked."

"Interesting that you would use that term - marked." Parker paced once again. "You both are unregistered inhabitants of the colony. And you're Epsilons, whom Cromwell is determined to make out as terrorists. In fact, Epsilons are at the top of Cromwell's most wanted list, regardless if you've earned the designation. How well do you think you'll both fare?" He focused his gaze on Jonas. "And you, Mr. Slade. What do you think will happen when Allistair learns that your memory has been... restored?"

Both former EWs sat in silence, both in deep pensive thought.

"After what transpired in the mining colony with Mr. Stroud – even though we all agree that it was warranted - this *is* Cromwell's colony. How do you think this will play out. Do you believe you'll be able to fly under his radar forever? And when you're found out, that he'll just turn a blind eye to the fact that you're both illegally here - and that you're Epsilons?"

Jonas and McGraw shared a tense moment of eye contact.

"So what's the plan?" Jonas finally said, before McGraw could open his mouth.

Parker raised an eyebrow and smiled. "So I have your buy-in?"

"We'll think about it," McGraw snarled. "But we hafta' know what we're gettin' into."

Parker lowered his chin to his chest and tapped a finger at his temple. "Fair enough," he announced after a moment.

He waved his palm over his opposite wrist – the pair of holographic heads dissipated, replaced by a growing, green vector image of the colony. It spun for a moment, and then upended to where they could view it from a birds eye. Finally, it zoomed onto the tri-pronged structure most prominent when viewed from on high in the observation tower.

"This," Parker explained with his back to the image, "as I'm sure you are aware, is the power core of Red Colony One. It provides not only the sole source of power for the entire installation, but also feeds life support to it as well."

Jonas fidgeted in his chair; an uneasy lump formed in his throat.

"The structure is entirely redundant in the fact that if any two of the three conduits are interrupted, the remaining will take on the load without effect to the colony. With one exception..." He turned and leaned back against the glass with a coy smile on his lips. A section of the display began blinking in red. "The executive enclave resides behind the rearmost conduit, and is fed exclusively by that conduit."

"Sounds like Cromwell is paranoid," McGraw observed.

"Cromwell is a genius. Or at least his daughter is. The design enables the colony echelon to survive in case anything should happen to the rest of the installation. The executive enclave is well fortified, and lies beyond the security enclave. But in his plan to keep himself safely ensconced, he introduced a fatal flaw."

Jonas leaned forward on his chair with a squint. "So what are you asking us to do, Parker?"

"Seal the executive enclave by taking out that conduit."

"But you just said it's impossible to get to because of where it sits..." said Jonas.

"Not impossible. Difficult. But, you are Epsilons, are you not?" Parker moved forward and looked upon them with silent derision. "I've heard my share of incredible stories of bravado from your outfit." He singled out McGraw with his piercing gaze. "And I would wager this is something a mercenary would find as a welcome challenge."

McGraw sprung from his chair and threw his hand in disgust. He turned towards the turbo-lift. "That's suicide, Bryce. Find another sucker."

Jonas looked to Parker with a hesitant flit of his eyes, then to McGraw before he followed suit.

"I'll await your word then, gentlemen," Parker continued smoothly, as if his plan had not just flown the coop.

"Not interested!" McGraw barked, waving his hand at the recessed panel next to the lift door.

"You may not have a choice, Mr. McGraw."

McGraw spun, strode like a bear across the room and stopped at Parker with a thick finger outstretched at the Brit's face. "You gonna turn us in?"

"And spoil any chance at removing this madman from power? That would be counterproductive."

McGraw narrowed his eyes.

"But it won't be long before they track you down. Mark my words. Punishment at the hands of Allistair Cromwell is a sight different than anything you've witnessed, I'm certain of that."

The burly EW ratcheted his eyes between Parker and Damon, whom stood quietly against the side wide of the chamber. "Why don't you do this yourself, then?"

Parker chuckled with a knowing look to Damon. "Cromwell is already suspicious of someone within his organization. You have the advantage of being outside of his inquisition. Besides, our talents are needed elsewhere. But rest assured, there will be a... distraction... that will provide all the opportunity that you both will require for success."

McGraw grunted and spun away. He stood at the doors as they slid open, grumbling under his breath. The pair of Epsilons stepped onto the waiting lift and glared back at Parker.

"We'll let you know..." McGraw said, just before the doors closed.

40:
The Temple Defiled

Mars. Red Colony One - Two days later

Mercury McGraw slugged back his mug of Dempsey's herbal brew, wincing away the distasteful sting on his tongue with a jagged sneer. He thunked the glass onto the table; Jonas Slade did his best to mimic the muscular Adonis, but spat out half a mouthful into his own mug after tasting the concoction. McGraw absentmindedly tapped his ringed finger against the glass.

Jonas squinted through the dim ambience of the sparsely filled pub, trying to make out the faces that had seemed so familiar for the past eight years - but now seemed so alien. The sweet aroma of cigar smoke wafted in from the slits of the overhead air vents - but knowing of the tobacco prohibition on Red Colony One, he saw through the simulation.

"So whaddya know about this Cromwell character?" McGraw grumbled. He cleared the weak suds from his square chin with a swipe of his hand.

Jonas shrugged. "I never really knew him personally. He was just my boss."

McGraw glared at the bartender, Dempsey, whom leaned on his elbows across the wooden bar.

"We're not really gonna do this, are we Merc?" Jonas asked.

"What do you think, Slade?" McGraw shook his head in disgust. "Got no reason to put ourselves out there. He's bluffin'."

"But what if he's not? What if he turns us in?"

"What're you worried about?" McGraw jabbed his finger with a heavy weight onto the table. Their glasses rattled. "No one knows your memory's back. All you gotta do is keep doin' whatever you were doin, and no one's gonna be the wiser."

"But what about you? They know you don't belong here."

McGraw snorted. "Don't worry about me, Slade. I know how to survive, and I ain't worried about Allistair Cromwell."

Jonas sat in silence, staring across the table at his former squad-mate.

"What?" McGraw snarled.

"Nothin', just can't believe you're a mercenary."

"Yeah," McGraw replied before swigging the last of the liquid in his glass, "well maybe one day you'll get back there and see that it's not the utopia you been used to here. Then you'll see why."

"So what're we gonna tell Parker then?"

"Not gonna tell him anything. You heard him, Cromwell's already sniffing around trying to figure out who the mole is. We sit back and let it happen and everything goes back to normal for us."

Jonas furrowed his brow. "You don't care about what Cromwell's been up to?"

Dempsey interrupted the pair, dropping a fresh glass of ale in front of the larger EW, before turning away and resuming his position behind the bar.

McGraw glared at Jonas. "How do we know what he's sayin' is true? You never seen any of that stuff, did you?"

Jonas shook his head. "But what if I did... and he wiped those memories, too?"

"Or maybe Bryce has an agenda all his own."

Jonas sat in silence for a moment, thinking over McGraw's wry observations. "What about the surveillance footage that he showed us? You think that's fake?"

"Anything can be faked, Slade." McGraw rose the glass and gulped another mouthful. "Especially if he's tryin' to advance his cause by usin' us."

Jonas bobbed his chin towards the pub entrance. McGraw rolled his eyes to the object of Slade's attention.

Parker's comm tech, Damon, strolled in through the opening, a tenseness hung tightly upon his face. He scanned the room, and after locating McGraw and Jonas, quickly strode to their table. Damon placed his fingertips onto the dark oak and leaned in.

"You gents need to come with me..." he whispered over the soft jazz emanating from the hidden speakers in the ceiling.

"Good timing, Damon. We were just about to come see you and your boss." McGraw leaned forward to clunk the latest empty glass onto the table.

Damon nervously glanced around. "Then there's no time to waste, let's move."

"It's a no-go on your boss's offer. You can tell him since he chose not to show up."

The Brit sighed and flattened his lips in frustration. "You don't understand." He looked around once again before leaning in closer to them. "Parker's been arrested... for treason."

McGraw flicked his eyes to Jonas, whom returned the knowing glare. The muscle-bound EW's eyes belied his harsh expression – he was all smiles inside. "And that's my problem... how?"

"It's all of our problems," Damon growled through his teeth. "This is much bigger than both of you." He backed up and scowled at them as if they were a pair of misbehaving teens. "I thought you two would have grasped the gravity of the situation."

"What are you getting at, Damon?" Jonas interjected.

"Parker needs to speak to you, there's not much time now."

Fifteen minutes later

The door to the small antechamber slid open. Mercury McGraw and Jonas Slade hesitantly stepped into the sterile pod, their eyes locking on the tube-shaped receptacle that made up the far wall. Damon, following the pair of EWs, ducked his head back out into the hall and scanned in both directions, before joining them in front of the isolation cell.

Parker sat with his back to the entryway, staring out at the vast expanse of barren Martian landscape.

The intercom activated at their presence.

"Parker, they're here," said Damon.

Parker leapt from his seated position and pressed his hands against the glass. "Epsilons..." he said with an excited breath, "I'm glad you've come. As you can see, things have changed somewhat for the worse."

"Sorry, Bryce," replied McGraw. "This isn't gonna go the way you planned. We're out."

Parker looked to Damon with a raised brow. "You didn't tell them?"

Damon stepped forward. "I thought it was important that it came from you."

"Very well." Parker exchanged a furtive gaze with Damon. He turned his attention back to the two EWs. "The situation has grown much direr than before. Much more than you can imagine."

"I can imagine quite a bit," McGraw said. "But we're still not interested."

Parker steeled his expression. "Show them Damon..."

Damon nodded his head, waved his hand over his wrist

computer. A teal hologram depicting a pair of surveillance images of McGraw and Slade sprung to life above his arm.

"What's this?" Jonas asked with an outstretched finger.

"The general alert that was sent out by the Prefect's office two hours ago, just after my arrest..." Parker began to explain.

McGraw stormed forward and pounded the glass with a balled fist. "You turned us in, you son of a bitch?"

"Listen to me, Mr. McGraw." Parker's demeanor seemed calmer than it should have been, considering his predicament. "Cromwell has taken the next step in ridding Red Colony One of Epsilon influence."

"Next step?" said Jonas, stepping forward to join McGraw at the glass. "What's that mean?"

Parker kept his eyes locked with McGraw's. "Like your counterpart, Stroud, he's seen fit to brand all Epsilons as terrorists. He intends to reshape your legacy in the annals of history to be in league with the Qadafi's, the Bin laden's, the Al Qaeda's, the American Reform Movement... and now the Epsilons. And because there are very few of your countrymen on colony, there's no one to offer an opposing viewpoint of his decree. After all, you Americans are not well looked upon outside of your wonderful Republic."

"So he's gonna have us arrested just for being EWs?"

Parker wagged his head. "No. He's going to make an example of you, by showing the rest of the colony just how dangerous you really are."

McGraw folded his arms in defiance across his bulging chest. "And how's he gonna do that?"

"*Going* to? Already *has*. Which is why it's of the utmost urgency that you be briefed on your mission. He's rigged the colony's power core with explosives," Parker replied. "And he's planning on blaming it on you Epsilons."

"How the Hell can he do that?" Jonas screamed, his arms akimbo.

"Mr. Stroud paved the way in the mines. He's simply following the logical progression that any colonist would beyond a reasonable doubt - as you Americans would say."

"So let him play out his little bluff... he'll lose," McGraw grunted.

Parker blinked once, his obsidian eyes reflecting the subtle glow from the antechamber like a lake at midnight. "It's not a bluff, Mr. McGraw. He *is* planning on detonating those charges."

Jonas put his hands to his hips. He shook his head. "I don't get it. Why would he blow up his own colony?"

"Critical thinking skills, gents," Parker chastised. "He's quite aware of the double redundancy that the power core conduit structures provide. He did design it, after all. So he's not blowing it up, per se. But enough to show that the Epsilons are an evil force that should be expelled from Red Colony One - one way or another."

McGraw and Jonas soaked in silence.

"But make no mistake..." Parker continued, "...if pressed, the man is mentally unbalanced, to say the least. He will sacrifice part of his domain to drive the nail."

"So why should we even bother then? He's got us dead to rights, no matter what we do," said McGraw.

Parker paused. Jonas's shuffling feet filled the stillness.

"There's a flaw in his plan. We've fed the locations of the charges into Darpa's analytical engine... and we've determined that despite the conduit structures, the power core will be irreversibly damaged – snuffing out all life in the colony within hours from lack of life support."

McGraw squinted at Parker. "How are we supposed to stop something like that?"

"You have an advantage."

"And that is..."

"You know the precise location of each charge, thanks to Darpa."

McGraw drew a deep breath, removing himself from Parker's gaze to pace the room in pensive thought. "Slade's probably got some contacts here in security..." he faced his former squadmate. "Right?"

Jonas pondered for a few seconds, nodded. "Sure, I can probably round up a few people over the next twenty-four hours..."

"No..." Parker interjected with authority. "You don't have that much time, and you can't count on assistance from anyone else because of the arrest decree for you two. You will be detained - or worse - on sight. And..."

McGraw forced his head over his shoulder to peer at the darkened detention cell. "And?"

"You have less than three hours to disarm the explosives... or all is lost. There are over a thousand lives at stake, gentlemen. I think we can agree that a handful of them are not our concern – but the rest..."

The bigger EW, his mouth agape, swapped glares with both Damon and Parker. He pounded his fist against the wall with a muted thud. He wiped the saliva from his chin and raised his ferocious gaze to Parker. "You're asking for the impossible, Bryce." He shook his head with deliberate pace. "Just show me the way to the portal. Time for me to head back to Earth."

Parker chuckled aloud. "There is no portal back to Earth, Mr. McGraw. I thought you realized that."

"Then how did Stroud get back?" McGraw growled.

A coy grin grew on Parker's lips. "He was the benefactor of a mechanism in place to deliver... *goods*... back to Earth. But that ship, as they say, has sailed. Literally."

McGraw let loose another fierce pounding on the wall. "How the Hell are we supposed to get out of this, Bryce?" he screamed, his spittle landing on the glass between them.

Jonas stepped forward and patted McGraw on the shoulder, but the burly EW jerked away and stomped to the other side of the small chamber.

"What if we just disarm the critical ones?" Jonas asked, with a calm designed to defuse the situation. "Would that work?"

Parker shook his head. "No, unfortunately. Those charges are linked."

"Linked?" Jonas tilted his head to the side.

"Yes. Regardless of their state, if one goes off... they all do."

Jonas could hear his own exhales in the din of silence.

"It's an all or nothing proposition, gentlemen." Parker waited for McGraw to face him once again before continuing. "I'd suggest you get moving. Damon will provide the required distraction to... thin out... the security population. Godspeed."

The glass in front of Parker dimmed to a smoky hue. Jonas turned to face McGraw, but could not get a return look. McGraw stood stoically silent with his hands in fists at his side.

Damon produced a pair of pulse rifles and offered them aloft.

"Not exactly high powered..." McGraw observed with a sneer.

"Don't be fooled. They pack a nice little punch. At close range, it's enough to scramble your internals."

The pair of former EWs took the guns and stowed them to their sides. Damon handed Jonas a small orb. With a furrowed brow, Jonas let the orb drop into his palm.

"I've downloaded the schematic of the power core. The locations of the charges are marked. Don't lose this."

Jonas, a slight hesitation in his comprehension, nodded.

"Come," Damon repeated. He stepped into the hallway.

40: THE TEMPLE DEFILED

Jonas and McGraw shared once last glance, and then followed.

Shortly afterward

Damon had taken his leave of the pair of former EWs, disappearing down an intersecting hallway a hundred meters before the triple-headed power core, en route to fulfill his function within the mission.

Mercury McGraw and Jonas Slade, moving with commando efficiency within the shadows available along each wall, took turns keeping watch behind them.

"Not that I care," McGraw said above a whisper, his thick legs carrying him ahead of his partner, "but you never did tell me how you ended up here."

"Not exactly sure of all the details, Merc," Jonas replied with a heavy breath, trying to keep up. "But I'm guessing through the portal like everyone else..."

"Nah," McGraw grumbled. "I'm talkin' about how you're still alive." He stopped and glared at Jonas. "We saw you blown to bits in Kalinigrad. How do you explain that?"

Jonas widened his eyes and shook his head. "I was never in Russia, Merc."

McGraw arched his brow into a skeptical bow.

"After they captured me in Portugal with you and Brig... I don't know. The brass..." Jonas held his head as if fighting off a growing migraine. "They came and got me out. Midnight raid... heli-jets. You name it, they had it. But they got me. Leveled the whole village where I was being held."

The pair poked their heads around the next corner and, seeing more empty hallways, strode into the next corridor.

"They took me to a secret base in Germany," Jonas continued, in-stride. "That's when the sedation really started. Next thing I know, I wake up in the med bay here in the colony. And I'm Emerson Winslow. Until three days ago. Crazy stuff."

"But why you?" McGraw placed one eye on the corridor ahead and the other seemingly on the pulse rifle that he fingered in his hands.

"Sorry, Merc. I don't know..."

"I'm not lookin' for an apology, Slade. So can it. I just wanna know why they came and got you, brought you here. Why not me or Stroud? What makes you so Goddamn special that you get taken out of that Hell hole back on Earth?"

"I..."

"Let me tell you, Slade..." McGraw poked a finger of steel into Jonas's chest. "We lost three of our squad on what you're tellin' me was a decoy chase. That doesn't sit well with me." He paused to let the steam subside. "And the brass knew? Bullshit..."

"I'm just tellin' you what happened, Merc, I..."

"Enough... there's the first conduit." He motioned towards the domed intersection ahead, and then held two fingers to his eyes.

As if engaging a silent switch deep within, the pair of commandos took to the sides of the wide corridor and inched forward, until they were at the lip of a bulkhead that stood out a meter from the main wall. The Epsilons brought their pulse rifles up to chest level.

Although Damon had dutifully provided them both with jumpsuits displaying the official security insignia stripes on their sleeves, McGraw's was woefully tight due to his size, and it gave him the appearance of a pituitary-mutated teen wearing a toddler's jumper.

Jonas craned his neck around the bulkhead, but instead of pulling it back as he had been trained, he allowed his upper torso to follow him around the corner.

"Slade!" McGraw strained in a high whisper, but his mission partner had stepped fully into view in the conduit vestibule.

Jonas motioned McGraw forward. "No one here, either." He relaxed his shoulders.

McGraw stepped from the shadows and entered the domed structure alongside Jonas. Both men side-holstered their pulse rifles and visually took inventory. McGraw eyed the empty security desk that lined one side of the hexagonal room.

"You'd think security would at least be here," he said.

"Must have been one Hell of a distraction Damon came up with, huh?" Jonas replied with a half-smirk.

"Lucky us..." McGraw grunted. "Now let's find that charge and get on to the next one."

"Hey! What're you two doing in here?" a voice from behind barked. His accent told them he was presumably another of Allistair's countrymen.

As McGraw's hand slipped unseen to his holster, Jonas stiffened and subtly shook his head. He slowly rotated to face the man.

"Winslow?" asked the man, also dressed in security duds. "Why are you here?"

"Uh, just doing a sweep, Crippen..." Jonas answered with a waver in his voice. "Boss told me and Mer... Michael here to check out each conduit arm."

Crippen narrowed his eyes. With a pursed lip and a wagging finger, he glared at Jonas. "There's something I heard about you. Now what was it?" He rubbed at his chin, before stepping to the security desk and typing in a quick set of commands. He paused and raised his eyes to McGraw. "And you look familiar, too, mate."

The set of surveillance photos listing the pair of EWs fugitive status came to life in front of him. His eyes bulged.

The room lit momentarily with a blinding blue-white flash, followed by a concussive 'ca-choom'. Crippen's mid-torso lit aflame in a globule of electric energy, before he flew backward against the wall, shattering his spine with a sickening crack. The stunned guard fell lifeless to the floor in a heap behind the console.

Jonas, unable to breathe for a full five seconds, spun to find McGraw standing with his pulse rifle at his side. He expelled the acrid stench of burning flesh from his lungs with a wheezing hack. "McGraw, what the Hell are you doing?"

"He was about to trigger an alarm." McGraw wore his trademark sneer. "We were as good as caught."

Jonas shook his head and pointed an angry finger. "I could've talked him down! You didn't need to do that!"

"You haven't changed. Wake up, Slade."

Jonas shook off McGraw's icy apathy, nodded to himself and fished the orb from his side pocket. Before he had released it onto his palm, it flared with red and green LEDs - firing a hologram upwards ten centimeters tall above his arm. With a sudden technical expertise and a stoic gaze, Jonas efficiently scanned over the translucent schematic hovering in front of him.

"There..." he said with a finger pointed into the ether, "...two access panels, one leading inward to this room, the other heads down into the conduit towards the core." He flicked his eyes away from the hologram. "Damon's map shows it's in the one headed to the core."

Before McGraw could display his usual brash bravado, Jonas pocketed the orb and dashed towards the low-ceilinged conduit tunnel that led from the room. He traded his pulse rifle with a thin tool on his belt, making quick work of the seamless panel on the wall just above his eye level. Within seconds, the panel dropped without sound into his waiting hand. He stepped back, mouth ajar.

"Holy shit..."

"What?" McGraw barked from behind, turning from scanning the hallway beyond.

"There's a bomb in here, Merc. There's really a bomb in here..."

"Well what'd you expect to find in there, Slade? A teddy bear?"

"I guess... I just was hoping this was all a ruse or something. It's Goddamn real."

"Yeah, so get back in there and disarm the fuckin' thing so we can get this over with," McGraw snarled. He shoved Jonas forward.

Jonas blinked at his brash partner. With a headshake, he gauged the explosive's environment with a thin LED that protruded from the sleeve of his jumpsuit.

"They're linked alright..." he said with his head half into the access panel. "This one's got a transmitter on it. Hope it doesn't set the others off when I do this," he said, before burying his hand behind the charge and producing a light 'click' that rendered the charge inert.

The pair stood for a silent moment and rolled their eyes to their surroundings, as if expecting the colony to burst around them. Jonas released a lungful of air and ducked his head into the small tunnel to his left.

"Dammit," he said, his voice echoing from within the enclosed space. "The containment walls have been activated down inside this conduit."

"Meaning what exactly?"

Jonas extracted the orb from his pocket and once again examined the holographic map. "There's three more charges inside this conduit tunnel, but behind the containment wall."

"Don't suppose the wall's retractable?"

"Doubtful from here," Jonas replied, ogling the small amount of controls at the vacant security desk behind McGraw. He traced his finger over the map again and then snapped his fingers with a victorious twirl. "There! Outside in the next hallway, there's a service tunnel that leads into the front portion of this conduit. Let's go!"

McGraw offered a skeptical glare to the younger EW, and then traced his motion out of the vestibule.

A few seconds later, as the sound of their footsteps died away into the next corridor, a shadowed figure, wearing a command red jumpsuit, emerged from behind a hanging wire umbilical and scanned the empty room. He stepped forward, reached his hand into the still-open access panel and produced the identical 'click' heard just moments before. The explosive charge snapped back to life with a small 'deet' and a blinking red LED. He exited the conduit end in pursuit of the EW commandos.

R. JAMES STEVENS

41:
Exodus

Mars. Red Colony One

Nadia Temple stood with a rigid spine at the fore of the turbo-lift, her arms obediently cocked near the small of her back. The subtle lighting of the car drew out the auburn locks flowing across the shoulders of her sparkling white lab jumpsuit. With a twinkle of her emerald eyes, she performed an integrated command that started the lift on its journey downward.

"I've downloaded the schematics that you will need into your wrist computer," she said, still staring forward at the wall of the cab. "You'll have approximately two hours and twenty seven minutes to disarm the remaining charges." Her voice sung over the mechanical harmonic of the car.

She did not receive a response.

Nadia raised her chin. "Cat got your tongue?"

Still no response.

"You're not worried about your health, are you? Because I can assure you that your vitals are normal – you are as healthy as you have been for years."

"I've been dead for three days..." came the voice with the Texas drawl, from the back of the car. "But that's not what's *botherin'* me."

Nadia tilted her head sideways to gather a look behind her.

Brigadier Stroud stood upright and ran his hand through his shoulder length hair.

"And what would that be then?" Nadia queried with a playful lilt.

"You're throwin' me with this... illusion... that you keep generating. Of..." He hesitated.

Nadia rotated with a feline grace on one heel to face Brig. "My apologies, Brigadier," she purred. "But illusions are just in the mind's eye. You have the power to discern illusion from reality. Perhaps all that matters is that you see me standing right here in front of you?"

Brig softened his scowl and stared through her. "Two and a half hours ain't a lot of time to get this done. Not alone."

Nadia did an about face once again. "You won't be alone."

"Who else knows?"

"A pair of Epsilons..."

"Epsilons?" Brig parroted. "But who..." His voice halted. He scraped his fingers across the stubble on his chin. "Jonas?"

Nadia bobbed her head in acknowledgement. "And a Mercury McGraw."

"I knew it..." Brig replied under his breath.

For the past few months, Brig had fought his own intuition about whether or not he had actually seen both former EWs on colony. He had chalked it up to his mind deteriorating from everything he had endured - or perhaps a wishful link to a past that he actually understood. Now, that past had rematerialized and was waiting for his turbo-lift to reach the ground floor.

"Where are they now?"

"They are already progressing in their mission. I'm certain that they will welcome your assistance."

Brig nodded and fell back against the rear of the car in thought.

The song of the turbo-lift filled the silence.

"Cromwell has her," Nadia offered after a moment.

Brig scrunched his brow. "Who? Steele? What do you mean he *has* her?"

Nadia lowered her gaze to the floor of the compartment. "She's being held in the same isolation cell that you were previously. She's in queue to have her memory blocked and remapped. She will forget everything that has transpired in recent months. The mines. The escape back to Earth." Her eyelashes fluttered. "You."

"That son of a bitch..." Brig growled. He pounded his fist on the wall beside his leg.

"I suppose you're..." Nadia began but paused. "...going to rescue her?"

"Well, yeah. Darpa, you know that I..."

Darpa gracefully rotated and offered an inviting smile. "You *can* call me Nadia..."

"But you're not..."

As if bound by a web of elastic bands at each end, the car came to a gentle crawl. Brig scanned the cab with a curious glare. Darpa stepped closer to him and gazed up into the renewed azure in his eyes.

Brig tensed. He had never seen Darpa's illusional aura up close and found it almost too brilliant to look upon.

"I understand," Darpa said, her voice a soft harmony upon itself. Suddenly, she boosted onto her toes, closed her eyes and brought her ethereal ruby lips to his.

Brig held his breath, not comprehending what was occurring. He shut his eyes. His heart told him that Nadia was indeed standing in front of him, but his brain could not release reality enough to make it so.

For the next few moments, the pair stood motionless. Darpa, her holographic mirage shining its brilliant aura as she kept a touchless contact with him, and Brig, his body stiff but welcoming the return of someone whom he had loved so deeply but had lost in such a heinous manner – even if it was a computer generated illusion.

Darpa fell back to her heels, covered her mouth with a bashful hand and flitted her sparkling eyes to Brig's. "Thank you..." A soul-deep want patterned her face.

Brig wagged his head once. "For what?"

Darpa dropped her hand to her side. "For allowing me to know life." She took two graceful steps backward and resumed her position at the front of the car. "Please be careful..." she added just above a whisper.

"I've gotta save her. She doesn't deserve that fate."

Darpa nodded mechanically. "There's not much time."

"But how can I get her out of that chamber? Parker was the only one that knew the codes."

Darpa lifted her head. "After some careful... surveillance... of Mr. Bryce, I managed to locate the codes in one of his data repositories. I've downloaded that to your wrist computer as well."

"Anything else I need to know?"

"Yes. His plan is to evacuate the non-security personnel in the colony to the Exodus platform."

"Exodus?"

"It's an emergency failsafe. Built in the unlikely circumstance of a catastrophic event that might render the colony uninhabitable."

The lift came to a gentle stop and the doors whooshed open. She stepped into the doorway and rotated to face him.

"Godspeed, Brigadier. Please be careful." She smiled, a strobe-bright gleam in her eye.

Steele lay on the frigid Broxium, her knees curled to her chest. She stared out at the Martian night.

The familiar rectangle of amber light filled the reflection on the glass. "Deja vu, huh sweetheart?" said Brig through the intercom.

Steele glanced at the image of the tall Texan's silhouette from the antechamber. She tucked her head into her arms. "Go away, Darpa," she droned. "Unless you're here to tell me Parker's on the way."

"It's not Darpa, Steele. It's me." Brig knocked twice on the glass to wake her from her trance.

Steele scrambled on the slick surface, her padded boots slipping as she tried to gain her balance. She pressed herself against the glass. "Brigadier! You're alive... but how..."

Brig chuckled. "Spent a couple days in a tub of jelly. And thanks to Darpa, I hear I'm as good as new." He tapped a sequence of numbers and gestures onto a wall-mounted pad. The glass between them released with a heavy 'thunk' and rotated upwards.

Steele dove from the raised platform into Brig's arms. "Oh my God, I thought I had lost you." She sobbed onto his chest.

Brig lifted her chin with a finger. "*You did.* But never again..."

Their lips met.

Steele released from the kiss, a sudden thought striking her like a piercing lance. "How are we going to get away from Allistair? He knows everything..."

Brig closed his eyes and rubbed at the back of his neck. "It's a lot worse than just him knowing."

"What does that mean?"

"He's rigged the power core with explosives."

"Are you mad? Why would he do that?"

"Seems he's got it out for us Epsilons. Gonna make us out to be terrorists by doing something crazy like blowing up half the colony."

"Dear lord." Steele brought her hand to her chin. She paced the small room in front of Brig. "Do we have a plan to stop him?"

Brig nodded. "Darpa's given us schematics to where the explosives are located, we just have to find 'em and disarm 'em before... well, you know."

Steele nodded a firm resolve. "Okay then, I'm no explosives expert, but I will do what I can..."

Brig put a loving hand on her shoulder. "By *we*, I meant me and two other Epsilons. In the meantime, we've got to get *you* to Exodus with the rest of the colony."

"But..."

"Back to the scene of the crime, huh Sampson?" called an Australian voice from behind them.

Brig pulled Steele to his back and spun to face the door.

Commander Greer stood in the doorway, wearing a satisfied smirk and his hand on the pulse rifle at his belt. And... *not dead.*

"Commander," Brig drawled. He nodded in mock respect. "I just had to come back, I missed your weekly visits so much. You're looking much less... electric... since I saw you last time."

Greer took a cautious step into the antechamber. "Well I don't know how you got out of here last time, and I don't know what you're doing back. But you're not gettin' out of here alive."

Steele stepped out from behind Brig and pointed an angry finger at Greer. "Commander! You are ordered to stand down, this man is not a prisoner!"

Greer's smile grew. He shook his head and continued to glare at Brig. "You already killed me once. I believe that makes you a criminal in the eyes of the Prefect. Not that I take orders from you, Dr. Fox." He flicked his eyes at Steele. "Aren't you supposed to be inside the cell anyway?"

Steele withdrew to stand partly behind Brig once more.

"Ah, you thought I didn't know about that? Get back!" Greer waved his pulse rifle at the pair.

Brig took a strong step forward and held his palm between himself and Greer. "Don't point that thing at her, she has nothing to do with this!"

Greer placed his finger on the trigger of the rifle.

However, as if Greer had been mired in molasses, Brig countered by diving forward and grabbing the rifle from the shocked Commander's hand. He followed his lightning attack by drilling Greer with an elbow to the throat. The rifle flew from Greer's hand and clattered across the floor, stopping at Steele's feet. Brig seized the advantage and began pummeling the beleaguered mining colony boss with vicious jabs to his torso.

Greer, struggling to maintain his balance, fell backward against a Broxium personal effects locker and flowed down to the floor.

"Even though I think it's cute that you call me a name I made up when I was a kid," Brig snarled, "my name is Stroud. Not that it matters where you're goin'..." Brig wound one leg and delivered a strong kick aimed at Greer's side.

Before it could connect, Greer spun and executed a scissor hold, sweeping Brig from his feet. The former EW's head glanced the tile floor, dazing him.

As Brig scraped at the tile with both hands, Greer regained his footing and snagged the pike from the corner of the room. He raised the gleaming, bloodstained shaft above his head with both hands and sneered victoriously down at Brig.

"You remember this, don't you?" he taunted.

The pole began its downward arc; a blue-white jet of lethal energy leapt across the room and buried itself in Greer's chest, tossing the stupefied Commander backward in a spiral until he landed with half his body lying in the external corridor.

Brig shook off the cloudiness in his brain and pushed himself to his feet.

Steele stood in front of the open pod door, a curl of white smoke wisping from the end of the pulse rifle in her shaking hands. Speechless, she lowered the rifle until it fell from her grasp with a rattle to the tile.

Brig pounced forward and wrapped her in a sturdy hug. The tears began to stream from her eyes.

"It's never easy, sweetheart," he reassured, his hands stroking her brunette tresses. "At least he won't be coming back this time..."

She pulled her head away from his chest and looked upon the motionless legs of Commander Greer in the doorway. "I've never..."

"I know. It's gonna be okay. We need to get to Exodus now."

Allistair Cromwell wore the expression of a hissing alley cat, hovering over his desk, toiling at the report General Rossi had just delivered. The General, silent in his smugness, stood a step to Allistair's right and peered through the gap in the Prefect's arm.

"Are you certain that the evacuation order did not come from your staff, General?" Allistair glued his eyes on the alerts lighting up across the holographic panel in front of him.

"No, Prefect."

41: EXODUS

"Darpa, can you confirm the evacuation order?" Allistair ordered into the ether above him, however he received no response. "Darpa, report please."

Rossi cleared his throat and leaned his two-meter frame forward. "Sir, communications appear to be down as well. Something is most definitely afoot."

"Blast!" Allistair boomed with a pounded fist on the translucent slab of a desk. "General, investigate the source of the order and get back to me at once!"

"Both of you, stand down..." Steele's voice called from the entry door.

The Prefect and his General spun in place.

Steele stepped forward, pulse rifle raised at the pair, the heels of her padded boots echoing off the polished walls of Allistair's executive office with each calculating step. Her hands remained steady and her lip warped upward at the sight of the surprised men.

"Steele, what in heaven's name... put that gun away before you hurt yourself," Allistair said with a derisive hand wave.

She inched closer and wagged the barrel of the gun. "Enough. Step back from the console or I'll be forced to use this."

Rossi's lip curled into a snide grin. "You're not a killer, Dr. Fox," he cooed.

"Sometimes people are what you make them, General." Steele refocused her gaze back to the Prefect. "Isn't that right... *father*? Or should I say... *Allistair*?"

Allistair chuckled under his breath. "Very good, Steele. Bravo for you. But your dramatics are for naught. The good General is quite privy to that knowledge already." He worked his way around the edge of the desk with an obvious caution in his gait. "I'm not certain how you escaped your cell, but I think it's time to end this little bluff of yours."

Steele glided her finger onto the trigger of the rifle. Allistair halted his advance. "It's not a bluff, Allistair. Your tyranny ends tonight."

"Tyranny?" Allistair mocked. "Search deep inside yourself, young lady, and I believe you'll find that you were with me every step of the way. If I am a tyrant, you were my willing accomplice."

Steele remained unfazed. "You *made* me your little soldier, I hardly had a choice in the matter." Her hand was as steady as her resolve.

The Prefect softened his expression. "So what's your plan here, Steele. Are you going to kill us?"

Steele paused, but remained stoic in her stance. "I'll do what I must to keep your influence from this colony." She arced the rifle to Rossi. "And General, you can release the emergency communicator in your pocket. I've blocked all communication inbound and outbound from the executive enclave."

Allistair nodded, as if impressed.

"I would ask you gentlemen to please keep your hands where I can see them and step together into the corner of the room."

After a brief glance between them, both men reluctantly raised their hands to their sides and paced across the room, until they reached a section of wall next to the large viewport.

As they faced Steele once again, a gentle rumble, like that of an approaching summer thunderstorm, shook the room. The lights within the ceiling, and those that shone up from the floor every few meters, flickered and then dimmed.

Rossi spied the holo-map of the colony along the far wall of Allistair's office. "Prefect, Exodus is online." He pointed at a flashing segment in the display.

Allistair did not waver his gaze from Steele.

Rossi ratcheted his eyes to her.

For a brief nanosecond, a warped spike traveled from her left foot and dissipated as it reached her knee. Then, as if she were an image from an antique television, Steele's entire body flickered before becoming normal once again.

"Blast. That's Darpa!" Allistair shouted. He stormed to his desk. He worked his hands with an efficient whir over the controls, but the small panel refused to respond.

"I told you, Allistair." A coy smile popped onto Darpa's face. "I disabled all communications."

"You!" Allistair screamed at Rossi with a finger point. "Gather your men and get to the Exodus platform at once!"

Rossi nodded and strode across the room. He stopped next to Darpa, looked her over from head to toe once, and then sneered. "Clever girl. But it won't work..."

Darpa smiled and disappeared.

41: EXODUS

As Brig and Steele sprinted along another of a seemingly endless series of empty corridors, Steele took the opportunity to point at the arched ceiling.

"There's been a security alert... and an evacuation order."

Brig, setting the quickened pace beside her, rolled his eyes upward. "How do you know?"

"The ceiling changes colors in accordance with the security alert level of the colony."

Brig shook his head with a brief smile that faded nearly as soon as it appeared. "Then we have to be extra careful. They've probably figured out you're not where you're *supposed* to be."

He glanced down at the rifle in her hand, which she now held as comfortably as a new appendage. *This* was the Steele that he knew, and he knew that she would do what she needed to adjust to any situation – no matter how dire.

Their padded boots echoed in the desolate halls of Red Colony One. They approached a nearby intersection.

"How far from the platform are we?" Brig shifted his eyes back and forth across the way ahead of them, once again allowing his EW training to guide his actions.

"It's just ahead to the right and through a small tunnel."

The pair reached the intersection of their current hallway and another. It sloped downward into a section of tunnel lit only by the same yellowish lighting that they had seen earlier on the ceiling. Brig, using Clarity to sense the way ahead, pulled up just past the corner and held his hand towards Steele. She stopped and leaned her head back against the wall with a faraway gaze.

"You okay?" he said.

She nodded and closed her eyes. "It's just odd. I'm a fugitive in my own home."

Brig squinted into the tunnel. "Well, it ends tonight, one way or another. Stay here in the shadows until I give the all clear." Before she could protest, Brig sprinted away down the ramp like a stealthy panther.

Moments later, he emerged from the opposite end of the tunnel. Twenty meters up from his position, within a hangar lit like a stadium whose domed top reached beyond the tunnel's ceiling, he spied a set of colossal tubes that resembled the open breeches of four cannons. A ceiling-mounted conveyer with massive hooks swung across the front of the tubes. Every few moments, a chassis, like that of a giant pod, lowered next to the opening of each tube.

Brig slowed and watched as more than twenty colonists stepped aboard each pod, an orderly procession to be sure, and one that Brig immediately recognized as a well-rehearsed effort. As the last colonist in each queue cleared the entryway of their respective pod, the doors swung shut and the hooks above the pods loaded their cargo into the tubes like hulking artillery shells. Within seconds of the tubes sealing shut, a dull rumble filled the chamber and the tubes opened once again to reveal an empty slot.

This process continued on, with each line growing shorter, until Brig snapped back to focus with the sound of a boot step behind him. He spun, but not in time to avoid two pairs of hands gripping him tightly around each armpit. A pulse rifle jabbed into the back of his ribcage.

General Rossi stepped from the shadows of the tunnel, his hands clasped behind his back and a victorious smirk across his face. "You're in much better shape than when I last saw you... *Stroud*," he purred, stepping fully into the light of the Exodus platform chamber. "I had a suspicion that you were behind this. Well, you and your co-conspirator..."

Behind him, seven armed security troops spread out on each side, their rifles at the ready. The end two guards pushed forward a familiar captive – Parker Bryce. With his hands locked behind his back, Parker held his head low and avoided eye contact with Brig.

The troops holding Brig released their grip and pushed him forward at Rossi. As Brig left their grasp, he spun and gripped one of their arms. The surprised guard stumbled across Brig's path. Brig deftly snagged the man with a hand hooked around the man's neck and the other holding the rifle forward. The pulse gun released a deadly stream of blue-white energy orbs in a spray pattern as Brig swung the guard back and forth, plowing through the scrambling security team with a searing carnage.

General Rossi, thrown to safety by one of his staff, peeked out from behind a nearby control panel and watched the Epsilon rain Hell upon his beleaguered guards. Ozone-rich white smoke billowed from the tunnel ceiling and into the Exodus chamber like an upward-flowing eddy.

41: EXODUS

As the pulse rifle in Brig's hand spent its battery, one of the colony guards caught Brig by surprise from behind, knocking him forward onto the hard tile. The guard jammed the muzzle of his own pulse rifle into the back of Brig's neck.

Rossi emerged from his hiding spot, stepping over several charred corpses that littered the tunnel entrance. He sneered down at Brig.

"Brigadier Stroud, you are hereby charged with treason." His voice flowed with a cold menace. Rossi flicked his eyes to the guard. "*Kill him.*"

"I'd advise against that, General," Steele interjected.

Rossi shifted his glare to the tunnel.

Steele stepped from the amber-tinted shadows, the sight of the pulse rifle next to her eye. "Order your guards... or what's left of them," she said, her voice registering with intense disdain, "to stand down and release both men."

The General's lip curled up with a wicked arc. "Ignore her," he commanded to the four remaining guards. "That's a hologram!" Rossi once again faced Brig. "Finish the job. Kill him now!"

The guard, with obvious trepidation, looked to his boss for confirmation.

The General glared a vicious snarl back at the guard, whom obediently lowered his gaze and jammed the rifle snout back into Brig's neck.

The tunnel boomed once more and lit with a bright aura for a brief second. General Rossi fell forward onto the cold floor, embers leaping from the cauterized hole in the center of his back. Two of the guards, momentarily dumbstruck, hurriedly disarmed Steele and forced her hands behind her back, while the other two continued to subdue Brig and Parker.

"Take these three to the Prefect, he needs to figure out what to do with 'em!" one of the guards ordered.

The others, nodding their agreement, brought their respective prisoners forward, and together they began to enter the tunnel back towards the colony.

Not three steps down the ramp, they were met with a flurry of activity from the darkness. Two groups of armed colonists quickly surrounded the remaining security detail and disarmed them before a shot could be fired.

Brig, Steele and Parker stared in disbelief.

One of the colonists stepped forward and allowed the light of the Exodus chamber to illuminate his face.

It was Granderson. Behind him, a small group, of whom Brig now recognized as the surviving freed miners, finished wrapping up the guards with electro-bands to their wrists.

"'ello, mate," Granderson said in a deceiving cheeriness to Brig. He offered an outstretched hand.

Brig took the Brit's hand, still amazed at the timing of the miners' arrival. "Granderson – how did you know?"

Granderson smiled and huffed out a chuckle. "Keeping our ear to the ground, as you Yanks might say." He pointed up at the ceiling. "That, and a friend led us to the proper spot."

Brig nodded his understanding. "Well, I – we - owe you big time."

"Nonsense, my friend. We're the ones that owed you this, and so much more. I doubt our debt to you will ever be repaid."

"But..." Brig argued, "...not everyone made it out of the mines. I think we're *more* than even now."

Granderson pulled Brig closer, grasping the Epsilon's shoulder with his free hand. "Tis better to die fightin' for freedom than to live as a slave, mate."

Humbled, Brig shook Granderson's gloved hand once more. "Then can I ask one more favor?"

"Anything..."

Brig rotated Granderson and pointed into the Exodus chamber. "Stand guard over this area and make sure everyone gets into an escape pod." He lowered his voice so that only Granderson could hear. "Somethin' bad's about to happen... *real* bad. And I'm sure more security'll be on the way once they realize what went down here."

Granderson nodded once. "Right-o, my friend." He stepped forward and waved his arm at his comrades. "Gents, this way. Our mission continues!"

The other miners shouted a series of cheers and stormed into the Exodus chamber.

As Brig proudly watched his rescuers take up defensive positions near the tubes, something in his peripheral caught his attention. Standing several meters away, against the wall of the darkened tunnel, Parker held Steele's hand and stroked the side of her face. And although she did not return his physical affection, she seemed calm.

Brig wrinkled his brow.

41: EXODUS

His initial reaction was to separate the two – to tell Parker to back off and never touch Steele again. Then, he noticed Steele's face - the lack of animosity that she showed Parker struck him most. After all that had transpired since Brig had first stepped foot on Red Colony One, the reality of it all had just surfaced once again.

Steele was *happy* with Parker – and that was something that he just could not change.

Brig lowered his head, rubbed the back of his neck vigorously with one hand. After a moment of pensive thought, he locked in his course. He spun and made his way to the entrance of the Exodus platform.

"C'mon you two, let's get in here before this place goes up!" he shouted back at the pair.

Embarrassed, Steele scrambled away from Parker and took up pace next to Brig. They entered the bright chamber. "Brigadier, I..."

Brig nodded, but did not look at her. "It's all good, Steele. Let's finish getting these things loaded and out of here."

Steele put a hand on his forearm. The two met eyes, his steely blue and her fathomless emerald.

Parker made his way into the chamber. "Your bravery is without reproach, Mr. Stroud."

Brig lowered an eyebrow and glared at Parker. "Not about to let a thousand people die just because some madman decided he was having a bad day."

"Indeed, and a good portion of the reason why I tasked you Epsilons for this mission."

Brig paused and continued to stare at Parker, hoping that more answers would come forth. Brig scanned the crowd of colonists readying to embark. "So where are the others?"

Parker glared into the empty tunnel. "Why... back performing the other half of this mission, of course."

Brig nodded.

One of the miners stepped forward and placed his hand on Steele's shoulder to gather her attention. "Time to go, mum..." he said with a polite bob of his head.

Steele looked to Brig. "On to our next adventure, then?"

Brig smiled. His gaze was distant.

"After you, Dr. Fox." Parker held a hand out in front of Steele.

She climbed the small ramp with Parker in tow. As the pair stepped onto the pod, the entry doors clamped shut behind them.

Steele spun and looked through the viewport at the back of the pod, shocked to see Brig still standing at the bottom of the ramp.

After a brief second, he turned and determinately strode towards the tunnel entrance.

The intercom in the Exodus bay came to life.

"Brigadier! Are you daft?" Steele called from inside the pod.

Brig did not respond - he hastened his gait away from the platform.

"Brigadier, stop this instant! That's an order!"

Brig slowed and then stopped, but did not turn.

"Are you going to explain to me just exactly what it is you think you're doing?"

He slowly rotated and stared at the viewport from a distance.

"You don't always have to be the hero, you know. You have nothing to prove here."

Brig wagged his head. "That's just the thing, sweetheart. All my life I always thought I had somethin' to prove. To my friends. To my squad mates. To my father. I thought that's what he wanted from me, to prove what a man I was. How I needed to prove I was as good as he was." Brig paused and gazed back at the tunnel. "*How I was such a big disappointment to him.*"

"But you're *not* a disappointment, Brigadier. Not to anyone... and especially not to me."

"I know that." Brig bobbed his head. "Someone opened my eyes to that recently. And I realized that I had him all wrong."

The intercom clicked open again. "Then you've done everything you can do. Now get onboard!"

Brig shook his head again. "I've got two of my brothers out there trying to save this place. I can't just let them sacrifice themselves while I step onto an escape pod and launch away from danger." His eyes fell distant. "I already lost one, I'm not gonna let it happen again."

"There's not enough time - you'll die trying, Brigadier!"

Brig took a step forward and gazed up at Steele. His face became calm as a summer lake. "I've died so many times in the past ten years that I don't know what dying *is* anymore, Steele. I'm not afraid of death. But I've gotta try."

Steele placed her head into her palms. "But... I need you, Brigadier. Everyone... needs you."

Brig spun and threw his arms out wide. His voice echoed in the grand chamber. "Look at this place, sweetheart. Just look. You did this. You created this! I'm not gonna let all of this just go up in smoke..." He rotated to face her one last time. "Besides, you don't need me. You're the leader that these people need now."

He did an about-face and took two steps towards the tunnel. Brig stopped and glanced over his shoulder. "Darpa, intercom off. *And launch now.*"

Steele looked on in silent panic as Brig stepped into the tunnel, the shadowy outline of his near-two-meter frame disappearing within the amber-tinted pitch.

The hatch closed. After a short second, the final pod rumbled and shot out of the Exodus tube.

R. JAMES STEVENS

42:
Epsilons

Mars. Red Colony One

Brig waved his hand over his wrist computer. With a subtle chirp, a three-dimensional schematic of the power core, and its associated conduit tunnels, sprang to life ten centimeters above his arm and began rotating in place on an invisible axis. A flashing timer reading '42:02' materialized next to the main display and wound backward, reflecting its brilliant blues and reds across his face.

With his head bowed, he closed his eyes and for the briefest of moments, let his mind wander from his task. Once again, he had managed to act as Steele's protector and shuttle her away from harm. The scraping feeling in his gut told him that it was *more* than that. Something about the split second when he witnessed Parker Bryce caressing her arm in the Exodus tunnel gnawed at him.

But why?

While Brig and Steele had grown much closer since their crash landing on Earth, deep inside he knew that the woman he *truly* loved – was not Steele. The something that differentiated Nadia from Steele – whatever miniscule trait that was not on the surface – was enough to cause him to push her away. But the farther he had gotten from the one in his heart, that heart was telling him something different now, and more than anything he longed to be sitting next to Steele on the Exodus pod – holding her hand in his and eventually making their way back home to Earth.

Brig shook off the conflict in his brain and focused with a vicious intensity on the map hovering like a firefly in front of him. A small red dot pulsed near his location on the schematic. Glaring through the display, he spied the access panel along the back wall of the domed hexagon that comprised the end of one of the conduit arms. He shook the hologram into nothingness and stomped across the room, stopping beneath the front of the panel. With two quick flips of the recessed release clamps, the rectangular slab of Broxium fell with a raucous clamor onto the tile floor.

The hidden explosive charge within immediately made its presence known, flashing out a small glowing beacon in the dark cabinet from behind a bundle of fiber optic cable. Brig stuffed his hand into the cabinet, more confident now than ever that this mission would end in success.

"You there!" a familiar Aussie voice boomed from the corridor just outside of the conduit head. "This is a secure area, how about you backing away from that panel with your hands where I can see 'em."

Brig paused. He extracted his hand from within the panel. He knew that voice. With his hands out to his sides, he slowly rotated in place.

Dempsey, the tapper from the pub in the entertainment sector, stood in a defensive stance at the entry to the conduit head, a pulse rifle raised in front of him.

The tension fell from Brig's face. "Dempsey! I'm glad to see you."

The Aussie scrunched his brow, but did not lower his weapon. "Sampson was it, right?" he said from behind the rifle sight.

Brig nodded and lowered his hands.

"Keep the hands out to the side, Sampson. No funny business!"

"This isn't what it looks like..."

"There's a general alert in the colony for a pair of Epsilons. Neither of them you. So why don't you tell me what this looks like?"

"First, my name's not Sampson. It's Brigadier Stroud. I'm an Epsilon, but I'm not a terrorist, if that's what they're tellin' ya..."

"Says the man who's standing alone suspiciously at the edge of the colony's power core..." Dempsey cocked his head and squinted at the open panel. His eyes widened. "Right in front of an active charge! You've got exactly three seconds to explain this mess... and I'm crazy for givin' ya that much!"

"Your boss planted a bunch of explosives around the core..."

"Bronson Fox? You're off your rocker, Stroud."

A pair of guards appeared from within the corridor and stopped behind Dempsey, each gripping the stocks of their own pulse rifles in defense of their colleague.

Brig pointed at his opposite wrist. "Can I show you?"

Dempsey narrowed his brown eyes, wagged the end of the rifle. The other guards fidgeted. Dempsey backed them down with a hand motion.

Brig waved his hand over his wrist, the map expanded once again. "See these dots? Those are the charges he's placed all along the conduits. And that timer is how much we've got left to disarm 'em all."

Dempsey took a hard glance at the data presented to him. "Why would the Prefect blow up his own colony?"

"Because we found out something he didn't want anyone to know," said Brig. "He's not who he says he is. And he's gonna make the Epsilons out to be the bad guys he's told everyone we are..."

Dempsey inhaled a deep breath, but did not take his eyes, or the aim of his gun, from Brig. "And I should believe you... why?"

"Because we've spent the past two hours disarming these little bastards all over the outer edge of the core," Mercury McGraw responded from behind the other guards.

Jonas Slade stepped up next to him, nodded in agreement.

"Now we've got a party, boys!" Dempsey exclaimed, rotating to the other side of Brig and alternating his aim between the three Epsilons.

"Not all of them, McGraw," said Brig.

"We got what was on the map, Stroud," McGraw growled.

"There's still a whole line of them starting at the south conduit."

"That can't be!" Jonas shouted. "That's where we started, Merc... I know we got all of 'em!"

Dempsey studied Brig's holographic map with a closer eye.

Brig bit his lip. "You gotta trust me on this, Dempsey."

Dempsey cast a doubtful glare to the Texan.

"I know you don't know me, but you know me enough to know I'm on the right side of things. If I'm wrong about who did this, then you're a big hero 'cuz you just captured three Epsilons." Brig looked around and shook his head. "But if I'm right, and we don't get these disarmed... we'll all be lookin' down on what's left of Red Colony One from orbit. And not a *good* one."

Dempsey pursed his lips and locked eyes with Brig. "Damn ya, Stroud. Doesn't look like we have much choice seein' as how everyone else has bugged out." He lowered his rifle to his side. "What's the plan?"

Brig raised his arm so that the hologram centered in the room, where everyone could see it. "Don't know what they told you two," he began, pointing at McGraw and Slade, "but these charges are linked. One goes... they all go."

"Right. But good thing we got most of them," Jonas offered.

Brig shook his head. "If any of 'em are lit, they light the rest – regardless if you disarmed them or not."

Jonas's face flushed pale.

"So we gotta split up. Me and Dempsey will finish up here, take the South conduit to redo those. Dempsey, your men need to head over to Northeast and confirm those are dark. McGraw and Slade, you're heading to Northwest – the executive corridor..."

"What? Are you crazy, Brig?" Jonas protested. "That's where Cromwell and his men are!"

"Knock it off, Slade," McGraw snarled. "Stroud's the senior officer here, you follow *his* orders."

Jonas blinked several times in rapid succession. In his time with the EW squadron, he had never seen Mercury McGraw agree with Brig let alone concede his higher rank. He nodded a hesitant understanding.

"Someone's gone behind y'all and reset these. Chances are, if it's Cromwell he's not in his lair," Brig reassured, although working from a hunch more than anything.

Dempsey patted the larger of the two guards on the shoulder. "Shaw, Lincoln... you've got our orders, head out... and make it snappy, we don't have a lot of time left." The pair nodded and sprinted away down the corridor, the thumping of their boots dying away as they disappeared.

Brig stepped back to the open panel, thrust his hand into the umbilical and deactivated the charge with an audible click. The red beacon extinguished. "One down..." he said with a head nod.

The four men entered the corridor. McGraw stepped in front of Brig and placed a forceful hand on his chest to stop him.

"No bullshit now, McGraw." Brig did not hide the exasperation in his tone.

"No bullshit, Stroud." McGraw glared down from his height advantage. "I don't need to tell you what I'm thinkin', nothin' you haven't heard before."

Brig sighed and watched as Dempsey and Jonas reached the next corridor intersection ahead of them. He clicked his eyes back to McGraw. "That it then?"

McGraw inched closer. Brig shook his head and pushed past the beefy EW.

"Stroud!" McGraw grabbed Brig's arm and spun him back.

As Brig turned, McGraw held out his arm in one-half of the Epsilon Warrior 'W' handshake.

42: EPSILONS

Brig, with folded brow, stared for a silent moment at the man whom had been his nemesis in the EW squadron for what had seemed a lifetime. He grabbed McGraw's hand with a vice-like grip to complete the oath.

"It's been an honor to serve under you... Major Stroud. Make *this count.*"

"You still never told me what you know about the Prefect that would make him to go suicidal like this, Stroud," Dempsey said, the pair jogging along a vacant corridor. "And who's Cromwell?"

Brig slowed and peeked around the next corner, the muzzle of his pulse rifle leading the way. "He's the one you know as Bronson Fox..."

"Where's the *real* one?"

As if they had worked together for years, both men took up positions on opposite sides of the hallway. "Back on Earth..." Brig replied, but then paused. "Well... he *was.*"

Dempsey scrunched his forehead at Brig.

"He died earlier this year," Brig said with a faraway gaze. He replayed the night at the power substation in his mind, pushed it away with a strong shake of his head.

"So who's this Cromwell character then? And how'd he end up in Fox's spot?"

"He's a lunatic, that's who. Long story, but he swapped places with Fox, and with the help of..."

Brig went silent again, suddenly picturing Steele in the pod somewhere out in orbit, looking down on Red Colony One – or perhaps already on her way through the portal back to Earth.

It's history, he thought.

"Bottom line is we got a guy that's insane - and powerful - controlling every aspect of life for a thousand or so colonists."

Dempsey glared long and hard at Brig for a silent moment. "You have anything to do with that ruckus down in the mines?"

Brig dropped his rifle to his side and stepped into the intersection. Dempsey yanked the former EW backward and threw him against the wall.

"The Hell?" Brig growled, pulling Dempsey's hand from his shoulder material.

Just as Brig shoved away the Aussie, a cadre of heavy troopers stormed by in the adjacent hallway, their brilliant malachite armor glinting in the emergency lighting. To their favor, the pack of commandos had not noticed Brig and Dempsey in the shadows of the intersecting corridor, and stormed onward to their target.

"Prefect's Guard," Dempsey rasped in a whisper. "If they're on alert, we're gonna have a fight on our hands."

Brig stepped away from Dempsey and halfway into the hall through which the troops had just passed. He scanned the subtle directional markers at the vertices of each entrance above him.

"They're headed to the northwest. Dammit..."

Dempsey took up a spot next to Brig and stared down the dim corridor. "Change in plans then?" He fingered the trigger guard on his pulse rifle.

A sudden wave of gunfire erupted from a distant intersection ahead, followed by a bright orange glare that flashed for a brief moment and dissipated. As the pair leapt forward to charge to the rescue of their comrades, a jolt rocked the complex, sending them off-balance onto their behinds. A deafening claxon, pulsating an alto drone like an enraged hornet, drenched the air. The lighting dimmed, replaced by crimson beacons at three-meter intervals along each side of the passageways.

Brig climbed to his feet and collected the rifle that had jumped from his hand during the clamor.

Dempsey clutched the wall and pulled himself upright. He studied the lighting for a moment, and then clenched his eyes shut in panicked thought. "That's a breach, if I remember my emergency protocols right."

Brig glared down both hallways, then at Dempsey. "Wanna bet that was the Northwest conduit?"

"Didn't you say those charges were linked?"

Brig nodded. "Which means we have zero time to get our part done, or..."

"Yeah... let's get going," Dempsey added, and both men dashed into the red-flooded haze.

Brig mopped the globules of sweat from his forehead with a swipe of his wrist. His other hand, buried within the access panel above the power core conduit entry, fished blindly for the switch at the side of the explosive.

"The one on the outside of the hall is taken care of, Stroud," Dempsey announced, jogging into the conduit head.

The Epsilon grimaced, his hand working at an inhumanly sharp angle around a wire bundle.

Another booming concussion shook the colony. Several ceiling sections above them splintered and rained down onto the gleaming floor. Brig craned his neck to glare at Dempsey.

"That sound like a detonation?"

Dempsey turned his ear to the corridor outside of the bulkhead. "More gunfire... we've got a full-on battle raging over there."

Brig, having successfully deactivated the final charge in their portion of the mission, swabbed a streak of blood from his hand across the chest of his jumpsuit. He waved his palm over the opposite wrist to recall the power core schematic. "Dammit..." Brig growled. "Still two lit down at Northwest. Those guys must be pinned down by the Guard."

Dempsey winked and patted Brig on the shoulder. "Good thing they don't know about us then, mate. Let's go save the day!"

An intense blue-white burst of light engulfed the hexagonal room. Dempsey jerked forward and fell to the floor, a spiral of thin white smoke corkscrewing from a charred mark on his back.

Allistair Cromwell stepped from the crimson-saturated hallway, a smoking pulse rifle raised at chest level in front of him. "I hate traitors..." he hissed. "Although I should have known *you* were behind all of this, Brigadier Stroud."

Brig stepped cautiously away from the open access panel. "Here to admire your handiwork, Cromwell? You're too late... we've taken care of all of the explosives. Your plan failed."

A queer smile grew on Allistair's face. "I've underestimated you, my boy. You've more lives than the proverbial cat. And this time you've brought friends, I see." He sneered down at Dempsey's motionless body.

With Allistair's attention snared, Brig eyed the pulse rifle that he had laid on the security desk two meters away.

A piercing chirp called from within the bundle of wires next to him. The charge – as with many along the chain - had rearmed itself. Both Allistair and Brig turned their heads at once.

Allistair's smile grew even wider. "A saboteur? Well, Brigadier, you've certainly sealed *your* fate."

A miniature hologram of a green-clad commando popped into view above the security desk next to the Prefect. "We've captured the two Epsilons in conduit number two, Prefect," the British soldier reported with a snap of his boot. "They put up a good fight... plenty of damage and we lost half our squad."

"Good work, Sinclair. Hold them, I'll be there presently to deal with the prisoners."

The hologram dissipated.

Brigadier, sensing a brief nanosecond of chance, leapt for his pulse rifle. The Prefect lifted his own and fired off a single orb of energy. The bolt ripped a chunk of flesh from Brig's hip and flung him against the back wall of the conduit head. Brig fell to the floor and grabbed at his smoking side.

"Always with the heroics," Allistair crowed. "But there's room on this colony for only one hero. *And it's not you.*"

"No one believes... you're... a hero, Cromwell." Each word strained from Brig's mouth, interspersed with blood-tinged spittle.

"You've lost, Brigadier. You and your merry band of outlaws have been exposed and detained for the terrorists we've all known you to be. Now, to retrieve... *my daughter...* and put her memory back where it belongs." Allistair pivoted away, allowing the sickening smirk to linger on his lips for Brig's benefit.

"You're too late," Brig said between short breaths. "Steele and the rest... of your precious colony have escaped... on the Exodus capsules. They're probably... halfway back to Earth already."

Allistair spun on a heel, slung the pulse rifle over his shoulder and snorted. "Silly boy. You don't believe that I'd create Exodus without the ability to recall the pods, do you? Steele will be back where she belongs - by my side - long after you are just a distant memory." He tilted his head and stared down at Brig. "Well, to everyone but Steele, that is. And if I can't... well... there's always the self-destruct directives."

42: EPSILONS

"You son of a bitch!" Brig gathered his remaining strength and attempted to regain his legs. He fell back to the ground in horrifying pain, not having the ability to lever himself with his shattered hip.

"I'll be sure to give your regards to my daughter." Allistair hummed to match his amused, but insane, smile. "A pity she won't remember *you*." With a final, wicked sneer, Allistair strode determinately to the bulkhead entryway.

"Nadia, seal the conduit!" Brig bellowed.

Allistair spun, his face contorted in confusion.

The hardened Broxium blast door dropped from the bulkhead seam above with a ferocity that sucked the excess air from the room. The startled Prefect tumbled to the ground, his shoulder fragmented by the impact from the failsafe gate. He howled and grabbed at his dangling arm, now fractured in three places along the Ulna.

Brig sat back against the bulkhead wall. He sealed his eyelids. A satisfied grin replaced his painful visage.

After a few moments, in which the only sounds in the room were the distressed breaths coming from both men, Allistair rolled himself over to his side.

"Don't think you've... won," he said with a grimace, all traces of Bronson Fox's smooth gait having fled. "My men will save me. And you..." He cackled. "You will finally get the reward you deserve. You have been the scurrying cockroach in my darkened kitchen. But now, as you freeze in the spotlight, I squash you under my boot."

Brig tore at his jumpsuit, gathering just enough material to stuff against the still smoking wound on his side. "I'm not gonna let you at this last charge, Cromwell. And that blows up your plan. Literally."

"What are you babbling about, you worthless cretin." Cromwell grasped with a painful wince at his own grotesque wound.

"Enough of the games," said Brig. "You made a mistake using linked charges. You miscalculated – now you're gonna pay with your life."

Brig's sacrifice was complete. He had saved the colonists. He had stopped Allistair. Most importantly, Steele was safe from Cromwell's influence.

This was the first day of the rest of *her* life.

Allistair released a maniacal whoop from his froth-covered lips. "Even in death, my legend will grow. While your notoriety as mankind's greatest terrorist will be etched forever. Even though we both know... *death is never final, is it?*"

"You're forgetting one thing. Steele knows exactly who you are. No legend's gonna outlive the truth."

Allistair shut his eyes and laughed once again.

"So who's the terrorist?" Brig added. "I'm not the one blowing up my own colony to settle a vendetta."

"Blow up the colony? Why, Brigadier, you *are* daft. I did nothing of the sort."

Brig scrunched his brow, unsure of whether Cromwell was still playing at his mind games. His mind clicked into overdrive, replaying and piecing together the events of the past several hours. "If you didn't set those explosives, *then who did?*"

Parker Bryce tugged at his restraining harness.

It had been nearly forty minutes since their Exodus pod had left its launch tube, and the weightlessness of space continued to turn his stomach. The rest of the pod remained hushed, as none of the occupants - nor the majority of the inhabitants of Red Colony One - were seasoned space farers. Moreover, they were still stunned at their sudden departure from a place they had called home for over a decade.

To his right, and in the center-most seat of the back row, Steele sat with her eyes fixated on the viewport. Their Areostationary orbit provided the rear occupants of the Exodus pod a stunning perspective of Red Colony One – her focus, of course, was the tri-pronged power core structure.

Parker leaned his neck forward and peered at Steele around the head restraints. "Watching it won't make things go any faster, Steele."

"I can't help it." Her voice quaked with a tinge of nervousness. "I just wish..." Her voice trailed. "...I had stayed."

"It's safer here." Parker fought the restraint to place a hand on hers.

Steele forced a weak smile. She patted the top of his hand.

"Besides," he added, "you'll get nauseous if you keep looking at it. We've a subtle motion, whether you feel it or not."

Steele glanced at her wrist computer. "Darpa still hasn't initiated the recall protocol. What could be taking them so long?"

Parker wagged his head in silence. "It'll happen." His tone was less convincing than a fox guarding a henhouse.

"I should be there. I could have helped..."

"Mr. Stroud is beyond courageous. And his friends as well."

Steele tilted her head forward to bring Parker's face into her line of sight. "Friends?"

Parker bit his lip. "The miners..." he said after a weighty pause. "They're all a very... courageous group. They'll get it done, Steele. Have some faith."

Steele pitched her head a notch - Parker offered a trustworthy grin. As she brought her head back, the flickering status light on her wrist computer begged for attention. "Oh bollocks, we've lost link with the central computer." She tapped with a futile persistence at the device.

She darted her gaze to the power core once again. The pod rotated several degrees, forcing her to angle her head sideways to focus on something she had not noticed before.

"What is that cloud near the northwest of the core?" she asked.

Parker, already spying the strange occurrence, remained silent.

Steele sucked in a breath. "My lord... is that *debris*?"

Suddenly, several massive fissures grew along the tops of each of the remaining conduits. As if a balloon popping underneath a mound of sand, the heads at each arm end ruptured and fell in upon themselves, spewing thousands of miniature particles skyward.

Steele gasped and wrenched forward in her seat, both arms grasping out into the empty space ahead of her.

"Oh God, no!" She tore at her restraints to no avail. "We have to go back! We can still save them!"

Parker grasped her wrist. "Steele! What are you going to do, jump out and float back to the surface? Get hold of yourself!"

She pulled her focus from the viewport to glare at Parker. "The recall protocol, we need to initiate it!" she screamed in a panic.

"Steele..." Parker's voice flowed like a soothing brook, "The power core has been destroyed. We would be heading to our deaths if we returned now." He rubbed her hand with a loving stroke. "And with no power, there would be no way to initiate the protocol from the central computer."

Steele forced her eyes shut. She wiped a tear from her cheek. Slumping back into her seat once more, the former DMST Senior Architect allowed her eyes to rest on the image of the dying colony below. She placed her hand over her heart, the racing that she could no longer control calling out to those lost.

Parker tugged at his restraint. As the Exodus pod and its sister crafts gained speed and raced from Martian orbit towards the awaiting Earthbound portal, he pondered the future with a fulfilled smile.

ABOUT THE AUTHOR

I find writing about myself in third person to be a very odd experience. This is about me, and written by me – so I'm forgoing the usual.

I was born in a tiny Western Pennsylvania burg – New Castle, to be exact. That's right - Cascade Park, 'the Hot Dog Capital of the World' and also similarly 'the Fireworks Capital of the USA'. While several very famous fireworks companies do call it home, I'm not certain how or when the hot dog moniker came into being (although I had been known to enjoy a Coney Island dog or two during my time there).

My family was not affluent, and as such, we moved around a lot. That's a misnomer – we moved around a ton. By third grade, we had already relocated (significantly – as in across town and into new school districts) no less than six times. So it should come as no surprise that I often found myself with not many friends to speak of – forcing me to be more introverted than I wanted. Subsequently, I developed quite an imagination. I spent a fair amount of time at the NC Public Library (as well as individual school libraries) and read more than my fair share of Science Fiction and Fantasy (my personal favorites) – I also found historical account novels fascinating.

Upon reaching my teenage years - and when we had finally started to solidify our residence to one side of town or the other – I took interest in what most average teenage boys do: sports, fun, girls. To my detriment, I strayed away from reading to any great extent.

However, I have to credit a couple of my English Lit teachers in high school for planting the seed of writing – despite my outside interests: Mr. Gryn and Miss McLaughlin. No one can force you to write, and no one can ingrain the ability to be a writer. These two, however, freed me up to put my imagination down on paper – without overly worrying about rigid storytelling structure. My most vivid memory was a day when Mr. Gryn came into the class, held up a Moody Blues album (hey kids, ask your parents what an LP is!) – and said simply "Write about this cover". No rules. No structure. Just... write.

This wasn't a one-time assignment, either. It continued. He would show us pictures, give us a setting, an event – and sometimes just a phrase. "Write about it..." he would say. Simple enough.

My assignments tended to be more on the odd side – many times macabre – and my peers would laugh at the strange stories I would concoct seemingly out of thin air. But I will never forget the day that Mr. Gryn read my paper aloud in class and followed the laughter by saying "This is a very profound story" – and he clapped. After class, he pulled me aside and said, "You have a gift – you need to keep writing!"

A fair amount of time has passed since those carefree days of my youth, and many things have drawn my interest away from writing. I served in the military during Desert Storm and met my wife near the end of my enlistment.

One day in 2003, I told my son-in-law, Karl, that we should make a comic book – knowing that he was a great artist in his own right, and after all, how hard could it be? He said "sure, but who's going to write for it?" Seven hours later, Brigadier Stroud was born. His remark to me woke up the writing spirit – "I never knew you had it in you..."

I do.

Catch up with R. James Stevens:

Facebook:	facebook.com/rjamesstevensauthor
Blog:	rjamesstevens.com
Twitter:	@RJamesStevens